This book is dedicated to my sister, Maureen.

You are braver than you think and more courageous than you know.

You have been my inspiration from the start, and my prayers are with you always...

All my love,

Kathleen

Pigtails and Potter's Field

When into existence we are conceived and birthed to life anew,
Life's playing fields are leveled for each helpless ingénue,
Soon placed in arms that will bear our weight,
And, in time, our sorrows too.

Innocence, innately beautiful, emanates from virginal hearts.
Soon toddlers that will run ahead, and on to youthful adventures embark.
There are no cares for the future or plans to be made,
For in this brief span of time, all in life is to play.
This is how life should be.

Yet, for daughters of turpitude, another course is set,
Where paper dolls and costume jewels in boxes are kept.
Their lids conceal treasures and worlds of pretend,
While tender hearts bear the scars violated by men.

A child's trust,
torn asunder,
by perverse appetence.

Adolescence is spent concealing depravity's mark.
The resulting behavior, a promiscuous heart.
Insecurity's role in her life will prevail,
Unless lascivious truth is expressed and unveiled,
And the deviant brought to justice for the crimes that took place,
So to transform images of intimacy long-thought debase.

As a young woman, the struggle for "normalcy" cannot be willed.
Anguished thoughts, habitually silenced, by pharmaceuticals or spirits-distilled.
Often depression and anger lead to crime and more strife,
For this tormented one, long hollowed, by the iniquity of life.

What began in childlike wonder did debauchery steal,
While those with knowledge feigned mute letting evil prevail.
When heads bow in remembrance, or under the weight of guilt kneel,
Shall they realize their silence filled the coffin now buried and sealed,
And grieving hearts are left to ponder on the bitter life that spanned

from pigtails,

to potter's field.

Contents

Prologue

Boston, Massachusetts, Fall 1998

IT'S ONLY BEEN A COUPLE of months...Staring blankly at the toddler in the cherrywood frame, she mindlessly twirled one of her sister's many bent pen caps, a lingering reminder of Caroline's quirky ways. It was the silence that brought her to her senses and to the end of another chaotic day.

Her going-away party, thrown by caring coworkers, had ended hours earlier. Suddenly, the office door burst open to reveal Liz, the receptionist, bubbling with her usual enthusiasm.

"Hey, Val! Sorry to disturb you, but I'm heading out. I've got a date tonight!"

Val rolled her eyes and smiled.

"Another one?"

"Well, yes!"

Liz circled the desk to give Valerie a hug.

"I wish you all the happiness in the world, girlfriend. I'm really gonna miss you!"

Backing up, she wiped at the corner of her eyes with her perfectly manicured fingers.

"Oh, look at me! I just spent twenty minutes fixing my makeup in the ladies' room, and now I'm gonna mess it all up crying over you!"

Quickly, Valerie pulled a tissue from the dwindling box on her desk and handed it to her.

"Oh, no you won't! I'm hoping to get you married off next!"

Liz smirked, then politely thanked her, as she carefully dabbed at her thickly mascaraed lashes.

"You'd think by now I'd know enough to use waterproof mascara on a day like this."

She fumbled with the crumpled Kleenex in her hand, not knowing what to do or say next.

"I'm gonna take lots of pictures at the wedding. He's gorgeous you know. You're so lucky!"

Val smiled warmly thinking of Warren.

"Oh, him! Yeah, he's all right, I guess ..."

She casually waved her hand in the air, purposely downplaying her compliment.

"Oh, right!"

Liz guffawed, which made them both laugh.

"It's good to see you happy now, Val. You promise to stay in touch, right?"

Val nodded, assuring her she would, and gave her a parting hug. Liz closed the door quietly, leaving behind the sweet, permeating scent of Revlon's Ciara perfume.

Similar sentiments had been echoed throughout the day. Numerous cards, memos, and telegrams had been delivered. No less than seven floral arrangements had been sent from the various branch offices. They echoed similar sentiments of good-bye, good luck, and best wishes for a happy marriage and prosperous future. Liz called a courier earlier and had the flowers delivered to Val's condo just a few blocks away.

Scooping up the bent pen caps, Val carefully placed Caroline's treasured toddler photo into her bulging shopping bag, heavy now with sentimental parting gifts.

Switching off the computer screen, she flung her purse over her shoulder. Sighing softly, she closed the door on what had been a rewarding and successful ten-year accounting career at Sidebar Magazine. Somberly, she entered the familiar elevator and began a thirty-six-floor descent to a new reality.

Val closed her eyes, letting her thoughts drift back to Caroline. *What might she be doing on a night like tonight if things were different?* It's what she kept coming back to: *What if things had been different?* Her only sister ... just twenty-eight years old. The circumstances surrounding Caroline's life were heartbreaking and incomprehensible. Val struggled with these new and conflicting emotions.

At thirty-five, she was about to embark on some major life changes. Not everyone at work was familiar with her story. When new employees entered her office, they often assumed that the child in the photo was her daughter. It was a stunning snapshot of innocence - a little girl dressed in a ruffled, orange and white-striped top with bright yellow shorts, extended a daisy toward the photographer. It was a perfect moment captured in time for eternity. Delicate white Mountain Avens blanketed the hillside. Wispy, auburn hair bounced freely framing her sweet angelic face. The haze that day muted the background, adding to the romantic surrealism of the scene. But it was real ... SHE was real, and it was the past.

"What! No good-bye for old Ger, here?"

A deep voice boomed from behind Val as she walked toward the revolving glass doors. Glancing over her shoulder, Val stopped in her tracks and blushed with embarrassment at her forgetfulness.

"Oh, no! Can you believe it? I'm so sorry, Gerry! I was just lost in my thoughts again. It's been such an emotional day."

The security guard nodded with understanding.

"We're all going to miss you."

Val walked toward the counter that surrounded his workstation, her high heels rhythmically clicking across the tiled floor.

"You know, I would have come back once I realized I'd left without saying good-bye to you."

Gerry always wore a smile and had an encouraging word for everyone he greeted. He had been standing guard in the lobby of Sidebar Magazine for as long as she'd been there. Val was familiar with his schedule, and on the rare occasions when she'd get into the office before 7:00 a.m., she'd bring him a cup of coffee. He had a caring manner about him and looked like a grandfather — round-faced, with deep wrinkles accenting cheerful, though, at the moment, serious, brown eyes. Were it not for two silver tufts of hair on either side of his head, he'd have been completely bald.

"I hear he's a good man, Valerie."

Pointing, the aging widower reminded her.

"And if it doesn't work out ... well, I'm still available for the taking!"

Grabbing his finger playfully, she leaned in and whispered.

"Old man, I could never keep up with you!"

Bowing, he turned her wrist gently and kissed the top of her hand.

"This is very true, m'dear."

His look was pensive as he hovered over the polished marble countertop encircling his security station. In a low voice, he spoke sensitively.

"Listen, kiddo, I know it's not been easy for you lately, but you've got a great life ahead of you! You're young, and, despite all that's happened, God is good! Remember that, okay? Enjoy life! I'll tell you truthfully, it goes by in a blip!"

He said, snapping his fingers.

"Suddenly, it seems like one day you wake up and, well, you're old like me!"

Val chuckled in spite of the tears welling up in her eyes. Gerry's hand clutched hers tightly. He offered her a freshly laundered handkerchief from his pocket. Nodding in thanks, she reached over the counter to give him a farewell hug and kiss on the cheek. She mouthed, "Good-bye," as no sound would come out. He squeezed her hand, as tears began to fill his own eyes.

"God-bless-you, sweetie. God bless,"

He whispered, then waved her on.

Stepping out into a very humid Friday evening, she sniffled again, and then set down her bag for a moment to peel off her suit jacket, tossing it absently over her shoulder. Heading down Boylston Street toward home, it was hard to believe that September had arrived. Indian summer had come to Boston, making it feel more like July than early fall. The unusually warm weather brought to mind a much happier memory.

*   *   *

Boston in July ... as picturesque a city as one could hope to find. In 1988, history mixed with youth as prestigious colleges drew in some of the nation's brightest minds. From within the heart of the city, Swan Boats animated the Public Gardens, while across Storrow Drive, a flotilla of tiny sails, launched from the docks of Community Boating, dotted the Charles River. Anticipation hung in the air, marking the beginning of the Fourth of July holiday weekend. Come Saturday, the MDC Hatch Shell would be teeming with people gathered for the annual Boston Pops concert on the Esplanade. The synchronized fireworks display brought massive crowds from all over New England as John Williams took command, conducting the world-renowned orchestra.

Val visualized herself with Caroline, and some of her old friends from college, queuing up to wait in line all night, anxious for the chance to stake their claim on the Esplanade. Come the early morning hours of July Fourth, the MDC Police would finally remove the metal barricades, allowing the crowds to rush in. It was first come, first served, and not a feat for the timid or frail. After sitting in the blistering sun all day, sweating profusely, everyone was physically drained come evening, and looked (and smelled) like wet dish rags.

Yet it was always worth it, for when the final strains of Tchaikovsky's "1812 Overture" signaled the church bells, and the sheer majesty and power of the music resounded across the Charles River, it was a holy moment. The sky would suddenly explode in crystallized color, showering slowly down to earth. Screams of delight were followed by a thunderous applause, as spirits soared heavenward. At that point, no one seemed to notice or care that the herd of spectators smelled like a bunch of goats. Everyone just kicked back, taking in the momentous occasion.

* * *

Thoughts of those days brought back other joyous and carefree memories. *Memories*, the word itself screamed "the past." Grateful for her background in finance, Val formulated many of her own opinions about life by way of the "Assets vs. Liabilities" theory. Trying to look at her own memories in this light, she concluded that, with lots of good ones, a person could count herself blessed (though chances are she might not always have a grip on reality). Too many bad ones, and life could be viewed as an existence to be endured. Neither extreme was good, and lately she wrestled to achieve balance.

Val knew she'd had her share of good times and bad. But all that was needed was one fifty-pound weight dropped from seemingly out of nowhere on the bad memory side, and the scales tipped dramatically. That's what had happened in her life just a few short months ago. She couldn't say if they would ever come fully into balance. Yet, she sensed that in time, justice and forgiveness would prevail, and life would, eventually, level out.

Chapter One

CAROLINE AND VALERIE SAT ON the edge of the dock, dangling their feet in the water of Otsego Lake, when, for no apparent reason, Caroline fearfully pulled hers up and tucked them underneath.

"What's the matter?"

Val was puzzled by her little sister's odd behavior.

"I don't want the sharks to bite my feet."

The naive seven-year-old replied.

Leaning forward, Caroline peered cautiously down into the water. Val instinctively put her arm out in front so that she wouldn't lean over too far and rolled her eyes.

"Sharks live in the ocean, silly ... this is a lake! The only thing that can get at your feet here are sunfish, and they don't have any teeth!"

She tried to reassure her little sister, but Caroline wasn't convinced.

"When I go fishing with Uncle Tim, he tells me I have to be really quiet and sit still or the sharks will get me."

She looked up to see Val's reaction.

"Well, Uncle Tim is only kidding with you. Next time, you tell him there aren't any sharks in lake water!"

Why'd he say that to her? At fourteen, Val knew better. *But Caroline was just a kid!* At seven years old, she still believed everything anyone told her. Caroline's voice became quieter.

"Valerie, I don't like going fishing with Uncle Tim. He makes me touch yucky worms and I don't wanna."

Val feigned a look of mock horror but felt a wave of aggravation at her uncle's insensitivity.

"Tell you what, when I see Uncle Tim, I'll tell him to bait his own hook, okay?"

Caroline didn't nod in agreement but remained silent; staring straight ahead, she seemed to focus intently on the horizon.

As the sun disappeared behind a large cloud, she turned and looked at her older sister for a moment, then bent her head, her eyes fixed on the darkened lake water. She often looked to Val for affirmation. Noticeably uncomfortable now, she broke the awkward silence.

"Would you touch 'em ... I mean ... if you had to?"

Val gave her another puzzled look, and then remembered she was still talking about the worms. Leaning over, Valerie splashed her hand on top of the water to scare away the tiny sunfish gathering at the dock's edge. She backed up and stood.

"NO WAY! They're slimy and gross!"

She wiped her hands on her shorts and tried to redirect Caroline's thoughts from worms to a nicer time.

"Do you remember when Daddy would take us fishing?"

Caroline watched Val intently, like she always did when their father was mentioned.

"He'd sneak a loaf of Mom's bread off the counter and bring it out to the dock here. We'd pick out the soft center and roll it into tiny balls to stick on the end of our fishhooks ... well, I mean, I would — you were too little — you'd just eat the bread slices. Daddy would put yours on for you. Once, you even chased after a duck when it grabbed a piece out of your hand!"

Val had managed to bring a smile to Caroline's face. She loved to hear people tell stories about her daddy. Of course, she couldn't remember those times, but she always said she did. Valerie felt bad that her sister never had the chance to really know him.

Suddenly, Caroline changed the subject.

"H'come you always get to go somewhere over the summer, and I have to stay here?"

Her lips quivered slightly.

Val knew she didn't like getting left behind when she went to summer camp. Caroline had to stay with Auntie Sheila and Uncle Tim at their summer home while their mother worked during the week. Grace had accepted a position teaching English to summer school students at the local middle school back home on Cape Cod. It was only for six weeks, and she saw it as an opportunity to perhaps attain a full-time teaching job later on.

"Caroline, I've told you a million times, I'm just going to a stupid camp for a couple of weeks. BELIEVE ME, I'd rather stay here!"

Caroline knew she was lying, but Val was trying to make her little sister feel better.

"Besides, you're not old enough to go yet. You have to be eight."

Val really liked going to camp, not because of all the outdoor stuff they did (she hated most of that), but because it gave her a chance to spend two full weeks with her best friend, Glynnis O'Brien, from Ireland.

*   *   *

Glynnis's family lived a few doors down from Granny and Granda in Ennis, County Clare. Valerie and Caroline played with her often when they went over to visit their grandparents and their dad's siblings, Uncle Sean and Aunt Siobhan. Glynnis had actually started out as their babysitter, which Val never did understand being that she was only two years older than her. She had actually resented Glynnis in the beginning. But Glynnis turned out to be great fun, so Val stopped complaining, and they became fast friends.

Glynnis was an only child, but thought she knew how it would feel to have sisters around when Val and Caroline were visiting. It was their mother who posed the idea of summer camp to Glynnis's mom, Mary.

"It'll give the girls a chance to see each other, and it will get Glynnis out of your hair for a little while. It'll be good for her ... lift her spirits a bit."

Mary was all for that, and made her husband, a wealthy attorney, spring for their daughter to travel to the United States during the month of August, beginning when she was twelve. She'd spend the first two weeks at summer camp with Val, and then another two weeks back at their home on Cape Cod. For Grace, it wasn't any trouble having another girl in the house.

The girls always had fun at camp, more from breaking the rules than keeping them. They'd narrowly escaped getting thrown out last summer for "borrowing" an abandoned golf cart from a nearby course. They'd gone there so Glynnis could sneak a cigarette. Val thought she was so cool because she smoked, until Glynnis offered her one and she nearly threw up from coughing so hard. Then she hated it immediately and thought Glynnis an idiot. Or "eegit," as Glynnis would say. Valerie always loved listening to Glynnis speak with her native Irish accent, and would often lapse into a brogue herself after they'd spent some time together.

On the night of the golf cart incident, the girls had stopped to sit on a stone wall that separated the camp from the private golf course. Glynnis was puffing away.

"I know how to drive one of those things, y'know? I go with my da golfing sometimes, and he lets me drive. Wanna give it a go?"

Val looked at the abandoned cart, and then back at Glynnis.

"Are you nuts? What if we get caught?"

Glynnis deliberately blew the smoke in Val's face; Val quickly waved it away.

"Naaah. I know what I'm doing ... trust me."

No one was around, and it was too tempting an adventure to pass up.

Glynnis flicked the cigarette quite a distance, and the girls hopped the wall. Glynnis jumped into the driver's seat. Turning the key, she rolled the lever beneath the seat like a pro and took off like a shot. Val nearly fell out of the cart, laughing hysterically in spite of how nervous she was.

Glynnis drove like a maniac, taking sharp turns and nearly tipping the cart altogether. It was Val's shrieking that alerted the staff and brought them out in pursuit of them. Two young guys shouted at the girls to stop the cart. Glynnis was up for the chase, and Val hung on for dear life, still cackling away.

"Let's see if they can catch us ..."

Glynnis floored the pedal.

"Pound down! Chase us for the rest!"

Val whacked her jokingly.

"They don't know what a 'pound' is. We say, 'Nickel down. Chase is on' here in America — get it right!"

Glynnis laughed and threw Val her cigarette pack.

"Light me another, would you?"

Val clumsily stuck a cigarette in her mouth while trying unsuccessfully to keep a bouncing match lit.

"The wind keeps blowing it out! You'll have to wait until we're in jail."

The cigarette dropped out of her mouth as they screamed with laughter.

"Is it true that, in America, they at least let you make one phone call?"

Val nodded.

"I think so ... but only locally, and I'm not bailing you out of this one — you're on your own! Won't your da love jumping on a plane and coming all the way to the US to spring you?"

Glynnis gave it some thought then slowed down. The young men quickly drove up alongside them, and she waved her fingers coyly, flashing them a huge smile.

"Ladies ... do you mind getting out of that golf cart now?"

They were average-looking boys, about eighteen years old. Glynnis was fifteen, but looked older since she'd started wearing mascara. Her Irish accent made her sound even more mature than her actual age. Val knew she was too young to hold their interest. Glynnis was in rare form.

"Gentleman, 'tis a fine day for a turnabout the countryside, wouldn't you say?"

They looked at her in amusement.

"Well, princess, here in the good ole U S of A, people get arrested for stealing things!"

They thought her accent was British. Glynnis sighed.

"Well, it's not really stealing, now is it? I mean, it's not like I took it off the property. I didn't pay for the ride, true enough. But if you lads would like to take me back to the club house, I'll gladly pay for my jaunt."

They looked at each other and shrugged agreeing that that should be okay.

"How much do they charge for a fifteen minute joyride these days, hmmm?"

They looked at each other and grinned. The freckled redhead elbowed his coworker.

"Where do you live? You're not from around here ..."

"We're at Camp Bretton, across the way,"

Val poked her head around Glynnis and piped in. They had forgotten she was even there.

"Did you get bored toasting marshmallows?"

The taller, crew cut boy directed his snide comment toward Val and then eyed Glynnis up and down, casually draping his arm around her shoulder.

"Tell you what, Mario Andretti here can ride with me, and we'll chauffeur you ladies back to 'Camp Bedwettin' — that okay with you, princess?"

Glynnis lit up another cigarette, knowing full well that he was checking her out. She daintily blew out the match.

"I wouldn't expect anything less from hired help."

He chuckled at her exaggerated sense of entitlement.

"Let's go then."

Glynnis winked at Val as she got in his cart and mouthed, "He's darling."

Val turned away so as not to let crew-cut see her laughing.

It was times like that, which made her summer adventures with Glynnis O'Brien so memorable.

* * *

Tears trickled down Caroline's cheeks.

"Val, I don't wanna stay here by myself! I wanna go home with Mommy!"

Standing, she stamped her foot on the dock and crossed her little arms. The pleading look in her eyes made Val wonder what was wrong. As far as little sisters go, she could be a real pain-in-the-neck. They argued a lot, but Caroline was no pushover.

"Listen, Caroline, Mom thinks you'll have more fun staying here while she's teaching at school. She won't be gone for that long. Don't make her feel bad, okay? Stop being such a baby!"

Caroline looked crushed. Val never understood what got into her head. One minute, she'd be fine; the next minute, she was a basket case.

"Listen to me, there's nothing to do at home. It's boring."

Val put her hands on her hips.

"Besides, I'll only be gone for two weeks. You can put up with anything for two weeks, can't you?"

Caroline lowered her head silently, looking helpless and defeated. Val tried to get her to look on the bright side.

"Hey! Listen! You'll know how to swim by the time I get back. Me, you, and Glynnis can have races out to the dock, okay?"

Val nudged her.

"Maybe you'll even win for a change."

Caroline completely ignored what Val said.

"Why can't I just stay home with Shelly and her mom? Her mother stays home during the summer. I won't get into any trouble — I promise."

She put up her hand like she was taking an oath and continued to plead with her older sister.

"Would ya please just ask Mommy for me, Val, huh? She listens to you."

Val didn't hide her sarcasm.

"Wanna bet?"

Suddenly realizing her sister had edged dangerously close to the end of the dock, Val grabbed her elbow to pull her back.

"Stay there and don't move. If you fall in and drown, Mom will kill me!"

Something was really bugging Caroline for her to be as hysterical as she was. Val didn't know what to make of it, so she bellowed from the dock, "MOM!" and started up the ramp to find her, glancing back once to make sure Caroline hadn't made a move closer to the edge.

When her mother suddenly appeared from around the shed, Val jumped.

"For crying out loud, Valerie, what are you hollering for? I'm right here."

She was holding large pruning shears in her hand.

"Mom, Caroline wants to come home with you for the summer. She's acting weird and doesn't want to stay here. I think you need to take her home and let her stay with Shelly and her mom."

Grace put down the oversized scissors and took off her gloves and sun hat.

"What's with the change of heart all of a sudden?"

Val shrugged.

"I don't know. Why don't you ask her?"

Walking toward the dock together, Val noticed, once again, how beautiful her mother was. Her dark auburn hair was piled on top of her head, held in place with the gold Claddagh barrette, a gift Daddy brought back from Ireland on one of his many trips home to visit with Granny and Granda. A few wisps of hair hung down the back of her neck. Her light blue eyes squinted against the sun as they walked down the ramp toward

Caroline, who was sitting, once again, with her legs crossed like a pretzel, resting her chin on her hand.

Grace took off her sandals and sat against the post, dangling one foot off the dock. She motioned for Caroline to come sit on her lap.

"What's up, honey? Val tells me you don't want to stay here? How come?"

Caroline shot Val a grateful look.

"Can I just stay with Shelly? I promise I won't get into any trouble at all."

She was twirling a piece of her mom's hair around her finger. Grace always turned to mush when she did that. The child twirled everything.

"Oh, honey, it's not that easy. You know I'm going to be busy teaching school this summer. Staying with someone who isn't family for six weeks is a lot to ask."

Caroline was quick to explain.

"But, Mom, Shelly's mother won't mind. She says we're like sisters anyways."

Grace was obviously confused at her daughter's sudden change of heart.

"But I thought you liked staying here with Auntie Sheila and Uncle Tim?"

Distress clouding her face, Caroline shook her head no.

"Listen, sweetie, Auntie Sheila loves to have you tag along with her shopping. She doesn't have a little girl ... and you keep her company! You know how much she spoils you when you're here."

She lilted, placing her hands on the child's shoulders.

Caroline didn't see her mother's hands motioning behind her to Val for support. Not finding any, she looked around Caroline's head, shot Val a look, and struggled on.

Taking Caroline's hands in hers, she clapped them together with each word.

"Not ... only ... that ..."

She held her hands still, together in hers.

"She's wonderful with arts and crafts, and she makes those little paper dolls you love so much, right?"

She brushed Caroline's bangs away from her eyes.

"She lets you play with all her clothes and jewelry any time you want ..."
Her voice trailed off whimsically.

Grace was giving it a good go, but Caroline, like the fish, wasn't biting. She was a pretty hard sell for a second-grader. Val stood still, staring at Caroline's back while their mother continued on.

"Honey, I can't ask that of Shelly's mom. Listen, I promise to call you every night, pumpkin, and I'll drive back on the weekends. There's so much for you to do here. Don't you like learning how to swim and fish?"

Val shot her hand up to try and stop the reference to the fishing part, but it was too late. She'd blown it. Caroline just crumpled forward onto her mother's shoulder and bawled.

This wasn't normal. Forever the drama queen, Val slapped her hand against her forehead, as Grace glared back at her with a stern "BE QUI-ET" look.

Val felt it her duty then to enlighten her mother as to their Uncle Tim's worm escapades.

"She hates fishing, Mom! Did you know that Uncle Tim makes her use real, LIVE worms for bait?"

Val stood there, aghast, with her arms crossed, tapping her foot.

"Why can't I just go home with you?"

Caroline pleaded.

"Please, Mommy!"

For a second, even Val felt bad for the kid. Grace's eyes filled up as she smoothed Caroline's hair with one hand and lifted the other as if in question or at a loss. She looked at Val for some sort of an explanation, and Val just shrugged her shoulders and silently mouthed.

"HOW SHOULD I KNOW?"

Grace gently lifted Caroline off her shoulder. She hated to leave her small daughter, but she had no choice at this late stage.

"Listen, honey, it's only for a little while, and when Val and Glynnis get back from camp, we'll all go home together, okay? You and I will plan a special school-shopping trip to downtown Boston. You're looking forward to school, aren't you?"

Caroline nodded. Grace cupped her tiny face in her hands and looked deeply into her watery eyes.

"Tell you what, sweetie. I'll talk to Uncle Tim and tell him that you only use bread for bait, and he can put his own worms on, okay?"

Caroline didn't respond and only sniffled, fingering the buttons on her mother's shirt. Grace bent to kiss her youngest daughter's sunburned nose.

* * *

Grace and the girls vacationed for a few weeks each summer with her sister Sheila and brother-in-law, Tim, at their home on Lake Otsego in central New York. When Grace was offered a temporary summer school position, teaching English for six weeks at the local middle school, her sister suggested the girls stay at the lake with them. Grace had never left her daughters with anyone before, and commuted back and forth on the weekends.

Sheila and Tim owned a large cottage built into the side of a steep hill. Uncle Tim would always direct them down the treacherous incline when they arrived.

"Okay, Gracie, just back her down slowly and turn the wheel hard. Go on. I'll tell you when to stop."

Val would close her eyes tightly each time they descended the narrow, vertical slope. It looked like they'd wind up right in the lake. If her mom was even a little nervous backing down in the huge, Ford Country Squire wagon (the thing was a tank, and it was even the same color green), she never let on.

Kathleen M. Urquhart

Auntie Sheila and Uncle Tim enjoyed having the girls around for the summer. They didn't have children of their own and genuinely looked forward to spending time with Valerie and Caroline. The families got together throughout the year, but summers in New York were special. Well, they were for a while anyway ... until Caroline started acting strangely.

Chapter Two

Chatham, Cape Cod, Massachusetts, Fall 1971

UNUSUALLY LONG LASHES ACCENTUATED NEIL Callaghan's penetrating blue eyes. At six foot four inches, the ruggedly handsome Irishman cast a protective shadow over his lovely wife and two young daughters. He attempted daily to comb back his curly, thick black hair. However, a few rogue curls would never submit to taming, and hung tauntingly about his forehead.

"They have a mind of their own," Grace would often say, twirling his hair with her finger as the two would chuckle and kiss. They were openly affectionate with one another, and Val loved watching them hug. Sometimes, when they were hugging, a lot, her daddy would ask her to go and check on baby Caroline. He'd give his eight-year-old daughter a quarter to sit there and wait quietly until the baby woke up. It was Val's job to come and knock on the door and tell them when she was awake. Sometimes, Caroline would wake up screaming, and Val didn't understand why they couldn't hear her themselves ... she'd often heard her daddy say that her crying could "wake the dead." Her mom would be the one to come out of their bedroom first, fixing her hair and adjusting her shirt. She'd pick Caroline up and gently hush her while Neil took a nap. Val was told to go and play quietly.

* * *

Grace Sullivan met Neil Callaghan in October of 1960. The United States was gearing up for its next election, and the country was rallying behind a young, charismatic senator from Massachusetts named John Kennedy. Grace was attending Wellesley College in Boston and majoring in

English while Neil was finishing up his Engineering degree at Dartmouth College in Hanover, New Hampshire.

The small, quaint New England town provided the perfect setting for love to blossom. Neil, forever quick with his wit, would say that he fell in love with "Gracie" the moment he first laid hands on her. It was a standing joke between them and always managed to bring a playful gleam to his eyes. Grace, ever modest, would tell him, "Shhhhhh, you! Be quiet." Then she'd playfully toss whatever she had in her hand at him, reminding him, "Little walls have big ears." She had a million of those sayings, which Valerie didn't understand at the time.

*   *   *

An amazing amount of information can be remembered from early childhood. Although Valerie only had her father in her life for nine short years, she could still recall every action, word, and scene as if it were just yesterday. It was like a lifeline to her past, which her mind would not surrender to time and circumstance. For example, she remembered a game that her daddy used to play with them called, "Shimmy Shoester." She'd stand on her daddy's shoes and hold on to his belt buckle, while he shouldered a giggling Caroline. Then he'd "shimmy" across the floor as Val stood on his feet. He really enjoyed playing with his girls like that. Then again, he was genuinely playful at heart. His laugh was deep, good-natured, and contagious. He went out of his way to accommodate "his girls."

Unlike her mom, he'd never get irritated if Val had to stop several times during the course of a long car trip to use the bathroom. Grace, in a rush to get wherever they were going, would be noticeably exasperated.

Neil would then gently remind her.

"Grace, y'know I'd take her, but how'd it look if a grown man took a young lady into the toilet?"

She'd sigh.

"I know, I know."

Walking quickly with Val to the restroom, she'd warn her through clenched teeth.

"I swear to God, Valerie, you're not having another thing to drink until we get there! Do you hear me?"

Val wanted to say, "Yes, Mom, and half the world can, too," but decided against it. Instead, she just nodded and rolled her eyes when her mom wasn't looking.

One time, Grace caught the eye roll, and Val knew she was in big trouble.

"Valerie Jean Callaghan, if you EVER do that again, you're going back home and staying there all by yourself!"

She then grabbed her daughter firmly under the arm, telling her to hurry up.

When they made it back to the car, Val found her father waiting patiently, but she was near tears, and Grace was exhibiting her "completely-put-out" look.

"Ahhh, Lord, what's the ruckus now?"

"Well, Valerie rolled her eyes at me when I told her that I was sick of stopping for potty breaks. I mean, Neil, at this rate, it'll take us a week to get there! She's not having another thing to drink until we arrive! She's developing a bit of an attitude …"

Neil looked back at Val in the rearview mirror, and saw her tear-stained face. He winked his "It's-okay-honey" look, and she smiled back and exaggeratedly rolled her eyes. He laughed out loud so that Grace knew she'd done something, but didn't see what. She glanced over her shoulder and gave Val a sidelong "What-am-I-going-to-do-with-you?" look. Val stopped sniffling and smiled at her sweetly. Then Grace reached over and playfully tussled Val's honey-blond hair.

All the while, baby Caroline sat bright-eyed in her car seat, feet kicking excitedly, as her daddy sang her his silly made-up song.

"Oh, I love you, Caroline Allison, yes, I do; I love you, Caroline Allison, y' know it's true; I love you, Caroline Allison, through and through; I love you, Caroline Allison ... I do, I do, I do."

He frequently sang that simple song to each of his daughters, changing their names accordingly. Val always loved that little tune, and found herself singing it to Caroline a few years later when she was restless and couldn't get to sleep. Caroline liked clapping and mimicking Val when she sang the *"I do, I do, I do"* part.

Chapter Three

Boston, Massachusetts, Summer 1972

NEIL WAS LEAVING LOGAN AIRPORT at seven o'clock in the evening for Shannon International Airport in Ireland. Val loved the drive into Boston and got so excited about seeing the airplanes. She'd been fascinated by planes all her short life, and had never once exhibited a fear of flying on their trips to Ireland.

By the time Val was eight, she was a seasoned traveler, having been to Ireland, at least, fifteen times. On the last flight, Caroline had thrown up all over Neil, and he smelled the entire way there.

Neil hailed from Ennis in County Clare. All of his family still lived there. He was the only one who had made his home in the United States. The girls loved going to Ireland to visit with their Granny and Granda, and their father's siblings, Aunt Siobhan and Uncle Sean. It was always a grand time, with lots of friends and distant relatives stopping by to visit and catch up with Neil and Grace, giving Val candy, and passing baby Caroline around like she was a pint of Guinness. Grace loved the people of Ireland.

"They're the salt of the earth."

Grace was of Irish descent (her roots, she discovered, went back to County Roscommon). Yet she proudly reminded them all.

"I'm an American first, Irish only by heritage."

Neil's family would have loved her no matter what her ancestry (although it didn't hurt that it was Irish), and they'd accepted her warmly.

As Neil was saying good-bye to his family at the airport, Val was hoping that he would surprise them and say they were all going with him like he did once before.

Her mother had been so thrilled; she was jumping up and down with excitement. Grace had assumed that she'd just be dropping her husband off, waving good-bye, then fighting the Southeast Expressway, Cape Cod summer traffic on the way back home to Chatham. She had Val and Caroline already bathed and in their pajamas for the long ride home, so she wouldn't have to wake them to put them to bed. But then Neil told her they were all going with him to Ireland!

Grace's excitement lulled momentarily as she started thinking about practical matters.

"But what about clothes for me and the girls?"

Neil just grinned.

"Not to worry love, you've got clothes aplenty already over there! And I packed up a travel bag for you, and extra clothes and diapers for Caroline."

Being confident in his ability to work any situation, Grace had learned to roll with the punches quite easily. She trusted his judgment.

"Okay!"

She shrugged her shoulders and kissed him suddenly on the lips. Smiling at her, he expertly kicked the brake release, collapsed the baby stroller, and handed it over to the baggage clerk.

"Grand! We're all set then!"

Producing all of their passports from his suit jacket pocket, he checked them in, and off they went!

Looking up at her father, Val sensed that this trip was different from that one, but she asked him anyway.

"Daddy, can we go, too?"

He gently transferred a sleeping Caroline into his wife's arms, and delicately brushed aside a lock of auburn hair from her forehead to kiss her good-bye.

"Upsy daisy, love."

He crooned as he gathered Valerie into his arms.

"I'm only going away for a few days this time, Vanilla Bean. I'll be back in two shakes of a lamb's tail."

Val had heard her parents talking about the reason for this trip, and it was something about a "will." Her Granny and Granda had asked if their oldest son could plan a short trip home, when convenient, to help them finalize a few legal matters.

As Executor of their Last Will and Testament, Neil needed to sign several documents. All young Val had been told about a will was that it was a piece of paper that needed to be filed with some lawyers when someone died. She thought it odd that Daddy had to fly all the way across the ocean to put a piece of paper away while her grandparents were still alive.

"Why couldn't Uncle Sean put it away for them?"

She asked her mother naively.

"You wouldn't understand."

Grace told her.

"Some things are not meant for children to know."

Looking down and poking playfully at her nose, Grace added.

"Children should be seen and not heard."

Val never understood that stupid saying either.

"Well, I have to listen to grown-ups all day!"

She shot back, smiling. Her mother laughed.

"Good point, Val."

Val would know all too soon what a will was, but at the time, the thought of Granny or Granda dying made her very sad.

* * *

Neil sensed his daughter's disappointment.

"You know, love, Aunt Siobhan and Granny bought you and your sister a couple of frilly dresses. I'm going to bring them home for you when I return, God-willing."

Granny and Aunt Siobhan loved to shop for the girls, and bought them the most beautiful lace dresses. Grace's friends at church often complimented her on how pretty the girls looked. They were often displayed in matching dresses, like twins.

Granny told Val that little girls in Ireland wore dresses every day ... even to play in the dirt! Grace never bothered to bring "play" pants for the girls when they visited. She did, however, let them wear shorts to play in the garden during the warmer summer months.

"Give us a kiss then, and on to Mam with you."

Valerie hugged him long and hard, until he made exaggerated choking sounds. She giggled, and he kissed her cheek several times. As Neil gathered up his bag and got ready to board the plane, he winked at his wife. Turning to Valerie, he made a promise.

"Now you be a good girl for your mam, aye?"

Val nodded.

"And I'll bring you home some more of that holy water y'like so much."

At that, both he and Grace roared with laughter, recalling Val's last tea party.

* * *

When Val was about five years old, she had a tea party with her dolls, the cat, and God. Because she had decided to invite the Divine, it seemed only right that she should make His tea with holy water. She went into her parents' room and took the bottle from her mother's drawer. It came from the blessed Knock Shrine in Ireland. Valerie proceeded to pour cups for the dolls, the Lord, and herself.

When her father got home from work, her mom was bragging about the guest list, and instructed him to go and peek in on the tea party. He knocked on the door politely and asked if he could join. Sitting awkwardly on the tiny chair beside his gracious host, he folded his hands in his lap and asked who the other guests were. Val named all her dolls, "Lucky" the cat (who'd just retreated under the bed), and, of course, God.

"God, y'say? What a splendid idea! Ummmm — did He just leave?"

Val shook her head no.

"He's still here."

Looking around the room, her daddy leaned in closer to her and whispered.

"Call me daft, love, but for the life of me, I can't see Him."

Placing her hands on her hips, Val smiled at him.

"Oh, Daddy, of course, you can't see Him. But He's there and here."

She pointed at the chair and then to her heart.

Her dad's eyes twinkled, and a smile lit up his face as he pulled Val toward him.

"Ahhh, love, that's right. He's right in here."

He placed his hand on her heart.

"I think it's an altogether grand idea to invite God to your tea parties."

Holding the little china teapot, Val gestured.

"Would you like some?"

Never one to refuse her offers for tea, he took the tiny toy cup in his large hands and pretended to take a sip.

"'Tis the most blessed cup of tea I've had in a while, Vanilla Bean."

Then he gave his Valerie Jean a big hug.

*   *   *

Sitting on his knee at the airport, Val suddenly grew tired. Reaching up, she began to unconsciously twirl his hair around her finger. He looked up at his wife in amusement.

"Funny how they both do that."

Grace, amused, nodded in agreement. Setting Val down, Neil held his wife for what seemed like ages, and then kissed her even longer on the lips. Val never took her eyes from them. It gave her a warm feeling inside to see them that way.

"Slán!"

He called out waving good-bye as he headed toward the ramp.

As her father boarded the plane, Val noticed that her mother's eyes looked sad. Val knew she worried about him when he traveled.

She didn't seem to pay attention to Val, who was pointing and asking a million questions about the different planes and talking to strangers. Instead, Grace watched intently as her husband's plane took off. Val stood by the window and waved frantically, yelling out to the plane.

"Bye, Daddy! We'll miss you!"

People smiled sweetly at her as her mother took her gently by the hand.

"C'mon, Val Jean, it's time to get you and your sister home to bed."

Val quickly hopped down from the window ledge. She knew then that her mom was going to be okay.

Chapter Four

THE FAMILY HAPPILY ADJUSTED THEIR schedules whenever Neil came home to Ireland. His parents, Pat and Ruth, notified friends and extended family in the event they wanted to stop by and say hello. Siobhan and Sean also made sure they would have some time to spend with their big brother, since they only saw him a few times a year.

Aunt Siobhan, as her nieces called her, took a few vacation days off from her job as a pediatric nurse. At thirty-three, her career was definitely the focus of her life, taking second only to her family, especially her nieces. She had no need to reschedule her social life — she was unmarried, with no prospects, and apparently no interest in the matter.

Siobhan never talked much about men. She'd been engaged once, for a short time, but it didn't work out. As the story went, her fiancé ran into a former girlfriend from university at a party one night and decided to take up with her for "one last fling," he joked with his friends. Still planning on marrying Siobhan, he didn't intend for her to find out. But a close friend of Uncle Sean's had been at the party and relayed to him the details of what happened.

After her brother warned Siobhan about the indiscretion, she confronted her fiancé with the allegation.

"She didn't mean anything to me. I was drunk." Followed by, "I don't even remember what happened!"

Rumor had it that Neil and Sean had a few words with their sister's cheating boyfriend one night after they spotted him coming out of a local pub. He left Ennis shortly thereafter for a job in England and never returned.

Neil's younger brother Sean, at thirty, was single as well, and worked as a programmer/analyst for a small computer start-up company in County Cork. He was a technology geek and never exhibited an interest in the family business.

Their parents had acquired considerable wealth building homes and developments on a vast amount of land that Pat owned in rural western Mayo. It was owned by Pat's father, who passed it along to his son when he died. Still undeveloped at the time, the land seemed worthless then, but became increasingly more valuable over the years.

Pat's company, which specialized in building retirement homes, was able to sell many of them to rich, nostalgic Irish-Americans who were anxious for a piece of the "old sod," having come to Ireland to find their roots and connect with their distant heritage.

Neil helped design the properties. When talks of rural renewal and the prospect of an international airport found their way into County Mayo's future development plans, the value of the Callaghans' land holdings soared, having come to the attention of powerful real estate development companies anxious to get in on the building frenzy.

Pat's solicitors scheduled a meeting in their Dublin offices to sort out the financial matters as they pertained to current retail property and the substantial amount of remaining land, which was still unsold. Legal documents had been drawn up which required Neil's witness and signature. It was all pretty straightforward: All assets were to be divided equally among the three children, with survivors' rights to their children in the event of an untimely death.

Valerie and Caroline were their only grandchildren. Generous trust funds had been established for the girls when they were born for their future educational expenses and a significant allotment would be awarded to each of them once they turned twenty-one. Granny and Granda wanted them to have a good start in life.

Granda, having come from very humble beginnings, heard too many stories of the great famine passed down from his relatives. He was determined that each member of his family would one day have the opportunity to own property outright.

"You know how we struggled in the beginning, Ruth. There's security in owning land."

"Lord above, don't I know! We didn't have a pot to pee in or a window to throw it out!"

"By God, my granddaughters will start their marriages in houses of their own! We helped Neil and Grace, and we'll do the same for them."

The Callaghan's did make one request of their children: if at all possible, they wanted the family residence on Bindon Street to remain in the family and not be sold.

Ruth would later say that she sensed something awful would happen once she signed off on their will. All of her husband's loving assurance couldn't stop her from feeling otherwise.

*   *   *

Neil was returning to Shannon Airport by way of a bus from Dublin late in the afternoon on Thursday, August 15th. He could have driven, but he actually liked taking the bus.

Once, while on holiday, Neil took Valerie with him to visit his longtime friends, Harry Donegan and his wife, Kathleen. He only told Val they were going on an adventure. At the next stop, a very dirty, unkempt woman boarded with a long thin stick in her hand and a young boy at her side. She kept the child in line with the switch, which Val thought very cruel. The boy looked terrified and dared not move.

Val's father explained to her that people like them were referred to as "Travellers." Val stared at the woman's hairy, bruised legs. Afraid to look at her for too long, she quietly whispered.

"I thought sticks were only used on slow horses."

Her father playfully patted the top of her hand.

"Well that, and fast children. So you'd best not try and run off!"

Then he made an exaggerated whip-like motion with his hand, startling her. It worked. She held his hand the entire ride and was "as good as gold" he told the family when they got home later.

Making his way back from Adare on that fateful day in August, Neil's bus was scheduled to make a half-hour dinner stop in Limerick. His flight back to the States was set to leave Friday morning at 8:00 a.m.

Not feeling particularly hungry, he decided to stretch his legs and walked to a nearby shoppe to purchase the evening paper.

The breeze was a welcomed relief on such a humid August night. Whistling the popular tune, "Horse with No Name" by the band America, he thought to himself how the climate in Ireland had been changing over the years, with summers becoming noticeably warmer. The fair-skinned people of Ireland weren't genetically predisposed for the intensity of the sun, causing many to wind up in the ER with second-degree burns.

As if to confirm his thoughts, a small group of badly sunburned revelers stumbled out of a local pub, obviously high in spirit and filled with false courage. They clumsily approached him, asking if he could spare a couple of cigarettes. Not breaking his stride, Neil replied.

"No, sorry. I don't smoke."

As he continued on, digging his hands deep into his pockets, he heard one of them slurring from behind.

"Listen, man, do you have a few smokes you can spare me an m'pals here?"

Figuring it best not to say too much, Neil chose to ignore them. He sensed their belligerence, and that they weren't taking "no" for an answer. They were drunk and seemed hell-bent on a confrontation.

"He's an odd one, ain't he?"

They mocked and laughed. One stupid fellow purposely pushed his buddy into Neil, who decided that keeping the peace might be worth a few pence, so he offered to buy them a pack of Woodbines around the corner. However, when he pulled his hand out of his pocket, one lout tried to grab his arm while another wrestled him for his wallet. Neil fought him off easily ... but that's when the others decided to pitch in.

According to witnesses at the scene, two of the men began throwing sloppy punches. With his height and strength, Neil held them off without much effort. When a small crowd began to gather, three of the attackers fled, leaving him with his knee on the fourth man's back, pinning him to the ground. Neil looked up at the gathering crowd, momentarily ignoring the man kissing the pavement beneath him.

"Someone call the guards!"

He shouted.

But as people in the crowd began yelling for the guards, a woman let out a bloodcurdling scream.

"NO!"

She had seen the pinned man reach behind into his pocket and pull out what appeared to be a small knife. In a split second, the man turned and caught Neil in the throat with a blade so small that it would have been laughable in a real fight. But the sharp edge was enough to put a two-inch gash in Neil's neck, puncturing his jugular vein.

White faced, in shock, he brought his hand up to his throat and felt the warmth of his own blood gushing through his fingers. Staring down in disbelief at the red liquid streaming through his hands, his last lucid thoughts returned him to Cape Cod and a gentle shoreline where his wife and two daughters were eagerly awaiting his return.

He uttered what someone later said was either, "God help me" or "Dear God," then slumped forward onto the ground.

The young murderer, eyes wide with terror, his shirt stained crimson, got up and ran. The guards apprehended him before he'd gone a block. They arrested him, and later, his companions as accomplices.

Neil's face was death-gray and his breathing shallow having lost a great deal of blood. He went into cardiac arrest in the ambulance and was pronounced dead at Our Lady of Mercy Hospital at 7:15 p.m. that evening.

Chapter Five

THE CALL ABOUT NEIL CAME in the early morning hours of August 16, 1972, the day he was to return to the United States. Grace was dressing Caroline when the phone rang.

"VAL!"

She shouted from the nursery.

"Can you get the phone, please?"

Val ran into the kitchen and picked up the receiver, mimicking her mother flawlessly.

"Callaghan residence. Who's calling please?"

She heard a familiar male voice on the other end. "Valerie?"

Immediately she recognized her uncle's voice and blurted out excitedly.

"Hi, Uncle Sean! Is Daddy still there?"

His voice weak, Sean tried hard to maintain his composure, purposefully avoiding her question.

"Aye, lass, you sounded so grown-up. I hardly recognized it was you. Is your mam about? I need to chat with her for a bit ..."

Valerie thought his voice sounded like he had a cold or something.

"She's dressing Caroline."

She looked down the hall to see if her mother was coming.

"Can I talk to Daddy now?"

After a short silence, and repeated clearing of his throat, Sean replied.

"He's ... aaaah, not here at the moment, love. Is Mam making her way to the phone yet?"

Val thought she heard him mumble, *God give me strength ...*

"What did you say, Uncle Sean?"

Rubbing his forehead and pacing aimlessly about the living room, Sean stammered.

"Ah, it's nothing, love. I just need to talk to your mam."

Valerie heard crying in the background.

"Uncle Sean, who's that crying?"

"Oh, uh, that's Aunt Siobhan, love. She's not feeling very well right now. Would you mind jetting down the hall and getting your mam for me, doll?"

His voice was strained and cracking.

Val loved her aunt Siobhan, and was concerned that she was crying.

"Okay, Uncle Sean, hold on. I'll go get her."

Putting down the phone, she ran back to find her mother.

"Aunt Siobhan is sick, and she's crying, and Uncle Sean needs to talk with you right away."

She said breathlessly.

Concern clouded Grace's face, and she quickly picked up Caroline and brought her out into the parlor. She reached for the box of Lorna Doone cookies left on the coffee table and handed one to the smiling toddler, then gently set her down in the playpen to watch Sesame Street.

"Val, keep an eye on your sister for a minute, will you? Make sure she doesn't take too big a bite and choke."

She went out to the kitchen and picked up the receiver.

"Hi, Sean, is everything all right? Val was saying Siobhan was ..."

Val went very still to listen because she noticed that her mother had become strangely quiet. She walked slowly and quietly down the hall, and peeked into the kitchen. Her mother's face held a serious look, and then grew pale as she fumbled behind her for the chair, sat down nervously, and listened intently.

Suddenly, she gasped.

"Dear God!"

She covered her mouth with a shaking hand.

"Oh, please, Sean! Please don't say Neil ... NO! Oh, God, no!"

She stood again, placing her shaking hand on her cheek, and began frantically circling the room, inadvertently becoming entangled in the telephone cord. A look of horror crossed her face as her voice rose in a shrill.

"My Neil ... oh, Sean! How! I mean, why? What happened! Dear Jesus, Sean, HOW did this happen?!!!!"

Val had never seen her mother so upset before, and ran to hug her around the waist. Instinctively, Grace put an arm around Val's shoulder, and then started wailing in a way Val had never heard before - like she was hurt. Caroline's whimper was heard from the living room, having realized she'd been left alone.

Val held on to her mother, who was bent over at the waist, holding her stomach like she was in pain. Val became frightened and started crying, too.

"Mommy, it's okay. Aunt Siobhan's gonna be okay. She's just a little sick. That's all ..."

Her mother collapsed with a thud and lay silently on the linoleum floor. Val struggled to free her mother from the cord that encircled her. She heard her uncle Sean's small voice calling from the other end. Val picked up the receiver in her trembling hands.

"Uncle Sean, pluh — please put Daddy on the phone. Mommy fell down, and she's hurt and ... and ... I need to talk with Daddy right now! Please, Uncle Sean!"

Val choked on gulping sobs. In the background, she heard her uncle.

"I should have called Father Bruce first, damn it!"

Valerie begged.

"Uncle Sean, please help me!!!"

She heard her uncle take a deep breath, then his suddenly calm and deliberate voice began to instruct her with a firmness she'd not ever heard from him before.

"Valerie, listen to me, love. I know you're a big girl. Now, I need you to go next door and get help for your mam. Is there a neighbor you can collect to come over and help you right away?"

Val nodded silently, hiccupping back tears.

"Valerie? Are you there, love?"

"Yes. I'm here, Uncle Sean."

She immediately thought of the Graziano's, a kind, older Italian couple that lived next door.

"Yes. Mrs. Graziano."

She wiped her face with her sleeve. She started to shake as panic rose from within.

"Oh, Uncle Sean, PLEASE put Daddy on the phone! Mommy's not moving."

Caroline's loud howls could be heard from the next room. Uncle Sean calmly repeated.

"Doll, you need to go collect Mrs. Graziano right now. I want you to put the phone down next to your mam and jet next door as fast as you can and ask her to come help your mam. I'll wait here on the line until you return. DON'T HANG UP! Alright, love?"

Val nodded silently, biting her thumbnail, her knees shaking.

"Are you there, Valerie?"

"Yes, Uncle Sean."

"Where is Caroline?"

"She's in the playpen."

"Grand. Leave her there and run and collect Mrs. Graziano. GO!"

Val knew enough not to question and did as she was told. Sean knew it was shock that had caused Grace to collapse, and he hated himself for not handling the situation differently. He wasn't thinking clearly at the moment either. The feeling of utter helplessness was maddening. He was thousands of miles away and couldn't reach out to his nieces, who needed him so desperately at this moment.

Val placed the receiver near her mother's limp hand, and bent over and whispered in her ear.

"I'll be right back, Mommy. Don't worry. I'll get Mrs. Graziano, and she'll help you."

Tears were streaming down her face.

She dashed out the front door and across the yard in the pouring rain. Sheltered under her neighbor's front porch, she simultaneously rang the bell repeatedly and banged on the door as hard as she could, yelling out for her neighbors.

"Mrs. Graziano, Mr. Graziano, are you there? Help! Please, help us! We need help!"

From inside, she heard a voice.

"Coming ... coming. No need to break the door down."

Mr. Graziano opened the door and peered down at her over his glasses.

"Val, what in the world are you doing out in the rain without a jacket on?"

Mrs. Graziano peered out from behind him, wiping her wet hands on her apron.

Without so much as a breath, the words rushed out.

"Mommy was crying really hard and fell on the floor, and Uncle Sean told me to come over and get you to help her."

Stunned, Mrs. Graziano looked at her husband for just a moment before rushing down the hallway and grabbing her raincoat off the hook. Mr. Graziano didn't bother with a coat, bolting out the door ahead of them. Using her coat as an umbrella, Mrs. Graziano shielded Val from the rain as they sloshed back across the yard.

"Oh, my God ..."

Mrs. Graziano gasped as they ran into the kitchen.

"I'll call an ambulance!"

Mr. Graziano knelt to listen to her breathing.

"Grace ... GRACE! Are you okay?"

She was coming to, but was inconsolable. Mr. Graziano sat on the floor holding her, and began rocking her like she was a baby.

"Shhhhh now ... it's going to be okay."

He motioned for his wife to pick up the receiver, still lying on the floor, from which a small male voice was calling, "Hello? Hello?"

Hesitantly, she spoke.

"Hello? Yes, yes, this is Joyce Graziano. To whom am I speaking? Can you please tell me what exactly is going on here? Valerie just came rushing over in a panic and —"

She was stopped in mid-sentence, recognizing the man on the phone as the girls' Uncle Sean from Ireland. He explained the tragic circumstances that led to Grace being on the floor. Mrs. Graziano hurriedly blessed herself three times in a row, and gasped as she brought her hand to her mouth, trying to contain her own shock.

"I see. Yes, of course, of course. We'll stay with them. I understand. I'll wait to hear back from you. Is there anyone I should contact immediately?"

She balanced the phone on her shoulder as she wrung her hands.

"Yes, very well. I'm sure Valerie knows her number ... I'll call her. I'm so sorry to hear about your brother, Mr. Callaghan. Yes, of course, we'll stay here with the children until she arrives. God-bless-you, too. I'll have Sheila call as soon as she gets here. I'm so sorry for your loss. Good-bye."

Slowly she turned and placed the receiver back on the hook. She didn't turn around right away, but stood staring at the wall for a moment. When she did face the group, with tears in her eyes, she managed a weak smile at Val and looked down at her husband, who was still on the floor rocking Grace and whispering soothing words. Her heart broke for her friend and neighbor. He nodded sadly at his wife, interpreting the dire situation without her having to explain.

Not quite knowing what to say, Mrs. Graziano inquired.

"Valerie, do you know your aunt Sheila's telephone number?"

A cry came from the living room. Caroline was letting everyone know that she'd had enough of her isolation.

Val shook her head no, and then remembered that the telephone book was kept in the drawer under the counter.

"It's in here somewhere."

She dug it out and handed it to Mrs. Graziano.

Suddenly, her mother spoke weakly.

"I'll call her."

Mr. Graziano stood and reached for Grace's elbow to help her to her feet. Val dragged a chair over for her. Suddenly, her mother's face looked really old. Her hair was sticking to one side of her tearstained cheek. She had a big red bump on her forehead from where'd she hit the floor. Mrs. Graziano saw the contusion, too, and rummaged through the freezer for some ice to put on it. She also put fresh water in the kettle on the stove to make Grace a cup of tea. Her matronly instincts kicking in, she turned to Val.

"Valerie, can you show me where your mom keeps the blankets? I'll check on the baby, Grace. You sit tight. Is she in the parlor?"

Grace thanked her weakly as she dialed her sister's phone number. There was no answer. Grateful for modern technology, she left a brief message on her sister's new PhoneMate answering machine.

"Please call me."

She hung up.

Val anxiously led Mrs. Graziano down the long hallway to the play-pen, not knowing what else to do or where to go. They found Caroline, sitting quietly for the moment, enthralled with Big Bird. She must have discovered another Lorna Doone cookie hidden in her playpen, as she had crumbs stuck all over her face and in her hair.

Mrs. Graziano chuckled at the adorable, though quite messy child, glad for something to do.

"Oh, gracious! I need to get a face cloth and clean her up."

She called out in the direction of the kitchen.

"I'll get you a blanket, Grace. Keep that ice on your forehead."

Val took her extended hand and directed her upstairs to the linen closet.

Val could hear her mother's voice hiccup, though she couldn't make out what she was saying as she relayed the details of the story to a sympathetic Mr. Graziano, who handed her tissues, and found he needed a few himself. Neil had been a longtime neighbor and friend. He'd miss him terribly.

The phone rang. Mr. Graziano motioned for Grace to sit. He answered it for her.

"It's your sister, Grace."

He handed her the phone, then walked toward the living room to give her some privacy. Standing in the doorway, he looked down at the playpen where Caroline sat, engrossed in the television show.

Grace began to wail again as she broke the news to Sheila, who started crying with her. Tim, her husband, had picked up the extension when he heard his wife's gasp. He sat on the edge of the bed, dumbfounded at the news of his brother-in-law's tragic and senseless death.

Mr. Graziano walked back and put his arm around Grace's shoulder for support. She didn't stay on the phone very long.

"They're on their way now. I'm sorry to upset you like this, Tony."

"Nonsense! That's what friends are for ... good times and bad."

Grace nodded and thanked him. Sheila and Tim would rush to get there as quickly as they could.

Val got a clean face cloth from the linen closet for Caroline and a blanket for her mother. She began to shiver, much from the chill of her wet clothes and the fear of knowing that something terrible had happened to her father, but having no one to tell her exactly what yet. Hearing her teeth chatter, Mrs. Graziano took Val to her room to find some dry clothes.

They took the blanket and face cloth and walked back downstairs. Mrs. Graziano picked up the baby and wiped her messy face and hands, while Val went out into the kitchen and tried to drape the huge blanket around her mother's shoulders as best she could. Mr. Graziano adjusted it and Grace thanked them, though she continued to shake.

Mrs. Graziano entered the kitchen carrying Caroline, who reached out her arms toward Grace and cried.

"No, Mommy do!"

Grace held Caroline in her lap and rocked her. Her eyes closed, and she began to cry again.

"Oh, Neil ... my poor Neil."

Caroline started to get upset, hearing her mother cry. Mrs. Graziano held out her arms for the child.

"Let me take her, Grace. I'll take the girls next door for a while."

Grace nodded.

"I'll make them some lunch and keep them for dinner, too, if you'd like. I'll call you in a couple of hours to see how you're doing. Tony will sit here with you until your sister gets here. Won't you, Tony?"

He nodded.

"Of course."

Grace nodded sadly, whispering, "Thank you." She kissed her girls, who were very reluctant to leave their mother in that condition. She was crying so hard it seemed to Val that she would choke.

Valerie finally let herself be lured away by the tempting offer to help Mrs. Graziano make her famous pizzelles. Val called them snowflake cookies, as that's what they looked like to her. She always made them with her neighbor around the holidays.

Mrs. Graziano hovered.

"You'll need some time to yourself to sort this out, Grace. I'm right next door, if you need anything, okay?"

Grace nodded and thanked her again. Val felt better knowing that her mommy wouldn't be alone.

"Are you girls ready to go and make some cookies?" Mrs. Graziano asked Valerie in as cheerful a tone as she could muster. She winked at Grace, who knew what she was trying to do.

Val nodded enthusiastically.

"Yep!"

Mr. Graziano readjusted the large blanket around Grace's shoulders, as it had started to slip on to the floor.

"Would you like a cup of tea?"

Grace nodded. Mrs. Graziano instructed him on where to find the cups. She hugged Grace before she left with the girls.

"I really am so sorry to hear about your husband, Grace — so very, very sorry."

Then she began to cry, too.

"Do you want us to call Father Moriarty and have him come over?"

Grace was too upset to speak yet, but nodded, yes.

He'd be their rock.

Before they left the house, Mrs. Graziano asked Tony to take the girls into the other room for a moment while she spoke to Grace. She passed Caroline off to him and directed him toward the parlor. Taking his free hand, Val went with him obediently. She glanced back over her shoulder still within hearing range.

Mrs. Graziano spoke in a hushed voice.

"What should I tell Valerie? She senses something is wrong, but I think she's afraid to ask, and I don't know what you've told her."

Grace nodded and brought her fingertips to her temples, like she was trying to rub out a pain or focusing hard to think.

"I need for Sheila to get here first. Then we'll break the news to her. We'll tell her together. I need my sister. I can't do this alone."

She broke down in sobs again. Mrs. Graziano held her hand, comforting her, and passed her another tissue.

"I know, dear. I know. Sheila will be here soon. Hold on."

But Val already knew. She knew something horrible had happened when Uncle Sean wouldn't put her daddy on the phone.

Chapter Six

Chatham, Cape Cod, Massachusetts, Summer 1972

EVEN THOUGH VAL WAS TIRED that night, she couldn't sleep. Cars had been pulling up in front of her house on and off throughout the day. People kept bringing food. Father Bruce Moriarty showed up at nearly the same time as Auntie Sheila and Uncle Tim, which seemed like just minutes after Mrs. Graziano had taken her and Caroline next door.

She watched her house from Mrs. Graziano's kitchen window all afternoon. She waved excitedly to Father Bruce when he spotted her at the window. He waved back before bounding up the front steps behind Auntie Sheila. The screen door slammed shut as it always did when it was let go.

Father was a regular guest at the Callaghan's home, and it was natural for him to be there. He was very close to the family and even had his own key to their house. Neil had asked him on several occasions if he wouldn't mind checking in on the house and cat when they'd gone to Ireland.

"Hang on to it. I trust you."

Her father would often joke with him.

Now, he held Grace tightly while she cried and clutched desperately at his shirt, trying to draw strength from him and the God they both served.

Mrs. Graziano brought the girls back home around eight o'clock that evening, after feeding them dinner and giving them baths so that they could slip right off to bed.

Father Bruce, visibly shaken, didn't leave the house until very late that night, and promised to return early the next morning. Before he left, he went upstairs to pray over Valerie and Caroline while they slept.

Val pretended to be asleep as she listened to him. He laid his warm hand on her head and whispered his prayers of comfort and peace to God, then leaned over and gently kissed her forehead before leaving the room, quietly closing the door behind him.

Val bounded out of bed and knelt at the window. Peeking out from behind the lace curtains, she watched him get into his car and drive away.

Slowly, she unclenched the delicate material she'd been gripping in her hand, and admired the intricate pattern, remembering a particular trip to Ireland when her mother and father took her to visit a convent in Kenmare, County Kerry, and her mother had bought the lace to make these curtains.

*   *   *

Grace gently examined the elegant tracery she held in her hands. Neil, chin in hand, leaned on his elbow watching her. He listened intently to his wife, ever the teacher, while she briefly explained the history of lace making to Valerie.

"Lace was originally called crochet in Ireland, Valerie. It was first introduced into an Ursuline Convent in County Cork during the great famine of the 1840's. During that dreadful time in Irish history, people recognized its value as an industry, and the nuns opened schools and taught young women how to crochet — that's what they called it back then. It was a valuable skill. If a girl knew how to crochet, she could earn money to help her family buy food. After the famine, it became an actual subject studied in convent schools. Because lace-making brought financial relief for many during a difficult time, lace was viewed as a symbol of hope and pride to the Irish."

Grace couldn't make up her mind about which pattern to buy. All the designs were equally beautiful; trying to choose just one was impossible.

Val admired them all, too. They finally settled on three patterns. Neil watched his wife, amused, as she fumbled through her purse.

"I can't find my note with the window measurements on it! I'm going to have to guess at this."

Neil eyed the size of the bolts and did some quick figuring in his head. Val sat in a chair and watched quietly as the employees brought out the large bolts of material, spreading it over the wide counter. Neil asked for a pencil and a piece of paper and calculated rough measurements for the cutter.

"Do you think I'll have enough, Neil?"

Grace asked doubtfully.

"No worries, love. I'll be surprised if the plane lifts off the ground."

"Well, good!"

She smiled and kissed her husband, knowing he'd factor in extra material.

After it was packaged up, Neil had to lug it all to the car and back to Granny's house, where she and Aunt Siobhan ooh'd and ahh'd over it while they were having afternoon tea.

"There's nothing like genuine Irish lace to adorn a home."

Granny stated.

She offered to have someone local make the curtains and have them shipped over to the States. Grace thanked her, but she was eager to take the material home and have the curtains made there.

*   *   *

Val tossed and turned in her bed, awaking very early in the morning. It was quiet inside her home, and she heard the rain falling gently on the roof. The weather seemed fitting for the mood that hung over their house.

Grace had yet to tell her face-to-face of her father's passing, yet she knew that was what had happened. She got up and went into the bathroom to take care of business and brush her teeth. When she opened the door to the closet to get the toothpaste, she caught the scent of her daddy's Old Spice cologne.

"I'm sorry for your loss, Mrs. Callaghan ... so very, very sorry."

Val recalled Mrs. Graziano's words from yesterday. She reached for the familiar bottle and held it closely, crying quietly to herself, realizing that he'd never wear it again.

Clutching the small white bottle, Val shuffled out into the hall and sat down on the floor just outside her mother's door. She'd wait for her to wake up. Soon, however, she lost control of her tears and began to bawl uncontrollably.

When her mother heard her, she jumped out of bed and opened the door. Hearing the commotion, Auntie Sheila quickly opened her door as well. Tightening her robe's belt about her waist, she scooped up Val and brought her into Grace's room, setting her down on the bed. Seeing Val clutching the familiar bottle in her shaking hands, Grace closed her puffy eyes and held her daughter close.

"Honey, I'm so sorry. I don't know how to talk to you about this ... about Daddy, I mean. Do you know what I mean?"

Tears streamed down Val's face and she shook her head no because she really didn't know why her mother hadn't talked to her about it yet. Grace held her daughter's head gently on her chest and stroked her hair as she recalled a story.

"Do you remember the time you had a tea party and decided to invite God to join you?"

Val thought that a strange question to ask at this time, but she nodded and looked up at her mother.

"Do you remember what you told Daddy when he came into the room and asked why it was that he couldn't see God?"

Val shook her head no. She couldn't remember anything, it seemed.

"You told him that, even though he couldn't see God sitting in the chair, He was still there. Do you remember now?"

Blinking back tears, Val nodded. Grace placed her hand on her daughter's heart.

"You told Daddy that God was right here, in your heart."

With that gesture, Val recalled his smile.

"Your daddy, sweetheart, has gone to be with God, but he will always be in our hearts because that's where we hold all of our love for him."

As she held Val close to her, all three of them broke down crying. Val had known he was gone, but she had needed her mother to tell her. She didn't ask how or why. It didn't matter.

It was one of life's darkest hours for their family, and it seemed that nothing in life could ever break their hearts so completely again.

* * *

Later, Val was sitting at the top of the stairs when she overheard her mother.

"I wish Ma were here."

Auntie Sheila's arms steadied Grace's shaking shoulders. It was the first time she'd ever heard her mother ask for her own mother.

Val didn't remember Nana Sullivan very well. She had died suddenly from a heart attack when she was only three. Her husband had passed away a year after Val's parents' first wedding anniversary.

There were beautiful pictures of her grandparents in her parents' wedding album and a tender photo of her grandfather in a gold frame in the living room. It showed a military man, about six foot two, his fine, short hair almost completely silver then, with a few traces of blond hair still visible. Val thought he looked very intelligent. His blue eyes twinkled as he beamed with pride on his youngest daughter's day of celebration. He commanded respect in his decorated Air Force uniform. No one ever questioned Grace when she asked him to wear his uniform instead of a tuxedo on her wedding day. She thought it made him look so handsome. He was.

Nana Sullivan never had to work outside the home. Her husband, a high-ranking official, made a comfortable living in the United States Air Force. They'd moved frequently over the course of his career, during which he rose to the rank of Colonel.

Grace had felt it a privilege to have the opportunity to live on bases in such interesting places as Riyadh, Saudi Arabia and later, Heidelberg, Germany. She was well accustomed to life on military bases; which is why she was so good at "going with the flow." It was her way of life growing up. She regarded her father's life of military service as noteworthy.

When asked why he continued his career in the Air Force, instead of retiring like so many others to pursue a lucrative career as a domestic airline pilot, her father would simply say he believed that, in this world, there were still some things worth fighting and dying for and his country was one of them. It earned him the respect of many, including a granddaughter he'd never know.

* * *

As the elder sister and coordinator extraordinaire, Auntie Sheila took over command in the Callaghan home during the devastating time following Neil's death. She and Uncle Tim had moved in temporarily to help out. The house was large and had no problem accommodating two more people.

Grace knew that Neil would want to be buried near his home in Ireland, and she made plans for Father Bruce Moriarty to perform a memorial service back in the States upon their return. Auntie Sheila took to answering the many phone calls coming in. She was in daily contact with Uncle Sean, coordinating the flights and burial arrangements.

Granny was kept busy reserving a hall for after the funeral, arranging catering, limousine transportation, and flowers for the service and cemetery. On the important matters, she consulted with Grace, who did make one request of Neil's parents in Ireland: that her husband be waked at a funeral parlor, and not laid out in the family living room as was the custom. She asked them to excuse her American culture and mindset; she just couldn't help but feel that if the children saw their father for the last time in those familiar surroundings, it might stick in their minds negatively and make them not want to visit their grandparents in the future. Truth be told, however, there wasn't anything that would have kept them away from their Granny and Granda for very long.

Grace wanted her husband presented in a suit that she'd bought for him during a recent trip they'd taken to New York, on their last anniversary. It was an Armani, and he had looked so handsome in it. He'd worn it that evening to the play, Miss Saigon, and Grace was so proud that he was her husband.

Chapter Seven

THE FIVE BLEARY-EYED FAMILY MEMBERS boarded the evening flight to Ireland the following Monday. The wake or "rosary and removal" as they'd say in Ireland, would be held on Thursday and Friday, with the funeral Mass and burial set for Saturday morning out of St. Peter's and Paul's Catholic Church in Ennis.

As the plane approached Shannon Airport early that morning, Val sat up and peered out the tiny sun-drenched window. She ordinarily loved the familiar view of the River Shannon and its rugged coastline, but this time her heart had a heavy feeling. It had been a long, quiet flight.

Neil's family met the somber group at the gate. Granda was the first to come forward with outstretched arms for Grace, who was holding a just-waking Caroline. He enveloped them in his strong arms, and both adults shook with grief. Granny then joined them, as Grace handed Caroline, who was getting upset, over to Aunt Siobhan.

Holding the fussy toddler, Aunt Siobhan bent to give Val a kiss, as silent tears streamed down her face. She was dressed in jeans and her layered, chin-length brown hair hung in a casual bob. Her eyes were puffy, but she still reminded Val of a china doll, with her creamy complexion and grayish-blue eyes. Her dark hair contrasted starkly with her fair skin. She rarely used makeup, as she was blessed with thick lashes that were naturally long and curled at the tips. Her current job as a nurse in the Pediatric Burn Unit of St. Clements Hospital had helped her develop nerves of steel, and she'd become a champion of children. She always made time for her nieces, calling them frequently, which made Val feel very special. She made trips to Cape Cod as often as she could. Very close to her brother, Neil, she had also become a dear friend to Grace and Sheila.

Uncle Sean offered to take Caroline from Aunt Siobhan, who reluctantly handed her over, so he could smother her face with kisses. Caroline reveled in the attention, and stopped fussing. Auntie Sheila and Uncle Tim offered to go and wait for the luggage in order to give the family some time with each other.

Uncle Sean, his eyes noticeably swollen, spoke to Val.

"How are you holding up, love?"

"I dunno."

Val shrugged honestly and looked around. She felt uncomfortable, like she'd forgotten something.

Caroline was fully awake and began to cry for her mother. Grace lifted her from Sean and gave him a kiss on the cheek at the same time. He put his arm around his sister-in-law, and they all headed down the long corridor toward Baggage Claim and the car that Granda had waiting to take them all back to the house.

They arrived at Granny and Granda's home tired and drawn. The delicious smell of fresh bacon and soda bread wafted through the hallway. One of Granny's helpers brought the suitcases upstairs.

Caroline and Val shared a large, well-lit bedroom, which was beautifully decorated in various shades of pink and cream. Little dolls sat propped up on miniature white chairs around a matching table that held a child's tea set. Cherished stuffed animals, which had been dragged over from the States, sat on Val's bed and in Caroline's crib, untouched since the last visit. Val's old, redheaded doll - Mrs. Beasley, whose hair she had cut off the year before, was still sitting where she'd been left — on top of the hand-painted Periwinkle's toy box.

Caroline's crib was done up with a tiny cream satin pillow, which she would throw out of the crib, and a shiny comforter to match. Val looked out the tall windows, all locked, that stretched from the floor to the ceiling, and thought to herself how comfortable she felt here, considering it her second home.

Neil's childhood bedroom was right next door with a bathroom connecting it to the girls'. The doors were always left open at night, so someone could hear the children if they awoke.

Grace and Neil shared his old room when they came to visit. It was very spacious, and had a huge mahogany canopy bed, a gift from Pat and Ruth for their wedding. Steps were needed to climb up into it. The heavy bedspread matched the drawn curtains. A beautifully carved armoire and matching secretary stood at opposite ends of the room. A lady's dressing table and chair had been added for Grace on her thirtieth birthday, a gift from Siobhan and Sean. Neil had gotten her a lovely silver brush and comb set which he saw her admiring at a local jewelry store. They were set on her dressing table, adding a feminine touch to an otherwise masculine room. During the winter, the fireplace would cast a blaze of warmth and soft light. Occasionally, the whole family would sleep in the large bed, with Grace on one side and Neil on the other, sandwiching the girls in. If one of them had fallen out of that bed, she could have broken her neck!

After breakfast, Val went and sat in the living room, with her shoes off and feet tucked up under her on the couch. She rested against Uncle Sean's shoulder and gazed idly into the crackling fire, yawning. Even though it was summer, Granny loved a crackling fire — any time of day.

"It gets rid of the damp."

She insisted.

The two uncles talked on about politics in the States, Nixon's trip to China, and the whole mess that was becoming known as "Watergate."

Closing her eyes, Val listened while Uncle Sean spoke, and imagined it was her daddy talking; they sounded so much alike. For just a moment, she allowed herself to pretend it was him, and that it was his shoulder she was leaning on, and that everything was as it was before.

Grace entered the room with Granny and Granda, followed by Aunt Siobhan. Auntie Sheila had gone up to take a bath, relax, and unwind. Uncle Tim mentioned that he'd like to go for a short walk and excused himself from the parlor. None of the adults were particularly hungry.

Val opted for soda bread with jam. Caroline, of course, wanted what her big sister was eating, so they shared bites. The conversation turned to the upcoming activities of the next few days.

"Will you have Valerie attend the wake?"

Granny looked concerned, but smiled weakly.

Trying to stifle an escaping yawn with her hand, Grace looked at her daughters sadly.

"Yes, Valerie will, at least, in part. She'll need it for closure, I think."

Granny nodded and delicately brought her handkerchief to her nose. Granda leaned forward on the couch; entwining his fingers, he addressed his daughter-in-law compassionately.

"You're welcome to stay here as long as you like, Grace. This is your home, and the girls'. I want you to know that. You're like our own daughter, and that will never change, aye?"

His voice cracked.

Grace smiled gratefully and nodded.

"I know, Pat. Thanks."

"We've asked Mary O'Brien's daughter, Glynnis, to help with Caroline and Valerie over the next few days. She's a love, that one. I'm sure she'll get along famously with the girls ... helping where she can. She's an only child, you know, but good with wee ones."

Granny gestured vaguely. She seemed so unsure of herself. It was hard for them to see her like this. She was a strong woman who generally "ruled the roost," but losing a child is heart wrenching for even the most steadfast of women.

Val yawned again, and Caroline quickly took a bite of bread out of her hand and got it all over her face. Scrunching up her nose, she made the funniest face, which made all of them laugh.

"Ahh, children. God-bless-them."

Granny would always follow a "God Bless" by making the sign of the cross on herself.

"Yes."

Granda agreed, smiling and lifting Caroline onto his lap. She offered him some of her soda bread, and he took a big bite, which made her grin. It was a much-needed spirit lifter, at which Aunt Siobhan made an announcement.

"All right, young lassies, time for a bath and off you go for a nap. C'mon."

She hoisted Caroline up onto her hip.

"I'll see to them, Grace. You sit with Mam and talk. I'll read them a story."

Grace thanked her, and the girls went around the room giving everyone kisses. Val trudged up the wide staircase behind her aunt and sister. She tripped going up the stairs and banged her shin.

"OUCH!"

Val rubbed her leg.

"Are you alright there, love?"

Aunt Siobhan reached back to help her up.

"You best be watching where you're going."

Aunt Siobhan ran the bath, adding in extra bubbles. It was an old-fashioned, freestanding, deep white tub with feet on the bottom. The silver faucet knobs looked like pinwheels with small, rounded balls on the end. They squeaked when you turned them.

Aunt Siobhan was getting Caroline undressed as Val sifted through her dresser drawers looking for a nightgown. Their clothes had already been taken out and put away and the dresses were neatly hung up in the closet.

Val ran into the bathroom, nude as a goose, and hopped into the tub. When she heard the door to her daddy's room open, she thought her mother was coming in to help. She was startled to look up and see her Uncle Tim standing in the doorway.

He looked surprised, too, but his gaze was steady. Val felt her face flush red, and quickly ducked under the cover of the bubbles. Uncle Tim remained in the doorway, his unblinking eyes penetrating as he seemed to stare right through his niece.

"What are you doing in Daddy's room, Uncle Tim?"

She thought it curious, him being there. Quickly coming to his senses, he turned around and mumbled as he exited.

"I'm so tired. I took a left at the top of the stairs and followed the voices down the hall to this room."

Understanding that he just took a wrong turn, Val called after him.

"That's okay, Uncle Tim. It's a really big house! Your room is down the other end of the hall."

She turned her head quickly when she heard Aunt Siobhan's voice.

"And who are you talking to, Val Jean?"

"Uncle Tim. He lost his way and came in the wrong room."

Aunt Siobhan gave Val a funny look as she went over to close the door to her brother's room.

"You're getting too old for anyone to be seeing you, love. You're not a little girl anymore. Make sure to close the door behind you. Modesty is everything in life, you know."

Her reminder was given gently.

"I know, I know — jeepers! You and Mom sound so much alike."

Val rolled her eyes, and Siobhan chuckled.

Lying on Val's bed, Aunt Siobhan cuddled her and Caroline and began to read to them from, A Handful of Love. It was one of Val's favorite stories, about a young bear cub that was leaving his mother to go to school, and how nervous and sad he was. His mom asked him to put out his paw.

She kissed the inside of it, and then gently curled his little claws around her kiss so that he could take it with him wherever he went.

It didn't take very long for Caroline to fall asleep in her aunt's arms. Siobhan tenderly lifted her up, kissed her chubby cheeks several times, and placed her lovingly down in the crib. She tried to pull up the crib rail quietly, but it made a hideous screeching and clanking noise. Val could hear her muttering to herself.

"Oh, for the love of God, this bloody crib!"

Caroline stirred for a moment but didn't wake up. Her aunt walked over and drew the heavy curtains closed, shutting out any seeping sunlight.

Val's eyes were already closing. She yawned loudly. Aunt Siobhan chuckled and went over to kiss her on the cheek.

"Shhhh, love. Take a nice nap, and I'll wake you in a few hours."

She turned on the nightlight and quietly closed the door behind her, deliberately leaving the bathroom doors between the two rooms open, so Grace could hear them if need be.

Chapter Eight

Ennis, County Clare, Ireland, Summer 1972

THE NEXT FEW DAYS WERE filled with preparations for the impending wake and funeral. Sheila went with Siobhan to help pick out flowers for the church altar, and for the cemetery. Granny was on and off the phone all day with friends, and the caterers, trying to estimate a head count for the gathering after the service.

Because Neil had always loved the sound of the harp and tin whistle, Sean, a talented flautist, was mustering up the courage to play at his brother's service. He was also on a quest to find a talented harp player.

"Ahhh, Lord-above, Da, how am I ever going to get through it?"

Pat put his hand on his youngest son's shoulder.

"Aye, indeed, it'll be rough. We'll light an extra candle before the Mass for strength."

Sean didn't know if Grace would feel up to playing the piano along with him, like they'd done on occasions in the past, or whether Val would want to play something on the violin, knowing how much her daddy had loved to hear her. He would ask them tonight. They'd performed together at various family functions and church events in the past, though for much happier times, to be sure. Uncle Sean remembered one of those events vividly.

* * *

Val showed great promise as a young violinist; she got her musical talent from her mother. As a young girl, Grace had learned to play the piano when her father was stationed in Germany. She'd studied under one of Heidelberg's finest teachers, Enrich Moeller, a critically acclaimed German pianist and much-sought-after instructor.

Valerie, however, took to the music of the fiddle. As a toddler, she couldn't stand still when she heard one playing. She'd jump around and clap her hands at many of the Irish festivals, delighting onlookers with her unabashed exuberance.

When Val was five, Neil bought her a practice violin, enthusiastically encouraging her to play. Grace approached one of her fellow ensemble members, Malcolm Wendelson, to see if he'd be willing to take her daughter on as a student. Malcolm welcomed the opportunity and was a patient instructor. Val, an eager student, picked up the technique quickly, and would practice for hours on end without having to be reminded.

Neil enjoyed clapping along, even when she was just practicing scales! When Val scratched out the first recognizable strains of "Twinkle, Twinkle, Little Star," at age five, he cheered for her. Only a few short months ago, he sat proudly in the school auditorium, his eyes closed, listening intently as she masterfully performed the music from Pachelbel. The crowd cheered her first flawless solo performance, having heard that she'd been chosen as one of the youngest members of the Chatham Bar Ensemble.

Grace beamed with pride and mouthed, "Thank you," across the crowded auditorium to Malcolm, who couldn't stop beaming himself at his star pupil. Father Bruce Moriarty led the standing ovation.

Sean was uncertain whether he should even bring up the question of asking her to play.

*   *   *

On Wednesday, Father Donnelly, Senior Pastor of St. Peter's and Paul's Catholic Church, stopped to check in on the grieving family to see how they were all holding up. He gave Grace a big hug. At Granny's urging, he stayed for lunch, and they talked over tea. He made some suggestions for biblical readings that could be recited at Neil's funeral Mass.

Pat, who earlier admitted to Grace that he'd not been to confession since he was about twelve, decided that it would be a good time to take Caroline and Val for a walk. Seeing them in their matching shorts sets, he smiled and asked Granny where he'd put his camera. She went into his office and found it quickly.

The afternoon was very warm and hazy. Granda was having the hardest time deciding whether to drive eastward toward Feakle, or stay local and venture over to Ballyallia Lake. Because it was so hot, Val would have chosen the lake without even thinking about it, but Granda finally settled on Feakle, thinking it would be nice to get away for a few hours and snap a couple of Polaroids of his granddaughters tromping through the heathery hills.

When Val was older, she'd laugh when she thought of the name of that tiny village, Feakle. Its name would certainly conjure up a different image "across the pond." But she thought it a lovely place, and would make it a point to visit on occasion when, later in life, she went to visit her grandparents.

Scouring the landscape, Val picked an occasional blossom to take back to her mother and Granny. She and Granda had to keep an eye on Caroline so that she wouldn't try to put the flowers in her mouth. Granda chuckled.

"I believe she thinks she's one of the sheep!"

"Or she stepped on some Hungry Grass."

Val smirked.

* * *

As it had been explained to Val, Hungry Grass was cursed grass that made anyone who stepped on it become terribly famished. It was an

Irish legend that came from the time of the Great Famine, when so many people died of hunger. Some believed that Hungry Grass grew over the unmarked graves of the destitute and ill who were too weak to carry on and were left to die where they lay across the land.

* * *

Running over to a small daisy that caught her attention, Caroline snatched it up and walked back toward Granda. Reaching up, she handed it to him as he snapped her picture. He bent and gave her an enthusiastic, "Thank you, love!" and a kiss. She giggled and ran away when he pretended to go after her for another.

Granda took Val's small hand in his as they followed Caroline. They walked without speaking he being deep in his thoughts. Val looked up at him at one point and saw a tear trickling down his cheek. He held his gaze steady and straight ahead, his eyes shielded from the sun by his cap. Val thought he might be thinking of her father, and how he should be the one walking these hills with his two daughters ... but now, her Granda would have to walk for Daddy.

As she looked around at the beauty of the land, she somehow knew it was a tender moment in life, one that should be treasured, one that she wished she could bottle up and keep forever.

When they got back to the house, Auntie Sheila took Granda aside.

"Have you seen Tim around anywhere, Pat?"

Granda shook his head no.

"With all that's been going on, I've hardly seen him since he arrived. Sorry, love. Are you needing anything?"

There was the slightest note of aggravation in his voice, due mostly to Tim's distant demeanor. Granda and the others often wondered aloud, but out of earshot from Sheila and Tim, what she saw in him.

Sheila reassured him.

"No, no, everything's okay. You know Tim, he feels like a third wheel sometimes and just thinks it's better to stay out of everyone's way and let people do what they need to do. He's probably just gone off for another walk."

Shrugging, she turned and headed back toward the kitchen. She hadn't stopped since she got the news of her brother-in-law's death. How could she? She had to be strong for her sister.

"A lot of nervous energy you've got there, Sheila ..."

Her mother used to observe as she set about a task.

As with everything Sheila did, she plunged right in and was a tremendous help to everyone. Granda muttered something under his breath that only Granny heard.

"That slacker of a husband of hers. So help me ..."

He mumbled.

To them, Uncle Tim was a loner and didn't appear to be highly motivated. He also wasn't interested in any sport, except hockey, which didn't endear him at all to the men folk. He rarely joined the other men in conversations about soccer or politics.

Sheila and Siobhan had hit it off well right from the beginning, and enjoyed catching up whenever they'd get together. Granda and Granny really loved Sheila and often remarked at how wonderfully she and Grace got along. They hoped Caroline and Val would, in time, become just as close, in spite of their age difference.

Neil's family just didn't care for, or try to understand, Tim. They weren't rude to him; they tolerated him for Sheila and Grace's sake.

One time, Val overheard Granny tell her father that Tim gave her "the willies."

"A pity he and Sheila never had any children of their own."

She'd said sympathetically one day thinking of poor Sheila.

"He's an odd one that one. Maybe it's just as well."

They snickered quietly, knowing they really shouldn't laugh at all.

"He's really not a bad guy once you get to know him."
Neil offered on Tim's behalf.
"Really, Mam, we shouldn't be talking about him like this."
"You're right, son, God-forgive-me."
She then blessed herself.

*   *   *

After lunch on Thursday, the first day of the wake, Grace went up to the girls' room and searched the large closet for the floral dress Val would wear to the afternoon service at the funeral home. It would be the only service she'd attend until the funeral Mass at church on Saturday. She would stay for a short time and then be taken back to the house to spend the rest of the day with Caroline and Glynnis, the babysitter, who was not that much older than Val.

The family had been debating about whether it was a good idea for her to go and see her father laid out like that. Auntie Sheila thought it might emotionally scar her for life. Uncle Tim, of course, agreed with her. Aunt Siobhan assured them that it shouldn't affect her negatively, so long as it was properly and lovingly handled. She had all the faith in the world in Grace's ability to explain things to her daughter and would be with them for moral support.

Glynnis O'Brien arrived just after noon to watch Caroline, while everyone was hurrying about getting ready for the first service. The wake would last two days with viewings from two to four o'clock, and then again from seven to nine.

Glynnis, a rather petite girl of eleven, had her straight, chestnut-brown hair held back with a headband. Her bright blue eyes sparkled with enthusiasm for her first babysitting role.

Grace called out from her bedroom.

"Valerie, honey?"

Standing in the next bedroom in her stocking feet and new dress, Val was pouring pretend tea for her dolls, Caroline, and their new sitter. Caroline threw her cup on the floor when she saw there was nothing in it. She didn't get "pretend" yet.

Their mother entered the room, wearing tall heels and a black dress adorned with the white pearls that their father had given her as an anniversary present.

"Did you find your shoes yet?"

Val shook her head and went on with her tea party.

"I know I packed them!"

She sounded exasperated and turned the light on in the closet to search again. Glynnis stood up.

"I'll help you find them, Mrs. Callaghan."

She crawled into the closet.

"OH ... here they are!"

She exclaimed, holding them up triumphantly.

"Thank you, Glynnis. You're a lifesaver! Here, Valerie, put them on quickly, sweetie. We've got to get going in a few minutes."

Glynnis offered to help Val put them on. When she adjusted the buckle a little too tightly, the nine-year-old winced.

"Ouch!"

Startled, and wanting to do everything just right, Glynnis quickly undid the buckle.

"Oh, I'm sorry. I'll fix it."

She assured Val.

Grace smiled at her gratefully and went back to her room to finish getting ready.

The family could have walked to the funeral parlor, as it was right around the corner from the house, and not far from the church, but they all piled into several waiting limousines instead. One of Grace's hands was being clenched by her daughter, and in the other, instead of her usual large pocketbook, she carried a small purse that held her tissues, gum, and a small pillbox containing a few aspirin. She sat and stared sadly out the window while Val leaned against her.

A small crowd had gathered outside their home when they saw the limos, anticipating a happier occasion. When Ruth, wearing all black, descended the stairs with Pat holding one arm and Sean the other, caps were removed, heads bowed, and women blessed themselves realizing that this was a family in mourning.

Turning, Grace rested her cheek on the top of Val's head.

"Valerie, when we go in, Daddy will be there."

Val's heart jumped! Seeing her look of excitement, Grace hurried to explain.

"But, honey, he can't talk to you. His body will be there, and he'll look like he's just sleeping. But he's really with God in heaven now and he can't talk."

Val didn't understand. Grace was second-guessing whether it had been a good idea to let her come after all. Aunt Siobhan quietly sniffled and offered her a reassuring look, encouraging her to go on.

Taking hold of Val's other hand, Grace tried to explain further.

"Do you remember that hermit crab you once had ... Sebastian?"

Val looked up at her and nodded.

"Remember how he had to carry his house around with him wherever he went? On his back?"

She nodded again and spoke.

"Yes, I remember, and when he died, he crawled out of his shell. I still have it in my room at home!"

Grace nodded and continued on.

"That's exactly right, hon. Our bodies are like that shell. When we die, our bodies are left, kind of like Sebastian's shell, but our spirit, that which makes us talk and laugh and gives us life, goes on to heaven to be with God forever. We'll all be together again one day. God promised us that."

66

Val was first struck by the strong smell of flowers as she walked into the funeral home. A sign displaying the deceased's name faced them as they entered, and several men in black suits, with sympathetic faces, held the door for the family and directed them into a dimly lit, pale-pink room engulfed with sprawling floral arrangements. Religious hymns played softly in the background.

Grace held her breath and shook slightly when she first saw her husband in that state. Uncle Sean rushed to her other side and held her arm. Val's heart leapt again, and she wanted to run to be near her father. Instead, knowing that something was very different about him, she walked slowly; looking up frequently at her mother for reassurance that everything was going to be okay and gripping her sweaty hand.

Honoring Neil's wife, Granny, Granda, Aunt Siobhan, Auntie Sheila and Uncle Tim stepped back to let Grace and Valerie spend time alone with him first. Grace stifled a sob as it rose in her throat, and tears filled Val's eyes when she heard her mother's muffled grief. She knelt next to her mother, and watched as she shakily placed her delicate hand atop her father's motionless hands, which were crossed on his stomach and entwined with rosary beads.

Her mother cried softly, her shoulders shaking, and then blessed herself. Val wanted to touch him, too. Uncle Sean stood close beside them, feet slightly apart, arms crossed in front, with his head slightly bent, staring over at his beloved brother. There was only enough room for two people on the kneeler.

"Mommy ..." Val whispered. "Can I touch his hand?"

Grace looked at her daughter through watery eyes, unsure at first, and then nodded slowly, managing a weak smile. Standing up on the kneeler cushion, Val reached over and placed her hand on his, as she'd seen her mother do.

"I think he's cold, Mom."

Grace couldn't speak and just stared. Val, also, looked at him for the longest time. She wanted to nudge him and tell him to wake up.

Looking at his large hands, she thought of the story Aunt Siobhan had read them the other day, A Handful of Love. She leaned further over the casket, leaving one foot dangling behind, and gently kissed her father's still hand. At first, her mother didn't understand what she was doing.

"Now you can take my kisses with you wherever you go, Daddy, and never be afraid because I'll always be with you."

Her mother swallowed hard several times, trying to gulp down a sob. Val stepped down slowly from the kneeler and began to cry for the first time since she'd come to Ireland. Aunt Siobhan dissolved into a flood of tears, as did the rest of the family at that point.

Granny buried her head in Granda's shoulder while Sean, collapsing onto his knees in front of his brother, held his head in his hands. Auntie Sheila went over and held Val close. She realized then that this would be the last time she'd see her daddy's handsome face, and that this was their final good-bye.

Seeing her sister so upset, and then her niece, Auntie Sheila struggled to maintain control. It was almost too much to bear. She asked Uncle Tim if he'd take Val back to the house. He could return for the rest of the service later. Val held on to her mother in a long hug, giving her a kiss before following Uncle Tim out to the car. She was still sniffling when he offered her one of his handkerchiefs. He opened the car door for her and she slid in. They drove back in silence.

At the house, Tim got out of the car quickly and went around to open the door for his niece. Glynnis opened the front door, struggling to hold a thrashing Caroline in her arms.

"Vl-rie!" she tried to say happily through a mouth filled with soda bread and jam. Val smiled at her, and gave her a little hug as she went by to go upstairs and change. She felt very odd leaving her daddy behind like that. She was sad for her mother, too.

When she went back downstairs, she asked her uncle Tim where Caroline and Glynnis were. He motioned silently with his thumb over his shoulder toward the backyard. Then he nervously lit up a cigarette, and began pacing in the hallway. Granny hated smoking in her house, and didn't normally allow it, but made an exception for company.

"Granny will yell at you if she sees you smoking. She doesn't like it." Val reminded him.

He opened the front door and flicked the cigarette out onto the sidewalk.

"Well, Granny's not here now, is she? And we won't tell her ... will we?"

Val smiled mischievously, feeling a part of his secret.

"Nope! We won't."

He smirked.

"Good girl."

She walked toward the back and out into the garden.

The garden was not very wide, but it was long. A small shed stood at the back, and a variety of colorful roses and assorted flowers lined the sides. The soft, perfectly manicured lawn was ideal for playing on. Granda had even built a small sandbox for his granddaughters.

Glynnis was blowing bubbles for the girls to chase when Uncle Tim called her to come inside and help him with the soda pop. A cold drink sounded heavenly being that it was so warm outside. Grace didn't normally allow the girls to have fizzy drinks, preferring that they have juice or water. Uncle Tim always let them have what they wanted, and saw no harm in a little soda now and then.

"Would you mind keeping an eye on your sister for a minute, Valerie?"

"Sure thing."

Glynnis happily bounced off in the direction of the house, once again eager to help.

Val sat on the grass in the "play" dress that her mother had laid out for her to change into. Caroline was clumsily trying to capture the bubbles Val blew, and laughed wildly at each failed effort, especially when she got sprayed with the slimy bubble soap. She nearly fell over with the giggles causing Val to chuckle right along with her. There was something about her laughter that could do that. It was contagious.

She ran over toward the sandbox and Val capped the bubbles and followed her. Val still loved playing in the sandbox, and Granny had provided them with all sorts of toys with which to build their imaginary worlds.

Caroline soon grew bored and made her way toward the back of the yard. She discovered Granny's watering can near the shed, and proceeded to pour the remaining contents all over her shoes. Val yelled for Glynnis, but got no answer. She'd been inside for a while, helping Uncle Tim with the drinks, and Val began to wonder what was taking them so long. It was really hot. She latched on to Caroline's hand and brought her into the kitchen, where she took off her wet socks and shoes and let her run around barefoot. Val saw no sign of Glynnis or Uncle Tim. The house staff was still attending the wake.

"Glynnis! I need your help! Caroline's socks are wet!"

There was no response.

"Wet, wet."

Caroline mimicked.

Val looked at her, amused. Being that she was only two, Caroline was really talking well.

"Yes, WET! WET!"

She made a yucky face. Val figured Glynnis must be in the bathroom, so she took Caroline upstairs herself to find some dry socks.

On the way back downstairs, Val stopped on the landing and noticed Glynnis sitting, very still and quiet, on the couch in the study. The glass doors were closed, and she just sat, staring straight ahead, her hands clutching tightly to the hem of her skirt as if to stop a strong wind from blowing it up. Val opened the door, and Caroline ran in and jumped up on the couch next to her.

"What are you doing in here all by yourself?"

Val asked.

Glynnis turned slowly and looked at her blankly before turning away again. Tears formed in her eyes, and she stared down at her feet, saying nothing.

"Do you want to get a drink now?"

She shook her head no. Val looked around.

"Where's Uncle Tim?"

Her head shot up startled.

"I-I ... dunno ... but I want to go home now."

"But you can't go home! Who will watch us?"

She turned away and sniffled.

"What's wrong, Glynnis?"

Val was curious.

"Nothing."

She replied quickly.

"C'mon. Let's get a drink then and go outside. It's too hot in here."

Val took Caroline's hand and led her out into the kitchen again.

Glynnis got up slowly from the couch, drawing her pastel skirt tightly about her, still clutching at the hem. She followed the girls into the kitchen, and then walked straight out the back door into the garden, without taking her drink. Val ended up juggling the cups for all of them. Glynnis sat down again, silently staring at nothing, as Caroline and Val went back to chasing bubbles.

When people started arriving back at the house, Glynnis didn't move from her lawn chair until Aunt Siobhan, looking very tired and drawn, went out back and asked her how the afternoon had gone.

"Please, may I go home now? I don't feel very well."

Glynnis's lip quivered.

"Oh, no, child, I hope you're not coming down with something."

Aunt Siobhan gently touched the girl's forehead.

Glynnis pulled back and began to cry.

"My heavens, Glynnis. Did the girls give you any trouble, now?"

Shaking her head no and wiping her eyes, Glynnis finally let go of the hem of her skirt for the first time in hours, revealing sharp wrinkles in the material.

"Well then, missus, let's be getting you home then. Girls, say 'thank you' to Glynnis."

Aunt Siobhan looked perplexed, hoping that nothing had happened which would cause the child not to want to babysit again. She knew her nieces to be very well behaved. It was hard to tell what was bothering Glynnis.

Aunt Siobhan put her arm around Glynnis's shoulder and walked with her up the long garden path that ran alongside the house. Glynnis told her she didn't want to go inside, to cut through. Sadly, she glanced back at her charges. The girls waved good-bye and yelled out, "Thank you!" again.

She turned away without a response, and didn't look back.

Chapter Nine

Ennis, County Clare, Ireland, Summer 1972

GRACE AND THE GIRLS STAYED with Granny and Granda for another week after Neil was buried. The adults had decided it would be okay for both of the girls to attend the funeral; Valerie was old enough to be a part of what was going on, and Caroline was too young to understand anyway.

The day was beyond sad. There was never a point where someone wasn't crying. Val cried out loudly when they put her father's coffin into the ground. She didn't want him to be afraid in there. That set everyone off, and people were barely able to collect themselves when it was time to leave the cemetery.

The mood back at Granny and Granda's house after the burial service was somber. The family began to talk of their plans for the immediate future.

Uncle Tim reminded Auntie Sheila that he had to get back home for work on Monday and that he'd be leaving on Sunday. He told her to stay as long as she wanted, and that he'd be okay and would look forward to picking her up at the airport when she finally got home. He didn't seem to like being with the grown-ups and much preferred talking and goofing around with the kids.

Tim was a dedicated, life-long employee of the New England Telephone Company. Beginning his career with them as a nineteen-year-old lineman just out of trade school, he'd worked his way up over the course of twenty years into a management position. He was no longer required to wear a uniform. It was a secure job with decent pay and excellent health and retirement benefits. Even so, Uncle Tim often complained that no one appreciated how long he'd been on the job, and that big companies didn't care so much about the "little guys" any more.

Auntie Sheila had her own real estate business. She had acquired an enviable reputation as an honest agent, selling many expensive homes in exclusive developments in and around Cape Cod. At this point in her career, she had the luxury of working only when she wanted to. Valerie loved how dressed up her Auntie Sheila looked when she worked. At least as tall as her five-foot-ten husband, she kept herself thin, but not too skinny, and was even taller than him in heels. Uncle Tim told her that he liked a little meat on her. Her wavy, strawberry-blond hair was layered in an attractive shoulder-length style. Nobody in the family could figure out what she saw in Uncle Tim, but what he saw in her was obvious, and he loved her dearly.

On Saturday morning, a day before the children's departure, Aunt Siobhan sauntered into the dining room while everyone was eating breakfast and held up a pair of girl's panties.

"Val, what in God's world are your knickers doing under the couch in the study?"

Val sat up straight and stared in horror, first at the underwear, then at Granda. She blushed mightily, her face hot with embarrassment.

"Those aren't mine!"

She quickly blurted.

Siobhan put her hands on her hips.

"Well, child, can you tell me then who else they might belong to?"

Seeing Val's embarrassment, Granda set down his paper and came to her rescue. Staring sternly over his glasses at his daughter, he admonished.

"Siobhan, who cares who they belong to. Quit embarrassing the poor child, will you? Just put them in the laundry and be done with it. Chances are they just fell out of a basket."

Aunt Siobhan felt badly then; she bent over to give Val a kiss and apologized.

"Sorry, love. I didn't mean to make you blush. I was joking. It did put a little color in your cheeks to be sure."

She giggled and gently pinched Val's cheek.

Granda, grinning behind the cover of his newspaper, whispered to Granny.

"Indeed, it's been a long time since any knickers have been found under a couch in my house!"

She froze him with a look that could kill.

"Bless-us-and-save-us, Pat, would you happen to be noticing that children are present at the table?"

He laughed out loud, and she grabbed the paper from him, folded it quickly, and slapped the back of his head with it.

Caroline and Val finished their breakfast and ran out back to play. Ruth handed the newspaper back to her joking husband.

"You know, I'm glad I took the girls walking in Feakle the other day."

Granda commented quietly as he followed Granny into the kitchen after breakfast. She took a pen out of the drawer. Without skipping a beat, as she began writing a note.

"Oh? And why is that?"

Granda relayed the story to her.

"The papers here say that the Guards are looking for a shady character who tried to coax a young lass away from Ballyallia Lake. She wasn't hurt or anything, the poor creature. She was smart enough to not go with him."

He shook his head, his voice trailing off in disgust.

Granny looked up at him and adjusted her glasses.

"God-help-us, Pat, the world's a treacherous place today, isn't it?"

He nodded in agreement.

"Faith! We never worried about such things when we were youngsters. I'm off to the chemist's. Would you be needing anything while I'm out?"

She shook her head at first.

"Just you be careful."

"Yes, yes, yes."

He repeated, as if, at his age, he still needed reminding. She turned suddenly.

"Oh, I just remembered. I do need something - a card."

"A card, is it? And whose birthday did we miss now?"

"Glynnis O'Brien...lovely little lass."

She gestured vaguely.

"It's not her birthday, but I've a little present I want to bring over ... you know, as a thank-you for watching the girls. Mary said she's been out of sorts lately."

Granda nodded.

"A thank-you card, it is. I'll soon be back."

He grabbed his cap and left through the front door.

*   *   *

Siobhan knocked softly on the door to her brother's room and ventured in at Grace's murmur. She quietly sat on the bed.

"All done packing?"

Grace sighed softly.

"No, not yet, only my stuff. I'll get to the girls' in a little while. I want to do some laundry before I go, so that I don't have to do it all when I get home tomorrow."

She folded clothes at the side of the bed, noting to Siobhan that they'd accumulated quite a wardrobe commuting between two countries over the years since they had Valerie.

Siobhan watched her for a moment, and then seemed to recall something and reached down into her own laundry basket.

"Speaking of clothes, do you know if these belong to Valerie?"

She held the underwear out for Grace to examine. Grace frowned at them and shrugged.

"They look kind of big for her ... but, you never know. We've got clothes all over the place here, and there are clothes in the drawers for the girls that I don't even recognize."

Siobhan nodded, chuckling.

"Mary O'Brien. God-bless-her. She sends a lot of Glynnis's old clothes over to Mam, thinking that the girls can use them when they visit."

Grace smiled warmly.

"Well, that's really nice of her to think of them. But panties?"

Both women tittered at the thought of hand-me-down underwear.

"Grace, whatever will you do now? When you go home, I mean?"

Grace stopped folding and sat down on the edge of the bed next to her sister-in-law, her eyes welling up with tears as she fumbled with a shirt.

"I really don't know. I'm trying not to think that far in advance ... just taking things a day at a time. No, a minute at a time. I dread it, you know? Going home to an empty house without my Neil. Thank God for the girls. But I feel like I'm abandoning him — leaving here."

She twisted the shirt into a knot and absently wiped her eyes.

"Sometimes, I sense he's standing right here next to me, Siobhan, and I just want to close my eyes and put my arms around him and feel his touch. I lie in his bed each night, and can't sleep. I mean, we made love here. Caroline was conceived here. Neil should ... I mean, it's his bed and ..."

Her voice trailed off, giving way to sobs. Siobhan held her, crying with her.

"Shushhhh, love. I know, Grace, I know. Faith! I wish he were here, too. God knows we all miss him."

Ruth peeked in then. She studied them for a moment, sizing up the situation, and then went in and used the steps to climb up and sit with them. She patted Grace's hand.

"We're just crying again, mam. It hurts so much."

Grace dabbed again at her eyes with the twisted shirt.

"God above, how well I know. I'm walking round here like I've lost my best friend. Crying at the drop of a hat I am, too."

She looked sadly at Siobhan.

"Your poor da doesn't know what to say to me anymore. God knows you're never prepared to lose a child. Not that your heartache is any less, Grace. So help me, I don't mean that. But when it's your own flesh and blood ... aahhh! I swear a part of you dies that can't be replaced. My Neil, he was my firstborn, God-bless-him."

She grabbed at the other end of the shirt still in Grace's hands and blew her nose. That was gross and made them all laugh. Grace threw the wet shirt at Siobhan.

"Wash it with the knickers."

Granny nudged Grace.

"Were they Val's?"

Grace shrugged.

"Don't know, mam. More likely than not, they're Glynnis's old ones that Mary sent over."

Granny nodded.

"Likely. She's a dear, isn't she? I'll be walking over there today. I've a little gift for Glynnis - to thank her for helping with the girls. Mary says she's been out of sorts lately."

"Still?"

Siobhan turned to Granny, eyebrows raised. Shrugging her shoulders. Granny replied.

"She doesn't know why. She says she's been acting very withdrawn. Mary's beside herself with worry."

"Oh, Mam, you know teenagers."

Siobhan waved away the concern.

"Could be anything or nothing then, aye? Kids' emotions - they're up and down, up and down! But she did seem sort of anxious the other night when I walked her home after the wake."

She remembered with another flap of her hand.

"Aahh! Girls can be so emotional. She's probably premenstrual. You remember me, don't you?"

Siobhan nudged her gently.

"How well I know! That's what I tried to tell Mary. She was scrapping with her sister on the phone the other day, and she reminded her that depression runs in their family, on the father's side mind you, and that she should have Glynnis checked out."

Siobhan looked aghast.

"Oh, no, she didn't!"

"Yes, afraid she did. Mary told her Glynnis wasn't depressed and told her to mind her own business and stop diagnosing her daughter. Can you believe it? Her sister got indignant then and told her she was only trying to help, and that she had her own daughter checked out years before, and she was glad she did."

"And did they diagnose her with depression?"

Siobhan's face tightened, and Granny waved her hand.

"NO! They told her it was all hormones and not to worry about it. She'd grow out of it and into something else in a few years!"

Amused, Siobhan shook her head.

"Are you seeing what you have to look forward to, Grace?"

Grace raised her hands in surrender, smiling sadly.

"I don't even want to think about it right now. Val already gives me a run for my money. She's rather strong-willed. But she's really good with the baby. Caroline just adores her."

Granny patted Grace's shoulder lovingly.

"Aye, I see that. That one's got a very protective nature about her, she has. Mind you, she gets that from her father, you know."

"Oh, is that so?"

Grace raised an eyebrow and smiled.

"Forget it, Grace."

Siobhan warned good-naturedly.

"Any good qualities in those kids, be sure, she's giving her son the credit for it."

Grace smiled at Siobhan.

"Well, I'll allow her that much ... but the looks: Hey, they're all mine!"

Sheila then knocked on the door when she heard them chuckling.

"Oh, it's so good to hear you laughing."

She climbed the steps and sat next to Granny on the crowded bed.

"It's so hard, Sheila. It'll take a long while to adjust."

Grace swallowed hard and sighed.

"Aye ... if ever."

Granny's voice trailed off.

Sheila got up and put her arm around Grace, gently squeezing her.

"I know, Gracie, but we all have to stay strong, for the girls' sake. They'll have lots of questions one day soon - Val before Caroline. But Caroline's day will come. Neil would want us to get on with our lives and not be whining over him. We all know that."

They nodded silently.

Caroline's scream suddenly pierced the room. Grace leapt from the bed and dashed down the stairs, through the kitchen, out the back door, and across the garden.

"What happened?"

Out of breath, she reached for Caroline, who was screaming hysterically.

Val tried to explain.

"She got sand in her eyes. She dumped the bucket on her head! She won't let me touch her."

Val stood, worriedly brushing the sand from her skirt.

"SIOBHAN!!!"

Grace hollered, only to turn and have her sister-in-law right behind her.

"Oh, thank goodness, you're here. She got sand in her eyes."

Siobhan scooped Caroline up and rushed her into the kitchen, where she ran the warm water she needed to flush out her eyes. Caroline's high-pitch screaming was painful to their ears.

"NO! NO!"

She screeched as if they were trying to kill her. Her hands flailed, and she shook her head violently, kicking all the while. Siobhan instructed Grace to hold the baby's arms down.

"Her eyes look really red. She's been rubbing them."

She tried to get a closer look.

"Caroline, can you open your eyes for Aunt Siobhan?"

"NO!"

She screamed, shutting them more tightly.

Grace was shaking.

"Do you think she could have damaged the cornea? Sand is pretty coarse."

Siobhan forced Caroline around to look at her eyes.

"I don't know, but she won't sit still, poor tyke. Let me ring the doctor's office. We could whisk her in, just to check."

Grace glanced at her wristwatch.

"That's a good idea. I can't have her screaming like this all the way home tomorrow. They'll throw us off the plane!"

Uncle Sean stumbled into the kitchen, still sleepy, and yawned loudly.

"What's with baby doll?"

He rubbed his eyes, trying to focus.

"Ahhh, she got sand in her eyes and won't let us touch her. She won't sit still long enough for me to take a look. They're really red, Sean. See if you can sneak a peek."

Siobhan passed the child to her brother.

When he took Caroline into his brawny arms, the baby went silent.

"Let's see those pretty eyes now, love."

She looked up at him - eyes wide open.

Sean grinned down at her.

"Now, that's a good lass!"

Caroline smiled at him.

Coyly, he asked.

"Do your eyes hurt you?"

He blinked at her widely and dramatically. She giggled and shook her head no. The women all stared at her in amazement.

"Why, the little vixen!"

Granny laughed with her hands on her hips.

"She had us all, she did."

Sean tickled Caroline's belly, and she pulled her shirt up for him to do it again. Siobhan motioned toward the sink. Holding up the water bottle and dangling it before Caroline, he asked.

"Can I wash that sand off your face for you now?

Caroline smiled and nodded. He carried her to the sink, and Siobhan ran the water. After they rinsed her off, he held her tightly as she laid her head on the towel on his shoulder.

In the parlor, he sat on the couch with her, rubbing her back gently, and she began to doze off.

"I think she's feeling Neil's loss in her own little way, poor lass."

He looked sadly at his sister.

When Siobhan tried again to look at the baby's eyes, Caroline's head popped up off Sean's shoulder, and she pushed her aunt away.

Granny brought in tea and set the kettle on the hotplate beside him. He passed Caroline to Grace and poured as he spoke.

"So, Grace, what time is your flight tomorrow morning?"

Grace shook her head and grimaced.

"Eight o'clock and I still haven't packed all the girls' things yet. There's a lot of laundry to do. I don't know that I'll get it all finished in time."

Granny held up her hands to stop her.

"That should be the least of your worries, Grace. Take what you want of the girls' things home and leave the rest. I'll take care to get it done. Lord knows I've got the help here. It'll be ready and waiting for you when you come back again."

"If you really don't mind, Mam. I think that's what I'll have to do. I just don't have the energy. But be warned, you've got two week's worth of dirty clothes piled up there. I hate leaving you with it all."

"Nonsense, girl! You've enough facing you when you get home. This is nothing."

Val slipped in and sat next to Granny on the couch. She put her arm around her granddaughter.

"Indeed, Val, you'll be needing to help your mother out now, you know, especially with Caroline."

Granny sat up suddenly.

"Ahhh, Lord, I nearly forgot again. I have something here for you."

She got up stiffly from the couch and shuffled to the bookcase. Holding out a small box, brightly wrapped in royal blue foil paper adorned with a silver bow, she offered it to Valerie.

"Go on, child, open it."

Val carefully took off the tiny bow and opened the paper, eager to see what it held. The blue velvet box contained the daintiest gold ring she'd ever seen. Granny instructed her to put it on her ring finger.

"Which way does it go, Granny, this little heart thingy here?"

"For you, darlin', it goes on the right hand with the heart facing out. It's a Claddagh ring, and wearing it that way means you're fancy free. Just imagine, then!"

Granny chuckled as she helped Val put it on the right way. Val turned her hand to look at it from every angle, and gave Granny a big hug and a kiss. Then she thought she'd better do that for everybody else in the room. They were a kissing kind of family.

"Now, child, don't be forgetting to thank your Granda, or he'll be mightily crushed, he will. I really should have waited for him to get home, but with all that's going on, I was sure to forget later. You know, we never made it over to the States for your First Holy Communion. You see, we were going to give it to you then."

Val had never heard of the weird name Granny had called the ring. She had seen it worn by adults, though, so she felt grown-up to have her own. She had to ask her again what a "clatter" ring was. Her grandmother kissed the top of her head.

"No, child, not 'clatter' — it's Claddagh."

She broke up the parts of the word, to help it stick in Val's mind.

"There's a folk legend concerning the Claddagh ring. But really, it's just the name of a small fishing village near Galway City. Of course, you wouldn't know where that's located, doll. Just trust your Granny. That's where someone designed the ring. Look close here; see how the heart's encircled by a pair of hands, and a crown on top of it? By God, it grew to be a gift that lovers or friends gave to each other."

She gently squeezed Val as she glanced at the others.

"Course, right now, darlin', you won't be minding that sort of thing. Later on ... a lot later on, child ... should you marry, then you'll be turning that heart facing in, toward yourself, meaning that you're spoken for. Better yet, if you were to slip it on the left hand, facing in, it'll tell all the world that you're happily married."

Val noticed that she wiped at her eyes. She was confused by the explanation.

"Spoken for? What does that mean, Granny?"

Ruth smiled, her fondness for her grandchild apparent on her face.

"Oh, child, it just means that some nice boy has stolen your heart."

She looked past Val.

"It'll happen, for sure. In time ... in time."

She winked rather sadly at Grace.

To Val, the ring signified a small piece of Ireland that she could take home with her. And it made her feel like a big girl.

Grace whispered, so as to not startle Caroline.

"C'mon, Val, old girl, we need to start packing. We've got an early day tomorrow."

She got up slowly from the couch. Caroline was sleeping soundly on her shoulder.

"I'm going to put your sister down for a nap. Want to help me?"

Val nodded and took her mother's free hand, reaching back to pick up Caroline's blanket. Granny watched Grace maneuver them both and worried over how they would manage not only the flight home, but also life without Neil once they were there.

"Mommy, can we come back to visit again?"

Val wasn't looking forward to leaving.

"Sure, we will, honey. We'll figure that out later though. Right now, I think we need to give Granny and Granda back their house, and some peace and quiet."

"Ahhh, no."

Granny shook her head.

"It'll be too quiet after you leave. God save us. I enjoy having you and the girls here. Indeed, maybe at Christmas you'll be returning?"

Granny asked.

"Think about it, Grace. No pressure, though."

"I know, Mam ... and thanks. We'll see how it goes. I just need to get through each day - each hour."

Grace glanced down, unsure of what to say next.

"I understand. Faith, I really do."

Granny put her arm around Grace and hugged her.

* * *

Uncle Sean offered to take Caroline upstairs and settle her down for her nap. Val followed him, as her mother decided to stay downstairs with Granny a little longer. He laid Caroline on Val's bed, instead of putting her in the crib. Val pulled the covers up over her and patted them down. He lay on one side of the toddler, and Val got on the other. She rested her head on the pillow next to her sister and tucked her blanket in between them.

"Is she in a bed yet at home?"

He whispered, as Val wiggled and adjusted herself.

"No, she's still in the crib."

Val whispered back.

"But I taught her how to climb out. She never stays in it anymore! Mommy was mad when I did that 'cause she said she could fall out and crack her skull."

Uncle Sean grinned.

"I see. Well, you didn't stay contained in your crib for too long either, come to think of it."

He nudged Val gently.

"I told Mommy I wanted her to get us bunk beds."

Val placed her doll next to Caroline on her uncle's side.

"Oh? And I suppose you'll claim the top bunk, too?"

Val nodded and smirked. She was impressed that Uncle Sean seemed to know so much about her.

"Mind you, your father and I shared a room for a little while, you know."

Sean's voice had risen to a low murmur.

"But we'd be scrapping with each other at night when we should have been sleeping, and one of us always ended up getting hurt, don't you know. Your Granny would holler up to us to stop. She said we gave her a horrible fright every time she heard a loud bump. Finally, she put her foot down.

'Enough is enough!!' She separated us and gave us our own rooms."

Val stared at him, puzzled.

"You and Daddy used to fight?"

He knew she loved to hear stories about the men as children.

"Well, that's when I was in short pants. Your da, he was always bigger and stronger than me. But we were hooligans we were ... got into loads of mischief. Drove your poor Granny crazy for a while, we did."

He shook his head, chuckling to himself, remembering some of their childhood antics.

They got off the bed slowly, so as not to disturb Caroline, and sat at the tea table. Sean folded himself awkwardly into one of the tiny chairs. Val sat across from him, eager to hear more.

"What did you do? You and Daddy I mean."

She pretended to pour him some tea.

"Well, one time we had a brilliant idea and decided to play in the sewer drains."

"Oh, God! That's gross, Uncle Sean."

He popped his head back, laughing.

"Why the smell didn't deter us is beyond me. We were daft and stinking wet, and knew we'd get bashed anyway, so we might as well just stay in the pipes — no need to rush back and get killed by your Granny. Had a grand time, too, we did! Surprised I am, we never caught a disease. Well, when we finally got home, Da nearly killed us both! Mam made us strip to the skin in the front hall, and she threw our clothes right out the front door and onto the street. She made us bathe for two days in a row! Said we stunk to the high heaven, she did. No laugh — it's true!"

Val could picture her Granny doing that, and giggled.

"Let's go downstairs and get some lunch. I've slept the morning away, and I'm famished!"

Sean propped pillows alongside Caroline and gave Val a piggyback ride downstairs.

"It's back to the grind for me in a few days, pumpkin. I'm going to miss you girls so much."

Val felt sorry for him.

"Don't worry, Uncle Sean. We'll be back soon, and I'll call you on the phone, okay?"

He patted her arms, strung around his neck.

"Of course, love ... of course."

Chapter Ten

Chatham, Cape Cod, Massachusetts, Summer 1972

GETTING TO THE AIRPORT EARLY Sunday morning required two cars. Granda drove one, with Granny at his side, and Grace, Caroline, and Aunt Siobhan in the back.

"Well, Caroline's in great form."

Granny noticed, smiling back at her.

"She seems a good deal happier."

The other car contained Val, Uncle Sean, Auntie Sheila, and the suitcases. Val stared at the fields as they passed - so peaceful and serene. She thought of many things: Glynnis and how sad she looked when she was sitting quietly on the couch staring blankly out the window, her room at Granny's, Daddy, and how he looked at the funeral parlor. She knew for sure that he wasn't coming home any more, and it made her sad to leave Ireland. Right then, she wished she'd ridden with her mother. She needed a hug.

Auntie Sheila broke the silence.

"You're awfully quiet back there."

Still staring out the window, Val replied.

"I'm just looking at how pretty the grass is. Everything here is so green - even the bugs! I wish I could stay here forever."

Uncle Sean glanced at Sheila and smiled.

"Well, you'll be starting lessons soon, love. Are you looking forward to that then?"

He was trying to lift her sinking spirits.

"I guess so ..."

Val rested her head on her hand on the armrest of the door and sighed. Hearing her despair, Sean looked at her in the rearview mirror.

"Hey, Val?"

She looked up at his reflection.

"Love you, lass."

"I love you, too, Uncle Sean."

They all stayed near the gate until the boarding call, which came an hour after they arrived. Val sat and colored with Caroline, who just scribbled lines all over the place. Val got mad at her for messing up her picture, and tried to show her how to color in the lines.

Granny sat across from them, talking with Grace and dabbing at her eyes with a tissue from time to time, nodding at whatever Grace was saying. Granda sat on the other side of Granny, patting her hand. Auntie Sheila checked her watch a lot, while Uncle Sean read the paper. Aunt Siobhan went off to the duty-free shop and picked out a couple of small sweatshirts with the green, white, and orange Irish flag on the front. She held one up for the girls to see. On the back it read, "Erin Go Brach."

"I know what that means! It's 'Ireland Forever' in Garlic!" Valerie cried out.

"That's Gaielge, love."

Aunt Siobhan pointed out, snickering and handed the bag to Grace.

"Just in case they catch a chill on the flight."

Val had a pin at home with that phrase on it. She got it the year before at the St. Patrick's Day parade in South Boston.

*   *   *

It seems it's always a very cold, gray day for the St. Patrick's Day Parade in Southie. But it was a tradition for Grace and Neil; they went every year. Grace's college roommate, Maureen, lived in a roomy first floor apartment off Broadway, where all the houses were stacked side by side, with her husband and three daughters: Megan, Moira, and Maeve. Grace and Maureen were pregnant at the same time with Valerie and Moira.

They'd all watch the parade together in the afternoon, and then run back to the house, where the fun went on well into the evening. Good food and Irish music abounded. The girls would play hopscotch out front until it got dark, and then continued to play under the street lights. The parents sat inside, singing loudly and off key.

Maureen's husband, Ian, played the fiddle, and the men would gather in the kitchen, drinking beer and talking sports or politics. The ladies would crowd into the parlor and smoke cigarettes. Sure enough, they'd get to feeling pretty good and would call the girls in to line up and dance for them. They wanted to see a return on all the good money they'd spent for Irish step dancing lessons, telling the girls that it was the least they could do for them.

The girls all studied under the same teacher, Mrs. Moran, from Cambridge, and they knew all the steps by heart. Ian would play the fiddle, and the men would join the women in the parlor to clap. The girls would take their bows when they were done, and each would receive a dollar. It was great fun, and they loved being the center of attention. They'd had many recitals at the John Hancock Hall in Boston, so dancing in front of a group of parents didn't bother them at all.

Neil's pride was evident when he watched his daughter dance. Val did her best to keep up. But Caroline would be the gifted dancer.

"Hop, one, two, three, four, five, six, seven — hop one, two, three, hop back two, three ..."

Neil helped Val keep her timing by clapping. On the weekends, their house was filled with the sounds of traditional Irish music programmed on AM radio - The John Latchford Show. When he heard just the right music come on the radio, he'd call Valerie in to come show him what she'd learned at dance class that Saturday. She grew up listening to the Clancy

Brothers. Forever after, when she heard "Four Green Fields," she'd think of her father and those early days ... sweet memories.

*   *   *

At the second boarding call, Grace finished gathering the crayons and coloring books.

"Okay, girls, give everyone kisses good-bye."

She picked up Caroline, who was blowing kisses to total strangers. Val gave Granda a long hug and a kiss on the cheek and thanked him again for the clatter ring. He kissed her fingers.

"Ahhh, love ... wear it in good health, God be with you. We'll be seeing you sooner than you know. Be good to your mam now."

"Grace, girl, if you need anything, you call me. We'll be talking soon."

Granny was all choked up. She could barely whisper good-bye. There'd been too many good-byes - but she managed to kiss Val on the cheek several times. Uncle Sean kissed his nieces again, and gave Val a gentle swat on the bottom, telling her to hurry up or she'd miss the plane. Auntie Sheila thanked everyone for everything a million times, and Aunt Siobhan cried, waving as the quartet turned and headed toward the gate.

Val held her mother's hand as they walked down the ramp and waited to get through the door. She got to sit next to the window; Caroline sat in the middle, and her mother on the aisle. Auntie Sheila sat across the aisle from them.

Val loved takeoffs and landings, but her mother always closed her eyes, blessed herself, and prayed. As the plane zoomed into the sky, Val watched the world below grow smaller and smaller. Before long, there wasn't much to see, and she started to get bored, so she entertained herself by trying to guess what they'd be served for lunch. Grace bought her juice from the serving cart, but she had to share it with Caroline. What she really wanted was her own soda, but her mom said no. Val took the rejection in stride, but Grace had second thoughts anyway, and told the girls they could share one with their meal if they behaved themselves.

Lunch was actually quite disgusting — some unidentifiable gray meat between sliced bread. The girls picked out the meat and ate only the cheese. Fortunately, Auntie Sheila pulled out of her large purse some soda bread with jam that Granny had one of her staff make for the long flight home. She knew that airplane food wouldn't be particularly appealing to youngsters, and that the only thing Val and Caroline would be interested in were the crackers the stewardesses passed out.

Grace stayed busy just trying to keep them halfway clean. Caroline eventually dozed off, as did Val. They both awoke a few minutes before the plane touched down at Logan Airport. Grace blessed herself again. Val asked if she could talk to the pilot and see the cockpit. Grace said no, children weren't allowed in the cockpit.

That annoyed Val.

"Someday, I'm going to marry a pilot!"

She glared at her mother.

"Good for you, honey. I hope you do!"

Grace replied enthusiastically.

"Well, I will. You just wait. Then I can see the cockpit any time I want to!"

Grace rolled her eyes at Sheila.

"Good, I hope she does. Then we can fly for free!" They both chuckled at that.

Tim was waiting anxiously for Sheila near the Baggage Claim area. He gave her an excited wave, and greeted her with a warm hug. Then he kissed Grace's cheek and gathered Caroline into his arms, playing with her. Tim had missed his wife. Their home in Carver wasn't too far from Grace and the girls. Given the circumstances, he was grateful they lived fairly close. The Graziano's had come to the airport to take Grace and the girls home so that Sheila could go home with Tim.

Auntie Sheila looked into her sister's eyes.

"Will you be all right, Grace? Want me to come home with you and spend the night?"

"Oh no, Sheila,"

Grace seemed to be somewhere else.

"You've been with us long enough. Go home to your husband or he'll hate us. Call me in the morning. Maybe come over for tea if you have a chance. We'll be ok. I promise. I'll call you if I need anything."

They hugged and separated.

Mrs. Graziano made small talk along the way, telling Grace about what was going on in town. She told Val that her cat, Lucky, had missed her terribly, and would cry and cry when she went over to feed her. Val was anxious then to get home to her. Mrs. Graziano told them that she'd made sure all the food that the people from church brought over was wrapped and dated and put away neatly in the freezer, and that Grace wouldn't have to cook for the next three months, if she didn't want to. She had collected the mail and put it on the kitchen counter. Tony had mowed the lawn, and she hoped Grace didn't mind, but she'd clipped a few roses from the garden for her kitchen table.

"They were so beautiful ..."

She smiled.

"Oh, don't even think about it. You can have roses any time you want. That's what they're there for. I just appreciate that you took such good care of the house and cat while we were away. Thank you."

"Oh, and Father Bruce stopped by to check in on you and the girls. He thought you were coming home yesterday. I told him that you were coming home today, and he said he'd stop by again tomorrow when you've had a chance to settle in. Sister Mary Margaret gave him Valerie's uniform to take over, so I hung it up in her closet for you."

Grace had been worried about coming back and not having even a gallon of milk in the house. She had also fretted about picking up Val's school uniform and the special blouses with the Peter Pan collar that were so hard to get. They might be all sold out if she couldn't get to the store in time to pick them up. Sister Mary Margaret had told her not to worry about a thing, and that she'd take care to get them and make sure Val's uniform was ready when she got home. It was. That was the beauty of being a part of a caring church community, led by Father Bruce Moriarty.

* * *

There were many people at St. Bridget's Catholic Church in Chatham who supported the Callaghan's during their loss. When Father Bruce and the congregation heard the news of Neil's death, Father immediately put the young family on the church's prayer chain and offered up a special Mass for Neil.

He was a young priest, new to the United States when he first met Neil and Grace. He came from County Mayo, Ireland, so he and Neil hit it off from the start. It wasn't too long before he was very much a part of the family, joining them for cookouts, birthdays, and holiday parties. Father Bruce was the kind of man who seemed to naturally draw people to himself, especially young kids and teens. As Caroline and Val grew older, they came to adore him.

* * *

The car ride home seemed to take a long time. Val challenged Caroline to hold her breath in the tunnel. She just pursed her lips and blew up her cheeks, but laughed at the face her older sister made, which made Val laugh, too.

"I won the game!"

Val exclaimed.

She was anxious to get home and see her beloved cat. As Tony offered his hand to assist Grace out of the car, Val jumped out the backseat and ran around the back of the house calling for Lucky. She could hear her meowing loudly.

"Hurry up, Mom! She misses us and thinks we left her for good!"

"Alright, honey. Hold on. I've got to find my key here."

She was searching quickly through her overstuffed purse.

"I'll get it, Grace. I've got the spare here with me."

Mrs. Graziano quickly produced the spare key from her pocket and opened the door. Lucky dashed out, and Val scooped her up and kissed her face as she purred loudly.

"Oh, Luckster! I missed you!"

Val nuzzled her so hard she almost squished her. Caroline, wanting a part of her, too, grabbed at her tail, causing the cat to flinch and jump out of Val's arms. That made Valerie mad.

"Don't do that! You'll hurt her!"

She shouted.

Caroline began to cry. Grace stopped, hands on her hips.

"Val, please don't talk to your sister like that, okay? We're just getting home, and she missed the cat, too. Be nice!"

Val scooped Lucky back up and turned her back on Caroline and muttered quietly.

"Well, she's MY cat!"

Tony brought in the suitcases, and Grace hugged him, then Joyce.

"Thank you both for all you've done. I couldn't have handled this without you. To be honest, I still don't know how I'm going to manage without him."

Mrs. Graziano teared up and shrugged.

"We didn't do much, Grace. If you need anything, please call, okay? Even if you want to just talk or have someone to sit with. We'll come right over."

They hugged again.

"I'm so sorry, Grace."

Grace nodded silently. She looked around the kitchen and found everything neat and clean, with the mail right where Mrs. Graziano said she'd put it. In the refrigerator, fresh lasagna, with a note, dated that day, with cooking instructions ... a salad in a yellow Tupperware bowl ... a loaf of fresh Italian bread on the counter - Valerie's favorite meal.

"Why don't you take Caroline out back to play on the swings? I'll fix us something to eat and open up the windows. It's a little stuffy in here, don't you think? There's a nice sea breeze outside. I'll ... ah ... be out in a minute, okay, hon?"

"Okay, Mom."

Val slowly walked out back, still clutching the cat, knowing with her child's intuition that her mother needed some time to herself.

Caroline ran to her favorite swing and yelled for Val to push her. The salt air smelled so familiar and comforting to them. Surprisingly, Val found herself glad to be home and safe in her own surroundings. She pushed Caroline a few times, then went and sat on the other swing. She looked up at the house to see her mother opening the windows. Lucky ventured off the porch and sat by the girls, acting more like a protective dog than a cat.

Grace walked slowly out onto the porch and sat in the wicker chair with a glass of wine in her hand. Lucky ran back to the porch and jumped up on her lap. She smiled and rubbed the cat's head mindlessly.

"Did you miss us, Luckmeister?"

The radio was mercilessly playing the song, "Without You" by Nilsson. She set her glass of wine down on the table and pretended to smile and wave at the girls, but it was hard for her to hold her composure. The song finally took its toll, and she turned her head as her shoulders began shaking, she grabbed hold of the lace curtain that had blown out the porch window.

Val felt deep sadness for her mother then. In the setting sun, Grace gazed out over the ocean and closed her watery eyes, resting her head on the back of the chair. Val wanted to run inside and shut the radio off; instead, she got down to push Caroline again until her mother went in to set the table for dinner.

Val, as well as her mother, knew that life was going to be different for them all, but Caroline didn't seem to know the difference. As Val thought it over, she did something that she felt strange doing outside of church or bedtime ... she prayed for herself, and thanked God for her family, and asked Him to watch over them and not take her Mom or Caroline or Lucky away, and she promised she'd be a good girl for the rest of her life.

Chapter Eleven

Ennis, County Clare, Ireland, Fall 1978

THE DISTANT SOUND OF SIRENS roused Glynnis, but was not loud enough to fully awaken her. The pounding in her head made her want to dig deeper under the covers. Whenever she drank and smoked weed, she suffered the following day. She put her hand to her forehead and dozed off.

Danny's friends, eighteen-year-olds — they could buy a case of beer for all of them ... not hard to do. They didn't really even check your card. She couldn't get caught at just seventeen — her father, a solicitor in Ennis, his only daughter picked up for underage drinking! Good God! He'd kill her. Her mother would die of embarrassment. The guards closed in around them, headlights glaring ...

She shot straight up, only to realize that it was just a dream. Reaching over for the alarm clock, she made sure it was off — no reason to get up early on a Saturday. She put her pillow over her head and shrunk back from the smell of her own breath, the taste sour from the beer and cigarettes. She worried that her mother would smell it on her. *Bloody hell, I don't care* ... but she couldn't stand the smell herself.

She dragged her tired body into the bathroom, aching all over from sitting on the cold rock wall. She felt like she'd be sick. Splashing hot water on her face, she remembered how Danny had kissed her for the first time last night. She replayed it over and over in her mind as the steam slowly cleared her throbbing head. She didn't want to let the feeling go. But as quickly as the steam evaporated, so did the fantasy. She'd led him on then abruptly shut him off. She popped two aspirins in her mouth and went back to bed.

Danny's good looks did not go unnoticed by most of the girls their age. At seventeen, his sandy-brown hair and green eyes (and having access to his father's car) reduced most girls to blubber. He had a flawless complexion, even as most of their friends were losing their war against acne. Danny was the youngest of the guys they hung around with. He was cool and had money. There were only a few girls in their crowd. Glynnis was the tallest and also the youngest of the three females. She conducted herself maturely and was, regrettably, still in school.

Clare's cropped, over-bleached blond hair showed a well-defined strip of black roots. At eighteen, she was no longer in school and had no idea what she was going to do with her life. She wasn't highly motivated and basically enjoyed bumming around doing nothing. At last conversation, she was leaning toward becoming a beautician.

Peggy was more of a mystery. A rather tough-looking teen, she appeared older than her stated years. Her eyes spoke of heartache and hard times. Strangely protective of her, the story the gang knew was that she was born in Ireland, had dropped out of school early, lived in England for a while with an invalid grandmother who had since died, and was presently on her own, rambling about the country with a group of questionable Travellers.

She displayed street smarts beyond her years, and for some odd reason, their misfit group was grateful when she adopted them as her friends. A rebel, she colored her hair pitch black and wore heavy, dark eye shadow and liner, enhanced only by the black matching lipstick. Her clothing would qualify as morbid. She liked gothic, punk fashion. Glynnis's mom was scared to death of her, and forbade her daughter to hang out with the "wild satanist."

"Jesus, Mary, and Joseph, don't that girl look like she needs an exorcism performed on her now!"

She had blurted out in the kitchen when Peggy came to collect Glynnis the evening before.

"Mam, quit embarrassing me, will you? You never have anything good to say about any of my friends. I'm sick of it!"

She spat back at her mother.

Exhausted from waiting up to confront her wayward husband the night before and sporting a migraine, Mary was in no mood for her daughter's flippant mouth. She didn't give a hoot that Glynnis' "night-of-the-living-dead" friend was within hearing range.

"So help me God, child, if you open your yap to me like that again, I'll send you sailing!"

In a show of defiance, Glynnis laughed at her mother's threat, openly mimicking her in front of Peggy. Her daughter's reaction enraged Mary, who lunged at her, slapping her hard across the face.

"GET OUT!"

Glynnis stood there in shock. Peggy grabbed her arm and pulled her quickly down the hallway.

"C'mon, let's get out of here. You don't need to put up with that! I'm deaf as a haddock on one side, and she nearly blew out my good ear!"

Glynnis, her cheek flaming with her mother's handprint, came to her senses and grabbed her denim jacket off the hook. They ran toward the front door.

"I'm leaving! I'm sick of listening to you rant! You don't have to ask me twice!"

She shouted back at her with fierce bravado.

Peggy laughed nervously as they bolted out the door, purposely slamming it hard behind them. They could hear Glynnis' mother yelling after them in the hall as they hurried down the front steps and ran down the street.

Tears stained Glynnis's swollen face as she approached Danny's car, where he was waiting at the corner. She was praying her mother didn't come running after her like a maniac and embarrass her even more.

Danny smiled and waved, watching her run toward the car with a slightly winded Peggy a short distance behind. As she climbed in, he could see she had been crying.

"What happened to you?"

Shaking her head, she scrounged in her bag for a tissue.

"Nothing. I just hate my mother that's all."

She mumbled as she blew her nose and examined her reddened cheekbone in his rearview mirror.

Peggy watched her wince.

"You should come and live with me, Glynn. You don't need to be putting up with that. She's daft!"

Glynnis nodded in agreement, but she wasn't sure she was ready for Peggy's bohemian lifestyle yet, even though the thought of running away from it all was tempting at the moment. She reminded herself that she had a longer-range plan.

Peggy didn't trust too many people. But she felt comfortable talking with Glynnis, and one night on the wall, she'd shared with her how she'd come upon the Travellers and her life with Bobby Burns and his former girlfriend, Leonore.

* * *

Peggy's father had abandoned her and her mother when she was a toddler. By the time she was twelve, her mother had run off with a security guard whom she'd met at a home for the elderly where she worked as an aide. Left behind in England to live with her uncle until age fourteen, she was placed in a children's home when he fled from British authorities after crimes of abuse had been leveled against him. Peggy ran away from the children's home at her first opportunity.

Feeling she would be safer in Ireland, and homeless at the time, she took up with a group of Travellers passing through Charlestown, County

Mayo. The small band, held together by their common bond of poverty, fended for themselves daily.

She met Bobby and Leonore when they came to Charlestown for the weeklong Rose Festival. A few of the single guys were hoping to meet girls. Bobby was always on the lookout for a new woman for his hotheaded brother, Stephen, who wasn't able to meet or keep women. He was a lot more tolerable to live with when he had a regular, willing partner. He spotted the young Peggy, intently drawing on a large pad of paper while smoking a cigarette. A small crowd had gathered around admiring her art.

* * *

Because she was close to her da, Glynnis felt comfortable talking to him about her odd and unlikely relationship with Peggy. He didn't freak out over her pals the way her mother did. He cautioned his daughter, however, to stay away from the Travellers, advising that her friend should try and get away as soon as possible. Not all Travellers were hoodlums and thieves, but some had reputations that preceded them.

As an attorney, Liam had established many contacts with the local law enforcement authorities over the years. Glynnis asked him if there was a way he could quietly check into Peggy's background. He did a little searching and was shocked to learn what had transpired in the young woman's life.

Keeping many of the more violent details from Glynnis, he only warned her that the authorities had received a tip that Peggy might be in Ireland. She wasn't wanted for any criminal activity but if the guards spotted her, they'd have to return her to the children's home in England until she was of legal age, just a few days away. He promised his daughter he'd not say a word to the authorities.

Glynnis's friends had kept a sharp eye out for the guards when Peggy was with them. Once, they hid her in the trunk of Danny's car. Mysteriously, and often without warning, Peggy would just up and be gone, leaving them with no word for weeks on end. When she did finally reappear, she'd always have amazing stories to tell.

Hysterically animated and articulate, she'd relay hilarious tales of their scamming skills. She told the story once of how when she was painting a house she had to find an unusual paint color and was told it had to be an "exact match." The homeowner was insistent on this. The problem was she had been given only a tiny paint chip of the color the owner wanted. Next to impossible to match perfectly, Peggy judged as best she could. When the house was finished, the owner marveled at how well it came out and complimented Peggy for her precise work.

When asked by her friends how she found the matching paint, Peggy replied that it wasn't too difficult, she just came as close as she could to the color, and then painted the chip! They all roared with laughter at her simple yet ingenious solution.

Peggy traveled with a rough crowd, vowing secretly to Glynnis that she was saving all sorts of money in order to get away from them one day soon. Peggy seemed to know so much about men, and life in general. Glynnis admired her determination and survival skills, but knew nothing, yet, of her gifts and talents.

* * *

"I can't believe she hauled off and whacked ya like that."

Danny glanced at Glynnis's face while working to keep the car straight on the road. Peggy looked, wide-eyed, at the lingering red mark. She was more shaken up than she let on having been on the receiving end of such slaps from Bobby herself.

"Ahhh, it's all my da's fault,"

Glynnis complained, trying to lay blame somewhere.

"He's never home anymore, and she's mad at him most of the time."

Danny shook his head.

"Don't worry, Glynnis. I'll get you something ... calm your nerves for sure."

She looked at him and smiled.

"Oh, now what might that be, Danny boy?"

She touched his cheek coyly, slowly feeling better since they'd put some distance between her and her mother.

"We'll be talking about that later now, love, won't we?"

He winked and stared ahead, his wide grin spreading. She couldn't wait to be alone with him, wanting so much for Danny to like her. He was finally showing an interest, and she didn't want to lose him.

He parked his car on the side of the road and turned off the lights. Peggy jumped out of the backseat and walked over to the wall to talk with Kevin Finnegan.

"Hey, Peg! Hold up! Would ya?"

Glynnis called out after her from the front passenger side window.

"Whadya say?"

"WHAT'S THE RUSH?"

Glynnis shouted to her.

"Well! Hurry up!"

Danny placed his hand on her arm.

"Hey, Glynn? Don't go yet. I want to talk to you alone."

His voice was sensitive. Reaching up, he turned her face toward him and kissed her cheek hesitantly in the darkness. Glynnis looked sadly into his eyes, and he drew her mouth to his. It was a moment she'd remember forever.

Suddenly, someone banged on the hood of the car, startling them both and causing her to jump, ending the feeling as quickly as it had begun. Danny wiped the moisture from the driver's side window with his sleeve, revealing Connie Sheehan's smirking mug.

"Hey! Give us the rest of the beer and you two can take off and fog up the windows all you like. Can I watch?"

Connie had a stupid grin on his face. He stood all of five feet high and his bright-red hair doomed him to never be taken seriously. Fortunately, his wit made up for his lack of height.

"Whadya say we stay for a short while, then we'll take off by ourselves?"

Glynnis smiled and nodded.

"Sounds grand! Drink quickly."

Danny hauled the case of beer out of the trunk, and walked it over to the grass behind the wall. He put his arm around Glynnis as they walked towards the group. Clare was sitting on the grass, peeling a label with her longest fingernail, and her mouth dropped open at the sudden show of affection.

"So, now I take it you two are going together, right?"

Danny looked quickly at Glynnis.

"Well, ahhh, I dunno. I mean, I never really asked you properly now, did I?"

Glynnis shook her head, jokingly admonishing him.

"Come to think of it, no, you didn't."

Glynnis tilted her head back and brought the bottle to her lips. Her long brown hair fell loosely about her shoulders. She knew she had his attention. He stared at her with open desire. One of her best features, she was told, were her eyes ... sky blue, accented by enviably long, dark lashes. They openly showed any emotion she felt.

Danny got up and brushed the loose grass from his jeans.

"You ready to go yet?"

He reached down with his free hand to help her up.

Glynnis shook her head.

"Nope. Staying for another. Need it to calm my nerves."

She winked at him.

"Remember? My nerves?"

Danny held her stare as he fished in his shirt pocket. Prolonging the suspense, he finally pulled out a joint and lit it. Passing it to her, he joked.

"Here, it'll help with those nerves."

She took a deep drag and held it in. She offered it back to him, but he waved it away.

"Keep it. It's all for you."

He lit up a couple more and passed them around to share with the group. Clare's jibe broke Glynnis's reverie.

"Oh, so now he's spoilin' ya, he is!"

"Yeah, true love, that."

Peggy nodded.

Glynnis felt the tension slowly leaving her body. The weed loosened her limbs and began to spin her mind around. *Don't need Mam's aggravation. What am I gonna do all next week during mid-term break? Ugh! That stupid school uniform. It makes me feel like a silly child. I can't wait to sit for my leaving certificate and just be done with that place!* She looked around at her friends, allowing herself to toy with Peggy's offer of freedom; it was a temporary mental escape from her family situation.

"You feeling any better, doll?"

Danny sat down behind her. Putting his lips close to her ear, he nibbled at her earlobe, giving her the chills. As he wrapped his arms about her waist, Glynnis dragged on the last of the joint. Pulling a clip out of her purse, she held the end to his lips. He sucked in the smoke and kissed her again before he exhaled. The trailing wisps hung in the night air between them. After minutes of tasting lips and warmth and sweet calm, they helped each other to their feet and staggered, hand in hand, back over the wall to his car.

Peggy called to them sarcastically.

"Have fun ..."

Glynnis turned and waved limply, her grin lopsided, having lost all fear of being alone with Danny. She wanted intensely to be with him; her stomach burned, and she trembled at the thought of getting close to him. She pictured herself with Danny, doing anything either of them wanted ... her desire building. *This time it'll be different.*

"Earth to Glynnis ..."

Danny's voice startled her, and for a moment, she looked right through him as if at a stranger.

"You're a million miles away, love. You feelin' okay?"

Glynnis rummaged in her purse, lit a cigarette, and blew the smoke out the window.

"Yeah, grand ... just grand."

"But I'll be even better with you."

Danny raised one eyebrow.

"You're pretty bleedin' frisky when you're high."

She chuckled, feeling more in control of the situation. She enjoyed the sense of power, knowing the effect her body had over men ... most men anyway.

She leaned over and laid her head on his shoulder. Danny took the cigarette from her and flicked it out the window. The autumn air was chilly, and a light rain had begun to fall. He grabbed an afghan from the back seat.

"Here. Put this over you. It's getting cold."

He wrapped the blanket around them and continued to kiss her.

Friday night, and Glynnis knew she had to be home by midnight. It was 9:30 p.m. - still plenty of time - but she grew restless and strangely uneasy. They had a bit of a drive to get her home. She quietly reminded Danny of her curfew.

"I'll have you home on time. No worries, love."

He was breathing heavily. She placed her delicate hand on his chest and felt his heart pounding. She initiated the next kiss and drew him with her as she lay back on the seat, wanting his body to cover hers. He fumbled with his pants. She felt herself responding beneath him and her breathing quickened. She wouldn't stop him and closed her eyes in anticipation. Then images, like bolts of lightning, assaulted her mind.

* * *

Babysitting ... Valerie and Caroline ... she went inside when he called her to help him carry the drinks ... It was warm, and she had been sweating, running around with the girls, blowing bubbles. She felt bad that the girls' father had died. The uncle had told her that, if she was hot, she should take off her top to get cool. That embarrassed her ... only eleven years old and had just started wearing a training bra.

He motioned for her to come inside the study with him. Then he shut the door behind her. The little ones were in the backyard, still blowing bubbles, happy, free from cares ... She heard their innocent laughter in the background. The uncle, seemingly so big, so much older, so strangely quiet, gently took her hand and led her over to the couch ... told her to stand in front of him and raise her arms. Numbly, she did what he asked, turning her eyes away from his penetrating gaze, his unmoving face. She brought her trembling hands up to cover her nakedness. He assured her she was beautiful and didn't need to hide her body. Then he drew her closer to him and kissed her lips. She stiffened, frozen in horror, shivering. She told him no - she had to go out back and watch the children. He told her not to worry, that he would watch them.

As he murmured his comforting words, he slid his hand up underneath her skirt. She could not bring herself to look at him while he explored beneath her clothing. He drew her in close, whispering that everything would be fine ... she weakly told him no again, but he slowly and firmly made her lie back on the couch. He wiped away her tears with his finger. She only stopped crying when he told her that he wouldn't hurt her. But he lied. It did hurt, and as she lay there, she prayed she wouldn't die and that the girls wouldn't come in to find her with her shirt off, knickers on the floor, and skirt up around her waist. She didn't want anyone to see what he was doing to her.

* * *

The weight of Danny on top of her made her feel like she was suffocating. She struggled to sit up, pushing him away.

"Stop, Danny. Just stop!"

"What's wrong?"

Her change of heart angered him.

"What the hell!"

"Nothing. I just want you to stop, okay? Take me home please."

Glynnis raked her matted hair with shaking fingers and knew she must have sounded daft.

"I've gotta get home. I'll get in trouble if I'm late."

Danny sat up and glared at her.

"You're a feckin' tease, you know that?"

He turned the key hard in the ignition and revved the engine, slamming the steering wheel with his fist.

"I'll take you home, I will!"

She sat there quietly, tears welling up in her eyes.

He shook his head angrily.

"What's with you? One minute, you're telling me you can't wait to be alone; the next minute, you're running like a scared rabbit. What the hell is up with you?"

His eyes blazed.

She didn't understand it either.

"I don't know! Just take me home, okay?"

She slumped against the door and stared out the window. Danny shook his head in frustration and drove. He didn't say anything on the way to her house. Glynnis snuck glimpses of his stony face. *Sure! He'll never want to go out with me again. Good going, Glynnis!*

At ten o'clock, they were in front of her house. He glanced unemotionally at her.

"G'night, then."

She was embarrassed and couldn't look at him, mumbling as she reached for the door handle.

"I'm sorry, Danny. It's been a rough night for me. You know ... the fight with Mam and all."

With reluctant compassion, he moved awkwardly and placed his hand over hers. She jerked it back suddenly. He shook his head.

"WHAT! It's not like I'm going to hit you ... geeesh, Glynn."

Something had spooked her. He wouldn't pursue it tonight.

"Glynn, forget about it, okay? I'll ring you tomorrow night."

He leaned over and kissed her quickly on the cheek. She got out of the car and ran up the front steps, her house keys jingling. She turned to wave good-bye, but he sped off, screeching his tires as he tore down the road. She sighed heavily - 10:00 p.m. on a Friday night! *At least Mam won't be screaming at me for not being home on time ...* She grimaced. *Small comfort that is.*

"I'm home, Mam!"

She called out in the hallway. She knew she needed to apologize to her mother at some point.

There was no answer. *Just as well ...* She climbed the stairs to her room, grateful that her father wasn't home — she hadn't seen him since Tuesday night.

Mam spent a lot of time alone in her room lately. Were it not for Ruth Callaghan's regular visits, she'd not talk to anyone. Glynnis wanted only to go to bed and dream about Danny, and what she might have done with him if ... She also craved another cigarette. *Do I dare sneak one? Maybe Mam's taken one of her tranquilizers.*

She knocked lightly on her mother's door, then peered into the dim room. "Mam, are you awake?"

She walked over to the side of her bed.

"Mam?"

Her mother's breathing was heavy and steady. She could vaguely make out a glass on the night table. She lifted it to her nose. *Hmmm ... thought so - it's the whiskey for you, is it?* She wrinkled her nose, shook her head. *Out like a light! She won't be waking up soon for sure.*

Glynnis walked back to her room, hustled a cigarette from the pack, and lit it, feeling rebellious. If her da came home, she wouldn't even try to explain, didn't think he'd care anyway. Her mind flicked to what he'd done in the last few months: hired a new secretary he did, and rumors from others were that he was having an affair. That didn't surprise her. It wasn't the first time.

She put her cigarette down in an ashtray and changed into comfortable sweat pants and a t-shirt. She looked around the room for something to do. It was too early for her to go to bed. She found her dreaded school uniform lying crumpled in a heap on the floor. With the smoldering cigarette dangling from her lips, she reached for the wrinkled skirt, flung the material over her shoulder, and tromped downstairs to iron it. Strangely enough, she enjoyed ironing.

She felt grown-up, smoking freely in the silent house. *Let 'em fuss, see if I care ... won't be long, less than a year until I'm outta here, leaving for university, for sure.*

The high from the joint still lingered slightly. She turned on the radio and set up the ironing board. As she worked, she thought about Peggy's offer. She utterly hated hearing her parents fight lately when they were home together. Nobody outside their house would ever suspect a thing's wrong. They can put on an act for everybody else. Her lip curled at the hypocrisy.

She knew, no matter what, that she had to finish school. Too many of her friends had dropped out and gone to work in low-paying jobs or, stupidly, had gotten pregnant. Her mind, once again, conjured up her dream: to be a nurse. She'd thought about it a lot more after talking with Val's aunt, Siobhan, who'd told her firsthand what it was like.

She made a mental note to call Siobhan to find out when Valerie and Caroline would be back over for another visit. She missed them. Being an only child, they'd become like her own sisters over the years.

Val was almost sixteen and pretty mature for her age. She considered her a best friend. Caroline always amused her. According to their granny, Caroline was becoming quite a handful for her poor mother. She'd overheard her own mother talking with Ruth Callaghan.

"A wild one she is ... Grace caught her smoking outside the library with her little friends!"

Ruth was concerned, saying that Grace was at her wits' end with the girl.

Glynnis knew, from early on, that she wanted to work with children. To her, Siobhan's job as a pediatric nurse sounded ideal. She thought kids were neat and hated to see them hurt. She searched through many different Nursing catalogs focusing on schools in England, and wanted more than anything to apply early. She had to be careful not to do anything that would divert her from her goal. Dropping out and taking up with Peggy's Traveller friends, though it was tempting when Mam exasperated her, was not an option. Even though she hated her life at the moment, she knew she had to stay the course and continue to get good grades, so she could get into the university of her choice. She told her parents straight out that she'd be living on campus in England. She wanted out of Ireland. Her mother didn't object.

She folded up the ironing board and brought her neatly pressed uniform back to her room. She clipped it on a hanger and hung it back in her closet. On her bed, now exhausted, she replayed the scene in the car with Danny. Each time, in her imagination, she'd let him go a little further. Her fantasy was vivid, and she could easily make it a reality, but she'd have to get over the thoughts that plagued her mind first ... and then get on the pill. She wouldn't risk getting pregnant. Peggy had told her where she could go if she ever needed to get a prescription.

"Go to a women's health clinic, fill out a form, get an exam ... and they'll give you three months of birth control free. They don't even call your parents."

Sounded easy enough.

She rolled onto her back making another mental note — *I may do that next week.* She knew Peggy would go with her if she asked.

Of course, the church spoke against birth control. *So what? Their stuff doesn't cut it with me any more. All those stories about priests abusing young boys and innocent students ... it's happening everywhere these days it seems.*

She recalled the snickers from the parishioners, a silent joke in the church, but it was hardly funny. She knew some of those boys who'd been abused. They were whisked away by their parents to unknown parts, and a new school — usually with a relative in the country to get away from the pitying stares and questioning glances of gossiping neighbors. Those bloody money-hungry barristers, of which her own father was one, drove the devastated parents to sue the church for thousands, if not millions, taking a hefty percentage for themselves.

Whatever path she took, she knew she'd have to be smart about it. She prided herself on being more mature than the other girls her age who still swooned when boys just looked at them.

Her demeanor reflected her sometimes-superior attitude, which didn't win her many friends at St. Joan of Arc, the private girl's school that daily imprisoned her spirit. She kept mostly to herself, achieved grades beyond what was expected, and left without so much as a word to her classmates.

Finally, she slept, without dreams of Danny or anyone else, stirring only slightly to the sound of sirens in the distance.

Chapter Twelve

Lake Otsego, New York, Summer 1978

"I BOUGHT SOME NEW BLANKETS to take with us to New York."

Sheila was making a last-minute check through the house to see if she'd missed anything.

"I figure we can always use them. I like to put extra blankets on the girls' beds. It gets pretty cold some nights. Don't you think?"

In the living room, half-listening to her comments, Tim concentrated on the end of a baseball game.

"Yeah, right ... gets cold."

She appeared suddenly in the living room.

"TIM! You're not paying attention to a word I'm saying, are you?"

She stared coolly at him.

He laughed and shook his head.

"Busted! Sorry, hon. You caught me! Hooked on the game. I'll make it up to you later."

She sighed dramatically, leaning against the doorframe.

"You owe me big time!"

He gestured, cigarette in his hand.

"You're right, I do. How about a diamond bracelet this time?"

"Nope. Got one. Thanks. But keep thinking along those lines. You're on the right track."

He laughed good-naturedly.

"You're all alike, you women!"

"Women?"

Sheila's voice turned to a fake shrill.

"You guys can't live without sports. God forbid you shut off that game and help me pack!"

She really didn't mind and was just giving him a playful hard time.

Painfully aware of how others viewed her husband, she'd overheard some of their comments when they thought she was out of earshot. They saw him as a loner, or a bit "off." She, however, saw his heart and found him good in so many other ways. She was secretly happy to see him making an attempt to cultivate an interest in another sport besides hockey.

He had finished high school and then attended trade school. He was great at fixing things. Growing up, what he really wanted to be was an auto mechanic ... maybe work for Ford or another big car company, but his mother adamantly refused to support him in that. He fell back on his second choice and studied to be an apprentice electrician instead. After he graduated, his brother Michael pulled some strings and got him into Bell Telephone Company, working as a lineman. It was a well-paying job with great health benefits.

He was a hard worker, and he doted on Sheila. Often, he, himself, wondered what she saw in him. They were so different. He hated being dragged into boring, intellectual conversations, but was a great listener one-on-one, holding his own when the talk rolled around to hockey or fishing. He preferred a simple life, though he was far from simpleminded. He cared for his nieces, Val and Caroline, as if they were his own daughters.

* * *

Sheila had met Tim by chance. She was in her mid-twenties, working as a legal secretary at a Boston law firm. It was a few weeks before Christmas, and she was standing in line at the bank, with the queue out the door - all those telephone workers cashing their Friday checks. Because she had to stay late to type a deposition, she'd missed cashing her check at two o'clock, after the lunch crowd, but before the end-of-day rush hour.

Now, at four o'clock, pinned in on all sides with the Friday crunch, she stood behind a young man wearing jeans, work boots, and a New England Telephone jacket. She leaned in and whispered.

"I hope there's cash left by the time we get there!"

She pretended to complain, but smiled at him good-naturedly.

He turned around at the sound of a female voice coming from behind him. He was surprised that such a pretty woman would initiate a conversation with him in line at the bank. He smiled and noted her long, strawberry-blond hair pulled up on the sides and held in place by a large, gold barrette. Her face was flushed from having been out in the stinging cold, then being confined to the warmth of an overcrowded bank with a wool coat on.

"I hope so, too, or they'll have a riot on their hands."

He chuckled in agreement.

"This is as good a reason as any to join a credit union, I'd say."

Sheila hesitated.

"I thought, if you worked for the telephone company, you're automatically in their credit union?"

He nodded.

"Yeah, I'm a member, but I'm going out after work, and this bank's closer to where I'm headed. I think just about any bank in Boston will cash a New England Telephone check."

"Oh. So, what are your plans ... tonight ... I mean?"

She couldn't believe she asked that. What if he thought her nosy? She was just trying to pass the time by making friendly conversation.

The young man seemed unfazed by her inquiry and shrugged.

"Heading over to Faneuil Hall to meet up with some of my buddies. Nothing great. We'll make the rounds ... typical Friday night, I guess. But it beats sitting home."

Another shrug.

Sheila wavered on the brink of asking him if she could join him. *No, I can't!* She shared his dislike of sitting at home alone on Friday nights, but she normally didn't go out of her way to meet men. It was out of character for her. Even though men had commented in the past that they found her attractive, dates weren't exactly beating down her door. She was "selective" she'd say to her sister, Grace, who would grin and tell her she needed to lower her standards to "breathing." That was easy for her to say. She had Neil.

There was something about this young man that was really holding Sheila's attention, something in his demeanor that made her want to continue talking with him. He wasn't attractive as far as handsome went. Actually, he looked rather on the thin side. But those dark, grayish-blue eyes lit up with enthusiasm when she spoke to him.

She had managed to convince herself that it was better to go out with men who weren't too attractive — they're not full of themselves. He was polite, if nothing else, and she liked his easygoing manner and approachability. He wasn't feeding her the standard lines. That was a nice change from what she was use to.

"What are your plans tonight? You doing anything fun and exciting?"

Tensing and feeling a little nervous, she blurted.

"Celebrating a birthday, I think!"

His eyes widened.

"Oh, yeah? No kidding! Happy Birthday! How old?"

Sheila shook her head and giggled, waving him off.

"No, no! I'm kidding. I mean, if we're here much longer ..."

She felt herself blushing.

"Then I'll be celebrating a birthday ... it's a joke. Sorry."

He shook his head and chuckled.

"So the girl's gotta sense of humor, too. A good thing - this waiting could drive you nuts."

Gaining in courage, he plowed on.

"Um, I know this might sound really crazy, but ... ah ... would you like to go out to dinner, IF we ever get outta here?"

Sheila blushed even more. Her blue eyes twinkled in the bright lights of the bank. Everything seemed to sparkle: the brass railings, the smooth, black marble floor. She surprised herself with her quick response.

"Yeah, I think I'd like that. But I don't want to mess up your plans with your friends. If they're waiting for you, I mean ..."

He waved away her concern.

"Don't worry about them. I can see them any time. To be honest, I'm bored with the bar scene. Same stuff, different day, you know? Do you like Italian food?"

Sheila grinned.

"Like it? I love it! There are tons of places to eat in the North End. Do you have a favorite?"

He shrugged.

"Well, I don't know, really. I don't go there much ... only been to a few places in and around Faneuil Hall, mostly for pizza. But we'll need some place where you don't need reservations ... or a suit jacket."

He grimaced and motioned to his work attire.

She couldn't wait to get out of the bank.

"How about Tecce's?"

She held her breath.

He nodded in agreement.

"Believe it or not, that's one place I have been to. They've got great Veal Parmesan ... and pizza!"

They both laughed.

"By the way, my name is Tim, Tim Hollis."

Extending her hand, she replied.

"Sheila Sullivan. It's nice to meet you, Tim."

Inwardly, she was somewhat appalled that she'd just made a date with a man whose name she hadn't even known! People within earshot turned and smiled at them.

They both seemed relieved. The line inched forward. He helped her take her coat off and glanced at the cream-colored, silk scarf wrapped loosely around her neck, held in place with a gold pin.

"That's a really nice scarf. It looks good on you."

Sheila flashed him a broad smile.

"Oh, thanks."

He watched her, becoming more smitten with each passing minute. *God! She's beautiful. I'm a nervous wreck! What am I going to say to her over dinner, anyway? I should run — now. What am I doing asking a total stranger out? What the hell ... she seems easy enough to talk to ... has a sense of humor. That ought to count for something. She did talk to me first...*

Talking about movies seemed to move the line along. Tim moved over into a line that looked like it might move faster. Sheila made it to a teller before him.

"I'll wait for you outside. I need some air."

She fanned her face with her hand.

He nodded in understanding and stepped up after her. Putting the cash into his wallet, he sauntered toward the door, pulling his jacket collar up against the frigid air.

"Whew! What an ordeal. I'm glad I only have to do that once a week."

She grinned. A light snow had started to fall, and delicate flakes clung to her eyelashes. She blinked them off dramatically. Tim watched her, amused. Seeking confirmation, she asked.

"Well, do you still want to have dinner with me?"

"Absolutely! I wouldn't have asked you if I didn't want to."

"Okay. Good! Me too. Let's go before we both chicken out and come up with excuses. This is so bizarre. Do you do this a lot?"

As they broached the curb, he offered her his arm. She grabbed hold, and they walked cautiously across the slippery street to the landmark Steaming Kettle.

"Well, I have to say, Sheila ... I, uh ... NO! I mean, this is a first for me. I've never just gone up to a woman in line at a bank and asked her out to dinner on the spot like that."

He groped for words that would sound more convincing. The dancing snow, now falling steadily, sparkled brilliantly in the surrounding florescent lights of Government Center. She shivered, but not from cold. She felt a coursing excitement run through her and wanted to egg him on a bit.

"Well, then, it's a first for both of us. I've never agreed to go to dinner with a total stranger before either."

She squeezed his arm.

"So what does that make us, huh?"

"DESPERATE!"

He announced jokingly as they continued laughing. She glanced at him while they trudged through the accumulating snow. *Very nice. He's fun. I can't wait to tell Grace about this ... of course, she'll laugh.*

As they walked along, Sheila nearly slipped and fell. His strong arm steadied her.

"Careful. If you fall and break your neck, you'll never want to go out with me again."

Sheila blushed, embarrassed that she'd almost landed on her behind, but happy that he was already considering asking her out again.

They both ordered the Veal Parmesan for dinner, and it was, as expected, delicious. They talked tentatively at first. He felt like an idiot when he forgot her name and had to ask her again. She didn't seem offended and repeated it graciously.

Slowly, the conversation moved toward family, generalities at first, testing the waters, sizing each other up. He inquired about her work at the law firm, and seemed genuinely interested in knowing more about what she did.

"Now, what about you, do you like working for the phone company?"

She watched his expression.

"Yeah ... sure. It's okay. I mean, I do okay there. I've been there a while. It's a good job."

Sheila nodded while sipping her wine, wondering what to say next. But he went on to tell her a bit about his family. His only brother also worked for the telephone company and got married two years ago. Tim loosened up gradually, perhaps because of the wine, and regaled her with snippets from his life: he'd grown up in Hyde Park ... came from a hard-working, blue-collar family ... his father was a retired Boston fire fighter ... they didn't have a lot of extras growing up, but Dad had been careful, and they always ate well, had decent clothes, vacations now and again. His mother never worked outside the home.

"But she worked hard in the home taking care of the three of us."

He emphasized that point. His parents still owned the large multi-family home he grew up in. He rented one of the apartments.

"Finding it hard to break those apron strings, huh, Tim?"

Sheila chided him.

"What? Are you kidding me? I've got it easy! I have my privacy AND get a home-cooked meal most nights. Did I happen to mention that Mom still does my laundry, too?"

He raised his glass to her and stuck out his tongue.

"OH, NO! You'll never move out! You've got it too good there!"

She laughed heartily.

"Damn right!"

He joked and told her more about his brother and sister-in-law.

"Well, they've been married a couple of years now and still don't have any rug rats. Why is it that mothers are always in such a rush for their kids to have kids, I wonder?"

"It's called ... revenge!!"

Sheila offered.

"You know, I think you hit the nail on the head! That's gotta be it."

Neither appeared to be in a rush to leave after they finished their meal.

Sheila felt very much at ease with Tim, a feeling no doubt helped by the wine. She asked him what he liked to do in his spare time.

"Well, mostly I catch up on sleep on the weekends, and I get out to a Bruins game when I can. Do you like sports?"

Sheila shook her head.

"It's not that I dislike them. I just don't know much about them. But I'm willing to learn!"

Her eyes lit up eagerly.

Tim smiled.

"It's a lot of fun once you understand the game."

"Hockey can be pretty rough, can't it? I mean, more fights than goals, from what I've seen of the Bruins on TV?"

Sheila asked.

"I guess that's part of the lure - for men, anyway. Brute beasts that we are."

She smirked at him.

"You're hardly what I'd consider a brute beast ... though I've met a few in my time."

Tim was a considerate man, not given to monopolizing the conversation. Their silences were comfortable, and the conversation was never forced. They shared their feelings and views on various topics and it flowed naturally, like they'd known each other for years. She sensed chemistry there and wondered if he felt it, too. Tim pointed to her empty wineglass.

"If you'd like more, I could order you another."

"Will you have one?"

She didn't want the night to end. He shook his head no.

"I'm done. I'm driving."

Sheila was surprised when she checked her watch. It was getting late, and she'd have to make her way home in what had become a blinding snowstorm. She got a little nervous at that thought, knowing that very few taxis would be on the road during a storm. Tim picked up on her anxiety.

"What's the matter?"

She motioned for him to look out the window across the room.

"I'm going to have a hard time finding a taxi to get home in this mess. I'm a little nervous at the thought of taking the train this late."

"You don't have to take a train. I'll drive you! Where do you live?"

"Commonwealth Avenue. It's not that far away."

"No problem, Sheila. I know my way all around Boston. Let me get the bill, and we'll walk back to the garage."

"Tim, thanks for dinner. I had a great time."

He smiled warmly at her.

"Me, too. Thank you, for saying 'yes' to a total stranger!"

As they left the restaurant, Sheila tried to stifle an escaping yawn. Tim nodded.

"Yeah, I'm kinda beat, too."

He yawned.

"See what you started ..."

She chuckled.

Taking hold of his arm, they trudged, heads down, into the raging snowstorm.

The garage was across from Government Center. Once inside, they easily found his car. Exiting the garage, they proceeded to fishtail down Boylston Street and onto Arlington Street. Fortunately, not many cars were on the road. They couldn't see more than a foot in front of them. What would have normally been a ten minute drive took over forty minutes. Maneuvering was becoming impossible due to the lack of visibility. Tim had to keep stopping to remove the heavy snow that clung to his windshield wipers.

"I must be living under a rock. I didn't hear anything about a snowstorm. Did you?"

Sheila shook her head.

"Nope, not at all. But then, this is New England!"

Tim reached out his window again to remove a clump of snow from the moving blades.

"You'll have to tell me where you live. I can't see a damn thing!"

Her roommate was gone for the weekend, and she had the apartment to herself. She loved living in Boston and the place she had on Commonwealth Avenue was a prime location. She couldn't believe her good fortune when she found it. It turned out that one of the attorneys she worked for owned the building, and gave her the second floor apartment at a reasonable rent. He was just glad to have someone responsible in there to keep an eye on things for him.

Sheila laughed nervously; the visibility was really bad.

"Listen, Tim, I know this might sound crazy, and I'm not trying to come on to you ..."

"Oh, no! Please do!"

Sheila good-naturedly slapped his hand.

"Knock it off. I'm trying to be serious here. My roommate is in New York for the weekend. The weather is awful, and you'd be nuts to try and get home in this. You could stay in her room. This is really white-knuckle driving. Oops! Here! Here! Stop. That's it,"

She exclaimed, pointing to her right. The car slid past her door.

"I may take you up on that ..."

Tim stopped the car in the rutted lane in front of her building and looked intently at her.

"Did you ever stop to think that I could possibly be a mad rapist or an ax murderer? You could be taking your life in your hands right now."

She held both palms up, weighing that.

"Well, you're right, of course. But I sense you're not. Besides, I'll have you know; I own a gun and know how to use it. I keep it under my pillow. How does that grab you?"

She joked.

"I love an aggressive woman ..."

The weather is horrible and, no doubt, it will take at least two hours to get home. Here is a beautiful woman offering for me to spend the night. Am I nuts or what?

He wouldn't dare take advantage of her by making any foolish moves. Besides, she seemed too refined ... not one given to messing around or casual sex, unlike others he'd been with. Sheila was different. He'd sensed that from the very beginning. He'd be on his best behavior. He wanted to go out with her again.

"Okay then. I'll take you up on your offer. How do you like your omelets?"

"Mushrooms and cheese with a hint of scallion. I think I've got eggs, milk, and cheese, but I don't know about the mushrooms or scallions ... and anyway, I'm sleeping until noon. You can trek to the store, if you want to, in the morning!"

Tim laughed, more relaxed with that decision out of the way.

"Okay, omelets for lunch then."

He maneuvered his car into what he thought was a parking space and pushed open his door.

"Let's hightail it. Oops!"

He assessed his awful parking and flopped back into the seat.

"Can't leave it out here in the road. I'll try to squeeze it in more."

"No, no."

Sheila instructed him to drive around to the back where she and her roommate's parking spaces were, off a public alley. Tim gave a quick shudder, as the air was biting cold, after the warmth of the car. They walked in through the basement and up to the main foyer and stairway. Sheila's hair was covered in snow from the short walk in to the building.

Gathering her mail off the table in the marbled hallway, Sheila commented.

"Oh, good! It's here!"

She picked up a large, bulky manila envelope.

"What's that?"

"Information I requested about a realtor course I want to take. I'm going to take classes in the evenings. It's something I've always wanted to do."

Tim admired her ambition.

"Good for you. Now I know who I can come to when I want to buy my own house. IF I ever buy my own house..."

He chuckled and nudged her.

"Oh! Do you think you'll buy a house any time soon?"

Sheila asked him as they climbed the old marble steps that led to her apartment.

"Well, not exactly. Remember, I'm going to live with my parents forever. Like most slackers do."

Sheila laughed aloud.

"Oh, that's right. I forgot."

"Seriously though, I'd like to buy one someday. It seems rather pointless unless you're married, don't you think? To own a big house by yourself?"

Sheila turned to him.

"Yeah, I guess so."

They sat on the deacon's bench just outside the door to the apartment and pulled off their boots. Sheila hung her coat on the ornate brass and walnut rack. Tim followed suit, hanging his coat next to hers, and followed her into the apartment.

It was more modern than he'd expected. The floors were natural hardwood throughout, and there was an exposed brick wall that appeared to run the length of the apartment into the kitchen. A large bay window with a built-in window seat overlooked the snow-covered park dividing Commonwealth Avenue. It was a pretty view, with the snow falling and the gas lamps glowing. He turned at the sound of her voice.

"Hey, I've got an idea! Are you really that tired?"

Sheila asked him excitedly, her eyes dancing.

Eyebrows raised, Tim shrugged.

"Well, no, not too bad. Why? What have you got in mind?"

"The Rocky Horror Picture Show! It's just a short walk from here, right around the corner really. It'll be fun to mush through that snow again, won't it? You up for it?"

Exhausted as he was, Tim wouldn't have disappointed her for the world.

"Sure. When's the next show?"

"I think eleven thirty. It runs pretty late. I'll call and check. Hang on a minute."

He watched as she sprinted into the kitchen, amused at her spontaneity and envying what had to be her second wind. He'd had a long day and his muscles ached. He walked around the living room, stretching his arms over his head, admiring the pictures on the fireplace mantle.

There were a few of her posing with a young woman with long, dark hair. The woman had brilliant blue eyes ... looking directly into the camera ... a stunning smiled revealed straight, white teeth. She resembled Sheila. He assumed it to be her sister. Sheila had mentioned how beautiful she was. He liked that about her ... her love for her sister — Grace, he thought she said her name was. He was close to his brother but didn't see him as much since he'd gotten married. His brother's wife was anxious to start a family. They made it a point to catch an occasional Bruins game together when they could. Tim never gave much thought to marriage. If it happened, it happened.

Sheila came back looking a bit deflated.

"Darn! We missed it. It started at eleven."

Tim put his hands up.

"Oh, well, it looks like we'll have to hang out here where it's warm and cozy and stare at each other's faces."

Sheila chuckled.

"Yeah, tough break. Anyway, I've got some spare sweats, if you want to wear them. I buy a lot of my kick-around clothes at Mickey Finn's. It's unisex. There's more wine and beer in the fridge if you want something to drink. Help yourself. I'll be back in a minute."

She seemed very comfortable with him and he liked that.

A large overstuffed beige sofa, with lots of assorted colored throw pillows, was set in front of the fireplace ... a single oil painting hung above it. A dark wooden desk was set diagonally in the corner. On top were pieces of Victorian-looking stationary, along with a brass pen and pencil set with a matching letter opener. Everything was neat and orderly. A large plant sat in the far corner, decorated in white lights, which added a warm glow to the room. The lights reflected off the satin-finished wood floor. *I've got to give her credit; she's got style.* He wondered if the fireplace worked.

Tim walked into the galley kitchen and opened the door to the refrigerator. He took out a bottle of wine, *Pinot Grigio* ... he'd have to remember that. Though they'd had merlot with dinner, he called out.

"Do you want me to open this bottle of white wine?"

Sheila opened the door to her room and went into the kitchen. She'd pulled her hair up into a ponytail, and stood before him with no makeup on and a freshly washed face. If possible, Tim thought, she looked younger and even more beautiful without makeup. She handed him a set of matching sweats.

"We'll be twins."

She smiled and took the bottle from him.

"I'll pour us a glass if you want to go change."

She reached overhead and slipped two wine glasses off the rack.

"The bathroom is down the hall past my room and to the left. The switch is outside the door."

Sheila waited in the living room, gazing out the bay window. She felt warm and safe with Tim there. She got up and lit the fireplace and the candles on the mantle.

For a moment, she allowed herself to imagine ... *I wonder what it might be like to have him around the house here permanently* ... and then laughed at herself. *Sheila, you dope! You just met him!*

He walked quietly back up the hall and stopped for a moment to stare at her, sitting at the window seat with her arms wrapped around her tucked-up knees, holding a wine glass. She looked so peaceful, in contrast to the storm howling outside. He joined her at the window, and she held up a glass for him. She patted the seat, inviting him to sit down. They sat in silence, watching the commencing nor'easter.

Looking around the room, Tim broke the silence.

"This is a nice place, Sheila. But, if you don't mind me asking ... how do you afford it? I'm sure you're a damn good secretary ... but a place like this? The rent's got to be outrageous."

Sheila didn't mind him asking, and she explained to him the situation with her boss, how he owned the building and wanted her to be there to keep an eye on it. She grimaced and sipped her wine slowly.

"Yeah, like I can control things, the big overseer."

She shared the apartment with a friend of hers from college, so the rent was reasonable.

"But I do have to do my own laundry. Imagine that! The injustice ..."

Tim grinned.

"I'll never hear the end of this. Will I?"

She tossed her head back.

"NOPE!"

They talked into the early morning, until neither one could stay awake any longer. Sheila got up first and stretched. She offered to take his wine glass, and he caught her hand gently and stared into her eyes.

"Thank you, again."

He kissed her lightly on the cheek.

She pointed him in the direction of her roommate's bedroom.

"Goodnight, Tim. I'm glad you're here and safe."

"Me, too."

Heading down the hall toward her own room, she closed the door, wishing she wasn't there alone.

Sheila woke to the smell of frying bacon and fresh coffee brewing. She got up lazily and stretched. Her hair was all over the place as she staggered down the hall to the bathroom to brush her teeth.

From the kitchen, Tim called out.

"You'll have to settle for just eggs and bacon. It's not fit for man or beast out there."

With the toothbrush still in her mouth, she garbled back.

"Is it still snowing?"

"Yeah, take a look. I bet there's more than a foot and a half out there! I can't even see the car anymore. It doesn't look like it's stopping any time soon either."

Sheila spit out the toothpaste and wiped her mouth on the towel. She loved lazy Saturday mornings. She went over to stand beside Tim at the window. Crossing her arms, she lamented.

"Oh, my God! I had no idea we were even getting snow, let alone this much! I'm glad you didn't attempt to drive home in this, Tim."

She tapped his back playfully.

"You'd better call your mother, so she's not a wreck worrying about you."

He looked at her warmly.

"They're down in Florida for the winter. THIS is why they leave."

He pointed outside.

"They're snow birds."

Sheila chuckled and reached for a mug to pour a cup of coffee. As she carefully sipped the hot liquid, she watched him.

"Okay, so, what's the game plan for today?"

Sheila shrugged.

"I don't know. I don't have one really. I told you, Saturday is laundry day. Not that you'd know anything about that ..."

She remarked coyly, bringing the steaming mug to her dramatically pursed lips.

"Do you want to catch a Bruins game with me? I've got season tickets. I usually give the extra one away, but since I didn't see the guys last night, I didn't pass it off to anyone."

Sheila loved the idea of seeing a game and nearly spilled her coffee. She'd never been to a live hockey game before.

"I'd love to! What time does it start?"

"At two o'clock, but we should leave here around twelve to get to the Garden on time. It looks like we'll be taking the train in."

Tim brought the breakfast plates into the dining room for them. The eggs were delicious, and the bacon was cooked crisp, the way she liked it.

"You made the bacon perfectly. I hate googly bacon."

He mocked her playfully.

"Googly?"

"Yeah, googly! You know, rubbery. I like it well done, kinda crunchy. Like this!"

He nodded in agreement.

"I do, too."

They made small talk and ate hungrily. She helped him clean up the dishes, and then he offered to carry her laundry basket downstairs for her.

"I'll take care of this if you want to go and take a shower. There are towels in the closet. Go on. I don't want you to see me washing my underwear. I barely know you."

Sheila joked and waved him off, but he followed her anyway.

Tim threw his head back and laughed.

"Right. I'm just the stranger you met in line at the bank and invited home to your apartment for the night, remember?"

Already it seemed like that was ages ago. She felt as if they'd shared so much already that it was hard to believe they'd only met the previous night. She closed the lid of the washer and followed him back upstairs.

He sang loudly and dramatically in the shower, and she laughed to herself as she poured another cup of coffee and leafed through her real estate brochures.

"I hope I didn't use all the hot water on you."

He had tried to use one of her razors to shave, nicking his face.

"I slaughtered myself with that razor of yours."

Sheila touched his face and assured him.

"I think you'll live."

He gazed at her warmly and slowly bent his head to kiss her. She didn't turn away and raised her mouth to his. He held her tightly as she leaned against the wall. Bringing her arms up around his neck, she held him close, smelling the clean scent of soap. He pressed into her and buried his face in her hair.

"Tell me more about this gun of yours."

"It's a .25 milliliter something-or-other."

She whispered in his ear.

"Hmmm ... I think you just described a high-powered water pistol."

"You scared?"

"Terribly. I'm shaking in my boots."

"Good. It'll keep you honest."

"It won't keep you very safe, I'm afraid."

Sheila snickered and ducked under his arms.

"I'm going to take a shower now. I'll make sure to lock the door."

She winked.

"You're a wise woman."

He said with a groan.

"If you'll excuse me, I'm going to go jump in a snow bank now."

Sheila laughed after closing the door.

The day seemed to fly by for both of them. Sheila lost herself in the excitement and intensity of the hockey game. Tim explained the different calls and rules to her, and she caught on quickly — even shouting out a few times, much to her own surprise. Tim laughed at her sudden outbursts and knew he was witnessing the birth of a future hockey buff. They stopped for pizza after the game, and hiked through a few snow banks on the way back to her apartment. The snow had finally let up, and the city snow-plows were out in full force.

Back at the apartment, she found him a shovel and watched from the window as he dug out his car. She saw his breath rising in clouds. The night was bitterly cold, yet crystal clear. She waved to him from the window. He smiled up from underneath the street light, waving back.

Finally, Tim came huffing and puffing upstairs. She handed him a cup of hot chocolate.

"Now would be a good time to consider giving up those cigarettes, don't you think?"

"Wise guy!"

He kissed her lips quickly. They were so warm.

"I've got to get going, Sheila. My brother is supposed to stop by tonight to pick up some books. I've had a great time. Would you like to go out again?"

"I would have been crushed if you didn't ask. I'd love to. Let me give you my phone number."

She turned to get a piece of paper off the desk.

"I'll give you mine, too."

In the foyer, Tim kissed her again and said good-bye. She ran back upstairs to wave again from the window. The back wheels of his car were spinning in place as he tried shifting to get out of the parking spot. Finally successful, he drove off, beeping the horn. Sheila ran to the phone; she could hardly wait to tell Grace about her weekend.

Chapter Thirteen

Ennis, County Clare, Ireland, Fall 1978

NOT LONG AFTER GLYNNIS AND Danny had driven off, the rain started in earnest and the rest of the gang finished their drinks and headed home. Connie offered Peggy a ride back to the halting site, and she took him up on it. Although she appreciated him giving her a lift, she insisted that he leave her at the end of the dirt road. It was pitch black outside, except for the headlights shining from his car. The air was cool. Seeing that she was only wearing a light jacket that was already wet, Connie insisted on driving her closer.

"No, this is fine. Really, Con."

Peggy insisted.

"They don't like strangers, and turn down the lights or you'll get the dogs barking. They'll wake the kids, and I'll catch hell for it tomorrow."

Connie quickly dimmed the lights and looked at Peggy. He didn't understand her living arrangement.

"Peg, how did you get hooked up with these people? I mean, they're knackers, right?"

Connie asked curiously. Peggy winced and shook her head at his callous reference.

"No, not exactly. We move around a lot to find work. Believe it or not, most of these guys are spoiled, English society dropouts. We like to consider ourselves artists of sorts."

Connie snorted at that.

"Yeah, right! They're a bunch of lazy thieves!"

"Not all of them, Con. It's not a life I would have set out and picked for myself – if I had a choice."

Connie sat and listened, intrigued.

"Well, what do you do for work? I mean, how do you contribute to this group?"

"You promise not to laugh?"

Connie nodded and mockingly crossed his heart.

"Yeah, go on."

"I draw, portraits, scenes with coal, or colored chalk. That is what I like to do best. Oh yeah, and I paint, too."

He sat up, genuinely interested.

"No kidding! What do you paint?"

Not one to draw attention to herself, Peggy was rather reluctant to elaborate, but seeing that his interest was genuine, she proceeded to tell him about some of the portraits and murals she had done, and how she painted houses during the summer to earn her keep with some of the men. There were more opportunities in the warmer months for house painting.

"I once painted a lovely scene on the wall of a nursery for a woman and she was so impressed that she told some of her friends. That's how I find work — referrals. But it can be feast or famine at times."

Peggy became excited when talking about her drawings.

"Wow, Peg! That's cool. I never would have guessed you were that talented. I'm going to have you draw something for me one of these days."

She laughed and promised him she'd sketch his mug for him one of these nights at the wall.

*　*　*

Certain things really bothered Peggy. The caravan she journeyed with ran into all kinds of trouble. Despised by some of the people in Ireland, Travellers, as they were referred to, would often take up residence on people's land or along the sides of roads until disgruntled landowners or locals would run them off, threatening them. Neighboring teens would occasionally throw rocks and holler obscenities at them, often unprovoked. It frightened the children and made them cry. The first time Peggy experienced the terror of such an encounter, it scared the wits out of her.

They had stopped at a designated halting site and settled in for a few days. A private property bordered the site. One of the dogs got loose, so Stephen headed off to bring it back. Peggy had been sleeping late and heard the women yelling to their husbands and boyfriends to get the kids inside. Leonore and a couple of the other women were running around screaming and pulling their still damp shirts and paper-thin towels off sagging, makeshift clotheslines.

Bobby banged on the side of the trailer, shouting for Peggy to get up. She shot upright, banging her head on the cabinet above her tiny bunk. He needed her help untying the rest of the animals. They hurried to get back on the road.

One of the families' dogs was shot and killed while the children looked on in terror. It was a horrible scene. The men wanted to beat the landowner for shooting the children's dog, saying that it could have been one of them that caught the bullet. The landowner yelled back from behind his stone wall that they had no right even keeping their children given the squalor and filth they lived in. There was nearly a donnybrook. Bobby grabbed Leonore and shoved her in the trailer, and they quickly sputtered off down the road.

Years ago, the Travellers were known for being tinsmiths of sorts that could fix just about anything. Some of the locals actually looked forward to their coming around to repair household items such as copper pots and metal buckets. They frequently bought and sold antiques and old horses but were most notably spoken of as swindlers who could talk the eyes right out of your head. They'd mull around well-known tourist attractions or holiday locations such as Salt Hill in Galway, or parts of Ennis, County

Clare, in order to play upon tourists' sympathies, begging coins to buy milk for their smudge-faced, runny-nosed children.

It was rumored that the Travellers would often hound local parish priests for baptismal certificates for fictitious children. These certificates were accepted and respected as well as any birth certificate in Ireland, and enabled them to apply for and receive a larger child allowance from the government. But again, Travellers were not the only ones that took part in such schemes — others on the dole committed similar acts. But the Travellers bore the brunt of society's disdain and were shunned because rumors were accepted as truth and no one cared to find out otherwise.

As an example, several years ago, there was a story all over the papers about a Traveller's child getting hold of a gun and accidentally shooting his sister, killing her. Though it could have happened anywhere, the episode set off yet another round of debate in the media about the capabilities of people with such itinerant lifestyles to properly care for their children. Could they even care for themselves, let alone provide for innocent children, when their perceived "ignorance" unnecessarily put them at risk?

It fed into peoples' hatred and blatant disrespect for a group of people who largely just wanted to keep to themselves and their own way of doing things and living life. It was later discovered that the people in the story were not even Travellers at all, but a young Irish family meandering across country on holiday. The child found his father's firearm, there was no safety lock on it, and it accidentally went off. Only one newspaper printed a retraction, and it was so small that it was entirely overlooked. It's a story many fell back on and referenced when trying to justify the country's mounting crime rate.

*   *   *

Connie stared at Peggy, sitting beside him in the car.
"Are you going to leave me hanging?"

"It's a long story, Connie."

She remarked unemotionally. He held up his hands.

"I've got time, if you want to unload."

Peggy stared at the small, metal trailers in the distance, their dull lights barely illuminating the side of the homes. She was embarrassed. True enough that it didn't look like much, but these people really had been her only source of support since she ran away from the children's home almost three and a half years ago.

Of course, there was a dark side; there was always a dark side. The man she found herself living with now, and his brother, who led the group, frightened Peggy. She was reluctant to talk about them, and was working hard to save up money on the side without getting caught. They had ways of finding out if you were withholding money from them, and there would be hell to pay if you got caught. It could be deadly. Not all were so tightfisted, but Bobby could be downright vicious. He found money once that Leonore had stored away in a sock. He slapped her around and accused her of prostitution. She took a horrible beating from him later that night - one of many. As Peggy's own private savings grew, the stress from worrying about getting caught was becoming unbearable, and she wanted to run away as soon as she was able.

Peggy felt no attraction to Connie. She liked to socialize and drink with her friends when her travels brought her back to these parts. They accepted her for who she was and didn't ask a lot of questions, until tonight. She had shared a bit of her story with Clare one night while drinking and feeling pretty good. Clare had sat and listened, dumbfounded.

It was Glynnis that Peggy felt close to and who she could talk with, if she ever had to unload. She felt drawn to her for some reason. She sensed somehow that maybe Glynnis held similar secrets, though the two had never shared personal stories in depth. There was a quiet strength to Glynnis that Peggy admired and connected with, even though they didn't know much about each other.

Their worlds were incomparably different. Glynnis's life consisted of crisp, white linen and fine-cut Waterford crystal. Peggy's reeked of mildew, and stained, chipped coffee mugs stolen from local eateries. Peggy often envied her friend's seemingly pampered life, then cringed at the confinement of it all. Freedom tasted good to her, even if it came at a high price.

Seeing Glynnis' mother slap her earlier brought out a protective nature in her and an anger that she'd not felt since she left her uncle. She'd wanted to lash out and strike Mrs. O'Brien right across her tight little mouth after she'd hit her friend. Her own experiences, far worse at times, lingered in the back of her mind; repressed memories of her own neglected childhood.

Connie sat patiently in silence, not wanting to push her too far.

"You don't want to hear the gory details, Connie. Take my word for it."

Peggy dismissed him with as casual a wave as she could muster. Had she been talking to Glynnis, she'd have never been let out of the car until every last syllable was pronounced. But Connie, being a guy, wasn't concerned about details, and just shrugged.

"Ok, but if you ever want to talk, let me know."

Had he persisted, even a little, Peggy probably would have spilled her guts. She was lonely, scared, and really did want someone to talk to. Instead, she thanked him for the ride and got out. She shivered from the wind and rain and headed down the muddy road, focusing intently on the dim lights ahead. Turning she waved Connie on, assuring him she'd be fine.

Peggy climbed the two flimsy, metal steps to the trailer, causing it to dip slightly under her weight. It was held stationary by two large cinder blocks. The dogs out back barked noisily.

"SHHHHH!!!"

The commotion woke a baby, who started crying in the trailer next door. She stood quietly, willing things to settle down, when a light went on. She turned to the screen door, badly in need of repair, which rattled in its frame as she tugged to open it. As she pushed the second small door open, the screen slammed shut behind her. She cringed. She'd hear about it for sure tomorrow.

Peggy could smell Bobby right away, and it disgusted her. She longed to leave the door open to let fresh air in, but it was cold and damp, and she didn't dare wake him. Bobby, vertically-challenged, exemplified a classic Napoleon complex. It ran in the family.

Leonore had been gone for a little over two weeks, and Peggy doubted she'd ever return. Bobby was furious when she didn't come back. In a fit of drunken rage over a dirty dish one night, he punched Peggy repeatedly, knocking the breath out of her and leaving large bruises on her back. She had to wear the same shirt for three days because it was too painful to pull the shirt over her head. He insisted she knew where Leonore was and that she wasn't telling him.

There was a small light on over the one-gas burner that acted as their stove. The stale smell of tobacco and sausages made the contents of her stomach rise in her throat. Dirty pans crowded the tiny sink, while plates with hardened egg sat untouched on the miniature counter top. The only ventilation came from a small window located in the broom-sized closet that was their bathroom.

The "bathroom" held a rusted toilet the size of a potty chair and a small sink that had to be covered in order to take a handheld shower. The showerhead had only five unclogged holes that let water trickle through. Peggy thought it a great tool for watering plants — useless for humans. The water leaked out from under the door if it wasn't shut properly; so the carpet was rotted with mildew and never completely dry. The floor beneath it had begun to sag.

She continued to tell herself that, as soon as she had enough money, she was going to find a small efficiency room somewhere, get a full-time job, and get out of this hell hole she called home. She'd accumulated a couple of hundred pounds in the last two weeks from a few painting jobs.

Though she contributed to their communal "kitty," she'd been skimming large amounts off the top for years and not telling Bobby the exact amount given to her for a job. He didn't appear to notice anything missing. They knew nothing of her savings from her many freelance portraits.

She'd be eighteen years old soon, and couldn't wait to leave this life behind. She often weighed the pros and cons of staying versus going back out on the streets. At least, on the streets, she knew of places to hide.

Bobby and Leonore had befriended her a couple years before, when she'd fled to Ireland, on the run from England's Child Protective Services and an abusive children's home they'd placed her in. She met them at a small town festival in Charlestown, County Mayo, where she was hanging with a rather tough-looking crowd of homeless kids at the time.

She'd learned how to survive on the streets, and realized she didn't need much. Staying at the train station or squatting in abandoned buildings often provided shelter during the winter months, while in the warmer months, she'd sleep under bridges or in an abandoned car.

At the festival, Peggy, who was only fifteen at the time, caught Bobby's attention. She sat quietly among the other kids, drawing on a pad of paper and smoking her cigarette. He and Leonore walked up behind her and watched as she used her tiny dulled pencil, and even some of the fallen ash from her cigarette, to create depth in a picture of a small bridge she was drawing. She looked older than her years, and was oblivious to those around her who danced wildly to the clamoring rock music. Bobby thought she might be a good match for his brother, Stephen.

Bobby and his brother stuck together. Stephen was the leader of the group. Bobby felt bad on occasion that his older brother didn't seem to have any luck with women. He was actually somewhat of an eyesore — a rather short, beefy bloke with rotting crooked teeth that he never brushed. He had an explosive temper, whether drinking or not, and was always up for a fight. He let his brown, frizzy hair grow long, and it hung lifeless down his back, giving him a caveman-like appearance. His seedy mustache and beard hadn't been cut or shaped in years.

Bobby thought Stephen might have a chance with the young, homeless Peggy. She was obviously talented and could bring in money, which was really all Stephen cared about. It would be cold soon, and Peggy might want someone to keep her warm. Bobby knew the street kids were broke and hungry. Spotting her new face in the group, he thought she might be just what Stephen needed. He could make life hell for everyone when things weren't going his way, and he hadn't been with a woman in a while.

Bobby and Leonore offered to buy Peggy a meal and a pack of cigarettes. She asked what they wanted before she accepted. They asked her if she had a job and a place to stay. She waited to hear more before she responded. She couldn't risk being set up and hauled back to England.

Leonore told her how, when she'd met Bobby, she too, was on the streets, and that after she moved in with him; they became one big family, sharing everything. Bobby explained that they had a small trailer, but offered out that she could stay with them in return for help with cooking, housekeeping, and watching the kids while the men worked. When she asked what else she'd have to do to earn her keep, Bobby replied.

"Nothing too difficult. Besides, you've got talent."

He pointed toward the grungy notebook she carried with her.

"You can get work doing odd jobs here and there. When any of us gets a job and gets money, we put it all in one big pot. That way nobody goes without. We watch out for each other."

Peggy convinced herself that it was sort of like a "nanny" job. Autumn wasn't too far off and it would be getting colder. She thought this opportunity might be her good fortune, and seized it, not wanting to freeze another winter. She told herself that she could do anything she wanted, and if she didn't like it, she could always leave. She was too innocent to have foreseen the many ways they could hold her captive.

Chapter Fourteen

PEGGY'S FATHER HAD DIVORCED HER mother when she was only three years old. She didn't remember much about him, only faint shadows, never a face. Her mother very rarely mentioned him, only to say that he had never provided for them. For financial reasons, Peggy and her mother were forced to leave Ireland and went to live with her grandmother and uncle in England.

After the grandmother's death, the house was left to Peggy's mother and uncle. When Peggy was five, her mother felt obligated to find a job to support them. There was nothing by way of money that came in from Peggy's father. Fortunately for Peggy, her grandmother's house was fairly big, and she had her own room. Her uncle took care to maintain the property. He enjoyed gardening and decorating. He loved young Peggy, and often bought her nice clothing and toys.

Increasingly bored and disgusted with her lot in life, Peggy's mother chose to work long, twelve-hour shifts each week as a care assistant at a local elderly home, leaving Peggy in her uncle's care. She left for work before Peggy got home from school, and got home after she went to bed. Peggy rarely saw her mother during those tender and formative years of her life.

She came to rely heavily on her uncle for the basic, day-to-day living needs. He cooked and cared for her, and did it lovingly. He made sure her clothes were clean and packed her lunch each day. Every morning, he walked her to school before he headed off to his own job at a local printing company.

While Peggy was still very young, her uncle's intentions toward her began to change. He still insisted on helping her bathe and dress, even as her body began to mature. When she was eleven years old, she protested some, but he assured her it was all very normal.

His hands would massage her in those delicate areas that she was told in school were "private." Her face would sting with embarrassment as he guided her hand to his private area. She tried to pull away, but his firm grip held her close. The act was mortifying to her at first, and she felt horrible guilt. Sometimes, on her way home from school, she'd break off from the rest of the kids and sneak into the church to light a few candles and pray to the Blessed Virgin for forgiveness. She never had any money to put in the box, but figured God to be quite rich, so he wouldn't miss it.

One night after her bath, her uncle helped her into her nightgown and invited her to sleep in his bed. He explained to her simply that his bed was bigger and much more comfortable. She'd sleep more soundly there than in her tiny bed. Once she lay down on the pillow, he reached into the drawer of his nightstand and took out a couple of girly magazines. He held up the pictures and had her look on with him.

Peggy was shocked, and blushed, yet was intrigued by what she saw. Those girls didn't seem the slightest bit embarrassed by a man's private parts. She couldn't even look at her uncle's when he asked her to, and would turn away, red in the face. He'd assured Peggy that other girls, not much older than her, would do the very same things to make men happy. He also told her that one day she may have a boyfriend, and that if she wanted to get married, she'd need to learn what men wanted. In her innocence, she always wanted to make her uncle happy.

From all outward appearances, he was very kind to his young niece, providing her with a loving, stable home environment, and she did love him dearly with a purity of heart he did not deserve.

Each night after her bath, he'd take her to his room and instruct her. Using the magazines as a guide, he'd tell her what pleased him, and continually assured her not to feel ashamed. It was their secret. He called it, "Our special, private time."

Her mother would never know. She was never home, and he made Peggy agree never to tell her.

"She wouldn't understand."

Uncle James would say sadly.

"She might think that I was hurting you. Do I hurt you, Peggy?"

She shook her head no, as he never did. Up to that point, he'd never penetrated her. He knew she was still too young, but he also knew how much she craved nurturing and attention. He'd bide his time.

Her mother was too busy and had recently become involved with another caregiver from the old folks' home where she worked. Eventually, she stopped coming home altogether. When Peggy turned twelve, a letter arrived from her mother.

She had written to tell her brother how grateful she was to him for taking such good care of her daughter over the years. She knew she wasn't a good mother, and said that she hoped Peggy would come to appreciate the things he did for her, and that one day she'd thank him for all of his love and kindness. She went on to explain how she had never really wanted children, but that her first husband had insisted and she'd conceded.

Two years after Peggy's birth, however, the marriage began to disintegrate. Her husband had left her for another woman and asked for a divorce shortly after that. She was finally finding the happiness that she wanted in her new relationship, and was leaving England for Australia with no plans to return. She asked her brother to continue to take good care of Peggy, as he was the only father she'd ever known. She left no forwarding address.

Peggy never saw nor heard from her again. James never reported his sister for abandonment, as he should have. He was very pleased with the way things were working out ...

In time, Peggy no longer needed a magazine as a guide, and the blushing that once accompanied their acts began to elude her. Her uncle had her experimenting and doing things she'd never imagined herself doing. She'd learned to please him immensely, and slept in his bed on a regular basis.

She knew somewhere in her heart that the arrangement wasn't right, but she felt helpless to do anything about it. Her uncle insisted, and she didn't protest too much at first. She was never allowed to have friends stay over, as that would mean she couldn't sleep with her uncle. He closely monitored her friends and relationships; no boys were ever allowed to call the house.

Her teenage years, however, brought about enlightenment and a new attitude, and on Peggy's fourteenth birthday, life took a dramatic turn.

Chapter Fifteen

Cariston, England, Fall 1974

PEGGY WAS EXCITED ABOUT MEETING up with her friends after school. They'd promised her a great celebration, complete with pints they'd hidden away for the special occasion, her birthday. It was Friday, and she knew her uncle had his own plans for her. He reminded her that morning before she left for school.

"I have a special, grown-up evening in mind for us tonight, Peggy."

He'd smiled warmly at her as he placed her cereal bowl in front of her for breakfast - like she was still six years old.

Turning away in disgust, she didn't care about his plans and wanted no part of it. He irritated her lately, and she was growing more rebellious by the day. Trapped in his home, but eager to get out from underneath his perverted gaze and away from his constant fondling, she had made her own plans for her birthday.

A young man, whom she'd met through friends at school, was interested in her, and she planned to sneak into town to meet him. Her jealous uncle couldn't know or he'd do everything in his power to make her life miserable. If he found out, he'd be furious.

Peggy got home that evening around eleven thirty. She'd seen no need to rush home after school, and hadn't bothered to call her uncle to explain. She knew she was already in big trouble, and asked Philip to drop her off a few blocks away from her house. She walked the rest of the way home alone, and stumbled slightly going up the front steps as she searched in her purse for her house key. It was hard to find in the dim moonlight.

As she approached the top step, the front door swung open as if on its own. He'd been waiting, and was standing in the doorway, hidden in the shadows, with only the moonlight illuminating his towering presence.

Peggy caught her breath and was visibly shaken. She knew his reaction was going to be severe.

She felt his bone-crunching squeeze about her tiny waist as she was hurled off the step in one quick sweeping motion and flung across the hallway. He slammed the front door at the same time her head hit the plaster wall, denting it.

Her head throbbed as pain coursed down the back of her neck. She heard his low, controlled voice addressing her.

"Do you have any idea what you've done?"

Measured rage dripped from every syllable.

"I had plans for us tonight, and you've seen fit to ruin them!"

Peggy tried to lift her head to look at him, but her neck hurt too much, and she was finding it hard to focus. He knelt down beside her, grabbed a fistful of her long, dark hair and violently snapped her head back.

"Tell me, who were you with?"

He demanded vehemently.

Peggy had never seen him so angry and struggled to pull away, but he was much too strong for her.

She heard a loud cracking noise at the same time she felt the agonizing blow to her mouth. He'd slapped her hard across the face, splitting open her bottom lip, causing blood to stream down her chin. The blow to her face came as a shock. She reached up shakily to feel the hot wetness on her swollen lips in disbelief. She hardly recognized her own voice screaming for help. When he'd lifted his hand again, the room went black.

James let her limp body drop to the floor and fetched a towel to clean up the mess. He felt the veins in his neck bulging. He knew he'd hurt her, and yet he wanted to do it again.

"How DARE she!"

He hissed through clenched teeth.

"I've given her EVERYTHING!"

Running the towel under cold water, he impatiently wrung it out and headed determinedly down the hall. It was dark in the house, and he nearly tripped over her lifeless form at the bottom of the stairs. He kicked her in the ribs to make her get up. She moaned. He roughly lifted her head and realized that she'd fainted.

Panic set in. Taking the cold cloth, he pressed it to her lips to wipe the blood as she winced in pain. When he saw that she was coming to, he impatiently got her to her feet. Peggy's knee buckled, and she collapsed again. Grabbing her under the arm, he dragged her upstairs. Once at the top, he let her arm go and ordered her to get to bed. He turned abruptly and went downstairs.

She leaned against the wall for support and held her ribs while she felt her way down the dimly lit hallway toward her room. Opening the door, Peggy could barely make out her bed. She could see only blurred images of her stuffed animals neatly arranged atop the single bed. It had been such a long time since she'd slept here. In response to the innocent surroundings, she began to cry.

Peggy closed the door softly and supported herself by holding on to the edge of her bureau. She reached out shakily toward the white chenille bedspread. She was barely able to lift her legs on to the bed when she heard the sounds of her uncle's footsteps climbing the stairs.

He headed down the hall toward his room. There was a moment of silence when he realized she wasn't there. Slow, determined steps plodded back down the hall, halting just outside her bedroom.

The door flung open and light flooded the darkness, causing her to squint and bring her hand to her eyes. She saw his shadow on the wall.

"Since when do you take to sleeping in here? GET UP!"

He demanded through clenched teeth.

Peggy physically couldn't move. She was in too much pain. She felt herself being hoisted off the bed, and then pushed down the hall toward her uncle's room. She tripped on the edge of the carpet and fell, hitting her brow bone on the wood floor. She held up her hand for him to help her and through tears cried.

"Please don't hurt me, Uncle James."

Aggravated, he once again reached down and yanked her up by her hair. He pushed her into his room and shoved her toward the bed.

"Do you remember what I told you this morning?"

Peggy could barely concentrate and felt herself going in and out of consciousness. It wasn't from the drinking. She'd been feeling pretty good before she got home, and was grateful for what was left of the alcohol's numbing effect. She heard his voice but couldn't understand what he was saying.

"Uncle James, I can't breathe..."

She gasped holding on to her ribs.

"Pity."

He said to her sarcastically.

"Don't worry, love. That pain will be replaced with something else."

She rolled over and curled into a fetal position. She hadn't changed out of her school uniform and still had on her blouse and skirt. She was trying to kick her shoes off, when she heard the familiar jingling sound of his loosening belt buckle. Turning over slowly, Peggy forced herself to focus on him. He couldn't possibly be thinking ...

"I had planned for this night to be so different, Peggy. I wanted it to be special for you, too. But you saw fit to change that, didn't you? Did you do with him all the things I've shown you?"

His voice was icy but controlled.

"I didn't do anything, Uncle James. I ... "

"Don't you dare attempt to lie to me, young lady!"

He walked toward her with a look of intense hatred.

She was terrified. In an effort to try and calm him, Peggy reached for him. He shoved her hand away. She was shaking. Her lip was seriously swollen, but no longer bleeding. In the darkness, she heard him unzip his pants, and then heard the metal buckle as it hit the floor. He stood quietly at the foot of the bed, his deadly gaze penetrating her broken body. His breathing was slow and heavy.

"Why did you do this to me, Peggy? To us? Don't you know how much I love you?"

His voice pleaded with her.

Peggy turned her head slightly and winced with the excruciating pain.

"I don't know what I've done to make you so angry."

Trying her best not to cry, as it took too much air to breathe, her voice broke.

"I didn't do anything with anyone, Uncle James. Honestly, I didn't."

He went to the side of the high bed and stood next to her. As he stared silently down at her weak and helpless form, she shook, frightened, in the cool, moonlit room.

As she lay back on the pillow, her head was level at his waist. He reached out and drew her to him. Knowing what form of pleasure he was expecting, Peggy attempted to quiet him orally, but her swollen lip split open, starting once again to bleed. She tasted her own warm blood and turned away.

"I can't. I'm sorry. It hurts."

She started to cough and felt like she was choking. The pain in her ribs was excruciating.

He pushed her aside, disgusted, and scoffed.

"Like I said, love, things could have been different."

He ripped at her clothing, and the buttons flew off her blouse and rolled across the floor. Her hands flew to her chest to try and stop him, but then he yanked at the zipper on the side of her skirt, lifting her slightly off the bed and roughly pulling it off from underneath. She stifled a cry of pain as he let her drop back on the bed. He carelessly threw her school uniform across the room, and then climbed on top of her.

Peggy was in no condition to do anything but weakly protest. Something was different tonight. He was taking the lead. She remembered the pictures from the books and magazines he'd shown her over the years, and the various positions from which a man could enter a woman's body. But he had never done that to her. He always told her what he wanted done to him.

As he knelt between her knees, she knew what he was going to do and was helpless to stop him. As he moved to position himself above her, she continued her mewling protests.

"Please don't do this. We shouldn't be doing this, Uncle James!"

Then she screamed at him and put her hands up to stop him, but he grabbed them both with one hand and twisted her wrists above her head.

She felt an intense searing pain rip through the lower part of her body as her tender flesh tore with his every thrust. She screeched at the sudden agony, and he brought his mouth down hard upon hers.

He continued to push his body forcefully into her. The blood from her lips mixed with his saliva as he moved rapidly within her. She heard him groan slightly then his motions slowed. He took a deep breath, then suddenly stopped. He lay very still atop her breathing heavily.

Peggy knew she was dying, and for a moment, hoped she would. She couldn't breathe. There was crushing pain in her ribs and chest where he lay on her. She was suffocating. She prayed quickly that God would forgive her and take her home. At that moment, she didn't fear death, but welcomed it.

When Peggy awoke, she was being tended to by a young nurse who was busy adjusting her IV pole while moving her bed around to make more room in a crowded hallway.

Shortly after the attack, her uncle had realized the severity of the situation and the fact that she could actually die, and he'd rushed her to the emergency room. James told the doctor that he'd been up waiting for his niece to return home and had grown concerned when it got late and she didn't call. It was her birthday, he explained, and he'd been holding off dinner and a surprise birthday cake, waiting for her to get home. She never checked in after school, and by 9:00 p.m., he suspected she was out with her friends, probably drinking and partying. When she staggered up the front steps later that night, obviously drunk, he saw her torn, bloody shirt and feared she'd been in an accident of some sort or, worse yet, raped. The doctor confirmed the latter to be true.

It was a brutal attack, the doctor informed him. Peggy had sustained two broken ribs, one of which had punctured her lung. The doctor ordered an MRI and several x-rays. Dr. Ferguson said that she was lucky to have escaped with her life after such a violent assault. She would be in need of rape counseling, and the Police would have to speak with her, at some point in order to fill out a report. He would refer a pediatric psychologist to her case before she left the hospital. James thanked him, keeping his shaking hands deep in his pockets.

"The Police will also need to speak with you, Mr. Burke. They'll want to perform a full investigation in order to find out who did this to your niece. They're sending over a woman police constable trained in sexual assault cases like this, to talk with Peggy when she comes to. This is a horrible thing to happen to a child."

James glanced warily down the hall at the men in uniform, and thanked the doctor again.

Peggy was to stay in the hospital for observation for a few days to monitor her concussion and punctured lung. When she regained con-sciousness, she vowed never to live with her uncle again.

Chapter Sixteen

England, Fall 1974

LAURA CAMPBELL SAT READING THE report of the brutal rape of the fourteen-year-old schoolgirl while she sipped Earl Gray tea at her desk. It was Sunday morning. She'd been notified by the station Saturday night of the assault, but was told not to bother coming in then, as the child was heavily sedated.

One of Laura's coworkers offered to drop the file off at her flat after his shift ended. They were still waiting for the doctor's notes and complete diagnosis for the criminal report. A more detailed medical evaluation from the A&E department would be forthcoming, pending final lab results and radiology findings.

The pictures were disturbing. There were swollen welts starting to bruise over her tender cheeks, eye, and chin. Her bottom lip had swelled to three times its normal size. Deep purple and red marks were visible on her chest and sides where she'd been kicked. The child reported severe pain in her head and neck. The MRI had shown she sustained a serious concussion. In addition, two ribs were broken, one of which had punctured her lung. The actual rape had caused vaginal tearing requiring stitches. The poor child had gone through hell.

Laura had seen abuse in so many forms and never found it any less disturbing. It was horrible when it happened to a grown adult woman. It reviled and enraged her when children were the victims. She knew their bodies could heal, but their young hearts and minds weren't so easily restored. The viciousness of the act would remain with them forever. Or worse yet, be blocked out entirely and reappear years down the line in some type of destructive behavior or addictive tendency. They could become their own worst enemies. Few would make a full recovery without counseling or a prolonged ministry of support. Many would suffer in silence until the day their memories finally surfaced and their dragons were faced.

Laura entered this line of work determined to help abused women find and prosecute their perpetrators, hold them accountable, and bring them to justice. The troubling part was that, in many cases, a woman knew her attacker but wouldn't turn him in. Laura would try to reason with the victim and assure her that she'd have far less to fear if he was caught and put behind bars. Therein, however, lay the little word that everything hinged on — IF.

Peggy's case, she sensed, wasn't a typical "date" rape as suggested in the Accident and Emergency report. For one thing, the attacker was very strong, deliberate. Whoever hurt her was angry and had the ability to inflict serious, life-threatening injuries.

Laura didn't think it possible that Peggy could have "staggered" home after an attack like that. She'd barely be capable of walking. The doctor should have asked more questions, but given England's national health care system and the shambles it was in, they were grateful to have gotten the patient's full name.

Laura glanced out the window and saw that it was raining. Peggy O'Malley was to be released from the hospital on Tuesday. According to the brief statement taken at the hospital, her uncle, James Burke, said that he'd been waiting for her to return home from school. When she didn't arrive around her usual time, he grew anxious but didn't want to alert the authorities prematurely. He said she staggered home "obviously drunk from being out with her friends and got in around one o'clock in the morning."

Laura looked over the medical report again. Her blood alcohol content, while confirming a slightly elevated presence, was not high enough to cause her to "stagger" home, and her physical condition would have made it nearly impossible for her to walk far at all without someone noticing her. The uncle went on to say that when he saw her swollen lip and the torn, bloodstained blouse, he immediately brought her to hospital, explaining that his niece had been attacked.

Laura took another sip of her tea and set the cup down while flipping through more pages. Why did the uncle bring her to hospital? Laura made a note to ask him about her parents. It had been her fourteenth birthday. She shook her head. It didn't make sense. If Peggy was with her friends, how did she get attacked? Where'd they go? Who dropped her off?

She searched through the file again to look for more information but there wasn't any. She found nothing substantial, probably because they weren't able to question the victim directly and had to rely solely on the uncle's testimony.

Laura picked up her keys, put her cup in the sink, and grabbed her coat. It was as good a time as any to go and visit with Peggy and question the uncle. She could have waited until Monday, but since her job was never nine-to-five, she picked up her bag, headed down three flights of stairs to the street, and made her way across town to St. Mary's Hospital.

Being Sunday morning, the streets were quiet, making it an easy drive. She was there in less than fifteen minutes. Since she was dressed in civilian clothing, Laura showed her identification badge at the front desk and asked for the patient's room number. She was familiar with the hospital and knew many of the nurses. She found her way easily. She took the elevator up to Pediatrics. The word, embossed in stainless steel next to the number two on the panel, to her meant babies, young children, someone much too young to endure the experience for which she must interview Peggy.

Laura checked in at the nurse's station. She recognized a couple of familiar faces and asked if Miss O'Malley's doctor was available for questions. One nurse stated that he'd gone home, but would be calling in around ten o'clock to check on Peggy's vitals. They told her they'd get her when he called. She thanked them and was directed to the patient's room.

Laura walked lightly and quietly on the freshly polished, tiled floor. She knew how the sound of heavy footsteps in the hallway could frighten children. She tapped on the door and heard a man's voice tell her to come in. Laura slowly opened the door and saw a weary looking man sitting slumped in the chair beside the bed. His hair was cut short and flat to his head. The growth on his face indicated that he'd not shaved in a day or more. The circles under his eyes told the story of a couple of rough, sleepless nights. Laura guessed the man to be Peggy's uncle.

James Burke was a relatively ruddy complexioned, yet kind-looking man, with sandy-blond hair and high cheekbones. When he stood, he was average in height — about 1.8 meters, and looked to weigh, at least 113 kilos. Laura held out her hand.

"I'm Officer Laura Campbell. I was hoping to speak with Peggy if she's awake and up to it."

She glanced over at the young teen lying in bed. She was awake, but her gaze was transfixed on the television on the wall.

"Hi, Peggy. I'm Officer Laura Campbell."

She walked around to the side of the bed so that Peggy didn't have to strain her neck.

Laura had an easy way about her, and her voice was confident and upbeat. Gently, she brushed Peggy's hair aside so she could see her eyes.

"How are you feeling today, Peggy?"

Peggy stared at her with uncertainty then glanced warily at her uncle, and said nothing. Laura caught the look and sensed Peggy's discomfort. She asked James Burke if he'd mind leaving them alone for a few minutes so as to let them talk privately. She told him she'd come and get him when they were done.

James stood up to protest slightly, but Laura firmly assured him she'd be fine and that it would only be for a few moments. He left the room reluctantly.

"Peggy, you can call me Laura. I know how hard this must be for you."

She was serious but in a way that let Peggy know she was on her side.

"You were nearly killed Friday night by whoever hurt you. I need to ask you what happened. Can you tell me what you remember and what you were doing before the attack?"

Laura looked compassionately into the teenager's doubtful brown eyes.

Peggy couldn't avert her sympathetic stare and burst into tears.

"Shhhhh, love."

Laura soothed her and held her hand.

"I know this is painful, Peggy. But I'm here to help you. Tell me what you remember, okay?"

Laura encouraged her, and Peggy nodded slightly. Her neck was still quite sore.

"Who were you with?"

Peggy answered slowly.

"I went out with some of my friends after school. It was my birthday, and we all pitched in to buy beer. We met up with some of the boys and hung out all night at the park."

"Go on ..."

Laura listened intently and without judgment.

"I knew I was already late, so I didn't bother to call my uncle. I didn't want to deal with him. So I just stayed out until everyone else had to go home."

Peggy's voice trailed off.

Laura thought it odd terminology that Peggy didn't want to "deal with" her uncle.

Peggy, on the other hand, was thinking of her friends and how they went home to normal houses, with mothers and fathers who'd yell at them to be sure, but didn't expect to have sex with them.

"Who else were you with?"

Laura reached into her bag for paper to take notes.

"Just some of the girls from school. A few of the boys came by later. I had Philip drive me home."

"Who's Philip?"

"He's a guy I met through a friend. I had him drop me off on another street near mine because I didn't want my uncle to see me with him."

"So you were able to walk? You weren't in too much pain at that time?"

Peggy looked at her oddly then shook her head no. Laura picked up on the discrepancy.

"Peggy, why didn't you let Philip drop you off at your house? Were you afraid of your uncle?"

Peggy became visibly shaken and didn't know how to answer. Tears began to trickle down the sides of her temples. Laura asked her point blank.

"Peggy, did Philip do this to you?"

Peggy shook her head no.

She wouldn't hide it any longer. She hated every second that he sat in that chair beside her bed in the hospital room. She'd asked him to leave on three occasions, saying that she was tired, but he wouldn't go. He'd whisper to her and cry softly when the nurses left the room, saying that he loved her too much and that he was sorry for hurting her and that he'd never do it again.

Peggy felt ashamed and sick to her stomach. All of the years that he'd made her do those things — since she was a little girl. Confined to the bed, she found herself lying to both doctors and nurses, all the while under her uncle's watchful and nervous stare. She didn't care anymore what happened to him. She just wanted him to leave her alone. She thought of her mother and suddenly felt an intense hatred for her.

"Peggy ... "

As if reading her thoughts, Laura asked.

"Where are your parents?"

Peggy was silent for a moment then responded weakly.

"My mom left me years ago. I live with my uncle."

Laura's eyes darted back to the chair where the man had been sitting. She knew it all then.

"Peggy, did your uncle do this to you?"

Peggy turned away, ashamed to even look at her then nodded and started to cry in earnest. Laura leaned over and held her close. It broke her heart. Peggy's tears and the intensity of her sobbing confirmed it all. A righteous anger welled up inside Laura.

"Look at me, Peggy. I have to act quickly here. But you need to know that we won't let him hurt you ever again. Do you understand me?"

She closed her eyes and nodded, holding her hand over her mouth to stifle the uncontrollable sobs. Laura handed the box of tissues to her. Holding Peggy's hand tightly in one of hers, she reached determinedly for the receiver with her free hand and phoned the nurse's station.

"This is Officer Campbell. Is Peggy O'Malley's uncle, James Burke, still roaming the corridor? Oh? Well, I need you to call security right away and find him. I don't want him leaving this hospital."

Nodding her head while staring sadly at Peggy, she held her hand and continued to delegate orders.

"Yes. Yes. Please call the station and tell them to send two armed officers down immediately. They need to send a car over to his home to check that out as well. Should he return, he is not allowed to reenter this room. Do you understand? I want Security called, and a guard assigned outside Miss O'Malley's door."

She hung up the phone and turned to Peggy.

"Can you tell me what he did to you, Peggy? I know it's not easy, but he's hurt you pretty severely to land you in here. I don't want him to ever do this to you again. Okay?"

Peggy nodded.

"Do you mind if I record this, Peggy? I'm not able to write all that fast."

Peggy didn't mind and watched as Laura pulled out a small recorder from her bag. She kept her note pad out to jot down important information.

Laura listened intently as Peggy poured out her sordid story of abuse. It started when she was six years old.

Chapter Seventeen

Ennis, County Clare, Ireland, Fall 1978

IT WAS IMPOSSIBLE TO ENTER the trailer quietly, and it seemed to Peggy she'd made more noise than usual. She cringed with every creak, knowing what Bobby would want from her if he awoke. Ever since she was a young girl, sex had been expected of her. She thought, at this point, she could prepare herself mentally and not make a big deal of it. Deep down, however, she held a rage so fierce that it could be deadly if ever let loose.

Peggy was exhausted. It was futile to try and change in the tiny bathroom. She was just too tall and didn't want to risk making any more noise. Lately, she'd taken to sleeping in her clothes so as not to entice Bobby in any way. She scrambled into bed quickly, praying Bobby was in another one of his drunken stupors and wouldn't wake up.

Bobby was a heavy drinker and smoker. Often, when Leonore had stayed out late working, he'd wake Peggy up in the middle of the night to keep him company. With the sound of sausages sizzling in the background, he'd demand that she get up and eat with him. Struggling to choke down the fatty meat at two in the morning, she'd beg Bobby to let her go to sleep. He'd take a few swigs out of a whiskey bottle and tell her to go on — after she ate; he wasn't wasting food. If she refused or complained, he'd hit her. Once, when she was sick and couldn't get up, he'd pounded his fist into the side of her head in another fit of rage. She'd noticed a slight amount of blood on her pillow the next morning and her ear rang for weeks. When the ringing stopped, she could hear nothing out of her right ear. Peggy knew that she'd heal from the physical pain, but what often followed on those drunken nights was more than she thought she could bear.

Before Leonore took off, she rigged up a sheet to act as a curtain for Peggy, to give her some privacy from Bobby's roving eyes. It did nothing, however, to muffle their sounds. The animalistic grunting embarrassed Peggy, causing her to cover her head with one of Bobby's old, saliva-stained pillows. Leonore would smile sheepishly in the morning and apologize if they'd been too loud. Bobby would whisper slyly to Peggy, when he thought Leonore was out of earshot, that he'd be willing to "teach" her one day. Leonore could not help but overhear and shot him an angry look. Then she'd peer cautiously, yet almost apologetically at Peggy. Peggy hated the way Bobby tried to stir up trouble between them. Leonore never held it against her for too long and once confided to her that she'd often thought of leaving him.

"One day, so help me God, I will."

Peggy's eyes sprung wide open when she felt the trailer dip under Bobby's weight as he labored to get out of bed and stumbled out into the tiny kitchen area. Cautiously, she followed his moving silhouette beyond the thinly tattered sheet. For a moment, he leaned heavily on the counter, dragging on a cigarette. The smoke swirled about his head. Turning, he flicked the cigarette carelessly into the filthy dishwater, making a short sizzling sound. He shut off the light above the stove and yanked back the sheet. He took a few steps toward her and slouched expectantly against the tiny bed.

Peggy held her breath and kept her eyes closed. She swore he could hear her pounding heart. He didn't say a word, but ripped the blanket off her, revealing her fully clothed figure.

"Get up and get out of those freaking funeral clothes!"

Peggy pretended she was asleep and didn't hear him, until he shoved her shoulder.

"I said get up and get undressed!"

Peggy had thought the punk clothes she dressed in might keep Bobby from coming after her. It certainly turned most people away in disgust, creating the desired perception that she was a freak. Glynnis's mother was scared to death of her. She had never wanted nor sought Bobby's attention. She didn't consider herself attractive as far as looks go, and purposely took steps to make herself even more unappealing by displaying her many body piercings and safety pins. Most people wouldn't go out of their way to talk with her. She preferred it that way.

She sat up. Bobby was drunk and wouldn't remember anything in the morning. He never did. He didn't care who she was as a person or what she looked like. He just wanted a body. An intense hatred rose in her as she considered picking up the pan close by and hitting him in the head with it. His foul breath nearly made her vomit. She slowly undressed in the dark as she heard his breathing quicken with anticipation. Long past tears and hardened by life's turns, Peggy dreaded the degradation she was about to endure. She coached herself into believing that she was simply a receptacle for Bobby's loathsome needs. She didn't talk about her experiences with the women in the caravan and kept mainly to herself. They gossiped among themselves and figured Peggy had simply taken Leonore's place in Bobby's life and that she'd become his girlfriend.

Peggy tried to dissuade Bobby from doing anything, informing him that she had her period. He didn't care. Closing his eyes, he fumbled between her legs and pulled hard on the string, yanking some of Peggy's pubic hair out with it.

"Damn it, Bobby! That hurt!"

She tried to back away but there was nowhere for her to move in the sardine can she called home.

Bobby held up the tampon like a prize fish.

"You can bury this out back when I'm done."

He mumbled and let it drop on the floor.

The trailer's toilet barely tolerated urine. Tampons would clog it. Hell, ordinary toilet paper clogged it. Bobby never seemed to notice the look or smell of the putrid bowl. He barely noticed that his own waste never fully flushed. The stench would gag Peggy when she needed to use the bathroom. She had taken it upon herself long ago to empty the waste tank whenever they made a stop at a rest-over. Leonore would have nothing to do with it. It was the only way Peggy could stand to live in that trailer. It didn't take much to stink it up, and there was no ventilation except for a few tiny windows, most of which were stuck shut.

The women who traveled in the caravan had a hard life. They did all the "grunt" work, literally digging shallow latrines to dump the contents of their trailer's waste tanks, which would infuriate the landowners on whose property they camped. Though they'd always try and cover it up, the stench remained. By the time a landowner would notice, the caravan would be gone.

Some of the men were truly ignorant and abusive. When drinking, they seemed to revel in humiliating their wives and girlfriends. Peggy recalled one especially degrading incident when one of the dogs resurrected a buried tampon. The mutt, almost grinning, sat wagging its tail as a muddied string hung from its mouth. The women were made to chase the dog and retrieve the revolting object from its teeth. The men then demanded that it be reburied — this time far beyond the reach of the tethered animal. Such was their lot in life. They didn't seem to hope for anything more in their daily existence.

Peggy smelled Bobby's sour breath on the back of her neck. There was no kissing involved, just meaningless thrusting until he let out a familiar grunt, which signaled the end. Bobby staggered back and fell on the torn, cigarette-burned cushion. Resting his head against the hollow tin wall, he lit up another cigarette.

"Go and bury the bloody tampon out back. Make sure it doesn't reappear. You freaking women are so stupid."

Believing what he said to be quite funny, he laughed to himself.

The rain was coming down hard and the wind made it raw. Having no warm socks to put on before she went out into the rain, Peggy wrapped her feet with toilet paper before slipping them into her clogs. She stumbled around in the dark, holding on to the side of the cold, metal trailer, until she found the shovel. Reaching forward, she could feel Bobby's secretion, mixed with her own blood, seep through her underwear on to her pants. The smell would be awful in the morning. She'd borrow a pair of Bobby's pants and ask Glynnis if she could do a wash at her house. She'd offer to buy her own detergent. She needed to purchase more tampons downtown in the morning, too. Peggy had hoped Leonore might have left some of her clothing behind, but that thought was rendered futile when Bobby declared one night after she'd left.

"There's gonna be a burning tonight!"

He took every last remnant of Leonore's clothing and tossed it into the campfire out back. Leonore had left with simply the clothes on her back. Peggy would probably do the same.

The dogs were running around wildly on their leashes and barking loudly, prompting a vicious shout from someone inside one of the trailers. Peggy carried the shovel up the road toward the trees. She could feel her heart beating within her chest as she dug into the earth. How many times had she done this humiliating task? She'd lost count. Her hair stuck to her face, wet from the rain, as she huffed heavily with each shovelful of dirt.

Tomorrow they'd move on. Rumor had it there was work in the next county. She wanted to see Glynnis before she left and tell her the whole sordid story, and decided she'd tell her about the plans she had made to leave. She didn't want to lose touch with her only friend. Peggy wanted a new life and was determined to make it happen. Something deep within compelled her toward a better existence. She'd listen to the voice within or die trying.

Although her eighteenth birthday was still days away, Peggy suddenly knew she couldn't take another day of the horrible, disgusting life she'd been living. She had tried to call home a couple of times over the years, but there was never an answer. The phone had eventually been disconnected.

She suspected that her uncle would never return to his house in England for fear of being imprisoned. Peggy had no idea where he was or what condition the house might be in. But it was part of her plan to find out. Her uncle had told her that everything he had would be hers one day.

No one would know any better. Peggy would concoct a story to appease inquisitive neighbors. She'd tell them that she went away for a while to live with relatives in the United States. She never told Bobby where she was from, so he wouldn't be able to track her down. Not that he'd even care to. After all, had he not tried for years to pawn her off on his sleazy brother, Stephen, whom Peggy despised?

Peggy had managed to hide her "freedom fund" from Bobby, Stephen, and the nosy caravan women. Knowing that he'd never empty the waste tank, which became her job, Peggy had concealed a container up underneath the hollow panels of the trailer where the tank was located. She was tempted to get at the money right then, but the light wasn't good, and the rain made it even harder to see. In any event, the dogs would bark continuously, causing someone to come out and whack them with a broom. She decided to wait until the morning. Though she'd never taken a chance at getting caught by taking time to count it, she had saved for years, and knew she had enough money to make her getaway. Her charcoal sketches and colorful chalk drawings brought in a handsome sum from the tourists.

Peggy was a talented artist. Her images won her accolades from amateurs and professionals alike. She had a keen eye for detail, and pulled expressions from the faces of people who showed none. She'd seek out well-known tourist areas such as Salt Hill in Galway, or set up near the Gap of Dunloe in Killarney. She'd create a simple seating station in which to sketch her patrons and, thoughtfully, applied less of her dark make-up so as to not scare off would-be customers. After she sat her first customer, people would gather around and watch as she brought life to paper. Tourists would be willing to wait hours for their chance to be sketched by her.

Americans were her best customers. They simply wanted to be able to say that they'd had their portrait done "in Ireland."

Peggy made small talk with those she sketched and learned quite a bit about the USA and other countries. She didn't say much, but people had a deep need to talk - some endlessly. Many shared personal experiences and thoughts. At times she found it quite amusing. For example, people from the United States were in Ireland "on vacation" and many were trying to "find their roots." Peggy wondered what the big deal was. Personally, she wanted to forget hers.

Peggy had been handed many business cards over the years from people asking her to contact them should she ever want help selling her work. A few were from England, some from the US. She would take and pocket them, but never did anything with them. She kept the cards in a box tucked in one of the tiny compartments she used for her few personal things. Bobby wouldn't know what to make of them should he find them. He couldn't read.

Her jaw was clenched tight as she finished the demeaning task of burying a tampon. Turning with a vengeance, she walked determinedly back to the trailer, clutching the shovel that would crush Bobby's head if he tried to approach her again. Resolute in her decision, there would be no more waiting. Tomorrow, she'd leave and begin her life anew.

Chapter Eighteen

CAROLINE WAS GRATEFUL FOR THE lull in the Emergency Room that evening. She fished for the packet of cigarettes in her purse and mentioned that she was heading outside for a smoke. Her actions prompted the usual responses from her fellow medical professionals.

"When the hell are you going to give up that filthy habit? We'll be treating you for lung cancer one day if you don't quit you know."

Such comments typically came from her friend, Karl Monroe. Karl was an unassuming man, unlike some of the doctors. He'd been with Puritan Medical Center for a little over ten years. Divorced with one child, he was a well-respected member of the medical staff, and a valuable asset to the trauma team at PMC.

Caroline leaned against the wall outside the ambulance entrance to the ER. It was a humid evening, and the sound of fireworks could be heard going off in the distance. Occasionally she'd catch a glimpse of one just above the tops of the buildings. She was working a double shift over the July Fourth holiday.

The emergency room had been bombarded in the late afternoon, and the last case to come in had thrown everyone for a loop. Even those who didn't smoke took time when they could to step outside, breathe in the thick, stagnant air, and try to clear their heads and come to grips with what had just happened a few hours ago.

Tom, from Security, joined her out back and lit up.

"It was pretty amazing, huh? The husband and wife thing, I mean. I still can't believe what happened in there."

Tom knew that she wasn't at liberty to discuss patient information, but would test the boundaries now and then.

Caroline just nodded in agreement, saying that it was the first time she'd witnessed anything like it.

"It sucks. I hope I never see it again."

"I guess you just never know when your time is going to come."

"Nope, you don't."

Caroline concurred and took a final drag on her cigarette before flicking in out into the street.

"Let's hope for a quiet night. See you inside, Tom."

He nodded and watched as she walked back inside the hospital.

Tom guessed Caroline to be, at least five feet eleven inches - tall, by his standards, for a woman. She was stunning to look at, with auburn hair and green eyes, and was a natural conversationalist, something Tom himself envied. She chatted easily with the many paramedics and law enforcement officers who usually followed the ambulances.

Tom overheard a great deal in the ER. The department had its own pulse and politics. The doctors often talked about the nurses, who they were dating or sleeping with, and the nurses in turn gossiped about them. No wonder so many TV soap operas were centered on hospitals.

Everyone liked Caroline. Unlike the many she worked with, she never talked about her personal life. During late night gossip sessions, she'd listen intently to others, lending a caring ear. The friendships formed were based on her kind nature, not on dramas revealed about her own life. Tom noticed her technique and was amused by her cleverness. She knew how much people needed to talk about themselves. A few of the veteran nurses were jealous of her. At twenty-six, she'd advanced quickly in the ER.

Whenever he heard her voice over the intercom calling "Security to the ER," Tom was one of the first to respond. She genuinely appreciated his promptness and would often write about his efficiency in her ER reports. The accolades had helped him receive a promotion to head of security on the nightshift.

Caroline was an energetic APRN, gifted and comical. She often played practical jokes on the staff. The patients found her easy to talk with. She refused to clump people into categories, and treated everyone with the same respect. She took her job as nurse supervisor seriously, but not superiorly.

Tom recalled one particular joke that Caroline orchestrated with the help of the other nurses and doctors. She was standing at the nurses' station, filling out orders. The counter was right above the secretary's workstation.

Pam, the secretary on duty and a long-standing employee, always got annoyed when lab technicians or nurses placed patient blood or urine samples on the counter above her head. She complained that if the vials ever rolled off, there would be blood and piss all over everything, and she'd be damned if she was cleaning it up.

Working in a hospital, Pam was obsessed with washing her hands whenever she touched anything. She found it easier to just wear latex gloves most of the time, to the amusement of the staff, who chided her endlessly. But they loved her, and she took it all in stride. Because of her diligence and commitment to her job, the staff considered her part of their team, which also meant she wouldn't be excluded from their practical jokes.

Looking over the counter at Pam, who was inputting orders on the computer, Caroline motioned to her friend, Dr. Monroe, to come over.

"Dr. Monroe, I don't like the color of this urine."

Caroline picked up the cup holding it out and directly over Pam's head, staring anxiously at its contents.

"Oh, God! Not again."

Pam looked up at the cup hovering over her head.

"How many times have I told you to put those over on that counter?"

She stood up and pointed to the area behind her.

"Look, I even put up a sign: 'Lab Specimens Pick-up/ Drop-off Here.' Can I be any more clear?"

Caroline looked at her sympathetically and continued on.

"Speaking of clear, Doctor, you really must see this. It's quite alarming," Caroline stated with great concern.

"It's a cup of piss!"

Pam reminded her with disdain.

Dr. Monroe played along with Caroline.

"What seems to be the problem, Caroline?"

She held up the bodily fluid and he, too, peered intently at the sample in the plastic cup.

"Here, smell it."

Caroline took off the lid.

Dr. Monroe put his nose deep into the cup and took a long sniff, wiping off the tip of his nose. Pam's jaw dropped and her eyes nearly bugged out of her head.

"Oh, that's just disgusting!"

To avoid smelling the urine herself, she pulled out her can of Lysol and sprayed.

Dr. Monroe gave Pam a stern look and stated very seriously.

"Sometimes, Pamela, we have to do things that appear odd or unusual. It may be our only way of diagnosing a patient's illness. This is another part of the puzzle in a complex medical history we're trying to piece together. In this case, it appears the patient may be spilling sugar."

Caroline, pretending to be concerned, asked.

"You think we've got a diabetic here?"

"There's only one other way I know of to find out ..." Karl stuck his finger into the cup and then into his mouth, sucking on it like it was frosting on a cake. Pam, holding her stomach, gagged and ran to the bathroom.

"I'm going to be sick."

All of the nurses, doctors, and various other staff (even some patients) laughed till they nearly wet their own pants. It was then that Pam realized she'd been the latest victim in their string of ongoing practical jokes.

"I hate you all!"

She shouted above the laughter from behind the bathroom door. When she finally made her reappearance, Caroline informed her, through her own watering eyes, that it was just apple juice. Pam whacked her in the arm and told her she was a jerk and that she was quitting ... again. No one took her seriously when she said that. They all knew how much she loved her job.

Pam chuckled whenever she caught a glimpse of Dr. Monroe and Caroline walking by, conceding that they got her good with their little prank. Pretending to snub them in mock anger, she was content knowing that she worked with a great group of people.

Recalling the joke, Tom felt somewhat comforted, in spite of the fateful events of that afternoon.

The emergency call had come over the two-way radio in the ER. A woman in her mid-forties was found lying unconscious in her upstairs bathroom by her husband, who had just returned home from work. The paramedics gave her vitals over the radio as Dr. Monroe took notes. The nurses gathered around to hear what was coming in, so they could plan their course of action. No one knew how long she'd been on the floor, but her breathing was shallow and her vitals poor.

Dr. Monroe had given orders to the nurses to prepare the cardiac room for her arrival. He continued to monitor the patient's vital signs in transit as they were radioed in. The well-oiled ER team sprung into action.

When she arrived, the paramedics were directed to the high-tech cardiac room; machines were quickly hooked up and the familiar beeping sounds filled the room. Pam began inputting the orders for routine chem panels and various other tests she knew they'd want. It was Dr. Monroe who caught sight of the distressed husband and quietly advised one of the nurses to call the on-staff grief counselors. He had a suspicion the woman wasn't going to make it based on her condition.

The husband was pacing frantically, trying to peer into the room where the team was working on his wife. Caroline, having been involved in dramas of this sort many times before, quietly approached the worried husband and gently suggested that he go and fill out some paperwork for his wife in Admissions. He was sweating profusely and looking rather pale himself.

Caroline whispered to Tom to go and get him a ginger ale. The man, however, reappeared within a matter of moments back in the emergency room pacing back and forth. Janet, from Admissions, followed him and notified Caroline that he was acting strange and mumbling incoherently.

The distraught man, rather thin with graying brown hair, sat on a chair just outside his wife's room. He bent over at the waist and cupped his hands over his face, resting his elbows on his knees. Pam went to get him a cup of water when suddenly he keeled over onto the floor.

She called frantically to Caroline as she rushed around the counter to his aid. The paramedics, who were nearby, dashed over to help lift him off the floor. Caroline reached for his wrist checking for a radial pulse.

"He's coding. Get him into Room C stat!"

Dr. Willis, who'd been paged to assist in the wife's code, and a few of the medical staff, stopped what they were doing and went next door to assist with the husband as pandemonium ensued.

Machines were blinking and buzzers sounding. After twenty minutes, the staff was unable to resuscitate the woman, and she was pronounced dead. A half-hour later, a strange hush fell over the ER as her husband was also pronounced dead. There was eeriness in the silence when all the machines were finally turned off.

Everyone was trying to come to grips with what had just happened. The grief counselor finally arrived and was as shocked as the rest to learn that both patients had just passed away. She, along with Drs. Monroe and

Willis, had the unenviable task of having to break the news to the grown children who had gathered in the private waiting room off the ER.

Caroline was worn out. Up until that point, she hadn't experienced anything so emotionally draining in her nursing career. It bothered her deeply, in a way that she couldn't express. The openly emotional children were slowly absorbing the tragedy of it all. Their desolate cries echoed in the halls of the ER.

Caroline chain-smoked during her early morning drive home. She was still numb, but was also exhausted from working a double shift. She was severely sleep-deprived. Yet she knew she needed to call Valerie. Her sister was her sounding board and pillar of strength. She shared almost everything with her.

Almost, however, was not everything. There was one secret Caroline had sworn to keep from her sister — for her own protection. She'd done it successfully for the last twenty years. She kept all the hurt and years of shame and disgrace to herself, telling her story only to Glynnis and Peggy, who shared similar experiences and understood her pain.

The prolonged abuse had manifested itself in various forms of promiscuous behavior throughout her teen years. As an adult, Caroline never knew when the past would rear its ugly head, but, after years of therapy, she was learning to recognize the triggers. Depression always followed after particularly stressful events.

If she'd made a mistake in choosing nursing as a career, no one would have an easy time talking her out of it. She considered the daily stresses of the profession; yet felt that it was a "healing force" in her own life. Somehow, witnessing others in the world whose situations were seemingly far worse than hers, motivated her to go on.

Her psychologist told her that this wasn't exactly a healthy perspective. She confidentially acknowledged to her therapist that it was a rather desperate form of self-preservation. Yet, when Caroline listened sympathetically to patients, she gained strength from those whose lives were shattered. When she'd compare her own life with theirs, she'd gain a sense of comfort and strength by telling herself that she was better off than many, and could thus go on. She needed those shots of affirmation as much as any drug she took, which was a red flag to her therapist, and something that they were just beginning to delve into during recent sessions.

Caroline had a deep need to nurture and protect others. There was no greater feeling to her than being able to bring a smile to the face of someone who was hurting. Her sense of humor was a welcome relief to many.

She had, over time, learned to deal with her reactions to stress in constructive ways, and the latest in antidepressant drugs. She'd been with the same therapist for the last two years; he knew everything about Caroline's life and what had shaped it, and how she'd become the woman she was. Not all of it was bad ... so she was told.

It was after this particularly stressful event, however, that Caroline started writing her own prescriptions.

Chapter Nineteen

Chatham, Cape Cod, Massachusetts, 1982

WHEN SHE'D GRADUATED FROM SIMMONS College, Caroline landed her first job fairly quickly at a small, senior care facility not far from her home on Cape Cod. She left the position six months later. It had been suspected by the staff that Caroline was taking medication from elderly patients in her care. She resigned before the nursing home officials could prove it and fire her. She told her mother and Valerie that she didn't like taking care of old people and had decided, instead, to get a job working with children.

Her family never learned the truth about her sudden departure from the nursing home. They did, however, recognize the signs of clinical depression that Caroline began to exhibit, and convinced her to seek professional help. The need for intervention was made evident after a near brush with death at a St. Patrick's Day party in South Boston.

Caroline had stumbled drunkenly out onto the back deck to have a cigarette and passed out. It was getting late, and no one had seen her go outside. It wasn't until her friend, Danny Keogh, went out back to shut off the porch light that he noticed her lifeless form. She was nearly frozen and her breathing was shallow. He recognized the signs of hypothermia and called for the ambulance. Dragging her into the house, he wrapped her in blankets and tried to keep her warm until help arrived. The combination of alcohol and cold temperatures could have killed her in a short time.

When she came to, she was belligerent, not wanting to be taken to a hospital. Danny, a medical intern at Beth Israel Hospital in Boston, insisted she get medical treatment and instructed the paramedics to take her to a local facility.

Caroline survived the ordeal, but it was recommended by the ER doctor who treated and released her that she seek treatment for alcoholism. She blew the idea off as ridiculous, insisting she was just having a few beers with friends and that it was hardly an ongoing problem. Both Valerie and her mother knew that wasn't the case. There was something else driving her, and someone had to help her figure out what it was before it was too late.

Grace often blamed herself for Caroline's bouts with depression and rage, thinking that perhaps she'd not given her enough attention in those early, formative years following Neil's death.

Grace had kept herself busy so as to not dwell on the loss of Neil. Money was never an issue as Neil was a partner in his father's business. She and the girls were well taken care of financially after his passing. Her in-laws were very generous paying for the girls' private elementary and high school educations, and retired the mortgage on their Cape Cod house after Neil's death. College funds were established for their future educational needs, and generous trust funds awarded when they were mature enough to handle it.

Grace needed a job more to occupy her mind, to keep her sane, and in touch with the real world. But all hell broke loose with Caroline in her teen years. Grace would often look back and refer to that period of time as the "black out" years.

In the early years following Neil's death, Grace stayed home with the girls and busied herself with charity events, the church, and her music. With Sheila and Tim's help, she made every effort to help the girls adjust to a life without their father. Grace didn't date, and didn't want to. She found life as a mother very fulfilling.

When Caroline, at age seven, began complaining about having to spend time alone with Sheila and Tim at their summer home in New

York, Siobhan and Ruth suggested the children come and spend a few weeks with them in Ireland. The arrangement worked for a good number of years. The girls would spend the early part of their summer vacations with their grandparents in Ireland and the remainder of the summer with Sheila and Tim at their lakeside home in New York. Grace would accompany the girls over to Ireland and fly back in time to teach summer school. Sometimes, Siobhan would fly back to the States with the girls, and spend a few weeks visiting with Grace, Sheila, and Tim. Pat's eyesight was getting progressively worse and his visits abroad had ceased. Granny, on occasion, would accompany Siobhan, leaving Uncle Sean to watch over Granda.

They followed a similar schedule throughout the girls' young lives. Until, that is, an adolescent Caroline began to put up such a fight about having her summers planned for her. She'd complain and rant on about wanting to spend more time with her friends, saying that she hated going to New York, and that Ireland was boring.

Grace had anticipated that most of her problems would lie with her oldest daughter based simply on her inexperience as a parent. But Val seemed to sail through her teens without many problems ... although Grace did catch her smoking in the bathroom one night after Val thought she'd gone to bed.

Caroline surprised Grace by continually fighting with her and her sister on seemingly every matter. Grace once had to physically separate the two sisters when she found them fighting in their bedroom over a watch. Sheila assured her that it was normal sibling rivalry, reminding her that they, too, had fought.

"Yes, but I never hit you! I mean, I wanted to, but I never did. Ma would have killed us both!"

Sheila agreed with Grace that Caroline did have a rather rebellious streak in her that no one seemed to understand. Only Tim seemed to have a way of getting through to her. Grace thought about how much time the two of them spent together over the summers, out fishing on the boat at the lake in New York. Sheila often encouraged Tim to talk with Caroline, reminding him that he was the most consistent father figure in her life.

When Caroline was fourteen, Grace made the decision to take her to a child psychologist. Siobhan helped her come to that decision through the many phone calls she made to check in on her and the girls. Siobhan's job included work with troubled teens, and she felt that Caroline was crying out for attention.

After five visits to the counselor, Caroline refused to go back, saying that it was her mother who needed the help of a shrink to "get a grip on reality," not her, and that she just wanted to be left alone. Grace was beside herself. Never did she wish she had her Neil back more than during those volatile years. Val was attending Boston University, and Grace felt their lives were in complete turmoil.

Grace was horrified to learn that Caroline was sexually active in the eighth grade when she discovered birth control pills hidden away in her bedroom drawer. At that point, she was beyond caring about her daughter's privacy, and was on a quest to find out what was causing such a dramatic change in her behavior.

Valerie told her mom she had no idea. But Val saw the changes happening, too, and one Sunday night, before she left to drive back to her college dormitory in Boston, she knocked on Caroline's door.

"Come in."

Caroline was listening to Led Zeppelin.

Val opened the door and poked her head inside.

"Oh, good! Your head's not rotating 360 degrees, and I see the crucifix is still affixed to the wall. Can we talk?"

Caroline looked at her sister in amusement. She could be pretty quick with the one-liners.

"Very funny ..."

Val sat on the bottom of the bed.

"Are you coming to watch me and Mom play next Friday night? There's a concert at the new Cape Cod Center for the Arts. It's a charity event for the new burn wing at the hospital."

Caroline hated Sunday nights and often withdrew to her room. Her sister left on Sundays to go back to college in Boston. She didn't do good-byes well. But she did love hearing her mother and sister play together. She'd always been a little jealous of Val's ability to play the violin so well. Whenever Caroline tried, the cat ran under the bed.

"I don't know. I might. It depends if I get a better offer or not,"

Val was openly hurt and angered by her statement.

"Why do you always have to be so sarcastic and mean? You're making life really hard for Mom and everyone else. Why don't you just go live with Auntie Sheila if you're so damn miserable here? Give Mom a break!"

Val got off her bed, slammed the door, and went to her own room to finish packing her bag. A knock sounded a little while later, and Caroline asked to come in.

"Screw you!"

Val had enough of her sister's cutting remarks and selfish behavior. Caroline opened the door and went over to where Val kept her violin. She picked it up and sat in the chair in the corner of the room, absently plucking the strings.

"Val, listen, I'm sorry, okay? I just want to live my own life like you, and have Mom stop telling me what to do. She nags me constantly when you're gone."

Val turned around to face her.

"She's a MOTHER! It's what they do. So get used to it!"

She paused and sat on the bed.

"Do you think I like the way she still tells me what to do? NO! But I let her say what she needs to say, and then I go and do my own thing. But I don't swear at her or openly disobey her like you do. You always make a scene of things. You can't just drink to get a buzz. You have to go and get smashed. If you smoke, it has to be grass and not just cigarettes. You take everything to the extreme. You're going to kill yourself one of these days if you don't knock it off, Caroline. I love you to death, but you're being stupid!"

Caroline looked at Val and started to cry.

"I'm pregnant."

Val's mouth fell open.

"Oh, no! Please tell me you're kidding …"

Caroline shook her head.

"Damn it, Caroline!"

Val shot up off the bed.

"How far along are you?"

She bowed her head.

"Only a few weeks, maybe a month."

"Shit!"

Val's eyes darted across the room to the telephone.

"We have to tell Auntie Sheila."

"NO! Don't. She'll tell Mom. They talk about everything. She couldn't keep this from her. Call Uncle Tim."

"Uncle Tim? Why him?"

Val asked skeptically.

"Because I know he'll help me out."

Caroline dialed the number, and her uncle answered the phone.

"Uncle Tim, it's Caroline."

She started to cry.

"What's up, Caroline?"

Tim sat up, concerned. Caroline didn't go into much detail, saying only that she needed to talk with him right away and that Val was there with her. Her voice was shaky.

"Yes, okay. Right. I'm on my way."

Caroline and Val continued to sit there, numb. Grace had tickets to their town's working theatre performance of Grease that night, and Auntie Sheila had gone with her. They wouldn't be home for another three hours. Val had declined the offer to join them, claiming she had studying to do and needed to get back to the dorm early.

Exactly half an hour later, the doorbell rang. Tim walked in and looked at the two of them.

"Okay, what's up?"

"Caroline's pregnant. We can't tell Mom or Auntie Sheila."

Tim stood there, poker-faced. He turned to Caroline and calmly asked her how far along she was.

"Only about a month."

Tim was inwardly devastated, but kept his tone even.

"Well, what do you want to do about it?"

Caroline stared at him coolly and unemotionally.

"I want to have an abortion."

Valerie gasped.

"YOU WHAT? That's murder, Caroline!"

Caroline glared at her sister with contempt.

"Val, just SHUT UP! This is hard enough, okay? I know it's not right, but I can't be a mother. I can't."

She collapsed onto the couch, sobbing. Tim went to her side and held her while she cried.

"Let me spend some time tomorrow looking into this. I think there are a couple of clinics in Boston where you could go. We want a reputable place, not some fly-by-night, back-alley doctor."

Caroline pleaded with her uncle.

"Please don't tell Auntie Sheila, Uncle Tim. She'll tell Mom, and Mom will kill me. No, this would kill her. Promise me, please."

Tim looked at his niece and felt nothing but compassion and love for her at that moment.

"Honey, I promise I won't tell your aunt."

Then he became serious.

"But, Caroline, when is all of this going to stop? I mean you're treading on thin ice. I can't always bail you out. You need to be responsible for your own actions. Do you understand?"

Caroline clenched her hands into a fist at her side and nodded her head. "Yes, Uncle Tim."

It was Tim who suggested to Caroline that if she was going to fool around, she'd better protect herself. When she went for her follow-up doctor's visit after the abortion, she was prescribed birth control pills and given a six-month supply.

In spite of Val's wishes for peace for her sister, the battles continued throughout Caroline's high school years. One Saturday evening, Grace heard a car pull up outside the house. Two guys got out and pulled a body from the backseat. That body was her daughter's. They carried her to the front steps, dumped her there, rang the bell, jumped back into the car and took off.

Grace's heart was pounding as she called out for Val to come help her. They both feared Caroline might be dead. They picked her up and placed her on the couch, ready to call for an ambulance, when Caroline mumbled something and then threw up violently, spraying the carpet, the couch, and all three females with her alcohol induced vomit.

Grace was livid. She made a frantic call to Father Bruce, who went over despite the late hour, and sat up listening to Grace as she cried and confessed what an awful parent she was. He assured her that she was a very good parent, and asked her if he could meet with Caroline, alone, to try and gain some insight into her behavior. Val piped in sarcastically.

"And if that fails, you can perform an exorcism!"

Father Bruce snickered quietly. Her mother, however, didn't find it one bit funny.

* * *

Grace often felt helpless in the face of her younger daughter's angst. After Caroline "resigned" from her first nursing job, Grace offered to contact some friends about getting Caroline a job in the school system where she worked. She ultimately helped her daughter secure an interview, and Caroline was offered a position as the school nurse in the same elementary school. It made Grace feel better, knowing she'd be near her complex daughter while they worked together in the same building.

Caroline wasn't thrilled about the idea of working with her mother. She still didn't know what specialty of nursing she wanted, but she was optimistic and looking forward to working with the youth.

What Caroline didn't expect after only a month at the elementary school was that she'd be bored out of her mind. One could only take so many runny noses and coughs. There was no challenge in it for her. Since she was grateful to her mother for having gotten her the job, Caroline held out for the school year, but declined an offer from the school department to renew her contract for the upcoming fall.

She went back to college and attained a Master's of Science in Nursing Degree. She'd had time to reflect on the type of work she'd like to pursue, and it was completely different from what she'd done in the past. After graduation, she interviewed for a job as an APRN in the emergency room at Puritan Medical Center in Boston.

She found her years working in the ER of PMC exhilarating, yet heartbreaking at the same time. The stress often wreaked havoc with her emotions. She was nearly fired from the hospital when, once again, someone suspected that she was taking drugs from the Pixus machine, the hospital's computerized medication dispenser. Her friend, Dr. Karl Monroe, a respected physician, came to her defense, writing it off as an error and helping her stave off that embarrassment. Quietly, he met with her.

She confided in him about her past. He sympathetically encouraged her to seek counseling for those childhood issues, which she assured him she was. Karl also suggested that perhaps she should consider an area of nursing that was less stressful than ER trauma.

Taking her friend's advice, Caroline interviewed with the Director of Pediatrics at PMC who saw within her compassionate strength, which she admired, and extended an offer.

The director said that it was Caroline's easygoing manner and nurturing instinct, coupled with her sharp wit, which convinced her that Caroline would be able to handle anything that came her way.

Chapter Twenty

Ennis, County Clare, Ireland, Fall 1978

GLYNNIS WOKE AT THE SOUND of the doorbell.

"MAM! Would you get the door?"

She yelled groggily, jamming her pillow over her head. When the bell rang a second time, she yelled louder.

"Mam! Someone's at the door!"

Flinging the pillow off her head, she listened for her mother's footsteps in the hall. Recalling the evidence found in her mother's room, she realized she wouldn't be up before noon. Chasing sleeping pills with whiskey didn't make for a chipper parent in the morning.

Glynnis threw off the covers and headed down the cold steps to the front door. She saw a figure through the decorative glass and opened the door to a shivering and out-of-breath Peggy.

"Hey! I hope I didn't wake you."

She smiled anxiously waiting for Glynnis to invite her in.

"No, I always get up at 7:00 a.m. on a SATURDAY!" She made sure to overdramatize the final word.

Peggy laughed nervously and apologized.

"May I come in?"

"Oh, yeah, sure. Sorry. I'm still in a bit of a fog."

"Late night last night with you and lover boy?"

Peggy taunted her.

"Ahhhh ... NO. As a matter of fact, it was a disaster. I'll tell you more."

She held the door wide for Peggy.

Peggy walked in holding a plastic bag. Her teeth were chattering, her hair was a mess, and she wasn't wearing her usual dark makeup. She looked tired, but strangely youthful, with her face flushed.

"What's in the bag?"

Peggy held it up.

"My laundry. I need to use your washer. Mind if I throw a few things in?"

Glynnis looked at her friend like she had three heads.

"You come over at seven in the morning on a Saturday to do your laundry?"

Peggy gave her an apologetic look.

"No, I've got to talk to you."

Glynnis figured there must be something else going on — not that she minded helping Peggy out. Pointing her friend down the hallway toward the kitchen she instructed her.

"Laundry is to the right of the sink. You throw that in, and I'll make us some tea. You want a sweater or something? You look half-frozen."

Peggy nodded and thanked her. Glynnis yawned loudly again and stretched.

"Did you happen to bring any cigarettes with you?"

Peggy called out from the laundry room.

"Yeah, in my sac! Help yourself. I bought a pack for you. I had to stop and get tampons and detergent at the store. There was no more water to take a shower at the camp. They're moving on today."

She was still shaking as she pulled her dirty clothes out of the plastic bag, recalling the events of the morning and the deadly fire that ensued.

*   *   *

In her rush to get away quickly without being seen, and to get her money out of its hiding place, Peggy got up at five o'clock that morning. She put on a thin shirt and a pair of Bobby's pants, threw her dirty clothes in a plastic bag, and headed out back. She didn't expect it to be quite so cool outside. Taking care to bring a few sausages with her, she tossed them to the dogs to keep them quiet. It worked, and they sat patiently waiting for her to give them more.

Peggy shifted the bag in her hand and lifted the broken panel that covered a hole in the side of the metal trailer near the waste tank. She held the loose panel with one hand and reached in and down to retrieve the container that held her secret savings of the last three years. She didn't hear him come up behind her.

"What have you got there?"

She jumped, startled. Her heart instantly sank to the pit of her stomach at the sound of his icy voice in her ear.

"What's in the box? You wouldn't be holding out on us now. Would ya, Margaret?"

He brought his body up close behind her and pressed his hips into her. "Hand it over."

His tone was flat as he grabbed the container from her trembling hands. She stood shaking with fear, knowing that she was in for the beating of her life.

Stephen's evil eyes lit up when he saw the contents of the box. His intense gaze bore into her and anger seethed from his hauntingly low voice.

"Were you holding out for some reason, Peg? Perhaps planning a little trip somewhere? So glad I decided to fill up the gas tank early this morning!"

He shoved the box back at her and picked up the heavy, red petrol container he'd set down when he'd come upon her. Jutting his face into hers, Peggy could see their breath mix as the vapors rose between them. He sneered.

"Let's tell my brother of this good fortune together, shall we?"

He forcefully grabbed her under the arm and led her around to the front of the trailer.

190

Peggy knew she was in trouble. You never hid money from them - ever. They were cutthroat about it. She knew she couldn't count on Bobby to come to her rescue. He'd beaten Leonore badly when he found £30 in her pants pocket, which she'd been trying to save to buy HIM a birthday present. He didn't believe her when she told him.

Peggy knew she needed divine intervention, a miracle, or her life was over. Even if she screamed or cried out for help, the other women might look out their tiny windows, but were too afraid to get involved for fear of being hit themselves. They abided by the group's code of silence. She started to cry softly, believing it to be the end. Stephen shoved her from behind, causing her to stumble. The dogs began to bark wildly, sensing the danger she was in.

"Hey, Bobby! Get the hell out of bed. I've got a surprise for you!"

Peggy stood shivering, with her head down still clutching the box that contained her life's savings. The wind blew the flimsy plastic bag hanging from her arm that held her semen-stained clothes. An empty rucksack hung over her shoulder containing only her toothbrush and soap. Stephen looked at her with contempt, sensing her fear and enjoying it. He'd kill her himself, but he wanted to watch her squirm for a while first.

Disgusted when he got no response, the only way his drunken brother was going to get up was if he went in and woke him. He shifted the heavy, plastic petrol container into his other hand, and then finally set it down on the ground at the base of the trailer steps. He approached Peggy and tapped his finger lightly on the box.

"I'll let you hold that for me for a little while longer. Don't try and run, Margaret. I'll let the dogs loose and when they catch you, they'll bring you back to me in pieces."

Turning, he reached for the door to the dilapidated trailer.

"Hey, you lazy shit! Get up!"

Stephen turned around in the doorway and caught a glimpse of his pathetic brother stumbling out of bed. He smirked snidely at Peggy, shaking his head. He reached into his shirt pocket for a cigarette and lit a match. The wind blew it out. Successful on the third try, he pointed and warned her again not to move.

Peggy looked down at the box that held her hopes and dreams. She was paralyzed with fear and couldn't move even if she wanted to. It was all over. Peggy couldn't breathe and felt like she was going to pass out. She needed to rest against something. Her heart was beating hard, pounding in her chest faster than she'd ever felt it before. Slowly she staggered backward to lean against Stephen's truck, making sure to stay in his line of view. She needed to steady herself. Stephen was smirking and blowing smoke rings while talking to Bobby. He never took his eyes off her.

She felt sick to her stomach and bent over to heave. Stephen was laughing, relaying the events to Bobby, who had a horrible hangover and was nodding in agreement to whatever his brother was saying to him. He could be mean as a snake when he woke up in the morning.

She laid her head against the truck, awaiting her fate, praying with her eyes closed. Stephen was right, she thought, it was useless to try and run. She was a lamb being led to the slaughter.

Bobby threw open the metal screen door. It swung back, crashing into the side of the trailer. He stared angrily at her, and motioned her over, yet she still couldn't move. What happened next was a blur.

Stephen and Bobby were both standing in the doorway of the small trailer when Stephen flicked his cigarette outside. Almost immediately there was a huge explosion and she watched in horror as a wall of fire went up the front of the trailer, forcing the two men to jump back. The cigarette had landed near the full petrol container Stephen had left on the ground, which he'd been readying for the journey later that morning.

There was some yelling at first as they tried to get out, but the heat continued to push them backward, trapping them inside. The flames quickly engulfed the trailer, and their panicking screams rose in what had to be excruciating pain as the fire singed their flesh. Peggy couldn't tell if it was Bobby or Stephen screaming; neither of them could be seen through the thick smoke and rising flames. Soon, the only sound she heard was that of the crackling fire and melting metal. The heat was so intense; she felt it begin to burn her own skin. It brought her to her senses, and she seized the opportunity to turn and run. No one saw her as she bounded for the woods behind the trailers.

She heard the shrill of women's voices as they fled from their own trailers and came to see what was happening. They kept the children away from the heat of the flames, crying in anguish as they assumed she and Bobby were both dead, burned alive in their sleep.

The fire leapt to Stephen's trailer, which soon became completely engulfed in flames as well, having been parked closely to Bobby's. Billows of black smoke could be seen rising up over the trees. Peggy ran for her life. She had asked for divine intervention and received it.

When she was far enough away from the caravan, she fell to the ground, gathering her composure and catching her breath. Her heart was racing. She said a quick prayer of thanks and blessed herself, asking God to give her the strength to go on and get away from the whole horrible situation.

She emptied the contents of the neatly organized box into her rucksack, stuffing a few of the bill rolls into her pockets as well. She had no idea how much money was there. She grabbed the plastic bag containing one pair of pants, a pullover sweater, a turtleneck shirt and a pair of underwear. Standing up with renewed hope, knowing that God was watching over her, Peggy headed for her friend Glynnis's house.

*　*　*

"Aren't you going with them?"

Glynnis asked as she reached for Peggy's satchel to get a cigarette. Peggy had her hand in the washing machine, swishing the clothes around to make sure they were saturated, when she heard Glynnis proclaim.

"Holy shit, did you just hold up a bank? Where did you get all of this money, Peg?"

Peggy poked her head out from the laundry room.

"No. I didn't rob a bank, so relax. Sit down. You're not going to believe what I'm about to tell you."

Peggy came out of the tiny side room and looked over at Glynnis, who was holding three of the rolled bill stacks in her hand.

"So where'd you get all of this?"

She asked again, peering into the bag and staring at her in amazement.

Peggy sat at the kitchen table and shook her head.

"I don't even know where to begin."

Peggy looked exhausted and drained.

"If you pour me a cup of tea, I'll fill you in."

Glynnis put the money rolls back in Peggy's rucksack and zipped it shut for her. Her mother wouldn't be up for hours, and her da hadn't even bothered to come home.

Glynnis filled the kettle with water and placed it on the stove. Pulling her hair back in a ponytail, she bent to light a cigarette off the burner flame. She handed it to Peggy, then lit another for herself.

"There's a lot I've not told you, Glynn."

Peggy blew a stream of gray smoke into the air and leaned against the radiator, grateful for its warmth.

"Partly because I'm ashamed and partly because I didn't want to get caught and dragged back to England."

Glynnis sat up in the kitchen chair, fully awake and a bit anxious about what Peggy was going to reveal.

"Peg, you're not on the lam or anything like that, are you?"

Peggy chuckled.

"Well, sort of, but not for long and not because I committed any crimes. Some of the guys I traveled with were criminals, but I'm not."

A relieved but puzzled look crossed Glynnis's face. She wanted to help her friend and sensed the seriousness of the pending conversation.

"Well, good, because my da, you know, the trustworthy, self-righteous barrister may have something to say about me harboring a fugitive."

Peggy assured her that, within a short time, she'd be of legal age and none of this would matter anymore.

She began relaying her story slowly at first, but soon began to pour out the events of not only that morning, but of her harrowing life to date, only pieces of which she'd shared with Glynnis and Clare in the past.

She told Glynnis about the deadly early morning fire which brought her to her doorstep at 7:00 a.m. Glynnis was horrified. Peggy then summarized how she'd come to meet Leonore, Bobby, and Stephen. She explained how she was homeless for a short time after she'd run away from the federal children's home in England, where she was cruelly treated, and that she made her way back to Ireland to avoid the authorities.

Peggy went back even further, recounting the story about her uncle and the abuse she suffered at his hands. She explained how he raised her after her mother abandoned her, and how he damn near killed her on the night of her fourteenth birthday. She described the beating and brutal rape she endured that evening when she returned home after partying with some of her friends.

Glynnis sat quietly and listened in shock and disbelief. Peggy, hearing herself tell the pitiful story, broke down and cried. Glynnis put her arm around her offering consolation. She could only imagine the years of hurt and pain Peggy must have endured.

Glynnis assured her that it was all over and done now and that she'd help her get her life back on track again. Glynnis quietly hoped those dirty bastards, Bobby and Stephen, were where they deserved to be, burning for a second time in hell, and that hopefully, Leonore was safe and living a better life somewhere far away.

To Glynnis, Peggy's ordeal made her own life seem like a cakewalk. All of her problems couldn't compare to what her friend had suffered. But Glynnis was smart enough to realize that all pain is relative. She was suddenly more thankful for the home she lived in and even for her own dysfunctional parents. Though her life was not perfect, she'd never been homeless, hungry, or without clothing. Her only experience with the Callaghan girl's uncle didn't seem so severe in comparison.

"Peg, I never would have guessed how tough things have been for you. I mean, I used to envy your freedom! You know, last night, when Mam hit me? I was seriously considering your offer to up and go with you and the knackers! I remember you telling me and Clare how you ran away from England, from the children's home, and I had questions, but I didn't want to pry."

Glynnis continued.

"My own family is pretty messed up. I was raped, too, when I was younger, but I never told anyone."

Peggy sat up and wiped away her tears.

"Who raped you?"

Glynnis lit another cigarette and slumped back in her chair.

"I was babysitting for Valerie and Caroline, friends of mine, but her grandparents were friends of my mother's at the time, just a few doors down. Their father had been killed, and I was asked to help with the girls during the wake and funeral. They were really nice kids and we're all good friends now. I'm pretty tight with Valerie, the older sister, even though her uncle is a pervert! She doesn't know anything about it. I never told her. Caroline is younger and has really gotten wild from what I hear. I've often wondered if their uncle ever tried anything on them. But I never asked. We still get together whenever they come over to Ireland to visit with their grandparents."

Peggy asked Glynnis about her experience and what happened.

"Well, like I said, I was babysitting the girls. They were out in the yard playing, and I came in to get us something to drink. The uncle called me over to sit on the couch. I thought it a rather strange request. When I sat down, he proceeded to run his hand up my thigh and put his fingers inside my panties."

Peggy nodded and bowed her head, knowing full well where the story was going. Glynnis stopped for a moment and squirmed in her chair.

"He asked me to lie back on the couch and then he kissed me. Peg, I was eleven years old! I didn't know anything about kissing or that kind of stuff! He kept whispering that I was such a big girl and not to be afraid and that this was just our secret."

Tears fell from Glynnis's eyes. Peggy reached her hand out and placed it over Glynnis's.

"Then he took my panties off and made me touch him. I tried to pull my hand away... but he was stronger than me and I couldn't! All I was worried about was that the children would come in and see me and get upset. Then he rolled on top of me and started moving against me, rubbing and prodding around. As I was crying, he got more demanding and kept 'shushing' me. I'll never forget his voice. Then there was this horrible pain ..."

Glynnis put her hands up over her face and pushed strands of her hair back, staring up at the ceiling.

"Anyway, when he did that, I screamed. I lay there literally thinking I was going to die. I could still hear the two little girls running around out back, laughing and playing, as if nothing in the world were wrong. Here I was, inside the house, laid out on their couch, as my freaking insides were being torn apart by this man. I bled for a week after that!

Peggy shook her head. Glynnis went on.

"Afterwards, that bastard took me upstairs and insisted upon cleaning me up and proceeded to give me a bath, saying that the worst part was over and that it would never hurt like that again. He gave me a pair of Valerie's panties and put a pad in it and left. I never wanted to go near that house or be alone with him again!"

"I'm really sorry that happened to you, Glynnis."

Peggy remarked sympathetically after they both regained their composure.

"What I experienced, Peg, is nothing compared to what you've gone through. Our bodies heal. It's our heads we've got to work on."

Glynnis continued.

"I've always wondered about Caroline and Valerie though – you know, if he ever raped or touched them."

Peggy gazed out the sun-filled window and asked.

"Did he ever try it again?"

"No. I never gave him the opportunity or chance."

Peggy glanced around the pretty kitchen.

"I had something like this once, you know. I went to a private school, had a nice house, pretty clothes ... and of course, china."

She motioned, holding up the elegant teacup to make her point.

"No one knew any different, Glynn. They had no idea what went on behind closed doors."

She shuddered. The two young women sat in the kitchen, smoking cigarettes and drinking tea, silent in their own thoughts, processing their emotional pain, and bound by the secrets of their troubled childhoods.

Chapter Twenty-One

Ireland, 1978

"So what are your plans now, Peg?"

Glynnis was concerned and felt somewhat more protective of Peggy since they'd shared their sordid stories.

"I think I'm going to try to get back to my uncle's house in England."

Glynnis sat up straight in her chair.

"Do you think it's safe?"

Peggy shrugged her shoulders.

"I don't know. I've tried to call the house a few times over the years, but the phone was disconnected a while ago. I don't think my uncle will ever come back there, knowing he'd be arrested on the spot. He did tell me long ago that everything he had was mine. It's written in his will somewhere in the house. I recall seeing the document with my name on it. I won't know until I go through the papers in the house."

"You will need those papers to prove ownership, so that you won't be evicted. My da can help you out with any legal matters. He'll do it if I ask him."

"Well, I know the house is paid for. But I'm sure there will be questions that I need to answer. I wonder if they're still looking for my uncle. No doubt they'll question me to see if I know anything."

Peggy smiled weakly.

"I guess I'll just head home and see what comes of it all. I don't know what to expect. I don't even know if the house is still standing!"

"Why don't you stay with me for a few days. You can calm down and plan your life. I've got a great idea! Let's launch a whole new you! Y'know, without your usual goth garb and dark make-up. Even Mam won't recognize you!"

Peggy liked the idea of looking human once again, shedding her dark persona for something warmer and more approachable. She wasn't dead anymore, but very much alive, and feeling inspired for the first time in many years. She needed to talk about what happened in her past. It brought closure and hope for the first time.

Glynnis got up to examine Peggy's head.

"What is your natural hair color?"

She picked through a few strands, trying to distinguish its origin.

"It's a deep brown."

Peggy ran her fingers through her matted coal black hair.

Glynnis perked up. Her eyes gleaming.

"We're going to seize this brand new day, my friend, and make some permanent changes!"

Grabbing a fistful of money and holding it out to Peggy.

"We're going to create a whole new you!"

Peggy rolled her eyes and blew out the smoke from her last cigarette.

"I'm not sure I'm up for this right now, Glynn. I'm just exhausted."

But Glynnis was too excited about the possibilities of a makeover and wanted to keep Peggy excited and engaged in the process.

"Nope! Too bad. You can sleep in the beauty shop chair. You're really very pretty, Peg. You just need to see that for yourself. I think you draw MORE attention to yourself dressed like this, with all the piercings and such. People won't recognize you if you're dressed normal. Besides, you don't want anyone from Ireland, I mean, your old life here, seeing you like this, do you?"

She continued.

"You're a lot classier than this, Pegster. I've known it all along!"

Peggy nodded her thanks. She didn't know who she was, or WHAT she'd become over the years. Survival instincts took over, and she did what she had to do, giving only an occasional thought to what she might actually *want* to do. She always had faith in her potential and future. She always knew, somewhere deep in her heart and soul, that she had the talent to become something wonderful and beautiful. What was it the Bible said?

"To appoint unto them that mourn in Zion, to give unto them beauty for ashes, the oil of joy for mourning, the garment of praise for the spirit of heaviness."

Peg began to think of the possibilities a total transformation could bring about. Suddenly, with renewed energy, she was eager for the change. She didn't want to be recognized. She hated the level to which her life had descended. She recalled the earlier years of girlish dresses, hats, and gloves. She pulled out her compact and moaned in despair at her reflection.

"HOW are we going to fix this? I'm such a mess!"

She motioned toward her broken and badly abused body.

Glynnis put her arm around her friend.

"I've not had my hair done in so many years. I usually just buy something cheap off the shelf and do it myself."

"No worries, Peg, ole' girl, leave it to me, and we'll get you fixed up. I'll call my stylist and make an appointment. Rumor has it she slept with my da, so I don't think she'll refuse me."

Peggy laughed despite her tears.

"Is there anyone that he hasn't been with in this town?"

Glynnis shrugged her shoulders.

"I don't think so, but in this case, we'll make it work to our advantage! She's never refused me an appointment."

They giggled.

"Let's get you some new clothes while we're at it ... a few nice dresses, some skirts for interviews."

Peggy looked at her in horror.

"Interviews? What the hell job do you think I'd qualify for? I'll need to go back and finish school first."

Glynnis put her pointer finger up.

"Exactly! Interviews for school, perhaps. Anyway, you should have a few nice skirts, and some pants, of course. Let's throw out and get rid of everything old. Leave nothing to remind you of the past."

Peggy listened as her friend continued to rattle off plans concerning her immediate future. She was grateful for Glynnis's endless chatter, as it helped her block out thoughts of the burning trailer and silence the screams of pain from Bobby and Stephen as the flames scorched their flesh.

After her laundry was done, Peggy was reveling in the warmth of a real shower, hoping the water could somehow wash off the dirtiness she felt inside as well as out. Glynnis went and got her friend's clean clothes out of the dryer. Handing them to Peggy through the bathroom door.

"When was the last time you wore a dress or a skirt?"

Peggy, dripping wet behind the shower curtain, had her head bent over while twisting a lilac-smelling towel around her head. She spouted off good-naturedly.

"Will you get off it! Probably not since I was in Catholic school. Years ago. Why?"

"Have you given any thought to what you want to do with your life now?"

Peggy wrapped her body in a second plush towel and pulled back the shower curtain. With hands on hips, she looked at Glynnis.

"I don't even know what I'm doing tomorrow! I don't know what condition the house is in, or if I even have a house to live in! I could be homeless again!"

Glynnis reassured her.

"No way! You've got to have enough money in that sack of yours to get your own flat. I'm sure of it. Besides, I don't think they can just sell it. I mean, if your uncle owned it and left it to you, it's yours. There may be some tax issues to resolve – but I'm sure my da can help you work all of that out. Set up a payment plan with the town administrators or something."

Peggy shrugged.

"I hope so. I had a key hidden out back under one of the garden pots for the longest time. Maybe it's still there, unless thieves found it and raided the place, which is a possibility, too."

Peggy had that glazed-over look on her face again. The morning had been a shocking nightmare.

"I just feel like I've gotten out of prison and been told, 'Here you go. Here are the keys to the world. Do what you will with them.' Only I'm not sure what to do."

Glynnis nodded sympathetically.

"I can't imagine how I'd feel if I were in your shoes, Peg. I think I'd try to look upon it all as an adventure, very sad at times, but hopeful now, don't you think? I mean, no more fear. They're gone, all of them, Bobby, Stephen, and your uncle. Now you're older and know better. No one will ever treat you like that again, unless you let them, and I know you won't!"

Peggy nodded in agreement and motioned her out the bathroom door.

"I've got to get dressed. I'm freezing. But you're right, Glynn; it was a nightmare I want to forget. So let's get going."

She looked around for her bag, remembering she'd left it in the kitchen.

"Do you mind bringing my rucksack up for me?"

Glynnis left to give her some privacy and went to retrieve the rucksack from downstairs.

Glynnis trudged back up the stairs, grabbing her jacket from the hook and a sweater for Peggy. Handing her the backpack and wool sweater, she reminded her.

"You'll need to buy a warm coat, you know. Winter's coming."

"I'm never going to be cold again, so help me. Are you ready to spend some serious money?"

Glynnis laughed.

"You know what? I don't even know how much I have!"

Glynnis gave her a funny look.

"You mean to tell me that you've never counted it?"

Peggy shook her head.

"No. When did I have the time or privacy to do that? I just kept rolling the bills and shoving every pound I got into the box when I could sneak away to stash it. There was no way I could count it without the risk of getting caught. I tried to save space by rolling them. There was always someone around watching. I had to be really careful. Now you know why."

Glynnis offered out.

"Let's count it then! You rolled them all very neatly and put hair bands around them. I'm impressed!"

Peggy smirked and felt the muscles in the back of her neck start to relax.

"Can I have another cup of tea first - before we count it?"

"Of course! You must be starved. Here, let's do this downstairs on the kitchen table. It's warmer in the kitchen, too. I'll make us some eggs and toast for breakfast."

The girls went downstairs. Peggy walked over to the stove and turned on the kettle while Glynnis searched through the refrigerator for eggs. She was curious to know what her hard work had amounted to over the years.

Glynnis still didn't know what to make of it all. She'd never known anyone to suffer the way Peggy had, and admired her ability to work hard and save. But she also knew it had been a matter of survival for her friend.

After they ate, the girls dumped the contents of Peggy's satchel onto the kitchen table. The pile of banded money rolled across the surface.

Glynnis joked.

"I think we should iron it out flat. What do you think?"

Peggy looked at her crazy friend.

"We're not going to 'launder' the money Glynn, we're simply going to count it."

Glynnis smirked and watched as Peggy pressed it out flat with her hand.

"Just do this. It will be fine."

They were quiet while counting and sorting, which took them almost thirty minutes. Glynnis reached for the pencil and paper by the phone.

She jotted down figures and began to stack the bills in order of denomination. Peggy did the same and wrote her figures next to Glynnis's. Both girls' jaws dropped at the totaled amounts.

"Peg, I've got a little over £8,000 here. Actually, £8,005 to be exact. What about you?"

Peggy smiled wickedly at her friend.

"How about £10,126?"

"HOLY SHIT!"

Glynnis exclaimed.

"That's over £18,000! You're bloody rich! You sure you weren't selling drugs? I'm kidding, just joking around."

Peggy assured her she never once did that and was beaming from ear to ear.

"Yeah, nice, huh?"

The girls hugged each other.

"Okay, let's be smart and think this through ... here's the deal,"

Glynnis began to brainstorm.

"You need to save money for your trip back to England and maybe to do some small repairs on the house. You'll need food and money to turn on the utilities."

Peggy put her hand up to slow her friend down.

"WHOA! Time-out here. Would you not go any further? You're scaring me."

She looked a bit overwhelmed.

"Sorry, Peg, don't worry. It's all going to fall into place. What I was getting at is that we don't want to spend it all in one day. You've got to hold on to enough to get you through until you figure out what you're going to do. That's all I meant."

Peggy nodded in agreement.

"But I do need some new clothes and shoes. I also want a good pair of boots and some heavy socks. I'm tired of my feet freezing!"

Glynnis got a fresh piece of paper.

"Okay, here's what we'll do. Let's make a list of all the things you've got to have right away ... beginning with number one, makeup!"

"You're joking, right?"

Glynnis shook her head no.

Peggy looked up at the ceiling and muttered.

"Now that's keeping one's priorities in order!"

Glynnis laughed and went on to item number two.

"Haircut and style. Don't laugh. This is very important. Remember it's all a part of the 'new you'."

Peggy began to put the money away neatly as Glynnis continued on with her list.

"You'll need new underwear and bras."

Peggy was embarrassed at the condition of her underwear; it was gray and worn out and offered no support whatsoever.

Glynnis stopped writing when it finally dawned on her that she hadn't even asked Peggy what she'd like.

"Peg? What exactly do YOU want?"

Peggy stared at her, amused.

"Oh, you mean, I actually get to put something on my own list?"

Glynnis laughed and apologized for her oversight.

"Yes, you sure do. Anything! What is it?"

Peggy began to think.

"Okay, here's my list. I want warm flannel pajamas in pink with a big, fluffy robe to match."

Glynnis wrote frantically.

"And some nice smelling things like candles or maybe perfume or powder or soaps."

"Get them all!"

Glynnis confirmed with a wave of her hand, writing like a demon scribe.

"You deserve it!"

The possibilities were exciting Peggy.

"This is like Christmas for most people, wouldn't you say?"

Glynnis nodded and smiled.

"I can't wait to get going!"

Peggy cautioned her.

"We need to set a limit though. How much do you think we should take with us for all of this?"

Glynnis took a moment to assess the list.

"How about we cap it all at ... oh, say, £2,500? We'll be good bargain hunters and get the most for our money, okay?"

The girls hugged and agreed. Grabbing their sweaters, they chatted animatedly as they headed out the door.

"We'll get nice stuff, not cheap, but well-made, so it lasts."

"How am I ever going to lug all of this back to London with me, on and off the trains and buses?"

"I'll loan you some suitcases and come with you to help you unpack and get settled into the house. I've got a school break coming up next week, and I'll just tell my mam I've been invited to spend a week in England at your parents' house. She won't mind."

"Brilliant! Do you think we can work in a really nice lunch some-where? It'll be my treat, for all of your help with my shop-till-you-drop excursion. What do you say?"

Glynnis smiled broadly.

"Sounds like a plan to me. Let's go."

They traveled downtown by bus. The wheels were still spinning in Peggy's mind.

"We'd better be careful when we take the money out. The shop owners will think we held up a bank. Let's make sure we do a lot of small purchases in various stores, okay? And let's take the money out before we get to the counter?"

Glynnis nodded in agreement. It was going to be a day they'd never forget.

Chapter Twenty-Two

Ennis, County Clare, Ireland, Spring 1998

SEAN WAS GROWING INCREASINGLY BORED with his job as a computer programmer. He'd been promised a sizeable pay increase, but was told that it would be paid out in the form of company shares once the new software turned a profit. However, the company's revenues weren't panning out as predicted.

Keystroke Technologies, Inc. was a relatively new software company that had met with great success in the early eighties and had shown great promise, according to Leading Edge Technology magazine. They launched their first release of the innovative Capture software in 1986. Capture was marketed to companies looking to increase their security and ability to monitor employee work habits and company data. The software enabled corporations to record every keystroke employees made on their computers. It also monitored e-mail and web surfing.

Sean considered it a compliment when family and friends referred to him as a "techie". He was highly experienced in his line of work. In the beginning, the company rewarded him with frequent raises and trips. His ultimate goal was to get involved in the marketing end of the business, and he was promised this opportunity during his last review. While Version 2.0 of Capture was being developed, however, his transfer was delayed. Then there was a management shake-up, and Sean was told they couldn't afford to let him transfer until beta testing was complete. In the meantime, a company from India had begun development of a product very similar to theirs, and was outselling them by offering more features and capabilities for less money, along with a 24-hour customer support center. Keystroke Technologies, Inc. was facing financial troubles as a result.

Sean wasn't too concerned about the company's financial situation. He tended to fall back on the fact that his family was well off. Not that he ever went to his parents for money. But it helped knowing that it was there should he need it. He still lived at home and found no pressing need to move out. His parents were getting older and in need of more help. He wasn't dating anyone seriously, which concerned his mother and father. They often pressed him on the matter. Sean overheard his mother ask Siobhan once if she thought he was gay. Siobhan laughed and said that she doubted it, but that she'd ask him if she really wanted to know.

"Don't you dare!"

Sean's father's approach was more blunt, asking him straight out one night over a pint they shared at a local pub.

"Son, I need you to answer me straight on this, and pardon my directness, but are you by any chance a 'puff'?"

Sean nearly snorted the liquid out his nose, not ever expecting to hear such a question from his da. But once he thought about it, he realized he'd be curious, too, if his thirty-something son hadn't brought home a woman in ages and showed no interest in finding one. Sean laughed, assuring his father he wasn't gay.

"Then where are the women?"

His da pushed him for answers.

"It's not like you're not handsome, son. Anyone can see that."

Sean cautioned his dad to lower his voice or the whole bar might think them both "puffs." Sean assured him that he'd just not found the right one yet. He went on to add that marriage wasn't for everyone. Then the subject was dropped and not broached again. Sean kept himself busy, tucked away, working a good deal of the time, and traveling on business.

Sean's room at his parent's home acted as his satellite office. He would often lock himself up in there for hours on end. His mother had learned early on not to bother him while he was working.

Often, Sean would leave his room in the middle of the afternoon and be gone until dinnertime. When his mother inquired as to his whereabouts, Sean would be evasive, answering, "Just out," or, "Off to corporate." She'd have his dinner waiting for him when he returned, and he'd sit and pleasantly chat with her about her day. He was thoughtful like that, even though his mother often referred to him as her "odd one." But Sean was always pleasant enough, and never asked anything of anyone. Siobhan and he had a great relationship, and they both adored their nieces and missed their brother terribly.

* * *

Sean had many fond memories of Neil, who had been a protective older brother. He and Sean had been joined at the hip during their early years, when their dad was often away earning the family fortune. Their mother made sure that both of her sons were brought up as good Catholics. They were educated in private, parochial schools, and both served as altar boys. Neil, at age thirteen, took the pomp and pageantry of the Catholic Mass in stride, often making light of his duties, much to his mother's chagrin. Sean, only being in the third grade at the time, however, was a nervous wreck when involved with the church services, but knew that he could never tell his mother how much he hated doing it.

School came easily to Neil, but was too stringent for Sean's taste. Neil worked well within the overabundance of guidelines and rules. Sean was more of a free spirit, preferring to find his own way of doing things. His attitude didn't sit well with the priests at St. Christopher's all-boys elementary school, who were often much too hard on the children for committing minor violations of school policy.

Neil once came to his little brother's rescue as a result of such an infraction. A young priest had warned the boys to stay in a straight line and file into the school quietly when signaled. Sean jumped out of line to retrieve a ball that was rolling away, when he thought the recess monitor wasn't looking.

Neil watched cautiously as the priest walked up quickly behind his errant brother and raised his pointer to strike him. Neil lunged at the priest, catching the stick with one hand, and twisted it away from him, breaking it over his knee then throwing it at his feet. The kids cheered Neil's bravery. Neil asked Sean if he was okay; his brother silently nodded that he was. Neil was a hero to their fellow classmates, but was punished by having to serve Saturday detentions for a month. His mother and father had no idea what happened, and the boys didn't tell them. Neil narrowly escaped being suspended for his actions but only because of his parents' generous contributions to the church and the scholarship fund they established at St. Christopher's. Had the incident involved anyone else, Neil's actions would not have been tolerated.

Neil dated frequently during his teen years, and often brought girls home to meet his parents. A good-natured young man, he worked two jobs. On weekends he helped out at a local stable, and during the harvest season he baled hay. Sean would join in on the task, more for the adventure than the money. The boys actually had great fun rolling and riding the big stacks. Sean enjoyed being with his older brother. Neil would often purposely aggravate him and they'd end up boxing or wrestling. They had a few rows, as was expected between brothers, but nothing that went on continually or with malice. They both liked a lot of the same activities and could be very mischievous. They played pranks on others and were considered partners in crime by their mother. Sean fought more with his sister, Siobhan, than with Neil.

*　*　*

Sean was alone in his room, surfing the web. He finished speaking with his contact in Seoul, South Korea, and sent off a confirmation e-mail, letting him know his date of arrival. Since his twenty-fifth birthday, Sean had been making regular trips to the country. After Neil's death, he'd gone more frequently, about every three months, telling his parents he was off again traveling on business. In actuality he visited the small country because it offered every sexual penchant a man was willing to pay for. Hoping to keep his taste for Asian women a secret, Sean never told anyone about his escapades abroad. His sexual appetite increased noticeably during stressful times, and if he couldn't manage a trip, he'd find a way to satisfy his desires locally, usually in England, which required yet more careful planning.

Neil was considered the smarter of the two sons, highlighted by the fact that he was named executor of their parents' will. Sean didn't want to admit it, but he was a little jealous of his brother. He had it all, a lovely wife, a beautiful home on Cape Cod in America, and two adorable and loving daughters. It was hard not to be envious of him.

After Neil's death, Sean wrestled with feelings of guilt and seriously considered escaping to Seoul for good. He wasn't sure that he could live up to his parents' expectations when his older brother was gone.

The flexibility that technology afforded him meant he could work remotely from anywhere in the world. Were it not for the fact that he wouldn't see his nieces, Sean would have done it. As it was, the girls' trips to Ireland had tapered off dramatically when Caroline reached her late teens. As they'd gotten older, it was Valerie who visited more frequently than Caroline. He'd watched and heard of Caroline's explosive episodes over the years — the late-night drinking binges, hanging out with a rough crowd, and dating a multitude of undesirable men. Grace had called his family for advice on more than a few occasions.

Siobhan offered a sympathetic ear and suggested counseling. She had suggested that Grace should check Caroline's room for drugs, as it sounded like Caroline could be using them, given her dramatic change in personality. No one could understand it. She was always treated with such love and admiration. The only thing that she seemed to stick with on any regular basis was her dancing. Sean recalled with pride her talent as an Irish step dancer, and his part in boosting her self-esteem when she won the Rose contest.

Caroline exemplified Celtic beauty. She'd been Irish step dancing since she was a young girl, and took it to a new level while Val was in college. She practiced at great length and went on to become an award-winning Irish step dancer who competed not just nationally, but internationally in Ireland.

During her early teen years, when Caroline wanted to escape summers in New York with Sheila and Tim altogether, she convinced her mother and Granny that she'd advance much more quickly in her dancing if she could spend summers studying in Ireland. Her Aunt Siobhan was all for the idea and encouraged Grace to let her come over. Everyone vowed to keep a close eye on her. True to her word, it wasn't long before Caroline became a well-respected and formidable competitor.

It was Uncle Sean's idea to enter Caroline in a Rose pageant when she was eighteen. The pageants were typically local contests held around the various counties. Val had flatly declined the offer, but Caroline, seeing no harm in it, competed and easily won the right to represent County Clare at the International Western Rose Festival held in Charlestown, County Mayo. A few ignorant folks complained that since she was from the United States, she wasn't eligible to compete. But Sean produced the government documents proving her dual residency and silenced her jealous critics.

Caroline outshined all the other contestants. Her physical beauty alone would have won it for her, but what clinched it was her outstanding performance during the talent portion of the program. She had asked her sister Val if she wouldn't mind fiddling for her while she danced. Val was happy to oblige and the two synchronized perfectly. Caroline took after Neil in height, and her perfectly erect posture and high kicking brought a thunderous applause. Later in the evening, she was crowned Ireland's "International Western Rose."

When word reached Ennis, Caroline was an instant celebrity. She often referred to it as her "15 minutes of fame." She was happy, and it was a great opportunity for her, but she didn't let it go to her head.

Caroline was special to Sean, and he'd told her that all her life — well out of Val's earshot. He'd never hurt Valerie's feelings. He loved her, too, of course, but in a different way than Caroline. Valerie, in Sean's mind, was more like her father. She was intelligent and analytical, possessing a quick wit with a rather dry sense of humor. She could be very engaging in conversation, and was comfortable entertaining guests or strangers, playing her violin or fiddling.

One night, when the girls were younger and had made the trip to Ireland for a visit, they went out with Glynnis and their new friend, Peggy, who'd begged Val to bring her fiddle. Val took her bored younger sister with her. Later, Sean happened to be walking across the street from the stone wall where the group hung out. He stood out of sight and listened. Valerie was playing a snappy tune while Glynnis and Caroline danced a jig, much to the delight of the boys, who were paying more attention to Glynnis's bouncing boobs than her feet. The other girls cheered them on and a few adults stopped to watch as well. The teenagers laughed hysterically when an adult, not realizing they were playing for their own enjoyment, tossed a couple of coins into Val's violin case. Then the boys offered to go and buy a few pints for them all.

Sean laughed to himself as it brought back his own youthful memories. He watched quietly as the boys good-naturedly complimented the younger Caroline on her dancing in an effort to make her feel special. Val was content to sit on the grass then with the other girls and play out quieter, more delicate notes on her violin. Afterwards, Caroline plopped down next to her older sister. Glynnis leaned her head against Peggy's while they closed their eyes and listened to the soothing music. Sean went unnoticed by the girls and continued on his walk home. He whistled as he walked, content in knowing they were happy.

Chapter Twenty-Three

Boston, Massachusetts, Spring 1998

VAL AND CAROLINE DECIDED TO meet for drinks after work. They'd not been able to steal away to dinner in weeks, given their ever conflicting and often hectic work schedules, and the fact that Val had just returned from another trip to Ireland. She'd also been keeping late hours since her promotion to Vice President of Finance at Sidebar Magazine.

She loved the challenge and traveled quite a bit. It was exciting and fast-paced. Although she didn't know much about the legal profession, and a lot of the legalese escaped her, she read her company's magazine from cover to cover every month. Val flew to the various branch offices around the country, conducting quarterly reviews and audits. Branch managers customarily took her to dinner when she visited, and they'd discuss recently published articles and schmooze over dinner about management practices.

Caroline hadn't changed after her shift at the hospital, and rushed into the bar dressed in her colorful Hawaiian scrubs still managing to look gorgeous with her auburn hair pulled up in an obvious hurried ponytail. Val sported a more conservative look in a white cotton V-neck shirt, silk stockings, and classic black heels nicely complimented her plum-colored business suit. Although they wore completely contrasting outfits, both of them were comfortable in their element, and neither was out to impress anyone. They didn't seem to notice the stares they received from admiring businessmen at the bar when they greeted one another with a hug. A couple of the men were seriously eyeing Valerie who was, as usual, oblivious to their interest.

Caroline had been curious about her sister's social life lately. Her career took up so much of her time; she hadn't given much thought to a serious romance in years. No one held Val's attention for very long, though Caroline had noticed her sister's distraction and happy countenance the past few days — another reason why Caroline had made it a priority to make time to catch up and find out what was going on.

Val was never at a lack for admirers. The problem was that she kept her life so full with work and her music that she didn't stop long enough to see who was noticing her. On her last trip across the pond, however, fate stepped in and made a loud announcement that even she couldn't ignore. She was anxious to tell Caroline all about it. But first she would listen to Caroline talk about her ER drama of the day ... Val always let her go first.

Though strong in words, Val knew Caroline to be emotionally delicate in nature. Easily hurt or offended, she longed to help anyone who was sick or hurting in any way she could. Too many men took advantage of her vulnerability.

"You know what, Val?"

Caroline sat back and yawned, putting her feet up on an open chair.

"It's so nice to just be able to sit and not have to run off and be any-where!"

She leaned forward and rested her chin on her hand, staring happily at her sister. She admired Val and the way she always managed to keep her life together. Caroline struggled in ways her sister suspected, but never really knew. She held secrets she'd never divulge, no matter how close she was to her sister. It was a promise she'd made to her uncle since she was a child. He'd never touch Valerie, he told her, if she'd comply and keep their meetings a secret. Caroline sought to protect her sister, even though Valerie was the older sibling. She'd done everything in her power to keep him from hurting Valerie.

"I really could use a drink."

Caroline scanned the dining room, looking for a waitress. Val nodded in agreement and signaled to an anxious young male waiter on the other side of the room.

"Don't worry. Just a glass or two for me."

Val waved her hand in the air, dismissing her sister's explanation.

"You're a big girl, Caroline. You make your own choices."

Caroline respected that about Valerie. Their mother could be over-bearing at times, but Val always made her look after herself and encouraged her to make good decisions. Once they determined to buy Sheila's condo together with part of their trust fund money, they discovered they made great roommates, and there weren't too many problems they couldn't work out. Only once could Caroline ever remember Val losing her patience. She'd thrown a fit that time. Caroline later admitted that she'd deserved it.

*   *   *

Val had had it with her younger sister, and told her she was fed up with her loose lifestyle. Every other night for the last two weeks, she'd come home and found Caroline in bed with some new man. She'd hear laughing coming from Caroline's room. Feeling like a stranger and uncomfortable in her own house, Val set out one night to reclaim her privacy and her sister's dignity.

She barged through Caroline's bedroom door and grabbed her latest conquest by the back of his head. She threw his clothes at him and screamed for him to get out of her apartment or she was calling the police and having him arrested for rape. He ran out the door half naked, getting dressed in the hall on the landing before running shoeless out the front door and down Commonwealth Avenue.

Val turned and shoved her finger into her sister's face.

"You're a whore, Caroline! How can you take such risks? You're a NURSE! You know what diseases are out there. I mean, AIDS, Caroline!

It KILLS you; it's not just something you live with! Not to mention a host of other diseases you're literally OPENING yourself up to!"

She shoved her sister back onto the bed.

"Where the hell is your head at, Caroline? Huh? One of these days, you might run across the wrong guy, a psychopath who could KILL you... or me if we're all in the same house! You never think of anyone but yourself!"

Caroline had been drinking.

"Just shut up, Valerie and mind your own business. I pay half the mortgage, and I'll do what I damn well want!"

Val was hurt. She was trying to get her sister to see how foolish and careless she was being with her own health.

Caroline was disgusted, for many reasons, but the fact was, Val was right. She pushed her out of her room, causing her to fall backward against the wall. Val banged her head and smashed her elbow, landing hard on the floor. Caroline immediately ran to help her up, but Val kicked her in the shin. What she really wanted to do was get up and punch her in the face.

Remembering the look on Paul's face when Val grabbed him by the head of his hair, Caroline suddenly burst out into wild laughter, followed by a stream of tears which she shed as she sunk down on the floor with her head in her hands, apologizing to Val.

She slowly got up off the floor and turned to go to her room, locking the door in spite of Val's pleas to open the door and talk things out. She'd cried herself to sleep that night after finishing off a small bottle of tequila, which she kept in her side drawer.

* * *

"Yo! Earth to Caroline!"

Val was waving her hand in front of her sister's face.

"How was your day? Bring any suicides back from the edge?"

Val reached for her wine glass and sat back, watching as Caroline devoured the spicy peanuts on the table.

"Naaah, just the usual ODs and cutters. Honestly, sometimes, I just want to show those poor bastards the proper way to kill themselves. I mean, if they're so hell-bent on doing it, and keep finding their way back to the ER, I feel bad that they keep screwing it up!"

Val laughed, only because she knew she shouldn't.

"Ahhhh, the voice of Mother Teresa speaks!"

"That's me!"

Caroline proclaimed, proudly popping another peanut into her mouth.

"What about you? How was Ireland?"

She sat back and lit a cigarette.

Val filled her in between handfuls of snacks.

"Let's see, the same, ummmmm ... different, and, well, ... new."

She let her words trail off, leaving Caroline hanging and wondering what she meant. She waited for Caroline to take the bait and for the anticipation to build. Val continued.

"Granny was concerned about Mary. Things are better between her and Liam I guess, but she misses Glynnis terribly and hates that she lives so far away in England."

Caroline sat up, as she was curious to know how their friends were doing.

"It's not like she's that far away, Val. I knew Glynn always wanted to live there. She and Peg are joined at the hip, those two. What about Peggy? What's she doing these days?"

"Peggy's doing great. She just started teaching an art class on Saturdays at her studio. But the best news is that she had a really successful grand opening at her new gallery, Panache. Don't you love the name? She got great reviews in the papers. Granny cut out all of the articles and saved them for us. I brought them home. They're on the counter in the kitchen, if you want to read them later tonight. She's going to be hugely successful. I'm so proud of her!"

Caroline smiled and agreed.

"Yeah, poor Pegster's had a tough life. I'm proud of her, too. I've got to get over there and see the new gallery."

She sat back, remembering some of the stories they'd shared over the years.

When Peggy confided in Caroline about the abuse she'd endured at the hands of her uncle James, Caroline had also shared her experiences and swore Peggy and Glynnis to secrecy.

"You know, you love to hear stories of how people like her overcome their circumstances. I wish the best for Peggy — she deserves it. I'll give her a call over the weekend. Had I known you were going over for that, I'd have tried to get the time off to go with you."

She looked down at her blood-spotted shoes. Her eye started to twitch slightly from fatigue.

"So what's the family up to over there?"

Caroline asked as she rubbed her eyes.

Val shrugged.

"Uncle Sean was off on another business trip. I didn't see him at all. He, Granny, and Siobhan are coming over here to visit Mom on the Cape in a few weeks. They're coming over for the benefit concert. Granny is going to donate the new library in daddy's name."

Caroline looked up, startled.

"What concert is this?"

Val shook her head.

"Do you ever listen to anything I tell you? The Harbor Lights Ensemble. I've only been practicing for hours every night. Haven't you heard me?"

Caroline tried to cover up her embarrassment. She really didn't remember her sister telling her about the concert, and Val was always playing the violin.

"I love listening to you play."

Caroline tried to smooth over her sister's wounded look.

"You're really gifted, sis. You should be playing for the Boston Symphony Orchestra or something — never mind working at a boring, legal magazine. Don't you think our family sounds great when they all play together? Mom is a concert pianist, Uncle Sean is masterful on the flute, and you are an exceptional violinist. I mean, we're such talented buggers!"

Valerie chuckled.

"Thanks for the vote of confidence."

She once again filled Caroline in on the details for the upcoming performance.

"The Harbor Lights Ensemble is hosting a charity concert to help raise money for the new children's library at Saint Bridget's Elementary School. Father Bruce will be conducting, of course."

Caroline listened intently. She'd been to many similar events over the years and thoroughly enjoyed them, taking pride in both her mother and sister's musical talents. But she was inwardly becoming concerned, as her memory lapses were happening with more frequency. She'd been having a hard time concentrating and focusing at work lately, and had been written up and given a stern warning a week ago for not paying attention to her supervisor's instructions. She'd prematurely discharged a patient, who later wound up back in the emergency room with a high fever because she hadn't received her prescription for antibiotics.

Val paid no attention to her sister's silence. She knew her mind wandered constantly. That was Caroline.

"Well, anyway, it's going to be held at the John Hancock Hall, right around the corner from our condo, so there's no excuse for you not to make it. I'm going to have a small gathering back at the house with a few old, and perhaps NEW friends ... so you'd best be there!"

Val demanded, pointing her finger at Caroline in a warning gesture. Caroline grabbed it and pretended to bite it. Val withdrew it quickly.

"We're also raising money for new computers and a reading room where local authors can come in and sign books and read to the kids. Sean offered to donate his time to get the computers networked."

Caroline regrouped and tried to focus again on what her sister was saying.

"That's nice of him."

"Yeah, he's good about such things."

Caroline changed the subject.

"So tell me, what's the same, different, and NEW in your life?"

Val perked up.

"SEE! You can be pretty sharp when you want to be. I was waiting to see how long it'd take before you got back around to that. I can't wait to tell you!"

"I sense a romance brewing ... at least, that's what I'm hoping you're about to tell me."

Val was beaming while Caroline continued.

"You know, I was beginning to think you'd become asexual or something. For the life of me, I don't know how you've gone this long without a guy!"

Val gave her a playful whack on the head.

"Oh, very funny! Unlike YOU, I realize the value in a friendship first."

She blushed. Caroline thought her adorable. Val quickly defended her position.

"There IS more to life than just men, you know. A fact you may want to explore at some point."

Val sat back and smiled warmly, recalling her time spent with Warren. He was all she could think about lately since her return from Ireland. He had promised to call her during the week, so they could talk about plans for his next four-day layover in Boston in a few weeks. Maybe they could catch a show at the Wang Center and have dinner at the Parker House. Responding to Caroline's comments, she went on.

"I know I've neglected some social aspects of life, but you, better than anyone, know how my life works and the schedule I keep. I just don't have time for intimate relationships. They're too demanding! Well, at least I thought so ... until I met Warren."

She became giddy and childlike in a way Caroline had not seen in years.
"DEAR GOD IN HEAVEN - he even has a name!"

Caroline dramatically set her wine glass out in front of her, bowing her head, offering a mock prayer of thanksgiving. Val gave her a wise crack.

"Oh, do shut up, brat, and let me tell you how I happened upon this fine, dark Irishman."

She recounted in her best Irish brogue.

Caroline smiled a wicked smile.

"I want to hear every last detail, and don't you hold out on me. Do you hear what I'm sayin'?"

Val quickly shot back.

"Oh, right, like your mind couldn't fill in the blanks."

Val smiled and Caroline gestured demurely.

"Qui, moi?"

Val had another glass of wine and proceeded with the tale of how she met Warren Cahill. Caroline leaned in, enthralled.

"I had an eight thirty flight Friday evening. I wanted to get to Ireland early in the morning to get a whole day in. I told Glynnis I'd call her when I got to Granny's. She was going to be at her mother's house on Saturday and wanted me to go with her to the opening of Peggy's new gallery in London that Sunday. Glynnis was visiting and had to pick up a few things she'd left at her mother's when she moved in with Peggy. Besides that, her Mom had been bugging her to come over."

"I didn't know Peggy was opening a gallery."

Val stopped in mid-sentence and stared at her sister incredulously.

"Caroline, I just told you that was one of the reasons I went over there! You really need to pay better attention. Are you okay?"

Caroline nodded. Val pointed out.

"I think you need to get off the night shift. It's killing what few remaining brain cells you have left!"

Caroline became quiet again. Val wasn't too far off the mark. A lot of her memory trouble lately stemmed from the fact that she worked so many hours with very little sleep. She took drugs to keep herself awake and then others to help her get to sleep. She was going to have to make some lifestyle changes soon.

"Anyway, Peg does fabulous work, as you know. She's the latest rage over there now."

Val reached for another handful of snacks.

"She was really disappointed that you couldn't make it over. She wanted me to tell you that you can have a private showing any time you like. She actually did a charcoal of you from a picture Granny gave her. Don't tell her I told you. It's supposed to be a surprise for your birthday."

"Well, thanks for keeping it a secret!"

"You're welcome."

Val quipped.

"It came out really nice, too. Granny was still obsessing over a frame for it when I left. I told her I'd look around over here and see what I could find. She was driving me and Aunt Siobhan crazy."

Val was off track until Caroline, ironically enough, abruptly brought her back around to the developing romance.

"Enough about Granny. You were in the process of telling me about this man who may very well be my brother-in-law one day?"

"Jumping the gun a bit there, aren't you? However, if I play my cards right ..."

She paused and looked hopefully at Caroline, about to continue, then threw up her arms.

"Hell! I don't even know how to play anymore. I don't do dating well! It's the one area where I feel so unsure of myself."

Both women laughed.

Caroline assured her.

"Oh, it's easy. You're just out of practice. Don't worry too much about it. Just go with it."

She motioned for Val to hurry up and continue.

"Okay, where were we? Oh, yeah, I left the office early and headed over to Logan to check in and grab a bite to eat. I decided to take a look around the Duty Free Shop and grab a few things for Granny and Aunt Siobhan. I bought a carton of Mary and Glynnis's favorite cigarettes and some snacks and reading material for the plane."

Caroline interrupted.

"Does Mary still smoke those Benson and Hedges?"

Val was amazed.

"Yes, how'd you know that?"

Caroline flipped up a peanut and caught it in her mouth.

"Whose cigarettes do you think Glynnis and I stole when we first started smoking?"

"You're shameless!"

Caroline wiggled her foot around and chuckled.

"And you're too uptight, sis ... but go on. We'll work on that."

Val went on.

"So I left the shop. I was starving, so I stopped at Legal Seafood and got a bowl of 'chowda' and a glass of wine, and started flipping through my magazine when in walks this group of pilots. They always look so incredibly handsome in their uniforms, don't you think?"

Caroline was on the edge of her chair, listening intently.

"Yeah, yeah ... go on. Don't tell me you met a PILOT?"

Val contained her excitement well so as not to reveal the answer too soon. She wanted to leave her sister guessing until the end. She watched as Caroline's foot bounce more quickly.

"Did I say anything about meeting a pilot? What ... was I going to just walk up to them and start a conversation? Nooooo. I finished eating and left the restaurant and headed over to the boarding area to sit and read for a while."

Caroline's look of anticipation deflated.

"You're a real blast, you know that? No wonder you can't meet men. Go on. I know this must get better."

Val blew her off.

"So I'm over in the boarding area reading my book, minding my own business, when, a few minutes later, a man sits directly in back of me. We were sitting in the last seats in the row, and I had some of my stuff on the little end table we shared. I was in the mood for a snack, so I reached over to the table for a handful of Tidbits. Do you remember those little cheese sticks from when we were kids?"

Caroline was growing impatient.

"YES! Now go on, you're eating Tidbits, and he's in back of you. What happened next?"

Caroline was waiting for the good part.

"Well, I put my book down and reached for my water. Then I saw him take a handful of my Tidbits!"

Val stated indignantly.

"Can you imagine that?"

Caroline looked confused.

'Sooo ... whadja do? Slap his hand, or what?"

"I wish I'd thought of that! But I found it very amusing — him eating my snack and not asking, so I tried to just shrug it off, but I started to giggle instead. He turned around to glance over his shoulder, and said, 'I'm glad you find this amusing.' Then he grabbed the bag and offered me some! I was nearly hysterical at this point. 'Don't mind if I do.' And I grabbed the bag back and pretended to cover and hoard it. He turned and asked, 'Do you mind sharing just a few more of those?'"

Val was laughing hard at this point. Caroline was laughing along with her. "WAIT, wait! It gets better!"

Val struggled to catch her breath and regain her composure. People at other tables were trying not to appear to be listening. Caroline was enjoying the sound of her sister's laughter; it was good to hear her letting loose.

"He reminded me of Daddy a little."

That thought sobered her enough to finish the story.

"I offered him the bag, and he took the whole thing back from me! Then he opened his newspaper and proceeded to read. I never thought him rude — but odd. I was waiting for him to laugh or something. I saw he was reading the Irish Times, so I continued to pretend to read my book, and asked him without turning around, 'What's new in the Times?' He responded without missing a beat. 'Same stuff, different day. Your book? Any good?' I still didn't turn around – we were seated back to back. 'Yes, it's very good, interesting.' Then he turned around so that his arm was touching the back of my neck. It sent a shiver down my spine. I could feel him staring at the back of my head. 'I bet that's a difficult book to read,' he whispered in my ear. His breath was so warm on my neck! 'No, no, not at all. It's an easy read.' Then he reached around me and turned my book right side up. I could have died from embarrassment! And now he was having a good laugh!"

Caroline was enjoying the story immensely.

"I wanted to die!"

Val blushed as she relived the memory.

"He knew I wasn't reading the damn book. Anyway, as it ends up, he was the one flying my plane."

At this point, people at the other tables had stopped pretending to look away and were avidly following along.

"He asked me if I was flying to Shannon. I joked and told him, 'No, Spain, I just like this boarding area better.' He pretended to be hurt, and I quickly assured him that yes, I was flying to Ireland. He handed me back the Tidbits, saying, 'Here you go. Enjoy. I've got to run and do my check-list. I'll stop by later when we're at cruising altitude.' Then he reached in and took another small handful of my Tidbits and popped them in his mouth. He had a fantastic smile, Caroline. It made me melt. I watched after him as he walked confidently toward the gate. He was grinning from ear to ear and waved to me before he headed down the ramp."

"So what happened next?"

Caroline was hooked.

Val put up her hand.

"Never in a million years will you guess. I got on the plane, found my seat, and settled in. Guess what I discovered once I was seated?"

"WHAT?"

Val adjusted herself in the seat; the wine was loosening her up a bit.

"After takeoff, I pulled my bag out from underneath the seat to get my magazine. When I unzipped the side of the bag, MY Tidbits were still in there. Caroline! I'd been eating his!"

Both girls were now howling, and some of the people at neighboring tables enjoyed a chuckle as well. Through her laughter, Caroline stammered out.

"Oh, God — that's precious! What in the world did you do THEN?"

Valerie was wiping tears away and went on.

"Well, I gasped so loud that the man in the seat next to me asked if I was okay, and should he call for an attendant. Then the attendant who was walking by heard him and offered me some water. Suddenly, this familiar voice comes over the loudspeaker to announce, 'Ladies and gentlemen, this is Captain Cahill, and I've got a few TIDBITS of information I'd like to share with you ...' I nearly peed my pants! The man seated next to me thought I was completely off my rocker. I don't remember what Captain Kangaroo said over the loudspeaker after that. I didn't even know his first name at that point."

Val was still flushed as she recalled her embarrassment.

"I wanted to crawl under the seat! I was mortified!"

Caroline was still chuckling.

"Did you see him when you touched down?"

Val put up her finger in a wait-a-minute gesture.

"I did better than that. I waited until we'd been flying about an hour and rang for the flight attendant. When she came around, I told her that the pilot was a friend of mine and asked if she wouldn't mind passing a message on to him. She said 'sure'."

"What was the message?"

"I sent my bag of Tidbits up to him, and asked the flight attendant to tell him that I'd found it in my bag and thought he might enjoy them."

Caroline teased her.

"That's it? You didn't offer to buy him a drink when you landed or something?"

Val looked dumbfounded and shrugged.

"We were landing at seven in the morning!"

This time Caroline shrugged.

"So what! You're in freaking Ireland. No one cares what time you drink!"

She asked the next obvious question.

"Did he send a reply?"

Val nodded.

"Yeah, the stewardess said she felt like she was back in school passing notes. He wrote that it was his pleasure to share his food with such a ravenous woman as myself. Then he asked if I'd share breakfast with him when we landed. Later, he actually came back to the cabin himself to get the answer! He was so handsome and good-natured, how could I refuse?"

Caroline sat back to take in all that her sister had told her. It was a great story, and she wanted to hear more, so over dinner she pushed Val for the details of the time she'd spent with this dashing pilot in Ireland.

Pigtails and Potter's Field

*   *   *

His name was Warren Cahill. He'd been a pilot for eight years, and was older than Val by five. He was tall — over six feet — and had dark, almost black hair with just the tiniest touch of gray at the edges. His eyes were brown, and Val had noticed he had marvelous lips. She wanted to kiss him immediately and couldn't understand why she was so instantly attracted to him.

He lived in Shannon, not far from the airport, and owned a house that overlooked a dairy farm. His idea of breakfast was for her to come to his house, and he'd prepare omelets for them.

"I'll be a perfect gentleman."

She felt completely at ease with the idea, and with him, as they found his car in the lot and proceeded out onto the airport road. They drove for a few miles before turning off the main road and up a steep hill toward his home. He asked Val if she'd like to come out to the hen house with him.

"You're going to have to come up with a better line than that!"

She answered. He laughed and led the way. The chicken coop was on his neighbor's land, and he assured her there was an agreement in place which allowed him to collect eggs without getting shot. He had actually helped his neighbor build the little enclosure.

She watched him reach in gently to retrieve the freshly laid eggs. Val had never been in a chicken coop, but it was fun gathering the eggs. On their way into his house, Warren grabbed two bottles of fresh milk and cream off his front step — a standing gift from his neighbors when they knew he'd be coming home from a trip. In turn, Warren would pick up American cigarettes, candy, and goods for them.

"It's an amicable tradeoff," he said. "I bring them back whatever they want to eat from the US, and I get all the fresh cream, butter, milk, and eggs I want. My heart will probably seize any moment now."

Valerie laughed. His sense of humor matched hers.

231

They'd talked for hours during and after breakfast. Suddenly, Val remembered that Aunt Siobhan and Granny would be worried because she'd not yet arrived at their house. She asked to use Warren's phone and called to say she'd met a friend at the airport, and was on her way. As it was, they still wanted to come and pick her up on every visit to Ireland. Val assured them she was a big girl and could find her way to her grandparent's house without any problems. Ennis wasn't that far from Shannon.

Warren asked where her grandmother lived and graciously offered to give her a lift.

"No, Warren, it's okay. You've been flying all night. You must be exhausted! I'll take a taxi."

"Are you tired?"

She shook her head no. She really wasn't. Instead, she felt energized. She was enjoying his company immensely.

"I'm not either. It takes me a little while to unwind once I land. Let me get the car then, and we'll get you over there. How long are you in town?"

Val told him only for a week this time, but that Ireland was her second home, and she visited her family frequently. As they walked to the car, he asked if he could take her out for dinner one night during her stay.

"Just ONE night?"

Val dared him.

Admiring her straightforward manner, he replied.

"Well, I'd like to capture you and keep you here all week, but that wouldn't be appropriate since we only just met. Perhaps we'll go for a few outings then. I've got some great ideas, but I'll keep it a surprise. How does that grab you?"

"Well, we'll just see how hard you work to impress me. Keep at it and I'll let you know how you're doing."

Putting on fake airs, she turned on her heel and walked haughtily to the side of the car, purposely waiting for him to open the door for her.

Giving him a playful snooty look, she put on her sunglasses, pushing them up the bridge of her nose in a deliberate manner.

"Okay, Lady Astor, get in the car."

He joked.

On the ride to her grandparents', they talked about Ireland and some of their favorite scenic areas. Valerie had told him how much she loved the Lakes of Killarney, specifically the place called, Lady's View. She then asked him if he'd like to join her in London for the opening of Peggy's new gallery on Sunday. He enjoyed art galleries, and accepted almost immediately. He inquired more of Peggy's work, and she filled him in. The chemistry was evident between them and both felt very relaxed and at ease. They spoke comfortably with one another, exchanging phone numbers at a stop sign.

Warren explained that he wasn't scheduled to fly for another week, as he'd met his monthly flight requirements. Valerie asked if Shannon-to-Boston was his regular route. He told her that it was, along with Shannon-New York, and went on to complain about how LaGuardia was an accident waiting to happen. Val nodded in agreement and explained that she flew there often herself on business. He asked about her work, and she told him of her recent promotion to VP of Finance. She pulled out a copy of Sidebar Magazine and left it on the front seat for him to read later.

He was impressed.

"Beauty and brains? You're the whole package, Val gal."

Then he smiled the most wonderful smile, melting her heart once again. She struggled to contain her excitement, and couldn't wait to fill Glynnis and Peggy in on the details. She wanted to pinch herself. She knew Granny and Aunt Siobhan would love him immediately.

Warren found Bindon Street without her directions, and they arrived in record time. Too short a time. Val thought to herself. Granny was watching for her out the window, and waved excitedly when she saw her granddaughter emerge from the black BMW.

"You look beautiful, sweetheart! You must be exhausted ..."
Granny and Aunt Siobhan gave her big hugs.
"Who's your driver?"
Aunt Siobhan whispered.
Val glanced over her shoulder nonchalantly and said loudly.
"Oh! Him? That's just James, my chauffeur. Pay him no mind."
She waved him off.
"He'll even get my bags for me, watch this."
Warren played the role of the dutiful and humble servant, bowing dramatically at her every command and seeming to enjoy the whole ruse.
"Will there be anything else I can do for you, Miss Daisy?"
All three woman burst out laughing at his perfect imitation of Hoke. Granny spoke first.
"I don't know who you are, sir, but you've got a great sense of humor - that'll carry you far. Grab the lady's bags then and come in for tea."
Granny smiled and shooed them both up the stairs. Warren laughed at the unfolding drama. Val looked over to see if he felt comfortable staying. He didn't seem in any hurry to rush off and bounded up the stairs with gusto, holding open the door for all to enter.
Val knew right then and there that he was going to be someone special; she just sensed it. One of Granny's real helpers met them at the door and graciously took the bags from Warren. Val reached out and grabbed his hand, leading him down the center hallway to the living room where they collapsed onto the couch to have tea with the family.

Chapter Twenty-Four

Fort Meyers, Florida, Spring 1957

AT AGE TWENTY-FIVE, HE WAS banished to a retirement community in Florida. Ten years later, feigning interest while Mrs. Loftus droned on with the all-too-familiar details for the next Christmas Bazaar, Father Rob Coughlin grew restless. It was only March for God's sake, and this wasn't something he needed to be thinking about right now.

"There is a lot of work that goes into putting something like this together each year, Father. We must start early if we want it to be a success."

He nodded. It was the same every year. He knew by heart how many tables needed to be set up and where. It was his job to secure the manpower to arrange the tables and chairs, and, of course, the cleanup — a job he resented. He reminded himself that it was a small price to pay in order to maintain the lifestyle to which he'd become accustomed. He hated the church Christmas bazaars. In his mind, it was just a bunch of old junk being peddled, and knit goods that no one ever wore. But the benefits of living there outweighed the boredom by far.

* * *

Father Coughlin had been a problem student when he was a youngster, unable to pay attention when his teachers were talking. His parents divorced when he was six, contributing to his emotional distance and immaturity.

His mother, Nora, was one of nine children. Cute when she was younger, she was, nonetheless, a very poor, repressed Catholic woman in Ireland. She'd learned survival skills born of necessity at an early age. Hungry most days, stealing and begging were acts she and her brothers committed regularly in order to survive. She didn't feel good about it and yet, over time, she rationalized that her dire circumstances justified the misdeeds. She feared God, but didn't understand how he gave so much to some and not enough to others. It didn't make sense, and at times, she was resentful. She wouldn't talk to her elder brother for years after he went on to become a priest, a job for which she saw no real rewards, until she was much older.

Rob grew up with the stories of heartache repeatedly told to him by his bitter mother. She'd dropped out of school after the tenth grade and married his father. She settled into motherhood immediately. His father, a tall and handsome man, worked as a bricklayer. He later abandoned his family for another woman and greener pastures in America.

Life was none-too-kind to a single mother with two sons. Were it not for the generosity of his uncle, who held an influential position within the Catholic Church, they'd have probably been homeless and hungry.

"Praise God for St. Vincent De Paul."

His mother would often say when handed a voucher for food or clothing.

His father drank frequently and was an avid gambler. Yet, no matter how bad things got, Nora stayed with him. In frail health herself, she put up with his drunken rages and beatings, because the alternative was to have no money to pay the rent, which was often the outcome regardless.

Rob heard her cry one evening when his da arrived home after having lost his entire paycheck at the track. He'd pushed Nora out of the way in search of his sons. His mother tried only once to stop him, suffering a tremendous blow to the head. It left her unconscious and bleeding. She'd sustained a number of concussions over the years, yet never went to a hospital for treatment. She suffered from frequent migraines, which only grew worse over time.

Rob and his brother, Richard, tried to hide the first few times their father called their names. But it was futile, as they'd only suffer more harm if he became enraged. It was easier to just endure the humiliation of being bent over the bed, than to be bruised outwardly, where people could actually see the results of his abusive actions.

Some things were best kept secret, to save themselves embarrassment and not have to answer anyone's questions. Their mother heard their muffled cries coming from the bedroom upstairs. She knew what he did to them and felt helpless to stop him. Each had to endure their drunken father's vile penetration. He'd always apologize afterwards and cry telling them how much he loved them and how he didn't mean to hurt them. He'd eventually slink off to his own room and collapse. If he remembered anything in the morning, he would never let on.

Ironically, it was their father who filed for the divorce. He told their mother she was a weakling.

"Like a ball and chain around my foot you are! You're always whining and complaining about all your ailments. You make me sick!"

His wealthy, American girlfriend bought him the divorce, and the boys never heard from him again. They only knew that he took off for America, and that they'd come close to losing their damp, four-room home on a number of occasions.

After their father left, their uncle, now Monsignor Alan Creedon, reached out to his struggling sister and young nephews with church donations of food, clothing, and fuel assistance. He secured the house for her by requesting from the church that her home be used as a local church food pantry, rescuing her from foreclosure.

He managed to convince the church officials that the arrangement made sense due to the fairly large population of poor Catholic families living in the area. It was a novel idea.

The Monsignor pointed out to church officials that people might not feel as intimidated seeking assistance if they could make arrangements to go to the home of an understanding neighbor discreetly in order to receive food assistance. This would eliminate the need for them to have to publically declare their poverty before a board, and thus preserve their dignity and the cause of Christ.

He pointed out that many proud families went hungry because of husbands who would not allow their wives or children to go before the St. Vincent De Paul Society and, in essence, have to beg for assistance. It plunged the people into depression and made the drink all the more appealing. He sought to encourage the people to continue to search for work. He'd personally oversee the budget and disbursement of food items so that it would be fair and equitable to all, promising to present the church with a monthly financial report which he'd prepare himself. The officials realized they couldn't argue the point further without sounding like Pharisees, so they let him proceed with his project on a trial basis.

Nora was hardly a fit mother, and took to becoming quite promiscuous after their father's departure. She became pregnant at one point, and didn't know who the father was, but lost the baby at four months, a blessing in disguise.

Rob was sixteen when she dragged him with her to his uncle's ordination as Cardinal. He really liked his Uncle Alan and was genuinely thankful for his generosity. The man had a good heart and helped them whenever he could. So when Alan suggested to Nora that perhaps Rob might want to consider entering seminary, Rob jumped at the opportunity. He didn't want to go to college, and the thought of being at home with his mother, any longer than he had to, made him cringe. From what he could see, the life of a priest was quite easy and comfortable. His uncle lacked for nothing. Going to seminary couldn't be that hard. In Ireland, at that time, it only required two years of study. He accepted his uncle's offer enthusiastically.

Strings were pulled, and before he knew it, his mother was celebrating their good fortune and bragging about her son becoming a priest. His neighbors laughed and gossiped openly about the hypocrisy, given their mother's loose lifestyle, and the rumors that quietly circulated about Rob's relationship with some of the younger boys in the neighborhood who came to request food from their house pantry.

Rob had been only thirteen when he took on the responsibility of overseeing the operations of the church food pantry while his mother worked cleaning offices. His older brother, Richard, would leave at odd hours and be gone for days on end. His mother never inquired into Rich's whereabouts. He always managed to find his way back home. Rob spent a good deal of his time alone, which he preferred.

At first he just fantasized about some of the younger boys who would regularly come to the house seeking food for their families. Before long, his thoughts escalated into a plan of action whereby he'd warmly welcome the boys into the house, and offer them sweets of bread and jam. Rob would listen intently to their stories, all the while openly sympathizing with their plights, and worked to set them at ease.

Many were already hungry and very grateful for the snack he provided, along with his promise of generous rations to take home. He'd compliment them, telling them how mature and grown-up they were for looking after the needs of their families. They craved his attention.

Once he gained their trust, he'd offer them a few sips of whiskey from his mother's stash, and shared a couple of woodbines with them. Once Rob saw the effects of the alcohol begin to set in, he'd move in closer to fondle them. A few of the boys thought it odd at first, but wouldn't complain too much, given their mildly drunken state and full stomachs. They enjoyed being in his company. He made them feel important. He never attacked them in a rough or brutal manner.

Rob's greatest thrill and one that he felt was even better than the sexual act itself, was his ability to make the boys obey him. He made a game of it, and didn't dictate in a way that was intimidating, but would make strong, leading suggestions, which they followed and never refused. He'd remind them of how generous he could be, promising them rewards of extra sugar or eggs so their mother's could make cakes for them. They considered their oral acts a small price to pay in order to feed their families.

Rob never rushed the children, but set about making them feel comfortable and protected. He'd reassuringly tell them that whatever they did together wasn't wrong and that it was their secret. No one else would know. The curtains were always drawn in the house. He'd ask the child if he could take pictures of them together — as friends. He'd have them hold a glass of whisky or a cigarette. They always said yes. If a boy appeared overly jittery or nervous he'd back off and wait patiently knowing they'd be back for food at another time, and not force him to do anything.

After each successful sexual encounter, he'd reward them in small ways. Each child was made to promise to keep their time together a secret. Rob would hold up the photos of them holding a whiskey glass or cigarette and suggest to them that he'd hate for their parents to come over asking questions and see the photos of them drinking or smoking. The boys, being utterly fearful of a beating from their parents, always promised to not say a word.

Rich came home unannounced one day and caught Rob under the covers with a neighborhood boy in his bedroom and threatened to tell his mother and the guards. Rich disappeared for a while after that. Rob became anxious, unsure of what he'd do when he returned. When Rich finally did come back, several months later, life at home was unbearable for Rob. His older brother continually blackmailed him. He wanted to run away from home, but his fantasies and desires had grown more demanding so he decided to stay. When Rich wasn't around, which was most of the time, the desires were quickly satisfied.

Rob had an idea of who God was, but didn't fear Him. His family rarely went to church, only on Christmas and Easter. He'd heard stories from his mother over the years about how lucky her brother, Alan, was and how she'd gotten the short end of the stick in her family. She'd rant for hours about her brother's lavish lifestyle.

"He lives in mansions as a priest! I'm struggling, and he's got servants cooking his meals and doing his laundry and all he has to do is sit in a box and tell people to say three Hail Mary's and an Our Father. Surely even you can do more than that!"

Rob would attempt to leave the room quietly, but she'd grab him and make him sit and listen.

"I live in this pit, and he travels the world preaching the gospel. I should have been a nun!"

The complaints never changed. In the months leading up to his departure to seminary, they became her mantra.

Rob was eighteen when he loaded his few personal belongings into the church car his uncle provided to take him to seminary. Uncle Alan was going to personally drive him and see that he got settled in and was comfortable. Rich, who'd been gone for two weeks, suddenly appeared and got out of a car that had pulled up behind his uncle's. Rich looked at the suitcase in his brother's hand.

"Did she finally throw you out, too?"

He half-laughed, and blew the smoke from his cigarette in Rob's face. Rob shook his head.

"No, I'm leaving for seminary."

Rich laughed hysterically.

"You're really going through with this, eh? Going to be a priest, are ya now?"

He glanced over at the front door to the house.

"You're not serious; I thought Mam was only joking all this time."

Rob was visibly angry and getting redder by the moment. He pushed past his obnoxious brother and made his way to the trunk of the car.

Their mother came running down the steps.

"Nice of you to finally make an appearance. Your brother's leaving for the priesthood - not that you care. You never stick around long enough to know what's going on. You're just like your father - here today, gone tomorrow."

Rich looked at his mother with contempt.

"I've come to get a few things of my own, and you'll never see me again. I'm off to America."

Nora's mouth dropped open at this announcement.

Rich was ruggedly handsome and knew it. He'd inherited his father's good looks and wanderlust. It was like déjà vu, as she'd heard the same words thrown in her face by her husband years before. Indignantly, she straightened up. Deeply hurt, she gathered her composure.

"Good. Then I'll finally have this house to myself and not have to pick up after either one of you!"

Turning on her heel, she went back in the house to pour tea for her brother before he took her remaining son away. Rob wanted to punch his brother in the face for hurting their mother like that, no matter how embarrassing their situation had become.

Rob didn't realize it then, but he wouldn't see his brother again until his mother's funeral six years later. He and his uncle would preside over the memorial Mass. There was never a time that he missed his brother in all those years.

* * *

The young priest nodded mechanically from time-to-time while the elderly ladies continued with their boring banter. Their ideas were none-too-original and a waste of his time. He had things to do. He allowed his imagination to wander yet again to the upcoming fishing trip to the Loxahatchee National Wildlife Refuge he had carefully planned and orchestrated.

He enjoyed the role of priest. He had access to some of the most lavish homes the Archdiocese had to offer locally, regionally, and around the world. There were beautiful coastal homes and glorious mountain hide-aways. His very first assignment in Ireland had him living in an old castle adjacent to the boys' school he taught at. The Vatican spared no expense during the renovation project. The property was breathtaking.

He was respected then, and loved the emotional power priests held over people - especially the students. It was explained to him after his ordination that from, time to time, the pressures of servitude demanded that one regroup in order to best serve the masses ... a perk he'd taken advantage of often. During times when he desired a warmer climate, he'd retreat for a week to one of the more exotic island homes available to the clergy.

His thoughts today, however, centered on the details for his upcoming trip to the northernmost part of the Florida Everglades. He was taking a few of his congregants' grandchildren on a fishing excursion.

He'd chosen his victims with great care, calculated the risks, and set about putting the plan in motion over a year ago. He got physically excited at the thought of what was to come, and had to adjust himself in his chair, grateful for the huge mahogany desk that shielded him from the gray-haired nemeses before him.

Once again, out of boredom from present company, his thoughts drift-ed to past relationships. He'd been sexually involved with hundreds of boys over the years, and found himself in a couple of sticky legal situations in Ireland due to accusations of abuse leveled against him. He'd been ratted out by a few of his young victims, and it had made local headlines. The church had managed to contain the initial frenzy at a local level and had bought the silence of the victims' families.

He'd been warned via form letter from the archdiocese's principal officer dealing with the growing clergy sexual abuse allegations that "canonical penalties" would be invoked, unless he sought treatment. He agreed and left Ireland at age twenty-four to enter the church's Canadian psychiatric treatment center, remaining there a year until the media frenzy died down. Predictably, he was cleared for service by a church therapist, and allowed to once again celebrate Mass. He was reassigned to the United States. He was grateful to his Uncle Creedon, now a Cardinal Bishop, who intervened with the church and exercised his power of persuasion on his behalf.

He'd mended fences somewhat with his older brother in the year following their mother's death. Rich knew his brother was a homosexual, and joked incessantly when he found out Rob was being reassigned to the US.

"Into the Vatican's Witness Relocation Program with you is it?"

Rich mocked him.

"When in doubt, move him out, aye?"

Some years later, he took pity on Rob. He knew they were both abused as children and thought it must have done something to affect Rob's mind. Rich knew his brother took a "vow of poverty," and he often sent Rob money, which, unbeknownst to him, would go toward the purchase of treats and rewards for Rob's future victims.

Father Rob Coughlin had a keen memory for names and faces and had long since burned his files and notes on some of the children he'd met and had contact with. He would gently end his relationships with them when they reached age eleven or twelve.

"Father Rob," as he let the kids call him, took advantage of his access to the youth of his parish. Children seemed to flock to him. He rationalized his actions ... these kids needed a father figure in their lives. They sought him out for comfort and love. They craved his undivided attention, and he gave it to them. God would want this for them.

His intentions were overlooked by some of the most steadfast and attentive parents. His plan of attack was quite simple, undetectable, and didn't differ from the way he'd worked from the very beginning ... he simply listened to the children. He showed an interest in what they had to say, making them feel important. Each child was made to feel as if he were the only one in the world, and that what they said to him was of value and mattered. He'd patiently listen as they spilled out their stories and dreams, and he'd encourage them to go on, often asking questions and offering encouragement and ideas. It was all so simple.

Most of the kids came from lower to middle working-class families that already had more than enough children to keep them busy. Still others were from divorced homes where remarriage and stepparents came into play, often making the children feel left out and uncomfortable within their new family circle. Such children were easy targets, as were those raised by single mothers who were often tired and overworked, anxious for anyone to watch their kids and give them a break for a few hours.

Father Rob often walked the neighborhoods and would show up at their houses, offering to take the kids out for something to eat or an ice cream, or to play ball during the summer months. The parents were always grateful and encouraged the children to go with him. He'd gain the child's trust but also, more importantly, the parents'. It wasn't too long before he'd receive dinner invitations to their homes or be asked to perform weddings for their relatives. He enjoyed the christenings and baptisms, but communion ceremonies were by far his favorite rite given that it was the age group he targeted.

"Father Coughlin."

Mrs. Loftus repeated. She was addressing him sternly. He sat up straight in his chair.

"I'm sorry, Mrs. Loftus. Can you repeat that? I was just making a mental list for the upcoming fishing trip."

She nodded understandingly and smiled sweetly.

"Well, we all have busy lives, Father, to be sure, which is why we are so grateful to you for taking the time out of your hectic schedule to hear us old biddies go on. We'll take our leave now."

The women cackled, and Father Coughlin laughed his fake laugh as he got to his feet.

"Yes, well, Mrs. Loftus, we'd not have such a great turn out at our events, now would we, had you 'biddies' not done your thing."

The women stood and chuckled again as he parroted Mrs. Loftus.

He reached for Mrs. Rice's decorated cane and handed it to her. The crumpled, elderly woman twirled silk flowers around the metal shaft. He found the custom of decorating and enhancing medical devices ludicrous, remembering his reaction the first time he'd observed a walker with tennis balls on the front feet. It was his Canadian therapist who recommended that he be assigned to a retirement community, rationalizing that it would be a safer venue, with less temptation, since the median age of the congregants was sixty-five. What his therapist didn't think about, however, was the abundant supply of grandchildren.

Chapter Twenty-Five

GLYNNIS OPENED THE DOOR TO the Cutting Edge hair salon. Fiona Mulcahey was waiting and greeted her and Peggy enthusiastically.

"So, this is Peggy!"

Glynnis smirked and nodded. Peggy, looking unsure of herself, glanced back and forth between her friend and the hairdresser. She couldn't imagine the woman being with Glynnis's father - although she'd only met him once, very briefly, as he'd rushed out the door to work.

Fiona observed the washed-out looking teen. Peggy had a pretty, almost childlike, face. She wore no makeup over her fair complexion, but had beautiful brown eyes. Her hair color was unnaturally dark for her face. She brought Peggy over to sit at her station, and pulled up a chair to assess the situation more closely.

"So what do you think you'd like to do today?"

Peggy glanced questioningly at Glynnis, who spoke right up.

"First, put her natural hair color back."

Fiona stood over Peggy and pulled at random strands of hair.

"Hmmm, let's see."

Fiona took out her hair color chart and held it up against Peggy's roots.

"HERE — here it is! What do you think?"

Glynnis examined the match and nodded in agreement.

"Yes, that's definitely it!"

Peggy examined the hair sample as she tried to remember how she looked in her natural hair color. She couldn't remember.

"What do you think Peggy? Do you like it?"

Peggy nodded and smiled self-consciously.

"Good! Well, that settles that. Now what do you want to do about a style? Leave it long, mid-length, short?" Fiona looked at the long mass of poorly layered hair, held back by a headband.

"I'd like it a little shorter, maybe shoulder-length, to make it even. I made a mess of it trying to cut it myself ... I'm not too good at this as you can see."

Fiona pulled a book from her shelf and pointed out a few styles that she thought might compliment Peggy's face.

"Here, what about this? It's a shoulder-length style that will bring all those layers to one length. What do you think?"

Peggy stared at the photo of the model. It would be a dramatic change for her. She was game. Glynnis agreed and Fiona set to work mixing the necessary chemicals.

The girls chatted about fashion. Fiona had a great sense of style, and made some suggestions about colors that might look good on Peggy with her new hair color. She pointed out a few of her own favorite shops in town. Glynnis knew them all. Fiona was touched that Glynnis seemed so concerned about her friend.

As she applied the thick solution to Peggy's hair, Fiona made small talk about current events.

"Did you hear about the fire this morning?"

The blood left Peggy's face.

Glynnis, sensing her friend's fear, tactfully changed the subject.

"Yes, I did. A pity, wasn't it?"

She paused only for a second and redirected the conversation.

"But getting back to Peggy here, I wanted to get some more wonderful suggestions from you, Fiona."

Fiona smiled at the compliment and went on with her recommendations. Peggy mouthed, "Thank you" through the reflected mirror. Glynnis winked.

"Well, what do you think, Fiona? Peggy is going to need some makeup with this new hair color of hers; she's never been one to wear much."

Glynnis smirked at Peggy, who rolled her eyes.

If Fiona only knew, and saw her even a week ago with her gothic makeup on, she'd have been in shock. Peggy burst out laughing and then stared intently at the thick brown molasses-like mixture being applied to her head.

Fiona's plastic gloves were a mess as she massaged the substance deep into the roots. She studied Peggy's face, trying to picture what would enhance those dark brown eyes of hers.

"Hmmm ... yes, I can see that. Makeup is supposed to enhance your looks, not cover them up. But I'm sure you already knew that. You've got a pretty face, Peggy. After we apply the color and I cut your hair, we'll look at some new makeup colors for you, and I'll show you a few application techniques. We've got a great line of products which, if you like them, you can purchase and take home with you today."

Fiona smiled warmly. Sensing a big sale, she knew exactly what to offer. She'd take her time and go over each step. She was one of the best hairstylists in town, with a wealthy, eclectic clientele. She was planning on opening another shop in England the following year ... with Liam's help.

Glynnis had been coming to Fiona's shop since she was a child, which was how Fiona eventually met Glynnis's father. Her mother hadn't been feeling well and asked her husband to take Glynnis for a trim before school started after the summer holiday. They'd struck up a rather animated conversation, and had really hit it off. After she was through with Glynnis's haircut, he invited her to join them for lunch, to thank her for the great job she'd done on his daughter's hair. Glynnis didn't know any better then, and was as talkative as could be.

Liam later made his own appointments for haircuts. He customarily took the last appointment of the day, and they'd go out for cocktails and dinner afterwards. That was many years ago, and they'd been seeing each other off and on ever since. Good friends as well as lovers, they were very discreet. However, Fiona knew that rumors would eventually surface.

Liam helped Fiona finance her house, in a location he helped her choose, well out of town. Over time, she'd paid him back every pound he'd loaned her for the down payment. In the beginning, he stayed with her often. She sensed that his wife, Mary, knew, but she never confronted Fiona.

Fiona spotted her only once about town while Mary was out shopping with Glynnis for school clothes. From what Fiona could gather from Liam's perspective, without prying, Mary didn't love him anymore. Fiona felt sorry for him. Mary was given over more to the drink and sleeping pills than worrying over her husband's whereabouts. He said he continued to pay the bills and kept his wife in a comfortable lifestyle, staying with her for the sake of their daughter. He said that Mary didn't question his regular absences anymore and seemed resigned to their way of life. He stated she had no real control over what he did with his time.

Fiona always cleared her calendar to accommodate Glynnis when she got older. The young woman never seemed bitter or resentful. Maybe she understood her father's frustrations at home. Liam would mention, on occasion, how pleased he was with the way she cut his daughter's hair. Fiona would do anything for him. She knew marriage would never be an option for them and was happy to have him in whatever way she could.

Peggy sat flipping through a tabloid magazine, admiring a picture of the young American star, Valerie Bertinelli, while under the hair dryer. She scratched carefully at the side of her head, as the heat made her itch. Her fingers came away stained an odd brown color. A towel flew at her from out of nowhere, startling her. Glynnis laughed and knocked on the top of the dryer.

"Hot enough in there for you?"

Peggy nodded.

"How much longer?"

Glynnis picked up the egg timer and turned it around.

"About four more minutes."

Peggy went back to reading her magazine. Fiona busied herself lining up her brushes and examining her cutting scissors, as a surgeon would an instrument tray.

"I think I'll add some bangs, rather wispy ..."

She held up a pair of scissors and made a quick snipping motion.

"I wonder if her hair has any wave or curl to it. I couldn't tell."

Glynnis tried to recall and remembered seeing a few gentle curls when Peggy's hair was wet out of the shower.

"I think it does have some body to it."

"No bother, we'll just see after I wash the color out."

Fiona's timing was perfect and the timer went off as she approached Peggy.

"All set. Let's wash you out and get to work, shall we?"

Peggy nearly jumped out of the chair. She was getting excited. Fiona took the water hose and rinsed the dark color out of her hair. She then squirted some luscious smelling shampoo into her hands and rubbed the liquid through Peggy's hair, massaging her scalp as she washed. Almost immediately, Peggy felt the tension leave her body. She gave in to the wonderful, relaxing feeling the personal attention brought. She closed her eyes and nearly fell asleep. When the shampoo was rinsed out, Fiona applied the conditioner, which had a melon scent to it. Peggy told Fiona she wanted a bottle of each to take home with her.

"You've got it."

They walked over to the chair, and Fiona began to comb Peggy's hair out. It fell about five inches below her shoulders. The color couldn't be defined yet as it was still dark and wet. Fiona pulled at various pieces of hair and held them up, trying to find the shortest layer to gauge where to begin cutting. She had Peggy tilt her head forward while she began snipping at the back. Peggy watched as long dark strands of hair fell on the floor at her feet. She couldn't wait to see the results.

The whole process took about an hour. When Fiona began to blow dry her hair, Peggy wanted to cry.

The color was perfect. It was like looking back in time. The warm, brownish color softened and elegantly framed Peggy's ivory face. Glynnis's jaw dropped, and she patted Fiona on the shoulder as she held the mirror up behind Peggy so that she could see the back. Everyone in the shop commented on how pretty she looked, even before the makeup went on.

Fiona then ushered Peggy over to the section of the shop reserved for makeup and nails. They also had a private room for eyebrow waxing, a service they had started offering only a few months back, but was immensely popular already.

Fiona set about picking out colors for lipstick, eye shadow, and blush. She was like a painter choosing her palette. Peggy would be her masterpiece ... after she plucked the girl's eyebrows a bit to even them out.

Glynnis sat in admiration as she watched Fiona instruct Peggy on the proper way to apply a light foundation and then a hint of blush. She then showed her how to enhance her eyes without using too much eye shadow. Fiona applied a little eyeliner and black mascara to Peggy's already long lashes. Glynnis thought that she could even go without mascara.

She was taking great joy in seeing Peggy transform right in front of her eyes. She hoped Peggy could see and appreciate the beauty Fiona had helped bring out in her. No doubt men would be after her soon. The thought worried Glynnis as she knew that Peggy needed time to heal. Men had hurt her for so long. Glynnis wanted to protect her, but didn't quite know how. She sensed that giving Peggy confidence in herself, would help defend her in the future.

Glynnis was lost in her thoughts when she heard Fiona.

"Well, what do you think?"

Glynnis looked up and was shocked! Peggy had the biggest smile on her face. Fiona was masterful with the colors she'd chosen. Peggy's eyes were stunning and her lips full, enhanced by the bronze gloss Fiona had applied. Her hairstyle changed the whole look of her face. Glynnis realized that had she not stayed to watch the entire transformation, she might not have even recognized Peggy afterward.

"I can't believe it. You look gorgeous, Peg!"

She got up and gave her a hug. Peggy stared in amazement at her reflection.

"Now don't start crying. You'll ruin the makeup!"

All three women laughed. Fiona set about collecting the makeup she'd used, and picked out a new one of each for Peggy to purchase and take home with her. She wrapped every product up in pretty blue tissue paper and placed it carefully into the shop's decorative bag. She put in a styling brush for Peggy at no extra charge. The girl was spending over £400 on her hair and makeover. It was the least she could do!

"Thanks, Fiona! I'll be back. Promise."

Peggy caught her reflection again in the mirror and couldn't help but stare at her unfamiliar countenance. Fiona chuckled and Glynnis affirmed.

"YES! It's really YOU!"

Peggy shook her head and felt the hair move easily, freeing her at the same time. She picked up her bag after paying Fiona, and left the store arm-in-arm with Glynnis.

The next stop was Paisley's, an avant-garde boutique featuring unique clothing, jewelry, handbags, and shoes.

The girls checked their bags at the door and were greeted by an effeminate young man, who looked Peggy over from head to toe and told her.

"Girlfriend, you need to lose those faded black jeans and heavy woolen sweater immediately!"

Both girls laughed. He scurried about, making a fuss, and clapping orders to the staff to find him various colors in skirts and dresses before he even consulted them about what they were looking for. He kept looking her over, though clearly not in a romantic way. He had them both go and sit at the cappuccino bar while he personally prepared their frothy delight. Both women were set immediately at ease with the delightful man who introduced himself as Joel.

The store was decorated in plum tones with touches of sunflower gold and sage green. The lighting was suspended from large bronze sconces, and a smooth jazz tune played in the background. It was safe to assume that Peggy would not find her flannel pajamas in this store.

The boutique was stylish – "chic" was the word she was looking for — and unlike anything she'd ever been in before. It occupied two stories of a converted mill building. The floors were all natural hardwood. The first floor contained clothing and the cappuccino bar, while upstairs exhibited accessories, shoes, and jewelry.

From where she sat, Peggy admired the artwork adorning all the exposed brick walls. She wanted to get up and look at the paintings more closely, but didn't want to appear rude by walking away from Joel, who was taking such an interest in helping them.

He looked at the tall, dark haired woman and inquired.

"Well, what exactly are you looking for today, and how can I help you?"

He was being dramatic, yet sweet, as he brought over the steaming cappuccino. Peggy was not used to this kind of attention and service and promptly blushed. She pretended to look away as Glynnis spun her tale of woe and took out the list from her purse.

"Well ..."

Glynnis filled him in.

"This is my friend, Peggy. Her house burned down the other day, and she's lucky to be alive!"

Peggy turned quickly, wondering in horror whether Glynnis was about to divulge the whole story. Joel's mouth dropped open.

"Oh, my God, NO!"

He fanned his hand in front of his face, then placed it dramatically over his chest and shook his head as if his heart had just stopped. He carried on.

"Did you hear about that fire this morning? At least, two people are confirmed dead! A group of Travellers, I heard."

He intended to continue, but Glynnis quietly acknowledged that she had heard, then whispered and motioned with her head toward Peggy that her situation was already traumatic enough, and that they probably shouldn't go on about it. Glynnis proceeded to read the list of items Peggy needed.

"Basically, she needs all new clothing. She lost everything - right down to her skivvies."

Peggy giggled. Unprepared for Glynnis's brutally honest comment, it was Joel's turn to blush as he put his hand over his mouth to stifle his own laughter.

"Well, it's true! She's now wearing a pair of mine, and I want them back!"

They couldn't contain their giddiness any longer, and all three burst out laughing.

Joel knew exactly what to do and sprung into action. He was dressed impeccably. Peggy was in good hands. He set down his cup and stood. He sized Peggy up, turning her completely around in a circle. She was not a small woman, certainly not fat, just rather tall. He estimated her to be about a UK size 14. She had wide shoulders, a moderate size chest, narrow waist, average hips, and long legs. She had creamy white skin, and he thought to himself, had he been partial to women, she was someone he'd ask out. She reminded him of his sister. He imagined her in that light, and dressed her accordingly.

He was in his element. Carlos, the store's owner, loved Joel's easy way with customers and hadn't thought twice about making him a managing partner in the business ... and in his life.

"All right, Margaret, my dear, let's get a good look at you."

He gazed at her approvingly.

"Give us that list and let's see what we can find for you, hmmmm?"

He quickly snatched the note out of Glynnis's hand and scurried off with it. He pointed out things that had just come in, then set about seeking help from the other associates.

He was like a commanding drill sergeant as he issued orders and had employees running all over the store, up and down stairs, so the girls wouldn't have to. Since there were only a few other customers browsing in the store that didn't need help, they had almost the entire sales team at their disposal.

Joel started with some stylish pants, shirts, and sweaters for her to try on. He had her try on a beautiful wool coat. She fell in love with it immediately. It was a deep shade of rust that accentuated her fair skin and complimented her new hair color perfectly. Joel picked a scarf off the arm of an associate, who looked like a curtain rod holding out armloads of silk and sheer, flowing material. The gold and brown hues in the scarf, deep enough to match Peggy's eyes, enhanced the total effect. That was set aside and she was led upstairs to the boots and shoes.

Joel made a few suggestions about footwear and let Peggy pick her boots out for herself. He was pleased with her choice, and they moved on to select a few more pairs of shoes for "work and play," including a pair of basic black pumps.

She'd never walked in heels before, and looked awkward and embarrassed. To everyone's delight, Joel put the shoes on himself and wiggled dramatically across the floor to show her just how easy it was. He bowed dramatically to the crowd's cheers, and assured Peggy that she just needed a little practice.

He then had her wait a moment as he picked out a stunning black dress for her to try on. When she appeared in the doorway to the dressing room everyone quieted and stared at her in amazement. She was simply a stunning figure.

"Margaret, you are model material."

Joel stated matter-of-factly.

"If I were straight, I might be aroused right now." Peggy choked and made an awful snorting sound that sent the rest of the group into hysterics.

"What the hell was that?"

Joel asked, turning to Glynnis. Peggy ran back into the dressing room, giggling and telling them that she was going to wet her pants from laughing so hard if they didn't stop it. Glynnis yelled back.

"You better not; those are my panties you're wearing!"

When they were finished choosing her new clothes, Peggy handed her old ones to Joel, who dramatically dropped them in the trash while pretending to say a prayer over them.

Peggy then threw Glynnis's panties over the top of the dressing room door, hoping they'd land on her head. Glynnis kicked them back under the door. Peggy was dressed in new clothing from head to toe. She had on a long, tweed skirt with a brushed wool sweater. Her leather boots went perfectly with the skirt, and she had enough panties and bras now to last a lifetime, not to mention an assortment of stockings and socks.

While Peggy and Glynnis waited for the rest of her items to be packaged up, Joel leaned into Carlos, who'd come in the door only moments before, and whispered something in his ear. Carlos nodded approvingly and Joel announced.

"Given the conditions which brought you to our store, Margaret, we are extending to you our 'Manager's Discretionary Discount' — 20 percent off your entire purchase!"

The girls hugged Joel as Carlos looked on appreciatively. The savings was significant, as they'd purchased over £1600 in merchandise. Peggy had everything she needed to wear but her flannel pajamas, and Glynnis assured her that they'd pick those up somewhere along the line.

The girls would have struggled to carry the bags around had it not been for Joel's suggestion that they leave the parcels at the store and come back for them when they were done. Since the bus they needed to catch to get home stopped just outside the shop, it would work out perfectly. Carlos and Joel promised to guard the goods with their lives. The girls waved and blew kisses as they walked out the door.

They meandered along the river walk and found a cute bistro called Hillary's. Peggy had passed by it before, and the aroma emanating from within always made her hungry. She sometimes set up her portrait stand along the wall nearby to draw sketches for the tourists, as it was a lucrative spot.

Hillary's boasted brick-oven pizza, the source of the mouthwatering aroma wafting through the street. Peggy's stomach was growling as they entered the restaurant. Both girls were famished. They asked for a corner table and collapsed into the chairs.

Glynnis stared across the table at her friend.

"Well, what do you think?"

Peggy just shook her head. She knew she should feel bad about the events of the early morning, but it was fast becoming just a bad memory. So many good and exciting things were happening to her that she couldn't process them quickly enough. She was finding it all blissfully hard to comprehend, but welcomed the changes wholeheartedly.

The waiter brought them menus, and the girls decided on a white pizza and salads, with ice tea. They also ordered salads to go for their new-found friends, Joel and Carlos. They were grateful for the transforming talents of Joel and Fiona. Peggy mentioned to Glynnis that the only other things she really wanted (besides her flannel pajamas) were some new art supplies and equipment. Glynnis set down her fork.

"Why do you need those things? Do you paint?"

Peggy nodded enthusiastically.

"As a matter of fact, I DO!"

Glynnis was in awe.

"I didn't know you knew how to paint! Why didn't you tell me? I thought you just painted houses."

"I dunno. It never came up in conversation, I guess. But it's what I love to do. I sketch, too, in pencil, coal, and chalk. I'll draw you some time."

Glynnis wanted to know more about Peggy's hobby and asked what she needed for supplies to get started. Peggy told her she wanted an easel, some proper drawing paper, and new charcoal and pencils. Peggy knew of the hobby shop further down the walk, and suggested that they might find some of what she needed in there — the rest they'd, no doubt, find in England. They ordered chocolate turtle cheesecake for dessert.

After eating so much food, they were grateful for the walk. As they passed a pharmacy, Peggy remembered that she, also, needed some personal toiletries.

"I left all of that in the trailer ... which is gone now."

Glynnis pulled her into the pharmacy and they set about gathering her necessities, including deodorant, scented soaps, hairspray, a hair blower, and a couple of brushes which Peggy would need for her new hairstyle.

Peggy paused before an assortment of perfume behind a locked glass door and stared at the various expensive, colored bottles. The sales clerk offered to open the cabinet for her. Peggy decided to purchase the green bottle she'd seen in an advertisement in the magazine she was reading under the dryer at the salon. She'd liked the way it smelled when she'd lifted the edge of the page to sample the scent. Peggy then asked to just sniff the bottle she recognized from her childhood — Charlie. Her mom had worn it. As she inhaled, a flood of memories swept through her mind. She handed the bottle back to the clerk and tried not to cry, as she walked away clutching her new perfume, Chanel No. 19.

Spying a bag of her favorite mint leaf jelly candies on her way to the counter, she added them to her basket. She met up with Glynnis in another aisle and made her sniff the perfume she'd picked out. They sparingly spritzed themselves with the floral yet woody scent, which eventually permeated the entire aisle. They paid for the items in the basket and headed further down the river walk toward the hobby shop.

Peggy was like a kid in a candy store, wandering about, touching everything. Glynnis didn't say much, as she didn't have any hobbies. She did enjoy arts and crafts in school and thought once or twice about learning how to sew, but she never did anything about it. Glynnis sat in a chair at the front, letting Peggy make her choices while she rested.

Peggy talked with a young clerk who directed her toward some easels and seemed to be making suggestions. He showed her an assortment of pencils and chalks in a myriad of colors and recommended something in a can that helped in setting a chalk drawing. Peggy asked to see their paper and chose her materials carefully. The man carried all of her materials to the front desk. He then asked Peggy if she had a portfolio for her drawings. She was embarrassed to admit that she didn't even know what that was. He smiled warmly and explained that if she wanted to display some of her work to prospective clients in a professional manner, she'd need a portfolio. He led her over to what looked like oversized briefcases and opened one up, explaining how it was laid out to display one's work. Peggy seemed enthralled by what he was saying to her, and she quickly chose a large leather portfolio in burgundy. She then quietly motioned Glynnis over.

"How much money do we have left?" she whispered. Glynnis replied she had a little over £700. Peggy sighed thankfully.

"I've been tallying this in my head and was hoping we'd have enough for bus fare home. I got everything that I wanted except ..."

Both girls said in unison.

"FLANNEL PAJAMAS!"

They laughed as they watched the young man carefully wrap up the chalk and then the pencils in brown paper affixing the shoppe's signature gold seal on each package and placed the supplies in various size bags.

"How are we going to carry this all home?"

Peggy was worried.

"We'll manage."

A confident Glynnis replied, grabbing one of the handled bags.

"Not to worry."

They each grabbed another bag as Peggy struggled with the awkward easel under her arm.

"This isn't going to work. We're going to be a target for thieves."

Peggy was growing more anxious by the moment, and Glynnis started to share her concern, as she hadn't thought of that.

They made it back to Paisley's and nearly dropped the men's salads on the floor. Joel tsk tsk'd them.

"How are you going to manage all of this on a bus? Even with the two of you it's too much!"

The girls really weren't sure of their plan any more. They didn't have enough money left over for a cab ride. Joel excused himself and went to talk with Carlos, then announced that he'd be glad to give them a ride home. They eagerly accepted his offer. He went across the street to the car park and drove his vehicle around, so they could load up the trunk.

The ride was pleasant, although the girls were hitting the point of exhaustion. Joel wanted to know where they got the money for everything. Glynnis, always quick with a reply, told him that the insurance company cut Peggy a check immediately for necessities after the fire occurred. Satisfied with that answer, he drove carefully while they conversed. Glynnis made a deliberate pouty face when she explained to him that they'd still not managed to secure a simple pair of flannel pajamas for Peggy.

"Ahhhh, well, no worries, love, on another shopping trip, for sure."

He patted Peggy's hand in reassurance.

As he pulled up to Glynnis's house, he was impressed with its stately appearance. He helped the girls get the packages out of his trunk and carried some up the stairs. Glynnis opened the door with her key and had him set them down in the hallway.

A small figure, dressed in a robe, peered out from the kitchen. It was Glynnis's mother, puffing on a cigarette.

"What have we got here?"

Glynnis appeared in the doorway behind Joel and smiled.

"Hi, Mam. Peggy and I did a little shopping."

Mary looked up in shock when Peggy appeared from behind Joel. She didn't recognize the young woman. Both girls laughed at her expression and told her they'd be back in a minute. They ran outside and hugged Joel, thanking him for his help, and promised to stop by the boutique again. He made them swear to return soon.

Mary waited behind the door, anxious to get another look at the woman her daughter referred to as Peggy. She switched on the hall light to get a better view.

"Oh, my God! Let me get a look at you."

Peggy could hardly stand still. She had to pee.

"WHAT did you do to yourself? So pretty. My God, why did you ever hide yourself in all that black?"

She smiled and turned her around, then offered to put on the kettle for tea. It was after four o'clock in the afternoon and she'd not gotten dressed yet.

Peggy excused herself to go to the bathroom. Glynnis apologized to her mother for her sharp words the night before and gave her a kiss. She carried the bags and packages upstairs to her room. It took three trips, and she was visibly out of breath. Glynnis, knowing her mother's short-term memory, wanted to get them out of sight so as to avoid her asking questions.

The girls sat and had a cup of tea with Mary, who seemed glad for their company. It was Peggy's suggestion that they order takeaway Chinese food for dinner later. They all agreed, and Glynnis's mother pulled out a menu from the drawer, so they could each pick their favorite dish. Just then, Glynnis's father came through the front door. He seemed to be in a rather good mood, sporting a smart business suit and tie. He was somewhat surprised to see his wife in the kitchen. Glynnis handed him the menu and told him to pick what he wanted. He glanced over it hungrily, making several choices. He then went upstairs to change and suggested that maybe Mary might want to get out of her robe and into more suitable clothes. She put her teacup down and followed him upstairs.

The girls went out back to sneak a smoke, even though it was getting dark and chilly outside. Inside they warmed themselves by the radiator. Glynnis's parents descended the stairs about forty minutes later, obviously in great spirits. Glynnis rolled her eyes, knowing what must have taken place, as her mam had showered and changed and put on some lipstick. It was an odd relationship. She looked at Peggy and shrugged.

Glynnis introduced Peggy to her father for the second time. He apologized for his lack of memory, adding that his job kept him so busy that it would be easy to forget his own name. Glynnis assured him they'd met a while ago and went on to describe Peggy before her transformation.

"You mean you were the one who frightened Glynnis's poor mother here to death?"

He asked, glancing at his wife and then at his daughter's attractive friend.

Peggy chuckled and nodded.

"Yes, sir, I'm afraid so. I was a bit frightening, I'll admit."

"Well, you certainly don't look frightening now!"

He exclaimed.

"Quite the opposite, to be sure!"

Peggy lowered her head and blushed yet again.

Glynnis nudged her father and joked.

"Enough, Da. You're not hitting on my friend."

"Could you blame me now?"

Even Mary chuckled as the doorbell rang.

Peggy got up to get the door and offered to pay for the food. Glynnis's father wouldn't hear of it, and pulled out his wallet as she reached for her purse. He over-tipped the young delivery boy. Lifting the full bag from his hands, Liam carried it down the hallway to the kitchen.

Glynnis and her mother were setting out plates in the dining room. Her father grabbed a Guinness from the refrigerator, and her mother poured wine into Waterford glasses for herself and the two girls. Acknowledging her husband's raised eyebrow, she calmly noted that Peggy was, in fact, just days away from turning eighteen, and that their only daughter was close enough to legal age for just one small glass. They sat and looked at each other across the table, and marveled at how time flies, and that it wouldn't be too long before their own Glynnis was of legal age and off to university.

The conversation made it around, once again, to the news of the fire that morning. Glynnis's father knew more of the details and filled them in on what the papers had said. Peggy was calmer after a few sips of wine, and Glynnis smiled at her in support and clenched her hand under the table. Peggy was relieved that she'd never told any of the Travellers her real last name. The papers simply mentioned that it was believed that three people were killed in the fire, two men and a woman. No names were released, pending notification of relatives.

Glynnis asked her parents if she could accompany Peggy back to London to help her back home with her things and stay for the week. Glynnis would be on a school holiday the following week and promised them she'd call each day. They planned to stay at Peggy's uncle's house. She'd tell her father the truth when they were alone. Her mother didn't protest too much, and she gave her father a silent wide-eyed look and a wink that let him know that she'd fill him in later.

Peggy ate her meal in peace, quietly thanking God in her heart. It had been a whirlwind of a day. She gazed at the foreign image in the mirror of the China cabinet across from her. Tomorrow she'd stop at the church and light a candle in thanks.

Chapter Twenty-Six

HE'D REMAINED IN THE FLORIDA retirement community for twenty years. His ability to remember not only the names of his congregation's sons and daughters, but, of course, their grandchildren as well, amazed his elderly parishioners.

Always calculating, he used the community to his advantage. He'd make quick notes on some of the families after service, and would remember to ask after their grandchildren following Sunday Mass. This personal attention gained him the respect and admiration of his congregation.

Starring the names of those grandchildren with particularly attractive attributes, Father Coughlin would note their height, hair, and eye color, as well as the dates of school vacations. He was partial to blond-haired, innocent blue-eyed, male children, and would make sure to secure an invitation to their family homes during the holidays. However, when he was forty-five, his name once again surfaced within the Vatican.

The delegation overseeing the sensitive matter of increased sexual abuse within the church was becoming annoyed with his repeated insubordinations and obvious refusal to abide by his oath. He was making matters difficult for them. The US Conference of Catholic Bishops didn't need anymore bad publicity, yet no one in authority was willing to risk their own future advancement by publicly denouncing the nephew of a cardinal. So they kept silent, reassigning him once again.

His last transfer found him in a remote, mountainous region of Montana. The congregation was very poor, and worship on Sunday turned out only a handful of the faithful. Those who made up his sparse congregation lived in archaic shacks with no plumbing or electricity.

Phones were a luxury afforded only to those few with steady jobs. There were a handful of children in regular attendance, and they sat with their mothers; hardly any men ever came to church. There were no programs in place for children. Father Coughlin sought to change that.

When he first arrived in Montana, he was immediately bored, and became increasingly more bitter and resentful of his decreased standard of living. Out of desperation, he called his brother Rich in California and asked him to come for a visit.

Rich reluctantly visited in 1996. They explored the rural area by horseback, and he was surprised when he fell in love with the rugged countryside. In fact, he was so enamored of the area; he impulsively bought a remote log cabin they stumbled upon in the mountains.

Once he'd made the place "livable," he left Rob a key, giving him permission to use it whenever he wanted. Rob agreed to keep an eye on the place, with other possibilities, of course, coming to mind. He felt that things in his isolated setting were finally looking up.

The cabin was not easy to find. There were huge open fields beyond the neighboring Indian reservation that went on for miles and stopped short at a thickly wooded area near the base of a mountain. Rich's property was located four hours off the main road by horseback. So dense was the forest that, if one became lost, there was a distinct possibility of never being found. The commanding view of the surrounding mountains was spectacular. Small rivers and streams, teeming with fish, meandered through the landscape.

One Sunday in June, after finishing up Mass in the stark, wooden cabin that served as his church, Father Coughlin was disrobing out back when the sad news was delivered. His uncle, Cardinal Creedon, had passed away.

The Vatican flew Rob over to Italy to attend his uncle's public memorial service. Father Coughlin was expected to participate in the elaborate ceremony for his most-celebrated uncle, and was asked to speak at the historic event, a task he dreaded. Many dignitaries, political officials, and hierarchal clergy members from numerous denominations would be in attendance.

As he stood to address the prominent members seated near the altar and in the pews before him, he realized with sudden clarity that he was now completely on his own in the church organization, without his benefactor's careful hand and influential position to smooth over his mistakes. He felt the blood drain from his face. This paralyzing realization took hold as he looked around the cold, ornate cathedral. The structure was unchanged and seemed to transcend time. He recognized a few faces who he felt purposely averted his stare. It made his skin crawl and caused his voice to falter.

Father Coughlin was visibly nervous throughout the ceremony. The Pope, bishops, and clergy from around the world who attended sat nodding in agreement at his well-prepared and heartfelt eulogy. To Father Coughlin, however, each one sat as a silent accuser, knowing full well the reputation of the man standing before them giving praise to one of their own. Archbishop Creedon had been well liked and respected.

After the ceremony, Father Coughlin was anxious to return to America. He thought it ironic how all the men in his mother's life had left Ireland for the United States.

He boarded a plane immediately following the burial ceremony and never looked back. He was, in a sense, forever cut off from that life, knowing that no one there would protect him anymore. He'd have to walk a very fine line with the church from here on in.

Once back at the modest two-bedroom rectory that he called home, Father Coughlin's mood was desolate. Depressed, he made himself several strong drinks. In desperation and loneliness, he called his brother to inform him of their uncle's demise. He'd had no time to tell him before the church rushed him off to Rome.

Rob cried after hanging up, realizing that his brother, whom he'd hated most of his life, was all the family he had left in the world — the only one who would know if he lived or died. With no friends to speak of and countless grown adult enemies, he began to feel quite sorry for himself. Even his imagination, still unbelievably vivid at times, could not offer him pleasure or solace through lewd visualizations; fantasies wouldn't even manifest. He'd relied on this form of mental escape all of his life when he needed comfort, and his inability to conjure up images frightened him in a way he couldn't understand. He lay down on his single bed in a drunken stupor, fell asleep, and didn't dream.

Chapter Twenty-Seven

Boston, Massachusetts, Spring 1998

AFTER DINNER, CAROLINE TOLD VAL she'd stop and pick up a few groceries on the way home. Val had to go back to the office to pick up a file she'd forgotten and needed to look over before her trip to Chicago. Caroline was still smiling as she thought about the story of how Val and Warren met. It began to drizzle when she ducked inside the Stop-N-Shop.

Caroline was relieved to get out of the rain. According to the weather report she'd overheard at the restaurant, it was going to downpour all night. She tugged at the shopping cart to pull it free from the row. Trying to picture Warren in her mind, based on Val's description, she browsed the aisles aimlessly.

She'd been concerned about her sister's inactivity on the dating front, which certainly couldn't be blamed on her appearance. Val was savvy, with flair and class. She dressed impeccably (under the strong influence of their Auntie Sheila). At five foot nine inches and about 130 lbs., she was fantastically proportioned, having more curves than most.

Caroline, on the other hand, could barely ever keep weight on her, and ended up feeling too bony and angular most of the time. Val's long blond hair and cool green eyes radiated confidence, which tended to attract strong, powerful men. They often admired her from afar. Caroline had been witness to the phenomenon, while Val herself was oblivious. She came across as somewhat serious at first, though after only a few minutes of conversation, and a flash of her bright smile, one could see she was actually approachable and down-to-earth. Val's only requirement of those she spent time with was a sense of humor. Her own laugh was infectious.

Caroline loved living in downtown Boston with her sister, and was relieved when a major food chain had decided to open up a store only a few blocks away from their condo. Of course, it really catered to college students from many of the surrounding dorms — one look at the displays told you that. The aisle end caps teemed with snack foods, just-add-water soups and, of course, macaroni and cheese. Caroline smiled as she reached for a box of the orange-colored food product — still one of her favorites.

Val said that Warren would be spending his next layover in Boston. Caroline thought it would be a good time to visit with her mom on the Cape and leave the apartment to Val, in case she decided to invite the new love of her life to stay with her. Caroline had also jotted down a note to herself while in the bathroom stall at Hillary's to remind her of the upcoming charity concert in which Val and her mother would be performing. Val had given her explicit instructions NOT to mention anything about her violin playing to Warren before the concert. She went on to explain that Warren had taken her to a performance at the new music center, The Glor, in Ennis. To her surprise and delight, he'd actually conducted the symphony! She confided to Caroline that it was then that she knew she'd marry him. It hit her that hard. Over in Ireland, Val made Granny and Siobhan promise after he left not to let on a word about her musical talents until she could surprise him.

"Turnabout's fair play."

She schemed with Caroline as they made plans for the upcoming benefit concert.

Caroline was making her way toward the produce section when she saw the elderly woman fall. She quickly abandoned the cart and ran over to her. Kneeling down, she asked her calmly if she was in pain. The woman was fearful and clung to Caroline's hand, shaking. She was having difficulty breathing and held her free hand over her chest.

Caroline suspected she was having a heart attack. The woman moaned in pain and then went unconscious and stopped breathing. Caroline shouted to someone nearby to call for an ambulance as she felt for her pulse and carefully positioned the woman's head to administer CPR.

A young man knelt down beside her, offering to do compressions while she did the breathing. A crowd had begun to form when a police officer arrived on the scene and cleared them back to make room for the paramedics.

Caroline was still wearing her hospital scrubs, and her Puritan Medical Center badge was prominently clipped to her pocket, confirming her qualifications. She heard mumblings in the crowd about how lucky the poor woman was that a doctor happened to be in the store.

When the paramedics appeared with the stretcher, the woman was just barely breathing on her own, and her color was still gray. Caroline wasn't sure if she'd make it, but she knew that her chances were greatly improved because of the immediate attention she'd received. She was acquainted with Dave, one of the paramedics who responded to the call, and asked to ride back with them.

Caroline's heart was pounding and her own adrenalin surging. She helped hold the IV line as Dave called in the woman's vitals over the radio to the awaiting emergency room physician. A couple of nurses met them at the entrance to the ER. Caroline, who was off-duty, hung back, and then waited around to see how the woman would fare. Hours later, she was finally stabilized and brought up to ICU. Caroline called a cab to take her home.

The rain pelted down with a fury as she stood outside, awaiting the cab. Caroline felt a wave of exhaustion overtake her as the lights from the taxi approached the curb. When they reached her condo, she lifted her hospital smock over her head to protect herself from the pounding deluge as she exited the vehicle. She was quickly soaked to the skin and her thin clothes clung to her.

Val was on the phone when she unlocked and opened the door. Turning around, Val balanced the phone on one shoulder and looked horrified at Caroline's soaked condition. She mouthed, "What's wrong?" Caroline waved her off.

Val cupped her hand over the receiver and whispered.

"What happened to you? I thought you were coming right home? I was worried about you!"

Val asked Warren to hold a moment while she got an abbreviated story from Caroline. When she realized how serious it was, she told Warren she'd call him back in a few minutes. Caroline was upset and crying. Val reached in the bathroom closet for a towel and handed it to her sister, who proceeded to dry herself off.

"So tell me what happened? This woman just collapsed in the store, and you gave her CPR in the produce section?"

Caroline nodded yes, sniffling.

Val sat down on the edge of the tub and put her arm around Caroline's shoulder. Caroline rested her head on her sister's arm and closed her eyes.

"So you went back to the hospital with her after that? But you already worked a shift ... or was it two again?"

She looked at her sister disapprovingly.

Caroline twisted the towel in her hands, trying to remember. She'd worked a double and met Val after that for dinner. She'd been up for over forty-eight hours, and Val knew her well enough to tell that she was exhausted and ready to crash.

"Never mind. Tell me later. You need to get to bed. You've done all you can do, and you've got to just let God do the rest, kiddo. You did a good thing ... it's out of your hands now, okay?"

Caroline wiped her eyes with the towel and nodded. She stood and pulled off her top as she headed down the hall to her bed. Val trailed after her, picking the wet shirt up off the floor, and the pants that soon followed. Caroline collapsed onto her bed. Val covered her with the down comforter and shut off the light. She called Warren back as she tossed Caroline's clothes in the hamper.

"Hi! Sorry to hang up on you so quickly like that. Caroline had a medical emergency happen right in the grocery store. Honestly, that girl always finds herself in the midst of trauma!"

She relayed the story to him.

"She was pretty upset. I think it was kind of a delayed reaction, but she's also exhausted. She's working too many double shifts lately and can hardly keep track of her days. She forgets things so quickly ... I worry about her."

Warren assured her that the memory lapses were probably just due to fatigue. He said he'd experienced it himself on occasion when he'd been flying for long periods of time, and that she shouldn't worry too much about it.

"You should suggest she take a vacation, go somewhere fun."

Val agreed that was a good idea. She'd mention it to Caroline tomorrow.

"By the way, I'm leaving for Chicago Tuesday morning"

Val mentioned.

"Yeah? What's taking you to the Windy City?"

"I'm doing a branch review, or should I say 'audit.' I try to hit all the branches quarterly. Chicago's a pretty cool city."

He agreed.

"But I love Boston. It's one of my favorites."

Val chided him.

"Awww ... you're just saying that 'cause I'm here. Who do you think you're kidding?"

Warren laughed.

"Well, that is true, but even before I met you I developed an affinity for the area. I just wish I could explore more of it."

"Well, we'll just have to do that when you get here. You'll love where my condo is located — one street over from the Charles River and three blocks from Copley Place, which has some of the nicest boutiques.

Caroline and I are Lord & Taylor buffs, so it suits us perfectly ... no pun intended!"

"What's Lord & Taylor?"

Val exaggerated her reply.

"What's Lord & Taylor? Only the most fantastic clothing store!"

"Oh, I see. Then it must be in the same category as those other high-priced American stores like, Needless Mark-ups."

Val burst out laughing.

"Oh, that's precious! You're very good! Caroline will appreciate that one. She's a big Neiman Marcus fan. By the way, I'd like to treat you to dinner at Morton's. They're known for their steak. Have you ever been there?"

"No, I can't say that I have. But it sounds great!"

Warren then asked.

"Well, now, have you given any thought to where you might like to go when I take you out for dinner?"

Val had to think about it. One of her favorite spots was Olive's Restaurant in Charlestown, after which they could pop into Sullivan's Tavern for a beer. Then of course, there was always Faneuil Hall in downtown Boston. He'd like Houlihan's. She and Caroline had taken Glynnis and Peggy there on their last visit.

"I'll give it more thought and let you know."

"Are you excited about my coming to visit?"

Valerie smiled and bobbed her head, even though he couldn't see her.

"Yes! Of course, I am. I can hardly wait to see you again. Caroline is anxious to meet you as well. I told her the 'Tidbits' story. It's already a classic, you know."

Warren laughed and shared how he'd told the story to a few of his friends, who also thought it quite funny.

He sat back in his reclining chair, taking in her voice as she continued.

"By the way, I'll have you know that Granny called my mother while I was en route back home, and now you're just the buzz of the family! She raved about you."

He chuckled and assured her he was looking forward to meeting the rest of her family.

"Now, how about you?"

He was lost.

"How about me what?"

"Are you excited to come and see me?"

He smirked on his end.

"You know, I know we've only known each other a week, but it went by so fast, Valerie. It's now a wonderful blur. I enjoyed meeting Peggy and Glynnis. They're really nice women — talented, too! I guess, well, I do really miss you ... and YES, I'm looking forward to seeing you again!"

He confessed unashamedly while swinging the telephone cord, knocking his glass over on to the floor. He felt like a gawky teenager and was glad she didn't hear the glass break.

Val felt that warm feeling in her stomach, which soon radiated through her entire body. She remembered his kisses and tender touch. He was a gentleman and hadn't sought more. She wanted to tell him by the end of the week that she loved him, but knew enough not to be premature about expressing her feelings. She'd wait it out and see what happened.

"Well, m'lady, we should be getting off the phone. We're going to be racking up some healthy phone bills in this relationship. I can tell."

Val laughed and allowed herself to grow excited as she hung on his words about "this relationship."

"Ahhhh, yes, dear Warren, but a small price to pay to hear my sweet voice."

He laughed at her imitation of his accent.

"Hey, you said that like a real Irish woman, Valerie!"

He was impressed.

She loved it when he called her by her full name. It sounded especially pretty when he said it.

"I AM a real Irish woman...safe landings, Warren."

She said softly.

"Always, m'love, always."

Val hung up the phone and walked down the hall to check on Caroline, who was sound asleep. Sitting on the edge of the bed for a moment, she stared down at her sister.

Something had troubled this beautiful young woman, driving her, haunting her for years. Val couldn't understand what it was and no matter how she tried, Caroline denied that anything was ever wrong. She felt like they shared everything, but there was a part that was closed off to her.

Caroline's life had been so erratic at times, followed by years of relative peace and sanity - almost normal. But lately, those moments were becoming few and far between. Whatever was driving her had escalated. Val genuinely felt that the pressures of her nursing career and the constant life and death ER dramas were getting to be too much. Her mother and aunt had tried to suggest other career alternatives, but Caroline wouldn't hear of it.

She had a "savior" complex — an innate need to help and protect others — somehow feeling responsible for the well-being of total strangers whom she came in contact with. Val knew that after the evening's drama, if anything happened to that woman in the store, another emotional crash might be looming. If anyone Caroline helped or assisted in a trauma situation died, she'd get depressed, more than most, and couldn't just "shake it off." There'd be nights of violent nightmares, followed by increased irritability and drinking. It was a clear and predictable pattern. Val was afraid it would kill her one of these days, drive her over the edge. No job was worth that much. She sighed as she stood and pulled the shade, leaving the room quietly.

Val changed into her sweats and picked up her violin. She placed her music on the stand and lowered it as she sat on the edge of the bed. Years before, she'd purchased what Caroline termed a "phantom" violin.

Because they lived in a condo and were surrounded by others in the building, and since Val often liked to play at odd hours of the night when she couldn't sleep, she'd bought an electric violin, which looked like the skeleton of a real one. It enabled her to plug in her headphones and play so that only she could hear. She kept her regular violin set up with another music stand by the bay window in the living room so that she could overlook the park while she practiced during the day.

Music was a part of her. It was her escape, a form of expression that she could not humanly convey or articulate. It had to be felt ... experienced. The violin breathed and spoke with a beautiful heartfelt sound which transcended time and space causing her spirit to soar — to cry out in praise or pain — an outlet for her many varying emotions. She felt it a gift to herself whenever she played, and took great comfort in the music, having done so since she was a child.

Val finished practicing her score for the upcoming charity concert. It was a difficult piece, and she'd need to work on it more. She'd call Father Bruce when she returned from Chicago and seek his help. Her violin instructor would coach her through the rest. She found it comforting that Father Bruce had always been there for her and Caroline and their mother. He was, in a sense, like their heavenly-appointed surrogate father.

Chapter Twenty-Eight

Cape Cod, Massachusetts, Spring 1998

THE UPCOMING CHARITY EVENT WAS serving more than one purpose. Undoubtedly, the school library expansion project would greatly benefit from the proceeds generated that evening. Grace, Sheila, and the girls were also talking over plans for a special surprise twenty-fifth anniversary celebration for Father Bruce Moriarty at the girls' condo after the concert. The ensemble was told and went to great lengths to keep the secret from him.

Grace sat in her kitchen, sipping tea, and talking with Sheila, when she first thought to do something low-key for him. A humble man, he didn't like being the center of attention.

"We should do something to acknowledge all those years of hard work and dedication. I know he's been a rock for me and the girls, not to mention the community at large. All the kids love him. Did you know that last year he was chosen by the Massachusetts Humanity Council and recognized for an award by the state for his outstanding contributions to youth leadership?"

Sheila nodded in acknowledgement.

"He deserves a medal for what he does. He's always gone above and beyond the call of duty."

"Don't I know it! Do you remember how he took care of us following Neil's death? I mean, he showed up here to cut the lawn, kept an eye on both girls in school. He even rounded up a crew to paint the house for us that following summer!"

Sheila reminded her.

"Don't forget about the roof he fixed. Remember how it leaked after that hurricane?"

"How could I forget? He came over that night to check on us since everyone was without power. He even brought candles! The girls and I were a little frightened. Well, not Val, but Caroline was scared to death. He lit the candles and stayed and talked with us while the winds were howling. I remember he prayed and asked God to watch over and protect our home from the storm. Other than a few shingles flying off, we survived it just fine. Did you see the Grazianos' house afterward? The poor folks needed a whole new porch after the tree fell on it."

"Sheila, you, better than anyone, know what we went through with Caroline. She was a holy terror as a teenager!' There was just no controlling her back then. I knew she was drinking, and then I found pot in her room. I called Father Bruce hysterical one night when she'd stumbled home drunk. He came over at one o'clock in the morning, and helped me get her to bed! I wanted to kill her. I was so embarrassed. I cried on his shoulder that night. I felt like such a failure. I told him that if Neil were there, he'd be so disappointed in me as a mother. But he assured me that God had his hand on her life, and that he'd not let her go. Sheila, he's been a 'literal' godsend to us."

Sheila and Grace were enjoying their girl talk.

"Val's still close with him, too. Of course, they share the same intense love of music."

Grace smiled.

"Do you remember how Valerie would get involved in those long discussions with him about God? He'd exhibit the patience of Job with her and all her millions of questions. She was so happy when he came over, on occasion, to have a tea party with her. He remembered how she used to do that with Neil all the time and missed it after his death. Father Bruce got a kick out of her serving the tea with the holy water from Knock Shrine."

Grace's eyes filled up with that memory. She and Neil had laughed about a similar experience he had with Valerie before he left on that fateful trip to Ireland. It seemed like ages ago.

"I don't know about you, but I think we need to skip the party and just have the man canonized!"

Sheila swallowed her tea with a gulp and laughed at her sister's comment.

"He's really gifted with kids, don't you think? I mean, the youth group has really grown under his direction. He gets right in there with them, goes to their track meets at school, shows up at their basketball games, and not just the kids enrolled at St. Bridget's either! There are kids that come to the youth group from some of the local high schools, and he just shows up to cheer them on. They really appreciate that and so do the parents! It means a lot to them since some of their own parents don't come. Didn't Caroline go on that hiking trip to Acadia years ago with him?"

Grace filled in the details.

"What started out as a handful of kids amounted to over fifty! They were scurrying to find chaperones. They had a blast and Caroline still talks about it! I think a lot of the church's success is due to him doing things like that ... setting up scholarships for kids who couldn't afford to go to college. I'm grateful we've had him around all these years. It's very rare that the church will keep a priest in one place for so long."

Sheila pointed out.

"It's very rare you'll get a priest who WANTS to stay in one place for so long!"

Without realizing that she spoke aloud, Grace whispered.

"I made the right choice."

Sheila looked quizzically at her sister.

"What was that?"

Grace jumped as if startled.

"OH! Nothing ..."

Sheila knew her sister was backtracking.

"No, no ... you said, 'I made the right choice.' What choice was that?"

Grace fidgeted with the cup in her hand. She couldn't get out of it. Sheila knew her too well and could tell when she was trying to hide something.

"I can't, Sheila. It's nothing really, and it was many years ago. Not worth bringing up really."

Sheila wouldn't let go.

"Grace, for crying out loud. What IS it? We tell each other everything!"

Grace shrugged her shoulders and preceded slowly, choosing her words with care.

"Well, it was something about Father Bruce and me ... years ago."

Sheila set down her cup, not taking her eyes off her sister for moment. She didn't even blink, trying to imagine what her sister was going to say next.

"Well, after another episode with Caroline, he'd stayed late into the night, and we talked."

Sheila gasped interjecting.

"OH! Don't tell me you and him ... "

"NO!!! Absolutely not! How could you think I'd ever do such a thing?"

"I'm sorry, Grace. I'll shut up. Go ahead. Finish."

Sheila made a motion like she was locking her lips with a key.

"Well, it's just ... we were talking and he shared some personal feelings he had toward me and the girls."

Sheila was dumbfounded.

"And ... what? What did he say?"

"He said ... I mean, he asked ..."

Grace stood and walked around the island in the kitchen, setting her cup in the sink and running a little water into it.

"He told me that, if I had feelings for him, he'd leave the priesthood to marry me."

Sheila gasped.

"You're kidding me!"

Grace put her hand on one hip and pointed.

"YOU are sworn to keep this secret, you hear me? You're to take this to your grave! The girls know nothing about this ... and they WON'T!"

Sheila crossed her heart and nodded.

"I will, I will. I promise. This is unbelievable! How come you never told me before?"

Grace felt guilty having told her at all, and shrugged.

"It was ages ago, Sheila."

Father Bruce had a nurturing instinct, and she often thought that was what overtook his senses that night. She loved and missed Neil and felt, at that time, that no one could ever replace him in her heart. That was what she'd told Father Bruce. She was flattered, of course. He understood, assuring her that he'd always be there for her and the girls regardless. That wouldn't change — and it didn't.

Sheila started laughing.

"Leave it to you to attract a priest, sis! Have you ever considered re-marriage? I mean, you're still attractive ... with the girls grown and gone, maybe you should revisit Father Bruce's offer!"

Grace rolled her eyes.

"Oh, do shut up, Sheila!"

Sheila held up both hands.

"Okay, okay, just a suggestion. You guys do get along quite well, now that I think about it!"

A dishtowel flew across the counter, landing on Sheila's head.

"What did I do?"

Sheila sat there comically with her hand up and left the dishtowel hanging over her face, causing Grace to laugh at her. She turned the water on to finish washing the cups in the sink and reached over to grab the towel off her sister's head.

"Let's get back to the party plans. Forget you heard this. It happened years ago, and I'll never revisit it again. You got that? You are not even allowed to tell Tim!"

Sheila groaned.

"Yes, yes, I've got it."

"It really is amazing that Father Bruce has stayed here so long. He's watched us all grow up and helped us evolve. We're the ones who are blessed. Bishop McLean thinks he's the greatest thing since sliced bread! He's Father Bruce's biggest advocate in helping him stay here this long. Father Bruce never wanted to be anything more than what he was. He never wanted a grand title. Do you realize that Val and Caroline received all of the sacraments from him? How rare is that? Well, all except marriage, that is ... I'm wondering when and if that'll happen!"

She sighed dramatically.

"I think I raised my daughters to be a little too independent! I'm still scared to death that Caroline will wind up pregnant without being married! Even though she's an adult and a professional nurse, the girl has no scruples!"

Sheila laughed.

"Not much you can do about that, sis. She's a big girl now. I wish Val dated more, though."

Grace piped in excitedly.

"Oh! That reminds me. Ruth called from Ireland and said Val met a nice man on her last trip! I've not talked to Val since she got back the other day. Oh, and you'll never guess ... he's a PILOT!"

Sheila's mouth dropped.

"That little prophetic scoundrel! She always said she was going to marry a pilot. Remember that?"

Grace nodded eagerly.

"I know! That's what I mean. He's coming to visit in a couple of weeks according to Ruth, and Val's going to take him to the charity concert. He'll get to meet everyone.

By the way, we're sworn to secrecy. We can't breathe a word about her playing the violin. Seems her new beau loves music and actually conducts the symphony from time to time over in Ireland when he's home. He volunteers at the Glor. Val wants to surprise him. According to her grandmother, she's quite enamored with him already. I'm looking forward to meeting him!"

"What's his name?"

Grace had to think for a moment.

"Warren, Warren Cahill."

She sat back and rehearsed.

"Hmmm ... Valerie Cahill. I like the sound of that."

Chapter Twenty-Nine

Cariston, England, Fall 1978

GLYNNIS HELPED LIFT THE SUITCASES out of the back of the taxi. Peggy paid the driver, and both girls stood silent for a moment surveying the slate blue home of Peggy's youth. The home had originally belonged to her grandmother; and was handed down to her uncle and her mother after her grandmother's death. Peggy's mother relinquished all rights to her brother when she abandoned her daughter. He, in turn, told Peggy he'd leave it all to her.

The house was over one hundred and fifty years old, and still very sturdy despite it being unoccupied for over four years. Peggy recalled that a new roof had been put on when she was eleven. She couldn't even imagine the house's value now. She breathed a sigh of relief and was glad to finally have a home of her own to come back to.

She still had a lot of details to work out. Looking a little worried, she glanced around to see if anyone was watching them. The girls dragged the suitcases up the stairs to the front porch. Peggy pulled the remains of the "Police" sticky tape off the doorway. She told Glynnis to wait while she went around back to look for the long-hidden key. Pushing her way through the overgrown briars, she reappeared moments later with a key in her hand, smiling nervously.

"Well, no one moved the flower pot, thank goodness. We've got to be careful, Glynn; there may be squatters in here."

Peggy put the key in the door and motioned for Glynnis to get the bags inside quickly. They shut the door and took a moment to adjust to the dim light. The house was eerily quiet and musty smelling. It would be dark out in a few hours. They stood silently, listening for noises in the house. The door didn't look as though it had been forced open at any time, and no windows on the ground level were broken that they could see.

It was Sunday, and the trip over from Ireland had taken nearly all day. They were exhausted after having lugged four large, heavy suitcases and several over-the-shoulder bags on and off the bus and ferry. The final taxi ride was a welcomed relief just to have someone else take over the carting of the luggage. Glynnis's mother had offered to ship Peggy's art supplies over once they notified her they arrived.

It was three thirty on a rather damp, gray weekend afternoon as they stood listening for sounds in the chilly hallway. The cool wind gusted outside. They proceeded cautiously. Peggy led Glynnis into the kitchen, where the windows let in a bit more of the pale fading light. A strange musty smell permeated the air.

"It's as if the house were dead."

Peggy observed.

Glynnis nodded and shivered and looked around cautiously. Nothing seemed out of the ordinary, yet it was obvious from the cobwebs and mouse droppings that it hadn't been occupied or cleaned in years.

"I dread opening the door to the fridge."

Peggy pointed to the appliance with a disgusted look.

"Well, I'm not doing it!"

Glynnis declared, scrunching up her nose.

"No doubt the police will be around soon. Once they see the tape removed from the doorway, or one of the neighbors calls to report us."

Peggy looked anxiously at Glynnis.

"What do we do now?"

Glynnis thought for a moment then suggested.

"Well, first, let's find the candles we packed and get them lit. Remember what my da said. If there are any problems with the police, call him, and he'll talk to them for you. Nice having a father that's an attorney, eh?"

She winked and reached in her pocket, pulling out a few of her father's business cards.

"He told me if anyone gives us trouble, we're to give them one of these. He's got business in London on Wednesday and said he'd stop by to check in on us. By the way, I promised to call him when we arrived. I need to find a phone or he'll send the authorities over himself to check on us. We also need to locate that copy of your uncle's will and any legal papers you can find so that he can get those documents transferred and drawn up for you. The police can't throw you out of your own house, Peg, so not to worry. There may be questions, but they can't evict you."

Glynnis looked at her friend and smiled.

"You know, I'm really glad you confided in my da. I've never seen that side of him before. I mean, he was almost human, sensitive, in a way I've not seen in years. I think he was horrified to hear what you've been through. I know he'll do whatever he can to help you, Peg. Your trailer nightmare is safe with him. My mom couldn't believe it either. I know she was nervous letting us come here alone. We'd better find a phone box and call them soon. But first, let's get this stuff up to your room."

The girls went out to the hall to collect the rest of the bags. Peggy screeched when a mouse scurried out from behind the luggage.

"Jesus, Mary, and Joseph!"

Glynnis jumped, putting her hand on her chest.

"For the love of God, Peg, you scared the wits out of me!"

Peggy reached cautiously for the suitcase.

"Remind me, please, that one of the first things I'm getting for this house is a cat!"

Glynnis cooed.

"That'll be nice. A kitten would be a good pet for you. Better yet, get two!!"

"I may just do that. The more, the merrier."

Peggy led the way up the stairs and down the long hall before she halted in her tracks. She turned and looked at Glynnis, realizing she was unconsciously heading toward her uncle's room.

"Sorry, wrong direction. Turn around. That way."

She nodded toward the opposite end of the hall.

"My room is the last door on the left. There is a guest bedroom across from mine you can take. The good Lord only knows what it looks like."

Glynnis turned in the direction Peggy was pointing. She set the bags down, opening the door to Peggy's room cautiously. The lighting was dim, yet she could make out the still rumpled bed and a few faded stuffed animals on the floor. A flood of memories washed over Peggy as she stepped through the doorway. The night of the rape was still vivid in her mind.

Glynnis brought the suitcases in and started looking through them. She took out a couple of votive candles and set one on the bedside table, another on the bureau, and one on the desk across the room. Soon, a light lavender scent permeated the stagnant air and the tiny flickering flames added a soft glow to the room. Peggy felt a chill run down her spine. The events of her last night here with her uncle were replaying in her mind. It felt odd to be back in her room.

"I need a cigarette."

Peg announced.

"How about you?"

"Yeah, I'll join you."

Glynnis reached into her bag and pulled out a pack, shaking a couple out for them.

They sat silently on the edge of the bed and looked around.

"This is a cute room."

Glynnis commented optimistically.

Peggy blew the match out and looked around for something to put the ashes in. She spotted a small jewelry dish on her desk and brought it over. It was a piece she'd made in a ceramics class in second grade, painted yellow with purple flecks.

"I think what we need to do next is find a phone, so you can call your parents. Then we can pick up a few things at the grocers and come back. Tomorrow, I'll contact the utility companies and see about getting the lights and everything turned back on. I hope the pipes are okay after all these years. I think the house is heated by oil."

Glynnis could see the wheels turning in Peggy's head.

"I just hope we don't freeze to death tonight!"

"Well, that's why God made sweaters!"

Peggy was calmer and was beginning to think more clearly. She really wanted to approach this whole new adult life thing as an adventure, and keep it all in perspective.

She felt certain that the guards wouldn't kick her out of her own house. Glynnis's father had confirmed that they wouldn't. He assured her that she wouldn't be arrested for having run away from the juvenile home years ago. She'd be eighteen years old on Monday and of legal age. The only problem she might run into was providing the authorities with more information about the night of her uncle's brutal attack. He investigated and found out that the case wasn't closed. They would still prosecute him if they could find him. They'd be looking to her for information on his possible whereabouts. She'd spend some time tomorrow looking for legal papers.

As if reading her mind, Glynnis asked.

"Do you think you know where your uncle might have put his will?"

Peggy nodded.

"I believe his papers may be locked in the desk in the living room. I'm sure the authorities must have searched through the house. Speaking of which, I think you and I should do a complete walk-through, and check this place out. I'll find the key to the desk later. If worse comes to worst, I'll just break it open."

Glynnis suggested.

"Speaking of breaking things open, let's grab something, should we need to defend ourselves."

They quickly scanned the room. Peggy got up and opened her closet door. Lying against the back wall was her baton.

"Will this do?"

She held up the rubber-tipped metal rod.

"Do you really know how to use that?"

Glynnis asked.

"Well, I used to."

She twirled it through her fingers and realized that, though her actions were a bit rusty, she remembered how to make it spin.

Glynnis was impressed.

"Did you happen to notice the cracked window above the front door?"

Peggy shook her head as she tried to toss the baton in the air. It landed with a thud.

"No. I didn't notice anything. But we'll take a better look at it in the morning. No doubt we've probably got some birds or bats in here, too."

Glynnis glanced around the ceiling of the room.

"Great! That's just what I wanted to hear!"

She remarked sarcastically.

The girls each picked up a candle to take with them. Opening the door to the guest room across the hall, Peggy entered first, setting her candle down on the table. The floor creaked as she looked in the closet and under the bed. She wasn't fearful with Glynnis there. At least, they knew there weren't any bats or birds in Peggy's bedroom.

Heading down the hall, a sense of dread came over Peggy as she opened the door to her uncle's bedroom. Her breath caught in her chest as she looked at the unmade bed. The sheets were yellowed and moth-eaten, and looked ghostly. A curtain blew gently in the wind and startled her.

"Is the window open?"

She asked Glynnis, who was standing by it.

"No, cracked and a small piece is missing, but no worries. Tomorrow is another day."

She checked the closet and Glynnis peered under the bed. Reaching underneath, she pulled out a stack of girly magazines.

Peggy's face flushed red.

"He read this stuff?"

Glynnis asked as she flipped through one.

Peggy grabbed them roughly from her hands. Glynnis was taken back by her abruptness. Peg softened her response.

"I'm sorry. It's just, well, he made me look at these things with him. I want to burn them!"

Glynnis gently took them back from Peggy and tossed them on the floor.

"Listen, tomorrow, I'll clean out this room. You busy yourself in another room, okay?"

Peggy thanked her and apologized again. Glynnis waved her off and told her not to worry about it. They shut the door and walked across the hall. There was a small sitting room across from her uncle's bedroom that he'd made into a study. It contained all sorts of books and more magazines, a small couch, and a chair. The curtains were well worn and faded. She found she needed to get outside and get some fresh air before she choked. The air actually tasted stale to her.

"Let's take a quick look around downstairs, and then we'll head out to the market, okay?"

They did a fast sweep through the dining and living rooms, running into cobwebs wherever they walked. When Peggy got to the fireplace, she reached for the metal handle that opened the flue.

"Hand me one of the candles, would you?"

Holding the flame up in the opening, she peered up and could see a little light at the top.

"Good. The chimney's not clogged. We can start a fire when we get back. At least, we won't freeze to death. This fireplace throws some good heat once it's up and running. It'll warm up the whole downstairs."

Dusting her blackened hands off on her new pants, she asked.

"Okay, what do we need to get through tonight?"

Glynnis thought for a moment.

"Well, I'd say a few more candles or maybe even a storm lamp, so we have light until the electricity is turned on."

"Wait!"

Peggy remembered something and went into the kitchen pantry.

"Can you come here with that candle for a minute?"

Glynnis cupped her hand around the candle's flame so as to not let the breeze extinguish it. She held it up high so that Peg could see. Standing on the step stool, Peggy reached up to the top shelf and pulled down an oil lamp.

"Ask and you shall receive."

Glynnis placed the small candle on the kitchen counter and took the lamp from Peggy. She blew the dust off.

"Let's see how well it works. I mean, it's an oil lamp so it should be fine after all this time I'd think."

She held the small candle up to the wick, and light burst forth.

Glynnis sneezed from the dust.

"God-bless-you."

Peggy offered out automatically.

"Let's go. I need to get some fresh air."

She then blew out the candles and oil lamp.

Peggy put the key in her pocket, and they grabbed their satchels. Walking down the road, Peggy pointed out various neighbors' homes.

"We're lucky we didn't have to contend with squatters! Other than a few broken windows and a lot of dust, it's in pretty decent shape, wouldn't you say?"

She looked at her friend optimistically.

"From what we can see in the dim light, it doesn't look too bad at all. We'll be able to tell better tomorrow in full sunlight."

Peggy thought that, perhaps, someone had kept an eye on the place over the last four years, but couldn't imagine whom. She didn't recall her uncle being that friendly with anyone. He'd always kept to himself; her circle of friends had been very limited because of him and their secrets.

The immediate neighborhood hadn't changed dramatically from what she could recall. She noticed a few of the houses were painted different colors. They walked along, breathing in and appreciating the fresh air. Peggy mentioned that just up ahead was the center of town. A few of the businesses had different names, and a couple of new storefronts had been added. Across from the little footbridge, there was a small café, which was open for supper. Peggy suggested they eat there after stopping at the grocers for a few necessities.

As they walked toward the store, Peggy noticed that Sherwood's Bakery was still there and had recently been whitewashed. It was a quaint town. Antique-looking gas lamps had been added along the cobblestone sidewalks, giving it an almost Charles Dickens-like appearance.

Located about forty-five minutes north of London, Cariston had become a very desirable area for London's business commuters. Peggy's house looked rather modest and a little run down compared to some of the more elaborate properties in the area. The housing market had soared since she left.

Peggy pointed out the phone box to Glynnis, who ran off to call her parents. When Peggy walked into the grocers, she didn't recognize the woman behind the counter. Gathering up some toiletries, bottled water, candles, and plastic bags, Peggy carried the items over to the register. She asked about the firewood, and the woman informed her that she'd have to pay for it here, and then she could take a stack from out back. An ordinance had just been passed that would not allow storefronts to keep anything out front. Some of the newer folks in town didn't like clutter and said it detracted from the quaintness of the village.

Peggy shook her head. The woman observed the pretty girl's reaction, thinking that she looked vaguely familiar. Peggy graciously thanked her for her help and told her she'd be back in the morning to buy some cleaning supplies. The woman told her that though she wouldn't be there, her husband would be more than happy to help her when she came in.

Glynnis bounded into the store like an excited puppy.

"My mam was a nervous wreck! She was so glad I called. Da got on the phone and told me he made a call to a lawyer friend of his in London. He's going to call the police chief himself tomorrow and explain the situation on your behalf."

She turned and leaned into Peggy so as to not let the woman behind the counter hear anything more.

"He won't mention anything about the trailer incident, though."

Peggy was visibly relieved.

"He said to expect a visit some time tomorrow, no doubt, but not to worry because you're not in any trouble."

Peggy was grateful for her friend's help. She felt positive again, and knew it was all going to come together. For the moment, however, she was hungry and getting tired. Peggy paid for her purchase and asked the woman if it was all right if they picked the wood up on their way back from dinner. The woman assured her that was fine. Peggy bought two large stacks of wood to get them through the night ... carrying it would be another story.

As the girls walked across the street to the café, Peggy pointed out the new Laundromat.

"I wish I knew that was here. We could have brought the sheets with us to wash while we ate dinner."

Glynnis shrugged her shoulders.

"We're just going to have to tough it out tonight. We'll take them outside and give them a good shaking and lay them across the couch in the living room with the fireplace. It'll be warmer than your bedroom. We'll work it all out in the morning. Let's eat. I'm starved."

The café was done in a Tuscan-style décor. Under her father's orders and with his money, Glynnis stated she was buying dinner and every other meal for them during her weeklong stay. Her da had given her more than enough money should they run into any problems, and told Glynnis he wanted her to buy food for Peggy once everything was settled. Her mother suggested she get her a nice house gift, too.

The whole Peggy "ordeal" had sparked something protective in her family, bringing them closer together in a way Glynnis wasn't used to. It was as if her friend's dire situation made them assess their own lives and count their blessings. Through Peggy's heartache, they were touched, and had become very thankful for what they had.

Dinner consisted of soup, salad, and penne pollo, a pasta and chicken dish with vegetables. They each had a glass of wine, and the tired waitress didn't question how old they were. The girls devoured everything and still managed to have room for dessert.

Returning to the grocers to pick up the two stacks of wood, Glynnis complained about the weight after trying to lift it.

"This is really heavy! I don't know if I can lug it all the way back."

Peggy noticed a wheelbarrow off to the side, and suggested they use it to cart the wood home. She wedged a note in between the doors of the closed grocery store and left her name and address, letting the owner know she'd return it in the morning. She had no doubt that was what it was there for.

It was dark when the girls returned to the house. They gathered up the wood and grocery bags, pushed the wheelbarrow off to the side in the front yard, and went inside. Peggy dropped the wood on the floor and sank to her knees. Glynnis lit the oil lamp. Clearing some of the cobwebs away, she leaned in to light the fireplace. Rolling a piece of paper bag up like a stick, she lit it with a match. She held the torch up inside the flue to start an updraft. She'd watched her uncle do it a thousand times. The paper went up in flames quickly, and she dropped it before it could burn her. Glynnis handed her a few pieces of the small kindling wood first. She laid it strategically in the fireplace. The larger logs were very dry, catching the flame easily. There was a little smoke at first, but a blaze of light quickly ensued from the paper wedged between the kindling wood. Soon the whole room was aglow in firelight.

Peggy sat on the couch as a yawn escaped her.

"Grab the lamp. I've one more thing I need to bring down from upstairs."

"What?"

Glynnis inquired.

"Promise you won't laugh."

She promised.

"Follow me."

They were a little nervous walking up the creaky, dark stairs.

"Before Granny died, my mom bought her a portable potty chair because she had difficulty walking. My uncle never liked to throw anything out. It may take a few days before we have running water back in the house, so I thought we could put it in the bathroom, just line it with plastic bags."

Glynnis stopped on the stairs, looking horrified.

"Hey, I know it sounds gross, but it's the only way I can think of unless you want to squat outside."

Glynnis groaned and shook her head as she helped Peggy reach in and pull the chair out from the crowded hall closet. Peggy lifted it easily and carried it down the stairs. They dusted it off as best they could before placing it in the bathroom. Another candle was lit and set on a plate, which they set in the middle of the deep porcelain bathtub so they could see where they were going should they need to get up and use the makeshift toilet in the middle of the night.

Peggy went back upstairs to pull the paper-thin sheets off her bed. It took her a few tries to open the stuck window. Finally the window gave, and she vigorously shook out the sheets. She also took a couple of sweaters out of their suitcases with which to bundle up. Returning to the living room, she blew out the oil lamp, as the light from the fire was more than enough. They each took an end of the large couch, falling asleep within minutes. Peggy woke up a few hours later to stack more wood in the fireplace. The living room was so warm that they shed their sweaters and immediately fell back to sleep. In the morning, they awoke to the sound of knocking at the front door.

Chapter Thirty

Montana, Spring 1998

RICH SAT AT THE END of the bar, casually observing his wait staff in action. They were a good group, very efficient, thanks to his diligent efforts. They often joked with him, telling him that he was obsessive-compulsive. His psychiatrist later confirmed the layman diagnosis, and recommended medication to alleviate the disorder. Rich declined. It was his business, his life, and he'd run it the way he wanted. His doctor advised him to lessen some of the pressure and stress in his life, suggesting he take a vacation in order to relax.

"Enjoy it while you can."

Rich lived in California, and it hadn't taken him too long to figure out that money was to be made catering to Irish-Americans longing for nostalgia. He'd opened several authentic Irish pubs with menus featuring basic fish and chips with vinegar. The food was purposely wrapped in newspaper like they did at home in Ireland. It became his trademark and, after he was written up in several local papers, and then national culinary magazines, people flocked to his pubs.

His most recent venture was in New York, and Rich found himself flying across the country a couple of times a month to monitor the opening and management of the new pub there. He visited for only a few days at a time, as he had to get back to California for business and doctor's appointments.

Rich had rules, lots of them. Employees were given explicit instructions on how to wash their hands after each and every meal they served. Tables shouldn't just be wiped down with a damp cloth; they were to be disinfected with a bleach-type cleanser using rubber gloves. Glasses were never to be left in the sink, but washed immediately after each use, by hand — no dishwasher.

He was meticulous with the liquor shelf. Bottles were displayed according to height, not brand or type. New bartenders who couldn't adjust, or complained excessively about his system, were shown the door. It made no sense to some of the employees, who remarked behind his back that all these rules were coming from a man who'd made his fortune by serving fried fish in newspaper!

His office was simple, yet sterile. It contained just the basic necessities, a chair, a desk, one telephone, a lamp, and a filing cabinet. Two sharpened pencils and two blue .5 millimeter pens occupied a cup holder next to the right-hand corner of his phone. His correspondence was arranged in neat rows and organized piles. Coins were evenly stacked according to denomination, and his filing cabinet was locked at all times. He always felt that someone was out to screw him.

Each morning he'd set his keys on a hook in his office and turn the key ring notched-side down so that each of his two keys would settle evenly into the metal nook and not jingle. He'd remove his shoes at the door, lining them up symmetrically along the edge of the floor mat.

He always sat when he urinated, wiping himself clean afterward. He would finish by tearing off exactly one new sheet of toilet paper from the roll, folding it in fourths to flush the toilet, making sure his fingers never touched the handle. With that task out of the way, he'd stand to adjust himself, taking great care to comfortably line up his appendage with the seam in his underwear. He was then free to center his belt buckle so that it was perfectly aligned with the top button of his pants. The entire bathroom process would end with an elaborate five-minute hand washing ritual.

With the precision of a surgeon, he'd work up a thick lather, turning the soap over and over in his hands — fifty times. He'd count. Then he'd cover himself in lather up to his elbows. Rinsing was done by turning his hands inward and moving his arms from side to side making sure the water cleared his hands, wrists, and forearms. He'd shut the water off using his elbow, and dry his hands with three paper towels, using a fourth one to open the door, which he'd hold open with his shoe as he threw the paper towel away in the wastebasket that had been placed next to the bathroom door for that purpose.

Sitting at the bar, exhausted, Rich sought to derive some pleasure from a pint of Guinness as he tried to figure out what was wrong with his brother, while dreaming about escaping to his Montana homestead.

*   *   *

He was stunned to learn that his only brother, a priest, had been assigned to rural Montana. At first, he felt somewhat reluctant to meet for a visit. After some persistent prompting on Rob's part, Rich conceded and agreed to meet him for a quick visit.

Rich's flight landed in Great Falls, and his brother met him at the airport, giving him a friendly, yet awkward, handshake. Rich had been relieved to see him dressed in regular clothing and not sporting his priestly frock. On the drive back to the rectory, Rich fell in love with the country-side. It was a part of America he'd never seen before.

The 1996 journey to his brother's remote church revealed some of the most beautiful terrain he'd ever seen — so rural, still much of it untouched. One could drive for miles without seeing any signs of human life. The majestic mountain ranges commanded respect, and imposing views could be had from every vantage point.

It was Rob who suggested a short camping trip, proposing they explore Glacier National Park. Rich was unprepared for the splendor the treasured land held. They rented horses and followed a trail called Soaring Eagle Falls. They spotted elk along the way and stopped to quietly observe a black bear as it slapped about the water's edge, hunting fish. Further up the river, they decided to stop and camp for the night.

During the next morning's jaunt, they came upon a deserted cabin. Located near the Blackfoot Indian Reservation, the structure was desolate and looked like a throwback from the 1800s. Rich got off his horse and walked around the property. The mountain views were spectacular. The land on which the cabin stood backed up to a very steep mountain range. It was many miles from civilization. Rich wondered how much land the house actually sat on. Rob had no idea, but said that people out in these parts usually owned considerable acreage.

Rich peered in the windows. It was a simple, large, one-room log cabin, with two windows in the front, a fireplace and a loft. The stone fireplace was the central focal point of the home. He could see a roughly carved table and two chairs. The floor was plank wood. There was a small alcove built into the corner of the room, containing space enough for a single bed, and what looked like either a makeshift couch or bench along the wall. No appliances were visible; the sink held a hand-crank spout. Rich thought it may have belonged to the reservation at one time, or was perhaps used as a shelter for hikers or campers. There was no bathroom, though there was a dilapidated outhouse, and no signs of electricity that he could see. He walked around to the back again. There was a stream not too far from the house where the water was crystal clear and seemed to be drinkable. He decided to inquire about the property when they reached the Blackfoot Indian Reservation.

The ride to the reservation took another few hours by horseback. Rich talked about the cabin and how perfect it would be if he could buy it, wondering if it was even available to purchase. Rob cautioned him about making an impulsive decision.

"You only live once."

Rich replied.

He'd always wanted a secluded place to which he could escape, a refuge where he could collect his thoughts. It would be just what the doctor ordered, a perfect retreat.

Upon arriving at the reservation, Rich spoke to a man whose name was Running Deer, who knew of the property they described and confirmed that it had been vacant for a number of years. It belonged to a man on the reservation. To the best of his knowledge, "anything" was available for purchase; the people of the reservation led a simple life and many were poor. He could put him in touch with the owner, Chris Bassett, reminding them that, due to its remote location, the cabin was inaccessible by car. Rich nodded and thanked him. To him, that was the beauty of the place.

Located, at least, fifteen miles in from any main road, the only way to get there was by horseback. An off-road type vehicle could drive within a few miles of the site; however, a horse would still be required to get through the rocky pass and swollen rivers and springs that dotted the landscape. Running Deer wrote down Chris Bassett's name and telephone number for Rich and pointed out the reservation's only public pay phone, located just outside the general store. The brothers asked where they might camp for the night. Running Deer, with his hands lifted in a way that looked like worship, turned around slowly in a complete circle.

"All of this is bestowed to mankind. The stars are your guide. You may find rest where they lead you."

Rob and Rich looked at one another and shrugged. Thanking Running Deer, they made their way to the general store to use the phone.

Rich heard the phone ring several times before anyone picked up. A raspy woman's voice asked him to wait while she went to find her husband. His voice was deep and calm.

"This is Chris."

Rich introduced himself and summarized the reason for his call. He told Chris of his interest in the property at the base of the mountain and asked if it was for sale.

Chris confirmed that the property was negotiable and offered to take the ride out with him and his brother in the morning. When Chris asked him where they were staying Rich mimicked.

"Wherever the stars lead us..."

Chris was silent as Rich explained Running Deer's comment about the stars.

"Actually, we brought our camping gear and were just going to pitch a tent somewhere close by for the night."

Chris told him that they were welcome to sleep in his barn that evening if they wished, and that he'd come and get them in the morning. His wife would make them an early breakfast before they started out. Rich thanked him for his gracious offer and accepted.

The three men rose an hour before dawn, and were treated to a hearty breakfast of bacon, sausage, eggs, and toast before they left for the cabin. They mounted on horseback just as the sky began to lighten, the sun's golden rays visible beyond the dark mountaintops.

Having lived in Montana all his life, Chris knew the land well. He chose a different route back to the cabin than the one Rich and Rob had come in on the day before. The new trail was, if possible, even more scenic, and he hoped the panoramic views would further entice them to purchase his grandfather's shack.

The sale of the old property couldn't come at a better time for Chris. His wife was expecting their fourth child, and he could really use the money. He'd let it go for well below market value if need be. He was stretched each year just to pay the taxes on it.

They'd stopped along the way to let the horses drink from the streams, and he pointed out the vegetation and animals that populated the area. Asked by Rich if he'd ever seen a grizzly, Chris laughed and told them that he'd be surprised if they didn't see one in their travels that day.

"They are a force to be reckoned with."

He warned them.

"It's best never to come upon them suddenly or try to get too close. This isn't Jellystone."

He advised Rich that if he had any pets it would be best to keep them inside at night, given the coyotes, wolves, and mountain lions that roamed the area. As they were meandering through a large field, Chris pointed out a stone pillar, which he explained marked the boundary of the homestead. They were still an hour's ride from the cabin.

The property being sold with the cabin totaled five hundred acres. Rich couldn't even comprehend how much land that was. It seemed endless to him, almost like possessing his own little country. He listened intently to Chris's explanations, asking many questions.

Rob rode behind silently, lulled by the rhythmic pace of the horses, lost in his own thoughts. Scanning the fields, Chris told Rich that if he did any digging or surveying of the land, not to be surprised if he came across bits and pieces of pottery. He explained how this area of the country was an archaeologist's dream. Shards of ancient Indian pottery littered the fields. Authentic, intact pieces brought in a handsome amount of money for many of his people on the reservation. If Rich unearthed anything, he could either keep it for himself, or let Chris know and he could find a dealer to sell it for him.

"So you're telling me I'm buying a giant potter's field?"

Rich laughed.

"In a sense, you are!"

Rich looked back for Rob, who'd stopped for nature's call. They waited and then forged ahead, approaching the cabin around noon. Chris unlocked the door and walked inside. He was quiet while Rich and Rob looked around. There wasn't much to see in the one, large room cabin, but Rich inspected everything. He ran his hand along the table and got a splinter. His brother headed cautiously up the rickety ladder to check out the loft. It was a fairly large space where you could put more beds if needed. He stood under the rafters looking down on the two men.

"You get another perspective from up here."

Rich climbed the ladder, and both men sat on the edge, letting their legs dangle over the side.

"I'm buying it."

Rich announced.

"How are you going to get to this place, I mean, to make it even livable? Aren't you use to all the comforts of home?"

"Yeah, but this will keep me humble. Besides, I won't change too much. The outside will remain as it is. I'll just have to figure out how to get things up here, but I'll manage. Give me a few months, and I'll have it all put together."

He looked around and mapped out the space in his head. *I will find a way to get a modern bathroom and running water in here. I'm not contending with any snakes in the outhouse!*

Rob hung back while Rich and Chris talked about the details of the deal. The place was going for a song, given the huge amount of land that came with it. Rich could well afford to dump some serious money into the place, adding a few upgrades and comforts, but he'd leave the fairly rustic appearance, as that was what gave it charm. Chris told them they were welcome to stay the night in the cabin. He'd come back with the papers in the morning for Rich to take back with him to California. The two men shook hands. The deal was done.

*   *   *

He stared mindlessly down into his almost empty glass, watching the tiny air bubbles fizzle to the top and disappear. He'd gotten a call from Rob late last night, but couldn't exactly recall all the details of the conversation. Rob told him that their Uncle Alan had passed away in Ireland. It was obvious to him that Rob had been drinking. He'd rambled on about how they'd all be out to get him now. Rich didn't know who "they" were, and in all honesty, he didn't really care. In some ways, he still harbored both disgust and apathy toward his younger sibling.

Rich had stumbled upon the knowledge that his only brother was gay when they were teenagers. He'd opened the door to their bedroom only to find one of the neighborhood boys in a compromising position with Rob. It sickened him. He'd never forget that scene. It was the first time he'd run away from home and was gone for months.

Rich was hardly a religious man himself, but still felt that it was sinful for Rob to even think about entering the priesthood. Rich had tormented his brother as a child and blackmailed him throughout their adolescent life, threatening to expose him to their mother and friends whenever it suited his purpose. Maybe that was why he'd been handed this fatal affliction — as his punishment for that torture.

He sensed all along that no good would come of Rob being a priest, and often wondered how he'd managed to stay in the order for as long as he had.

Rich's many years of drinking and carousing had finally caught up with him. His recent cancer diagnosis was unsettling. He was glad, however, that over the last two years, he'd at least tried to mend fences with his younger brother. According to his doctor, his death was certain. He was getting his business and financial affairs in order. He still hadn't told Rob about his diagnosis. He'd explain it to him in person on his next visit. Only his business partner knew the extent of his illness, and he'd been sworn to secrecy.

Rich felt no emotional connection with Rob, despite the time they'd recently spent together. He'd bought the place in Montana a few years ago with the intention of using it as a peaceful getaway when he needed to regroup and take stock of his life. He'd hoped that the cabin might provide an opportunity for him and his brother to work out their differences. He'd soon realized, however, that those differences were probably too great to overcome in his shortened lifetime. Too much time had passed and too many memories still haunted him.

Since they'd gotten older, they were different, estranged. Shame had divided and conquered each of their lives in different ways. Perversion had carved its path deep into Rob's life, and Rich sensed his brother was on the road to destruction. Rich decided he didn't want to get to know Rob any better for fear of what he might discover. It was painful and awkward when they did meet. Their encounters silently forced them to come face-to-face with their shared past, and the humiliation and degradation of their father's abuse. It made both men very uneasy. The only way they were able to speak freely with one another was when they were drinking. Even then, neither spoke comfortably about what happened when they were kids. But it was always there, looming in the recesses of their broken and depleted hearts. Their lives, "a cross to carry," Rob once remarked sarcastically.

In the beginning, Rich trekked back and forth between California and Montana frequently to his cabin retreat. He paid his contractor through the nose and pushed him hard to get it all done quickly. The contractor hired a work crew of twenty-five illegal immigrants to haul in the materials for plumbing, and heavy generator equipment to provide electricity for the well pump. Rich gave the workmen stern warnings to dig carefully.

It was during the excavation for the septic system that they discovered several pieces of pottery still intact. Rich kept them all. After gently cleansing what he felt might have been water jugs, he set one on either end of his floor-to-ceiling stone fireplace. The two remaining pieces, plates, were also delicately cleansed, and placed on the mantle piece. It was a natural setting for the earthenware, and they blended perfectly in the rustic cabin.

The fireplace and a coal-burning stove heated the house. The hurricane lamps, when lit, gave off more than enough light in the evening, and with the installation of a new picture window, sunlight streamed in most of the day. He hadn't any time to waste. Rich enjoyed every phase of the construction.

Hurricane lamps were mounted to the inside beams and walls on both sides of the cabin. Another was placed outside, a few feet from the front door, as he didn't want the bugs, which were attracted to the light at night, getting into the house. He'd accumulated a good year's supply of lamp oil, which was stored in the freshly carved cabinets. The new coal-burning stove would be stocked with coal from one of the local mines in the region, and the large surface area could be used for cooking. A huge kettle was kept on top, which he used to make tea. He had additional cabinets mounted for dishes and cups.

The plumbing and septic design cost a fortune. He had wind turbines shipped in and assembled to generate electricity. An addition was added which contained another room and new bathroom. He had the carpenters sand down and shellac the original table and chairs left with the property. Insulation had been added underneath the floorboards, which were filled in, sanded down, and shellacked to match the other furniture in the house. Trees that were close to the cabin had been cut down, the logs sized, and the wood stacked in a shed built just for the purpose of sheltering it from the elements. The local loggers warned him to watch for snakes when gathering the wood in the warmer months, since they liked to make their homes in woodpiles.

A large picture window, which had been added on the backside of the house, showed off a panoramic view of both the river and mountains. Rich also had the carpenter build two beds into the loft and had a sturdy, permanent staircase attached to the rafters leading up to it. He used woven Indian blankets bought from the reservation as area rugs on the floors of both the main cabin and the loft.

Finally, Rich asked to use Chris's address, to have a couple of final furniture pieces delivered. He'd picked out a comfortable couch and chair and had a couple of new mattresses delivered for the single beds in the loft.

He asked Chris to hire some men on his behalf to haul it out to the cabin. It looked quite homey when it was done, and Rich found it a therapeutic respite from the demands of his business life.

He'd come back on many occasions, not bothering to notify his brother of his arrival. He just wanted some time to himself. But his energy and his quality of life were quickly deteriorating, and before long he wouldn't be strong enough to make the trek out by way of horseback any longer. On his next journey, he'd meet his brother at the cabin and inform him of his fatal medical condition and his plans concerning the homestead.

Chapter Thirty-One

Cariston, England, Fall 1978

PEGGY JUMPED AT THE SOUND of knocking at the front door. She shoved Glynnis to wake her up.

"Someone's here! What do we do?"

Her face held a panicked look.

Glynnis shot up, trying to run her fingers through her matted hair.

"Well, answer it. Remember what my da said. You're not in any trouble."

Peggy reached for her sweater. She didn't even remember taking it off, but the house had grown chilly with the fire nearly out. Cautiously, she opened the front door.

A small, portly gentleman smiled at her.

"Good morning, miss. I got your note on the door when I went to open the store this morning. I've come to collect my wheelbarrow. I need to deliver some wood to a customer."

Peggy felt the tension ease as she smiled at the kindly man, and apologized.

"I'm sorry, sir. I planned on bringing it back this morning. We got in late last night, and needed wood for the fireplace. I saw the wheelbarrow and hoped you wouldn't mind my borrowing it. The wood was just too heavy for us to carry home. I hope you understand."

She felt badly that he had to come out to the house to pick it up.

The little man smiled at her and assured her that it was fine.

"Thank you for leaving a note. Some of my customers take off with it, and I don't see it for days on end. It always winds up back at the store, but I was grateful to locate it so quickly this time. Well, I must be going. Thank you again for your patronage."

Peggy and Glynnis followed him down the steps and unloaded the remaining logs, carrying them into the house. Peggy immediately stoked the fire and placed more wood on the fading embers.

"Well, that certainly woke me up."

Glynnis remarked, yawning.

"Oh yes! Happy Birthday by the way. You're finally legal!"

"Thanks! I don't feel any different being 18."

Both girls took turns using the makeshift potty in the bathroom. They brushed their teeth and washed up with the bottled water. Peggy started planning.

"First things first. I say we head into town and get some breakfast, then off to the store for some cleaning supplies. I'll call the utility companies from the pay phone when we're done shopping."

It was a brisk morning, and the girls walked quickly into town. The streets were coming alive as they entered the café and ordered tea and eggs with toast. They devoured their meal and used the bathroom.

"I never thought I'd be so grateful to hear the sound of flushing water."

Peggy joked.

They whisked through the store, picking up ammonia, lilac scented floor cleaner, trash bags, bleach, rubber gloves, and carpet freshener. They needed wood polish for the furniture and a special cleaner for the hard wood floors, along with lots of paper towels and window cleaner. They bought a bucket, a mop, sponges, and rags. When they approached the checkout counter, their morning wake-up man was, once again, smiling at them.

"You've a lot of work to do back there, I see. How long have you been gone?"

Peggy shifted uncomfortably, not knowing how to answer.

"I've been gone for about 4 years now. Today is my 18th birthday."

The man smiled sympathetically and looked surprised. He remembered the young girl who often came in with her uncle. The entire town was enraged to hear of his brutal attack against his young niece. Frank's heart went out to the beautiful young woman standing before him.

"Well, I'm glad you are back and are well, Margaret. Welcome home, and I'm sorry for your troubles. Happy Birthday by the way! What a nice way to start off the week. If you'd like to take the wheelbarrow again to cart all of this home, you're welcome to it. If you need more wood, I can drop it off for you tonight."

He offered.

Peggy was taken back by the man's kindness and for his recollection of her birth name.

"Thank you. I don't know what to say. You can call me Peggy. I will probably need the use of that wheelbarrow again at some point! I'm going to call the utility companies now and see about getting everything turned back on so I can settle in more comfortably."

The man ushered her around the counter and wrote out the numbers for the various companies, telling her to go ahead and use his phone in the back office. He offered to load up their items in the wheelbarrow while they made their calls. Peggy and Glynnis thanked him.

"What a nice man he is."

Glynnis observed.

Peggy sat at the desk and called the telephone company. After a brief explanation of events, the company scheduled someone to go out there by Wednesday to check the connection and turn on the telephone. That was only two days away.

The electric company was another story. It took her fifteen minutes and four transfers to reach the man who'd eventually take pity on her and put in an emergency request.

"You mean you're living in the house with no electricity now?"

He asked.

"Yes, sir, and it's getting cold and dark early."

The man assured her that he'd get someone out there by three o'clock that afternoon, telling her that she should plan to be there to let them in. She assured him that she'd not leave the house until they arrived.

With that task done, the next call was to the water company. She once again explained her story.

The customer service representative asked a number of questions; she confirmed her uncle's name and explained that he was deceased. The woman apologized and told her she'd put a rush on the service call and that they should have running water by morning, explaining that the serviceman would have to come into the house and inspect the pipes before turning on the main line from the street. Peggy thanked her for her prompt response.

The other remaining task was to make sure there was oil in the tank. She walked back into the store.

"Sir, by the way, if it's not too forward of me, what is your name?"

The man held out his hand.

"Frank Doucette. Please call me Frank. You probably don't remember me."

Peggy smiled.

"Thank you, Frank. It was a long time ago. Listen, do you happen to have the name of a local oil company? I don't know what's in the tank at my house, or if it's even advisable to use it after all these years of it just sitting there. I think they'll have to do a major cleaning and servicing before I chance it."

Frank reached for a magnet on his note board.

"Here, this is the oil company I use. Let me call them for you. I know a few people there and they typically respond very quickly. I'll see what I can do for you. I've got your address here on this piece of paper."

Peggy was grateful to let him take care of the matter for her. She listened while he talked on the phone.

"Judy? Good morning. This is Frank Doucette ... yes, yes. No she's fine ... we're all well. Thank you. Listen, Judy, I was hoping you might be able to help a friend of mine. A lovely young lady has just moved back into the neighborhood after having been away for a while. She's getting her house back in order and has yet to try the furnace."

He cupped his hand over the mouthpiece and whispered to Peggy.

"How long has it been since the furnace was last used?

Peggy held up four fingers.

"Judy, she says it's been about four years. Well, I'll give you the address and let her know not to touch it until someone gets out there. If you can, could you make this a priority call? I mean, the poor thing is in the house and had to sleep in her sweater all evening. Thanks, Judy. I'll let her know you'll have someone out today. Thank you very much."

Frank gave Judy Peggy's address.

"THANK YOU, JUDY!!!"

Both Glynnis and Peggy chimed in unison.

Frank replaced the receiver.

"Well, I guess you'd best get home now. You've quite a few people visiting you today. Here's my card for the store. Let me know if you need anything else, and I can run it up. Would you like me to put this on your account, Peggy?"

Peggy gave him a funny look.

"But I don't have an account with you."

Frank nodded his head.

"You do now. You're part of the neighborhood!"

Peggy felt uncomfortable, and offered to pay for the purchase right then.

"Not to worry. I'll send you a bill at the end of the month."

Peggy hesitantly put her money back in her pocket. She'd never had an account anywhere before and was feeling pretty grown-up. She walked out of the store with a smile on her face.

"Well! Isn't that just lovely? *Just put in on my account, daahling...*"

Glynnis good-naturedly joked.

"Oh, be quiet, you."

Peggy chided, chuckling at her friend's snobby imitation.

The girls were grateful to Frank for all his help, and for the use, once again, of his wheelbarrow. They took turns pushing it back to the house. As they were unloading the items, a police car pulled up with flashing lights. Two guards got out of the car.

"May we help you, ladies?"

Peggy had expected their visit, and was strangely calm.

"Thank you, officer. My name is Peggy O'Malley and this is my friend, Glynnis. This is my house. I returned here last night."

The officers motioned for the girls to stay put for a moment while one guard went back to the car to call in her name. He was gone for almost ten minutes.

When he returned, he stated.

"Ms. O'Malley, if you don't mind, we've a few questions we need to ask you."

Peggy motioned for them to follow her into the house as she pulled out her key. They helped pick up the remaining grocery bags, assisting her into the house and setting the bags on the floor while they looked around.

"You haven't seen any signs of occupants or forced entry, have you?"

Peggy shook her head.

"No. As a matter of fact, I kind of feared we'd be fighting squatters."

The officers told her.

"No, we've been keeping watch over this house for years. We've been waiting and hoping your uncle might return. He's still a fugitive and wanted on serious charges, which is why we want to speak with you."

Peggy offered them a seat, apologizing.

"I'm sorry I can't even offer you anything to drink. I'm just getting settled back in."

They assured her that they wouldn't take up much of her time.

"Ms. O'Malley, do you remember Officer Laura Campbell?"

Peggy recalled the protective woman who was by her hospital bedside years before, just days after the beating. It was all a blur.

"Not all that much, but I remember she was kind to me when I was in the hospital."

The officers took a moment to fill her in.

"Ms. O'Malley, Ms. Campbell has had us watching this house on regular daily patrol with hopes that either he'd return, so we could arrest him, or that you'd return one day and be able to help us locate him. We're hoping you can do that now."

Peggy sat and offered what she could.

"I don't know where my uncle is. I just got here last night."

Glynnis pulled up a chair next to her friend.

"When I was released from the hospital, I was immediately placed in a children's home. The people there were hostile, and the oldest boy was always putting his hands on all the girls. He'd gone further with some ..."

Her voice trailed off.

The officers knew it was uncomfortable for her, and were sympathetic to the lovely young woman explaining her own disappearance years before.

"Ms. O'Malley, we know this is difficult for you. You ran away from the home. Where did you go when you left?"

She looked at her friend Glynnis who spoke up.

"She came to Ireland and basically was homeless for a few years. Recently, she's lived with me and my family."

The officers assured them they weren't in any trouble. According to their records, the girl just turned eighteen. Laura would, no doubt, stop by to talk with Miss O'Malley herself at some point.

"Can you tell us where you think your uncle might have gone and fled to?"

Peggy was at a loss. The last correspondence from her mother had come from Australia. She knew the address might be somewhere in the house.

"My mom left me with my uncle when I was very young. She went to Australia ... that's all I know. There may be an address around here somewhere, but I don't know where to begin to look for it. I've not even begun to unpack and clean yet."

The officers apologized for the unexpected visit.

"Ms. O'Malley, if you don't mind, Constable Campbell will probably want to speak with you sometime over the next few days. May we tell her it's all right to stop by?"

Peggy nodded.

"That would be fine, and thank you – for keeping an eye on the place."

The older officer spoke up first.

"Your uncle committed a brutal crime against you as a child, Peggy. Aggravated rape and assault with intent to kill are not minor charges. He's a felon on the run from the law. We want to find and prosecute him."

Peggy's blood went cold. She looked pale, and Glynnis held her hand.

"Peg, don't worry. My da will be here in a few days. He'll help you out."

Glynnis looked up at the officers.

"My father is an attorney. He's offered to help Peggy in whatever way he can."

The officers left her with their names and phone numbers and told her to call them when she found her mother's Australian address.

"I'm glad that's over with. I guess he's in a lot of trouble still, huh?"

Peggy exhaled after they left. She was shaking.

Glynnis retorted.

"I hope they find the bastard and kill him!"

Peggy winced at the severity of her words.

"You know what, Glynn? This might sound really strange to you, but I really loved my uncle. Not in the perverse way he loved me, of course, but he was all I had as a child. I didn't understand why he tried to hurt me or why he wanted me the way he did."

Peggy started to cry.

"I didn't do anything to entice him."

Glynnis held Peggy.

"Shhh, I know. He was sick, Peg. He didn't think like a normal man. Grown men aren't supposed to have sex with children! It's not right. He violated YOU, abused you when you were young and vulnerable — and dependent on him. He should have known better. And piss on your mother for leaving you as well! The bitch ... I hope they get the both of them!"

Peggy cried on her friend's shoulder.

"I'm sorry for saying 'piss on your mother'. I just get angry thinking that a parent could just up and abandon her child and never want to see her again. What's wrong with people, Peg?"

Peggy stared blankly out the window.

"I don't know."

She got up suddenly at another knock on the door. The electric company had arrived with a bucket truck, and was busy working on the lines outside her house. She directed the man with the electric torch in hand to the basement.

The girls were unloading some of the cleaning supplies when an odd humming sound echoed through the house. A few of the lights flickered, and then went off again. The man hollered up.

"Did anything come on?"

Glynnis yelled down the stairs.

"Yes! But only for a moment! Now they're off again."

She heard him swear.

"Blew a fuse ... hold on."

He wiped the cobwebs off his shirt as he walked back up the stairs.

"I need to get something out of the truck."

The girls set about putting a cleaning plan in place.

"Well, I think we should work together, room by room. Let's start here in the kitchen."

Glynnis moaned at the thought of emptying the fridge. Both girls stood before the door, afraid to open it.

"Go ahead."

Glynnis urged Peggy.

Reluctantly she opened the door. To her wonder and surprise, there was nothing in there.

"Who would have emptied the fridge?"

They looked at each other with relief.

"Maybe it was that woman constable they mentioned ... Laura?"

Peggy shrugged.

"Well, let's get to work in here first, then we'll tackle the bathroom."

They worked diligently and meticulously as a team, tackling the kitchen. Everything needed scrubbing.

Not five minutes after they'd started, there was another knock at the door. It was the man from the water company. He couldn't do anything, however, until the power came back on, as the water pump required electricity. He followed the man from the electric company down to the basement to wait.

Within a few minutes, the humming sound was back, and the lights stayed on without flickering. A radio blared out from the living room, and Peggy, startled, ran over to shut it off. It was still set to her favorite rock station.

The man from the electric company showed her the burnt out fuse he'd replaced, and left her with another brand new one in a box. He advised Peggy.

"You might want to pick up a few of these at the ironmonger's to keep on hand."

She took the box from him, thanking him. He sat at the table and took out a form for her to sign, and asked if she was able to make the first month's payment. She reached for her new wallet and handed him cash and signed the form. He signed after her and gave her a receipt. Her first bill in her own name ... it was a start.

The man from the water company was downstairs swearing. Peggy and Glynnis were trying hard not to laugh too loudly at his language.

"Are you all right down there?"

Peggy yelled.

"Yeah, the handle is just stuck. When was the last time this was turned on?"

"Four years ago!"

"GRAND!"

He replied sarcastically.

Peggy set about wiping down the kitchen cabinets. They were filthy, and the counter tops were littered with mouse droppings.

"This is disgusting!"

Peggy grimaced.

Glynnis called out from on her knees in the bathroom.

"I know, but we'll get it done. Make sure you use the rubber gloves."

She threw a plastic package at Peggy. Both girls jumped at the loud thumping and squeaking of the old pipes.

"TRY THE COLD WATER!"

Commanded a voice from the basement.

Peggy went to the kitchen sink and turned on the faucet. The water sputtered and spit out a black mud-like substance.

"Oh, gross!"

She jumped back from the sink too late. It had splattered on her new sweater.

"This is turning into an ordeal, I'll tell you."

She reached for the paper towels to try and remove the mess from her sweater.

The man trudged up the stairs.

"Best leave it running for a while. Is there water in the toilet?"

Glynnis, emerging from the bathroom, shook her head.

"Dry as a bone."

He walked toward the bathroom and the girls quickly expressed embarrassment about the potty chair. He didn't seem to care and moved it easily out of the way in order to manually fill the tank.

"I need a bucket."

The girls stepped aside. The water flowing in the kitchen sink was black. The man said it would take a day for it to run completely clear, advising them to drink bottled water until then.

He gave them a couple of new washers for the faucets, and showed the girls how to install them. He then hauled a bucket of dirty water into the bathroom and filled up the toilet tank and the bowl. When he flushed, the pipes sounded like they were strained and about to burst, but the water went down, albeit very slowly. He assured them that that was a good sign. He flushed a second time, and the water went down quicker.

"You may have to manually fill it a few times until the water pressure comes back up. I'd give it a few hours before you try it again. Just add water each time and you can flush. It'll fill up on its own eventually. Call back if you need anything else. You'll be hearing a lot of noises. Nothing to worry about, just some remaining air in the pipes working itself out."

The girls thanked him. They felt good! It was only eleven o'clock in the morning, and they already had water, albeit dirty, and electricity. Peggy said a quiet prayer of thanks. All they needed now was the oil company, gas company, and British Telecom to turn on the phone.

The afternoon flew by. The girls turned the radio back on full volume and danced through the living room. Peggy found the vacuum and began to suck up the seemingly endless cobwebs and mouse droppings. They were everywhere. She tied a handkerchief over her nose and mouth so as not to breathe in the dust as she vacuumed the furniture. She struggled to open the old windows and let fresh air circulate through the rooms. It was chilly out, but they were working up a sweat and the cool air felt good.

"I better get some mouse traps. What do you think?"

She asked Glynnis as she dumped the contents from the dustpan into a trash bag.

"Well, I like the cat idea better. Then you don't have to see the critters or touch them!"

"Where am I going to get a cat?"

Peggy asked.

"We'll find one. Not to worry. We can go to the animal shelter."

The girls took down all the old, faded curtains and threw them out.

"I'll get new ones, eventually. We'll just have to pull the shades for now."

Together they set about cleaning the windows. Peggy took the inside and Glynnis worked the outside. They moved quickly and efficiently. The kitchen was done and sparkling, and the water was beginning to run a little clearer, more steel gray than black but still nowhere near drinkable.

The bathroom sink and tub had been disgusting before Glynnis started scrubbing with bleach and a vengeance. They vacuumed and washed the wood floors with a solution that smelled like pine. They rolled up all of the area rugs and moved them outside to vacuum and let sit over the railing to air out for a while.

Moving upstairs, they started in Peggy's room. They immediately pulled the curtains off the windows. The remaining linens were stripped from the bed and thrown away, along with the old pillows. They vacuumed the floor, and the two of them struggled to drag the mattress outside to air it out. They set about polishing the furniture, leaving a pleasant lemon scent lingering in the room.

The guest room across the hall received the same treatment. The front porch, crowded with mattresses and rugs, was getting more than a few stares from passersby wondering what was going on in the long-vacated house.

"You're going to need new sheets and pillows."

Glynnis noted.

"I know."

Peggy nodded.

"Let's head into London tomorrow. I'd like some new curtains for these rooms also. Something cheerful."

Glynnis took charge as they moved their cleaning equipment down the hall toward her uncle's room and study.

"Okay, downstairs with you! I told you I'd take care of this room."

Peggy put her hands on her hips.

"No, no, Glynn. You don't have to do this. It's my responsibility."

Glynnis was adamant.

"It's no big deal to me, but I know how hard it is for you."

Peggy acknowledged her discomfort with the room in its current state. Seeing the bed made her shudder. But she held on to quiet resolve, telling herself it was over and feeling a sense of conquest since she now owned the house.

"I've an idea. Why don't we just get rid of this bed altogether and move the settee from the study in here, and I'll make this my art room. I'll make it a place of beauty and creativity once I get it painted and spruced up!"

Glynnis thought that a great idea, and she admired Peggy for her courage and positive frame of mind. They set to work breaking down the bed. They dragged yet another mattress downstairs and out on to the front porch.

"I need to find out when the garbage truck comes around here. Do you think they'll take all this junk we're throwing out?"

Peggy asked.

"They'll take a small Volkswagen if you give them a few pounds."

Glynnis remarked.

The girls were on the front steps when the large oil truck pulled up in front of the house. A good-looking young man climbed out and asked if he'd found the O'Malley residence. Peggy told him he had, and she led him inside and down to the basement. Peggy told him that she had no idea what condition the furnace was in, but was sure it needed a thorough cleaning after so many years of unuse.

"Everything else needed cleaning in this place!"

She exclaimed.

"Well, it doesn't look so bad at first pass."

He commented offhandedly as he looked around quickly with the handheld light.

"I'll leave you to assess the damage."

Peggy went back upstairs leaving him to work in the cellar.

Glynnis told Peggy to go and busy herself elsewhere in the house while she took the rest of her uncle's room apart. She closed the door to the room and opened the windows to air it out. She shivered — more from the history of the room than the chill.

Her first task was to collect all the dirty magazines. Angrily, she shoved the pornographic material into a dark heavy-duty plastic bag. She'd put them on the curb to go out with the other trash and stained mattresses. Next, she opened the closet door and gathered up all of the uncle's clothes. Glynnis searched through the pants, finding twenty pounds in one of his pockets. She'd inform Peggy of her lucky find. She then emptied the contents of his bureau drawers, which looked as though they'd been rifled through, no doubt by the authorities searching for clues to his whereabouts.

Glynnis opened the bedroom door and dragged the heavy bag downstairs and outside. She called to Peggy to come up and help her move the bureau across the hall. They both shimmied the heavy desk over from the study into the now vacant room. The yellowed shades were pulled from their brackets. They kept one to use to measure for new ones. Peggy wanted shades with scalloped edges like she'd seen in Glynnis's bedroom.

Finally, with the last of the vacuuming done, they washed the wood floors upstairs, making them shine. They wiped the upstairs mirrors and windows with glass cleaner, noting those few that were cracked or in need of repair.

"Maybe Frank at the general store can recommend someone to fix the window panes, a handyman of sorts."

At this point, the girls were exhausted and starving. The oilman trudged up from the basement complaining about how filthy the furnace had been.

"Never mind what I said before. It's the worst I've seen in years!"

"I'll try not to take offense to that!"

Peggy joked with the harried young man.

"Yes, well, it's clean now and seems to be in good working order. Not the oldest I've seen, but certainly the dirtiest."

He went outside and dragged the long hose from the oil truck over to the side of the house and began filling the tank. Upon returning indoors, he adjusted the thermostat and waited for the heat to kick on. A long, grinding noise erupted from the basement, and a spoon on the counter rattled slightly from the vibration.

"It'll take a little while for it to get cranking, but it will warm up soon."

A burning odor reached their nostrils.

Pointing to the vacuum he explained.

"You probably need to take that and Hoover the heating elements. That's just old dust you smell."

The girls set about sucking up the source of the dust smell. They were getting hot with all of the activity and asked the young man to actually turn the heat down a bit. So far, everything seemed to be functioning as it should.

After he left, the girls sat on the couch in the living room listening to the various strange sounds in the house. It was waking from its slumber. The baseboards played tunes. High-pitched pings and twangs echoed from various places around the house. The sounds brought back childhood memories. Peggy closed her eyes to rest for a while, and before she knew it, both she and Glynnis had fallen asleep.

When they awoke, it was dark outside. Peggy nudged Glynnis. The sound of the water running in the kitchen sink made them have to use the bathroom.

"You first."

Peggy handed Glynnis the bucket, filled with semi-clear water.

"Gee, thanks."

She took the heavy lid off the top of the tank and poured the water in.

"Hey, it's nearly full. Let's give this a try."

Glynnis pushed the handle and the toilet made normal gurgling sounds, then started to refill on its own.

"Oh, thank God!"

The girls laughed as Peggy turned to leave Glynnis to her business. She dragged the humbling potty chair out of the bathroom and left it by the back door to put out on trash day.

"I can't leave that on the front porch!"

She said aloud, snickering to herself.

Peggy lifted the receiver of the phone, momentarily forgetting there was no connection. The phone company would be there on Wednesday. The gas company was needed to get the stove hooked up. That should do it for bringing the house back to functioning normally.

"Well, all in all, it has been a very productive day, wouldn't you say? We've got water, electricity, and heat. I'm happy!"

She called in to Glynnis, who was washing her hands in the sink.

"Yep. Me too! I'm also starved. Let's say we get a pizza. I'm buying! There's still a little time left to celebrate your birthday!"

She proclaimed.

"That sounds good to me!"

Peggy hollered back.

The girls made their way up to the center of town to the pizza shop, and brought a few extra slices home with them, along with a couple of sodas.

"I love cold pizza in the morning, don't you?"

Glynnis asked as she put their dinner away in the refrigerator. The fridge was immaculate after Peggy had finished scrubbing it clean. The only items in there now were leftover pizza slices, bottled water, and soda. They'd need to do some food shopping soon. There was plenty of time to do that. They'd accomplished an amazing amount of work in just one full day. Both girls were determined to make it as livable and comfortable as possible. Then they could rest ...

They stayed up late, listening to the radio and talking about what they wanted to do the next day. Neither even thought to turn on the television. They slept in the living room again that evening, since there were still no clean sheets for the beds. They'd get new ones on Tuesday when they ventured into London by bus. They decided not to set the alarm figuring they needed their rest for the hard work ahead. Dozing off quickly, they slept soundly until nine fifteen the next morning.

Brilliant sunshine flooded the living room. The house was warm, and the water in the bathroom and kitchen, which they'd left running all night, was finally clear enough to drink and bathe. Both girls were eager to take showers. Peggy produced a new bar of lemon-scented soap from her suitcase, along with the melon-scented shampoo and conditioner she'd bought at Fiona's salon. They brought towels with them, and found a new set of sheets, still in the package, in the hallway closet.

"Great! All we have to do is wash them downstairs and we're all set. I still need another set, however – for your room."

Peggy mentioned to Glynnis.

They were excited for their shopping trip to London. Peggy needed new pillows for the beds, a couple of pretty bedspreads, some new cheerful curtains and scalloped shades for the upstairs bedrooms. She also wanted a couple of colorful area rugs for the bathroom, living room, and hallways. She needed a new laundry basket to carry clothes down to the washer and dryer in the basement, and a new hamper for her room, as the mice had eaten holes through the old wicker one.

"Listen, Peg, you could blow through a lot of money here. My da gave me money, and Mam told me to buy you a house gift and birthday present from them. So why not let me get the curtains, rugs, bedspreads and pillows for you, okay?"

Peggy was grateful and accepted her parents' generous offer.

"I'll write your mother and father a nice thank-you note. Please remind me to pick up stationary and extra pens while we're out, okay?"

"Are you kidding me? I've got my own list going on in my head! You better write it down, or we'll both forget!"

Peggy added the items to the list she was compiling. She did want to be careful with her money. She still had plenty left, but wanted to make it last until she found a job. Then she'd be all set for a while. All the utilities that were turned on were paid for a month ahead of time, and she felt confident she'd find work soon. Once her phone was turned on, she was going to start calling the people whose business cards she'd collected over the years and let them know she was starting her own painting and art business with the hopes of opening her own gallery one day.

She really didn't like the idea of using credit at the grocers, but wanted to show Frank she was trustworthy and build a friendly relationship with the local businesses in her neighborhood. She'd pay him off promptly and in full at the end of the week.

They got ready in record time, as they were anxious to get into town. They first went to talk to Frank about getting a handyman to fix the windows and finding someone who could cut away the mass of thorns and briars on the front and back lawns and mow the grass. The hedges were in desperate need of trimming and shaping as well.

Frank took notes, and Peggy inquired about garbage day.

"Ahhh, yes. That would be Thursday. They come this way around 7:00 a.m."

Frank was kind enough to answer their other questions, beginning with the handyman referral.

"Well, I've a few good ones I know and have used personally. PJ Johnson's son is still in school and a good, strong lad, about seventeen years old, I'd say. He could do the mowing and basic landscaping to clean up the front and back lawns. He'd like the work. I can call and ask for you. He's got his own mower and trimmers, too. His father can help with the replacement of those broken windows, and they could also cart away any old junk you're getting rid of too. Are all your utilities turned on yet?"

Peggy smiled and told him that everything was up and running for the most part except the telephone, and that she needed the gas company to come out and turn on the line in order for her to use her stove.

"Speaking of telephone, I'd better give my mam a call again."

Glynnis was prompted.

Frank told her to use the phone in his office.

"But it's to Ireland. It'll cost money."

Frank waved her off.

"Well, just don't talk for too long."

He then advised Peggy.

"British Telecom, well, they take their time fixing anything ... it shouldn't be too much longer. Feel free to use our phone again if they're not out by tomorrow. The gas company can be pretty responsive. Just call and tell them you moved back in and smell a gas leak. They'll be out in no time at all!"

Peggy laughed and thanked him once again for his help, and told him that, if PJ were available, any day that week would be fine with her to get started on the yard work and windows. Frank assured her he'd get someone over there to help her out.

"Thanks, Frank. We'll be back for a rather large food order later."

Peggy smiled.

"Write out a list and leave it with me. I can deliver it over to the house since you've no vehicle yet."

"You're amazing, Frank. Thank you so much. I'll get my list to you tomorrow - PROMISE!"

He waved to them out the window.

The girls waited at the end of the road for the bus. Frank had given them a copy of the bus schedule, and told them it ran, on weekdays, every hour on the hour up until eight in the evening. He told them to be careful in the city. They assured him they would.

They stopped at the café across the street from the bus stop for a croissant and a cup of coffee to go. They had fifteen minutes left before the bus arrived. Both young women were excited to be out and about.

With the heavy-duty cleaning behind them and creative decorating ahead, they looked forward to their city adventure.

It was a glorious day. Peggy was grateful for the sunshine, having her home back, and what seemed to be very caring neighbors. She was most grateful for her best friend, Glynnis. The girls locked arms as they walked across the street to wait for the bus.

Chapter Thirty-Two

Boston, Massachusetts, Spring 1998

"SHE'S ALWAYS LEAVING ME, Uncle Tim."

The childlike voice on the other end mewled.

"I hate it when she goes away. I don't like being alone."

Her voice kept rising in pitch until she finally broke into sobs.

Tim anxiously paced the floor.

"Caroline ..."

"She's going to leave me for good when she marries him. I know it's going to happen."

She choked out.

"In a way, it's good. You know why, Uncle Tim?"

Tim sighed sadly.

"Why, Caroline?"

There was a slight pause.

"Because then I don't have to protect her anymore. I let it happen, so she wouldn't have to go through it."

The phone went dead.

He stared in dismay at the silent receiver in his hand, and then stubbed out what must have been his third cigarette since his niece called him. There was something about the sound of her voice this time that he really didn't like.

"Sheila, I've got to head into Boston. The office called. I'll be back later."

He didn't wait for her response.

He felt like a heel lying to her and couldn't even think of what he'd say when she questioned him on his return. He thought to himself, *she's such an angel; she probably won't even ask.* Sheila trusted him completely. His wife was a gem, and he knew it. It pained him to keep secrets from her.

The drive into Boston was tedious. It was a two-hour trek on a day without traffic, due to the ever-changing traffic patterns. The Central Artery Project cut the city to ribbons. Getting *to* it, let alone *through* it, was a white-knuckle experience. According to reports, the driving wouldn't get any better for many years. The expressway expansion project was the most expensive ever undertaken in the country, but the plans were a mess, and it was already over budget. *No wonder taxes in Massachusetts are so high,* he thought as he fought to get ahead of a confused driver.

He had once known Boston like the back of his hand. He prided himself on being a veteran of the city. Even with the detours and one-ways, he was familiar with the side streets and back roads. That evening, however, he found himself stuck on Charles Street, reading an annoying sign that screamed, "If You Lived Here, You'd Be Home Now." Hell of a lot of good it did him! He'd tried a different route unsuccessfully, and ended up going straight through downtown Boston to get to Commonwealth Avenue. He took the first open space he saw, deciding not to waste any time trying to find something closer. He'd walk. No, he'd run.

Not slowing even as he reached their building, he took the front stairs two at a time, jabbing repeatedly at the bell. No answer. Pulling the spare key from his pocket, Tim unlocked the front door and headed upstairs to the girls' condo. He knocked and waited. There was no answer. He used his key to open their door.

"Caroline?"

He yelled as he headed down the hall toward her room. He knocked on her door.

"Caroline ... it's Tim ... are you in there?"

He knocked louder, and then opened the door. She was lying across the bed at an angle. Tim walked over to her and shook her.

"CAROLINE?"

She moaned slightly at his voice but didn't move or open her eyes. Although it wasn't dark outside, the room was gloomy, with the shades pulled. Tim flipped on the light and glanced around. There were no visible signs of alcohol, and he couldn't smell any on her breath. He didn't see any prescription bottles. He grew more concerned at the second prospect, knowing of her past addictions.

"Caroline!"

Slowly, she turned over.

"What?"

She whispered with her eyes still closed.

He breathed a sigh of relief.

"I want to talk to you. I'm putting on the coffee, and we're going to talk. Do you understand me?"

She rolled back over and didn't respond.

Tim walked out into the small galley kitchen. He knew every nook and cranny of the place. He and Sheila had spent their first two years of marriage living there before they built their house on the South Shore. Tim hadn't objected to Sheila wanting to live closer to her only sister. He admired their sense of family and their devotion to one another. Grace's daughters displayed the same attachment to each other.

From the time Caroline was a baby, Tim had seen the close bonds develop between her and Valerie, who was away on a business trip to Chicago and wouldn't return until Wednesday evening. Warren was arriving on Thursday to spend a week with her, and the whole family was anxious to meet him. Ruth, Siobhan, and Sean were to fly in on Friday morning for that evening's Harbor Lights charity event at the John Hancock Hall.

Valerie told Sheila she didn't know how she'd find the time to practice before Warren arrived. He would be staying at the Omni Parker House Hotel near Beacon Hill. He received a generous discount on personal travel, and the hotel was a short cab ride to Val's condo on Commonwealth Avenue.

Tim thought it odd that Val didn't want him to know she played the violin. He'd heard that Warren voluntarily conducted back in Ireland and shared the family's love of music. He promised Sheila he'd not breathe a word and give away Val's surprise. He didn't always understand women. But he'd go along with it; he had no choice! Warren sounded like a good guy, and he looked forward to meeting the man who'd captured his eldest niece's heart so quickly.

At the moment, he had to try and get inside the heart of his troubled younger niece. He poured the steaming liquid into two cups and hollered into Caroline.

"Sit up! I've got hot coffee coming."

Tim gently opened the bedroom door with his foot and saw that Caroline hadn't moved at all. Still in her work scrubs, she had removed only her shoes before lying down.

"Caroline!"

He set down the mugs and rolled her over. She pushed him away.

"Uncle Tim! I'm tired. I need to sleep, ok? What are you doing here anyway? Just go away! We can talk later!"

She was irritable.

"You called me, remember?"

He stood and paced beside the bed.

"You called and were crying, telling me that no one understands what you're going through. You said that you can't cope and are sick and tired of this "Facade" was the word you used. What exactly does that mean, Caroline? Tell me! I rushed all the way up here from the Cape half-expecting to find you dead! What am I supposed to think?"

Caroline put her hand over her eyes to shield them from the overhead light. He went on.

"Why do you continually push me away? Why won't you let me in on what you're thinking? I mean, you go along fine for a little while, and then BOOM! You explode and it affects everyone!"

Caroline opened her eyes and stared blankly at the ceiling, but her head was reeling. She didn't want to talk to him. She felt trapped and desperate and didn't remember calling her uncle or saying anything to him that resembled what he'd just told her, though "facade" was a word she used often. *My whole life is a facade ... and I'm tired of being used. It all comes down to sex — that's all it is,* she thought and closed her eyes, falling immediately back to sleep.

Tim tried to wake her, but it was obvious she was exhausted and couldn't keep her eyes open for more than a few minutes at a time. He mumbled to himself.

"What the hell are you on now, Caroline?"

He propped the pillows up behind her head and spoke to her, hoping she could hear him.

"Listen to me. I'm here for you - we all are. Val's frightened for you and doesn't know what to do anymore. She loves you. You're working too hard, and you can't remember important dates. You know what you're like when you get tired; you get depressed and run down. You're killing yourself, kiddo, and all of us who love you are dying right along with you!"

Caroline opened her eyes and struggled to sit up. Her hands trembled as she tried to lift the mug Tim was offering her. He helped her take a sip.

"Careful. It's hot."

The sedatives were wearing off, and she knew she'd get the shakes unless she took more soon. Lately, she needed speed to get up and sedatives to get back down. It was a cycle she knew she had to break free from and was planning on breaking it soon. She couldn't go on like this indefinitely.

She threw her legs over the side of the bed and told Tim she needed to use the bathroom. Making a side trip to the dining room to get her purse off the table, she proceeded down the hall and locked the bathroom door behind her. She wished he'd go home.

Sitting on the edge of the tub, she looked at her pathetic reflection in the mirror. What the hell was happening to her? The face peering back at her looked old. When she lifted her shirt, her bony ribs reflected a skeletal frame. Deep down, she knew what she was doing, yet she seemed helpless to stop herself. She took a couple more Valium to calm the trembling she felt coming on, and flushed the toilet.

Caroline crawled back onto the bed. She was still groggy; her words slurred slightly when she spoke.

"Listen, Uncle Tim, I'm sorry if I worried you, and made you come all the way up here for nothing. I know I've been working crassy ... ummm, I mean crazy hours. I promise I'll take better care of myself. I've just got to sleep now, okay?"

Her head fell back on the pillow like a lead weight. She closed her eyes, looking almost angelic in her dreamy state. Not knowing what she'd taken, he left her propped up on the pillows and headed to the bathroom. He noticed her purse on the floor and picked it up, bringing it to the dining room to empty the contents out on the table. The first thing he saw was the prescription bottle of Valium.

He sat quietly at the dining room table, unconsciously tapping the half-full prescription bottle on the smooth surface. Glancing around at the spacious living room, he remembered how he and Sheila would sit on the couch in front of the fireplace and talk for hours on end.

The apartment held a lot of family history. He and Sheila talked about their future and about having children, a dream that had gone unfulfilled. Tears filled his eyes. Instead, they treated their nieces as if they were their own children. They loved them both dearly. He'd felt twinges of remorse over the years that they had been denied the privilege of parenthood - it was his fault.

He reminisced about the summers when the girls would come and spend time at their lake house in New York. He loved the peace and solitude of fishing, and although he could always talk Caroline into going with him, he couldn't get her to actually enjoy the sport no matter how hard he tried. Val, on the other hand, didn't seem to mind fishing. He'd taught them both how to swim and how to change a car tire. He'd always tried to be a good male influence in their lives — even more so after Neil's death, leaving his sister-in-law and wife to teach them about style, color, and instilling in them confidence and a sense of class.

Tim recalled the years following Neil's death. They'd all taken it very hard, but they pulled one another through that most difficult time. Tim and Sheila had often brought the girls over to their house, giving Grace a much-needed night off or a weekend to herself. They couldn't have loved their nieces more than if they were their own children. They'd changed their diapers, given them baths, and read countless bedtime stories. They even added an addition on to the house when the girls were young to give them their own bedrooms when they stayed over.

Tim prided himself on his surrogate parenting skills, but questioned whether or not he'd have made a good father. The girls, however, felt very comfortable with him. When they were little, they were completely uninhibited about getting undressed in front of him to get into the tub or for him to change them into their nightgowns. They had a second set of parents in Sheila and Tim.

When he and Sheila babysat for the girls, Grace would go into Boston to meet up with some of her college friends from Southie, or head into town to see a play. She needed those times in order to regroup. Tim was surprised she'd never remarried, given her good looks and great attitude towards life. But she said her heart would always belong to Neil. She was accepting of her single life and never complained. She had her beautiful daughters, her sister's companionship, her music, and unconquerable faith. Caroline confounded and frustrated her, and she'd often remark to Sheila and Tim how she felt that somehow she'd failed her youngest daughter.

Tim took the prescription bottle and put it in his shirt pocket. He called Sheila and told her a partial truth. He didn't want to alarm her when he left, but he'd come to check on Caroline, as she hadn't sounded well when she'd called, and Val was away. He'd decided to stay the night to keep an eye on her; she was asleep but seemed somewhat depressed.

Sheila offered to drive in and stay with her so that he could get to work in the morning. He assured her he had more than enough time to do the turnaround in the morning, and could afford to take a day off, if necessary.

Sheila was thankful that her husband was so attentive to her niece's needs; most men would not have become as involved or been able to deal with a young woman with so many emotional issues. There was something about their bond that enabled Caroline to trust him in situations where she just would have ended up fighting with her mother or aunt.

Tim set his jacket on the back of the chair. He took off his shoes and socks and walked quietly into Caroline's bedroom. She was out. He'd always come, whenever she needed him. Even as a little girl, there was nothing he wouldn't do for her. He sat gently on the edge of the bed and reclined next to her.

"Will you lie down with me until I fall asleep?"

She'd say to him when she was younger.

Theirs was a special relationship. Val never had a problem falling asleep on her own. Caroline, however, needed the extra comfort of knowing someone was there. He'd rub her back and tickle her head, playing the "letter" game on her back. He'd write a large letter from the alphabet on her back and she'd have to guess what it was, telling him repeatedly to "write it again." He would, and she'd fall asleep by the fourth letter.

He sat in the dark, listening to her shallow breathing. Every now and again, she'd jerk suddenly. He wondered what was going through her mind during those moments. He laid his arm across her waist and cuddled her close. He'd protect her.

Always.

Chapter Thirty-Three

Boston, Massachusetts, Spring 1998

VAL TOLD THE DRIVER TO slow as they approached her building. On nights like tonight, when she was in a rush, she was grateful not to have to fight for a taxi at the airport. The company's limo service was waiting for her curbside, holding a sign at Baggage Claim with her name on it. She never took her car into Logan Airport anymore. It was a welcomed relief to sit back and let someone else fight the midweek traffic.

She was anxiously counting the hours until Warren arrived the next day. The limo slid to a smooth, gradual stop in front of her building. Val signed her name to the corporate voucher. The driver opened her door and placed her bags on the sidewalk. Val thanked him and walked up the steps to the front landing. It was a hot and muggy May evening.

Caroline was sitting in the living room, looking over some brochures. She jumped up when she heard her sister come in, and hopped over to give her a hug.

"Good to see you! How was the trip? Catch any one dipping into the till?"

Val rolled her eyes.

"NO ... everything was as it should be. How 'bout you? The place doesn't look like it fell apart while I was away."

She smiled at Caroline, who still looked tired to her.

"You okay?"

"Yeah, I'm fine. I've got good news though!"

Val set her luggage down on the floor beside the dining room table and walked over to the refrigerator to get a bottle of water.

"I'm going on a trip!"

Caroline announced proudly. Val looked surprised.

"No kidding! Where to?"

Caroline was like a little kid.

"SPAIN! I've decided I want to take a bike trip. Uncle Tim convinced me that I need to take some time off from work and clear my head. I made all the arrangements today."

"When are you leaving?"

Val asked, pleasantly surprised.

"Sunday night. I wanted to stay and see your performance on Friday. Do you think for one moment I'd leave before meeting the infamous Warren Cahill? I wouldn't miss this for the world! Besides, you know how much I love hearing you play. I can't wait to see his face when he sees you on stage."

Val squeezed her hand.

"I know! I don't think I've ever been so nervous! You know me. I'm usually pretty collected, but I want to surprise him! I'm making myself sick thinking about it. Stupid, huh?"

Caroline shook her head.

"No! It's not stupid. You obviously like this guy, and he means a lot to you. I'm really happy for you, sis! I don't think you have to worry too much about impressing him. I think he already is. He called and left five messages in three days."

Val looked surprised and jumped up from the couch to go and listen to his messages. She called back to her sister.

"I'm glad you're taking this trip. It'll be good for you! I'm going to change and unpack. I want to hear more about it. Do you feel like Chinese food tonight?"

Caroline catapulted off the back of the couch to retrieve the menu from the drawer. Val bellowed from the hall.

"Get the usual! You know what I like - mushroom beef chow yoke. NO water chestnuts. I hate those crunchy things in my food!"

Caroline hollered back.

"How about some Crab Rangoons, too?"

Then muttered.

"And chicken fingers, AND some veggie fried rice, and boneless spareribs ..."

After phoning in the food order, she went into Val's room and bounced on to her bed.

"Don't tell me, about thirty minutes?"

Val guessed from behind the silk dressing screen, throwing her clothes over the top.

Caroline chuckled as she hung her sister's blazer up for her in the closet.

"Yep, as always."

Val asked about the details of her trip.

"So tell me, are you up for long-distance biking?"

She emerged from behind the screen in jeans and a t-shirt and heaved her suitcase onto the bed, then hung up a new garment bag in the closet.

Caroline rephrased her question.

"What you really mean is, am I in shape to do this? Ummmm, the answer to that would be a resounding 'NO,' and I'll probably hyperventilate and die along the route. But I had a choice to either travel with a group or go off on my own to see other places. I may do a little bit of both. If I go with a bike club, they usually come with a van. If I get tired, I'll throw the bike in the back and ride with them in an air-conditioned vehicle. I'm so pathetically out of shape it's not even funny."

Val looked at her sister.

"You actually need to put some weight ON, lady. You're looking emaciated."

Caroline tightened the belt of her bulky sweater, painfully aware of her dwindling frame. She was always cold lately.

Val was still asking questions.

"So where in Spain are you biking? Are you going the hostels route?"

Caroline snorted.

"Are you kidding me? I could do those years ago, when I was eighteen. Nope, no bare-bones accommodations for me anymore. I'm thinking more along the lines of five-star paradores!"

Both girls laughed.

"I'm twenty-eight, Val. I refuse to rough it. I'll fly into Madrid, put my bike together at the airport, and head out down the Paseo de la Castellana."

Val was impressed with her Spanish pronunciation.

"What is that?"

Caroline handed her a brochure.

"Here, it's the equivalent of Paris's Champs-Élysées. It's lined with gorgeous French-style palaces and townhomes. Anyway, I'm taking the train up to San Sebastián. There's a really cool cultural center there formed out of sea-green glass that appears to float over the Bay of Biscay. Here, look."

She tossed Val another brochure.

"They've spent a ton of money over there on art centers and beautifying public spaces. Peggy would love it! San Sebastián is a marvelous city filled with fancy buildings, ornate bridges, and great food! I plan on eating my way through it while cycling around the little fishing villages and basically just touring the Basque Country."

She'd done her research.

"Well, it sounds like you'll have a great time. How long will you be gone?"

Val was unpacking and sorting her dirty laundry.

"About three weeks, I think. Will you miss me?"

Val threw her bra at her.

"Of course, I will. I'll be totally jealous! How'd you get the time off from work?"

Caroline smirked.

"Well, I threatened to quit, of course."

342

Val stopped pulling the dirty clothes out of her suitcase.

"You what?"

Caroline looked smugly defiant.

"I'm kidding. I had a meeting with my supervisor and told her I was burned out and needed a few weeks off for some R&R. She agreed. She also happened to be working on the schedule that day, so I caught her in time. I'm taking a full month off, and when I come back, I'm transferring out of the ER for good."

Val breathed a sigh of relief.

"I am so glad you're doing that. It is a burnout job there. I think it'll make a world of difference for you, Caroline. I really do."

"I've already interviewed internally for another job and accepted a position up on Pediatrics when I return. Aunt Siobhan will be so happy to think I'm following in her footsteps. I haven't told her yet. By the way, did I tell you that the woman I gave CPR to died?"

Val looked at her sympathetically.

"I'm sorry. How'd you handle that?"

Caroline shrugged.

"The way I usually do. I was depressed, worked myself into an anxious tizzy, and nearly collapsed."

Val shook her finger at her.

"You know ..."

Caroline grabbed her finger.

"I KNOW, VAL, I KNOW. I'm going to take better care of myself. I promise. This trip is part of my whole new healthy approach to life. I'm gonna pull it together this time."

Val backed off and smiled at her warmly.

"Good for you!"

The doorbell sounded and Caroline ran downstairs to pay for the Chinese food. The phone rang. Val picked it up.

"Hey there! How are you? How's Peg? Good ... good. No, my flight just got in a little while ago. I'm unpacking and sorting my laundry as we speak. Do you want to talk to Caroline? I'll call you later. Promise. Okay? I just need to get myself settled in and have a glass of wine. Here she is."

Val set the phone on the back of the chair.

"It's Glynnis."

Caroline picked up the phone and immediately launched into the announcement of her impending trip to Spain. She then recounted her plans to switch her nursing specialty to Pediatrics. Val let the two nurses talk and lifted a chicken finger from the box as she went back to her room. She scooped up an armload of dirty clothes to toss into the washer down in the basement.

After starting her laundry, Valerie went back upstairs. Opening the fridge, she reached for the unopened bottle of Pinot Grigio. Sliding a wine glass off the overhanging rack, she offered one out to Caroline, who shook her head "no" and continued with her conversation.

"So how's Peggy these days? Keeping busy? Val said her gallery is amazing. I can't wait to get over there to visit. Tell her I apologize for not having made the grand opening. I was busy working myself to death. Did she get the flowers I sent? Good, good. Is she there now? Put her on the phone for a sec. I want to say hi."

Val sauntered up next to Caroline, who had the phone balanced between her head and shoulder. Reaching for a Crab Rangoon, she leaned into the receiver.

"Hey, Picasso, how's things?"

Val didn't wait to hear her answer, she just wanted to let her know she was thinking of her.

"Tell her I'll call her later. You talk. I'm exhausted and need to practice."

Glynnis and Peggy had been housemates for years. Soon after Peggy moved back to Cariston, Glynnis sat for her leaving exams in Ireland. She received her acceptance to Kingston University's Nursing Program at St.

George's Hospital Medical School in London. The school came highly recommended by a doctor Siobhan Callaghan had worked for. Siobhan had written a letter of recommendation on Glynnis's behalf, and with her high test scores, she was quickly accepted. It took her just three years to complete her course of study in child health. Later, she added mental health to her list of specialties and resume.

Glynnis lived on campus while attending nursing school. She spent her weekends at Peggy's in Cariston. She had her own key and a permanent guest room. They became full-time roommates after her graduation.

At just 18 years of age, and not long after settling back into her home in Cariston, Peggy, too, sought to finish her education. Once her exams were successfully completed, she applied to the City & Guilds of London Art School. She was scrutinized during the interview, and her work carefully evaluated by top instructors who, after recognizing her obvious talent in the area of "Life Drawing," recommended her as a candidate for discretionary awards and grants.

While attending art school, Peggy earned money offering private painting lessons from her home. She later drafted a proposal and secured a meeting with the manager at a prestigious London hotel. After showing him her portfolio, she sold him on the idea of allowing her to have a small portrait-sketching kiosk in the main lobby of the opulent London Gardens Hotel. Both guests and staff were very happy with Peggy's unique service offering, and her reputation spread by word-of-mouth.

Prestigious hotel guests, as well as the general public, regularly sought her out. It proved to be a very lucrative business for Peggy, and her confidence grew through the many affirmations and endorsements she received. She chatted up strangers with ease and skill, and was amazed at what people would pay to have their portraits done.

Peggy was gifted in seeing the best in people. If someone were rather homely or plain, she'd find his or her greatest attribute and play it up, bringing a smile to the face of her satisfied customer. She brought out the best in everyone.

Glynnis worked as a nurse at St. George's Hospital for eleven years after she'd graduated. Eventually, the daily commute to London from Peggy's home in Cariston wore her down and became a burden. At Peggy's suggestion, she decided to cut back her hours and worked only a few per diem shifts a week, keeping her hands in nursing and helping Peggy more at the gallery on the weekends.

Theirs was a comfortable union; Glynnis enjoyed being a homebody and stood behind Peggy one hundred percent, encouraging her in her blossoming art career. They balanced one another out and were satisfied with their relationship.

Caroline hung up the phone and bluntly questioned Val.

"Do you think they're lesbians?"

Val pondered the question.

"You know, I never really gave it much thought. They're just 'Glynnis and Peggy' to me. They've been our friends since we were young. I guess they could be. Peggy went through hell as a teenager, and that whole ordeal with the Travellers must have been a nightmare. I certainly couldn't blame her if she didn't want anything to do with men! But you know what's amazing? After all she's gone through, she's not bitter. I just don't get that from her at all. You know what I mean?"

Caroline nodded in agreement.

"I think they're both just really content in their lives, and are comfortable with where they're at."

Val concluded.

In a matter-of-fact tone, Caroline stated.

"I think I'll just ask them straight out next time I talk to them."

Val chuckled at her sister's nerve.

"Would it bother you if they were?"

Caroline thought about it for a moment.

"You know, they've been our friends forever. It wouldn't change how I feel about them one bit. I love them both dearly. I could see how it could happen though. I mean with Glynnis being abused as well ..."

Val set down her wine glass and looked incredulously at Caroline.

"What do you mean? Glynnis was abused, too?"

Caroline had unconsciously revealed a long-held childhood secret, and couldn't backtrack to get out of it. It had slipped out accidentally. She was visibly nervous and wrung her hands. She'd always been supremely careful. She had to be!

"I can't believe I said that. I just broke a promise! Please, Val, please don't ever say a word to Glynnis about this. She'd never forgive me. I swore an oath to her I'd never tell a soul. It just came out."

Val put up her hand to calm her sister's growing anxiety.

"Wait, wait! Relax, Caroline. I promise I won't repeat it. Just tell me what happened to Glynnis, would you?"

Val sat at the dining room table as Caroline stood, purposely turning away from her sister. She took a deep breath, closing her eyes for a moment. She had to stay calm. She was in uncharted territory and had to tread carefully, lest she give her own secrets away. She'd lie to Valerie if need be.

"Years ago, when Glynnis was young, she was babysitting and the kids' uncle molested her."

Val was in shock.

"You mean she was raped?"

Caroline nodded slowly.

"Oh, my word ..."

Val's mouth dropped.

"And she NEVER reported him?"

Caroline shook her head.

"No."

"Why the HELL not?"

She shouted in anger.

"Listen, Val, she was young. She was afraid she'd get in trouble. She doesn't like to talk about it, okay? So just don't bring it up. You promised."

Caroline had to somehow move past the topic quickly.

"Val, she never told anyone - not even her mother. She was too scared and embarrassed. She just kept it to herself. She's been to therapy and has worked through it. But, well, you know ... it's been rough for her when she's with guys. The whole intimacy thing freaks her out and brings back horrible memories."

"I think, in her relationship with Peggy, they both kind of support one another, you know? It's like they understand where the other's at and just sort of ... pull in the wagons to protect themselves. You know what I mean?"

Val was dumbfounded at first, and then hurt.

"Well, yeah, but how come she never told me about it? I mean, we're close. I've shared personal things with her. Doesn't she trust me?"

Caroline assured her.

"Glynnis and Peggy both trust you with their lives, Val! No, no, I think she just doesn't want anyone to know. To her, it was humiliating. You know, shameful. She only told it to me after she'd been drinking quite a bit one night. It's nothing personal, Val. I'm sure of it."

"I wish I could have helped her."

Caroline assured her.

"There's nothing anyone can do, Val. It's kind of a personal, silent pain you go through. C'mon. Let's eat. I'm starving. Glynnis and Peggy have both moved past this and so can we."

She set a plate in front of Val.

They picked their food out of the various cartons, taking turns scooping out the rice with their chopsticks. Val broke the silence.

"I've got to practice for a few hours tonight. It's the only time I've got before the concert, and Warren gets here tomorrow!!"

Her countenance brightened at his name.

"I'm so excited about seeing him. HEY! By the way, did Mom and Auntie Sheila get back to you with any details about the party yet? It's only two days away. I wonder how the plans are coming along for Father Bruce's twenty-fifth anniversary celebration. Before I left, I told her to invite the ensemble back here afterward. The whole family will be here, too. We can have Tecce's cater it, from the North End. Everybody loves Italian food."

Caroline perked right up at the mention of the party.

"You know what? I know this sounds crazy, but what if we call Glynn and Peggy back and see if they can come over for a few days? I know it's last minute and a long trip - God knows we've done it enough times ourselves. But they love spur-of-the-moment stuff like this! It's only Wednesday. They could get here by Friday."

"Great idea! I'll call them."

Val walked toward the phone, looping a Lo mein noodle into her mouth with her chopsticks.

Their number was programmed into their phone's speed dial. Caroline went over to the desk to grab a pen and paper and quickly began writing a list of things they needed for the party. They had a lot to do if they were going to pull everything off in just a few days, and she wanted to get organized.

Val waited while the phone rang.

"Hey, it's me. I've got a proposition for you and Glynnis. If you're up for it."

Valerie proceeded to fill her in on the upcoming activities.

"It's going to be a whirlwind weekend. Do you think you two can steal away for a few days?"

Peggy was willing and eager. Glynnis hadn't heard the proposition yet as she was too busy burning a perfectly good English grilled cheese sandwich in the background. Peggy was sure she'd say yes, too.

"Here's the series of events. I've got a performance Friday night here in Boston, right around the corner from my condo. Remember when you were here last year, and I pointed out the John Hancock Hall to you? Well, Mom, Uncle Sean, and I are performing in a charity concert with the ensemble. Yes, Sean's playing, too."

"Warren's coming over from Ireland tomorrow and staying for the week. Did I tell you that already? I'm taking some time off from work to show him around and will probably take him down to my house on the Cape for a few days. Here's what Caroline and I were thinking. After the concert on Friday, we're coming back to the condo and having a party for Father Bruce's twenty-fifth church anniversary. So do you think you and Glynn can dust off those passports and come over for a long weekend? I think Granny and the others got a flight out tomorrow. I know Warren will arrive late afternoon. Have you got anything special going on at the gallery this weekend?"

Peggy told her nothing this weekend, but the following weekend she did have a new exhibit opening up. She told Glynnis to douse the grilled cheese and go pack.

Glynnis shrieked with delight in the background when she heard.

"I love spur-of-the-moment adventures! I can be ready in an hour!"

Both women were as giddy as schoolgirls. Peggy promised to get right back to her.

"Let me see what I can do about flights. I'll call you as soon as I get the details."

Val nodded and gave the "thumbs-up" sign to Caroline who was jumping up and down on the couch.

"Caroline's running through her gymnastics routine on the furniture. She so excited! Don't worry about a hotel room. You can stay here. Warren's got a room at the Parker House all week."

The women talked for a little while longer, certain that they could pull it off.

Not needing much in the way of an excuse to travel, Glynnis and Peggy loved historic Boston. It was an old city, but young at heart. They had so much fun when, in the past, they'd visited and explored Faneuil Hall Marketplace. The four friends loved eating at the outdoor café on Rowe's Wharf, where they'd managed to get quite tipsy one summer night before they boarded the elegant yacht, Odyssey, for an evening of dinner, dancing, and yet more drinking.

Val hung up the phone in much better spirits.

"Let me make out this list, and I'll go shopping tomorrow for everything." Caroline offered.

Val put her hand up to stop her.

"No, Florence Nightingale, I'll do the shopping tomorrow. God knows I don't need you performing open heart surgery in the dairy section!"

Caroline managed to laugh at her sister.

"You're quite witty when you want to be."

Val left Caroline to organize her list, and then headed back into her bedroom to practice quietly on her violin. She found the music in her bag and propped it up on the stand.

"Come out here and practice!"

Caroline shouted from the living room. The neighbors never complained. She liked to believe they enjoyed hearing her play. A few of her neighbors had complimented her when they passed her in the hall or saw her collecting her mail. She always tried to be conscious of the noise and didn't want to play too late at night, or early in the morning. She'd have to warn them about the party on Friday night. They were pretty cool about things like that. It wasn't like she and Caroline had these get-togethers every weekend.

"Which piece are you playing?"

Caroline asked.

Val explained the music. It was a new multi-rendition of Pachelbel.

"It's the same basic score I've played for years, only dramatically enhanced and more emotional - very beautiful on many levels. I think you'll find it rather moving."

Caroline encouraged her to play, wanting to hear it for herself. Val placed the music on the stand near the bay window. It was a familiar view, comforting, prompting her to utter.

"It's good to be home."

Caroline reclined on the couch as her sister perfectly positioned the bow on the strings. She'd seen her do it a million times. Slowly, yet masterfully, Val gracefully worked the strings. It was a delicate piece, as she'd said. Val rarely made mistakes, and she played naturally, with such ease, it was as if she'd played the tune every day of her life. She made it appear effortless, like breathing. Only Caroline knew the years of study and practice it had taken to get her to this point.

She remembered when they were younger, how Val would scratch out choppy little songs and make the chords screech, causing the cat to run under the bed. Caroline laid still, her head resting on a couch pillow as her spirit absorbed the richness of each note. She felt at peace. It was as if the music spoke to her soul, bringing comfort and healing.

Elegant sounds resonated through the large, regal room. Caroline admired Valerie and told her that often. Val would return with a compliment, insisting that she wished she could dance as well as Caroline.

When she'd finished the score, Val announced.

"It still needs a lot of work. I wish I had time to run through it once with Malcolm, or if I could have Father Bruce just listen and point out any weak areas."

"I wouldn't worry about it, Val. I think it sounded great. Practice a little more tonight. You'll be fine. What time is the ensemble meeting at the hall on Friday?"

Val twisted the bottom of the bow to loosen the tension and placed it back in her case.

"The concert starts at eight. I think they'll arrive around four. You know Father Bruce, he likes to get everyone into place, check out the acoustics, and run through a few scores. I didn't even stop to think of how to entertain Warren while I'm gone for Friday's afternoon rehearsal. You up for the task?"

Caroline assured her she'd take care of him.

"He's going to be floored when he hears you play."

Val gave her sister a seductive look and hinted.

"He's going to be floored when he sees what I wear!"

Caroline got excited.

"Did you buy something 'to die for' when you were in Chicago?"

Valerie nodded.

"I most certainly did. This little number cost me over eight hundred dollars!"

Caroline jumped off the couch.

"You've got to show me!"

Val shook her head.

"Nope. You'll have to wait to see it as well. It's perfect for the concert, sexy, yet elegant. It's a dress that'll make him fall madly in ... lust with me."

She winked at her sister.

Caroline caught the gleam in her sister's eyes. She was sure Val was falling in love.

Chapter Thirty-Four

Boston, Massachusetts, Spring 1998

VALERIE REACHED OVER TO SHUT off the source of the high-pitched beeping. She slapped at the snooze button and quickly fell back to sleep. She dreamt of her reunion with Warren. Her dreams took her to Ireland.

They were walking up a hill that overlooked a farm near his house. They walked for miles it seemed, hand in hand, stopping when they came to the edge of the cliffs. Cautiously, they peered out over the roaring ocean. Her face was flushed from the brisk walk, and she enclosed herself in Warren's arms, shielding her from the wind. Gazing out at the sea, both watched as storm clouds quickly approached the rugged coastline and the sea began to churn violently. Val clung to Warren as the wind whipped about their bodies. Walking was difficult, and it was getting harder to see as the rain blew sideways, lashing at their faces with near hurricane force. Slowly they made progress as Warren held her tight, guiding her back to the safety of his home ...

Val groaned when the alarm sounded again. Sitting up slowly, she felt every bit her thirty-five years. She never slept well when she flew on business, and was exhausted today. The fatigue soon gave way to renewed anticipation, however. It was Thursday morning, and Warren would be flying in that evening. She had so much to get done before his arrival. She had set her alarm early to get in an hour of practice before she had to get ready for work. Still in a fog, she fumbled about for her violin and bow, warming up with her eyes still closed. She opened her blurred eyes and stood, trying to focus on the sheet music in front of her. She got a head rush and sat back down on her bed.

After a moment, she got back up again and began to play softly. There was a knock at the door. Caroline entered with a cup of coffee, bright-eyed, showered, and looking fabulous.

"Good morning, sunshine!"

"What's with you being up so early? You've no right to look that good at this hour!"

Val sarcastically, yet playfully replied.

"Are you a little grumpy, miss? But how can that be! The love of your life is en route to his beloved fair maiden. I'm so excited, I can hardly stand it!"

A very chipper Caroline set the steaming mug down on the bureau.

"Do you want to hear my plans for the day while you're at work earning an honest living?"

Val nodded and yawned again.

"Go on ..."

"Well, first off, I'm going to the pharmacy to pick up a few things for my trip. Then I'm heading over to the party shop. Mom told me Father Bruce's favorite color is green, so I'm going to get a bunch of green decorations. Tecce's was contacted, and they'll cater for us. They'll deliver the food and set up around 9:30PM Friday night. I based it on a count of forty people; it's going to cost you your next bonus check, so I'll be sure to lead a toast to your impending poverty. I'll ask Helen downstairs if she'll let the caterers in, and see if she wouldn't mind keeping an eye on things until we get home from the concert."

Val was intrigued by her sister's banter. She hadn't seen her so focused in a long time, and complimented her on her organization skills.

"You're doing a great job! Do you have any idea how many people will actually be here for the party? That sounds like a lot of food."

Caroline shook her head.

"Nope. Mom and Sheila are calling a few more people today. Keep in mind there's like 22 people in the ensemble alone, plus some friends from your work and mine. I'll head over to the liquor store when I'm done running around and have them deliver everything Friday morning. What kind of beer does Warren drink?"

Val didn't miss a beat as she finished playing her score.

"Sam Adams Summer ... but of course."

Caroline jotted on her piece of paper.

"Okay. I'll clean up around here after you head off to work. There's not much to do. We keep the place fairly neat. Oh! Glynnis and Peggy couldn't get a flight out of London until Friday. They'll arrive at Logan around 5:00PM. It'll be tight with traffic, but they should make it in time for the evening performance at 8:00PM. I told them the tickets will be held in Peggy's name at the front desk if they should run really late and can't get here first, and they just laughed when I asked them if they were a couple, and told me to mind my own business."

Valerie nearly spit out the coffee at her unexpected confession.

"You SHOULD mind your own business!"

Caroline just shrugged and went on. It didn't bother her.

"They won't have a moment to rest! Mom and Auntie Sheila will bring the cake for Father Bruce, and we'll have him do the honors of cutting later in the evening."

She stopped and took a long dramatic breath.

Val was amused with her little sister.

"Well, I think it's just a grand idea having a cake for Father Bruce. He deserves it, having put up with the likes of us all these years."

She set the violin down in its case and drank carefully from the still-steaming mug.

"I've got to get in the shower and get going. I've a meeting at 11:00, and I'm leaving the office around 3:00 for the day. Warren's going to call me when he gets to the hotel. I think that should be around 6:30PM or so."

Caroline jumped off the bed and told her sister she had to run, too, and that she'd see her later in the afternoon. She told her to call her should she think of anything else they needed.

356

After her shower, Val pulled the plastic off her dry cleaning and twisted the top of the hanger in order to hang it from the molding above her door. She dressed quickly, and, of course, put a hole in her new nylons. Cursing, she threw them on the floor and grabbed another package. She wanted to get in a little early to go over a few reports before the senior staff meeting. She only had a couple of hours in the office before beginning her weeklong vacation with Warren. She sighed and told herself she could only do what she could do. Grabbing her Coach bag, a gift from her company on her fifth year anniversary, she bounded out the door for the office.

* * *

Warren had grown fidgety sitting for so long, even with a book to distract him. He wasn't used to being a passenger and wished he could take a walk up to the cockpit and talk with his associates. However, FAA regulations wouldn't allow it. He smiled graciously at the elderly woman sitting next to him. Staring out the window, he thought of Valerie and how they first met.

He had first spotted her in the Duty Free shop through the window. He had arrived early for sign-in, and had some time to kill before his preflight checks. The crew he was flying with liked to meet up at Legal Seafood for a bowl of New England Clam "Chowda" before the flight home.

In his travels over the years, he'd seen and met many beautiful women. Valerie was no exception, yet something about her was different. She was certainly very pretty, but it was the quiet confidence she exuded which attracted him. She walked with the elegant posture of a dancer, or someone who was comfortable being in the public eye; he hated it when women slouched. When she'd entered the restaurant and sat to eat a bowl of chowder by herself, he was taken by her easygoing manner and way in which she engaged the wait staff. Not many women liked to eat alone in public. It didn't seem to bother her as she ate her meal and drank a glass of wine while scanning through her new book.

Warren would never forget the snack incident. It was certainly "one for the books" as Val put it. He'd found himself laughing heartily in the cockpit while he ran through his preflight checklist. He couldn't resist alluding to it over the cabin speakers when he made his welcome announcement. He'd hoped she'd have a sense of humor. She didn't disappoint him.

Warren was forty, and if he had to take a guess, he'd estimate Valerie to be in her early to mid-thirties. He'd not married, having focused on building his career. He'd been rewarded with a promotion to captain at the age of thirty-eight.

When he was home in Ireland, he kept himself busy volunteering and conducting at the Glor in his free time. He was also active in his airline's community outreach program often spending time speaking to students in local primary and secondary schools. The boys loved hearing him tell stories about flying planes, and the girls always asked about becoming flight attendants. He'd come equipped with little goody bags for the students provided by Aer Lingus, which contained a postcard with a picture of their fleet of planes, a miniature model airplane, a deck of playing cards, and candy. The children loved the goody bags. He'd stuffed one in his suitcase to give to Valerie.

Recently, on one such school visit, he'd spotted a quiet little girl in the second row who reminded him of his younger sister, Susie, who had died of leukemia at the age of nine when he was just a boy. He'd realized then just how much he wanted a family of his own and had sent a prayer heavenward asking God to bring the right woman into his life. He wasn't a player in any sense, but prior romantic relationships just never led to the altar.

Warren enjoyed talking to Valerie on the phone. They never seemed to be at a loss for words or conversation and occasionally would talk over each other in their excitement to share a story. They'd already felt comfortable sharing some personal details about their lives that might only be divulged to a longtime, trustworthy friend. They laughed easily and often and felt an instant connection with one another. The chemistry was there, with both responding to the other's kiss in a way that left them both longing for more. They'd not been intimate, as Val made it clear to him that she felt it important to get to know one another first, and not "muddy the waters" by jumping too quickly into a physical relationship. He respected her position on that matter.

His anticipation grew as he glanced at his watch. Three more hours until he landed in Boston. He found himself a little nervous about their meeting and the upcoming time they'd planned together. He was looking forward to meeting the rest of her family and attending the charity concert. He secretly hoped that Val loved classical music as much as he did. She seemed genuinely surprised and enjoyed watching him conduct that evening at the Glor on one of their evening outings. That was important to him as music was a big part of his life.

They still hadn't planned exactly what they were going to do once he got in, but he suggested to Valerie that perhaps she might want to join him for dinner at the hotel. The Omni Parker House was in a great location, near enough to Valerie's home on Commonwealth Avenue, and a stone's throw from the historic Boston Common. They planned on taking in the sights and sounds of the city over the course of the next week, and Val had promised him a special private tour of Cape Cod. She thought it might be nice to spend a night or two at her family home in Chatham.

* * *

Val didn't end up leaving the office until after four o'clock. It was later than she'd wanted to stay. The weather was warm for early May. She was sweating and in need of another shower before she met Warren. Her phone rang at six forty-five.

"Hello, Val?"

Her heart raced at the sound of his voice.

"Hi there! Are you all settled in?"

She asked excitedly.

"Yes. It seemed like a long flight. I realized I'm not a very good passenger."

She laughed.

"You didn't try to wrestle the controls from the pilot, did you?"

Warren chuckled.

"No, though I was tempted to during a bit of turbulence. It feels good to be on the ground. So tell me, m'love, have you eaten yet?"

Val smiled at his term of endearment, a common phrase in Ireland.

"I've not, and I'm starved! I got out of work later than I'd hoped."

Warren, in a mocking English accent, commented.

"Would you then do me the honor, Valerie Jean Callaghan, and join me for dinner at this fine establishment that I've checked into?"

Val, in like, replied.

"I will, indeed, kind sir."

She told him she'd be there in about twenty minutes and that she just had to hail a cab.

Warren's voice was gentle and serious on the other end.

"I can't wait to see you Valerie. I've missed you."

"Me, too. I'll see you in a bit."

She hung up the phone as Caroline walked in the door. Setting a few bags on the dining room table, Caroline let out a long cat whistle.

"Oh! Do you look gorgeous! He's never going to let you come home. I guess I'll be by myself again."

She put her hands on her hips and pretended to be hurt.

"No, I'll be home. I just don't know what time. I'm meeting him for dinner at the Parker House. I can't wait for you to meet him. I'm calling a cab now."

Val picked up the phone.

"I'd offer you a ride over, but I just found a parking space out front, and I hate to move the car and lose it!"

Val told her not to worry about it; that a cab was easier all around.

"Where did you get that little number?"

Caroline admired her dress.

"It's adorable!"

Val had chosen a flirty, flutter-sleeve silk georgette dress in a spring geranium floral. Her matching leather sling backs complimented the dress for head to toe perfection. Caroline nodded approvingly.

"You're a vision!"

Val laughed at her sister.

"And you're a nut. Don't wait up for me."

Caroline began to unpack the groceries.

"Oh, remember, Cinderella, your mop and bucket will be awaiting your return. We're cleaning tomorrow morning. I didn't get to it all today unfortunately."

Val sighed dramatically.

"Yes, yes, killjoy!"

Picking up her cream leather clutch, she went to wait on the stoop for her taxi to arrive.

Once inside the cab, her excitement began to build. She pulled out her compact and touched up her lipstick, admitting to herself that she looked good. She'd not been this excited or felt this much anticipation about anyone ever before.

As the car turned the corner, she spotted him standing on the carpet under the awning to the hotel. The taxi pulled to a halt and she waved. His face lit up as he bounded for the door and handed the fare to the driver. He held out his hand to assist her, and in one swoop, pulled her to him to kiss her hello.

"God, you look gorgeous, and smell wonderful! What's that you're wearing?"

Val looked at him deadpan.

"In America, we call this a dress."

He smirked and rolled his eyes.

"I guess I asked for that! I was talking about the perfume. What is it called?"

She smiled and gently nudged him.

"It's Coco by Chanel, dahling. It's one of my favorites and just a tad spicy, like me."

He raised his eyebrow.

"Don't go there, my love. Don't go there."

She snickered and took hold of his arm as the bellman opened the door for the handsome couple.

Parkers Restaurant was made famous as the birthplace of the Boston Cream Pie, The Parker House roll, and Boston scrod. The upscale dining area was decorated with rich oak paneling, and the lobby boasted Waterford Crystal chandeliers. They were seated at a simple, white linen table. Val ordered a glass of Pinot Grigio while Warren chose Bordeaux. They admired the stately elegance of the room. He reached across the table and took her hand.

"You know, it's so perfect sitting here with you. I feel very comfortable. I've really missed you."

Val leaned in and kissed his lips. It was a natural response to his tender words.

"I know. I couldn't concentrate at work today. I kept looking at my watch, envisioning you on the plane, and couldn't wait to get out of that place. I sat and daydreamed through the entire two-hour team meeting this morning."

The restaurant wasn't crowded, it being a Thursday evening. The waiters were very patient, not wanting to interrupt their intimate conversation. Two hours and a bottle of wine later, they finally ordered their meal. Val chose their famous scrod and Warren opted for swordfish.

"I'm thinking that you'll want to sleep in tomorrow."

He shook his head.

"Are you kidding me? I'm not letting you go home!"

She smiled at his playful possessiveness.

"So tell me, Valerie Jean, what are some of your other hidden talents that you've not chosen to share with me yet?"

He stared at her fingers, which he held in his hand.

Val looked at him quizzically. She'd not said a word about her violin playing and doubted that anyone in her family told him. She decided to reveal to him her private love for poetry.

"The Irish are known poets and wordsmiths. Have you written any poetry yourself?"

Warren asked.

"I have, and even had a couple of pieces published in anthologies. Would you like to hear one?"

Warren was impressed. He smiled and leaned forward nodding.

"Please. I'd love to hear you recite a poem to me."

Val felt very much at ease. She and Warren were the only two left in the restaurant.

"All right then. This poem is called, 'Toll at Sea'."

Warren interrupted her.

"Wait, you wrote a poem called, 'Toilet Seat'?

Val burst out laughing and playfully threw her napkin at him.

"You nut! I said, 'TOLL AT SEA'!"

Val sat back and looked into his eyes.

"I wrote this not long after I'd heard that a friend and coworker of mine's private jet went down. He and his wife were returning from a business trip. It was tragic."

Warren nodded sympathetically — a stark possibility he lived with daily.

Kathleen M. Urquhart

"Sitting atop warm grains of sand, knees drawn up, chin in hand, I bask in this universal place of solitude, as the ocean's shores draw men.

To clear one's mind and contemplate life, or to simply let hearts mend.

A gift to us, no charge is asked, to meditate in blissful peace on land.

Tranquil breezes, rhythmic waves, wash gently over nature's boundaries drawn. Off depths of blue, does morning's sun glisten and calm. Its temperament is placid, tame, raw beauty that does charm.

Till storms and winds do churn its depths and unleashed fury spawn.

Of respect and fear does it demand, this powerful dichotomy.

From its waters men draw resources, over its vastness travelers roam.

At times the price for passage is the life to us on loan.

A watery grave, the toll to pay, from an unremorseful sea.

As inhabitants above the earth, we are alien to the world below.

Our sight limited by the horizon, while the imagination ponders what lay beneath. Its many conquests not divulged, nor its victories bequeath.

For its silence offers comfort, its only sympathetic show."

Warren's heart was touched, and he knew then he'd ask her to marry him one day soon. Her poem was thought provoking and revealed to him yet another side of this multifaceted jewel. She was fun, witty, intelligent, and beautiful, inside and out. He couldn't wait to discover all that there was to the woman sharing the table across from him. He spoke after a few moments.

"I'm dumbfounded. I've never had the ability to even think like that, let alone write. I can picture myself sitting at the ocean's shore and thinking those thoughts, but never being able to express them in such an eloquent way. It's truly a gift you have."

Val blushed, and he chuckled, causing her to turn a deeper shade of red.

"Okay, that's enough. I'm embarrassed. Let's say we stand up and get the blood circulating to the legs, shall we? We've been sitting here for hours."

Warren stood first and pulled out Val's chair.

"Who says chivalry is dead?"

Val whispered and flashed him a great smile. Just then, their waiter approached once again to thank them for their generosity.

"I'm glad you enjoyed your meal. The table you were sitting at is pretty famous, you know."

Val listened incredulously as he explained that John F. Kennedy proposed to the lovely, young Jacqueline Lee Bouvier at their exact table, table number ten.

Warren slightly bowed to the waiter.

"I'm honored, sir. Thank you."

They walked lightheartedly out to the lobby.

Warren tried unsuccessfully to stifle a yawn.

"I'm sorry. This day is catching up with me I think."

Val turned to him and took both his hands in hers.

"You, my dear, must get some rest. I'm going to catch a taxi out here, and head home myself. Call me when you get up tomorrow, but no rush. Sleep late. Warren, I had a wonderful evening. I'm glad you are here."

He drew her to him and hugged her tightly. He bent his head and inhaled the scent of her hair and kissed her. Her kiss was the sweetest he'd ever had, leading him to steal another, and she let him.

"Pleasant dreams, love."

When he opened the door of the taxi for her, Val wanted to pull him in and take him home. Instead, she waved good-bye and sat back for the short ride home. She closed her eyes and replayed every detail of their first romantic evening together in Boston.

Chapter Thirty-Five

Montana, Spring 1998

FATHER COUGHLIN PLACED THE SPARKLING new silver dollars in a black velvet bag and pulled on the drawstrings. The coins would be parceled out to the boys as rewards after they'd completed all he wanted them to do. He'd been planning this excursion for weeks and had no time to waste.

Recently, he'd been informed by the Archdiocese that, due to monetary constraints, they were closing his small, rural church in Montana. Within a month's time, he would be relocating. The details of his next assignment were sketchy and still being worked out. He'd been asked to delicately transition his congregation.

He'd waited until after Mass on Sunday to speak with the boys' parents. It wasn't hard to gain their trust or permission. The idea had already been presented to both children weeks before, a special fishing trip with just the three of them. He explained to the boys what he envisioned, and told their parents that a weekend teaching retreat was required by the church in order for their sons to receive the sacrament of Confirmation.

Grateful for the church's willingness to finance and expose their children to the wonderful outdoor world that God created, the parents encouraged their sons to go, telling them that opportunities like this didn't come around too often, and that it would leave them with a lifetime of memories ...

Father Coughlin promised the boys a fun week, filled with fishing and adventure. He bought each boy his very own fishing pole and tackle box, complete with a variety of colorful lures. In return, the boys were expected to fulfill their end of the agreement.

Rob had "groomed" them both over the years. They no longer tried to resist his advances or demands. At age ten, they only understood that his treatment of them was just part of being his friend. He controlled not only their bodies, but also their minds.

His pattern was consistent: Select and isolate a potential victim, gain his trust, get him to do or say something he knew the parents wouldn't like and would probably punish the child for, then use it as blackmail to get them to do things they'd never normally do. Pouring small amounts of alcohol into their sweet drinks, he'd invent games that would get them to gradually expose themselves, introduce them to self-stimulation, and eventually coerce them to perform oral sex — first with him, then with one another.

Rob never allowed himself to feel guilt. He saw himself as a man who was deprived of a normal life while growing up in Ireland. He was the victim, not them. He felt cheated in many ways and had convinced himself that he had the right to pursue happiness in whatever way made him feel good. If having physical relations with children was wrong, he refused to believe it. He never personalized the act or got emotionally entangled. In fact, he was of the opinion that the children actually enjoyed having sex with him. They never made any attempt to stop him, and greedily took whatever rewards and treats he offered them afterward. He had put from his mind any feelings of helplessness that he had as a child at the hands of his degenerate father.

Somewhere deep in the recesses of his mind, he'd always thought himself a coward. He'd hated school and never interacted with other children for fear of rejection or being hurt. In fact, he hardly played at all as a youngster, which led him into periods of depression and self-pity, resulting in self-imposed isolation throughout his young life. It was during these long periods of being alone that he comforted himself through self-stimulation on a regular basis, and began to sexualize every aspect of his life.

As far as he was concerned, his present state was his parents' fault. If he'd had someone, anyone, in whom he could confide, someone to talk to who'd say, "yes, this is good" or "no, that is bad," maybe life would be different. As it was, his world was one of hypocrisy and violation by both parents, albeit in different ways.

They had left him alone to all but raise himself as a child. What he needed most then, he rationalized he was giving to his victims - time, attention, affection, affirmation, compassion, patience, and a willingness to listen.

In his summation, his family drove him into the lifestyle he led. He fed into that victim mentality over the years when it suited his purposes. It enabled him to commit horrific acts for which he felt no shame or remorse. It was only during those episodes of abuse that he felt powerful and fully in control. His heart raced with excitement when he was able to convince someone young and vulnerable to do his will by just speaking suggestions that they would carry out.

When he was young, his sexual fantasies allowed him momentary escapes from the reality that was his troubled youth. Over time, however, he found that even his most heinous fantasies were not enough to "get him there." He needed more, and began to orchestrate situations that put him in the company of trusting and defenseless children.

Occasionally, if he felt the physical rewards would be worth his time and effort, he'd pursue a child who had initially refused him. The challenge: to dominate that child's will and break his spirit to the point of total submission. Such had been the case early on with one particular child back in Ireland.

He thought back, recalling his first intimate encounter as a priest with a young boy from his parish in County Clare. His duties varied in those early years as a priest, but he spent a good deal of his time teaching at the church's private school. Though he was not certified to instruct in the core competency subjects, Father Coughlin was qualified to teach Christian education to students. He taught a religion class for several years to primary and secondary school students. It was from those classes that Father Coughlin would choose the children he'd personally train as altar boys to assist him with Mass at church after school.

The child came from a wealthy family. His older brother was a model student, who had actually humiliated Father Coughlin once in front of an entire schoolyard of children. Father Coughlin knew enough to not approach the eldest child, yet sensed that the younger one might feel inferior in the shadow of his overachieving older brother. The younger boy feared Father Coughlin.

Father changed his tactics with the child and apologized for his harsh reactions and started showing him more interest, time, and attention. He granted him greater freedom in his class, and would often choose him to erase the boards or clap the erasers outside, or pass out books and papers to the other students. The child responded by opening up to him, and would often seek to stay after school for extra help in order to spend more time with him. It came as no surprise when Father Coughlin asked him to become an altar boy.

The child needed much coaching, however, as he didn't fully embrace the idea of serving Mass. When his parents learned of his selection, they were insistent upon his compliance, and assured Father Coughlin of their son's full commitment, whether he liked it or not. To them, serving Mass was an honor, which played well into Father Coughlin's plans for him.

Father Coughlin began by having the boy come to the rectory after school. On his first visit, he showed him around the palatial building. The child had never seen the inside of a "priest's house." He was amused when the boy's face dropped at how sparsely furnished the residence was.

"Are you poor?"

He'd asked innocently.

Father Coughlin patted the boy's shoulder.

"God supplies all our needs."

He then led him unsuspectingly upstairs, to his bedroom.

Father Coughlin made the child sit on his bed, and he purposely sat across from him in a chair. The child sat on his hands at the edge of the bed, nervously dangling his feet. Father told him that he thought they'd have more privacy up here to talk and that he should feel very special to visit the priest's private room. Not all children were allowed this privilege. He told him how much he trusted him and what a good student he was. The boy's face lit up.

The next step was to test the child's trustworthiness. He did so by purposely letting his language slip to see what the child's reaction might be, and if he'd tell his parents when he got home. For sure he'd hear about it if that were the case. However, the child answered as he'd expected.

"It's okay, my da slips up sometimes, too."

That was what the priest wanted to hear.

Father Coughlin was eager to begin with his new protégé and told him that, in order for him to participate in the Mass, he'd have to be outfitted with a brand new vestment. Father Coughlin instructed the boy to strip down to his underwear in order for him to get the exact measurements for his robe. The boy was very reluctant to do so at first, until the priest assured him that it was okay and that his parents were fully aware that this needed to be done in order for him to be outfitted.

The boy awkwardly stripped down to his underwear and stood there, red-faced. Father Coughlin smiled, assuring the child he had nothing to be embarrassed about and that if it made him feel more comfortable, he'd do the same. The child watched in horror as the priest defrocked in front of him.

"See, I've got the same parts as you. No surprises here."

Father Coughlin then had the child lie back on the bed while he took out a measuring tape from his top drawer. The boy lay there, frozen, not understanding what exactly was taking place.

I just want to snatch up my clothes and run out that door. It's not far. I can make it. I don't want to be an altar boy! Mam is waiting for me. If I'm late for dinner, she'll kill me. It's getting dark. I really gotta go. This is weird, and I don't like it!

The priest then took off his own underwear and lay down next to him on the bed. The child wiggled his foot nervously and stared straight at the ceiling pretending he hadn't seen what he just did. The priest didn't say anything to the child but set about rubbing his legs and inner thighs, slowly moving his hands over the child's body and lingering at his midsection.

Oh, God! What is he doing?? He's got no clothes on, and he's touching me there! I'm going to get in trouble ... I can't tell Mam and Da, or they'll kill me for sure! I don't like this. Oh, God!!! Please help me ...

The child shivered in fear. The priest assured him he had nothing to be frightened about, and covered him with a blanket he had folded at the end of the bed. The child was very still, frozen in place. The priest assured him that no one would come into his room, as the door was locked, and that his parents would never punish him for being with a priest.

The child's breath caught in his chest when the priest lightly touched between his legs.

"How does that feel?"

I can't talk ... I can't even breathe. Please someone knock on the door. Mam call the rectory and tell them I have to come home for supper. Please, Mam! The street lights are on ... it's getting late.

The boy was obviously reluctant and embarrassed to say anything and chose to remain silent.

"You can tell me the truth. It's okay to enjoy this. It makes me very happy. Do you like this feeling?"

How can I like this? He's not supposed to touch me THERE! It sort of feels weird, but it doesn't hurt. Maybe if I tell him "yes," he'll stop. I'll tell him I have to go home. If I could just talk ...

"Yyyes ..."

Came his weak reply.

"Well, I enjoy making you feel good."

Sitting up, Father Coughlin lifted him slightly to remove his underwear. Tossing them on the floor, he kneeled over him and stared down.

"There's nothing to be afraid of. I'm not going to hurt you. You're special to me, which is why I chose you. Other alter boys have done this same thing. They know that I like to play little games with them. We have fun together. It's our secret. Now, I want you to relax. No one will know."

Is this what the other kids do with him? What kind of games? I don't think it's much fun! I can't get off the bed now because he took my underwear. Mam will kill me if I come home late and am missing my underwear. My brother will notice for sure when I get dressed for bed. I just want to go home ... OH, GOD! What is he doing? Please stop ... please stop!

He watched for the child's response and was close to coming himself, but held back. The boy was focusing on the ceiling, arching his back and gripping at the chenille bed spread with both fists as he tried to resist the priest's oral stimulation. He didn't cry out and didn't know what to expect, being only ten years old. Father Coughlin kissed the child on his forehead afterward.

"You're a good boy."

The priest got up and walked across the room to the chair. His arousal was evident, and he motioned for the child to come over to him.

"I want you to kneel."

Thinking it to be a call to prayer, the child did as he was told.

What is he trying to make me do? Oh! I can't do this. I can't ...

The child tried to pull away from him at first, but Father Coughlin firmly held his shoulders in place until he stopped resisting. He was careful to not be too forceful. He didn't want to scare him. The boy didn't know what to do or expect.

That was gross! I'm going to be sick. I have to get out of here. I hope nobody saw me. I don't think anyone did. The shade is closed. What if my da finds out? I'm gonna be in trouble for sure. I'm never coming back here again!

The priest pulled out a piece of paper and pretended to write measurements on it.

"You'll make a fine altar boy, son. We'll spend more time together. Your parents will be so proud to see you on the altar at your first Mass. Now, we can't tell them about your actions here, however. They would be very angry and punish you for taking your clothes off in front of a priest. They wouldn't understand. I won't tell them. We'll keep this just between you and me."

Reaching inside his pants pocket, Father Coughlin pulled out a few pieces of hard candy and gave them to the child.

"Here, it'll take that taste out of your mouth."

The boy, grateful, unwrapped the piece of butterscotch candy and eagerly popped it in his mouth. He thanked him and the priest nodded.

NOW can I go home? I think he's going to let me leave. I'll have to run home for sure. I know I'm late ...

Over the course of a few weeks, Father Coughlin spent more time alone with the new boy. Because his parents wouldn't listen to his protests about being an altar boy, he had to go to the rectory every day after school. The boy resigned himself to the priest's treatment and was never at ease. They'd undress in his room, and the boy would lie on the bed. The priest would teach him about his body and what it could do, and how it would respond to certain types of stimuli. He'd bring him to the point of climax and then withhold, causing the child to writhe in discomfort and anticipation.

I don't like this. How do I make him stop? Sometimes it feels good, but I know I shouldn't like it ... I wish I could stop coming here but he'd tell my parents and they'll get mad at me for disobeying a priest. I have no choice. I'm stuck! I'll just let him do this quickly, and I'll go home. It's not so bad ...

Father Coughlin took a sash from his robe and told him that he was going to play a game of "kidnapper" with him, and proceeded to blindfold him. He then put a handkerchief in his mouth and positioned the boy in front of him.

He's getting weird ... I can't see what he's doing. He likes to play really strange games. I don't like the feel of this.

The child tried to pull away. But Father told him that he needed him to be cooperative as it was all part of the game. He reminded him that the other boys played this way and that he'd get use to it. He just needed to breathe and relax. The pillow muffled the child's screams while his rhythmic motion increased in speed and intensity.

I'm going to die. This hurts so bad. Why is he doing this to me? I can't get away from him. I should have never come here. I hate Mam and Da for making me become an altar boy. Please, God, make him stop!

The priest groaned for a moment, then went still. Still connected to the child, he withdrew slowly, quieting him with words of false reassurance and love. Before he took off the sash and blindfold, Father Coughlin cleaned up a small amount of blood with a towel and then helped him get dressed.

"I know that seemed a little crazy to you, but come over here. I want to show you something."

Father Coughlin led him over to his bureau and pulled out a magazine hidden under some clothes.

"Other boys do this with each other and me all the time. We're not the only ones who play these kinds of games. See ... look here."

Father Coughlin pointed to the pictures of men fondling one another. He then showed him a photo of what he just did to him.

"You're very grown-up for a boy your age. We're doing what these men do and you're so much younger. I knew you were very mature."

Tucking the magazine back into his drawer, Father Coughlin gave him a piece of candy and took him downstairs to get a soda. The child asked to use the bathroom and was gone for some time. Father Coughlin felt an immense sense of satisfaction and drank his soda happily as he leaned against the kitchen counter, waiting for him to emerge.

The boy exited the bathroom quietly.

"Are you alright?"

The boy nodded and took the soda offered to him.

"Tomorrow I'd like for you to meet me at the church after school. You can tell your parents you'll be there for a few hours for practice. I want you there on time. We need to walk through the entire ceremony, so you'll be ready for this Sunday."

The child nodded slowly and looked at the clock. It was just about five o'clock, and he had to get home for dinner. Father Coughlin thanked him for coming and told him to get his homework done, so he could go outside and play after dinner. The child picked up his book bag and flung it over his shoulder. As he stepped outside, he looked around cautiously, hoping no one saw him. Play was not something he felt like doing tonight.

Father Coughlin watched as the boy crossed the street and pulled up the hood of his sweatshirt. He felt euphoric. The more risk involved, the more intense his orgasms. Tomorrow would be a first for him. He'd never attempted anything like it before with one of his boys. But the fantasy kept coming to him over and over in his dreams. He'd thought out every detail, and planned the occasion, so it would not coincide with any event at the church.

The next day, he'd found it hard to concentrate in the classes he taught. When the child entered his class right before the end of the day, he found his hands sweating with excitement and anticipation.

Father Coughlin told the boy to meet him downstairs in the lower church. He thoroughly scanned it for stray parishioners. When he saw none, he locked the entrance doors and told the child to go out back and change into his altar clothes, making sure to leave his own clothes off underneath. The boy knew what this meant and did so reluctantly and without protest. Father Coughlin's heart, once again, began to race at the thought of the act he was about to commit.

The child sat quietly in the pew where he'd been directed. The priest stared down at him and smiled. He walked over to the confessional box and opened the middle door. He looked around again. Satisfied that no one was there, he motioned for the boy to come inside with him. The child rose slowly and followed the priest into the small, confined quarters. Once he shut the door, blackness enveloped them. He lifted the child's vestment. He was silent. No words were spoken as he ran his hands up and down the boy's small frame. The priest held the child firmly in place until he thought he was past the point of sensitivity. The child still winced in pain. The priest came within seconds then hurriedly withdrew. Father Coughlin let his vestment fall to the floor covering his own nakedness. He told the boy that he'd exit first and that he should wait a few minutes before meeting him up front. They'd then run through an abbreviated "Mass" in preparation for Sunday's service

He directed the sullen child to take his place at the kneeler to his right. Father Coughlin stepped up to the altar, centering himself in front of the tabernacle, and lifted his hands in worship. The child kept his head bowed low and rang the bells at the appropriate time. Father Coughlin instructed him about the order in which to present the gifts, and the child performed the task perfectly. He went back to the altar and turned toward the cross.

"Let us go in peace, to love and serve the Lord ..."

The child looked at him in bewilderment.

How does he do that? How can he hurt me and do dirty things to me and then turn to God and ask for his blessing? Why is God silent! I hate God because he lets him hurt me! I hate him!

Father Coughlin turned and looked down at the boy, who was defeated. He then went around the church shutting off the lights. He told the

376

boy to hurry home, and that he looked forward to seeing him on Sunday for the nine o'clock Mass. He assured him there was nothing to be nervous or worried about. He'd be there to help him, and they'd get through it together.

Chapter Thirty-Six

Chatham, Cape Cod, Massachusetts, Spring 1998

Tossing and turning, Father Bruce finally got up out of bed. It was early, and he was restless and troubled in his spirit. Recognizing what might be the Lord waking him to pray, he dressed quickly and went across the street to the church.

Father Bruce had been roused from sleep on several occasions in his life. God would place an emotional burden on his heart for someone, and he'd know to go and pray on their behalf, often not even knowing the person's situation. Tonight, he asked the Lord whom he was to pray for. Immediately, Caroline Callaghan's face emerged in his mind's eye. Over the years, he'd placed her on the Lord's "altar" many times.

A lovely, intelligent young woman, Caroline had been in and out of the grip of various addictions and depression for years. Father Bruce had a tender heart toward her from the time she was a child. She had not known her loving father for very long as she was quite young when he died.

Father Bruce had grown quite close to and protective of the family in the years following Neil's death, and he adopted both Valerie and Caroline as his spiritual daughters in his heart. He would have gladly adopted them in real life had Grace seriously considered and accepted his offer of marriage. Having grown incredibly fond of her over the years, he'd have left the priesthood to marry her.

During her teens, when Caroline was giving her mother a great deal of grief, it was he who stepped in and would, as needed, correct her. She respected him and what he stood for, and would never mouth back to him as she did her mother. She'd made a strong attempt to change her ways initially, but it was always a struggle for her. He knew that among Valerie's stated reasons for not getting romantically involved was her sense of responsibility and obligation to help her sister.

Father Bruce knelt in a pew and rested his forehead against his hand.

"Lord, please tell me how I can help. I've tried for years to find out what's driving her. Please, show me how I might reach out to her. Grace is a good mother. She's been faithful to you. She never remarried, and has honored your covenant, loving her husband far beyond his death. She's suffered so much heartache already. Please don't let her suffer any more. She has dedicated her life to her daughters. Valerie is a beautiful young woman. She, too, has been faithful in serving this church and you through her music. Please be with her. Grant her and her mother wisdom in how to help Caroline. Reveal what's bothering her. Caroline has a loving heart, but is deeply troubled and none of us know why. Please bring all deeds done in darkness, out into the light."

His eyes watered as he sat in silence. At that moment, a vision came to him like a movie. He sat transfixed as the scenes unfolded.

They were on a city street. Caroline, Valerie, and their mother were getting out of a parked car. He pulled up behind them. Another priest, and the girl's uncle, rode in the back of the car with him. As the women got out of the vehicle and began walking, the uncle had glanced behind them, and shouted for them to run. A pack of what appeared to be wild dogs or wolves came from seemingly out of nowhere, bounding toward them and gaining on them quickly. They locked hands and ran toward a staircase that led up to a federal-looking building and safety. Caroline was lagging slightly behind as the animals closed in, nipping at her heels as she scaled the steps, baring their ferocious teeth.

Father Bruce sprinted toward the front of the monumental structure and opened its large door pulling a very frightened Grace, Valerie, and their uncle into a large foyer as they screamed for Caroline to hurry. The other priest rushed past Caroline to save his own life leaving her fatefully behind. The women pleaded with Father Bruce to go after Caroline and help her. Father Bruce had to physically restrain Val from running back to rescue her sister, warning her that she'd be torn to pieces if she left the building.

Valerie was helpless, shaking, and holding on to her mother crying as bloodcurdling screams were heard outside coming from Caroline, who was quickly overtaken by the pack, their savage teeth tearing at her clothes and flesh.

Father Bruce realized there was no human way to help her. He wanted to pull the door shut on the selfish priest who ran past Caroline to save his own life. Instead, he reached out and pulled him in and quickly hurried the traumatized group down the wide main hallway trying locked doors along the way.

Suddenly, the front doors burst open and the animals raced down the hall towards them. A door he tried opened and he quickly ushered them all in. He felt along the wall for lights and found a switch. The room was illuminated and they found themselves inside an empty courtroom. Just then, the largest wolf in the pack, with flesh still hanging from its teeth, lunged toward the slightly open door. The three men rushed back to pull it shut. The animal had managed to half wedge itself inside the door, making it impossible for them to close it. It was growling and barking, its eyes wild, rabid-looking. The animal was strong as iron and seemed resistant to pain, even as Father Bruce kicked at its head while the other two men tried to pull the door shut in an effort to crush its skull, succeeding only in infuriating the beast more.

With increasing strength, the animal forced its way into the amphitheater-styled room. Valerie and her mother were standing huddled against the back wall while the uncle and priest ran down to the front. Father Bruce stood protecting the women as a shield. He'd give his own life if need be.

The animal seemed to not take notice of them and focused solely on the uncle and the other priest who were holding each other and cowering at the end of the aisle in front of the judge's desk. The pack moved slowly in unison encircling the trembling pair. Father Bruce seized the opportunity and motioned them toward the door. The animals were transfixed on the two men up front now trapped and panicking.

Narrowly escaping death themselves, they ran back down the hallway and outside. Ambulances had arrived and crowds were being held back from the horrific scene. The street was ablaze in flashing blue lights. Blood had puddled in the spot where Caroline's body lay on the court steps.

He put his arms around the women and turned them away from the gruesome scene, comforting them in their grief. The police, with guns drawn, surrounded the building where the wild animals were still penned up inside with the two men. Suddenly, gunshots rang out as the beasts were destroyed.

The paramedics entered the building and brought out the body of the priest. The girl's uncle was miraculously alive but badly wounded. It was unclear whether he would live or die.

Father Bruce sat up soberly. His hands were shaking.

"Lord, please, I beg your mercy on this family and especially Caroline. I know you love each and every one of them. Those whom you love are often sought out and pursued for destruction by the enemy. Satan hates anyone you cherish or deem special. That's why he rages against your children and wants to bring heartache and death upon them. Satan has been stalking Caroline's life for a long time."

Father Bruce stood. He was shaking, angry, and began to walk the long aisles of the empty church, praying with passion, intensity, and a sense of urgency.

"In the name of our precious Lord and Savior, Jesus Christ, I command the demonic realm to release her!"

He railed against the powers and principalities of darkness.

"Father, I ask you to grant her peace. Set a hedge of protection about her. Free her from all that has tortured her these many years. Only you know, Lord, only you know. Please give me the wisdom and knowledge that I need in order to help them. I ask this in your precious name. Amen"

Father Bruce sat back down. He took out a handkerchief and wiped the sweat from his brow. His hands were still trembling and his heart raced.

He didn't know God would call him to intercede this night. He considered himself a servant, and would follow God's leading. This was a spiritual battle between unseen forces of good and evil. He'd experienced it before, but never with such intensity as tonight.

He stood up and walked over to the rows of candles set before the statue of Jesus. He reached inside for the lighting wick and lit a candle for Grace, Valerie, and Caroline.

Chapter Thirty-Seven

Montana, Spring 1998

RICH DOZED OFF TEN MINUTES into the flight. This would be the last trip to his beloved Montana homestead. He simply did not have the physical strength to journey there any longer. He was tired. Visiting his brother also drained him of what little emotional energy he had left. The new medication made him sleepy, and his stomach was upset most of the time. He had to force himself to eat.

Montana had brought him so much in the way of peace and relaxation over the last couple of years. He knew that Rob didn't have any money of his own, given his self-proclaimed vow of poverty. He'd encouraged Rob to use the cabin whenever he needed to get away, and had given him a key. Rob was good about calling ahead of time to see if he was planning to be there. Rich was actually grateful to have someone keep an eye on the place during his long absences.

He awoke when the plane touched down, and was in a bit of a fog, trying to remember where he was actually landing. He'd traveled quite a bit over the last month, getting his life in order, and it had taken its toll. He'd spent the last few weeks tending to legal matters and transferring ownership of his assets. He'd willed to his business partner of twenty years the California and New York restaurants. He would inform Rob on this trip of his plans to leave him the Montana property. He hoped to have enough energy for one last horseback ride out to the cabin. He wanted a final opportunity to sit and view the majestic mountains from his front porch. On this trip, he'd finally reveal to Rob the details of his terminal illness.

Rob was waiting for Rich in the Baggage Claim area and almost didn't recognize him. Were it not for the familiar Yankees baseball cap he'd worn faithfully, Rob would never have recognized him. Rich had lost a lot of weight since his last visit. He was gaunt and his eyes and skin appeared somewhat yellow. Rob hoped his brother's haggard appearance was due to a rough flight, given the torrential winds and rains now assaulting the state. His flight was nearly canceled.

Rob reached out and shook his brother's hand.

"You're looking a bit under the weather there. You all right?"

Rich nodded and told him that it was just a long day, and that he needed a good night's sleep. Both men struggled against the gusts as they made their way through the deluge to the car. Rich began to shiver uncontrollably when he got inside the vehicle. Rob stared at his brother's face in the florescent light of the parking lot. He looked ghostly.

"You sure you're okay? You look like you're coming down with something."

Rich assured him that he'd be fine and that he just needed something to drink and a decent night's rest.

"Well, lean your head back. The seats recline. We've a two-hour ride ahead of us."

No sooner had he spoken than Rich fell asleep, resting beneath a blanket his brother had produced from the backseat.

When they arrived at the church, Rob helped Rich out of the car and took his bags. Rich thanked him and asked him to make them both a cup of tea.

"Tea? You mean you don't want a drink? C'mon now! I went out and stocked the refrigerator! I'm just hoping I don't get a surprise visit from the Bishop. I'll have a lot of explaining to do!"

Rich chuckled and started coughing. The pain was excruciating, and he put his hand on the table to steady himself. Rob helped him into the chair, then got him a glass of water and turned to put the kettle on the stove.

Rich motioned toward the fishing equipment piled in the corner.

"Are you going on a trip?"

Rob was confused by the question, until he noticed the direction of his brother's nod.

"Oh, those! Yes. As a matter of fact, I am. I'm taking a group from church fishing next week, and I thought I'd use your cabin, if that's okay?"

Rich waved his hand in the air.

"As a matter of fact, that's what I came here to talk to you about."

Rob poured the steaming liquid into cups and handed one to Rich, taking a seat across from him.

"Listen, there's no easy way to say this, so I'm just going to tell it like it is. I was diagnosed with Hepatitis C years ago. About six months ago, they discovered I had liver cancer. The prognosis isn't good. I feel it more now, and as you can see, I'm failing rather quickly. I came here to tell you that I'd like to give you my cabin. I can't think of anyone else who'd enjoy it more. I also wanted to ask that you bury me on the mountain, and well, you know, maybe say a few words or something ... when the time comes."

Rob sat very still, shocked by his brother's revelation. It seemed to him that his entire world was slowly slipping away from him. He'd never felt particularly close to Rich, but over the relatively short span of time since they'd reconnected, they'd found a different path with one another and had drawn some solace from the fact that they weren't totally by themselves in the world. Without Rich, his worst fear would come to pass. Rob would be completely alone.

"I don't know what to say, Rich. I mean, I'm grateful that we were able to finally connect as adults and well, you know, what we went through I mean."

His eyes watered as he sat across from his only brother.

"I can't take the cabin."

Rich looked at him in surprise.

"Why not?"

"Well, I mean, it's yours. I should pay you something for it."

Rich laughed.

"I'm giving it to you! What would I do with the money at this point anyway?"

Rob shook his head.

"I wish I could give you something for it. I mean, you don't have to do this."

Rich leaned forward.

"Well, if it'll make you feel better. How much have you got on you right now?"

Rob looked over at the velvet bag containing the payout silver dollars.

"About thirty dollars."

Rich watched as his brother walked over to the pile of fishing gear in the corner and retrieved a small, black bag.

"You just bought yourself a cabin!"

Rob studied him and then tossed the bag of coins at his brother, who caught them with a smile. He dumped the contents onto the table and admired the brand new silver dollars.

"Why do you have these?"

Rob told him he was planning games and contests and using them as prizes. His brother immediately wanted to give them back.

"No, you keep those. I have other rewards I can use."

Rich stood up.

"Well, I've got to get some rest. This new medication is wreaking havoc on my system, and I really don't think it's doing a damn bit of good!"

He motioned for Rob to hand him his bag and took out a prescription bottle, downing two pills with the last of his water.

"The doctor has me finishing these up. They do little to alleviate the pain really. His next drug of choice is morphine."

Rob shook his head in disbelief.

"I'm sorry, Rich. I wish you didn't have to go through this. Is there anything more you can do? I mean, chemo or radiation or something?"

Rich shook his head.

"No, I opted out of that. I had a friend go through it, and she was sick as a dog. It didn't do too much to prolong her life either. What little time she had left was miserable."

Rich became very quiet as he recalled a personal and intimate memory.

*   *   *

Her name was Amanda, and Rich had met her shortly after coming to America. He'd developed a reputation amongst his male and female co-workers as a "skirt chaser" and king of one-night stands. His business provided him with a steady stream of attractive young waitresses, and he took full advantage of his position.

Many women had expressed their love for him over the years, but he never stayed with anyone for too long. Those who did manage to capture his attention for a time; he'd eventually cheat on. When they found out, there was always a lot of screaming and tears, but it never shook him. He had trouble with commitment.

Amanda was different. Unlike most women he was exposed to in his profession, she deplored alcohol and wouldn't be caught dead in a bar. She was a woman of high moral standards and zero tolerance. She was a Physical Therapist who worked with disabled children. He met her by chance while walking to work one afternoon.

A small school bus had pulled up, and she was having trouble maneuvering a wheelchair onto the ramp. One of the brakes wasn't released and one wheel was off the track. She didn't want to reach too far over and risk tipping the poor child out of the chair. As he was passing by, she called out to him.

"Hey! Excuse me, sir, but would you mind giving me a hand here for moment? I can't reach the lever to unlock the brake. Could you just push that down for me?"

Rich rushed over to help release the brake. He then helped her lift up the other side and guide the chair back on to the track and into place. The child they were maneuvering was actually a teenager and wasn't light.

"Boy, you must have some great muscles doing this every day."

He commented with a smile.

"As a matter of fact, I do! Thanks for your help. I appreciate it."

She thanked him again and waved goodbye.

He didn't know what to say next so he wished her a good day and continued on to the bar. He'd never noticed her before and wondered how he'd let her get by him since he took the same route every day. He'd made it part of his exercise routine to walk to work each day. He was in good shape then, and had been told he was very handsome.

Amanda was tall and lean, with blue eyes and brown hair, which was twisted in a bun on top of her head. She wore athletic shoes and a US Navy warm-up suit. Her image called to him, and he started making it a point to look for her every day from then on as he walked to work. Eventually, he got up the nerve to ask her out. She was attractive, athletic, cheerful, and self-assured. What attracted Rich, for the very first time, was her goodness and kindness of heart.

Rich had fallen in love with Amanda hard, and theirs was a whirlwind romance. She knocked him off his feet. Before too long, he was attending church with her on Sundays, and leaving the bar early so as to have quiet dinners with her at home. She never let him sleep over her house and refused to be intimate with him. It drove him crazy most of the time, but he knew, without marriage, she was off limits. He bought a ring and was going to propose to her on Valentine's Day.

In December, Amanda had taken a serious fall, landing her in the hospital. After weeks of physical therapy, with Rich at her side encouraging her through it all, she was concerned that she wasn't getting stronger more quickly. Her doctor then confirmed through tests that she had leukemia. The diagnosis was devastating to both Rich and Amanda. On Valentine's

Day, he still proposed to her. She, however, wanted him to have a full life, and knew she'd not be able to give that to him. She told him she couldn't marry him, although she loved him with her whole heart. Rich cried openly at her bedside, and she comforted him in spite of her weakness. Five short months later, she died holding his hand. He was inconsolable.

Rich stood slowly facing his brother, sobered by the thoughts of his beloved Amanda. He was now anxious for death with the hope that it might usher him into her presence once again.

"I experience horrible pain from time to time, more so recently, but I'm not so sick that I can't get up and move ... at least, not yet anyway. I have good days and bad. But I'm afraid the bad days are becoming more and more frequent."

He smiled weakly.

"But let's look on the bright side, I'm here to enjoy my favorite place on earth. I would have never found this place had we not hooked up. I'm sorry I took so many years to get back to you. Growing up, I hated you. We were such a dysfunctional family. But I'm grateful to be able to see you and tell you this in person, before anything happened."

Rob wiped the tears from his eyes and went over to hug his brother, who didn't stiffen or pull away for once. Instead he just sighed.

"It's going to be okay. I'm not afraid to die, Rob."

He nodded and lifted the suitcase, leading the way upstairs to the bedroom.

"Are you feeling well enough to ride out to the cabin on horseback? I mean, it's not an easy journey."

Rich nodded.

"We may just have to make a few more stops than usual to sit and rest along the way, but I think I can make it."

Rob nodded.

"Good night, Rich."

Rob slowly turned away and went to his room. He wouldn't tell his brother, but he cried most of the night. Never once did he even think to pray.

The early morning sunlight streamed in through the bedroom window. Rich got up first and walked downstairs. He took his medication and put on the kettle for tea. He'd let Rob sleep. While pouring, Rich noticed the black velvet bag of coins on the kitchen table. Quietly, he opened the back door of the kitchen and walked around the house to the wooden cabin that served as Rob's church.

It was a simple structure with a small granite altar. Crossbeams held the functional lighting. Rich walked down the center aisle and placed the velvet bag of coins on the altar. He looked around the empty church and wondered what his brother would say about him when he died.

Through the picture window, he curiously observed a couple of squirrels happily chasing each other up a tree. *Their lives are so carefree,* he thought. He walked back to the house, entering quietly through the back door. Rob was surprised to see him up so early and asked him where he'd gone.

"Just checking out your church."

"How are you feeling this morning?"

Rob inquired.

"So far, so good. Why don't we get a move on? I'm rather anxious to get out there while I still have some energy."

The men had their tea and started out on the familiar journey.

Rob had packed all that they needed, and loaded it into the car. They drove to the reservation, where they traded their vehicle for horseback and began the long trek out to the cabin.

Rob's eyes teared up at several points along the way when Rich would point out his favorite views. He was visibly tired when they stopped for lunch near a wide stream. They still had hours of riding ahead of them before they reached the homestead.

Rob helped him down and set up a mini-campfire so he could prepare the food. He rolled out the mat and sleeping bag he'd brought for Rich, knowing he might need to rest for a little while. After they'd finished eating, Rob told him that he'd like to do a little fishing. When he looked back, he saw that his brother's eyes were closed. He was far enough away that Rich couldn't hear him crying. The sobs that escaped him were drowned out by the sound of rushing water. He stood for what seemed like hours and didn't catch a thing.

After making his way back to the site where Rich slept, he pulled off his wading boots and packed up the rod, then made sure the campfire was completely extinguished. Rich awoke to the sound of the horses neighing.

"What time is it?"

Rob checked his watch.

"It's 2:35. Do you feel okay?"

Rich needed help standing but appeared steady once he was on his feet.

"I'll be fine. It's only a few more hours until we reach the cabin."

He looked around and walked off in the direction of a cluster of trees. Rob rolled up his brother's bed and loaded it on the back of his horse, then helped Rich up in the saddle.

At the highest point of his land, not far from the stone property marker, Rich pointed out to Rob where he would like his ashes scattered. Rob hated hearing him talk about his imminent death, but knew he needed to and agreed to carry out his final wishes.

As the cabin came into view, Rob hung back as Rich, in one last burst of energy, urged his horse to a full gallop surging ahead toward his beloved homestead.

Chapter Thirty-Eight

Boston, Massachusetts, Spring 1998

GLYNNIS AND PEGGY COULDN'T SIT still on the plane. They kept giggling like a couple of schoolgirls. They'd not done anything so spontaneous in their lives, and they'd never heard Val play in a professional concert before either. Their exposure to her music consisted of house parties and stone wall gatherings when they hung out as teenagers with nothing to do. The girls, led by Caroline, would line up and dance various reels or hornpipes while Val fiddled. Peggy was new to the group then, and had quickly become a part of their clique. Adults now and in their thirties, both women still felt like kids. Caroline, at times, still acted like one.

* * *

Only Glynnis and Peggy knew of Caroline's dark secrets and what it was that often sent her over the edge. Caroline made them swear never to tell a soul, especially Valerie.

The abuse Caroline sustained at the hands of her uncle was revealed in Ireland one night after Peggy had shared her own brutal experiences while they sat on the wall sharing a Guinness and smoking cigarettes.

Caroline, then seventeen, was staying at her grandparents' house that summer studying dance. Both Peggy and Glynnis were home from England visiting with Glynnis's parents.

Glynnis was suddenly put on the spot when Peggy absently mentioned, how all three of them could relate to one another.

"Glynn, you too? What happened?"

Caroline was extremely sensitive toward her, and it broke Glynnis's heart.

"I can't tell you, Caroline. I just can't."

"Glynnis, you can tell me. We can swear here and now never to tell another soul."

Caroline assured her.

Glynnis put her hand anxiously on her forehead and paced.

"You'll hate me, Caroline. You'll just hate me! You may not even believe me."

Caroline looked at her perplexed.

"Why the hell would I hate you? I don't get it, Glynn. What are you trying to say? Just say it! We both did."

She looked over at Peggy for support, then back at Glynnis.

Glynnis walked over and sat next to her.

"It happened at your grandparents' house, many years ago, when I babysat you and Val during your da's funeral. Everyone was out of the house at the service when your uncle came home ... now he's wrecked your life, too, and it's all my fault. I should have told somebody."

She burst into tears.

Caroline was furious, but not at Glynnis - like herself, she'd been an innocent victim.

"I can't believe this! I swear I'll kill him."

She comforted Glynnis with a re-assuring hug and assured her that she was not mad at her - not ever at her.

Glynnis choked back sobs as Caroline told her of the years of painful abuse she'd experienced since the time she was little at the hands of the supposedly "trustworthy" father figure in her life. Caroline repeated how ashamed and sorry she was that he was a member of her family, and that she'd like to see him in prison for what he'd done to them both.

"Maybe if I'd have said something sooner ... maybe it would have saved you from him. I should've, but I was so scared and embarrassed. I

just wanted to forget about the whole thing. But I never could, you know
... it still haunts me! I'm so sorry, Caroline."

Glynnis sobbed.

"How could you know, Glynnis? How could I know? We were so
young. He's such a pervert!"

They talked well into the night, sitting on the wall, sharing their personal, tragic stories. It was like an all night therapy session, complete with
tears, laughter, and emotions running the gamut. In the end, they vowed
to keep their secrets amongst themselves.

Peggy was the one to ask.

"Do you think he's tried anything on Valerie?"

Caroline looked at her squarely and firmly shook her head "no".

"How can you be so sure? I mean, how can he do it to you and not her?"
Peggy was skeptical.

Caroline told them how, from the time the abuse started, her uncle
would call her his "special" niece, and that as long as she remained *special*
to him he would never do to Valerie what he did with her. Caroline stayed
glued to Val to the point of being a pest. She never wanted her to be alone
with him. She promised to be quiet if he wouldn't hurt Valerie. He'd used
that to control her all those years. It wasn't until she was a teenager that
she began to openly rebel, telling him that she'd turn him in to the police
and have his pathetic life thrown into jail if he ever even looked at Val in
a lustful way.

Valerie, Caroline knew, could take care of herself. She'd probably rip
him apart with her bare hands if she ever knew what he'd did to her. Truth
be known, he was afraid of Val. She had a very close relationship with her
mother and aunts, and he couldn't trust that she wouldn't say anything to
them. He'd gotten to Caroline when she was still very young and easy to
manipulate.

* * *

When the pilot announced they were passing over New York, Glynnis and Peggy could hardly contain their excitement. They'd be in Boston in a little over an hour! Tucking up their trays, they took turns running to the ladies' room to freshen up and stretch their legs. They held hands during the descent, as they were both a little nervous about the landing.

Once the plane arrived at the gate, they were free to run. They had packed lightly taking only one piece of carry-on luggage each. Peggy glanced at her watch and announced that the concert was still three hours off; they should have enough time to stop at the condo, unload their bags and run down the street to the John Hancock Hall.

After clearing customs, they ran through Baggage Claim and jumped into a waiting taxi. Giving the driver the address, the girls asked him nicely to hurry as they were in a rush and didn't want to miss the concert. The driver sped off, admiring the pretty women in back through his rearview mirror. Anxious to impress them with his navigating abilities, he had them at the condo in thirty minutes. They hurriedly paid him, leaving him with a generous tip. He told them his name and said he'd be more than happy to take them around Boston should they need a taxi again. The women smiled and waved, thanking him, rolling their eyes as he sped away.

They ran up the steps and rang the bell. In response to the questioning voice on the intercom, both girls shouted to be let in. Caroline's voice could be heard screaming with delight. Instead of buzzing them in, she ran downstairs in her bare feet and nearly knocked them both over. They all hugged in the foyer.

"Where's Val? Has she left yet?"

Caroline smiled and shook her head.

"No, she's just getting ready. She's a nervous wreck! I've never seen her this *high strung* before ... no pun intended!"

Her play on words made them chuckle.

When they entered the dining room, Val's voice was heard from her bedroom.

"I'll be right there!"

The women set down their luggage and looked around at the dining room, decorated with lively green and gold colors.

"You throwing us a party? You shouldn't have ..."

Glynnis remarked coyly.

Caroline laughed.

"As a matter of fact, we are!"

"It'll be a combination Twenty-Fifth Anniversary, Welcome Warren, Peggy, Glynnis, and Bon Voyage party. I think that covers it!"

The girls laughed at her dramatic run-on sentence.

"You see, we have the whole family here."

She shot Glynnis a reassuring look and whispered.

"Don't feel uncomfortable. I'll make sure you-know-who is on his best behavior. If not, for entertainment, we'll publically castrate him."

Her comment made them all burst out laughing. She explained how she, Val, her mother and aunt threw the party together rather last-minute given that everyone was going to be in Boston and in a festive mood from the concert.

Val suddenly appeared in the doorway wearing a beautiful, one-shouldered lilac chiffon dress, which was laced with delicate beading and fell softly to the floor. Her swirl-strapped silver heels completed the look, making her appear statuesque. Draped around her back and arms, she held a matching beaded shawl. Her blond hair was pinned up elegantly on her head, with baby's breath laced throughout the back; long wisps of delicate curls hung softly about her face. Her graceful white arms were warmed by the pastel color. She looked like a Greek goddess and was radiant.

The women let out a long collective whistle.

"I can tell you're out to impress him."

Peggy said admiringly as she gave Val a hug delicately, so as to not mess up her hair or makeup.

Glynnis followed suit and touched the strands of hair flowing down her back.

"You look beautiful!"

"Thanks!"

Glynnis and Peggy caught sight of the time and hurriedly rushed to put on their own standby "little black dresses." Nylons were quickly pulled on, and empty packages thrown on the floor. Dress tags littered the coffee tables as each one helped zip up the other. Caroline wore a glamorous cream-colored cocktail dress with a plunging neckline. She ran about in her stocking feet telling them not to worry, that she'd pick everything up before the guests arrived. The women moved quickly in and out of various rooms, using mirrors for hair, makeup and touch-ups.

With a few minutes to spare, they sat in the living room looking beautiful.

"So tell us again how you and Warren met."

They picked up their wine glasses and listened intently. Val's face lit up as she happily relayed the tale. They almost had to redo their make-up after laughing over the Tidbits story again. It was funnier the second time around. Val stood nervously awaiting his arrival.

"I think the best part of all is that he LOVES music and voluntarily conducts when he's not flying!"

Val told them enthusiastically.

"I'd say it couldn't get any more perfect!"

Caroline chimed in, beaming at her sister's good fortune and raised her glass with a wink.

Val reminded them that they had to get to the auditorium soon. Caroline had briefed them over the phone about Val's plan to surprise Warren on stage at the concert. She reminded them that he had no idea she was a violinist. They all felt rather wicked about their deceptive roles, yet privileged to be a part of the plot. They asked Val to cover the details with them one more time.

"Well, here's what I thought. We'll all go into the hall together and get seated. I have my concert dress already hung up in the dressing room, so I'll just slip into it there."

She was interrupted by Glynnis.

"Wait, wait, wait. You mean to tell me that you're not keeping this dress on? Why change?"

Val smiled slyly.

"Because I have another dress that's going to take his breath away when I walk on stage."

Glynnis shot Peggy and Caroline a surprised look.

"Oh!"

Val stood and put her hands on her hips striking a seductive pose.

"You see, in this, I'm his 'respectable' date, but on stage, I'm going to be his dream."

"Aaaahhhh..."

They all sighed in unison.

She sat back down and crossed her legs primly.

"Besides, he attends quite a few of these events at home in Ireland. This look is something he'd see all the time."

She pointed to her flowing dress.

Glynnis shrugged her shoulders.

"Maybe so, but I still think you look stunning in it."

She drained the last sip from her wine glass.

"Isn't he supposed to be here by now? Will you run through the plan once more while we're waiting? I don't want to screw anything up."

Val stood behind Glynnis, who was sitting on the couch, and placed her hands on her shoulders.

"All right, now listen closely. Once we're all seated, I'm going to tell Warren that I forgot to tell my mother something. I'll leave you guys to talk with him until the concert begins. Make sure he doesn't look at the program, or he'll see my picture! I almost forgot about that. When the lights flicker, Caroline, since you'll be sitting next to him, open the brochure and make a snide remark like, 'Oh, she's playing again.' He'll then probably ask, 'Who' and you'll have to come up with something clever. But don't give it away just yet, okay?"

Caroline nodded. Val couldn't stop smiling.

The three women were sitting on the edge of the couch, engaged in the plot, when the doorbell rang.

"Oh my gosh!!! It's him!"

Val jumped.

They all got up at the same time and stood at the door, looking dumbfounded. Realizing how stupid they looked just standing there, they tried to go in different directions to make it look like they weren't waiting. Val headed downstairs when she realized she'd forgotten to put the music stand away. It was still set up in the living room.

"CAROLINE!"

She yelled up in a stage whisper from the middle of the staircase.

"WHAT??!!!"

Came her anxious reply.

"Go and put the music stand away in my bedroom, I forgot."

"RIGHTO!"

Caroline closed the door, and her footsteps could be heard scurrying across the living room.

Val took a deep breath and descended the remaining stairs gracefully. She smiled through the glass and waved at Warren. He looked irresistibly handsome in his tuxedo.

Warren, holding a dozen long-stemmed Sterling roses, couldn't stop staring at the vision before him. The roses matched Val's dress perfectly.

"How did you know what I would be wearing?"

She reached for him and they exchanged a passionate kiss. Warren drew her closer to him and kissed her again.

"If we keep this up much longer, we'll miss the concert."

Val warned breathlessly.

"You look striking, Valerie."

The spell was broken by the sound of her sister's quickly pattering footsteps overhead. She closed the hall door. Smelling the roses, she thanked Warren for his thoughtfulness.

"The roses are what made me late. I was waiting for the concierge desk to call me when they arrived."

She took his hand and led him upstairs. Caroline was just then digging into the dip with a chip when they walked through the door. She'd just placed the loaded chip in her mouth and couldn't smile or reach out to greet him because she had dip on her hands. She tried, once again awkwardly, to smile, and put her hand up to cover her mouth. She chewed quickly.

"Sorry about that. It figures I'd meet you with my mouth full."

Glynnis and Peggy appeared from the kitchen and waved.

"Warren, this one, munching away, is my sister, Caroline."

Caroline quickly wiped her hand on a green napkin and extended it, smirking with her mouth still full.

"You remember Glynnis and Peggy. They just arrived from England a little while ago."

Warren was delighted to be in the company of such enchanting women. Each one was uniquely different and beautiful.

"I'm going to be the envy of every man in the concert hall when I appear with all of you lovely ladies."

The women laughed and told him jokingly that they were planning to walk on the other side of the street.

"Good, good. I was waiting to hear something like that. Now I'm back in my rightful place."

"They won't let you get away with anything, you know."

Val reminded him.

"I can see that. But you can't fault a man for trying."

He walked around the table to where Caroline was standing and, taking the chip she'd dropped on the table, scooped the dip from the bowl.

"Is it as good as it looks on you?"

Caroline turned in the mirror and saw the dip on her chin.

"Oh, that just figures! You can dress me up, but you can't take me anywhere!"

She took Warren's napkin from his hand and wiped her chin, placing it back in his hand when she was done.

He stared after her.

"Is she always this formal with everyone she meets?"

Val shook her head.

"Only those she doesn't know."

Patting him on the back, Val announced.

"Ok, we've got to hustle here. Are we walking or what?"

The women decided that it was a beautiful night for a walk to the John Hancock Hall, especially since it was right around the corner and would only take a few minutes.

Caroline knocked on their neighbor's door on the way out to remind her to listen for the caterers, who'd be arriving around 9:30PM.

"It's going to be a great night, Warren. I think you're going to really enjoy this."

Warren was already in high spirits and held out both his elbows to Val and Caroline, who each locked hold of one arm.

They talked animatedly as they walked. Men looked after them as they passed by, and Warren was enjoying his enviable status. A few people stopped, thinking it a model shoot for a magazine.

As they approached the front of the auditorium, Val heard her mother's voice from within the gathering crowd. The Harbor Lights Ensemble bus was out front and members of the group were getting on and off, fixing strings and tuning their instruments. The men were making adjustments to their tuxes while the ladies, dressed in white blouses and black skirts, helped them straighten out their bow ties.

"Valerie!"

An elegantly dressed woman approached and gave her a hug. She then went over and gave Caroline a kiss on the cheek.

"I've got gorgeous daughters, don't you think?"

Warren nodded in agreement and put his hand out.

"With that hint, you must be the illustrious Mrs. Callaghan."

She curtsied and replied.

"And you must be the heart-stopping Mr. Cahill my daughter has been talking about incessantly."

Warren turned to Valerie with a surprised look.

"Incessantly? Really! All good I hope?"

He turned to Grace for affirmation.

Val tugged at him gently on the arm.

"Of course, it's all good! Now let's hurry and get our tickets or we'll all be late."

Warren gave Grace a quick kiss on the cheek, telling her it was wonderful to meet her and that he looked forward to talking with her more after the concert.

Val was anxious to get inside before someone from the ensemble asked her why she wasn't dressed. Little did she know that her mother had already announced to the entire ensemble on the bus ride up from the Cape of Val's secret plan. No one would dare say a word. Over the many years, they'd become like one big family.

Caroline held the tickets and their group headed over toward the snack bar, which also offered beer and wine. Val declined, while the other women opted for a glass of wine. Warren picked up the tab.

Val watched as the members of the ensemble began to file down the back hallway and waved at her. The curtain was drawn, and she knew they were all taking their places backstage to run through warm-ups and sound checks. The audience wasn't allowed to enter the hall yet. A crowd had begun to queue outside and Valerie was nervous; a shudder went through her. Warren offered her his jacket, but she politely declined.

She spotted Father Bruce, who waved, then walked over. She prayed he wouldn't say anything.

"Well, good evening to such a bevy of beauties. Don't we all look exceptionally fetching tonight."

The women thanked him, and each gave him a quick kiss and a hug. He looked at Warren and held out his hand.

"I'm told you're Warren. A pleasure to meet you."

Warren shook his hand and smiled at Valerie, who introduced them.

"Warren, this is Father Bruce Moriarty. We refer to him as Father Bruce. You can call him something simple like 'Your Eminence'. He'd love that ... "

She playfully poked at Father Bruce.

"Is she always such a clown?"

Warren asked Father Bruce.

"Afraid so, but you'll get used to it. She kind of grows on you - like moss."

Warren laughed at the analogy.

"Well, I just wanted to say hello. I must go and rally the troops. We'll see you inside."

He winked at Val as he turned to leave.

They were all standing around chatting when some of the staff from Puritan Medical Center spotted Caroline and went over to talk with her. Caroline pulled Valerie along to introduce her to some of her coworkers. Peggy and Glynnis were chatting up Warren, who looked to be in the middle of telling them a very animated story.

Valerie had just begun to relax when the lights started to flicker. She stiffened up when Caroline announced, "Show time!"

They got everyone in their party together and walked down the aisle to find their seats. Warren stood aside to let the women enter first. Val stood last at the end of their row motioning him to go in before her so she could take the seat on the end.

The concert hall clamored with patrons. Val's company, Sidebar Magazine, was one of the many sponsors of the event and had several rows of seats reserved for the VIPs and their families up front. Val waved excitedly to her aunt and grandmother, who sat above them in a private balcony. She quietly pointed them out to Warren, who waved up at them. While he waved, she gave Caroline the thumbs-up sign.

"Warren, would you excuse me for just a moment? I need to quickly go and tell my mom something about the party. I'll be back in a flash."

Warren squeezed her hand.

"You'd best hurry up, or they won't let you back in."

Val dashed up the aisle, dodging guests. Once out of site behind the entrance door, she took off her high heels and sprinted down the long corridor that led backstage. Pulling hairpins out of her hair, she let it fall freely in gentle waves.

Her mom was anxiously awaiting her arrival.

"Where have you been? We all thought you got lost. Father Bruce is having a fit. Hurry up! I've got the dress. C'mon, I'll help you get into it."

Val was ushered into a small room and was surprised to see her Auntie Sheila there. She gave her a hug.

"Hurry up, will you!!!! Father Bruce is getting ready to make the welcome announcement already!"

Sheila helped Val pull off her "date" dress. Her mother removed the elegant black bustier Nicole Miller column dress from the garment bag.

"Would you look at this?"

She held the dress up for her sister to admire.

"I've not been able to fit into something like this in over fifteen years. Oh, to be young again."

She smiled at her daughter.

"You'll be a dish! Let's get this on, shall we? Did you tune your violin, I hope?"

Val nodded. Her hair got stuck on the zipper.

"Oww!"

Sheila apologized as she zipped up the back of her dress a second time, and then stepped back in admiration. Val let the rest of her hair down and the soft curls fell about her face. She stood confidently in front of the mirror and turned to her mother and aunt.

"Well! What do you think Warren will say?"

She turned to look at the back of the dress in the full-length mirror.

Her mother assured her.

"He won't be able to take his eyes off you, honey."

"Neither will the other men in the audience."

Auntie Sheila pointed out.

"Come to think of it, you may even give Father Bruce second thoughts."

They all burst out laughing at her irreverent comment.

It was exactly the look she wanted, classy, yet sexy.

Grace kissed her daughter and told her to "break a leg," and slipped out to take her place behind the piano. Sheila blew her a kiss as she ran back to her balcony seat.

Val set her violin on her shoulder and played softly through the scale for a moment, then left the dressing room and walked over to the edge of the stage. Hidden by the curtain, she stood directly behind her mother, who sat at the piano at the stage's edge. Grace motioned behind her back for her to come in a little closer and whispered.

"Are you okay?"

Val reached out and squeezed her hand. She waved to her uncle Sean, who made a motion like he'd just touched something hot. All the men turned and nodded in agreement. Val curtsied to them.

Back in the audience, Caroline leafed through the program.

"I hope your sister hurries up, or she'll miss the opening set and won't get back in."

Warren looked anxiously up at the back for her. Caroline glanced over at Peggy and winked.

"Oh, look! SHE's playing again."

Warren was too concerned looking around for Valerie and missed her cue.

"No worries, Warren. She wouldn't miss this for the world."

Peggy leaned over and assured him.

The women straightened in their seats as the lights were brought up. The crowd applauded when Father Bruce appeared on stage.

"Thank you."

He smiled broadly at the audience.

"First, I would like to thank all of you for joining us tonight, and to express my sincere appreciation for your generous contributions. As you may know, tonight's performance will benefit the addition of the new Neil Callaghan Memorial Children's Library. It is through the generosity of family members, friends, church members, and corporate sponsors, that we are able to bring you such an inspirational music event this evening."

"Tonight's performance features the music of Pachelbel in a unique way that not many have ever heard before. We have compiled a list of music, which we believe you'll find entertaining and delightful. It is my pleasure to introduce to you this evening a young woman whose first public performance with the Harbor Lights Ensemble occurred when she was just twelve years old. She has studied violin for many years under Malcolm Wendelson and remains a faithful member of the Harbor Lights Ensemble. It is my pleasure, ladies and gentlemen, to introduce to you, Miss Valerie Callaghan."

Pigtails and Potter's Field

The curtain opened to Grace's gentle piano introduction. Caroline watched as Warren's gaze was transfixed on stage. Valerie was breathtaking in her new dress. Her movements were slow and precise.

Warren was completely captivated by her. The background light illuminated her slender figure and her blond hair glistened. She spoke to him through her music. Caroline thought she saw his eyes water slightly, and knew at that exact moment, he'd fallen instantly in love with her.

She elbowed Peggy, who then nudged Glynnis to look. They observed with amusement the trance-like state Warren was in. He was enthralled, studying her every move. Valerie, if she was the slightest bit nervous, didn't waiver a note. He glanced over at Caroline, Peggy, and Glynnis who couldn't help but grin stupidly back at him. He wagged his finger at them.

Sean entered the score playing a perfect accompaniment. The two knew each other's timing instinctively and harmonized beautifully. Warren closed his eyes in order to take in the passionate sound of Valerie's violin, enhanced by the delicate flute tune. When he couldn't keep them closed any longer, he awoke as if from a dream and wanted to pinch himself.

She was more than he could have ever imagined, the definition of class. He knew then that Valerie Callaghan would one day become his wife. He couldn't wait to talk with her about what music she liked and the various arrangements she'd played. It would be his privilege, one day, to be able to conduct while she played.

Warren shook his head slightly, knowing he'd been set up, and squeezed Caroline's hand.

"She's amazing."

Caroline gazed up at her sister with pride and uttered quietly.

"I know."

Chapter Thirty-Nine

Boston, Massachusetts, Spring 1998

WARREN LED THE STANDING OVATION. The program ended after two curtain calls. Valerie made several bows and was presented with a beautiful floral arrangement at the concert's conclusion. She waved to her grandmother and aunt in the balcony and blew a kiss to Warren, who smiled and signaled back at her. Val couldn't wait to run off the stage and jump into his arms. At the concert's end, when the curtain finally closed, everyone backstage was in a joyous mood.

Val explained to her mother that she wanted to get back to the house quickly to check on the caterers and make sure that everything was in order and ready when people started arriving. Not all the members of the ensemble could make it back to the house for the party, and a handful took the bus back home after the concert. Those who wanted to attend the party had driven their own cars into Boston.

Grace and the rest of the family had made reservations at the Parker House where Warren was staying. They wanted to enjoy the celebration in Boston and not have to worry about driving two hours back to the Cape late at night. They'd hoped to have a leisurely Saturday morning sleeping in, and a late breakfast, before getting back on the road. However, Sheila was boasting of a "surprise" to be revealed only to those willing to get up early and meet her for breakfast in the restaurant the next morning. Grace had also reserved a room for Father Bruce, only he wasn't aware of that yet ... another surprise they'd spring on him later.

Val exited quickly through the stage doors and immediately spotted Warren, who was leaning against the wall, waiting for her to appear. He approached her and smirked.

"All I can say is ... touché!"

He kissed her forehead.

Val smirked and pointed at him.

"Aha ... and I got you good!

He kissed her hand.

"Yes, my love, you did just that."

Putting his jacket over her shoulders, he inquired.

"Where's your violin?"

Val told him that either her mother or her uncle Sean would bring it back to the house. She wanted to get home quickly and change before the guests started arriving. Warren good-naturedly offered to help. She rolled her eyes and led him out a back door.

Within moments they were on Commonwealth Avenue, and a stone's throw from the condo. He couldn't wait to get five minutes alone with her.

Val took the key out of her purse and climbed the stairs. Helen yelled up from downstairs that everything looked good, and she told her she'd placed the desserts in the refrigerator.

"Thanks, Helen! Come on up for something to eat in a little while."

Val offered, stopping to look down over the railing at her.

"Thanks! I'll do that!"

She waved and headed back into her apartment.

When they were inside, she turned to Warren, who'd removed his jacket from her shoulders and beheld her in her gown. She was delectable.

He led her into the living room to sit on the couch. Removing her sandals, he rubbed her feet.

"Oh! That feels wonderful."

She lay back on the couch, gazing into his deep blue eyes.

"I'm so glad you came into my life, Valerie. Tonight, when I saw you up on stage, I was filled with so many different emotions. I mean, I was proud, and amazed, and, dare I say, fell head over heels in love with you!"

Val sat up quickly and stared intently at him. Gradually, she leaned back against his shoulder to let what he just said sink in. She didn't say anything in return. He tipped her chin up to kiss her.

She was floating. It was a Cinderella moment. They played with each other's lips, giving and receiving quick kisses, and were becoming entangled in a passionate embrace when they heard the sound of women's laughter on the landing below the living room window.

"They're here!"

Val jumped up to straighten her dress and hair.

Warren stood to open the door.

"Just in time, too. I couldn't have been held responsible for what might have happened next."

Val shot him a sly smile and told him to behave.

He headed out to the kitchen to pour her a well-deserved glass of wine. Opening the refrigerator, he snatched a miniature éclair from the dessert tray before carrying it to the dining room and placing it alongside the coffee on the server.

"I'll stand by and guard these tonight."

Val laughed and kissed the sweet frosting off his lips just as the other women entered the room.

"Well, maybe we should have knocked first. I hope we're not disturbing you."

Caroline exaggerated.

"Well, you know you ARE, but you live here too, so I'll make an exception in your case."

Val nudged her.

"Great job tonight, sis. You were marvelous as usual."

Peggy and Glynnis offered similar compliments, then headed straight for the dessert tray Warren had taken out of the fridge.

The doorbell rang and people started drifting in. When someone announced that Father Bruce was only a few yards away, they all hid as best they could. Father Bruce loudly announced halfway up the stairs to Val that he was dying of thirst.

"Well, hurry on up here then! We have all sorts of things to drink!"

She yelled from the landing, and then snickered quietly, shushing the people to be quiet.

When he entered into the dining room, everyone jumped out.

"SURPRISE!!"

Father Bruce saw the anniversary cake on the dining room table, along with the festive green streamers, and smiled at them all.

"Thank you so much for remembering. It's been an honor to serve with all of you!!"

He thanked them whole-heartedly.

"Now ... I want someone to serve me a piece of that cake! I'm starved!"

Everyone clapped and cheered for a few moments. Warren asked what he wanted to drink, and Father Bruce opted for one of Warren's Sam Adams lagers.

The men stood in the kitchen talking, drinking a brew, and eating cake. Warren complimented him on the concert and went on to explain that he, too, conducted, at the Glor in Ireland on occasion. Father Bruce had heard that from Grace, and expressed his enthusiasm at having found a fellow conductor. They were engrossed in their conversation, and it made Val feel very comfortable that Warren fit in so naturally with her friends and family.

Sheila and Tim were helping to carry all of Valerie's gear back to the house. She met them at the door and took the violin case from Tim, who congratulated her on another amazing performance. He offered to put the instrument in her bedroom for her. Val hugged her grandmother, and took her shawl.

"You looked and sounded enchanting tonight, lovey. My heart was filled with pride. All those lessons finally paid off!"

Val laughed and asked her to pick her poison. She opted for Baileys over ice. Tim appointed himself bartender for the evening. He took orders and set about making drinks in the kitchen for all who asked.

The food smelled delicious and people dug right in. Caroline turned on the stereo and music drifted from the living room into the large dining room and kitchen. A few of the men from the ensemble sat at the window seat in the living room, balancing plates on their laps and drinks in their hands. A couple of women shared the piano bench, sipping daintily from their wine glasses.

The piano belonged to their Auntie Sheila who had bought it for Grace when she came to visit. Sheila thought the girls would enjoy keeping it in the condo. It got a lot of use when Grace was there. It provided for some wonderful mother/daughter moments for her and Val. Caroline was their captive and always enthusiastic audience.

Val had borrowed some folding chairs from work. Many of her co-workers stopped by for drinks and a bite to eat. They were happy to finally meet Warren, and he had his arm around her waist as he grilled them about what she was really like at the office. Liz, the receptionist, replied.

"What you see is what you get! She's great!"

Warren made a face of dramatic relief.

Val wanted to get out of her evening dress and headed down the hall to her room. She opened the door and was startled to find Tim lying across her bed.

"Oh! Gosh you scared me. Are you all right? What are you doing in here?"

He assured her he was fine and that he was just a bit tired and thought he'd lie down for a few minutes. He said the long drive was catching up with him. He motioned for her to come and sit next to him. She sat and asked him to unzip the back of her dress, instructing him then to turn around, which he did when she went behind her dressing screen.

"Well, you can't fall asleep! I'm throwing on a pair of jeans and plan on doing a little fiddling later if you're up for it. We'll get a few more glasses of wine into Caroline and she'll become a dancing fool."

Tim laughed. He never tired of watching Caroline's step dancing, she displayed such liveliness and energy. Everyone in the family had been a bit disappointed when she'd turned down the offer from the Song for Ireland Theatre Company to become a part of their American Troupe, but Tim had understood that mentally she would probably not have been able to withstand the grueling demands of a traveling life. Caroline slipped easily into depression when she was tired.

Val tossed her gown on the bed and took her violin out of the case. She attached her chin rest and wiped down the strings with a silk scarf. Taking an emery board, she scratched it across the hard, rosin block until she saw it powder. Then she ran the block up and down along the bowstrings.

"I'm good to go!"

She stated after testing it out.

Tim threw his legs over the side of the bed.

"Let's go. I'll feel better after another drink I think."

Val smiled at him and opened the door, escorting him out.

Upon returning to the living room, she didn't see Warren. Setting her violin down on the coffee table, she headed back to the dining room to get some food. Warren was in the kitchen, talking animatedly with Glynnis and Peggy. He waved at her from across the room as she filled her plate with an assortment of food.

Warren was clearly enjoying himself. Val, starving, sat to eat for the first time that day. Her mother brought out the sliced cake and had everyone gather in the dining room while she presented Father Bruce with his gifts — a signed picture of the entire ensemble and tickets to an upcoming performance of the Boston Symphony Orchestra at Tanglewood. She also informed him of the room reserved for him at the Omni that evening, so that he could stay as late as he wanted and not have to rush to get home. He gave an appreciative "thank you," and everyone took turns either hugging him or shaking his hand. Val got up and gave him a kiss on the cheek, as did Caroline. He hugged them both warmly, thanking them for the nice surprise.

Warren excused himself from the women's company and went to sit beside Val. She cut off a piece of the veal Parmesan with her fork and fed it to him. He smacked his lips and opened his mouth for more. Val stuffed it with rigatoni, causing sauce to drip down his chin. She laughed, handing him a napkin. The house was filled with animated conversations and laughter. She heard the screeching sound of her violin coming out of the living room. Malcolm, her violin instructor of many years, was beckoning her into the crowded living room to come and play.

"I haven't even finished my dinner!"

She whined loudly and was pulled off the couch to her feet. Malcolm placed the violin in her hands.

Soon, Uncle Sean joined her on the flute, filling the room with a lively tune, getting the guests to clap along. Grace was involved in a serious discussion with Siobhan, but Sheila soon dragged her over to the piano. Tim and Granny talked amicably on the couch.

After the music ended, Val picked up her plate, grabbed Warren's hand with her free one, and led him back into the crowded living room where everyone had gathered. Her uncle Sean had lifted the plate from her hand again and replaced it with her violin.

"Oh, come on, guys. I just want to finish eating."

She droned.

The crowd wouldn't hear of it and told her to eat later. Caroline turned off the stereo. At Sheila's urging, Grace played a simple, snappy tune. Val playfully fiddled along. Uncle Sean joined in once again on the flute as Caroline tried to pull Glynnis up off the floor to dance with her. Glynnis declined, telling Caroline she'd sit this one out and just watch.

Caroline, who'd lost her shoes when she'd come in the front door, did her best River Dance reenactment. Val, having memorized some of the music from the show, fiddled furiously as the two kept in sync with one another. Shouts were heard from across the room as the men got to their feet. Warren couldn't take his eyes off Val, and was equally amazed at her fiddling ability.

He joined in the festive mood and clapped heartily, adding a few whooping calls of his own while Caroline danced. Taking a quick breather, Val spotted her hair clip on the mantle and used it to pin her hair up, then placed the violin back on her shoulder. She changed the pace of the music. Warren stood, and to her surprise and delight, danced a reel with Caroline, Siobhan, and Peggy. Father Bruce later was coerced into dancing a hornpipe and did a fine job, holding his own. Caroline clapped for him when she was done. Glynnis seized the opportunity to shout to Caroline that she needed to quit nursing and open her own dance studio, a thought she'd toyed with off and on over the years. Many in the room nodded in agreement.

When Val complained that her arms were killing her, and that she couldn't hold the violin up any longer, Sean took over playing a couple of solemn, dirge-like songs. The room quieted as people relaxed and took in the haunting sounds of the tin whistle. Grace accompanied him on the piano. The time was well after midnight when Granny announced that she needed to get back to the hotel and get to bed. Siobhan asked Val to call them all a taxi as the rest of the guests took their cue and agreed that they should be getting along as well. Grace tried without success to stifle a yawn.

Val thanked everyone for coming. She encouraged them to take platefuls of food home with them, as there was still quite a bit left over. Sheila reminded Val and the women that they were all meeting for breakfast the next morning at the hotel before heading home to the Cape. Turning to Warren, Sheila commanded playfully.

"And you'll have no excuse for not being there, Mr. Cahill, since we're all staying at the same place."

Warren told her he'd set his alarm and wouldn't dare miss it. Sheila then baited them.

"Remember, I've got a huge surprise for those of you who show up tomorrow morning for breakfast."

Peggy assured her.

"Okay, okay! We'll be there. What time?"

Caroline sighed.

"How about ten o'clock?"

"Nope. 8AM and no later! You'll see why tomorrow."

"8:00AM!!! Are you nuts?"

Caroline protested.

"Suit yourself. It'll be your loss if you don't make it."

Sheila warned, piquing their curiosity further.

Finally, everyone reluctantly agreed, warning Sheila that it had better be a damn good surprise to get them out of bed that early on a Saturday. They kissed and hugged as they filed out the door.

Peggy, Glynnis, and Caroline set about clearing the dining room table. The caterers would be back in the morning to pick up the serving trays. The women packaged up the remaining food into whatever containers they could find. Warren tried helping but got caught up in the plastic wrap. Val freed him, so he could continue to pick at the pastries. Glynnis and Peggy gathered up the various wine glasses and cans from around the house, dumping the empties into a big trash bag. She handed the bulging garbage bags to Warren and asked him to take them around back to the dumpster in the alley, a job she hated.

When he returned, Peggy and Glynnis had moved down to the other end of the house to talk with Caroline in her room, leaving them with a few minutes to themselves. Val collapsed on the couch and Warren lay down next to her. They cuddled in front of the fireplace until Val felt herself dozing off.

He ran his fingers gently through her hair, kissing her ear and neck, giving her the chills. She sighed contentedly with the wonderful, relaxed feeling that streamed through her body. All tension dissipated as he massaged her scalp. She held his hand under her chin, kissing his fingers. Taking one of his fingers in her mouth, she playfully tickled his finger with her tongue. She quickly felt his response against her back, and chuckled softly as he quietly moaned.

"You're testing my resolve, Valerie Jean Callaghan. You do realize that?"

Val returned his demanding kisses.

"You are a beautiful woman, in many ways."

Warren whispered and nuzzled his face in her hair, inhaling the light floral scent.

"Thank you."

She softly replied, and reluctantly suggested.

"I think we should call you a cab now."

Warren nodded.

"Yes, a wise move. I rather enjoy taking cold showers at two in the morning."

Val rolled her eyes but encouraged him gently.

"I can assure you, Mr. Cahill, that it'll be worth the wait ... someday."

He smiled at her broadly.

"You don't say, but how about we just practice a little, you know, so we can become REALLY good."

Val threw a pillow from the couch at him, which he caught easily. Placing it back on the couch he got up and grabbed her arm and hugged her tightly.

"OOOOOHHHHH ..."

They were caught kissing by the women who'd come to stand in the kitchen.

"We were hoping to see a little bit more action than that!"

Warren laughed.

"Yeah ... me, too!"

Val picked up the phone to call him a taxi. They walked downstairs together and waited in the darkened hallway. The light from the street lamps filled the foyer as they leaned against the wall, holding one another tightly. Warren laced his hands around her waist and stared deeply at her in the evening light.

"I can't wait to see you tomorrow and spend some time alone."

Val nodded.

"We will. I promise."

The taxi pulled up and beeped. They shared one final embrace before he climbed into the cab.

Upstairs, the women were seated at the table eating the remaining Tidbits out of a bowl.

"Oh, and whose clever idea was it to get those? I didn't even see them!"

Glynnis pointed at Caroline.

"Who do you think?"

Caroline raised her hand while yawning and announced that she was going to bed.

"I've got to start packing up all my gear tomorrow. My flight leaves Sunday evening at eight. Do you have any idea what Auntie Sheila's surprise is? If this turns out to be one of her all-day things, I'm never going to be ready in time."

Val shrugged her shoulders.

"Who knows? I guess we'll all just find out in the morning."

Peggy and Glynnis were to share the pullout, queen-sized couch in the living room. Val grabbed a set of sheets, and extra pillows from the linen closet. She'd opened the window wider to allow a breeze in.

They all said good night, and Val shuffled down the hall to her room. Removing her clothes and slightly dampened panties. She sank beneath the down comforter and immediately fell asleep.

Chapter Forty

SHEILA'S SURPRISE WAS MORE THAN any of them could have expected. They all sat blurry-eyed at the breakfast table set for a party of eleven. Everyone was anxious for coffee.

"So tell us, Sheila, what's your big surprise?"

Warren was the first to inquire. Yawning, he reached for the sugar and passed the creamer to Caroline.

"Glad you asked, Warren. Here you go."

She was so bright-eyed and chipper. She passed out small envelopes to each one at the table.

"Oh, my GOD!"

Caroline was the first to exclaim.

"Carly Simon tickets!!!"

The women screamed with delight as hotel guests from other tables looked over.

"How did you ever get your hands on these?"

Sheila was delighted with their response.

"Let's just say that I've got friends in high places."

The concert was scheduled for that evening, on Nantucket.

"How are we all going to get there? We need ferry reservations."

Sheila had taken care of all the details. Friends of hers on the Cape, who vacationed on Nantucket each summer and had a slip reserved for the season, would ride them over in their large cabin cruiser. Sheila had given them tickets as well, and admitted to having planned the event months ago.

Knowing how much her nieces enjoyed Carly Simon, Sheila had pulled some strings with a few of the locals, and secured fifteen tickets for the event. It had cost her a small fortune, but she knew it would be well worth it. Val and Caroline got up from their seats and went around the table to give their amazing aunt a big kiss.

Sheila laid out the plan of action.

"We've no time to waste. Finish eating and then you gals head back to the condo and throw some things in a bag. Drive down to Dock Ave in Hyannis, and we'll meet you at the Yacht Club. The guard has a list of our names, and we'll just park and walk over to Alan and Audrey's boat. They're expecting us all to arrive no later than two. It'll take us a couple of hours to get out to the island."

Warren was very excited. Though he'd heard about Nantucket Island, he'd never been there. His vacation was turning out to be more exciting than he'd imagined. He squeezed Valerie's hand, announcing that dinner on the island was his treat.

"We've got to move quickly. If we all get on the road by ten, we can be at the Yacht Club in time to have lunch. Do you think you can all pull it together that quickly?"

Everyone assured her they would hurry. They rushed through their meals. Granny picked up the tab for breakfast and was a little anxious about the boat ride, saying that she'd probably need a Dramamine, as she was prone to seasickness. Caroline told her she had some at the house and would bring it along.

"Not to worry, Gran. You can just hurl over the side. You'll be fine."

"Thanks, Caroline, that's just what I wanted to hear during breakfast." Sean responded sarcastically.

Caroline wondered how she was going to get all of her stuff together in time for her trip to Spain Sunday night. Peggy and Glynnis assured her it would all work out; they'd help her pack when they got back Sunday afternoon. Carly Simon had been one of Caroline's favorite singers since she was a kid. She'd move heaven and earth to get there.

Val went up to Warren's room to help him throw a few things in a bag. Warren tackled her on the bed and she offered no resistance. She felt a tingly, luscious electric current rush through her body at his touch. He devoured her with his kisses.

"Sweetie, we've got to get going or we'll be late - much as I'd like to stay here with you forever."

Warren smoothed her skirt out.

"I can't have you looking like I just tackled you."

Val laughed.

"But you just did."

He tossed his bag over his shoulder and grabbed his wallet off the bureau.

"Let's go. Who'll drive?"

Val told him that they'd not all fit in one car, so she suggested that Caroline take her own car and ride with Peggy and Glynnis, and that she and Warren would drive down in her BMW.

It was a gorgeous May day and was expected to touch into the low eighties. Warren put on his sunglasses. Caroline, Glynnis, and Peggy had already left the hotel, and Warren and Val jumped in a waiting taxi. They made it back to the condo in record time, and Val bounded up the steps. The house was a flurry of activity. The caterers had taken the trays, leaving the table clear. Val ran back to her room and instructed Warren to grab a few bottled waters out of the refrigerator. Caroline, Peggy, and Glynnis were ready to go and shouted that they'd meet them there.

"Drive carefully. I'm SO excited!!!"

Caroline was giddy.

Warren waited in the living room, admiring the many photos of Val and her family.

They were all beautiful women. Even their mother was still very attractive. He stared amusedly at Sean in a goofy pose with Valerie in front of a horse-drawn carriage; he thought they might be at the Gap of Dunloe, in Killarney, County Kerry. Siobhan held a wiggling baby Caroline in another photo. There was a picture of Grace and Sheila leaning against a tall, gray-haired man whom he assumed was their father. He stopped short when he saw the picture of Neil with Valerie as a young girl, balancing a toddler, Caroline, on his shoulders at the beach.

"Are we all set?"

Val dashed out of her room, wearing a floral sundress with a big white hat.

"Well, don't we just look like the queen!"

Val gave him her best version of the royal wave. She searched through her bag for her keys.

"Let's be off then!"

They rushed down the steps. It was 10:05AM when they loaded the trunk of her car and sped off.

The roads weren't that crowded in downtown Boston, and it wasn't long before they were coasting toward the south shore and the split off Route 28. Val turned up the music, pulled off her hat, and put down the top to her car. She looked rather chic in her oversized white sunglasses, singing along to the radio. Warren talked with her about music and asked about life growing up on Cape Cod. Val mentioned a few of her favorite spots to visit and have dinner. Warren asked after her father, and Val spoke warmly about him. She shared some of her favorite childhood stories. Warren listened intently without interrupting. He admired her devotion to his memory.

Val got excited as she entered the circle before the Bourne Bridge.

"This is it, Warren. Leave your cares behind. I love going over this bridge. You know you're really on the Cape when you get to this point."

She turned up the music and pointed out various things along the Cape Cod Canal. The bridge was expansive, and Warren's heart was filled with anticipation. He looked across as Valerie drove and leaned over to kiss her on the cheek.

"What was that for?"

She smiled and touched his hand, then quickly shifted gears.

"I don't need a reason, do I?"

She shook her head.

"Nope ... never!"

They followed the road for what seemed like miles without seeing much of the ocean.

When Val put on her directional and turned off toward Hyannis, she picked up speed in an effort to gain some time. She beeped as she approached the Yacht Club, and gave her name to the guard who motioned her in, where she pulled up alongside Caroline's car. The three women were getting their bags out of the back.

"How are we getting home tonight?"

Caroline asked.

Val suggested they all stay at Grace's house that night and head home in the morning. Glynnis and Peggy's flight was scheduled for eight thirty Sunday night, and Caroline's flight to Madrid was set for 8:00PM. They could share a taxi to the airport. Val mentioned that she and Warren might stay a few days longer with her mother on the Cape as she wanted to show him around and visit some of the local lighthouses, perhaps do some biking along the Salt Marsh rail trails. Caroline could already feel her sister being pulled away from her.

"HEY!"

The women turned to see Sean waving them over.

"We're up here."

Warren carried the water bottles, and Val helped Caroline get a few things out of her bag.

She put her white hat back on. Their mother and aunts were sitting on the deck of the club, eating sandwiches and sipping something frosty from wide-rimmed glasses with fruit sticking out of them.

"You should grab something for lunch before we get going."

Sean suggested.

Alan gave Val and Caroline a hug, as did his wife, Audrey. Val introduced them to Warren and they all started talking excitedly about the concert. The waitress took their drink orders; Val ordered fried clam rolls for herself and Warren. Caroline had her usual turkey club, and Glynnis and Peggy ordered grilled chicken sandwiches.

They watched as the seagulls squealed and swooped from the telephone poles. The sounds were perfect in their natural surrounding. Val loved the Cape and enjoyed every opportunity to come and visit.

Grace sat next to Warren, and the two talked easily with one another. Grace had put her hand on his arm as she appeared to be explaining something to him. Audrey filled Val in on her daughter, Faye, who was now an attorney. She'd been in the newspaper recently, having passed the bar exam, and was getting married that fall. Sean was talking with Caroline and her friends and bought them another round of tropical drinks. Alan paid the bill and announced that everyone should start boarding.

Val sipped the last bit of her piña colada and kissed Warren unexpectedly on the lips.

"Now, what was that for?"

She shrugged her shoulders.

"No reason. I just felt like it."

He held her hand as they walked across the lot to the ramp.

Warren helped Alan untie the boat from the dock. Alan climbed the steps to the bridge and made radio contact with the marina, transmitting his coordinates and destination to the harbormaster. He let out a long siren sound as they left the channel.

Maneuvering through the tricky waters of the Cape Cod Canal posed a challenge to even the most experienced of captains. The water converged from three different sources and made for a very strong current. Warren stood up on the bridge with Alan, holding on to the rail above, warning him of impending markers.

"You've got one coming up at three o'clock."

Granny sat with a pleasant smile on her face as Audrey and Sheila ducked in and out of the cabin, bringing drinks to those gathered on the deck. The stereo system from the cabin boomed loudly, creating a party-like atmosphere. Caroline, Glynnis, and Peggy were sprawled out on the bow, working on their first-of-the-season suntans. When they stripped down to their bathing suits, Alan sounded a long whistle. In response, Caroline displayed a quick grinding motion and Valerie threw an ice cube at him.

Tim was off smoking a cigarette, leaning with his arms over the side, staring in the direction of the young women. Sean was below, cutting up cheese and busying himself with putting a cracker tray together. Audrey stood next to him, slicing carrot sticks while Sheila whipped up a sour cream and onion dip. Father Bruce had declined the offer to come along, stating that he needed to get back to prepare for Mass on Sunday.

Val eventually joined her sister and friends sunbathing on the bow. Sean's head, popped up through the hatch, scaring the women to death. He passed out frozen strawberry daiquiris in festive tropical glasses, complete with cherry and orange wedges. Alan yelled down that they were all beginning to look like lobsters and threw down a bottle of tanning lotion, which they took turns applying.

They arrived at the Nantucket Boat Basin by 4:15PM. Walking up the ramp, they made their way to the White Elephant Hotel for dinner. The waitress seated them out back on the deck and told them they were lucky to get such a great table, given the number of people expected to attend the concert later that evening on the grounds of the hotel. She pointed out that cars had already started to line up. They informed her that they, in fact, had tickets to the concert but would be watching it right from their boat - pointing it out to her from their table. She was envious and told them how lucky they were to get such a close slip with a great view.

Val and Warren scanned the menu, deciding upon the New England clambake. It consisted of a cup of chowder, steamers, corn, coleslaw, and two boiled lobsters with lots of drawn butter. They were outfitted in traditional plastic bibs and laughed at one another when each got squirted trying to break apart their lobsters. Caroline could barely stomach watching them eat the lobsters, and went on to tell the story of how she and Val tried, unsuccessfully, to set the lobsters free when they were young.

* * *

Neil had brought lobsters home for dinner from the fisherman's exchange. He put them in the bathtub with cold water. The girls learned of their whereabouts and were playing with them, pushing them around in the tub with a ruler. It was Val's idea to set them free, and she told Caroline to get the laundry basket. She loaded them up and each girl took an end of the basket, carrying them down to the water's edge.

Grace watched her daughters with amusement and called to her husband to come quickly. She laughed hysterically as Neil chased after them down the beach. He gathered up the creeping crustaceans and brought them back to the confines of the tub.

He and Grace ate them during a late night dinner after the girls were put to bed. Granny loved hearing stories of her eldest son. Grace had tears in her eyes recalling the tender moment.

* * *

It was seven o'clock when they'd left the restaurant. The streets were teeming with tourists lined up to hear the concert. The group pushed their way through the crowd and showed their credentials at the marina gate. Looking across the water, they could see the equipment in place for the concert.

It was a warm evening and the breeze was gentle off the ocean. Val's face, slightly red and freckled from the afternoon's sun, gave her a healthy glow. Her green eyes sparkled in contrast. A few members of the band performed a sound check on the instruments. The crowd cheered in anticipation. Val could see the figure of a woman off to the side wearing a green ruffled dress.

"I think that's her!"

Audrey handed Valerie the binoculars. It was Carly. She was talking to one of her guitarists and smiling. Val could see her every facial movement. She called Caroline over and let her peer through the binoculars.

"This is so cool! I can't believe I'm looking at Carly Simon!"

Warren laughed at her excitement and took his turn staring through the binoculars. He handed them back to Val. Caroline ran to get her camera out of the cabin and Val followed after her to use the bathroom.

"Hurry, Val! You don't want to miss this!"

Caroline urged her from the doorway. Val quickly washed her hands, wiping them on her dress since she couldn't find a towel. The music started, and Val screamed as she opened the door and rushed out. The music was the hit song, "You're so Vain." It brought the crowd to their feet. Val and Caroline appeared on deck and did an impromptu staging of the music's lyrics. Val seductively pulled her large brimmed hat down over one eye, pulling a slinky scarf from her neck. Caroline pointed at her and sung out.

"You're so vain ..."

Warren laughed at their display. People from other boats cheered them on as Val danced in a somewhat sexy manner along the boat's edge.

Watching her, Warren threw his head back in utter defeat. Grace laughed and nudged him gently in the arm. Peggy and Glynnis joined Caroline, who'd moved to the bow. Their dancing brought a round of cheers from the men on the boats docked next to them.

It was a beautiful evening filled with good music and laughter. When the concert ended, Alan started the boat and they began their journey back to the mainland. There was a flotilla of ferries and boats leaving at the same time, and the harbormasters sailed about, keeping order.

The wind had shifted and Val pulled her cotton sweater over her head. She rested in Warren's arms, sitting on the cushions on the deck.

"It was a wonderful evening, don't you think?"

Warren asked Valerie.

She nodded in agreement and yawned.

"Yes, it was. It was great of Auntie Sheila to do this. I'm getting pretty tired though."

He let her nuzzle into his shoulder and cuddled her close, resting his chin on her head. The others had opted to go inside since the breeze was chilly off the water. Glynnis braved the elements to sit with them.

Once back on shore, they thanked their host and hostess and everyone kissed good-bye, then made their way back to Grace's house. Granny, Sean, and Siobhan were going to spend the night at Auntie Sheila and Uncle Tim's. Valerie, Caroline, Warren, and the girls would stay at Grace's house.

Their home was a classic, expanded Cape saltbox with a huge porch that spanned the back of the house. Neil had put on an addition shortly after they'd moved in. The house contained four bedrooms, three of which overlooked the ocean. Val showed Glynnis and Peggy to one of the guest rooms, which contained two single beds. Val shared her sister's queen-sized bed and let Warren have her childhood room. Grace left the women to sort through the details, explaining that she could hardly keep her eyes open any longer. They kissed her goodnight, as did Warren, and she climbed the stairs to her room.

They all slept late Sunday morning, yet managed to make it to the eleven o'clock Mass at St. Bridget's. After service, Grace greeted Father Bruce with both her daughters and their friends in tow. He warmly shook Warren's hand and told him it was good to see him again. He then pulled the family off to the side once the crowd dispersed.

"Caroline, you're off to Spain, I hear."

She nodded and smiled. He looked at her friends.

"Peggy and Glynnis, you're heading back to England tonight?"

They nodded.

"Would you mind if I say a prayer for you ladies for a safe journey?"

They welcomed his blessing joining hands.

"Lord, I thank you for bringing this family together. We are grateful for the joyous time we've shared this weekend. We thank you for friendships both old and new."

Warren, with his eyes closed, squeezed Val's hand.

"I place these precious children into your protective hands, and ask that you grant them traveling mercies. Be with Warren when he flies keeping him and those he's responsible for safe. Watch over Caroline as she ventures to a new and exciting country, and please watch over Peggy and Glynnis as they make their way back home. We thank you for your faithfulness and protection. Amen."

The family all replied "Amen," and blessed themselves. Grace thanked him for his prayer. Father Bruce waved to them as they drove off in their cars.

Caroline's carload followed Val back to their mother's house. Peggy, Glynnis, and Caroline went up to their rooms to gather their bags. Grace had made a spinach and cheese quiche and told them to have a quick bite before they got on the road. She set up dishes and lemonade out on the back porch. Caroline ran through the list of things she needed to get done before they headed to the airport that night.

"I can't wait!"

She exclaimed and proceeded to talk shop with Glynnis, telling her about her plans to switch specialties in nursing, and how she'd interviewed in Pediatrics and had gotten the job.

"I'm looking forward to the change when I get back. I had to get out of the ER."

Everyone gathered in the circular driveway for good-bye hugs. Val told her sister to have a great time and not to push herself too hard on the bike trails. Caroline responded by good naturedly warning Warren.

"Take good care of her."

He assured her he would. Grace waved as Peggy and Glynnis drove off with Caroline. She had tears in her eyes. She hated good-byes.

Val and Warren followed Grace into the house, then continued out back to the yard and collapsed into the white Adirondack chairs overlooking the ocean. They sat, lazily gazing at the water, watching in silence as a few lone clouds passed briefly over the sun.

"So what are your plans this week?"

Grace sauntered over to the couple. Val, resting her head against the back of her chair, nodded toward Warren.

"I'm planning on taking him tomorrow to see a few lighthouses, and then out for dinner."

Warren looked at her in surprise.

Grace perked up.

"No kidding! You'll love Chatham, Warren."

"Remind me to make reservations for us at the Chatham Bars Inn, will you? It's such a nice place. The food is excellent. It's a classic Cape Cod establishment."

He was looking forward to it.

Grace stood and told Val she was heading over to Sheila's. They were planning on taking Granny and the gang out for dinner and she didn't know exactly what time she'd be back. They were more than welcome to join her if they wanted to. Val looked wearily at Warren and he left it up to her.

"I think I'll pass, Mom. It's been a whirlwind weekend so far, and I just want to crash for a while."

Grace asked Val if she had her house key, and she assured her mother that she did. She told them to have fun. They heard her footsteps across the porch, then the motor from the car as she drove off.

"Do you want to go for a walk along the beach?"

Warren stood up and helped her out of the sunken chair.

"I'd love to."

He followed Val on the narrow path that led down to the ocean.

"Watch your legs, the ticks here are horrible."

He glanced down at his hairy legs.

They walked at a leisurely pace and took their shoes off at the water's edge. Val always lost her balance when she stared down at the moving surf. The water was so cold it took her breath away.

"My God!!! It's so cold it's making my feet ache!!"

Warren told her that the water never warmed up in Ireland either. They moved away from the flowing tide and walked casually hand in hand. Warren pulled Val onto the warmer sand further inland. She reclined between his legs as the two stared out at the ocean.

"This is better than I'd ever imagined, Valerie. Your family is great! I felt comfortable with them almost immediately."

She smiled.

"I know. They felt the same way about you, too. I can tell."

"Tim's a little on the quiet side but Sean seems to be the life of the party."

Val chuckled.

"I know. Uncle Sean is definitely the more outgoing of the two. But Uncle Tim is nice. He just doesn't like crowds too much. He's not a total recluse however."

They talked about Glynnis and Peggy, and Caroline's trip.

Warren moved Val around until they lay on their sides facing the ocean. She curled herself into him. There was no one on the beach, and they felt like they were on their own private island. Warren placed her head in the crux of his arm and kissed her warmly. She put her arms up around his neck and held him close.

"I want to make love to you."

She placed her hands in the center of his chest.

"I know. I want you, too. But we can't ... I mean, not here. I couldn't relax thinking someone might see us."

Warren chuckled.

"I didn't mean here. I want you to feel completely relaxed when that time comes."

She quickly assured him that the time would come, but that she wanted to take it slow, and not jump into a physical relationship just yet.

"Warren, it's obvious that we're attracted to each other. Let's just let it build gradually, okay?"

He told her he'd try to be on his best behavior, but that it wouldn't be easy.

Val stood up.

"C'mon, I know just the thing to help you."

She ran toward the shoreline and he chased after her. Once she hit the water, she screamed from the shock of it and turned to kick the icy water at him.

"This will cool you down!"

He tried unsuccessfully to block the splashes, shivering from the cold.

"Well, you're right ... it worked!"

He stood before her with his hands on his hips, staring at his midsection. Valerie pulled him out of the water, laughing. They headed up the winding path to the house.

Chapter Forty-One

Cariston, England, Spring 1998

THERE IS NO STATUTE OF limitations in cases of rape in England. Add in a charge of Grievous Bodily Harm and one could be looking at a possible fifteen-year-to-life sentence, which Peggy learned when she returned from the United States.

Long past ever thinking she'd see her uncle again, Peggy was stunned to hear Constable, now Detective Inspector, Laura Campbell's voice on her answering machine. She'd not heard from her in many years.

"I'm leaving this message for Peggy O'Malley. This is Detective Inspector Laura Campbell. Please contact me immediately regarding James Burke. Thank you."

Peggy's blood ran cold and her heart sank at the mention of his name.

"Why do you think she's calling?"

Peggy asked Glynnis nervously as they listened to the message a second time.

"Well, it could be that he's dead, or it could be that they've found him. In which case, they'll prosecute and send him to jail for the rest of his pathetic life!"

Glynnis was angry. It still bothered her, knowing how he'd abused Peggy as a child. She'd like to see justice prevail in this man's case.

"Do you think I should call her back now?"

Glynnis nodded.

"I would. Just to know what it's all about. Personally, I think she's calling to tell you he's dead."

Peggy sighed and picked up the phone.

"Let's hope that's the case."

Peggy called the number Laura had left on her answering machine.

She got her recording and left her own message.

"Laura, this is Peggy O'Malley. I'm just getting back from a trip to the US, and returning your call regarding my uncle, James Burke. Please feel free to contact me tonight or tomorrow. Thank you."

She hung up the phone slowly. Her hands were shaking.

Glynnis put her arm around her friend.

"Listen, hon, there's nothing that man can do to you now. Either he's dead or they caught him. In which case, the Royal Prosecution Service will try him. My da would love to be there to nail him!"

Peggy nodded her head, but she was still frightened. So much time had passed, and her life was calm now, routine, and her business successful. Her home reflected her creative and artistic touch. She and Glynnis had renovated it from top to bottom over the years. She didn't want anything to disrupt the peace she'd struggled so long to find. She set about busying herself.

The women carried their luggage upstairs. Peggy's legs felt like lead weights. She closed the door to her room and collapsed on the queen-sized bed. It felt good to be home. She looked around her pale yellow and sage green room and smiled. This was her home and it felt good to be back.

Glynnis knocked quietly on the door.

"Come in."

She went and sat on the bed next to Peggy. Staring down at her friend, she moved a piece of hair that had fallen across her eyes. There was a gentleness in her touch that comforted Peggy. Glynnis got up and went around the side of the bed. She lay down next to Peggy, putting her arm over her. Peggy closed her eyes and drifted off into a peaceful sleep. Glynnis felt she needed a nap and dozed off as well.

Peggy's body instantly tensed at the sound of the telephone, knowing it to be Laura Campbell. She reached for the phone near her bedside.

"Hello?"

Peggy answered nervously. Glynnis got up and sat in a nearby chair, giving her space to walk around.

"Peggy O'Malley, please?"

The voice on the other end inquired.

"This is Peggy."

She stood still with her hand on her hip.

"Peggy, this is Laura Campbell. It seems we've been playing telephone tag. How was your trip?"

Peggy felt a little bit better as Laura's voice was light and sounded more human when she asked about her trip.

"It was exciting! A rather spur-of-the-moment, whirlwind weekend you might say. But a lot of fun."

Laura's voice was calm and positive.

"Good! Peggy. I'm calling because there have been some developments recently in your uncle's case. We found him. It seems he's been living a rather tough life in Australia over the last few years, and was recently picked up on an attempted rape charge. Due to the paperwork process, we've not been able to extradite him until now. We saw no need to alarm you until we knew for sure that we could get him back here to the UK to prosecute."

Peggy couldn't seem to find her voice. She cleared her throat. Glynnis got up from her chair and went to sit beside her.

"Peggy, your uncle is in our custody, and will be put on trial in the next couple of weeks. He's being charged with rape and grievous bodily harm. We're pretty sure we can put him away for at least fifteen years, and perhaps life, if we can prove he's a danger to society. Given his violent tendencies in Australia, and his past violations against you, it shouldn't be hard to convince a jury of a life sentence."

Peggy paced nervously, taking deep breaths.

"What do I need to do?"

She asked Laura.

"The Crown Prosecution Service will be spearheading the case, Peg. If you have a lawyer, he can help the team sort through old records, photos, and lab tests. Your uncle's DNA results, from years ago, will be matched. Your attorney will add a more impassioned plea that could help sway the jury to a heavier sentence if he's any good."

Peggy assured her she had sound legal counsel.

"You know, Laura, after all these years, I never thought I'd ever have to lay eyes on him again."

Laura sympathized with her.

"I know, Peg. But think about it. This is your chance to see justice administered. This man hurt you, not just physically, but mentally as well. Because of his actions, your life was set on an uncharted and dangerous course. There's a reason why you survived and have become as successful as you are. I believe there is a God-ordained purpose for all that we go through. You're one fortunate woman. By following through with this, James Burke will never be allowed back into society to hurt another child again. We need your testimony, Peg. Can we count on it?"

Peggy looked at Glynnis, who gave her the thumbs up and mouthed, "I'll call my da."

Peggy affirmed her decision.

"I don't ever want him in civil society again, Laura. He doesn't belong here."

Laura sighed thankfully.

"That's my girl. I'll be in touch with more details in a few days. We'll need to get together with your attorney for a few meetings to go over the evidence and chart a plan of action."

"Peggy, we've got pretty compelling evidence. I want you to know that this isn't going to be easy for you. You'll need to get yourself into a positive frame of mind for this. It's going to mean reliving a lot of your painful past. Everything he did to you will be told to the jury, and no doubt a watching public. But I promise, in the end, he'll not ever hurt you or anyone else ever again."

Peggy thanked Laura for all of her hard work over the years and hung up the phone. She knew what she had to do. Boldness seemed to come over her and she smiled at Glynnis, who was confused at her friend's sudden change of disposition.

"I won't let him hurt anyone else, Glynn. I want him put away for good. I guess you need to get your da on the phone. Tell him, I'll pay him for this one. It's not a freebie."

Glynnis rolled her eyes.

"You know he wouldn't take anything from either one of us. So forget that idea. I'll call him now."

Glynnis jumped off the bed and took the phone. She called home and after exchanging pleasantries with her mam, asked to speak to her da.

"He's not home right now, love. I'll have him call you in a little while. He just stepped out for the paper. He'll be back in a few minutes."

Glynnis looked frustrated.

"Thanks, Mam. Just ask him to give us a call as soon as he gets in."

"Is everything all right?"

Glynnis assured her that they were fine. She didn't feel like getting into the details as she'd have to answer a million of her mother's questions. She told her that she had a legal question she needed an answer to.

"Did you enjoy your trip to Boston?"

Glynnis told her about the Carly Simon concert and how Caroline was on her way to Spain, and that Val had a wonderful new boyfriend.

"Do you think they'll get married? I've not been to a wedding in ages." Mary remarked.

"I don't know, Mam. It's too soon I think, but they very well may."

Not wanting to get dragged into a conversation about marriage, Glynnis made an excuse to get off the phone.

"I've got to go and unpack. I'll talk to you soon, Mam. Love you!"

She hung up.

Peggy changed into her nightshirt and hung up some of her clothes, then threw the dirty laundry into a basket.

"I'm heading down to do the laundry; you want me to throw some of your things in?"

The women walked across the hall to Glynnis's room and sorted through her clothes. With the basket quite full, Glynnis offered to take it downstairs.

"Why don't you go and pour us a glass of wine and put on the fireplace."

Peggy gave her a quick hug.

"That's a great idea. I'll order a pizza, so we can eat in and wait for your father's call."

Peggy set about filling the wine glasses and picked up the phone to call in the order when she was startled by a man's voice on the other end.

"Hello?"

"Peggy? It's me, Liam."

Peggy chuckled.

"Hi! I was just getting ready to call out for pizza, and POOF! There you are! Hold on. I'll have Glynnis talk to you first."

Glynnis dashed down the stairs and took the phone.

"Hi, Da. Yes, I'm fine ... we're both doing well. Yep, had a great time. It was good to see the girls again. Listen, Da, there's a matter that's come up, and we need your help."

Glynnis motioned for Peggy to pick up the other phone in the living room.

"I'm going to have Peggy get on the other line so we can all talk, okay?"

"Sure."

Liam paced the floor, wondering what could be the problem.

"Da, it seems that Peggy's uncle has reappeared after all these years. The Crown Prosecution Service is bringing his case to court. They've extradited him from Australia and are planning a trial over the next few weeks."

"No way!"

Her father's voice seemed genuinely surprised.

"How the hell did they find him?"

"Laura Campbell said they've been keeping an eye out for him. Seems he got into some trouble in Australia. Attempted rape down there, I guess. Peggy's going to testify. She wants to do this."

"Peggy."

Liam's voice was compassionate.

"Are you sure you want to do this? It'll be dredging up a lot of old and painful memories."

Peggy assured him that she felt compelled to testify. He confirmed his commitment to help her.

"Well, not to worry then, love. I'll be in touch with Ms. Campbell first thing in the morning. I'll make a special trip to London by the end of the week. Don't mind if I stay with you ladies a few days, do you?"

Peggy and Glynnis assured him that he was always welcome in their home.

He'd helped both his daughter and her friend when Peggy decided she wanted to add Glynnis's name to the deed of the house ten years ago. They'd both invested so much time and money into its refurbishment, Peggy said it was as much Glynnis's as it was hers. Besides, if anything ever happened to her, she'd want it to go to Glynnis. She had no one else.

"Peggy, he won't get away this time. You've no idea what they do to pedophiles in prison. The inmates have their own system of justice."

Peggy felt a twinge of pain in her heart toward her uncle. She quickly brushed it from her mind.

"Please try not to worry, Peggy. I'm glad you called me. I've been hoping something like this would come about one day. He should be made to serve time for what he did. He also needs psychological help."

"I'll leave that for the court to decide. I trust you."

He assured her that he'd gladly assist Laura on the prosecution team.

"We'll get through this together, Peggy. Go about your normal business and try to keep to your routine. It'll keep you sane!"

Peggy laughed.

"Good advice. I'll go and paint. Take care, Mr. O'Brien, and thank you again."

Peggy hung up her extension.

"Thanks, Da. Yes. I'll be here tomorrow. Call me when you know more. Okay. Bye."

Glynnis hung the phone up.

"It's all going to work out, Peg."

Peggy felt unusually calm. She knew in her heart that justice would prevail. More than anything, she wanted to prevent her uncle from ever being able to hurt another innocent child.

Chapter Forty-Two

CAROLINE FELL ASLEEP QUICKLY ONCE she was settled on the plane. The busy weekend and all the rushing around had knocked her out. She'd taken a Xanax when she left Boston to calm her flight jitters. She rested soundly, and awoke when the plane was half an hour from landing at Charles de Gaulle Airport in Paris.

Yawning, she got up to use the bathroom, taking her small bag with her. She brushed her teeth and gargled, then splashed the tepid water on her face, drying her hands and face with the course paper towels. She fumbled through her purse for some lip balm and came up with tinted lip-gloss instead. She finished applying her makeup when the "Fasten Seat Belts" signal flashed then sounded. They were beginning their descent.

She sat back down and buckled in. In a daze, she watched the flashing red lights reflect off the wing of the plane. It was a beautiful city, Paris, though there wasn't much to look at in the early morning darkness. She almost wished she could disembark and stay for a few days. On this trip, she would just change planes and head on to Spain.

She sat back, smiling to herself. She was excited about the journey. It far surpassed any of the nervousness she originally felt about going it alone. Somewhere deep within, she knew this was something she had to do in order to clear her mind, confront her fears, and gain a firmer grip on life. Her new job in pediatrics awaited her return.

It was a dream come true, a goal she had accomplished. She finally admitted to herself that the drama in the ER was too much. It wore her down. She did, reluctantly, give in to her ER supervisor's pleas to stay on per diem for another two weeks when she returned until they could hire a replacement. She was looking forward to her new role caring for children and young adults. It was the least she could do for her supervisor given that she gave her a month off.

The change of planes in Paris went smoothly due to the lack of crowds at that early hour. Caroline was grateful for the opportunity to stretch her legs. Needing a sugar boost, she bought a package of cookies and bottled water from the lone open kiosk. The flight to Spain would only take another two hours.

As she stood at the gate waiting to board the small plane to Madrid, she stared out at the place where the sun, which had not yet peaked above the horizon, would soon rise. Hues of pink and blue could be seen in the distance and it looked like it was going to be a beautiful day. She couldn't wait to get on her bike and go. According to her map, the hotel wasn't that far from the airport. There, she'd settle in and take a leisurely day to explore the city. She wanted to rest before the "bone-shaking" train ride she'd take from Madrid to San Sebastián.

She browsed through the in-flight magazine, which was all in Spanish. She was surprised at how much of it she actually understood. Of course, the pictures helped. It was a fairly small plane; no one was seated next to her. She put up her feet on the adjoining seat and read for a while.

Disembarking from the craft proved to be a lesson in patience. They had to wait for a skycap to be called to assist an older disabled woman in the first row. Caroline stood waiting, with her large backpack slung over her shoulder. Everything inside was neatly rolled in order to conserve space and time.

Once she cleared Customs, Caroline searched the board to find her baggage claim area. She gave a big sigh of relief when she finally spotted her bike box. She'd put a bright pink sticker on it to make it stand out. Biking was a common pastime in Spain and all the boxes looked alike.

Caroline pulled her container off the conveyer and went off to the side to begin piecing it together.

Once the bike was assembled, Caroline adjusted the panniers making sure the weight was evenly distributed. She stored her bike box in a locker and carefully placed the receipt in her pack. She clipped a handlebar bag on the front and removed from her backpack her sunglasses, sunscreen, wallet, a few energy snack bars, and her map. She adjusted and tightened her helmet and backpack then shook the bike to make sure everything was secure and walked it out front. After consulting with an airport employee, she set off toward a busy highway that connected the airport to Madrid.

Spain catered to cyclists and motorists treated them with respect. They held their own bike race each year, called the Vuelta à España, just a step down in prestige from the Tour de France. The law in Spain required motorists to clear cyclists by a meter. Not doing so resulted in a hefty fine.

She had not chosen a grueling bike trek on this trip. Instead, she opted to be with her cycling group in part, and would settle into a comfortable hotel each evening. She'd factor in time for sightseeing, a day or two at the beach or shopping, and browsing around museums and galleries. She told herself she'd be part athlete, part tourist, and part patient taking care to enjoy some much-needed R&R in this unfamiliar yet picturesque landscape.

Caroline pedaled at a leisurely pace down the elegant Paseo de la Castellana. After stopping at a café to buy more water, she found her hotel situated amid French-style townhouses and palaces. She checked in, and then immediately headed up to her room to shower and change. The hotels in Spain graciously accommodated cyclists, and no one seemed put out when she wheeled her bike onto the elevator.

She guided the bike into her hotel room, unloaded her backpack, and jumped into the shower. The water felt invigorating after the long flight and bike ride. Getting ready took no time at all. She put on very little makeup and left her hair to hang free and dry naturally. Clipping on her fanny pack, she added her wallet and passport to its contents.

She was wheeling the bike out of the room when the pedal got stuck on the doorjamb. A man in a business suit was walking by and offered his assistance. Once she cleared the door, she thanked him as they walked to the elevator together. He inquired about her trip and introduced himself as Miguel del Mar. She smiled and held out her hand to introduce herself. The elevator chimed, and he held the doors for her as she walked her bike on. She thanked him when they reached the ground floor. He told her to enjoy the day.

With her damp hair blowing in the breeze, Caroline cruised along the city streets. She stopped at a quaint-looking outdoor café and ordered a light tapas lunch along with a draft beer. She sat contentedly taking in the sights and sounds of her new surroundings, enjoying every moment of it. There was something invigorating about being on her own, a feeling that was new to her.

Caroline was unaware of the admiring stares she was receiving from male patrons and passersby alike. Her hair, which had dried along the ride, now hung in gentle waves down her back. She reached into the handlebar bag on her bike and took out a clip. Twisting her hair, she pulled it up into a bun on the top of her head and then applied sunscreen to her face and arms. She was wiping her hands on her napkin when another draft beer was brought to her table.

She questioned the waitress, as she'd not ordered it. The waitress pointed out a man, a few tables away, who was lifting his glass to her. Caroline flashed him an appreciative smile, raised her glass back at him and mouthed, "Gracias." She didn't feel the need, however, to go over and talk with him. She finished only half of the glass before getting back on her bike and continuing on.

Having stocked her panniers with water bottles, Caroline set off exploring narrow streets and bustling marketplaces. She tooled about the city and stopped to browse in a couple of shops. She purchased a small, fourteen carat gold, scallop shell charm and gold necklace for Valerie.

Caroline asked about the significance of the scallop shell, as the symbol seemed to be everywhere. The woman, carefully wrapping her sister's gift, explained the legend to her.

"In Spain, the scallop shell is the symbol of St. James, the Apostle of Jesus. For more than a thousand years, Roman Catholics have made the grueling, mountainous pilgrimage to the northern Spanish city of Santiago de Compostela, enduring great difficulties such as thieves, foot sores, and attacks from wild animals, in exchange for a heavenly promise. According to church doctrine, those who made the trek to the tomb of St. James shorten their time in purgatory."

Caroline leaned in.

"I think I may have to change my route then!"

The woman laughed.

"If you've a bicycle built for two, I may join you!"

Caroline thanked her and said good-bye.

After stopping to take a few pictures and eat one of her energy bars, Caroline headed back to her hotel. She stopped out front and snapped a picture of the building, which was a tenth century castle that had been converted into a luxurious period-style hotel. The owner loved cyclists she was told.

When she entered the lobby, she took the clip out of her hair letting it fall about her shoulders. She was sweaty and wanted to take another shower and relax. The man who'd helped her earlier that morning sat in the lobby, reading a newspaper. He got up when he saw her enter, and approached asking her impression of the city.

"Oh, it is beautiful. I hate to leave!"

He motioned for the bellman and, in Spanish, gave him her room number and asked him to take her bike up to her room.

"Oh, he doesn't have to do that. I'm heading up to shower. I'm a sweaty mess."

She blushed.

Miguel directed her to the bar.

"You must be quite thirsty, Caroline. Come, I want you to try a cold glass of our world-famous sangria."

She admitted that she was thirsty and took him up on his offer.

The man at the bar seemed nervous waiting on them. Caroline picked up on his tenseness.

"What is it about you that makes them all jump so quickly?"

She nudged him gently.

He smiled.

"I am the owner."

Caroline looked at him, impressed with his hospitality.

"Well, that's nice to know. Tell me, should a well-respected hotelier like you be seen in the presence of a sweaty American cyclist? Certainly that can't bode well for your reputation, no?"

He laughed heartily.

"Ahhh, a sense of humor as well. This is good!"

They sat and shared a small pitcher of Sangria. Caroline had to admit that it was like nothing she'd ever tasted before, delicious and refreshing.

Feeling somewhat more relaxed, Caroline told him a little about herself — how she was a nurse back in Boston and was touring Spain by bicycle for the first time in her life. He was impressed that she'd decided to make the trek on her own and asked where she was headed.

Caroline ate the orange wedge, realizing suddenly that she was very hungry.

"North — San Sebastián, Bilbao then west on to Cantabria province. There's so much that I want to see, yet I want to try and keep it simple, too. I may have to make another trip."

He smiled.

"San Sebastián is a food lover's paradise! They eat six meals a day there!"

Caroline pretended to smack her lips.

"It sounds like a place I'll really enjoy then! I'm starving!"

He reached over and put his hand over hers.

"Please join me for dinner. I would be honored."

Caroline looked down at her present state of appearance.

"You'll have to give me an hour to shower and change. I assure you, I clean up fairly well."

He leaned over and kissed her hand.

"Thank you. I'll meet you in the lobby at eight o'clock. Is that enough time?"

Caroline drank the last of her sangria.

"Yes, more than enough time. I'll see you in a little while, Miguel. Your hotel is truly a work of art. I'd like to see more of it. Perhaps you can give me a tour?"

He bowed gallantly

"It would be my pleasure."

Caroline smiled as she walked to the elevator. He was a very handsome older man. She'd guess him to be in his mid-forties and she was looking forward to having dinner with him.

When she opened the door to her room she was surprised to find two dozen yellow roses set on her bureau. The note read:

"May your days in Spain bring you great peace and joy. Sincerely, Miguel."

Caroline set the card down and smiled again. *He is simply charming!* She quickly sifted through her backpack and found her "little black dress" that she took with her whenever she traveled. It was perfect for most occasions and could be easily dressed up or down. The best thing about it was that it was "wrinkle-free." She could simply unroll it, shake it out, and slip it on.

Caroline got in the shower again, taking time to shave her legs, and used the hotel shampoo and conditioner. She blew her hair dry, and carefully applied her makeup. After donning the dress, she put on her platinum earrings and matching bangle bracelet, gifts from her uncle, Sean. It was the only jewelry she'd brought with her. She slipped into a simple pair of black sandals and adjusted the straps, then stood back to check the results in the full-length mirror. She was happy with what she saw. Her face had a healthy glow from being outside all day in the sun. Even with sunscreen, however, her face was a little red.

She checked the clock, and it was almost eight. Before she left the room, she reached into the crystal vase and took a rose with her. When she got off the elevator in the lobby, she saw that Miguel had changed into a cream-colored silk shirt and casual dress pants. His Bali shoes gave him a tailored yet relaxed look. He approached her with a big smile.

"You look gorgeous!"

She thanked him and pointed the rose at his nose.

"Thank you for the roses, Miguel. That was very sweet of you. You know, you didn't have to send me two dozen. One would have been enough."

She tapped him on the head with it.

"I feel badly that I won't be able to enjoy them for very long. Promise me you'll give one to every beautiful woman who registers at your hotel. That way none will go to waste."

He gave his word.

"Good. Now let's eat."

Caroline took Miguel's arm as he led her away from the hotel restaurant and through a hallway that led to his private residence. They walked through the marbled foyer and out to a stately portico within a private courtyard. At the center of the courtyard was a magnificent lighted fountain. Miniature rose bushes grew all around the courtyard, permeating the air with their sweet smell. Candles had been placed on an elegant table set for two. A violin player was in the distance playing music that Caroline recognized as Handel.

"My sister plays the violin. What a nice touch! You've gone all out, Miguel del Mar. You didn't have to do all this. I would have been happy with a steak and a salad."

Miguel pulled out Caroline's chair, and then sat down across from her. There was a bottle of wine on the table and he poured them each a glass of the deep red liquid. He lifted his glass, said "Cheers" and winked. Their glasses clinked together and Caroline asked him to tell her more about himself.

Miguel was a hotelier whose business extended into the Basque province. Caroline was thrilled to learn that she was, ironically, booked into another one of his hotels during her stay in San Sebastián.

"You will find my hotel there even more opulent."

He went on to describe the famous five-star parador located in the same square as the 1499 Cathedral built by the Roman Catholic monarchs, Isabel and Ferdinand.

"Tell me more about your travels. Where will they take you? Perhaps I could offer some suggestions."

Caroline thanked him and went on to explain her itinerary.

"Well, tomorrow I'll board at Chamartin Station to catch the overnight train to San Sebastián ..."

Miguel stopped her.

"That's a horrible train ride, you know. It's cramped, and you'll get very little rest. I can assure you. You bump along the whole way. The tracks are old. It's nothing like our AVE trains that are much faster. Let me fly you there. I must go there myself anyway."

Caroline was speechless. She'd never met anyone who had their own plane before.

Miguel went on to explain.

"I've got to head that way this week. I spend most of my time flying back and forth between hotels. I was planning to fly on Wednesday. I'll adjust my plans and go a day earlier."

Caroline looked at him incredulously.

"Tell me, dear sir, what is it like to have your own plane and be able to jet set about the world at a moment's notice ... hmmmm?"

He smiled.

"You will see. I enjoy life. But I've worked hard. This business was not handed down to me. It took a lot of work to attain this. Now, I enjoy the fruits of my labor. I would be happy if you'd join me."

Caroline nodded.

"Well, it certainly doesn't sound like I'll be missing much if I don't take that train ride."

Miguel shook his head.

"No, for sure it is an experience you can do without. I would be pleased to show you around once we're there."

Caroline interjected.

"Miguel, do you have a bike?"

He dropped his head back and laughed.

"Yes, and I'll have you know that I've biked many of the famous routes. I recently finished a 500-mile coastal trek along the Bay of Biscay."

"That's one of the routes I'll be taking — not the full 500 miles, though. I'd never make it that far. This is a rather leisurely bike trip for me. But I wanted to see the Bay of Biscay. I've heard it's breathtaking."

He concurred.

"It is truly remarkable. You'll see for yourself when we arrive."

Dinner was delicious. He saw to every detail. Around ten o'clock, Caroline unconsciously let a yawn slip, a culmination of jet lag, biking, and the wine. She was suddenly quite tired, so she excused herself, assuring Miguel it was not his company. He took no offense and offered to walk her to her room.

As they walked through the lobby, Caroline asked if he was married.

"I know this may sound pretty straightforward, but I know European men have a different set of ideas about women and relationships. I just want you to know that if you're married, I'm not traveling with you. I'm not a husband stealer."

Miguel admired her for being so forthright.

"Your honesty and integrity are refreshing. No, I'm not married. Widowed, actually, my wife was killed in a car crash several years ago. In her absence, my work has kept my life quite busy."

He stared at Caroline with a mixture of admiration and longing.

"When I saw you, you looked so happy and youthful; I just wanted to meet you. I'm not asking for anything more. I enjoy your company. Every now and again I remember how lonely life can be ... when I stop long enough to consider it."

Caroline stopped outside her door and turned to Miguel.

"I'm very sorry for your loss, Miguel. That must have been devastating for you."

He nodded.

"It was. But if there is a heaven, I know she's there. She was a remarkably kind and devout woman."

Caroline gave him a gentle kiss on the cheek.

"Thank you for a perfect evening."

He kissed her hand.

"Good night, Caroline. I'll call you later in the morning."

Once she entered her room, Caroline observed that all the wet towels had been removed from the floor where she'd dropped them. New towels had been placed in the bathroom. All of her clothes, which had been quickly removed from her backpack, were meticulously folded and arranged neatly on the top of the bureau. The bed had been turned down for her, with a chocolate left on the pillow. She smiled as she unwrapped it and popped the sweet candy into her mouth. She brushed her teeth before slipping comfortably into bed, falling asleep within moments.

The following day was a flurry of activity beginning with a tour of the hotel and later a quiet breakfast in Miguel's private courtyard. They continued talking easily with one another. He pointed out routes on her map that would yield her the best views. She was heading west after she left San Sebastián, and he marked the N-634 coastal road with a highlighting pen.

"This will take you to Bilbao and, if you follow it long enough, into Galicia."

He pointed out that there were fishing towns along the way and that if she had the chance, she should check out the picturesque Lequeitio while there.

Miguel once again saw to all the details. While they ate, the hotel staff had packed up everything in her room and loaded it on board the plane. Miguel walked arm and arm with her out to the front of the hotel. His car was waiting to take them to the Madrid airport to board his jet for San Sebastián.

Miguel pointed out various businesses along the way and told her stories about some of the architecture. She found him to be very kind and knowledgeable. When Caroline arrived at his hotel, she found that its ancient architecture and intricate designs were truly breathtaking.

Her days spent in San Sebastián were filled with a mixture of group biking tours and lone excursions. She and Miguel spent a few days biking together as well. At one point in their journey, high above the ocean on the coastal road, Caroline stopped to take in the beauty laid out before her. They pulled their bikes off to the side to venture near the edge of a cliff. Caroline asked Miguel if he'd mind taking a few pictures of her with the ocean in the background.

The sky was a glorious blue, and the aquamarine ocean seemed to glow. Caroline took off her helmet and smiled at the camera as a breeze gently blew her hair. Miguel was delighted with her, and took pleasure in having her strike various funny poses. When they were done, Caroline turned to gaze peacefully at the ocean. Unbeknownst to her, Miguel had snapped another photo that she'd discover later. It captured her spirit and the whole essence of her trip. She was rested, eating regularly, and exercising. Finally, she was healthy, relaxed, and happy. Her skin, slightly tanned, highlighted her blue eyes, which were dazzling in the setting sunlight.

Caroline parted company with Miguel a few days later. She hugged him warmly, thanking him for his hospitality.

"You know, I came here by myself. I mean I knew I'd meet a few new people biking and maybe strike up a casual friendship. But I never expected to meet someone like you, Miguel. You've made this trip so enjoyable. I can't thank you enough."

She had tears in her eyes as she reached over and hugged him for a second time.

Miguel held her close.

"It is I who should thank you, Caroline. You made me feel young again, alive. I hope I get to see you again one day."

Caroline let him kiss her. She felt passion stir within her, yet slowly pulled away.

"I hope we see each other again, too. Please stay in touch. You have my contact information."

Miguel nodded. Somehow, he sensed he'd never see her again, but he was grateful for the time he spent getting to know her. He knew she was fun loving, yet complex at a deeper level, which made her all the more intriguing.

He presented her with a small box. Caroline looked at him in surprise. She took the gift and opened the package. Smiling, she lifted a delicate gold chain from which hung the familiar scalloped shell of St. James. Miguel took the necklace from her and undid the clasp, he placed it gently around her neck. Now, she and Val had similar jewelry.

"Thank you, Miguel. I don't know what to say. It's truly beautiful. I will cherish it."

He smiled.

"You are beautiful, Caroline."

Caroline put her helmet on and fastened the chinstrap.

"Adiós, mi amigo."

She didn't let him see her tears as she pedaled away from the hotel, and purposely didn't look back.

Chapter Forty-Three

Montana, Summer 1998

FATHER COUGHLIN LED THE TWO boys over smooth rocks as they rode their horses along the shallow riverbed. The youngsters talked endlessly about fishing, but Father Coughlin, sullen, tuned out their animated conversation, his sour disposition becoming more evident as he purposely ignored the young boys' questions. They looked at one another and shrugged at his silence. He urged them to go on up ahead of him.

It was a trail he'd ridden with his brother on more than a few occasions. The news of Rich's imminent death had dampened his plans, and he was depressed. He was angry that Rich hadn't told him sooner and ruined his fishing trip. To make matters worse, he received word from an Archdiocesan official that he was once again being transferred. As anxiety about life mounted, his depraved mind contrived ways to alleviate his present frustration.

Rob had been notified of the church relocation the day before his fishing trip. In order to buy some time, he lied and told them he was leaving on a youth outreach expedition and wouldn't be back for a couple of weeks. He'd made so many preparations for this "mission" trip he was determined to see it through.

The church magistrate wouldn't divulge too much information over the phone about his new location. He was pointedly reminded that he was to have no contact with the young adults of the new parish. Rob stifled a yawn over the phone, knowing that these threats never deterred him for very long.

The boys talked amongst themselves, looking back frequently to make sure they could see Father Coughlin. He stared at them from behind as they bounced along in the saddle. He comforted himself with sadistic thoughts of what he had in mind to do, and prided himself on how well he'd groomed them both over the years.

As the cabin came into view, his heart was heavy with the knowledge of his brother's impending death. He was questioning his own miserable existence and wondered why he'd ever gone into the priesthood. He sure as hell didn't put his faith in God, and blamed him for the monster he'd become.

He and the boys tethered their horses and carried their gear into the cabin. The boys dropped their new tackle boxes on the floor and excitedly looked around. Their first venture was to climb the stairs to explore the loft area. Rob was overcome with memories of his brother's presence in the place. Rich wasn't dead yet, but he felt it haunting him nonetheless.

He barked at the boys to find a spot for their gear and meet him outside in a few minutes. Father Coughlin produced a container of bait and headed off in the direction of the rushing water.

The sound of the boys' laughter lightened his heart some, though he still remained aloof.

"Father Coughlin, look at the size of this, would you?"

Billy was struggling to reel in his catch. The priest rushed over to help him and scooped it up in the net. He took out his camera and took a picture of the boy proudly showing his prizewinning catch. He encouraged Matt to be patient, as his turn would surely come at some point. No sooner were the words out of his mouth than his own line jerked. The boys were jumping with excitement, and Father Coughlin smiled at his own good luck. The fish didn't want to get caught and fought him furiously.

"Get the net! I'll bring him in closer, and you scoop him up."

He ordered to Matt.

With the familiarity of a pro, Matt gathered up the fish when it was in close, but he had a hard time lifting the net. Father Coughlin grabbed it roughly from him with his strong arms and tossed it over onto the riverbank.

"Well, that should be more than enough for dinner."

The boys nodded in agreement as they waded back to the riverbank.

Rob enjoyed cooking outdoors over an open fire. He threw a bunch of orders at the two boys, who were kept busy running in and out of the cabin, bringing him various cooking tools and utensils.

He gutted the fish, wrapped them in tinfoil and placed them on the makeshift grill. The boys eyed him from the front porch while playing cards. He loved the thought that they were totally alone and dependent on him for their survival. Thinking along those lines electrified him. He stopped before entering the cabin and stared down at the two innocents playing cards.

"I have more games planned for us tonight. You haven't forgotten your promises, have you?"

The boys looked up at him quickly and then solemnly back down at their cards, shaking their heads.

"Good. I've got some great prizes ... if you do all that I ask."

The boys glanced warily at each other and then determinedly focused on the cards in their hands. They knew the types of games he liked to play.

The children devoured their dinners hungrily. Father Coughlin had brought along a bottle of rum to lace their soda. It took the edge off the pain and killed any inhibitions they might have. The children, without realizing, drank it happily. Being small in frame, they felt the effects rather quickly.

"Hey!"

Matt squinted his eyes.

"I think he gave us those funny drinks again. I feel kinda weird ..."

"Yeah, me too."

Billy replied a little nervously.

"You know what that means."

Matt nodded and became quiet.

Father Coughlin instructed them to go inside and wash up, and then to strip down to their undershorts. They slowly turned and did what they were told. There was no point in arguing with him. Father Coughlin felt another jolt shoot through him as they submitted to his orders without question. He stepped out onto the porch to have a cigarette and kicked dirt on the dying campfire. He returned to the cabin after a few minutes and bolted the door.

Though there wasn't a living soul around for many miles, he pulled the curtains shut. He heard the children whispering upstairs in the loft and called for them to come down. He lit a few of the oil lamps that hung on the beams, casting a flickering glow on the wide, open room. He poured himself and the boys another rum-laden soda and lit the fireplace. They drank and were nervously awaiting his instructions. They'd long since resigned themselves to the fact that they couldn't stop him from doing what he wanted to do, so they didn't fight him. Tonight was different, however. They noticed he wasn't laughing or joking as much, and he didn't take time to explain the specific games he wanted them to play. He was eerily quiet.

Father Coughlin pulled a camera from his bag. He suggested they take off their underpants and proceeded to position them. They did as they were told reluctantly and without complaint. Only Matt still exhibited a slight amount of apprehension.

"What if somebody finds the pictures? We'll get in trouble for sure."

Father Coughlin had no patience left, and exasperatedly told him that he'd not let them out of his sight. Seeing the boy's hurt expression, he softened his tone slightly.

"Don't worry. These are just for me. No one else will see them."

Seizing the opportunity to play upon their sympathies, he confessed.

"I want to have some pictures to remember you by. I'm leaving when we get back, and I may never see you again."

The boys were stunned and quiet.

"You've been my best friends while I've been here. I'm really going to miss you. This trip is special for me, and I hope for you, too."

He put his head down and they approached him to put their hands on his shoulder.

"Do you have to go?"

Billy piped in. Rob assured them that he had no choice. It was for a new job and he had to go. They told him that they'd miss him, too.

Father Coughlin was convinced the only thing they'd miss was his money and the prizes. That quick thought made him angry, though they both looked convincingly sad at his news. Again, he felt a current rush under his skin, giving him the goose bumps. His excitement grew at their nearness to him.

"That's why we need to make this time special and memorable for all of us, okay?"

The boys nodded as he poured them another small drink.

The children were getting pretty drunk and were completely uninhibited. Father Coughlin chuckled as they stumbled about. He directed them over to the couch and snapped pictures of their nakedness. He lined the photos along the mantle above the fireplace. When he was satisfied with his photographs, he set his camera down on the table.

Father Coughlin, like a shark circling its prey, walked around the back of the couch and looked down upon the naked boys. They smiled up at him trustingly. Rob leaned over and encircled his arm about Matt's waist and hoisted him off the cushion. Positioning him over the back of the couch, he freed himself from his own clothing.

The child was unprepared for the sudden violent penetration. He cried out in pain as the priest tore into him. Billy, startled, quickly scurried to the other end of the couch. Matt's arms were flailing, frantically clawing at the air, begging his friend to help him.

Billy felt sick to his stomach and was paralyzed to reach out. He closed his eyes so as not to watch and felt the couch lurch with each thrusting movement. He listened in horror to Matt's terrifying screams.

Billy was helpless and ashamed of his own cowardliness. He quickly drained the last remaining drops of alcohol from his cup on the end table. He curled up into a ball and locked his arms around his knees, rocking himself while his friend whimpered during the last of the rhythmic pounding. Father Coughlin, having consumed vast amounts of alcohol, was having a hard time finishing the job, which only prolonged the child's suffering.

When he finally withdrew, Matt whimpered and slowly sank to the floor. Father Coughlin went into the bathroom and emerged with a towel. Billy saw him disappear behind the back of the couch. Matt protested slightly as the priest assisted him. Billy saw the blood on the towel when it was tossed carelessly into the corner. Matt was still wiping tears from his eyes when Father Coughlin told him to sit and handed him another drink. He motioned for Billy to come over and stand in front of Matt.

"Your friend's upset. I want you to help him."

Father Coughlin seated himself in a comfortable leather chair across from the two boys and watched with lascivious contentment as Matt's body contorted against the conflicting sensations applied by Billy. When Billy had successfully completed all that he was required to do to his friend, Father Coughlin handed him another soda.

Seeing them both shivering, he tossed them a blanket that was hanging over the back of his chair.

"C'mon! Get up. I got a little carried away. I think I've had too much to drink."

The boys were drunk and half-heartedly accepted his apology. Grateful that it was over for the time being, they huddled together under the blanket, shielding their nakedness from his perverted stare.

462

Father Coughlin suggested they take a shower and he watched them from the doorway. He was tired and sent the boys upstairs to bed with strict instructions not to talk, as he didn't want to hear them while he tried to sleep downstairs.

The days progressed at a morbidly slow pace as the week dragged on. Rain moved in, dampening their fishing plans, leaving them to spend most of their time indoors.

Like a man possessed, Father Coughlin's game playing escalated to include heinous acts using blunt objects. When the children had stopped crying after each episode, he'd shift the attention back onto himself, taking full advantage of their natural, child-like instincts to forgive, tearfully telling them how sorry he was if he hurt them. On every occasion, the children, predictably, wound up feeling bad for him and did whatever they could to try and make him happy.

Father Coughlin cut the weeklong trip short and took the boys back home a few days early. He felt that if he stayed holed up with them any longer, he might, in a drunken rage, kill one of them. He'd grown unusually aggressive and forceful in his lustful bouts.

It was still raining when they left on horseback for the reservation. During the car ride home, he bought their future silence with blackmail. He warned them to never speak to anyone about what happened during those few days at the cabin. If they did, he'd show the pictures to their mothers and friends.

Both boys nearly burst into tears and begged him not to. They swore they'd never tell anyone. He assured them that the photos would remain safe with him, so long as they never talked about their secret. The boys promised never to tell a soul, and Father Coughlin smiled to himself. He knew they wouldn't.

He dropped them off at the dilapidated shacks they called home. Father Coughlin told their mothers that because of the rain, they had to cut the vacation a little short. At their mothers' urging, the boys were told to thank Father for his kindness. He waved to the children as he pulled away down the dirt road.

Father Coughlin stood beneath the waterfall streaming from the roof. He was getting soaked as he tried to work his key into the rusted lock. He finally got the creaky door to the rectory open, cursing the rickety old building. He was angry when he punched the button on the answering machine. An unfamiliar voice, claiming to be a friend of his brother's, asked him to call back when he got the message.

Father Coughlin dialed the number.

"This is Rob Coughlin. I was left a message concerning Rich."

The low voice on the other end introduced himself as Rich's business partner. He went on to tell Father Coughlin that Rich had passed away four days ago and that he'd tried to reach him without success. Father Coughlin was silent on the other end. The man went on to add that Rich had asked specifically for his ashes to be spread over his property in Montana.

The man offered to have the cremation company professionally ship the remains directly to Father Coughlin, who, for some reason, thought that statement rather funny and started laughing. Rich's business partner seemed baffled by the response. Father Coughlin told him that shipping the ashes would be fine and that he appreciated his efforts to get in touch with him.

Father Coughlin slumped into the chair beside the phone in the hallway. He'd come back early only to pack up what few belongings he had and get ready for his move. Rich's friend said that the package containing his brother's ashes should arrive by Saturday. Father Coughlin would take the ashes with him as he wouldn't get another chance to get out to the cabin for a while. He would fulfill his brother's wishes and spread his ashes when he took a vacation later in the year.

Father Coughlin left his luggage in the hall and went upstairs to his bedroom. He didn't bother to turn on any lights or even change; he just lay on his bed, went to sleep, and didn't cry.

Chapter Forty-Four

England, Summer 1998

GLYNNIS SAT IN THE ROW directly behind her impeccably dressed father, who sat next to Peggy as part of her legal team. Glynnis held her mother's hand as they waited for the trial to begin. The two encouraged one another, talking quietly back and forth. Peggy turned around to look for reassurance from Glynnis.

"It's going to be all right, Peg. We'll nail him!"

The judge entered the courtroom, and they were all motioned to rise.

Peggy felt a wave of nausea sweep over her. Liam O'Brien put his arm around her shoulders to steady her. He'd done that when he'd led her through the crowd of photographers amassed outside the courthouse as well.

Television and newspaper articles had spread the story of the attractive young artist who'd been brutally raped by her uncle as a child. They detailed the story of her subsequent life of homelessness and wandering following her escape from an abusive children's home in Cheshire. Neighbors and friends from Peggy's hometown were interviewed and spoke only kind words about her, one going so far as to say he'd give the bastard a life sentence, and another older woman who graciously offered to castrate him with a butter knife ...

Peggy's breath caught in her chest as she saw the frail, elderly, handcuffed man led into the courtroom. His face was wrinkled and darkened from years of hard labor in the unmerciful Australian sun. Life had not been kind to James Burke.

Kathleen M. Urquhart

He'd spent many years on the run, as a migrant worker doing menial tasks on farms, living hand-to-mouth, never staying in one place too long. He'd often wished for death to come, and had even purposely placed himself in dangerous and life-threatening situations, but somehow death avoided him causing him to continue on in this miserable existence.

On two occasions he'd volunteered to wade into murky waterways containing crocodiles, in order to lay pipelines. He stared right into the eyes of one and it swam off. On another occasion, he positioned himself next to a poisonous adder while digging, but it slithered away. To him, these were signs that he was meant to remain suffering on earth.

Giving up all fear of getting caught, he took deliberate chances. One day he finally gave himself over to his growing lusts while boarding at a house with other workers. He'd spotted two young blond girls, daughters of his boss. They played innocently in the grass near their home, while the men worked setting fence posts in the distance. He fantasized about their youthful white skin and imagined how soft it would be to his touch.

The sun, burning his head through his hat, made him dizzy, and the next thing he knew a post had been dropped on his hand. He was driven to the main house for medical treatment, and was told he should probably go to the hospital to have it set and looked at. They were sure a few fingers had been broken. He refused to go to the hospital, choosing to deal with the pain. He was given a room at the main house for the night and told to rest. It was during his recuperation at the house that he raped the older child while her parents were away in Queensland.

The children had been left in the care of their nanny. The young woman was smitten with one of the male workers and was off flirting with him when James talked the eldest child into coming to his room to help him, using the excuse that he couldn't move his hand too well. The child, feeling sorry for the injured man, willingly agreed to help.

466

He ushered her into the room and locked the door behind them. Spare bandage wrappings had been left on the night table, and he shoved them into the child's mouth to stifle her screams, using the other to tie her hands. He forced her onto the bed and raped her repeatedly over the next eight hours.

The nanny didn't even notice she was missing. James threatened the girl by telling her that he'd kill her parents if she told anyone what he did. He undid her restraints and left her cowering in the corner of his room, sneaking out of the house under the cover of darkness.

The child became emotionally withdrawn, and her concerned parents took her for psychological counseling a month later, where it was discovered she'd been raped. Soon his phony alias and composite sketch was all over the news in Australia. It was broadcast around the country and abroad, eventually leading to his apprehension.

James Burke stood and stared at his niece while the Crown Prosecution Services read the list of charges to those gathered in the courtroom. She took a deep breath and stared back at her uncle, whom she barely recognized. The only thing Peggy felt was contempt and a very slight amount of pity. How had he ever become this monster? She asked herself as tears welled up in her eyes.

The jury listened to hours of testimony by both the prosecutor and defense counsel in the case concerning James Burke and Margaret O'Malley. Glynnis's father stood and read his statement. Peggy gave her testimony, and the jury listened intently. One of the female jurors cried as Peggy struggled to maintain her own composure. Liam nodded sympathetically while listening to her story; they'd gone over it a number of times.

Peggy told them what she could remember. Laura Campbell produced old medical photos for the jury. The child's face was barely recognizable from the raised bruises and swollen lips. In one picture, her ribs were exposed to show the kick marks. Laura pointed out what was clearly a deep puncture wound in one spot. The photos horrified the jury. It proved to be too much for one woman who was overwhelmed with emotion. The judge called for a short recess.

Peggy, shaking, was led back to her seat.

"I don't think this will take too long, Peg."

Liam assured her.

"Given what they've got on him in Australia, and the overwhelming evidence Laura and the team preserved, we're going to push for a life sentence."

Peggy nodded as Glynnis reached over to touch her friend's shoulder in support.

The jury was given the last remaining bits of evidence, and the DNA results clearly confirmed James Burke as the rapist. Peggy was embarrassed as the information was read to the jury and she bowed her head in shame. They, in turn, looked away, so as to not make her feel uncomfortable. A man from the jury, his jaw clenched tight, glared intensely at James.

The jury was done with their deliberations before noon the following day. Peggy sat anxiously next to Liam as the judge read the verdict. The court found James Burke guilty on all counts. The lawyers gathered at the bench for a brief conversation with the judge, who told the court that he'd deliver his sentence later that afternoon. Court was dismissed until two o'clock.

Glynnis gave a huge sigh of relief, and her father shook hands with the Crown Prosecution Services team, thanking them for their efforts on Peggy's behalf. Laura, Glynnis, and Mary O'Brien sat with Peggy, sharing quiet words of encouragement with her, shielding her from the curious stares of those still left in the courtroom.

The women walked to the back of the courthouse, thinking they'd be able to sneak outside to catch a breath of fresh air. They were not far from the building when photographers spotted them and swarmed, snapping pictures and shoving microphones in Peggy's face. Glynnis tried to shield her from the onslaught of questions and flashing bulbs. A local news station caught them on camera.

"Ms. O'Malley, how are you feeling right now?"

"Do you still have feelings for your uncle?"

"Where's your mother in all of this?"

"Do you feel you've been vindicated?"

The question about her mother caught her off guard, and she began to cry. Officers quickly came to their aid leading them back to the courthouse while holding the newshounds at bay. The whole scene made for a heart-breaking opener on the evening news.

The next day Peggy's face was plastered on the front page of newspapers all over England. For a day, she was even more famous than Princess Diana.

When the court resumed, silence fell over the room as the judge pronounced his sentence. He told the packed courtroom that, based on what he viewed as a progressive disposition toward violent and destructive behavior, it would be for the safety of society that Mr. James Burke serve out a life sentence in the case against Margaret O'Malley. In addition, his name would remain on a sex offender's register for the remainder of his life.

The courtroom broke into a thunderous applause. The judge in this case seemed unusually gratified to be handing down the sentence. Peggy turned and looked away as her uncle was led out of the courtroom. She sat back down in the chair and sobbed as Glynnis and her mom held her tightly. Glynnis's father protectively shielded them from curious onlookers.

The jury appeared pleased with the job they'd done. Justice had been served. One man from the audience called to her on his way out.

"Don't let the bastard get you down, love!"

The jury knew in their hearts it was the only sentence James Burke deserved. Some wished it could have been a death sentence.

Peggy wiped her eyes with a handkerchief and started toward the lobby with her entourage. Ropes held the reporters and photographers back so that she could get outside to the waiting car. She and Glynnis sat inside the vehicle as Liam O'Brien read a well-prepared statement on her behalf.

"Ms. O'Malley, as you can imagine, is overwhelmed by the events of the last few days."

He paused to clear his throat.

"As a young girl, Ms. O'Malley struggled to survive on the streets. James Burke, her uncle, sought to control and destroy her through heinous acts. However, by the grace of God, she has gone on to become a successful artist, curator, and responsible citizen. She is anxious to get back to her work now and resume a normal life, knowing that justice has been served. Her London art gallery, Panache, is a unique success story and testimony in its own right. Many of Peggy's sketches are done in vivid colors depicting her eternal optimism toward life, and her hopes for a bright future."

He'd hoped that by providing this cleverly worded pitch about her business, people would go and view her work for themselves and experience the beauty she brought to the world through her pain.

"Peggy views today's decision with both relief and remorse. She understands her uncle is a sick man, and hopes that the time he spends in prison and therapy will help him come to terms with whatever demons have driven him to become the dangerous pedophile that he is. She is grateful to the court for ensuring that he will never again be allowed to hurt innocent children, and calls upon all of those who have knowledge of such crimes not to be silent. Silence is what allows crimes like these to continue. We are all guilty when we turn away and neglect to expose those whose acts and deeds hurt others."

The crowd clapped and waved to Peggy as the car slowly pulled away. Peggy sat back in the seat with a sigh of relief. It was over. She closed her eyes and again thanked God that justice had been served.

Peggy stared out the window at the highway ahead as cars flew past her. The sun was still shining as people finished up their busy workday. Life had not stopped on her behalf. The world, she realized, had its own agenda, but she was, finally, at peace.

Chapter Forty-Five

IT SEEMS TO BE EVERYWHERE, like an epidemic, Val thought to herself. She was watching the local news while packing when the face of a beautiful little girl appeared on the television screen. Her name was McAllister Bingham ("Callie" to her family and friends). She was eight years old and had disappeared while playing at Olmsted Park in Brookline, Massachusetts not far from her home. She'd been missing for over twenty-four hours. Her parents, both well-educated attorneys, were frantic with worry. They'd let her go and play under the care of a family friend. In front of the cameras, the mother, held by her equally distraught husband, made a desperate public plea for their daughter's safe return.

Val clicked off the television. It was too much for her to handle in light of the recent events in Peggy's life, and what she'd recently learned about Glynnis's as well. She was heading to Ireland to see Warren, visit with her family, and check in on her girlfriends after the dramatic reappearance and subsequent prosecution of Peggy's uncle.

Val and Caroline were both shocked at the news of the trial. Caroline, after returning from her trip to Spain, had enthusiastically thrown herself into her new career in pediatrics. She'd wanted to fly to England to support Peggy through the crisis, but because of her new job, she couldn't take any more time off. Val, on the other hand, received five weeks of vacation a year and was in a better position to go.

Val hauled her suitcase off the bed and called for her sister. The still tanned and smiling woman appeared in the galley kitchen, sticking a bobby pin in the back of her ponytail to hold back annoying wisps that wouldn't stay put.

"Are you heading out already?"

Caroline asked.

"It's only four o'clock!"

Val nodded.

"Yeah. I don't want to run into Friday night traffic on the way to the airport. Are you going to be okay?"

Caroline smiled reassuringly.

"Yes, sis, I'll be fine. My old supervisor asked me to do her this one last favor. It's my last stint in the Emergency Room. I promise. It's not even a full shift - just 7:00PM to 11:00PM. I'm pretty sure I can handle it."

Val was glad, too. The stress from the ER had nearly put her sister over the edge more than a few times.

"Well, let's pray nothing catastrophic happens. I'll be back in a week. I'll call you in a few days and let you know how everyone's doing. I can't wait to see Warren! Give us a hug then ..."

Caroline gave her only sister a big bear hug and then decided to walk downstairs and wait with her for the taxi. Val felt an instant chill go through her body as she stared up from the sidewalk at Caroline leaning against the rail on the landing. She looked amazingly relaxed and healthy. Val shook it off rationalizing that it was just the dramatic change in temperature having just left the coolness of the air-conditioned apartment into the humid summer heat.

"Tell Mom I'll call her later in the week, and remember, don't work too hard!"

Val pointed and warned as the taxi approached. Turning, she waved lovingly before climbing into the backseat.

Caroline smiled and waved goodbye before bounding up the steps to put her watch on. She had plenty of time before she needed to be at work. She packed her lunch bag, not knowing if she'd get a chance to eat or not. In the ER, you were at the mercy of the ambulances. She grabbed an apple and sighed. She really didn't want to work the shift at all, but her old supervisor called begging her for this one last favor.

When she left the house at 6:00PM, traffic wasn't too bad, and she managed to pull into the hospital garage twenty minutes before the start of her shift. She made her way across the walkway toward the ER. Looking down at the entrance, she saw that several ambulances were already in the bays. She sighed to herself, hoping that wasn't an indication of how the evening would progress. She was surprised to see several TV trucks and their crews near the entrance as well. She assumed some VIP must have been admitted, and headed inside, purposely avoiding the media frenzy.

She'd barely put her purse in the locker when she was quickly summoned to assist in the trauma room. They had just transferred a young girl from the ambulance. She heard screams coming from the room and hurriedly threw her lunch bag at Sherry, the ER secretary, asking her to put it in the fridge for her. Caroline automatically grabbed at the box of latex gloves and had a chart shoved into her hands. The doctor had just arrived. The child was hysterical, screaming in pain. There was blood seeping through the sheets.

"What the hell is going on?"

Caroline took a clean blanket out from the metal blanket warmer and proceeded to pull back the bloodstained sheet. She was unprepared for the horror underneath. The child had a jagged stick protruding from her vagina and was bleeding profusely.

"Mother of God ..."

Caroline whispered to herself. The doctor rushed over and ordered an IV. In addition to the trauma team, he requested they summon the OB/ GYN on-call doctor. A pediatric surgeon was also en route to meet them in the OR. Caroline had to choke back the contents of her stomach. She calmly covered the child, who was shaking and blanched white.

"We've got to get her typed quickly."

She whispered to the lab tech already at the child's side. Caroline tried to comfort her while they drew blood. The little girl screamed hysterically when the lab tech inserted the needle. She was thrashing about as the other nurse helped gently pin her down. Caroline kept talking softly to her, reassuring her they were there to help her and that she'd try her best not to let the next needle hurt like that again.

She moved about mechanically as she readied the tubes and untangled the awaiting IV line. Caroline went over to the counter and extracted a vile of Lidocaine from the overhead cabinet and affixed the sticker to her shirt. She'd numb up a small area of her arm in the area where the IV line would go.

Caroline tapped the needle out of view from the little girl. She glanced down briefly at the chart and was shocked to read the name, MCALLISTER BINGHAM — the little girl from the news report. Teenagers who heard her crying in the woods near Larz Anderson Park had discovered her. Her parents were on their way, being led by a police escort. Caroline remembered from the news report that they called her "Callie."

"Callie ..."

The child's screams were changing over to short cries and whimpering. She seemed to listen and focus on Caroline's soft voice.

"Honey, I know this is really scary ... but we're going to help you and make you feel better okay?"

The child was crying for her mother. Caroline's heart was breaking for her, yet she had to remain focused. Time was of the essence, as they were going to quickly bring her up to the operating room to remove the embedded object.

"Honey, I'm going to give you some more medicine, and we have to put another very tiny needle in your arm to do this. But here's the deal, I promise you that it's only going to feel like a little pinch and then you won't feel anything at all, ok?"

Caroline nodded to her associate, who kept her hands on the child's hand so as to not let it flinch. Caroline's recent training in pediatric IV's proved invaluable. The doctor watched in admiration at her speed and precision. The child "oww'd" softly at the Lydocaine injection but was soothed by Caroline's voice. She was getting visibly weaker.

"There. It's all done! If you look at that really funny-looking doctor over there, you'll never even know it's in."

Everyone was too stressed by the situation to laugh at her comment, but the doctor smirked at Caroline, and it helped calm the child for a moment before she let out an agonizing scream as another spasm gripped her lower body.

"My tummy hurts!"

She cried out.

Caroline looked over anxiously at the ER doctor. She felt they weren't moving fast enough.

"Did you order an abdominal ultrasound yet?"

She asked him.

"Yeah. Radiology's on their way now."

Once the IV was in, the doctor ordered heavy-duty antibiotics and pain medication. Callie's parents were ushered into a private waiting room off the ER and briefed on their daughter's condition. An anesthesiologist was taking down important information and vitals. Callie's mother's frantic cries to see her daughter were heard from behind the door. They were assured by the team of doctors that they could see their daughter as soon as she'd been prepped for surgery.

The father, understandably angry, hurt, and shocked, shouted a stream of obscenities at the one who was responsible for the vicious crime. The police in the room assured him they were hot on the trail and leads were pouring in from witnesses all over the city. They were determined to find the criminal. They made it a point to add that they could sympathize with him, as they, too, had daughters Callie's age.

Callie was feeling the effects of the pain medication, drifting in and out of consciousness. A second IV was put in her other arm with no resistance after she'd drifted off to sleep. She needed a blood transfusion, as her pressure was dipping dangerously low. Security had been called to guard the doors from the prying news stations, which had set up a small camp in the parking lot. Callie's mother was borderline hysterical, and the ER doctor prescribed a mild sedative to calm her while they made final preparations for Callie's surgery. Both parents were told that they'd need to gather their wits about them for their daughter's sake before they'd be allowed in to see her.

Mr. and Mrs. Bingham managed to pull it together as they walked into the intimidating trauma room, where beeps from the various machines alerted the medical personnel of their daughter's dire condition.

Caroline stood off to the side, gathering up the important papers needed for Callie's chart which would accompany her up to the OR. The parents had a few precious minutes with their beloved daughter, holding and kissing her tiny hands and forehead while she slept. Caroline looked at the clock. She'd have to interrupt them in less than two minutes. Mrs. Bingham touched her daughter's angel-like hair and kissed her cheek. Her husband kissed her head repeatedly. Caroline turned so as not to let them see her own tears.

Caroline discreetly wiped her eyes and walked over with an encouraging smile.

"We've got to get her up to the OR now. We'll show you to the waiting room."

Caroline gave instructions to the secretary to summon a transport attendant to walk the Bingham's upstairs. She wedged the x-rays and medical chart into the side railing of the bed and moved the IV poles. An attendant rushed to help her. They quickly ushered the child upstairs. Two of the attending doctors were on the phones in the glassed-in room off the trauma room, giving orders to the awaiting OR staff upstairs.

Caroline handed off the charts to the operating room nurses and went over the medications with the anesthesiologist. After the transfer, she left to walk back to the elevator. She began to shake. The pain and horror that child must have endured caused a well of rage to rise up within her.

"Where the hell is the elevator?"

She shouted loudly, banging the panel button a few times with her fist and pacing before the closed doors. The nurses at the OR desk heard her, but didn't react or comment. They were unified in their emotions and understood what was bothering Caroline. They heard about the case.

Callie was in surgery for over six hours. They removed the stick from her after they'd taken gruesome pictures to be used as evidence when and if they caught the person responsible. Callie's mother was told that her daughter would never have children. The jagged object used to violate her had punctured the uterus and tore the vaginal wall in several places. Though they'd managed to repair everything necessary to control the bleeding and keep her alive, reconstructive surgery would be needed in the immediate future. The biggest fear now was infection.

After she'd been stitched up and stronger antibiotics had been administered, the doctors sat in silence, stunned that any human could inflict this much harm on an innocent child. Callie was brought to intensive care, where they'd monitor her closely before transferring her to Pediatrics.

After a traumatic start, the rest of the shift was a blur. The nurses tried to shake it off and busied themselves with patients who had the usual complaints of back pain, a persistent cough, a broken ankle, and other non life-threatening ailments. Caroline had to bite her tongue to not tell one obnoxious woman to shut her fat mouth, after she complained incessantly about the long wait she'd had. She had a "horrible migraine headache." Caroline stayed on longer than her intended shift leaving the ER in the early morning hours. She vowed she'd never work in that department again.

She went home and turned on the television. Her young patient dominated the airwaves. A sketch was displayed of the rapist believed to be the abductor. Various interviews with people in the area at the time of the crime gave the detectives more leads, and they publicly vowed to hunt down her attacker.

Caroline turned off the TV. She was off the next day and hoped to go biking along the Charles River with a friend from work. She lay in bed for hours, but couldn't sleep. Glancing at her watch for the twentieth time, she decided to call Valerie in Ireland.

Val had arrived at her grandmother's house just a half hour earlier. Siobhan was already up and in the kitchen, putting the kettle on for them to have a cup of tea when the phone rang. Val picked it up.

Caroline apologized for the early morning call and quickly relayed the tragic details of the night's events to her and Aunt Siobhan, a pediatric nurse veteran, who was invited to listen in on the other line. They talked in medical terms Val didn't fully understand, but she could glean from the situation that things weren't good.

"That poor little girl ... I can't understand how anyone could do that to a child! If I got my hands on him, I'd neuter him myself!"

Caroline and Siobhan were both surprised to hear Val talk like that. Caroline knew she wasn't supposed to talk about private patient information but was finding it hard to process it all. It was grounds for firing.

Val asked Caroline if she'd be okay.

"I'll be fine. I'm just a little shaken by the whole thing. I couldn't sleep, so I thought I'd give you a call. I'm getting tired now though."

Val switched to a lighter note, telling Caroline that Uncle Sean was taking them all out for dinner that evening, and that she and Warren had tickets to another concert at the Glor.

"It's becoming one of our favorite places to go when I visit here now."

Caroline told her to give him a kiss for her when she saw him and to have a great time.

"Thanks! I'll do that."

Val assured her enthusiastically.

"Listen, sis, I've gotta go and get some rest. I've not been to bed yet."

Val encouraged her to get some rest. Caroline hung up the phone and fell back onto the bed, undeterred by the midsummer sizzle that gripped the city of Boston in its first official heat wave of the season.

Caroline stirred at the sound of the phone ringing the next morning but let the answering machine pick up. She just didn't feel like talking to anyone and wanted to sleep in. When she awoke again, the early afternoon sun was streaming in her window. The humidity caused the sheets to stick to her body. She kicked off the strangling covers and staggered out of bed to close the windows and turn on the air conditioner. On her way to the bathroom, she filled the coffeemaker in the kitchen, so it would be ready when she emerged from the shower.

The cool water brought her body temperature down, and she slowly began to feel more alive. She reached for a plush plum-colored towel, wrapping it around herself as she moved into the kitchen to fill a mug and listen to the answering machine. It was her new boss. She explained that they were shorthanded because someone had called in sick and she wanted to know if Caroline could come in and work.

Caroline called her back, eager to show her new supervisor that she was a team player. Though she had the day off, she agreed to work the 3:00PM to 11:00PM shift. Caroline called her friend and moved their biking date to another day, explaining that she had to be at work by three. She'd slept until one thirty and had to rush to get there on time.

It was a gorgeous day as she drove to PMC with the top down on her car. People were lying along the banks of the Charles River sun tanning and playing Frisbee. Tiny sails were seen bobbing beyond the BU Bridge. A Redline train crossed over the bridge in the distance.

Caroline pulled into the employee parking lot and put the roof up on her car. Aside from the condo and trip to Spain, her Saab convertible was the first real gift she bought with her grandparents' trust fund. Turning off the blaring AC/DC music, she locked the vehicle and made her way to the elevator flashing her badge at the front desk. She waved to a few of the nurses huddled at the station, and made her way out back to change. Her supervisor went back to talk with her before her shift began.

"I heard you were in the ER last night when they brought the Bingham girl in. Good job. Dr. Sever was really impressed with you."

Caroline nodded while slipping on her clogs.

"Yeah. It was really tough going there for a while. The child was in agony. Have you heard how she's doing?"

Her supervisor sat down on the bench beside her.

"Well, she's holding her own and battling a fever. It's still touch-and-go. But they're transferring her out of ICU later this afternoon and up here to us. I want you to cover her."

Caroline's eyes widened.

"She'll be your only patient. I know you're new to this, but when Dr. Sever heard that you worked on this floor, he suggested Callie might feel less frightened if she sees a familiar face when she comes to."

Caroline nodded, but wasn't quite sure she could handle it. The case was very high profile and would require her using every bit of knowledge and skill she'd ever learned. She was somewhat reluctant, nervous, and more than a bit anxious.

"So long as you won't be too far away should I have questions. I'm happy to help out. She's a beautiful child. This should never have happened to her!"

Her supervisor nodded in agreement.

Callie was settled into her new room directly across from the nurses' station. Dr. Sever explained to Caroline that internally Callie was still a mess. It would take months for her to heal physically, and even longer, if ever, to recuperate emotionally.

He requested another MRI, handing the orders off to an eager young nurse just out of school. He prescribed an even stronger antibiotic for Callie hoping that it would attack the infection and bring down the fever. After glancing at his watch, he jotted a few more notes in her chart and spent a significant amount of time going over the complicated case with the young doctor up next on duty.

Callie's fever was persistent. All attempts were being made to bring the infection under control. The doctor assured Mr. and Mrs. Bingham that due to the severe nature of her injuries; it wasn't unusual for infection to be present. Callie was hooked up to various machines, which were monitored closely at the nurse's station. Caroline was her primary nurse for the remainder of the shift, and she paid diligent attention to the child's every need. Her mother and father never left her side, taking turns sleeping on the extra bed that had been brought into her private room for them.

The young nurse was anxious for her shift to end and quickly gathered up her mounting paperwork. She placed it on top of Callie's chart and seemed frustrated that she'd not be able to get it all done before it was time for her to leave. The supervisor told her not to worry and to go on; she'd sort it all out. The young woman was grateful and thanked her.

Caroline sifted through the paperwork to get at Callie's chart. Her vitals needed to be taken and meds were due soon. She set off in the direction of the child's room, armed with another intravenous bag. There were stickers all over her smock that needed to be transferred onto Callie's chart for accounting purposes.

Caroline talked quietly with Callie's mother and father, who were watching the news and waiting anxiously to see what, if anything, the Brookline Police Department had to say about the latest on the search for Callie's abductor. They were careful to keep the volume low while she slept.

Caroline reached for the child's wrist and was surprised at how warm she was. Without warning, a machine alarm sounded, startling all in the room. Callie didn't move. Caroline reached over and quickly shut off the source of the high-pitched beeping. She was concerned about the reading and excused herself from the room to inform her supervisor. The alarm sounded once again from Callie's room, and a warning light flashed brightly on the console at the nurse's station. Callie's temperature was rising quickly.

The doctor on duty immediately went into the room to assess the stats for himself and ordered yet another round of medication to help bring her temperature down. Caroline punched her code into the dispenser and opened the cabinet drawer to get the medication. The doctor sat nervously at the desk, tapping his foot and flipping through her chart. It was going to be a long night.

Caroline's supervisor finished up her notes and talked by phone with the next supervisor on duty. Caroline went into Callie's room to remove her blanket in an effort to keep her cool. She pulled the curtain around them to check on her catheter and empty the attached bag. Caroline noticed a slight amount of blood on the sheets, not unusual after the type of surgery she had, and reached for the overhead light. She pressed the button on the side of the bed and her supervisor quickly answered the call. Caroline pointed and whispered so as to not alarm the parents, who were just outside the curtain. The supervisor quietly left to go get the doctor.

Callie's parents were asked to kindly wait outside their daughter's room. The pediatric surgeon consulted on the phone from Callie's room with the OB/GYN doctor. He covered the phone with his hand and asked Caroline if the MRI results were back yet. Caroline didn't see a Radiology slip in the child's chart.

"I don't see an order here."

She flipped through the paperwork.

"Damn it! It was ordered three hours ago! You mean to tell me that it hasn't even been called in yet?"

Caroline was taken back by the severity of his voice and was visibly shaken. The nurse supervisor took her aside as they both searched through the files left by the student nurse. The surgeon called the MRI in himself — STAT.

Caroline looked over at a pile of papers still stacked up on the other counter and searched through them. She recognized the pink Radiology slip. It had been accidentally placed in the chart of a ruptured appendix patient down the hall. It clearly had Callie's name on it. She showed it to her supervisor, who vowed to look into the error later.

It took over an hour for the radiologist to get to the hospital, due to a severe thunderstorm that had blown in. The surgeon complained to him that it took far too much time, given the fact that he lived only fifteen minutes away. Callie was taken down to Radiology for the procedure, which would take over an hour. She slept through the entire test. Caroline waited outside, listening to the familiar clicks and beeps. The radiologist was standing at the ready to read the images as soon as they were available.

The MRI showed that a few small fragments of splintered wood were still embedded deep in the child's tissue. They needed to get her fever down before they could perform another surgery to remove the slivered pieces gone undetected in the vaginal wall. Callie's father was furious that the splinters had not been found earlier and vowed to sue the hospital should anything happen to his daughter. His wife was trying to calm him down as he paced the floor, anxiously combing his hand through his hair as he walked. Caroline called for Security to come up and be near in the event things got out of control.

More monitors sounded once Callie was brought back and settled into her room. The doctor was securing permission to move her back to the Intensive Care Unit when a scream came from Callie's room. Her mother had pulled back the covers and saw that her daughter was lying in a pool of blood. The parents were quickly ushered out of the room as a code was called for their child. Her body convulsed from the fever. The small room was quickly filling up with lab techs drawing blood, and doctors hovering while monitoring her vitals and deciding what to do next.

Within a few hours, Callie succumbed to the infection. Shock waves rippled throughout the hospital. Callie's parents were devastated. The pediatric ward was abuzz with people coming and going. Caroline sat at the nurses' station, hugging the child's chart to her chest and staring blankly as various relatives arrived to comfort Callie's grieving parents. Caroline had been warned to use another door when leaving the hospital after her shift to avoid the reporters who were gathered outside awaiting a news conference.

Caroline couldn't help but feel responsible. Had she seen the MRI orders earlier, maybe they could have saved precious time and found the embedded fragments and operated sooner. Her nurse supervisor assured her it wasn't her fault. Caroline rubbed at her forehead and tried to come to grips with the reality of what had just happened. She stayed well past the end of her shift in order to go over all the details with the doctor and nurse supervisor. No doubt a full hospital investigation would be ordered. Caroline worked silently alongside the nurse supervisor to disconnect the tubes still attached to the child's lifeless body.

Callie's face looked so peaceful. Caroline tried to pretend she was still just asleep but gave way to tears when she reached up to lift the IV bags off the overhanging hook. Her supervisor patted her shoulder, telling her to go home, that she'd take care of it. It had been a difficult night for them all.

Caroline walked numbly out into the hallway and back to the nurse's lounge. She took a soda out of the refrigerator and retrieved her purse from the locker. Security offered to walk her to her car. She shook her head no, walking past them with a distant and blank look in her eyes. They knew it had been a rough night for her.

Opening the door to her apartment, Caroline felt an overwhelming sense of loneliness. She looked at the pictures in the living room of her, Valerie, and her mom. She passed by the blinking answering machine registering the number 4. Changing into a T-shirt and shorts, Caroline filled a glass of water and walked calmly back to her room. She threw her head back as she swallowed, and the pills went down smoothly.

The phone rang once again, but Caroline was helpless to move. Her spirit had already begun to separate from her body. She floated above the lifeless form lying across the bed and then hovered about the apartment, lingering for a short time in Val's room. She reached out and gently touched her sister's violin, then turned to begin her final journey home.

Chapter Forty-Six

Ennis, County Clare, Ireland, Summer 1998

VALERIE TURNED OVER AT THE sound of the telephone but didn't fully awaken. Glancing briefly at the clock, she noticed it was 1:30 a.m. She was very comfortable in Warren's guest bedroom, snuggled beneath the comforter. She could faintly hear Warren's voice next door, his footsteps in the hall, then felt him sit beside her on the bed. His hand moved gently over her back to waken her.

"Valerie ... hon."

She struggled to open her eyes, having slipped back into a strangely restless state. Warren gathered her hand up into his. She smiled up at him trustingly. He spoke to her softly.

"Valerie, I just received a phone call. It was your mother ..."

His voice was a little hoarse, and she thought she noticed a tear trickling down his cheek, illuminated by the light from the hallway. Val sat up, alarmed and fully awake.

"What is it, Warren? Tell me ..."

Panic rose within her. Warren didn't know how to say the words gently. He struggled with how to say it at all. Finally, he spoke what needed to be said as sensitively as he could

"Valerie, it's Caroline, love. She overdosed on some pills and, well, your uncle Tim found her body a few hours ago. I'm so sorry, darling."

Val stared at him blankly, her expression devoid of emotion. Her mind was struggling to understand the words her ears heard. Warren knew she was in shock.

"I guess there was an incident at the hospital Saturday evening, and she just couldn't handle it. Something about one of her young patients dying."

Val listened numbly to the words he spoke but found the whole story surreal. She couldn't speak as she tried to process all that he was saying to her.

"Valerie, are you following me, love? I know this is hard to come to grips with."

He gently squeezed her hand.

Val looked up at him and nodded. As it all sank in, tears sprung from her eyes. She whispered something he couldn't quite make out as her head fell forward onto his chest, and then the words came tumbling out.

"I knew this would happen one day! I'd hoped it would never come to this. But I knew it would. I sensed it. I didn't want to leave her, Warren. I felt it on the landing at our house ... when I was waiting for my taxi with her. I had this thought that it might be the last time I saw her. I shoved it from my mind. I've always worried about her."

Her voice trailed off.

Warren's strong arms embraced her. Her body shook while she sobbed. After several minutes, Val wiped at her eyes and put her hand to her mouth, trying to stop the guttural sounds that emanated from deep within.

"Does Granny know yet?"

Warren nodded sadly.

"They wanted to come and get you, but I told them that I'd take you over to the house later this morning. It's only about 2:00 a.m. right now. I'm going to see what I can do about getting us all on a flight back to the US. My airline is good in emergencies like this. They'll do their best to help me out."

He looked down at her delicate hand in his.

"Valerie, I'm so sorry."

Remembering something, she leaned over and kissed him sweetly on his cheek. He looked at her somewhat puzzled.

"I promised Caroline I'd give you a kiss for her."

She broke down into tears and buried her face in the pillow as uncontrollable sobs once again wracked her body.

Warren lay down next to her. His own quiet tears mingled with hers as he rubbed her back.

"I know, hon. I know."

He didn't know how else to comfort her at a time like this. His heart ached for Valerie and her family. Though he didn't know Caroline all that well, he felt like an old friend when they'd met. The love between the two sisters was evident and endearing. The days ahead would be difficult ones for the entire family.

Valerie lifted herself up onto her elbow. Her nose was stuffed up, and she couldn't catch her breath. Warren offered to get the tissues and make her some tea.

He heard Valerie moving about upstairs and knew that she was gathering her things together to pack her suitcase. After putting the kettle on, he called his work's twenty-four-hour employee hotline, identifying himself as a pilot and reciting his ID number to the supervisor who took the call. She was sensitive, understanding, and extremely helpful, telling him she'd look into flight options for all and call him back.

Warren heard the bathroom door close and the shower turn on. He bit his lip when he heard Valerie once again sobbing in the shower. He felt helpless, and it broke his heart to hear her so sad. He wanted to run to her, and yet knew she needed some space and privacy to work through her emotions. The phone rang again, and it was Sean. He apologized for calling in the middle of the night. Warren assured him that he was already up and expressed his sorrow to Sean for their loss. Sean asked how Valerie was holding up.

"She's distraught, and I think she's still in shock."

Warren told him that Val was taking a shower and would call him back a little later. He assured Sean of his devotion to Val and would help her through this. Sean thanked him for being there to comfort his niece.

He informed Sean that he was looking into flights back to the US for the entire family. Sean's voice faltered as he thanked Warren for his help before hanging up.

Valerie trudged downstairs. Her hair was wet, yet combed out, and she wore his navy blue bathrobe. She looked pretty even in the face of grief. She sat at the kitchen table, her eyes puffy, and cradled the hot, steaming mug in her shaking hands.

"Warren, Caroline was always driven by something. I never knew what it was."

She pulled her knees up on the chair, tucked the bathrobe beneath her, and struggled to make sense of it all.

"It was as if something gnawed at her constantly. I mean most days she was 'normal.' But whenever she was under a lot of stress, she'd take these emotional cliff dives. She'd always deny anything was wrong when I'd ask her. But I knew something was there, just lurking beneath the surface."

Warren pulled out a chair to sit and listen.

"I didn't know her very well, Valerie. But I know how much she loved and admired you. I saw it in her eyes the night of the concert when she watched you perform."

Val nodded her head and smiled, then started crying again. She buried her face in her hands; she couldn't believe they were talking in the past tense. A sharp pain jabbed her deep in the stomach, leaving her slightly nauseous. She took another sip of tea to try and calm herself.

"She did love listening to me play."

She whispered mournfully.

"I don't know how I'll ever pick up the violin again without completely losing it."

He wiped her tears as they fell. She struggled on.

"When I play, I'll think only of her. I don't know how I can ever separate the two ... all my life, I'd play; she'd dance."

Her slight chuckle gave way to tears yet again.

Warren held her hand.

"Love, you don't have to separate them. Your love for music and its powerful expression will pull you through. It can be very soothing, therapeutic. It transcends language, ministering deep into the soul. You just need to let it flow from you. Draw strength from it. It'll bring you peace. I believe it will help you heal. You know Caroline would never want you to stop playing. I dare say she'd come back and haunt you!"

His attempt at humor made her smile weakly.

Valerie got up and sat on his lap, draping her arms about his neck and burying her head in his shoulder. He took in the sweet smell of her body and the scent of her freshly washed hair, and was disgusted at his body's reaction to her close proximity — especially during this time of grief. He apologized awkwardly and was more than a bit ashamed. Valerie laughed softly, assuring him it was okay.

"So, you are human."

She joked and kissed him slowly on the lips. She hiccupped and pulled away slightly as tears once again started without warning. He hugged her close and gently rocked her.

Valerie wanted him to make love to her. She led the way up to his room and slipped out of his robe before sliding beneath the covers. Warren exercised amazing restraint upon seeing her body. She was beautiful. She pulled him to her, and he groaned, returning her passionate kiss. He lifted himself up on his elbow and traced her nose with his finger.

"Valerie, you know that I love you. You've a lot of emotions swirling around in your heart right now, and you're struggling to make sense of it all. I want for us to make love when it's the right time. As much as I could devour you this instant, I know that I shouldn't. I want your mind free and clear and your heart not burdened. I never want you to feel regret, it would only add to your sadness. I don't want our first time to be over shadowed by guilt."

490

She knew he was right. He gently kissed her lips and held her until she rested in his arms. He awoke feeling his hand at her breast. Slowly he removed his hand and painstakingly inched himself away from her, wanting to let her sleep.

He escaped to the confines of his glassed-in shower stall and turned on the cold water, stifling a shudder at the shock of the frigid water hitting his body. He washed quickly and headed downstairs. Turning down the volume on the answering machine, he listened to the message left by the woman from Employee Relations.

All of the reservations had been taken care of and they were scheduled on an 11:30 a.m. flight. Warren glanced at the clock. It was already 7:30 a.m. He called Sean and informed him of the departure time. Sean assured him they'd be ready to go and would meet him and Val at the airport at 9:30 a.m.

Val appeared, wrapped once again in his bathrobe, and told him that she wanted to call her mother now that she'd had time to digest the information. Warren offered to leave the room while they talked. She told him he didn't have to. Val's voice was tender as she addressed her mother.

"Hi, Mom. It's me ... Val."

She started to cry when she realized how that must have sounded. Now there was no other. Her mother cried when she heard her eldest daughter's voice. There were no words for a few moments between them as mother and daughter mourned together. Val spoke first.

"Mom, I'm on my way home. Warren was able to get flights for all of us. We'll be taking off in a few hours. Is Auntie Sheila there with you?"

Her mother assured her she was, along with Tim. She mentioned that Father Bruce had stayed up with her through the night as well. Val asked her to give them her love, and then told her mother to try and get some rest. Finally, she told her how much she loved her and hung up.

Val's next call was to Glynnis and Peggy at their home in England. Glynnis answered the phone with a groggy voice. Val choked back the sob that rose in her throat. She cleared her throat.

"Glynn?"

"Yeah ... Val?"

Glynnis sat up in bed.

"What's up? You sick or something? You sound horrible!"

"No. Umm, I'm okay ... sort of. Glynn, it's Caroline. She's ..."

Val couldn't speak the words and looked helplessly up at Warren. Shaking, she held the phone out to him. He went to her side, taking the receiver. Val turned away, unable to speak without sobbing. She ran to the bathroom where she threw up the tea she'd just finished drinking. Warren asked Glynnis to hold on for a moment and dropped the phone to go help her. He reached for a face cloth and ran it under cool water, using it to wipe her face. Taking her puffy face in his hands, he assured her.

"You're going to get through this, darling. I promise. Please hang in there."

His tears were a reflection of hers.

He helped her to her feet and walked back to the kitchen. Warren apologized to Glynnis for dropping the phone on her. He went on to calmly explain what had happened. Val was still too distraught to speak.

Peggy had walked into the room and could be heard in the background asking Glynnis what was wrong. Glynnis couldn't believe what she was hearing. Her voice shrilled.

"Oh, my God, Warren! When did this happen?"

Glynnis was crying uncontrollably. Peggy had no clue what was going on and was trying to piece the story together from her hysterical friend; she finally just pried the phone from Glynnis's hand.

"Hello?"

Warren's strong voice responded.

"It's Warren, Peggy. I've got some bad news I'm afraid."

Peggy walked across the room and sat deliberately in the chair, bracing herself for what was to come.

"Go on, Warren. Tell me. Glynnis is hysterical. I'm afraid to ask."

She sat on the edge of her chair, listening intently as Warren relayed the story of Caroline's death. Tears began to drip steadily from her eyes and onto her pajamas.

"Is Val with you now?"

She asked in a controlled voice.

"Can I talk to her, you think?"

Peggy stood and paced back and forth while Warren brought the phone to Val. She could hear Val blowing her nose in the background.

"Val, it's me. Peggy. I'm so sorry."

Peggy sat on the floor beside Glynnis, and the three women cried together over the phone. Val repeated to her what little she knew, and that she wasn't sure what, if anything had been done yet in the way of arrangements.

"No doubt Auntie Sheila will take care of those matters."

She mentioned that she, Warren, and her family were flying home from Ireland later in the morning and should get into Boston around seven that evening. She couldn't talk without having to take deep, hiccupping breaths, and told her friends she had to hang up and go pack.

Peggy understood and assured her that they'd make their flight arrangements immediately and would meet up with her either in Boston or on the Cape in a few days. Val invited them to stay at her apartment when they finally arrived in Boston. She was having a hard time keeping track of the travel details in her own life and didn't know if she was going to head straight to the Cape later that night to see her mom or stay in Boston and head down on Tuesday morning. It just depended on how everyone was doing. She told Peggy that if she wasn't there when she arrived, to just get the spare key from Mrs. Brohmien on the first floor. She'd call her to let her know they were coming.

"Val, don't worry about us. We'll catch up with you when we get there. We'll call your mom and let her know."

Peggy decided to close the gallery for the week.

"Valerie, you know that we're here for you. We love you and Caroline so much."

Peggy's voice cracked as she thought of her friend being gone forever.

"We'll talk to you soon, okay? Please hang in there."

Val nodded silently on the other end and gingerly hung up the phone. Warren had gone upstairs. They packed quickly and got ready to head to the airport. Val pulled her hair up in a ponytail and put on big sunglasses. She wore no makeup and was grateful that she didn't feel the need to have to impress Warren. He accepted her for who she was.

Val felt weighed down by many concerns on the way to the airport. She dreaded seeing her grandmother and aunt and uncle upset.

"Warren, how are you managing the time off from work to come with me? They've got you scheduled already ..."

Warren assured her he'd worked it out. He'd spoken with his employer and told them a close friend had died, and that he needed some time to help out with the funeral arrangements. The company would give him a week's bereavement leave, and he would take an additional week of vacation. They'd cover his schedule. He was a long-standing employee with over eleven weeks of vacation time. They even encouraged him to take more time if he felt he needed it.

"You don't have to do this, Warren. That's your vacation time. I feel horrible having you use it for something like this. I mean, it should be for fun ... not like this."

She turned away, so he couldn't see her crying again.

"Please, Val. No worries, love, okay? I could take months off, if I needed to. Before I met you, I worked constantly and very rarely took any time off. I've stored up quite a bit for myself. Unlike a lot of companies today, mine lets me accumulate my vacation days. I don't 'lose it if I don't use it'."

494

He rhymed, and smiled, putting the matter to rest. She didn't bring it up again and thanked him, leaning her head on his shoulder.

Thinking out loud, she said.

"You know, there's a musical piece I think I'd like to play at Caroline's funeral, if I can muster up the strength to do it. I'll have to talk with Father Bruce when I get back and see if he can bring it together in such a short time. It keeps playing over and over in my head. Caroline would have loved it. It would require the whole ensemble helping out, however. They'll do it for her. I'm sure of it."

"Do you remember me telling you how Caroline had won an Irish Rose Contest years ago when she was a teenager? Uncle Sean, without her knowing, signed her up for it. She wanted to kill him but she won it hands down. She thought it a talent show of sorts. Anyway, there's this beautiful piece by a composer I love - Tim Janis. He's extremely gifted. It's a piece called, 'Somewhere Still the Rose'."

Val wiped away her tears.

"Just hearing it in my mind makes me want to cry. I've played it by ear, and I know I could get my hands on the music for the ensemble, if I have to call Mr. Janis myself, I will. Maybe you could help me work on it, too. I just don't know if I can get through it without a complete melt down. It's such a moving piece. Caroline would have loved it."

She repeated and hiccupped back another sob, struggling to regain her composure as Warren pulled up slowly to the automatic gate at the airport.

"We'll work on it, and you'll do a beautiful job. I have faith in you."

Granny, Sean, and Siobhan met them at the Irish Tourist Board counter not far from their departure gate. They hugged and consoled one another. Val was worried about her grandmother. She was getting up there in years, and Val was afraid the trauma from this tragedy might be too much for her. Granny told her not to worry about her and that they needed to save their strength to help her mother through this. She asked Val how she was coping.

"Granny, I still can't believe it. I'm just so sad! I worry about ... well, when I go home and walk through the door of the apartment. She won't be there. I'm so used to her bounding down the hallway. She was like a puppy! Bouncing along with those crazy pigtails of hers."

She laughed for a moment, and then started to cry, burying her head in her hands. Her grandmother reached out for her and held her heaving shoulders. People walking by tried politely not to stare. Others, upon seeing the group in tears, removed their hats in acknowledgement of their grief and obvious loss.

Warren returned with all of their tickets and told them that they'd be seated ahead of the others in first class. He sat down to talk with Siobhan. Sean sat with his back to them all, alone, staring out at the plane they were about to board.

The trip seemed long and very quiet. Val dozed somewhat on the plane, thanks to a mild sedative Siobhan had given her. She declined anything to eat for fear she'd be sick. Her grandmother and Siobhan talked nervously about funeral arrangements the entire flight. Sean, seated by the window, stared blankly at the water far below, barely even blinking. He said nothing the entire trip. Warren felt sorry for him. It was obvious how much Caroline meant to them all.

They had lost not one, but three significant members of their family in their lifetime, Val told him. Neil, her father, when the girls were younger, her Grandfather Callahan, just two short years ago, after a bad case of pneumonia, and now Caroline - in the prime of her life. He could only imagine how they felt and sent up a quick prayer for comfort. He'd light a candle for each of them at their church in Chatham when they arrived. He wanted to talk to Father Bruce about helping with the music at Caroline's funeral. Val's idea of a special selection would be a fitting tribute to such a beautiful young woman.

Assuming that Val and Warren would stay in Boston when they arrived, Sean had ordered a limousine to take him, Granny, and Siobhan directly down to the Cape. Val asked if she and Warren could squeeze in with them. Suddenly, she realized that she didn't want to go to her vacant apartment. She quickly explained that she had clothes with her and at her mother's house. Warren was unconcerned with the sudden change in plans, sensing her discomfort at going to the apartment. At that moment, she wanted desperately to see and be with her mother. She was grateful that her auntie Sheila and uncle Tim were already there with her - and Father Bruce. At that moment, she felt so grateful for her family; they were really all that mattered. Love, that's what it all came down to.

Sean offered to have the driver stop to get them something to eat. No one was particularly hungry, and Siobhan told them that there'd be plenty of food at Grace's house. Grace had told her that the people from church had, once again, gone all out in her time of need.

"Your mom said she can't fit it all in the refrigerator and had to put some in the Grazianos' refrigerator next door."

Granny smiled.

"They're such a generous parish! You're very fortunate, you know, Val. You've a real gem in that Father Bruce ... too bad we didn't have more like him!"

Val nodded.

"This is going to be hard for him, too, Granny. He loved Caroline dearly. She was like a daughter to him, if that's possible. He told us both that many times."

When they pulled up to the house, it was close to nine o'clock. The driver had a hard time finding a spot to park, as the driveway was filled with cars and people. Someone yelled to Grace that they'd arrived and she ran out, with eyes looking only for her daughter, squeezing her tightly.

Everyone was in tears. Val noticed her elderly neighbors: Mr. Graziano had his arm around his wife's shoulders as she brought a handkerchief to her nose. Father Bruce went out and huddled around the two women offering a quiet prayer of comfort. He warmly embraced Granny, Siobhan, and Sean, shaking Warren's hand and patting him on the back. Tim was standing off to the side and went over to give Val a quick, though awkward, hug. His jaw was set; no tears were visible. Val knew he was trying to be strong for Sheila and Grace.

The men took the luggage inside and then upstairs. The ladies went into the dining room. Val removed her shoes and walked barefoot into her childhood home. It was a hot and humid summer evening, and a small sea breeze started blowing in off the ocean. She looked around at all the friends that had gathered. There were ladies from the ensemble working in the kitchen, setting up pastries, and making coffee and tea. They'd not even had the wake yet, and the turnout in support was overwhelming. Val thanked them all for helping her mother and told them what wonderful friends they were. They each hugged her and told her how sorry they were.

Sean sat in one of the Adirondack chairs outback overlooking the black ocean. When Val went out to get some air, she noticed him and walked over. He reached for her hand and squeezed it gently.

"I wish I could roll back time, Vanilla Bean."

Valerie wiped the tears from her face at the mention of her childhood nickname. He sounded just like her dad when he said that. All of a sudden, it dawned on Val, a revelation of sorts.

"You know what, Uncle Sean? This is all very sad, but what's good about it is that Caroline is finally with Daddy. I mean, she never really knew him, and now she's with him!"

Sean cried openly at his niece's ever-hopeful outlook.

"Aye, it's true, love. He'll give her a heaven's welcome, for sure."

Val got up and told Sean she'd leave him to his thoughts. She set off in search of Warren. As usual, Warren fit right in and was sitting comfortably on the couch in the living room, talking with Father Bruce, who was nodding with him in agreement about something. Val went upstairs and found her mother in Caroline's room. Val sat next to her on the bed. They quietly held one another's hands and wiped at their tears.

"Uncle Tim found her."

Her mother spoke softly.

"That little girl, you know, the one on the news, the one that had been abducted and raped? She died from an infection at the hospital. I guess Caroline was her nurse the night she died."

Val closed her eyes, knowing her sister's response in cases like these. Her mother choked back tears.

"I'm guessing she somehow felt guilty. You know how she was about these things."

Her mother's voice trailed off. Val patted her hand as they sat quietly in the darkened room.

"I wish she'd never become a nurse!"

Her mother spouted angrily, then put her hands up to her mouth to stifle a cry.

"Mom, Caroline was a unique individual, so complex and vulnerable at the same time. Tell me something; do you have any idea what it was that drove her to be like that? I mean, such extremes? I asked her so many times and she'd just deny anything was ever wrong. But there was something wrong! Damn her for not telling me!"

Val was angry, too, and clenched her fists as she walked across the room to look out the window. The moon danced on the ocean currents.

Her mother fiddled with the tissue in her hands.

"I know what you mean. I asked her that same question many times, and she just always told me I'd never understand. Of course, that's what all girls say to their mothers, like you think we're idiots or something ... incapable of feelings. But we DO have feelings. Damn it!"

She threw up her hands in frustration. Val went to sit beside her mother again as they tried to talk it out.

"Mom, I don't know what I'm going to do without her. I don't know how I can go back to our condo. She's everywhere there."

Her mother looked into her older daughter's eyes.

"I know, honey. You'll have to be strong."

Her mother suggested.

"Why don't you go downstairs and get something to eat. See if Warren wants something, okay? I just need some time alone."

She paused and smiled at Valerie.

"He's a good man, Val. That Warren. I'm very happy for you, despite all that's happening right now. I somehow know you two will be very happy together."

She glanced over at the photo of Caroline and Val as children on the beach.

"Just give me a few minutes to myself in here, would you, sweetheart?"

Val rose to leave. She turned around before closing the door.

"I love you, Mom."

Grace smiled at her daughter.

"I love you, too, Valerie."

The crowd downstairs was thinning out. Auntie Sheila stood at the doorway, saying good-bye to people as they left. Tim was out on the back porch smoking a cigarette; Sean still sat quietly staring into the night over the moonlit ocean. Val sat down beside Warren on the wicker loveseat on the porch. She was restless. He had his head back and eyes closed. She tucked up her feet and leaned against him. He put his arm around her without opening his eyes.

"Are you hungry?"

Val whispered to him. He made a "so-so" motion with his other hand.

"Why don't I get us both something to eat?"

Warren wanted to make sure she ate something, so he got up and followed her into the kitchen. Everything had been wrapped or tucked away in Tupperware bowls. She pulled a bowl out of the fridge.

"I love this stuff. Auntie Sheila makes the best macaroni salad."

Val got a spoon out of the drawer and put some on plates for them, while Warren lifted lids and sniffed at the packaged contents. He pulled out an assortment of food, and they heated some things in the microwave.

"These are the best inventions don't you think? Microwaves?"

Val smiled and dug in. She hadn't realized how hungry she was.

Sheila entered the room, sighing.

"So how are you two doing?"

She went over to give Val a hug, and they both teared up yet again.

"It's so unbelievable, Auntie Sheila. I can't imagine what life is going to be like without her."

Sheila sat down at the table. Tim stood beside her, putting his hand on her shoulder. She reached up and patted it without looking up at him. Tim seemed like he wanted to talk. Warren started the conversation.

"Tim, how'd you know? I mean, to go see her? You found her, right?"

Tim nodded sadly.

"When I heard the news about the little girl, I knew Caroline would take it hard. She'd called and told Sheila she'd taken on an extra shift Saturday night and that there was a possibility she could find out more about the young girl who'd been abducted that she assisted with in the ER the night before."

"I know how Caroline is with these kind of things, and when I heard the news on the television of the child's death, I tried calling her, and there was no answer, so I drove up. I just sensed something was wrong. We keep a spare key in case of ..."

He paused for a moment to maintain his composure.

"In case of an emergency."

Val took a sip of her soda and couldn't swallow it. She waited for the bubbles to subside. She felt like she was trying to swallow a rock.

"She had overdosed. I found the bottle in the bathroom. What was the drug called again?"

Sheila closed her eyes, trying to recall.

"I think it was Equanil - something like that. We'll know tomorrow. The coroner's office will call us with the results. Then we can pull the arrangements together, once they release her body to the funeral home."

Val choked on her macaroni salad. Tim pounded her on the back. She couldn't swallow. Eating was just too hard for her at the moment. She set her plate on the table, resting her chin on her hand.

"This just isn't happening. I mean, we're talking in past tense! It's not right damn it!"

She pounded her fist on the table and got up to head outdoors. Sheila started after her, but Tim held on to her arm.

"Let her go, Sheila. She needs time ... "

Warren watched as she cut across the yard and down the sandy path to the beach. He'd go after her in a bit.

Val walked briskly down the path to the shoreline. The wind was cool off the water. She ran along the water's edge until she was out of breath, then let forth with her frustration and anger.

"HOW could you do this to me? To Mom? Caroline!!! You know what she went through losing Daddy! You're always so damn selfish. You know that?!"

She kicked at the sand. Warren watched as she raged against heaven. She didn't see him standing in the shadows of the long shore grass.

Val ran far down the beach, then turned and ran back eventually slowing to a walking pace. Warren watched and waited silently. He saw her bend over at the waist to catch her breath, resting her hands on her thighs. Finally, she collapsed to her knees and stayed there. Warren walked toward her.

She was exhausted, kneeling in the surf. The humid air dulled the moon's light, and it was quite dark. He could barely make out her crumpled silhouette at the ocean's edge. As he drew nearer, he could hear her crying. He counted the lights from the houses on the cliffs above them to use as a guide back. As he drew closer, he could hear her breathing heavily.

"Why? I mean WHY, Warren?"

He bent to help lift her from the sand, gathering her into his arms.

"C'mon, love. It's time to go home."

Val staggered for a moment, unbalanced by the motion of the receding tide. Warren steadied her. They held hands as they walked back to the house in silence.

Arriving at the quiet house, they noticed that Sean had gone to bed, Granny was upstairs talking with Grace in her room, and Sheila and Siobhan sat drinking tea quietly in the dining room. Random sniffling could be heard. Tim had driven home, telling them he'd be back in the morning. The women had the details for Tuesday already mapped out and were planning on taking Grace to talk with the funeral director in the afternoon once the coroner's report was in.

Val asked if they'd mind if she didn't go with them. She wanted to meet with Father Bruce to go over music for the service.

"Warren's going to help me pull together a really beautiful tribute to Caroline."

They nodded.

"It's what you do best, sweetie. Go for it. We've got it covered here."

All the bedrooms were taken, and Warren volunteered to sleep on the couch, but Val told him she had a fairly comfortable futon in her room that he could sleep on. He questioned whether her mother might mind them being in the same room. She assured him it would be fine.

"We're adults, Warren. It's the furthest thing from her mind right now."

Val went into the bathroom to change and wash her face. She caught a glimpse of herself in the mirror and turned when she saw Warren's reflection in back of her.

"Thank you for being here. I can't tell you how much this means to me."

He hugged her tightly.

"I'm exhausted. How about you?"

She yawned in response and nodded.

"Climb into bed, and I'll tuck you in."

Val told him she would in a minute. She walked down the hall toward her mother's room and knocked softly on the door. There was no answer. She quietly opened the door and walked over to the bed, staring for a moment at her mother's sleeping face before bending to give her a kiss good night. "Sedative Siobhan" had struck again, giving her mom a prescription-strength sleeping pill so she could finally get some rest. Val quietly left the room without her mother so much as stirring.

As she climbed into bed, she heard the water running in the bathroom sink as Warren washed up. Pulling the covers up around her neck, she fell asleep almost immediately in the security of her childhood surroundings.

Warren dried his face and shut off the light. Seeing that Val was already sound asleep, he quietly shut the door to the bedroom. The sheer curtains fluttered in the gentle breeze. He loved the cool salty smell of the ocean air.

Lying down beside her, he placed his arm over her waist and kissed her forehead staring intently at her. He memorized the lines of her brow and smooth curve of her lips. Her breathing was quiet; she was, for the moment, at peace. He got up and went over to the futon she'd pulled out and set up for him. She'd made sure the new sheets were carefully tucked in and had given him two new pillows. He marveled that she could be so thoughtful even when heartbroken. He fell asleep to the sound of her rhythmic breathing and the ocean's gentle waves.

Val rose early, and went and knelt beside the man she knew she loved. She kissed him on the cheek, causing him to stir slightly. She headed for the bathroom to wash her face and brush her teeth then went downstairs for coffee.

Sean, with his hair disheveled and face unshaven, was already up sitting in a chair on the back porch, reading the morning paper. He looked up when she came out, greeting her warmly.

"Have you had your coffee yet?"

She asked.

"Yes, two cups, thanks. Is Warren still asleep?"

She yawned and nodded.

"He's exhausted."

Sean smiled and stared out at the ocean. There was something special about mornings on Cape Cod that he loved. Sean and Val both chuckled as Granny shuffled out onto the porch in her old terrycloth robe and dirty slippers.

"Here she is, the Queen Mary."

Sean joked.

"Mother, when will you ever buy a new robe? That one is falling to pieces, and you look like you're wearing two dead rabbits on your feet with those gray slippers!"

She told him to keep his comments to himself.

"You don't have to wear them, so what is it to you?"

Sean laughed.

"Yeah, but I have to look at them! You look like a pauper, Mam."

She wiggled her finger out of the hole in her pocket and wagged it at him. The rest of the household was slowly waking up.

Sheila was busying herself in the kitchen, making scrambled eggs for everyone. Val looked up from the porch to her room's window when she heard Warren's loud yawn.

"C'mon down and have a cup of coffee with us!"

She shouted up to him. He stuck his head out the window. His hair was a mess, and he looked blissfully bedraggled.

"You look as good as the rest of us!"

Granny waved to him.

"You can be a part of our elite bedhead club ... c'mon down."

Soon, everyone was on the back porch drinking coffee and eating scrambled eggs off paper plates. Warren sat on the steps in his T-shirt and shorts, balancing the plate on his knees while sipping from his mug. The air had dried out, and it was sunny and warm.

Tim stopped by and brought Sheila some more clothes. Grace was the last one to come downstairs, and sat quietly in an Adirondack chair at the end of the porch drinking her tea. She waved as Father Bruce pulled up and parked his sedan. He joined them, perching his leg on the edge of the railing with his coffee mug in hand.

Val talked to him about her idea for music, and everyone agreed it would be a fitting tribute. Her mother and Sean agreed they'd like to try and be a part of it. Both voiced the same concern as Val as to whether or not they could make it through the music without breaking down. Father Bruce said he'd get in touch with the members of the ensemble to see if they could gather for a few quick rehearsals on Wednesday and Thursday.

"I can't guarantee we'll get everyone there for both rehearsals ... some folks are away on vacation. We've reached everyone with the news, and I know they're all trying to make their way back for the service on Friday."

Val nodded understandingly.

"I have to drive back to Boston to get my violin and pick up some clothes today. Glynnis and Peggy should be there at some point. I'm not sure what they were able to get for flights out, but I need a dress for the service. Speaking of which, Mom?"

Grace turned away from the ocean's hypnotic lull upon hearing her daughter call to her.

"Are you having the wake for one or two nights?"

Grace told her only one. It was too painful to drag it out. She always thought two nights to be an emotional burden. Everyone agreed.

It was only Tuesday and they decided to have the wake on Friday with the burial on Saturday morning. Val excused herself and went to use the phone to call her apartment in Boston to see if Peggy and Glynnis had arrived. She then called their home in England, with no answer.

Everyone sprung into action, anxious to keep busy. Val took a shower and put on fresh clothes. She didn't wear any makeup and pulled her hair up on her head. It was going to be hot and she hated leaving the cool ocean breeze for Boston. The city would be stifling. Warren took a shower after she was done. Uncle Tim tossed her the keys to his Trans Am.

"Val, just so you know, I cleaned up a bit around the condo and stripped the bed in Caroline's room. There are no surprises when you get there. The place wasn't a mess or anything. You'll just need to take the sheets out of the dryer. I washed everything."

Val thanked him and gave him a big hug.

"Thanks, Uncle Tim. I appreciate it. I promise to return your car in good shape."

Val winked at him and hopped into the driver's seat after giving her mother a kiss good-bye; Warren climbed into the passenger side. It would be a busy day for all of them. Val's job was to hit the florist on her way back to Boston and order the flowers for the funeral home and church. She was grateful for the busyness of the days ahead. The owner expressed his deepest sympathy when she entered the store and told her that he and his wife would stop by on Friday to pay their respects. Val thanked them, trying hard not to cry.

The Callaghan's had known the owners of Kerrigan's Florist for many years. Val had graduated high school with their only daughter, Mindy. Val focused their discussion on the various seasonal flowers available. She wanted vibrant colors, feeling they would best express Caroline's personality. She made some suggestions and told them she'd check back in with them soon.

As they were driving to Boston, Warren sifted through Uncle Tim's music collection in the glove compartment.

"Wait! WHAT is this? He drives a Trans Am and listens to the Carpenters? There's something fundamentally wrong with that!"

"The CARPENTERS?"

Val laughed.

"Caroline and I used to make him play that music over and over when we were young. We loved it!"

Warren popped the tape into the cassette deck. The song, "We've Only Just Begun," played out gently and Val's eyes teared up. She remembered how she and Caroline used to sing the song as kids. Warren apologized and turned the stereo off.

"Do you want me to drive?"

He asked cautiously.

"No, no! Turn it back on. I want to hear it."

She sang along.

"White lace and promises ... a kiss for luck and we're on our way..."

Warren dramatically sang the chorus with her, and she chuckled at him - grateful for the joy he brought her at such a sad time in her life.

They arrived at her condo in Boston and there was, miraculously, a parking space right out front. Val had a sinking feeling in her stomach as she put the key in the door. She sighed, and her eyes filled up when she saw Caroline's bike still in the hallway. Normally, she'd expect to see her pop her head out the door at the top of the stairs. Instead, it was the downstairs door that opened, and Mrs. Brohmien approached her with open arms, crying.

"Oh, Valerie! I'm so sorry. She was such a beautiful girl!"

Val cried, too, and patted her neighbor's back.

"I know. It's so sad."

They spoke briefly, and she pointed out to Valerie the beautiful silk floral arrangement on the table in the center of their foyer. It was an elaborate array that must have cost a fortune. The residents of her building had pitched in and bought it in memory of Caroline.

"Thank you."

Val said appreciatively, admiring the beautiful silk arrangement done up with Sterling Silver roses - her favorite flower.

Warren carried the bike up-stairs and put it in Caroline's room. Everything was in order, as if she'd just stepped out for a moment and would be right back.

She went over to the answering machine and saw that there were twenty-three messages. She sighed and told Warren she'd listen to them later. She took off her shoes and headed to the kitchen for a soda, switching on the air conditioner in the dining room along the way. She offered a can to Warren and wondered where Peggy and Glynnis were. Val led him to the window seat overlooking Commonwealth Avenue and they watched the gray clouds gathering overhead.

"We'd sit here for hours, Caroline and I, just talking and staring out this window, especially during snow storms. I love this spot."

He smiled at her.

"Are you a little more comfortable now?"

She took a sip of her soda, not understanding what he was saying.

"I mean, now that you're here, in the house. How do you feel?"

She looked around the living room.

"I'm sure, when I'm by myself, I'll sit in this very same spot and cry my eyes out ... and perhaps I'll feel a little lonely. But I feel her presence here. It's weird. I don't quite know how to describe it. I don't know how long I'll keep the condo though."

"You mean, you want to move?"

Warren asked her.

"In time, yes. This condo's been in my family for a long time. It belonged to my Auntie Sheila originally, you know. Caroline and I bought it from her a few years after Caroline graduated from college. But I won't make any rash decisions. Now's not the time for that."

Warren told her that was wise. Val stood up and took his hand. She led him to the back of the house, to Caroline's room. She opened the door and stared in. Warren put his arm around her.

"I wonder if she was scared ..."

Val asked quietly. She turned and buried her face in his chest. He kissed the top of her head.

"I don't know, love. I'm sure her emotions were all mixed up ... but she's at peace now."

Val nodded and took his hand, leading him downstairs to get the sheets out of the dryer.

"Would you mind helping me make up her bed? Glynnis and Peggy can stay in her room. That is if they're not too weirded out by it all."

Warren turned and asked Val.

"Are they lesbians?"

Val chuckled, remembering how Caroline asked that same question.

"You know, it's funny you should ask that. Caroline asked me the same thing not long ago. She asked Peggy straight out and she told her it was none of her business! But, who knows? They've always been dear friends of ours and always will be."

Warren helped her pull the sheet corner over the mattress. He reached out to Val and pulled her down on the mattress to hug her. She let him roll on top of her and kissed his lips repeatedly.

"Now this is a switch!"

She stated matter-of-factly.

"What's that?"

Warren asked.

She laughed and explained how usually it was Caroline she caught in bed with a guy ... not her. Warren smiled and joked.

"I always take up with the wrong sister!"

Val pretended to push him off. He rolled off to the side and playfully tossed a pillow at her.

Val walked back to her own room and looked at her violin on the bed.

"That's odd."

Warren stood in the doorway.

"What?"

"My violin. I always keep it in its case. It's never out on my bed."

She looked puzzled. She reached for it and slid the bow across the strings. It was in perfect tune.

"Well, THAT never happens either!"

Warren sat on the edge of the bed.

"Play me something."

Val picked up the bow and set the violin on her shoulder.

She began to play the Tim Janis piece she wanted to perform at Caroline's funeral Mass. The music would be powerful in that old church, resonating off the arched ceiling. Warren closed his eyes, taking in the sweet, yet often-dramatic notes. He could hear the orchestra in the background and raised his hands as if he were feeling out how he'd conduct it. Val watched him for a moment, then closed her eyes and continued to play, letting the music pour forth from her heart. He opened his eyes and watched her, motioning to the flow of the music with one arm.

"Look at me while you play."

Elegant sounds emanated from the instrument. She let it say all that she couldn't put into words. Warren felt her emotions through the notes.

When she was done, he smiled at her.

"I know exactly how I'll conduct this. We'll need the sheet music for the rest of the ensemble. Do you think you can get it in time?"

"I secured permission from his company this morning. I can make the copies needed. I really want to do this for her, Warren. This music IS Caroline ... it's as if her spirit is compelling me to. I can do it now. I know I can."

"I know you can too, darling. With the ensemble backing you up, it'll be a powerful and moving piece. It can be a tribute from all of you. Do you think your mother has the strength to get through it?"

Val said she hoped so, and that she'd talk to her more about it when she got back down to the Cape. She only hoped it wouldn't be too much stress for her to try and learn the new music with all that was going on already.

Kathleen M. Urquhart

Her mom was a quick study and could typically run through a piece a few times and nail it, the same way Val could on her violin. Keeping busy and focused learning the beautiful new score might be a welcomed diversion from the inevitable sadness of the days ahead.

Chapter Forty-Seven

Montana, Summer 1998

FATHER COUGHLIN ANSWERED THE DOOR to the rickety rectory. He couldn't wait to leave the dump of a house he'd called home the last twenty or so years. His brother's cabin was far more inviting than the shack he lived in, which leaked and smelled of mold. He signed for the nondescript package.

He didn't know what to expect when he opened the mailing. Styrofoam packing material surrounded a small wooden container engraved with his brother's name, date of birth, and date of death. It seemed very strange to him to be holding all that remained of his only brother in his hands. He began to cry as he stared at the sealed oak box.

Having already packed his suitcase, he carefully wrapped his brother's ashes inside a thick towel and placed it amongst his meager belongings. He heard the car horn and hurriedly gathered his things together. He didn't bother to lock the door and didn't look back. The photos of the boys had been burned in a barrel out back the night before. He left no incriminating evidence.

The trip to the airport took a long time. He was anxious to be gone from this part of the country. The colorful flora, which once brought him so much joy, seemed lifeless to him now. He thought he'd feel better leaving Montana, but suddenly realized that what he really wanted to do was leave the priesthood altogether. How could he possibly do that? He had no marketable skills.

Earlier allegations about his "improper behavior" were behind him, with no recent mention of them by any church officials. He felt confident that the boys he'd molested in Montana would keep his secret, their silence having been bought with blackmail.

In the eyes of the church, Father Coughlin was a reformed man. He'd repented of his sins and had gone on to "serve dutifully for many years in a spirit of love, humility, and kindness." He snickered to himself recalling the pompous magistrate's exact words when he'd called to tell Rob of his fortuitous new assignment.

In all honesty, he had to admit that his life wasn't all that bad and things seemed to be looking up. His next parish was located in an affluent seaside community in Massachusetts. He was nervous that Boston's Cardinal, Charles Leonard, had requested that he come to his residence to spend a few days with him before heading off to his new assignment. As he worried over the reasons for such a benevolent invitation, he began to wish earnestly that it was him in the box, instead of his brother.

The landing at Logan airport was rough due to rain and wind. He motioned to a slowing taxi and got ticked off when two young women, obviously in a rush, brushed past him as he turned to lift his suitcase, jumping into the backseat ahead of him. He cursed as the vehicle spun off, and he had to wait in the pouring rain for another cab to appear. *The least thing the damn Archdiocese could have done was sprung for a car to pick me up,* he muttered to himself.

He handed the address, written on a small piece of paper, to the Indian driver. It soon became apparent that he didn't know how to read well or know where he was going. He apologized, explaining in broken English that he'd only been driving in the city a week. Father Coughlin eventually lost his patience and yelled, telling him that he'd never been to the damn city before either and that perhaps the driver should get on his two-way radio and get directions before it cost him a bloody fortune! The driver, not caring that his passenger was a priest, spoke what Father Coughlin was sure was profanity in his native language. Eventually, they pulled up to a gothic stone structure that looked like something out of a horror movie.

The driver took his money and, without giving him back change, sped off, splashing him in the process. Father Coughlin cursed after him.

He walked up the narrow front steps of the darkened stone mansion. There wasn't a light on and the place looked deserted. A stern-faced woman opened the door and inquired after his name. She nodded her head when he answered, telling him that he was expected, and showed him to what would be his room for the next few days. She made no attempt at conversation.

The room was the same as virtually every other room in which he'd spent his nights as a priest ... a picture of Jesus in the hallway, a cross above a single bed. The hard mattresses, he swore, were bought in bulk. The décor consisted of one simple bureau, one chair, a dim reading lamp on a small bedside table, on which lay the customary Bible. The rooms, it seemed, were always painted some shade of pale pink. He looked around and felt nothing but disgust.

Father Coughlin's meeting with the Cardinal the next day unfolded as a complete surprise. It started with an elaborate lunch in his honor. After many prominent guests left, Cardinal Leonard invited him into his study to sit and chat privately.

"I understand you've had a number of assignments over the years, Rob. Due in part to your *weakness*, shall we say?"

He raised his eyebrows, staring squarely at Father Coughlin over his glasses.

Rob shifted awkwardly in the chair. Sensing his uneasiness, the Cardinal sat calmly in the opposite chair with his hands folded on his desk.

"Please know that I forgive you. Christ forgives you. He keeps no record of our wrongs ... and neither do I."

Rob nodded, looking down at the floor, avoiding the Cardinal's penetrating gaze. His superior stood and rested his hand on Rob's shoulder, assuring him that what was past was past. Rob stiffened at his touch.

Cardinal Leonard went on to thank Rob for his commitment to the service of Christ and the church. He made no other mention of Father Coughlin's past offenses, and congratulated him on his new role as head pastor of one of Massachusetts' more prominent and affluent churches.

Rob was speechless, and couldn't even remember the name of his new parish. Cardinal Leonard went on to explain that the youth pastor of the church had been a faithful man, loved by the congregation, and had earned a trustworthy reputation in the small coastal town. Rob disliked him immediately, feeling threatened before he even met him.

The next day was filled with administrative tasks pertaining to Father Coughlin's transfer. The reason for the visit to the Cardinal's residence in Boston had become apparent. His Eminence's residence held all the paperwork on his sordid background, and the Cardinal assured him that he guarded the Archdioceses' legal documents diligently.

Father Coughlin was to serve Mass with the Cardinal, and was anxiously pouring over his sermon for the next day. It was on forgiveness and reconciliation. When he looked at pictures of his new church and the rectory where he'd soon live, it was so much more to his liking than his previous residences. It was an elaborate, regal structure set near the ocean. He was told that due to the size, it had several housekeepers. He'd also have his own secretary. He was nearly giddy with excitement. He couldn't believe his good fortune.

As head pastor, he was given the church's financial statements, which listed the yearly contributions of the prominent families to which the Cardinal had referred. Their giving was significant, and certainly worthy of his special attention. He was impressed with a recent donation by one Ruth Callaghan of County Clare, Ireland.

A recent charity concert, given by the church's own Harbor Lights Ensemble, had been held in Boston raising over $250,000 in contributions for the school's new library. Mrs. Callaghan contributed the remaining amount needed for the building. They would break ground the following spring. One of his first "official" duties would be to speak at the dedication of the new library when it was completed. It was donated in loving memory of Ruth's eldest son, Neil. It was strongly suggested that Father Coughlin should meet with Neil's widow, Grace Callaghan, to gain a bit more insight into the man's life.

He made a mental note to check in with the widower after he settled into his new church located in Chatham, Massachusetts.

Chapter Forty-Eight

Boston, Massachusetts, Summer 1998

VAL HUGGED GLYNNIS AND PEGGY when they arrived Tuesday evening at the apartment.

"We were in such a rush to get here, we actually cut off a priest and took his taxi! God, forgive us!"

Val laughed when Glynnis quickly blessed herself.

"I'm not sure, but I think I actually heard him swear!"

Peggy shrugged her shoulders.

Warren gave each of the women a hug and welcomed them in. He was heating something in the kitchen for dinner that smelled wonderful. Warren and Val had decided to stay at the condo Tuesday night and wait for the women to arrive.

They joined Valerie in her bedroom as she tried to decide what to wear to the wake and the funeral. She scanned through her wardrobe twice but just couldn't concentrate, and sat on the bed next to her friends. They held hands and cried.

Warren gave them their space, opting to spend time in the living room reading a magazine while listening to Bach at a low volume on the stereo. Every now and again, he'd hear laughter mixed with the sound of weeping. He knew that Val would pull through: she had a strong support network of friends and family. The church was amazing in their outpouring of prayers and support. Warren knew that what he wanted to say to her would have to wait. She needed time.

"Ladies."

They turned and smiled warmly at his sudden appearance in the doorway.

"May I interest any of you in something to eat?"

They followed him into the dining room and marveled at the table he'd set.

Warren accepted their compliments on the table setting but denied any doing in the meal itself.

"This meal is brought to you by the culinary abilities of Mr. and Mrs. Graziano of Cape Cod, Massachusetts. I had nothing to do with it, which is why it will taste so good."

The women laughed, and Val went on to explain how much food had been dropped off at her mother's house once the news of Caroline's death reached the congregation.

"She has no more room in her freezer, and since she knew you'd be here, she loaded me up with food to take back. I think she's afraid I'll wither away."

Warren poured each of them a glass of wine. Glynnis and Peggy asked about the night of Caroline's death, and Val struggled through the details. She was able to get through the account without crying, which she thought a good sign. Talking about it definitely helped.

Warren smiled encouragingly at her across the table. Glynnis and Peggy's eyes both filled, and Glynnis wiped at her tears with her napkin. Val went on to describe the music they planned to play at her funeral, making it a family affair, with her mother and uncle participating. Glynnis excused herself and went into the bathroom. Peggy looked after her, concerned.

They all helped clear the table and clean up. Val suggested they try and get some sleep, given their early morning ride to the Cape. She asked her friends if they minded sleeping in Caroline's room. Val told them that if they felt odd about it, they could have her room, and she'd sleep in there. They looked around at the familiar brightly colored room and told her they were fine with it and didn't feel uncomfortable at all. Warren took the couch in the living room.

They started off for the Cape early Wednesday morning. Warren drove; he dropped Glynnis and Peggy off to get settled in at Val's mother's house before taking Val back to the florist to make her final selections. She was pleased with what they'd suggested. The colors made her smile. Val also ordered white balloons to be brought to the cemetery. She thought that they could all release them at the close of the graveside service as a symbol of Caroline's spirit being set free. Her eyes watered as she explained her plan to Mr. Kerrigan. He squeezed her hand and told her that the balloons would be his gift to the family.

Warren waited outside against the wall. He knew she wanted her sister's good-bye to be special. He put his arm around her as they walked back to the car. They spotted Father Bruce across the street and called out to him. He waved and trotted over to greet them.

"Good news! I got in touch with all the members of the ensemble, and everyone will be here tonight for practice. A few hadn't heard the news about Caroline and were understandably shocked. Some are making a special trip back just for the service. We'll rehearse tonight and tomorrow, say from five to nine. How does that sound? Did you make copies of the music yet?"

Val nodded and replied.

"Yes, I have the sheet music. But if you could make more copies at the rectory for everyone, that would be great. I want to get back to Mom."

Val took the keys from Warren and walked over to the car. She unzipped the pocket of her violin case and pulled out the sheets Father Bruce would need.

"This is the only copy I have so ... DON'T LOSE IT!"

She ordered him jokingly.

"I won't. I promise."

He looked over the music with Warren, and they pointed out and acknowledged areas that would need special attention. Father Bruce commented to Warren.

"I think you should conduct."

Warren nodded.

"Aye, Val asked me to."

Father Bruce smiled encouragingly at her.

"I'll be there to assist and for moral support for all of you then. Warren, the ensemble is made up of an amazing group of dedicated professionals. They'll do a great job."

Father Bruce shook Warren's hand and had to rush off to take care of other things in preparation for the ceremony.

When they entered the kitchen at her mother's house, Glynnis and Peggy were having tea with Grace and Auntie Sheila. Val went up behind her mother and gave her a hug and kiss. Warren gave her a kiss on the cheek as she patted his arm.

"The flowers will look great, Mom. I think you'll like them. I ordered balloons, too."

Her mother looked a little surprised at that.

"Balloons ... what for?"

Val drank a large glass of water. It was getting hot outside.

"Well, I thought it would be a nice send-off for Caroline. At the graveside, that's where it'll be toughest for everyone. I thought that as we set the balloons free that it would represent our letting her go ... setting her spirit free. Sort of a celebration of her life. Do you know what I mean? That's what I hope to accomplish, even with the music. You don't think that's too silly, do you?"

Her mother got up and went to her.

"I don't think it's silly at all. It'll be perfect!"

They all tried to smile through their tears.

Kathleen M. Urquhart

Part of the day was spent talking to various friends who stopped by to express their condolences. Glynnis and Peggy took Granny and Siobhan out shopping for dresses for the funeral. Val went with her mother to pick out a dress for Caroline.

They cried as they held up the various dresses. They found what they were looking for in a small boutique on a side road, whose owner closed the shop to give them the privacy they needed and who personally helped them with the details. They decided upon a pale yellow chiffon biased cut dress with a shear floral overlay. It would go beautifully with Caroline's hair. The owner expressed her condolences and hoped they would come back to visit again on a happier occasion. She squeezed Val's hand as she left the store.

Val changed into a skirt and tank top before she and Warren drove her mother to the church for rehearsal. Before they started, Father Bruce thanked everyone for coming and said a few words about Caroline; there wasn't a dry eye in the church. They held hands and prayed for strength and comfort for Grace and her family. Warren bowed his head in prayer, squeezing Valerie's hand. She looked up at him and mouthed, "thank you".

Father Bruce passed out the music, and everyone took out their pencils to mark splits and crescendos. Father Bruce talked about the piece for which they had only two days to prepare.

"Now, we all believe in miracles here, don't we?"

He asked them with outstretched arms.

They all laughed, then set about studying the music in their hands. They were unified in purpose. A few hummed the tune; others asked questions about various notes and rests. Father Bruce motioned for Warren to come up front and join him. Warren went on to explain how he would direct the music. He then took a moment to share his personal impression of the chosen score with the talented musicians gathered.

"When I first heard Valerie play this on her violin, it tore at my heart. It's extremely moving and powerful. Its ability to minister to broken hearts will be evident. We, on the other hand, will have to draw strength from it by focusing on its ability to heal, inspire, and help us let go. It's the only way we'll get through it. I can see how she felt it would be a fitting tribute to Caroline."

He turned to address Valerie's mother and uncle.

"Sean and Grace, you'll each be adding your own unique contribution to the piece: Sean's flute will speak, Grace's piano keys will respond, and Valerie will lead with the violin. I envision you all communicating with one another - not with words, but through the notes. Let your instruments speak to one another. No words are necessary. Music has its own language."

"Every heart present will understand without explanation. I promise this will be a moving experience, not just for you, but for all those who'll sit out there on Saturday - your family, friends, and loved ones. I believe Caroline's memory will be blessed by all your efforts here over the next couple of days."

Val kissed him on the cheek, thanking him for so eloquently conveying what she'd wanted them to experience and understand.

Father Bruce clapped his hands for everyone to get started and had them break off into sections to study their parts. There was a new energy in the church. Malcolm broke off with Valerie and the stringed instruments. Warren went over and listened closely while they practiced, stopping to point out things he heard that needed addressing and correcting.

Father Bruce worked the melody with Sean on the flute. Grace practiced her delicate piece on the piano with ease, stopping on occasion to blow her nose. After an hour and a half of study and individual practice and run-through's, it was time for them to try it all together.

Warren stood at the podium and ran through warm-ups with the various sections. Father Bruce leaned against the rail behind him, closing his eyes to listen and point out those areas where they were off even just the slightest. Mistakes were recognized, corrected, and not repeated. Father Bruce read the music as they played along and conferred with Warren on various notes. They'd stop in places to highlight changes and make adjustments.

Val drew strength from the support of the other ensemble members who were learning with her. She loved them all dearly. Seeing their dedication on behalf of her family, she counted herself blessed. Grace was momentarily relieved to be at the practice session, in order to refocus her mind on something else for a little while. Friday's wake and Saturday's burial would be like a knife in her heart. Tears trickled down her face and onto the ivory keys, causing her finger to slip and miss a note. She looked up and apologized to everyone. Val, standing next to her, gave her a hug. That simple act of tenderness toward Grace seemed to energize the ensemble, adding greater inspiration to their efforts. They played the piece as one. Warren was impressed with their obvious talents and abilities. Father Bruce continued to stand at the railing with his eyes closed, taking in the beautiful sound, and praying.

Warren called Valerie, Grace, and Sean together during a quick break.

"Grace, your playing is delicate, soft ... your part introduces the melodious story. Valerie, the violin is the 'narrative' so to speak. Sean, the flute piece, echoes or mirrors the violin's sentiment. It's like you're pleading with one another for forgiveness. Both of you will lead the ensemble into each crescendo. This will happen twice. You'll lift and guide the music, then simply let it soar. It may be tough for you, but simply allow the music to come underneath and support you both."

Sean nodded in understanding. Grace agreed with the interpretation, as did Val.

Father Bruce called everyone back together for a few more runthroughs. He pointed out a couple of tricky areas to listen for and told the members to note these things on the staff, more for tempo. He asked if anyone wanted to run through a specific section again. They'd been practicing for a little over three hours by that point, but no one seemed to notice the time or mind.

Sean wanted to try his entrance, blending in with Valerie again. They did it in perfect harmony. Warren congratulated them and told them, in closing, that he knew it wouldn't be easy to get through the song without tears.

"All I can say is to watch me, I'll cue you in. Draw your strength from the music."

They all thanked him for his help. Father Bruce said goodnight, reminding everyone of the final practice the next night at the same time. He stayed behind to help tape down some of the cables and turn off the amplifiers. Warren told him he had a great music ministry. Father Bruce appeared rather distracted.

"It's my privilege to be a part of this group. They're all very talented. Which makes my job very easy at times. But I dread going home now."

Warren looked puzzled.

"Why is that?"

Father Bruce's emotions were displayed in the sadness of his eyes.

"Now I have to go and write one of the hardest eulogies of my life."

Warren looked at the man behind the frock. He was flesh and blood. A man, like himself, with real feelings and a tender heart. He wasn't feigning sadness. He felt the family's pain as if it were his own. He loved Caroline.

Warren didn't envy Father Bruce's position. Placing his hand on the priest's shoulder, he acknowledged that it was a very difficult task.

"I'll pray for you, Father. God will give you the words. It's going to be hard on everyone."

He glanced across to Val, who was loosening up her bow and placing it back in the case.

Friday dawned with bright sunshine. It was defiantly cheerful, given the sadness which lay ahead later that afternoon and evening. The household activity level in the early morning was surprisingly low. It seemed as if everyone were suspended, waiting for the right time to get ready. When the waiting got to Val, she asked Warren if he'd take a walk with her. They walked quietly, hand in hand along the shore. Children's laughter could be heard, as well as dogs barking at flying Frisbees.

"Funny how life just goes on, huh?"

Val mused, while gazing out at the ocean, then back at people enjoying themselves at the beach. She watched as a baby sat at the water's edge, kicking her feet excitedly. It made her smile. She thought of Caroline at the dock in New York and how she was always afraid of the sunfish biting her feet. Warren held her once again as she shook and cried. He looked up toward the cloudless sky and prayed for God to somehow comfort her.

The limos began arriving at twelve forty-five to take them to the funeral home. The family would be alone for an hour, then the parlor would be open to the public from 2:00 p.m. to 4:00 p.m. and then again that evening from 7:00 p.m. to 9:00 p.m.

Mr. Sawyer, the owner, greeted the family at the door. He took Grace's arm and led her slowly into the viewing area, patting her arm in support. Val's stomach lurched. She stood beside her mother as the two knelt at the railing. Warren stood off to the side admiring Caroline's beautiful face. She looked very peaceful.

Val and her mother said nothing to one another, just stared, letting the tears fall. Warren turned when he heard Ruth begin to wail. Siobhan and Sean held her tightly. Sheila looked like she was about to faint and had to sit down. Tim left to get her a glass of water. Mr. Sawyer, accustomed to seeing grief, stood stoically nearby.

Father Bruce soon entered the room and immediately walked over to stand behind Valerie and Grace. Placing his hands on their shoulders, he prayed.

"Dear Heavenly Father please be with us now. We need your strength. I humbly ask that you send your Holy Spirit, the great comforter, to be poured out upon this family during their hour of need. Give us courage during this difficult time. We pray that our precious Caroline is now resting with you."

He set his gaze toward her lifeless form lying in the casket.

"She was a beautiful young woman, a gift to all who knew and loved her. We don't always understand your ways, but help us to accept this, too, from your hand. We pray that she is with you now and her spirit at peace."

With heads bowed and hearts heavy, the mourners gathered whispered replies of "Amen."

Val got up to use the bathroom. Glynnis and Peggy arrived in another car, and both girls were heard crying upon viewing their beloved friend. Val could hear their sobs through the bathroom door, then a light tap, followed by Warren's voice.

"Val, are you alright?"

Val told him she was and that she'd be right out.

"No rush, just checking on you."

He walked back into the parlor to kneel and pay his respects after all the family members had finished. The air was thick with grief.

The afternoon wake went by quickly. Grace had moments where she seemed to hold it all together well. Then someone would appear in the condolence line that would trigger a specific memory and a whole new flood of tears would follow. Such was the case when a group of women came in who had danced with Caroline as teenagers. Their presence brought back many happy memories for Grace. They were young; some were married with their own children. She cried again when she realized that her daughter would never have that opportunity.

The family left the afternoon service and went home for a few hours before the final evening service. For the first time in her life, Val wanted to take one of her uncle's cigarettes and smoke. She had tried it once as a kid and hated it, coughing to the point where she nearly threw up, but she was feeling somewhat reckless and defiant, and extremely agitated.

She busied herself in the kitchen with Peggy and Glynnis, making sandwiches, and snapped at her uncle Sean when he asked where a pen was. He left the room quietly and went out on the back porch. Warren kept an eye on her. Valerie wasn't acting like herself, but he knew it was because she was deeply troubled.

The evening service opened wounds again as more and more people showed up. The line was well out the door and beginning to form down the sidewalk and around the corner. Val was becoming more comfortable in her sister's silent presence. It was odd, yet comforting at the same time, standing beside her, stealing glances. What she dreaded was the final closing of the casket. It would be the last time she'd lay eyes on her sister's beautiful face.

After the last guests knelt to pay their respects, Mr. Sawyer locked the door behind them. His associates brought out coffee to the family as he went over the details for the next day's burial. They'd meet at the funeral home at eight o'clock for the family's final viewing before the procession to the church. Val and her mother knelt again to say "goodnight" to Caroline. Val kissed her forehead, as did her mother.

Saturday morning dawned hazy, hot and humid. Val was the first to rise. She'd showered and made coffee by 6:30AM. When Warren came down they sat on the back porch, sipping silently. Val looked at the wispy clouds streaking the sky and stated flatly.

"I hate this day already. I just don't know how to say good-bye to her, Warren."

Warren set his mug down and went to stand behind her rubbing her shoulders.

"I know, love. We'll get through this together. I promise you."

At the funeral home, they gathered around the coffin that held Caroline snugly. Val was holding Glynnis's hand tightly; both were crying openly. Father Bruce prayed and wiped at his eyes as the coffin was finally closed. Grace suddenly reached out her hands for her youngest daughter and let out a horrible cry as Sheila struggled to hold her up.

Mr. Sawyer went quickly to her side and led her to a nearby chair, whispering comforting words. Father Bruce sat next to her, holding her hand, until it was time to leave for the church. Warren put his arm firmly about Valerie's waist and walked her out to the limousine. The cars were lined up out front, and Val sat with her mother alone in the first car.

"How are we ever going to play at her service, Mom? I thought this was a great idea at first, but now I don't think I can even lift the bow without bursting into tears. I mean, I wanted to stop Mr. Sawyer from closing the coffin, too. I don't want her all sealed up like that! Mom, she shouldn't be in that damn box!"

Grace knew exactly what her daughter was feeling and hugged her.

"I know, Val. But we've got to be strong. Remember what Warren said. Just watch him and play with your heart. Caroline will be there, I believe, in spirit, to give us strength."

Upon seeing each other's tears, they both reached for tissues at the same time. The air-conditioning in the car felt good, a relief from the staggering humidity outside.

The family was led into the church and seated in the front pews. The church was soon filled to capacity. The organist played soothing music while Father Bruce stoically prepared for the service out back. He lifted the vestments presented to him by the altar boys and kindly thanked them for their help. They left to take their places.

When everyone was seated, he appeared on the altar to receive Caroline's coffin. Carrying her body were six pallbearers. Two of the men were former coworkers from the hospital. The next two were friends from college. Lastly were her uncles, Tim and Sean. Glynnis and Peggy could barely contain their anger at watching the hypocrisy unfold as the man who had tormented their friend carried her coffin.

As Father Bruce descended the steps, everyone in the church stood in respect while Caroline's coffin passed down the center aisle. Father Bruce clutched his Bible in one hand and incense in the other as Caroline's draped coffin was set down in front of him. Tears openly rolled down his face. He felt like he was saying good-bye to his own daughter.

The organist stopped playing as Father Bruce walked around the casket, swinging the powerful incense. He set it down on the steps and turned around to face the mourners. His was a personal approach. He chose to stand close to Caroline's body while he addressed the family and friends that had gathered from the aisle.

"I want to thank you all for coming, not only to pay your respects, but to be here as a sign of support to Grace, Valerie, and the entire Callaghan family during this time. I know they appreciate your love and support and thank you."

"A little over twenty-five years ago, I had the privilege of coming to this church. Just new out of seminary, I was very green and didn't know what to expect from my first assignment. Many of you went out of your way to introduce yourselves and welcome me. I've 'grown up' with the best, and worst, of you ..."

The audience laughed at his offhanded comment.

"Shortly after my arrival here, the Callaghan's suffered a significant loss with the untimely death of Neil Callaghan, Grace's husband, the girl's father, and my friend."

Father Bruce glanced over at Ruth and proceeded gently.

"Neil was a strong family man, and a devoted son who loved his wife, children, parents, and siblings as much as any man could. I did, at times, look at him and question whether I'd made the right choice in becoming a priest. Seeing him with his happy family, I realized that that would be one of the biggest sacrifices I'd ever have to make - not having a biological family of my own."

"Following Jesus is never an easy calling. But where God asks for sacrifice, there is always great reward. Not in monetary or material ways, but in terms of fulfillment. When he asks something of us, to those who answer that call, he always equips us. Such was the case with Valerie and Caroline. As young children without a father, and here, me, with a father's heart and no children, God filled my life with offspring. I had the joy of watching them grow in life and in their faith. I attended many of their birthday parties ... tooooo many birthday parties!"

The audience snickered.

"Yet, at each stage of their development, I was able to share and observe their personal growth. They allowed me into their lives, their hearts, and into their family. To that end, I want to say thank you to the Callaghan family. You allowed me the opportunity to have the family and children I never thought I'd have, and I couldn't be more proud of all that you've accomplished."

The crowd applauded in agreement.

"To tell you the truth, I dreaded this service today. Here I'm called to perform a religious duty for the Church, and yet still manage to somehow hold it together on a human level. Not an easy task, and I ask God's grace to be with me as I talk to you."

"Caroline was a beautiful young woman, whose desire to help others was evident when she chose to make nursing her career. Her heart of mercy led her to help those who were hurting. She knew and responded to God's call on her life - to help the sick, sometimes pushing herself too hard. We all knew this about her. She was one of the rare few who gave her entire heart to those in her care. She struggled to keep emotional boundaries between patient and caregiver. Despite those guidelines and warnings, she often found herself emotionally attached to those she cared for. Some might be quick to say, she cared too much, and it cost her her life. I'd like to believe that she had a compassionate heart that was willing to risk being broken in order to bridge the human divide."

"Now, I want to address Caroline's suicide. This is an uncomfortable point to touch upon, as there are some strong views held about this in the church. But today, here and now, I am speaking to you from my human side, and will try, with God's help, to explain this as best I can."

"I know that many believe that those who commit suicide go straight to hell. I can only imagine how this line of thinking would increase the grief of family members and friends who live on after a loved one who's died in this manner. Allow me this, I believe strongly that God knows the hearts and minds of those whom He created. I believe He sees deep into the soul in ways that we cannot."

"The Bible says that the Lord is near to the brokenhearted and that he hears their cries for help. I believe that only God knew what was in Caroline's heart at the time of her death. She must have struggled tremendously. I know how much she loved her mother and sister. I believe, somewhere in her heart, she felt pain and empathy for others at a level many of us have never felt. This burden, if any of us were to try and carry it, may have similar consequences."

"I cannot and will not judge the condition of any man or woman's heart. I've not walked in their shoes. I've not lived their life, and I don't claim to know the whole story. They may carry burdens and afflictions the likes of which we may never know!"

Father Bruce walked over and put his hand on Grace's. Glynnis and Peggy bowed their heads.

"Grace, you are a good mother. You raised your daughters the best way you knew how. They are well-liked, well-educated, respected and admired, as evidenced here today by the outpouring of so many friends and loved ones who have come to support you in your grief."

"Valerie, you are a successful business woman, loving sister, a devoted daughter, granddaughter, and niece. You had a beautiful relationship with your sister though it may have seemed strained at times — but who hasn't felt some tension in any relationship? C'mon, let's be honest here."

The congregation nodded.

"There were times you probably wanted to slap her."

Val piped in.

"I actually did once!"

The people chuckled at her confession.

Father Bruce smiled.

"But you loved her with all of your heart, didn't you?"

Val's eyes teared up as she nodded and bowed her head, fumbling with the tissue in her hands.

"Do you know that that's God's heart toward us? I've no doubt there are days that we all deserved to be 'slapped upside our heads' ... yet, he still loves and forgives us and gives us that second chance. He tells us continually that when we've done something wrong that offends or hurts him, if we simply come to him and tell him we're sorry, he will forgive us. He can do that because of Jesus. Jesus was the one who made the sacrifice for us all. He took it upon himself to carry our sins because no man was ever going to be good enough to earn their way into heaven. We all get in the same way, belief in Christ, by faith - period!"

"I believe so strongly that Caroline did not want to really hurt herself, but wanted more to escape the excruciating emotional pain she was feeling at the time. In a moment of extreme weakness, something we've all experienced at one point or another, she'd gone too far to turn back. I do believe she had a personal relationship with Jesus and a healthy fear of God, respecting his word and his promises. If she expressed her sorrow and remorse for what she'd done before she drew her final breath, God, in his infinite mercy, would find it in his heart to forgive her."

"I hate the term 'funeral' because it sounds too much like 'final.' Because on one level that is exactly how it appears. But this ..."

He pointed toward her casket.

"Is not where it ends. This casket is closed, but this is not the last time we'll see Caroline. You see, unlike many of the teachings circulating out in the world today, there is only one that I know of who actually rose from the dead. That man is Jesus Christ. He gave us a promise, and it's so simple that many trip over it. He told us that if we would simply humble ourselves, come to him in private, and confess our shortcoming which we know offended or hurt him, ourselves, or others, that he would forgive and heal us. But we need to let him know that we want him governing our lives, our actions, and our decisions. He wants to hear us say that we need him and desire that he might come and dwell within us! He wants to enter in to our broken lives and hardened hearts so that he might reveal his nature in and through us. You see, God doesn't want a 'religious' people. Does that shock you? It's true! He doesn't. A "religious" mindset is impersonal, kills, and destroys."

"But it's different when you're in a relationship with someone you love. It gets personal quickly and the heart is engaged. It will affect you directly and, as a result, the world around you - positively. It's that simple. When we come to the end of ourselves and finally admit that we're not the 'master and commander' of our own destiny, only then can we experience the hope that he alone offers. This hope comes with an eternal promise of a changed, resurrected, and eternal life with him. We WILL see Caroline again in the fulfillment of time!"

Resounding "amens" echoed throughout the church.

Father Bruce turned and walked up onto the altar. He looked over the marble edge and saw Valerie's violin resting on the corner. He motioned for the members of the ensemble to come forward.

"At this time, ladies and gentleman, I would like for you to sit back and enjoy a beautiful musical tribute to Caroline Callaghan. Her sister, Valerie, along with her mother, uncle, and the other members of the ensemble, have prepared a moving piece in remembrance of this lovely young woman who meant so much to all of us. Under the direction of Warren Cahill, the Harbor Lights Ensemble will play a selection from composer, Tim Janis, 'Somewhere Still the Rose'."

Valerie stood to the side of the pew to let her mother proceed first. When Grace got to the foot of the altar, she paused briefly and kissed her daughter's casket. Val was choked up and kept her eyes focused on Warren, not knowing how she'd find the strength to not cry. A tear slipped down her cheek, and she quickly brushed it aside. Grace sat at the piano as Valerie perched the violin on her shoulder. Warren stood at the podium and motioned for her to turn so that she could look directly at him. Sean sat off to the left side of the altar, adjusting the microphone.

The entire church was silent. Warren smiled tenderly at Grace, signaling for her to begin. She softly touched out the beginning notes. Valerie came in right on cue, holding the violin firmly. Sean joined in on the flute. Together they played what their voices could not express. They spoke to one another through the chords. Warren directed Valerie's attention and mouthed to her to watch him when he saw her hand begin to shake slightly.

Val led with the first few stanzas. She briefly gazed past Warren to her grandmother and friends as she let the bow slide across the strings. Sean played alone for a moment, then Grace expressed soothing notes from the piano. Val conveyed Caroline's life through a song without words while Sean accompanied her. The ensemble elevated the composition giving flight to the melody.

Warren conducted masterfully and all were in perfect harmony. The congregation smiled, some bowing their heads. It was the song of angels, inspired in heaven, and played out through the faulty and unworthy hands of men, ministering directly to each individual's heart and soul. Val actually made it through with only a few tears.

Father Bruce stepped down and went among them in the aisle.

"Ladies and gentlemen, this is not good-bye. It is a difficult transition but one where we can say with all confidence, 'Caroline, I will miss you, and with God's help, I will direct and live my life in such a manner that I know I will see you again.'

"Dear Lord, please accept Caroline into Your beloved and most holy kingdom. As much as we love her, we know that You, Father, love her more. Comfort us who remain. Help us to give of ourselves, like Caroline did, in the service of others, for that is where our greatest rewards will be found. Amen."

Father Bruce walked before Caroline as the pallbearers lifted her casket. He humbly represented Christ, going before mankind to prepare a final resting place for them.

Valerie held her mother's arm and led her slowly from the church. They were silent during the ride to the cemetery, which was located on a hillside from which the ocean could be seen. Valerie turned to watch the long procession wind through the center of town. Many shop owners came out and took off their hats, bowing their heads. Everyone in town knew the family. It was a very sad day in Chatham.

The police officers on duty downtown stopped the summer traffic to allow the lengthy procession to pass. One officer took off his hat as they went by, holding it solemnly against his chest. Valerie cried when she saw the unified show of respect for her sister. The young police officer, she remembered, had once wanted to ask Caroline out, but never got up the nerve. He bowed his head as the hearse containing her body rode slowly past him.

The heat was unbearable. Val stood beside her mother and grandmother. Someone came up from behind to hold a large umbrella over her mom and grandmother in order to shield them from the sun's rays. Sheila was behind them as were Sean, Siobhan, Tim, Warren, Peggy, and Glynnis. They each held a single white rose and a balloon. Father Bruce stood at the foot of the coffin, which was positioned next to the newly dug grave, ready to be lowered when everyone left.

Gazing upon her sister's final resting place, Valerie broke down into uncontrollable sobs for the first time that day, having held her emotions in check throughout the service. Father Bruce walked over and held her tight, whispering words of strength in her ear. He wiped her tears as his own fell. Warren bowed his head. His heart broke for her. He wished there were some way he could take away her pain. Father Bruce spoke while holding her hand.

"Holy Father, we cry out to you. Letting go is never easy. Please instill in us the hope we need to carry us through this time of sorrow. Replace our tears with joy and let us look forward to the day when we will all be together again. We release our sadness to you, Lord; please give us your joy and your strength this day. Amen."

Val was the first to release her balloon, and soon the sky was filled with white balloons. The group stared up at the sky, watching as they drifted away and disappeared out of sight. Val stopped crying and leaned forward to set her rose on Caroline's casket. She paused briefly in order to whisper to her how much she loved her and gently stroked the earthbound casket.

Tim supported Grace as she bent to kiss the casket and place her rose beside Valerie's. She didn't linger. Sheila walked over to her husband, and they too kissed the casket and touched it lovingly. Tim wiped the first tears from his eyes with a handkerchief.

Val stood off to the side, being held tightly by Warren, who leaned against a tree that supported them both. Her face was buried in his shoulder as it had been so many times over the past few days. Peggy and Glynnis each placed their roses on the casket and returned to their car weeping.

Val spoke quietly to Mr. Sawyer, the funeral director, and thanked him. She told him that she'd like for him to collect some roses from the various displays and a few of the white roses from the casket, as she and her family would like them to dry and press in books as a keepsake. He told her he'd drop them off at the house later in the afternoon and hugged her gently.

The outpouring of support was moving. The many guests all found their appetites when they were invited to return to the church reception hall for a meal. Many had planned on just stopping in to say farewell, and ended up staying on to talk and eat. Grace was laughing with a couple of her old friends from South Boston. It warmed Val to hear her mother's laughter.

Sean picked up his flute to play as a small crowd gathered around his table. It was a peaceful tune that offered solace. Glynnis got up to go outside and Peggy followed her. Val sat next to Warren and ate a little bit of salad and drank some iced tea.

"Do you know what I want to do when I get back to the house?"
Warren shook his head.
"No, what?"
"I want to go swimming."
Val's response surprised him. Warren raised his eyebrow.
"You want to go swimming, eh?"
She smiled at him.
"Yes, I do. Would you like to join me?"
Warren smiled at her.
"It's certainly hot enough, though I didn't bring any trunks with me."
"Just use your shorts."
They ate quickly and said good-bye to some of the guests who were leaving.

By two o'clock, most of the people had left. A few women from the church offered to stay and clean up, urging Grace and Val to head on home and rest refusing their offers to help.

"It's been an emotional day, Grace. Go home and get off your feet. Make yourself a pitcher of ice tea and sit in the shady breeze."

Grace said she'd do just that and thanked them for all of their help. They kissed her and waved her off.

Grace gave Father Bruce a big hug and a kiss on the cheek. He held her for a little while before releasing her. It dawned on him that soon she'd be realizing yet another anniversary - that of her late husband's death. It seemed too much for one person to bear. He'd pray in earnest for her.

As soon as they got back to the house, Val kicked off her shoes and peeled off her nylons, to the amazement of everyone, in the front hall. Warren laughed at her as she nearly fell over trying to get her foot out.

"Mom, I'm going swimming!"

Her antics didn't seem to surprise Grace one bit. She knew how much her daughter enjoyed the ocean.

"Good for you, honey. I'll be down to join you in a little while."

Everyone looked at them in amazement. Warren just shrugged his shoulders.

"Well, I guess I'm going too. Anyone else?"

He looked around at the others. Peggy and Glynnis grinned and shrugged and went to find shorts and t-shirts. They hadn't thought to pack bathing suits for this trip. Sheila said she'd come down and watch. Granny was going up to her air-conditioned room to take a nap, and Sean said he was doing the same. Tim packed up a cooler and filled it with a variety of drinks and snacks.

Grace arrived downstairs wearing a shift over her bathing suit. Val descended next, wearing a sheer patterned wrap about her waist that matched her suit. Warren did a double take. She pulled her hair up, managing to look rejuvenated.

Tim took one end of the large cooler and Warren took the other as they walked down the sandy hill, making their way to the water's edge. Sheila spread out a blanket and sat down to snack on strawberries and grapes. Val took off her wrap, unveiling her trim figure. Warren had borrowed a pair of Tim's shorts and waded out next to her.

"Does this water ever get any warmer?"

He winced against the frigid temperature.

"Depends on where you stand. Come here. Feel where I am. It's pretty warm."

Warren walked toward her, and she vigorously splashed him with water. He jumped and lunged for her, causing her to scream with delight. Grace was already submerged up to her neck, taking in the refreshing feeling of the cold water on her overheated skin. It made her happy to hear Valerie laugh. She watched delighted as her and Warren frolicked about.

Glynnis and Peggy waded in slowly hating the shocking cold water. Tim sat with Sheila on shore. He was applying sunscreen to her back as she held up her hair. In the distance, Siobhan was making her way down to the beach, carrying a couple of folding lawn chairs. The sun broke through the overhead clouds and haze, and the next white puffy batch seemed far off in the distance, allowing them direct sunshine for a while. For Val, being in the water felt good for her soul — it seemed to inject new life back into her exhausted body.

She and Warren stayed submerged as she sat leaning against him, letting her body rise and fall with the waves. Peggy and Glynnis joined them now floating in cool water, talking about the rest of the weekend. They all decided to return to Boston the next morning after church. Val was planning on taking some time off from work. She'd talked to her boss briefly at the church after the funeral. She'd take another two weeks. Warren had another week before he had to report back to work. Siobhan joined them in the water.

"Oh, this does feel good. It's much cooler here. A great idea, Valerie!"

Val smiled.

"Thank you. I needed this as much as anyone. It clears your head, doesn't it? Caroline would have done the same thing!"

They rose to get out of the water, and each found a towel with which to dry off. The clouds were slowly shifting and the air temperature was changing quickly. When they arrived back at the house, Val suggested that they could each take turns rinsing off in the outdoor shower.

"There's hot water and soap and shampoo. Dad hooked this up years ago. We use it all the time in the summer. There's something rather liberating about showering outside."

They all laughed, and Warren smirked at her.

Granny couldn't sleep after all, and had come downstairs and made two pitchers of iced tea for the crew. She set out more food, which they all picked at. Val appeared from the outdoor shower, wrapped in an overly large towel, and picked up a handful of blueberries as she headed into the house to change. She returned some fifteen minutes later wearing a pretty floral strapless sundress. She managed to look youthful and refreshed despite her grief.

Warren returned from his shower, still in Tim's swim trunks, toweling off his head, and kissed her on the lips.

"You look lovely!"

She curtsied and replied demurely.

"Thank you."

He went in to change as the others took their turns rinsing off. Sean was nowhere to be found. He'd gone off for a walk somewhere. They lit citronella candles and moved to the expansive back porch where they all sat, relaxed, talking late into the night about love, life, and Caroline.

Val felt stronger after a good night's sleep and was looking forward to returning to her home in Boston. It was Sunday, and Peggy and Glynnis would stay on for one more night before leaving to go back to London on Monday evening.

Sheila and Tim announced that they were taking Grace away to their place in New York for the remainder of June once everyone went home. Warren planned to stay a few more days in Boston before heading back to Ireland with Valerie. It was his idea that she come back with him. She needed time to gather her thoughts and plan what she was going to do now with the rest of her life. Warren questioned his own timing ...

Chapter Forty-Nine

Boston, Massachusetts, Summer 1998

VAL PULLED INTO THE BRIGHT, sunlit Alley 53 behind her condo. She didn't mind parking out back during the day. At night, however, she was always on guard when getting out of her car, given that vagrants and thieves occasionally meandered through the back alleyways.

Some years back, she had convinced the other tenants in her building that they should install sensor lights. Because her back bedroom overlooked the alley, they used to startle Caroline occasionally when they suddenly lit up the night, usually due to someone or something rummaging around in one of the nearby dumpsters. Because of the bars that had been installed on the windows near the fire escape, they'd never experienced any break-ins.

Once they were settled in, Peggy and Glynnis told Val they were going for a walk along the Charles River and then into Faneuil Hall for dinner. They asked if she and Warren wanted to join them.

"I don't think so. But thanks for asking. I think I'm going to just lay low here for a while. Warren can join you if he wants to."

She motioned to him.

Warren thanked them politely but declined.

"I'm looking forward to a little downtime myself."

It was a beautiful summer afternoon. The humidity had finally broken, and it had reached well into the eighties. Val took a nap, with Warren curled up beside her. They snuggled under the covers, as she had put the air-conditioning on high. She loved sleeping with the covers pulled up under her chin. When they awoke, it was after five o'clock.

Val felt refreshed, and took a long shower before deciding on where to go to eat. She wanted to take Warren to dinner at Joseph's on Newbury Street, an elegant bistro right around the corner from her condo. Peggy and Glynnis hadn't come back yet, so she assumed they'd found some place to eat downtown.

Warren took a quick shower and needed only a few minutes to get ready. He dressed in a pair of wrinkle-free khaki dress slacks and a long sleeve, blue Oxford shirt with brown Bali shoes. His black, wavy hair was combed back and left to dry naturally. Val took care getting dressed and put on a cute, halter dress - navy blue with white polka dots and matching navy sling-back heels. She also put on makeup for the first time in days. After drying and styling her hair, she managed to look both rested and eye-catching for their first night out since Caroline's death.

It pained her heart, and she winced when she thought of her sister in that manner. Caroline would often come into the bathroom and put the lid down on the toilet seat to talk with Val while she put on her makeup. Her eyes watered for a moment, but she didn't cry. This time, when she looked up, it was Warren who appeared in the doorway, smiling at her.

"You look gorgeous, love. Are you ready to go? I'm famished!"

"I'm ready if you are!"

They walked hand in hand to the restaurant one street over. Warren was immediately impressed with the establishment's black and white marble foyer, as well as the impeccably dressed maître d' who greeted them warmly upon their arrival. The restaurant wasn't crowded and they had their choice of tables. Val asked to be seated at the center table, by the window that overlooked Newbury Street. The maître d' lit the candle in the miniature hurricane lamp casting a gentle, peaceful glow around them. Val's eyes, though alert and sparkling in the flickering light, still registered sadness.

Warren looked at her lovingly and smiled.

"You know, Val. I want to talk to you about something. I'm hoping that my timing isn't horrible, given all that's happened."

Warren was calm and held her hand across the table.

Val lightly squeezed his hand and smiled.

"I already know what you want to say to me."

Warren cocked his head to one side.

"So you do, do you?"

She smirked and nodded.

"But go on. I still want to hear you say it."

Warren kissed her hand.

"I love you and want to marry you."

Val smiled brightly.

"I knew that was it! Warren, dare I say that I would have said yes to you only a week after we met. I knew, then, that I wanted to marry you, too."

Warren brought his chair around to her, placing an elegant blue velvet box in front of her. Valerie had tears in her eyes, this time from pure joy.

"When did you have the time to do this?"

He smiled.

"In Ireland. I had the ring made there, though I must admit that I bought the diamonds from the Jewelers Building right here in Boston during my last layover. I designed it actually."

Val's hands were shaking as she opened the box. Her mouth dropped at the sight of the ring. It was a large, princess-cut diamond in an antique platinum setting. There were two triangle-shaped diamonds accenting what must have been, at least, a two-carat center stone. It shimmered magnificently in the candlelight.

Val's eyes teared even more as she held out her hand to let him place it on her finger. The wait staff had quietly gathered in the corner to watch him propose to her, and clapped when they saw Valerie kiss Warren and accept the ring. Val and Warren smiled and waved to them. She was so excited. She couldn't stop looking at the beautiful promise that had just been placed on her hand.

"When did you know? I mean, that you wanted to marry me?"

He thought seriously about it.

"When you stole my Tidbits at the airport!"

Valerie laughed heartily.

"You've got to admit, that really was a classic. I just wanted to die when I looked in my bag and found them."

He chuckled.

"Well, it worked for us!"

Val looked at him seriously.

"Warren, this is a difficult time for me. I'm still a basket case. I know I'll pull through it, but ..."

Warren shushed her.

"Love, I know. Take all the time you need. We don't have to get married any time soon. I'd actually rather wait until you work through this."

He switched to leaning on his right elbow and asked while reaching for a roll.

"But I was hoping that, well, now that we're officially betrothed, can we at least have sex?"

He playfully ducked as Val pretended to whip her napkin at his head.

"I knew there had to be an ulterior motive!"

Val squeezed his hand. She knew there was probably some element of truth behind his joking. She felt the attraction, too. But she knew she wanted to do this one thing in her life right before God, and she'd do her best to try and hold off the temptation for intimacy until they were married. It wouldn't be easy.

"I asked Father Bruce to bless your ring. He told me he was honored."

Val looked at the ring again with admiration.

"Wait, you mean, Father Bruce knew about this?"

Warren nodded and took a bite of his roll. Val was amazed.

"He never let on."

Warren smiled.

"That would have kind of ruined the surprise, don't you think?"

He enjoyed kidding with her.

"Is there anything you haven't thought of?"

She was so impressed and in love with him. It warmed her grieving heart knowing that she was his alone, that he loved and wanted her.

"You know, I can't wait to meet your parents and family."

He put up his finger.

"We may be able to fit that in when we get back to Ireland. You'll have the whole house to yourself while I'm working the second week, to think or read or take long walks or just sleep! I'm usually gone for about three or four days in a row when I fly. But I do look forward to having you there waiting for me when I get home. I'm wondering already how I'll make do without you."

Val sipped her wine and day dreamed.

"Can we look ahead into the future and imagine what our life will be like?"

Warren agreed, but added a stipulation.

"Only if it involves sex."

She rolled her eyes.

"Do men ever think of anything else?"

He leaned in and kissed her and then pulled back, pretending to really think about what she'd just asked.

"Ahhh, that would be NO. But I must tell you, you really appeal to my carnal side, darling. Get used to it."

She winked at him.

"Okay, I'm changing the subject now. Where shall we live?"

She asked him curiously.

"I was thinking in a house ..."

He said with a poker face.

Val shook her head and burst out laughing. It really felt good to laugh, and he made her momentarily forget the sadness of the past week.

"Would you for ONCE be serious? You're a nut! I'm planning my future with a nutcase!"

He chuckled and told her he'd be serious.

"Okay, okay, tell me. Ideally, what would you like to do? I'm really open to living anywhere, but I must tell you that I'm partial to Ireland."

Val thought about it. They were fortunate in that they could have the best of both worlds. Val had grown up in the States, but had spent a considerable amount of her life in Ireland. Both countries were intricately linked in her heart. Ireland was the home of her beloved father, Neil, and she had family there and was, herself, a dual citizen.

"Warren, I hope what I'm about to tell you won't shock you."

He shook his head.

"Not possible. Go on."

"Well, I've been in corporate America a long time and I've done well. I'm really happy with all that I've accomplished in my career to date. But it's been lonely at times and demanding in many ways. When it was just me, I could manage it. But now, when I think of marriage, my priorities are changing. Caroline's death has put a lot in perspective for me. What I really want is a more traditional type of marriage."

She was silent for a moment, waiting to see his response. He asked her to define "traditional".

"Well, in a nutshell, I want YOU to go to work. I'll kiss you good-bye when you leave on a trip, busy myself with our children and housekeeping, and make time to go to lunch with friends once a week. I'll get involved in some sort of musical group, so I can still play my violin. Warren, I want to be a wife and mother and say good-bye to the business world. What do you think of that?"

He stared at her in amusement as she continued on.

"I know it all sounds rather antiquated, given women's lib, and the 'I can do it all mentality' that prevails today."

Val stopped to take a breath when she saw a big grin cross his face. "What?"

She asked him suspiciously.

"I scared you, didn't I? I knew it. You don't believe me!"

He kissed her hand.

"Valerie, what man, in his right mind, would ever object to that request? I couldn't have written a script for a wife any better! I want all of those things too. Our life will be very comfortable. But, back to the question of location and where to live, I'm based out of Ireland. Could you live there?"

Val nodded without hesitation.

"Oh, yes! Of course. It might actually work out well if I did decide to keep the condo in Boston then. It's not too far from the airport, and you could stay there during your layovers. I can come home and visit with Mom frequently. I'd be reluctant to move if she didn't have anyone here, but she's got Auntie Sheila and her friends from church. I know she'd miss us, but I also know she'd come to visit with us regularly. We could turn Caroline's room into a nursery when we're here."

Her eyes welled with tears.

"I wish she were here so I could run home and show her my beautiful ring. I'm sure she's watching and is very happy for us."

Warren held her hand.

"You know, this is a confirmation, hearing you talk like this. It's amazing how God works out all the details in life and lets us think we have a part in it all. I was thinking along similar lines, and I'm looking forward to our life together."

He looked lovingly into her eyes.

"By the way, when we get back to Ireland, there's going to be a party in our honor."

She looked at him in surprise.

"Well, there will be once I call my mother and let her know you accepted my proposal. Your refusal might have put a damper on the plans."

She laughed as he filled her in on the details.

"I told my family that I was going to propose to you. This was before the news about Caroline. They sent their condolences, by the way, and a floral arrangement to the funeral home. I don't know if you got a chance to see it."

Val shook her head.

"No, I'm sorry. I didn't take much notice of anything, I'm afraid. I will get a nice note off to them, however. I am going to take care of that job for my mom, writing out the thank-you notes. I could do that back in Ireland when you leave for work."

He spoke to her tenderly

"I love you."

"I love you, too, darling ... and I'm very happy at this moment."

She smiled, looking at the glittering diamond on her hand and wiggling her fingers.

He ordered a bottle of Dom Perignon and toasted to their future. The waiter offered to let them keep their glasses as mementos, and wrapped them in tissue paper, putting them in an elegant bag for the couple to take home.

Val held her hand out, staring at her ring under the streetlights.

"Warren, this is a truly lavish engagement ring. I'll be afraid someone would want to steal it!"

They playfully swung their arms as they walked.

"You're welcome. Might I say, you look rather regal with that rock on your hand?"

"Oh, you're just saying that because you want to jump into bed with me."

He nodded.

"This is true."

They were laughing as they climbed the steps to her home.

Once in the apartment, the lights flipped on, and Glynnis and Peggy both jumped up and down excitedly, asking to see her ring.

"YOU KNEW ABOUT THIS, TOO?"

They looked at Warren and giggled.

"We sure did! Had the whole thing planned."

Warren shrugged, acting as if he'd not done a thing.

"Who else knows? Did you tell my mother?"

Warren shook his head no.

"I did leave that for you ... only my family, Father Bruce, Glynn and Peg here."

Val immediately ran to the phone and called her mother with the good news. Grace was ecstatic for her eldest daughter.

"Oh, honey, I'm so happy for you. We needed this good news. It's like a shot in the arm. I'm going to call Auntie Sheila and Uncle Tim. Granny's here. I'll let you tell her."

Grace put her mother-in-law on the phone.

"Hi, Granny! Guess what? I'm engaged!"

Val couldn't help but bubble over with excitement. Her grandmother was extremely happy for her.

"See, child, life does go on ..."

Siobhan got on the phone to congratulate her. Val asked if Uncle Sean was there to tell him. Siobhan told her that he decided to catch a flight back home early, and had left hours ago, saying that he needed to get back to work. Granny was in the background speaking.

"You know men, they need to work."

Siobhan explained how she and Granny had been talked in to going to New York with Grace, Sheila, and Tim, and planned to stay on another week in the states. Val told her mother that she'd be heading back to Ireland with Warren for two weeks to meet his parents and unwind.

"They've already planned an engagement party for us, Mom. Can you believe it?"

Her mother told her to have a great time and that they'd be planning something on this side of the Atlantic when she returned.

"Mom, don't worry, please. Just get through this time. Don't worry about me. I'm happy. Don't put any pressure on yourself, okay? We'll plan a nice, simple wedding."

Grace assured her daughter she'd be fine and to have a wonderful time with her new fiancé. Val liked hearing that term.

"Thanks, Mom. Love you!"

"Love you, too, sweetheart. Congratulations and give Warren a kiss for me."

Val hung up the phone and gave Warren a kiss.

"From Mom."

He smacked his lips.

"Well, thanks, Mom!"

The women gathered around her in the kitchen to marvel at the impressive ring. They demanded a role in her wedding, to which she assured them they'd each have a major part.

"We've not set a date yet. I've got to move past this first."

They headed into the living room to sit and talk for a while. It was a nice change to talk about something positive and upbeat. Warren washed a couple of glasses in the sink and went out to join them, sitting beside Valerie and holding up her hand to examine his gift to her. He was really pleased with how the ring had turned out. It suited her perfectly.

It was after eleven when Glynnis and Peggy got up to go to bed. Warren was getting comfortable and settled onto the couch. Val walked down the hallway to turn down the air-conditioning before going to bed. She was just outside the door to Caroline's room when she overheard Glynnis and Peggy talking.

"I couldn't stay in the same room with him."

Val leaned in closer, wondering, in shock, if they were referring to Warren.

"I mean, after everything that man did to poor Caroline over the years, and there he was pretending to be so sorry about the whole thing. It made me sick to my stomach. I swear I left the room every time he came near me. I didn't want to get into a conversation with him. My skinned crawled just being near him."

Val hesitated, and then tapped lightly on the door before entering the room.

"I'm sorry. I was just eavesdropping. Who are you talking about?"

Peggy looked shocked and Glynnis was dumbfounded.

"Ahh ..."

Val went in and sat on the bed.

"You weren't referring to Warren, were you?"

They both stared at each other and shook their heads no. Glynnis looked at Peggy for help. They couldn't lie. Val needed to know the truth.

"Oh, God, Val, I never meant for you to hear that. Not now."

Val was staring very intently at her friend.

"Glynnis, out with it. What's going on? Who were you talking about, and what did he do to Caroline?"

Warren walked down the hall when Val hadn't returned. He heard the tone of Val's voice change.

"Is everything okay in here?"

Glynnis stood and Peggy went and sat beside Valerie on the edge of the bed. They were both nervous. How were they ever going to tell her? They just buried her sister yesterday; she just had the most beautiful marriage proposal and was so obviously happy.

"This sucks!"

Glynnis spat out, her nerves getting the best of her.

"I'm going to be sick."

She ran to the bathroom and vomited. Peggy asked Val and Warren to come out and sit in the living room.

After handing Glynnis a towel, they walked down the hall. Glynnis's hands were shaking because of what was about to be revealed. Glynnis paced and Peggy sat opposite Val and Warren.

"Valerie, you've been through so much already. The last thing in the world we want to do is see you hurt again. Tonight was such a happy time. I mean you and Warren. God! I just don't want you to hate us ... but you need to know. You should know. This timing just sucks."

Val looked at Warren, puzzled, not knowing what to expect. He drew Val close.

Glynnis spoke up next.

"Val, we weren't talking about Warren. We were talking about your uncle."

Val looked at them, not understanding at all what they were getting at. Glynnis sat on the edge of the coffee table in front of her and put her hand gently on Val's knee.

"You've said for a number of years that you thought there was something wrong with Caroline, right? Like there was something driving her. Well, you were right."

She paused to think about how she was going to tell her.

"Valerie, this is so hard for me to tell you."

She looked up at Warren, who was rubbing his forehead and bracing for what was to come next.

"Caroline, throughout her childhood, was abused. By your uncle."

Warren could not believe what was being revealed. His grip tightened on Val's hand.

"What do you mean 'my uncle'?"

Val looked at her incredulously, searching for understanding.

"Which uncle? What kind of abuse are we talking about here?"

She asked with trepidation.

Glynnis turned away, knowing that there was no turning back now. She got up nervously and walked over to the mantle, looking down at the floor, she shook her head.

"It was your uncle ... Sean."

Val blinked hard. The information wasn't registering with her. Shock was not allowing her to process the revelation. Glynnis sat back down on the couch, giving the news time to sink in. After a few moments, she leaned forward.

"Can you explain what you mean, Glynnis, by 'abuse'?"

She nodded sadly.

"Valerie, me, Peg, and Caroline all shared similar secrets and experiences."

This time, it was Glynnis who sank back into the couch.

"Do you remember many years ago when your father died and I baby-sat you two for the very first time?"

Val nodded silently.

"Do you remember how I was all excited to watch you and then after your uncle came home I was really quiet and you found me in the living room sitting on the couch, not wanting to move?"

She let out a rather muffled moan.

"Your uncle Tim had dropped you off and stuck around for a little while before he left to go back for your mom and Auntie Sheila. He didn't seem to want to leave you girls. Sean, however, came back unexpectedly while I was in the house getting us some drinks. He told your family he forgot something at the house and needed to go back home for a moment."

"Your uncle Tim seemed a little anxious leaving us, and wanted to stick around while Sean was home, but Sean and he had words over Tim's smoking in the house, and Tim stormed out, angry. He didn't like Sean."

Val nodded, having sensed the tension between them over the years but never understanding why.

"While you and Caroline were out back playing, Sean led me into the living room."

Glynnis stood and wrung her hands and Peggy went over to support her, putting her arm around Glynnis's shoulder.

"He raped me, Val ... on that couch in the living room."

Valerie's jaw dropped, horrified. She stared at Glynnis in disbelief. Glynnis was openly crying, with her head buried in her hands. At first Val wanted to hit her and shout that she was a liar. But the words wouldn't come out. She could see her friend was heartbroken. Why would she make up a story like that? Why now? Oh, God, in her heart of hearts, she knew it had to be true. What else would drive Caroline to behave like she did?

Glynnis went and knelt in front of Valerie.

"Val, I know what you're thinking. I can see it on your face. I would never make something like this up. That would be cruel. I would never do that to you. Caroline confided in me one night when we were all out at the stone wall."

Warren stood and ran his hands through his hair.

"I can't believe this."

Val stared at him.

"Do you want your ring back?"

Then she burst into tears.

Warren rushed over to her.

"Oh, love, NO, that's not what I meant. I just can't believe all this is coming out now. I mean, I'm shocked. Sean is so friendly and outgoing. He's the life of the party!"

He continued.

"Not for nothing, but if I had to guess which uncle were a pervert, I'd have picked Tim. You know the quiet, reclusive one. It's just a damn, pitiful shock!"

Val paced the floor, clutching her arms.

"Please tell me what happened to Caroline."

She stood and walked over to her mother's piano bench, seemingly distracted and touching the keys so lightly that they made no sound.

"Your uncle first began touching her when she was about six years old."

Val shook her head without taking her eyes off the piano keys. Glynnis continued.

"It happened in Ireland."

Val looked up incredulously.

"But we shared a room at Granny's. How could he have done that when I was right in the bed next to her? I don't ever remember seeing him or hearing anything."

She struggled to try and remember the past.

"My mom was always in the next room. She'd have caught him for sure."

Glynnis explained how it typically happened when her mother was out visiting with friends and Sean babysat. She told Val the story Caroline had relayed to her about how on one occasion, it happened when all the adults were downstairs watching TV late. He snuck up into their room and carried a sleeping Caroline back to his room and fondled her until she woke up.

Val closed her eyes, not wanting to envision the scene. She struggled to understand it and couldn't get the images of Caroline and Sean out of her mind. Her world was collapsing around her. She was taking measured deep breaths.

"As she got older, Sean told her that she needed to keep their secret from your mom because she wouldn't understand and Caroline might get in trouble. He bought her silence by saying that your mother would get mad and would never let you and her come back to visit them in Ireland anymore. He told her that your granny and Siobhan would cry and be very sad if they couldn't ever see you girls again."

Glynnis looked to Peggy for confirmation. She nodded.

"Wasn't Caroline about twelve, Peg ... I mean, when he first, you know, entered her."

Peggy looked away in disgust and nodded.

556

Val slammed the piano cover with a loud crash, causing everyone, including Warren, to jump.

"Val, she never told you because later Sean threatened her!"

Val stared right through them, her anger rising.

"He knew he was losing control over her as she got older and feared she'd tell on him. It was then he said to her that, if she didn't meet his demands, he'd do the same thing to you."

Val collapsed onto the floor.

"Mother-of-Christ!"

Warren exclaimed and shot off the couch to help her. He scooped her up gently into his arms. She was mumbling something unintelligible. He looked at Glynnis and Peggy, visibly angry.

"She can't take too many more shocks like these, ladies. It's going to put her right over the fucking edge! Would one of you go and get her some water please?"

Peggy ran off to get a cool face cloth. Warren walked her over to the couch. Glynnis sat at the window seat, sobbing. She buried her head in her knees.

"I'm so sorry. I never meant for her to hear us, Warren. I would have taken this to the grave with me. I swear I would have. But I couldn't lie to her when she overheard us. I just couldn't."

Warren walked over to her and put his arm around her shoulder.

"I know, Glynn. I'm sorry for yelling at you. It's not your fault. None of this is. It's all so sordid and sick. I mean, Caroline's death, now this revelation."

His voice was low as he whispered.

"I honestly don't know how she's going to recover from this. I'm really worried about her, Glynn. I don't know what to do to help her."

She nodded and turned away and looked out at the street below.

He went back to Val's side as Peggy placed the cool cloth against her forehead. Warren whispered.

"Valerie, you've got to just tough this one out, love. It's a shock, I know. But you ARE going to be okay. None of this is anyone's fault. Do you understand me?"

She turned to face him.

"It's Sean's fault, Warren. It is his fault that my sister is dead!"

There were no tears. She stared at the ceiling without blinking; noticing for the first time the tiny speckled flecks glittering in the light. She sat up slowly to face her friends.

"I don't know what to say right now, except that I'm sorry Glynnis. That man, MY UNCLE, should be behind bars for these crimes! I had no idea and no knowledge that he ever did this to you and Caroline! I feel so betrayed and ashamed."

She went to sit at the window seat.

"I'm even mad at Caroline! She should have told me! I would have defended her."

She started to cry then. The girls went over and put their arms around her.

"There's nothing you could have done, Val. We were all very young. You know how kids are with adults. They believe everything grown-ups say. We were brought up that way."

Glynnis stated.

"Why didn't you tell your mother, Glynn? Did he threaten you, too?"

Glynnis answered no, and that it only happened that once. She never allowed herself to be put in a situation where she was alone with Sean again.

"I was afraid my mam would be mad at me, too, when I told her I wasn't going to babysit for you guys anymore. I went home that day clutching at my dress and afraid that if my mother found out, she would kill me! Isn't that sick? I was ashamed, Val ... and embarrassed."

Valerie put her hand to her head to stop the pounding. It was too much to process. She wondered if her grandmother and aunt ever suspected anything, or if her mom did. Chances were they didn't. They'd never allow that!

Val asked Warren.

"When are we leaving for Ireland again?"

Warren looked at her questioningly.

"Tuesday."

He was wondering what she was thinking.

Val stood and paced.

"Let's see if we can get a plane out tomorrow. Sean flew back home today. Granny and Siobhan are here with Mom for another week. I have to confront him, Warren. I want to hear what he did, right from his own mouth."

Glynnis and Peggy were amazed. The Callaghan girls never shied away from a confrontation.

"Are you sure you want to do this, Valerie?"

Warren cautioned her.

"Emotions are running very high right now. Don't you think you should wait until you're a bit stronger?"

She shook her head.

"No, Warren. I have to do this! Don't you see? He can't get away with this. How dare he do this to my sister and Glynnis... and who knows how many others!"

She ranted and held her hands clenched in a fist as she paced the floor.

"He's the one who killed my sister! I need to know why he did this. What would make him prey upon little girls like that? It's for my own peace of mind, Warren. I've got to confront him, and I want to do it while Granny and Siobhan are still here in the states and away."

"This revelation is going to rock my family when it gets out. It could very well shatter it! How the hell am I going to break this news to my mother? Granny could have a heart attack over this whole mess, and Siobhan will personally castrate him if I know her."

Warren clenched his jaw.

"Valerie, I insist on being there when you talk to him. I won't let you do this alone. Your emotions will be running amuck."

The women agreed that if Val felt she must confront Sean now, then it was a good idea to have Warren there with her. She agreed and reached out shakily for his hand. He was reeling from the news, and disgusted to think of what Sean did to not just one, but two innocent young girls ... perhaps even more. The thought made his blood boil. He'd have to restrain himself from punching him in the face. It was all so sick. He'd have never figured Sean for a pedophile.

Val hugged Glynnis and Peggy and told them how sorry she was. She assured them that she didn't blame or hate them in any way. She knew it all now, even poor Peggy revealed some of the suffering she'd endured at the hands of her own uncle as a child. Beyond just being angry, Val was in awe of how these women survived such horrible ordeals and went on to become so successful. They were her hero's. She thought of Caroline and what she must have endured, and it made her nauseous.

Val told the women she was going to her room, and that they should all try to get some rest. Warren followed her into the bedroom.

"I don't know what to say. I'm in shock, as you are. I'm very worried about you, darling."

Val went behind her screen to change into a yellow cotton nightshirt.

"I'm worried about myself too, Warren, believe it or not. I don't know what I'll say to him. I'm just numb. I'm still sad for Caroline, but I'm angry. I feel so betrayed!"

She whipped the polka dot dress over the top of her screen, almost tipping it over. Warren lunged to keep it upright.

"Warren, this man, whom I've loved and trusted all my life, turns out to be somebody I don't even know! I mean, he's been a lie my whole life! He took advantage of us! He betrayed Daddy's trust, Mom's, even his own parents! What goes on inside the mind of somebody like that? He should be in jail!"

560

Warren nodded.

"Hurt people HURT people, Valerie. Who knows what he experienced in his life. We just don't know yet."

She went and sat beside him on the edge of the bed, putting her hand on his.

"That's why I've got to get to the bottom of this. I've got to talk to him and find out what caused him to do this. I need answers. Caroline kept silent all her life, and it eventually killed her. Once he explains, and HE WILL EXPLAIN, maybe then I can let it rest and figure out how or if I should even mention it to my mother. I may just decide to keep it with me and that's it. I don't know if she could handle it."

Warren and Val had the worst night's sleep ever. There was no chance of temptation that evening. Neither one could rest. The next morning, Peggy and Glynnis confirmed their night was the same. They looked at each other's puffy, bloodshot eyes.

"Okay, so we're all pathetic messes. Who wants coffee?"

Warren summarized for them all.

Val stood in the center of the dining room with her hands on her hips.

"Isn't this family just the picture of dysfunction? I mean, if you asked me a month ago, I would have thought my family fairly normal. Well, you can toss that notion right out the window!"

Peggy asked her.

"Do you feel better now ... having said that?"

Val took the mug of coffee Warren held out to her.

"Yes. I certainly do!"

She quipped, and turned on her heel to sit at the dining room table.

Warren couldn't help but admire her legs in the short nightshirt. Val stared at her engagement ring and smiled. Warren caught her smile, and it warmed his heart. Val knew she still had many blessings to count. She had the man of her dreams, who'd become her fiancé.

"I still love my ring, you know."

He smiled.

"I'm glad. I just hope it keeps you smiling through this next ordeal."

He had booked their flights to Ireland with his airline early that morning, taking full advantage of his employee benefits. They were scheduled to depart at eight o'clock that evening out of Logan Airport. They decided to leave the house around four o'clock, so they could all have a leisurely dinner at Legal Seafood in the airport before they had to board. Glynnis and Peggy's flight left shortly after theirs for London.

Val didn't even remember what she threw into her suitcase for clothing. It still contained a few items from her last trip to Ireland. She took a quick shower and threw on a pair of jeans and a casual navy and white striped top. She also grabbed a light summer sweater from the drawer, as the flights tended to get cold. She put on a pair of sneakers, wanting to be comfortable for the long trip. Warren carried the luggage downstairs and set it in the hallway to wait for the taxi.

Glynnis and Peggy gave them both a parting hug after dinner, before heading for their respective airlines. The women apologized again for all that had transpired, and talked about how their next visit together would be for a much happier occasion. They admired Val's ring one more time and squeezed her hand before turning to head toward their gate.

Val held Warren's hand at the check-in counter. The woman behind the desk commented on Val's diamond when she handed back her license and passport.

"What a beautiful ring. Best of luck to you!"

Val thanked her and beamed at Warren.

"We're going to spend a lot of time at airports, I can tell."

Warren nodded.

"Would seem so with the transatlantic life we're planning. I don't mind. I'm quite used to it now."

They stood in line patiently waiting to board. Warren leaned down to whisper in her ear.

"But soon I'll have the pleasure of knowing that when I come home, you'll be there."

Val put her arm around his waist and patted his stomach.

"I'll have to learn how to cook better. The only thing I know how to make is reservations."

He chuckled at her joke as they boarded the plane. Both fell asleep halfway through the flight. Val woke with a blanket that Warren must have placed over her. They were in first class thanks to his status with the airlines, and were able to recline comfortably. It was a quiet flight. Val enjoyed looking out the window as they descended. She'd always been fascinated with landings, especially at Shannon Airport. The coastline was so ruggedly untamed.

"Does it ever scare you?"

She asked without turning.

"Landings, I mean?"

Warren was shaking the cobwebs out of his head and yawning. He leaned forward and gazed past her out the tiny window.

"Only when it's windy. It's a beautiful morning today though. I can't wait to get home."

There was something about the way he said "home," which included Val now that touched her deeply. The comfort of that thought was short-lived as she felt a sinking sensation in the pit of her stomach, dreading the impending confrontation with her uncle Sean.

Warren had left his car in the employee car park and found it quickly. His house was only twenty minutes from the airport. Pulling into the driveway, Val admired the front of the house from a new perspective — one that would have her living there soon.

The house was new. It still needed some landscaping, but the view from the hill was spectacular. She was actually looking forward to the daily routine of collecting fresh eggs from the hen house. Warren encouraged her to walk around a bit. Tired as he was, he told her he'd often go for a quick jog when he got home, just to stretch his legs. He needed to check in with work to get his schedule for the following week. Val told him she'd make breakfast.

"I'll get the eggs!"

She offered graciously.

Warren pointed her toward the cabinets that contained the bowls.

"Do you think we could call your neighbors to get some fresh milk and cream?"

Warren said they'd do better than that. When he was done with his call, they could walk down the hill and visit with them in person. He was looking forward to introducing her to them.

Val found a bowl in the cabinet and headed out to the hen house, which desperately needed cleaning. She stepped around carefully and reached into the hay, feeling around for the warm eggs. She tried to picture herself doing this daily chore. What a difference from reaching for the New York Times and a hot cup of coffee on her way in to work in the morning.

She liked the pace of life here and thought it would suit her perfectly. She collected more than a dozen eggs and walked back to the house to wash them off. Warren reappeared and asked if she was ready to walk down to the Kelly's dairy farm.

"Watch where you're stepping though. We'll need to get you a pair of boots for around here."

Val laughed and tread very carefully. Warren walked her around the back of the house and down the hill. Brian was talking with a woman out in front of his truck and waved when he saw Warren and Valerie descend the hill.

"Look who's back!"

Brian held out his hand to warmly greet his neighbor.

Warren turned to Valerie.

"Brian, I'd like to introduce my fiancée, Valerie Callaghan."

Brian, clearly thrilled by the good news, removed his cap and smiled broadly, telling her it was a pleasure. He also expressed that he was sorry to hear about the loss of her sister. He explained that Warren had called and filled him in.

Brian turned to the woman next to him to introduce them.

"Valerie, this is my wife, Maggie."

Maggie held out both of her hands, and her mouth dropped when she saw Val's ring.

"My God! It's a stunner! Just like you!"

She smiled and gave her a hug. The Kelly's invited the couple into their house for tea.

They sat around the kitchen table as Maggie busied herself making a pot of tea and setting out the soda bread and butter.

"My future bride wants to know if you happen to have any fresh milk and cream handy."

Val blushed and they all laughed.

"We've plenty, love, and we'll load you up on the way home. Fresh butter, too."

Val thanked her new neighbors.

"Running a dairy farm seems like an awful lot of work, Maggie, is it?"

She smiled at the younger woman. They were only six years apart in age, but Maggie's face looked older.

It wasn't always easy, but Maggie swore that it was rewarding.

"Ahhhh, it's not so bad. It's what we know and can do well."

A young girl bounded into the kitchen.

"Good morning, Mr. Cahill."

She smiled up at him sweetly.

Warren, tipping his cap to the child, responded.

"Well, top o' the mornin' to you, Eileen. Were you busy helping your da out there?"

She nodded, still smiling.

"That's lovely."

She exclaimed, pointing to Val's ring.

Val held it out to her, so she could get a closer look.

"Do you want to try it on?"

Val offered.

The youngster nodded excitedly as her mother put her hand over her anxious heart.

"Oh, mother-of-God, if she ever loses it, Valerie, I could never replace it!"

Val put her hand up.

"Not to worry, Maggie. I'm right here. She just wants to try it on."

Val set the child on her lap and took off her ring. She placed it on Eileen's pointer finger and told her to make a fist.

Eileen did as she was told, looking at her hand from all angles.

"Can I wear it?"

She asked innocently.

Val kindly explained to her.

"Well, Mr. Cahill gave that to me as a gift because he wants to marry me. I think he'd be sad if I didn't wear it."

"Even more sad if it got lost..."

Warren added playfully.

Eileen reluctantly gave the ring back. Val placed it on her finger while Warren watched, amused by his fiancée's first interaction with his neighbors' daughter.

Maggie was clearly relieved to have the ring safely back where it belonged.

"Okay, now that that little bauble is back in place, let's have tea, shall we? Are you two just getting in?"

They sat for a while and chatted. Maggie placed her hand on Val's and expressed her apologies over the loss of her sister.

"You poor thing. I'm so sorry about your sister. What a tragedy. I'll remember you in my prayers, Valerie."

Val looked down into her teacup. It still seemed foreign to her to hear Caroline talked about in past tense.

When they were about to leave, Val told her she'd bring her some eggs later.

"Oh, no need. We can run up and grab them ourselves when we need them. Now that we know you're back, we'll leave you milk, cream, and butter in the morning. Let me know if you need anything else."

Warren and Val were loaded up with dairy products for their trek home. Val was huffing as they climbed the hill.

"It didn't seem this steep on the way down."

Warren chuckled, seeing her flushed face. She stopped for a moment to catch her breath and look around.

"Warren, I love it here. I really do. Brian and Maggie are such nice people — salt of the earth. Their daughter, Eileen? She's just adorable. Did you see how her eyes lit up when she saw my ring?"

"I did indeed!"

He nodded.

"See! It's innate. Women are born to love diamonds!"

He could see her breath in the cool air. It made him happy to hear her enjoying her stay already.

He set the bottles down on the top step and opened the door to the house. She stopped him in his tracks with her authentic brogue and scolded him.

"Ahhh you, look at ya now. Off with those dirty boots. They'll be no tracking of filthy manure into my kitchen!"

Warren laughed at her skillful impression.

"You know, you actually sounded like a real Irish housewife then. No doubt you'll be talkin' to me like that soon enough. It'll happen, y'know, once you're here long enough."

She knew it was all too true. When she'd return to the States after a summer visiting with Granny and Granda, she could skillfully mimic the Irish people, and would amuse her friends and teachers with her impeccable brogue. She often entertained the girls at school when they'd ask her to "talk Irish" for them. That memory still made her smile.

She set about finding things in Warren's kitchen and told him she was making a list of utensils she'd need if she were going to mutilate anything worthwhile in the kitchen. She could borrow some of the more immediate things from her grandmother.

"Don't go robbing your grandmother's house. I'll buy them. We'll need them anyway."

He admonished her.

Val patted him on the back.

"Oh, you're such a proud man, Warren Cahill."

Again with the Irish accent.

He snuck up behind her a moment later and pinched her on the bottom. She jumped and screamed, then turned to put her arms up around his neck.

"I love you."

He bent and kissed her. She responded instantly and stepped back, somewhat surprised at her body's sudden reaction to him.

"I've, um, got to scramble these eggs here."

He bit her on the ear and remarked.

"Very well."

Val blushed under his gaze. She wanted him more than he could ever imagine.

Val spent the better part of the morning exploring the house and envisioning some changes. She asked his opinion on things, and he told her to feel free to decorate any way she liked. All he cared about was his office.

She could do whatever she liked with the rest of the house.

"Well, all right, if you must keep it as is."

He playfully tossed an eraser from his broken pencil at her as she tried to straighten out some papers on his desk.

"When do you want to talk with Sean?"

Warren asked her over lunch. Val narrowed her eyes.

"Never, really."

He watched her cautiously.

"No, no, I know I must. I'm thinking tomorrow. Part of me wants to avoid it, the other part of me just wants to tackle it head-on and be done with it."

She looked out the window with a distant gaze.

"It's sad, Warren. I mean, I loved my Uncle Sean. I just feel so hurt and betrayed ... and ANGRY! Caroline might still be alive right now if she wasn't so messed up emotionally by him. I always knew there was something she was hiding. Don't get me wrong. I don't want to see the man dead or anything I just ..."

She sighed.

"Well, I just want to find out why he did this. He needs help Warren, or he could do this again to someone else. I think of someone like little Eileen down the hill there ... can you imagine him doing that to her?"

Warren's grip tightened on his chair at the thought of it and warned her.

"I can tell you one thing right now, Valerie, he'll not get within a meter of our children. I'll rip his head off!"

Val nodded in agreement.

"Darling, I probably wouldn't stop you. They'd have to lock us both up!"

After lunch, Warren put on an old pair of pants and boots and went out to clean the hen house. Val made a list of items she needed at the store. He was out of everything, and would be home with her for the rest of the week before returning to his schedule the following Sunday. She'd have most of the following week to herself. That would probably be a good time to go and pick out curtains for the living room and kitchen.

She walked into the dining room and pulled up the shade to let the sunlight in, and was momentarily taken back by the stunning view. It was breathtaking. *I wonder why this isn't the living room?*

Kathleen M. Urquhart

Warren didn't have a dining room set in there yet, and she saw that the room was clearly as big as the one he was using as his "living room." She made a mental note to talk to him about switching them around. But later, she was getting tired, adjusting to the time difference.

Val went upstairs and brushed her teeth. Then she walked over to the henhouse to ask Warren where the nearest store was. He told her down the road "a bit" on the right.

"You're going to be talking in metrics soon, too."

He informed her.

She wanted to go pick up some things for dinner.

"I thought I'd take you out tonight. We've several places right around here to choose from. There's Fitzpatrick's Hotel right down the road here. Or, if you're feeling adventurous, we can go to Bunratty Castle. A tourist trap – but fun."

Val told him she'd be happy going to Durty Nelly's for a beer and a sandwich. It, too, was a tourist spot, but they had great food. They settled on that and Warren commented on how he'd enjoy a cold beer later.

"They've usually got live music there, too."

By one o'clock, Val needed a nap, and fell asleep on Warren's bed. He washed up, changed out of his clothes and lay down beside her. When she awoke, she played with his hair, waking him gently. She put one eye near his nose and fluttered her eyelashes, tickling him and causing him to smile without opening his eyes.

"Those are called 'butterfly kisses'."

She whispered to him, and did it again.

He opened one eye and crinkled up his nose.

"You keep at that and I'm going to sneeze on you!"

"Oh, gross!"

She whacked him on his behind and told him to get up. Val picked up her suitcase and flung it on to the bed; unzipping it, she pulled out a casual denim skirt and colorful knit top. The air was cooler here than in Boston, and the nights had a chill to them. Val announced she was getting into the shower.

As the warm water cascaded around her, she suddenly felt his warm hands caress her shoulders and slowly make their way down to her breasts. She stuck her face under the water in order to rinse the soap off, then turned to look at him.

"Fancy meeting you here, Mr. Cahill. Tell me, what brings you into my shower?"

He didn't respond verbally but brought his mouth down on hers. He reached for the soap and began to rub it over her body, sending shivers down her spine. She took the soap from his hand. Kissing his neck, she reached lower. He moaned at her touch.

"Do you think this was such a good idea, Mr. Cahill? I mean, now that we're both all hot and bothered?"

Warren smiled at her encouragingly. She looked down and commented.

"You're quite ... how shall I say this? Admirable."

He touched the tips of her breasts.

"So are you, Ms. Callaghan. So are you."

With that he turned on the cold water, causing her to scream.

"WARREN CAHILL! SHUT IT OFF! SHUT IT OFF NOW!!! It's freezing!"

He laughed and jumped out of the shower.

"That's payback from your little Cape Cod escapade the other day!"

She laughed at him as she adjusted the water to warm. He poked his head into the shower once again, commenting.

"Nice nips, love."

She playfully threw the wet face cloth at him and told him to get out and stop bothering her. He laughed again as he shut the door behind him and purposely turned off the light.

"WARREN!!!"

She mumbled something under her breath about getting him back.

Dinner was relaxing and enjoyable. They met up unexpectedly with a few of Warren's friends at the pub and congratulations were expressed on their engagement.

"Speaking of which ..."

He turned to Valerie.

"Remind me to call my mother. I have to get the details for the party."

"Who's coming to this party?"

Val asked, after taking a sip of Guinness. Warren entwined his hand in hers.

"Ah, well, it's not a huge engagement party, just a few members of my immediate family: brothers, sisters, cousins, aunts, uncles ... I estimate it to be only around two hundred people, give or take a few."

Val looked shocked.

"I'm kidding love ... but there will be a houseful to be sure. Are you looking forward to meeting them?"

She told him she was.

"Tell me. Are they all as crazy as you?"

He nodded.

"Of course. Every last one of them."

Someone bought them another round of congratulatory drinks. The crowd was warming up, singing before there was music. Warren waved to a member of the band whom he recognized from the Glor, and they went over to talk to him.

"Nice to see you, Warren."

The men shook hands.

"Jared, this is my fiancée, Valerie Callaghan. Valerie, this is Jared Walsh."

Jared congratulated them on their engagement.

"What a great surprise! We love weddings!"

"Thank you!"

Val laughed and shook his hand.

Warren had his arm about her waist as he and Jared talked about some of the upcoming performances at the Glor.

"I hope you like Celtic music, Valerie."

Val nodded and winked at Warren.

"Valerie's no stranger to it. She's quite an accomplished violinist herself, not a bad fiddler either."

Jared raised his glass to her.

"Well, then, maybe we'll get you up on stage later tonight."

She shook her head no, but Warren warned her.

"Now that he knows, you'll never get away!"

Jared excused himself to head up to the small stage.

Val said hello to the women who accompanied Warren's friends. They admired her ring and congratulated her asking what she did for work in America. They inquired if she was going to move to Ireland, and she told them that was their plan. Promises were made to have them over for dinner soon. Val was very much at ease in the company of her fiancé's friends, and they all left the bar for a table together to sit, eat, and listen to the music.

Val ordered a toasted ham and cheese sandwich with chips. She didn't want anything too heavy. She and Warren laughed when the waitress brought them out one ham sandwich and one cheese sandwich. The waitress didn't think it funny at first until Val assured her that it was fine, and explained that in America the ham and cheese were served together on one sandwich. The waitress took the halves of the sandwiches apart and placed one on top of the other.

"There you go. No problems, love!"

Val burst out laughing. Warren made sure to give the waitress a good tip.

They were so busy talking that Val missed her name being called from the stage. Jared was making a toast to Warren and Valerie's engagement and called her up to play a song with them. Val looked at Warren, who put his hands up.

"I'd get up there if I were you. These folks get pretty nasty when the music stops."

Val tapped him on the top of his head as she passed by. All the women and men at the table cheered her on. Warren was wincing, pretending she'd hit him hard. She made a face at him.

Jared decided to have a little fun with her.

"So, Valerie, with a name like Callaghan, you're what … Italian?"

She shook her head.

"No, no, American. Irish-American, though."

The crowd cheered.

"My father's from Ireland and my mom is second-generation."

"Well, we've heard this rumor that you're a pretty good fiddler. Is this true?"

Val pretended to glare over at her fiancé, who was enjoying the entertainment.

"I think I can hold me own."

She said in her best brogue, to the delight of the onlookers. She took and positioned the fiddle Jared handed to her.

"Catch me if you can!"

Val took off with lightning speed to a popular song the band struck up. Warren was the first on his feet, clapping as she gave the musicians a run for their money. The rest of the crowd quickly followed suit, getting into the spirit of the song. A couple of the women at their table got up on the floor to dance a jig.

Val's fiddling was superb and lots of whooping calls went up during her solo parts. When she was done, she made a quick bow, to the delight of the audience. Jared told her that for that performance she'd be provided with free beer for the rest of the night. The bartender lifted a glass to her.

"Well, that makes you a cheap date!"

Warren laughed as he kissed her on the lips when she returned to their table.

"That was precious, love, absolutely precious."

Val sat, somewhat winded, but exhilarated. It felt good to play like that - cheerful music.

She and Warren walked up the hill toward home sometime after midnight. The cool night air felt good and the walk cleared her head from the smoky room. Bright stars brilliantly lit up the cloudless sky.

"How come the stars are so much brighter in Ireland?"

She sat on his front steps and looked up at him.

Warren stood on the steps above her, searching for the right key in the dim moonlight, then gazed at the sky.

"I don't know. I guess I never looked at the stars that much in the States. I'm used to them here. They're beautiful for sure ... as are you."

She looked at him and smiled.

"Awww. That's so sweet. Warren?"

"Yes, love."

"I want to make love with you tonight."

He walked down the steps and kissed her lightly.

"Ahh, I've got a bit of a problem here."

Val looked at him, concerned.

"What?"

"Ya see, my house keys are in my pocket, and I can't get at them at the moment, as there is something blocking the way."

Val let out a howl.

"Oh, you are priceless. Get the darn key out, or I'm going in after it!"

Warren smirked mischievously.

"Well, that's what I was hoping you'd say."

He produced the key after much drama and opened the door.

"Remember to take your shoes off!"

She warned him.

"Yes, dear..."

He mumbled humbly.

"And so it begins."

Val giggled as she bounded up the stairs to his bedroom.

She went into the bathroom to brush her teeth and wash her face. Warren followed her. He put his arms around her stomach and kissed the back of her neck while she had her mouth filled with toothpaste. She spit it out and took a sip of water. Then she breathed in his face.

"How's my breath?"

He told her it smelled minty fresh.

"Good. I'll leave you to brush your own teeth."

He looked after her comically and mimicked.

"I'll leave you to brush your own teeth" ... Thank you, darling!"

Val giggled as she undressed, thinking how fun it was to tease him. Warren shut off the bathroom light and climbed into bed beside her. He was wearing a pair of boxers and no shirt. She quickly had him go under the covers with her, as she was freezing. He cuddled her close.

"Valerie, Valerie, where to begin with you?"

He kissed her passionately and suddenly stopped. She looked at him, puzzled. He remembered his promise.

"You know, when I had your ring blessed by Father Bruce, we had a discussion."

Val rested her hand on his chest.

"What did you discuss?"

She asked softly.

Warren, tracing the profile of her face with his finger, answered.

"In a nutshell, celibacy ... waiting until we're married."

Val pulled back in amazement.

"CELIBACY! Really now, tell me more."

She shook her head and chuckled.

"Well, Father Bruce asked me to honor you and the laws of marriage, and wait until we were married. I'm not kidding. He did. He went on to tell me that that is what God would want."

Val asked him.

"Do you really think we can do that? I mean, I know we should. It's the right thing to do ... but do you think we can?"

Warren nodded reluctantly.

"Listen, Val, I could devour you this very minute. However, I did make him a promise, and I've got to stay true to my word. Our time will come."

"You need to sleep in my guest room, love. I'll not trust myself with you here in my bed. I hope you understand."

He gazed at her longingly as his body began to defy his pledge.

At first, Val felt a twinge of hurt, but then, she was strangely honored that he'd be so strong as to follow through on his promise to Father Bruce. After they were married, she'd make a mental note to playfully chide Father Bruce on his Godly advice.

He held her close and kissed her good night. She moved seductively against him until he could take it no more.

"GO ... NOW!"

Val saluted and nodded obediently.

"Yes, sir."

She grabbed the pillow and made her way into the guest room down the hall. She smiled as she closed the door. Warren woke during the middle of the night with desire coursing through his veins and thought, for a moment, of tiptoeing down the hall and sneaking in beside her.

"Lord, help me ..."

Instead, he got up and went downstairs to drink a glass of cold water.

Chapter Fifty

Ennis, County Clare, Ireland, Summer 1998

VAL DREADED THE THOUGHT OF meeting her sister's abuser face-to-face. She no longer viewed him as her uncle. A vital tie had been severed. She was apprehensive - not trusting her own reactions. Part of her was afraid she might try and kill him; another part didn't want to hear his sob story and then feel sorry for him. He was responsible for her sister's death! She didn't know what he could possibly say to make her forgive him. She would not extend that to him. He didn't deserve it.

Warren put the top down on the car for the drive over to her grandmother's house. Val grew quieter as they neared Bindon Street and he reached for her hand. The house looked quiet and the front shades were drawn. She rang the doorbell.

Shellie, Granny's longtime helper, answered the door and was surprised to see her, as she seldom arrived unannounced. She welcomed her boss's granddaughter and asked if she'd brought any luggage with her on this trip. Val smiled and told her no and that she was staying with her fiancé. She turned and introduced Warren. Shellie's eyes lit up with excitement as she stared up at the handsome Mr. Cahill. She congratulated them happily.

"Shellie, can you tell me if Sean is home?"

Shellie informed them that he was upstairs, locked in his room, working on his computer. Val thanked her and told her that since she and Warren were staying for a while, she could have the afternoon off.

"I'll let my grandmother know. It's not a problem. Enjoy this nice weather we're having."

Shellie looked a little unsure about taking direction from her boss's granddaughter. But something in Val's voice prevented her from protesting. Instead, she admitted it would be a good time to go home and get some weeding done in her garden. Val watched her go and shut the door.

Val asked Warren to wait downstairs for a moment. She assured him she'd be right back down. As she made her way up the circular staircase, her legs felt like lead weights. She heard the frantic clicking of a keyboard before she knocked on the door. A tired voice responded.

"Shellie, I'm very busy right now. I don't want to be disturbed. Whatever it is, it can wait until I'm done. Thank you."

Val took a deep breath.

"This isn't Shellie. It's Valerie. Please open the door."

She heard Sean mumble.

"Valerie?"

He opened the door and smiled.

"What a surprise. What are you doing here? Mam and Siobhan stayed back with your mom."

Val stopped him in mid-sentence.

"I'm aware of that. Please come downstairs. I need to talk with you."

Sean stared after her, and then followed her downstairs to the study. He said hello to Warren, who held his gaze in an unflinching stare. Sean's concern grew.

"Have a seat."

Valerie demanded more than requested, as she motioned toward the couch. Sean looked at her and his heart sank. He knew, then, that she knew.

"Sean, what happened on that couch on the day of my dad's funeral?"

He hung his head in shame, folded his hands, and shook his head. He couldn't believe what was happening.

"ANSWER ME!"

Val shouted at him. Warren sat up straight when her voice rose.

"Listen, kiddo…"

Val sprang up and stood in front of him.

"I am not a kid, Sean. Glynnis was a kid when you raped her on this very couch!"

She turned and walked toward the fireplace.

Warren kept his eye on the fireplace poker, ready to grab it from her should she pick it up. He didn't like the way this was going. He sensed that Val might lose control. Silently, he watched her pace about Sean like a lion about to attack its prey.

"How old was Caroline when you began molesting her? Say five, maybe six years old? Does that sound about right? Do you remember exactly how old she was when you started fondling your only brother's daughter? Your NIECE?"

Her voice rose icily.

Sean couldn't bring himself to look at her. It was his worst nightmare come to pass. He knew he deserved her fury, and was speechless.

Val stood before him.

"Sean, I want you to look at me."

Her voice was dead calm. He wouldn't raise his head. Val grabbed him by the head of his hair and whipped his head back.

"You BASTARD! You are responsible for Caroline's death! Do you understand that? You blackmailed her as a child after you repeatedly raped her for years. You're sick!"

Warren watched as Sean offered no resistance to her verbal assault. Val pushed his head to the side.

"I came here today because I have questions that I need for you to answer. You owe that to me. You OWE that also to my mother, Granny, and Aunt Siobhan. It's a good thing that my father is dead because I know he'd kill you with his bare hands! Maybe if he were here, you wouldn't have had the balls to try this!"

She slapped him across the face.

"I trusted you! Damn it!"

Val went and stood stiffly by the window. Warren stared at Sean, who half attempted to wipe at his lip. Sean wished he had a gun, so he could end it all for himself as soon as possible.

"Val ..."

She spun and glared at him.

"What?"

"I'm sorry. I'm so very sorry."

He held his head in his hands and shook with grief and remorse. Val went and sat beside Warren. In a deliberate voice, she pressed him.

"Sean, what made you become like this?"

He looked away as tears fell from his eyes. Val wrung her hands in her lap.

"Tell me! Don't you see? Caroline did exactly what you're doing. All her life she kept these secrets within her, and it ate at her, like a cancer. Little by little it sucked the life right out of her until she had nothing left to give. What happened to you, Sean?"

She pleaded with him.

Ashamed and defeated, he picked at a thread on the hem of his shirt, avoiding their eyes. Then, in a low, monotone voice, devoid of emotion, he began to tell her what she desperately needed to know.

"When I was a boy, Neil and I attended a private, all-boys Catholic school. Neil was always the strong one, and smarter. I sometimes resented him always sticking up for me. I told him that I could fight my own battles. I was kinda jealous of him."

He paused.

"Don't get me wrong. I loved Neil. There were times when I wished he were there to defend me. He was a great older brother. He was everything I wanted to be. At school, I'd try to distance myself from him though. I needed my own space, my own identity. Not always 'Neil's little brother.'"

Sean rubbed at the growth on his chin.

"There was a young priest, new to our school, Father Rob Coughlin. He taught religious studies. Anyway, he was always very nice to me and told me that he had an older brother that was a lot like Neil when he was younger. He told me that he didn't always get along with his brother either. He befriended me, and soon he had me pegged for an altar boy, which I didn't want to do."

A sarcastic tone crept into his voice.

"Mam and Da thought it grand, and a privilege, that I was asked, and therefore, in their eyes, I couldn't say no to the priest ... to the church."

Val stared at him. Warren's eyes never left him.

"Valerie, I know this may be hard to understand, but I was raped over and over for years by that priest. He took me to the rectory after school and obtained my parents' full permission to stay late in the evenings in order to 'practice mass.' There was nothing that he didn't do to me. As time went on, I found out that he did these things to other boys as well. Some years later, in school, a couple of the guys I chummed around with used drugs; two of them committed suicide. They couldn't live with the truth of it anymore. I never told anyone and kept it to myself. Eventually, some of the braver kids came forward with their accusations, and he was reassigned to another church. I don't know where they sent him."

"I know this doesn't make any sense as to how I could do this to Caroline. Anything I say is going to sound like an excuse. I hate myself every day of my life. I know it's sick! I just don't know how to stop. I'm not gay. I don't go after young boys. I know that going after young girls doesn't make it any better or easier to understand. I suck at adult relationships with women, which is why I never married. I'm not a man who stalked about looking for little girls to drag off and kill in the woods. I know you don't know what to believe right now. But that's the truth."

Val started crying the minute he said Caroline's name.

"Why didn't you stop when she told you to? Didn't she cry when you hurt her? I mean, she was a baby, Sean! An innocent little girl ..."

She stood, and Warren firmly grabbed her arm.

"Valerie, don't love. It won't help matters. Sean needs help. He's sick."

Val turned and looked at the pathetic, broken man in front of her. He was beaten down and probably suicidal. She would not allow herself to take pity on him, however. She still wanted to scratch his eyes out. She wanted to kick him over and over until he cried out in pain.

"So what now, Sean? Are you just going to stay in your room and waste away doing God-knows-what on that computer for the rest of your life? If you need help, why don't you go and get it? There are clinics for these sorts of problems. In your case, money is not an issue."

Sean rubbed the palms of his hands together.

"I've already called a few clinics. That's why I came back early. I'm waiting for them to get back to me. I am committing myself. Caroline's death made me aware of the depth of my problems. It was in the works before you arrived. If I don't do this, I may go the same way as she did."

His statement was matter-of-fact, not a threat.

Val started crying again when he alluded to suicide.

"Sean, don't. Please don't. I can't stand you at this moment, but we've all had more than our share of heartache in this family. I can't take much more. Your death, much as I'd like to administer it right now, would serve no good purpose, except to kill Granny with a heart attack, and leave Aunt Siobhan all by herself."

She actually found herself mad at Caroline at that moment for committing suicide.

"Sean, I'm heading back home at the end of next week. If you haven't heard, Warren and I are engaged."

His eyes brightened then suddenly turned sad. He'd not have a future role in her life, and he knew that now. He sensed Warren's invisible hedge of protection about her already. He had no right to ask anything of them, and quietly congratulated them.

"Before I leave here, I want to see either documentation or speak to someone who can confirm that you are officially registered in a reputable clinic. You will be the one to tell Granny and Siobhan what you did. I can't bear to see their faces, and I hope, for your sake, that poor Granny doesn't drop dead where she's standing. I have to go home and break this news to my own mother, who's already grieving. She never loved anyone but Daddy and now has lost her youngest daughter. This is devastating to all of us! Your actions didn't just hurt Caroline and Glynnis, Sean. It has a rippling effect and will hurt our whole family! I just hope the bonds we've established hold through this next revelation. This could shatter our family!"

"I want to see proof that you're in a rehab of some sort before I leave. I mean it, Sean."

He nodded silently.

"If I don't see that you are actively involved in ongoing therapy, I will encourage Glynnis to bring charges against you. You belong in a registry for sex offenders."

He stared at his feet. Val went on.

"Her dad, as you know, just defended our friend, Peggy, and won. He'll go after your jugular for hurting his daughter. You didn't blackmail her like you did Caroline; but you did manage, however, to buy her silence all these years through shame. But Glynnis isn't afraid of you anymore. She had to go through years of therapy to work through all the crap your selfish actions caused. You've managed to not only screw up yourself, but others as well. Get help, or Glynnis is waiting at the ready to tell her father, who will haul your sorry ass off to jail. There is no statute of limitations here on rape, Sean, and I'll testify on her behalf! Do you understand me?"

Sean nodded. What she'd said was true. Val suddenly pulled a small tape recorder out of her sweater pocket. She'd borrowed it from one of the attorneys she worked with a long time ago and had forgotten to return it. She had packed it for just this purpose.

"Just in case you don't think I'm serious, I've got your full confession on tape, and I'll use it if I have to."

Sean was shocked. Even Warren raised his eyebrows when she produced the recorder.

"I'm here until the end of next week. I want you admitted, and in a rehab program before I go. You will confess everything to Granny and Siobhan, and you will call me to let me know when it's safe to come and talk with them."

Val turned to Warren and placed the recorder in his hands. He put the recorder safely in his pocket. She didn't look back as they left; Sean stood alone in the living room. Warren closed the door carefully behind them.

He opened the car door for her. Val waited until they were a few miles from the house before she cried.

"I don't like swearing like I did. I sounded like a longshoreman!"

Warren patted her hand.

"They were all very well-placed, darling. You handled it better than I thought you would. Remind me never to piss you off. Where did you come up with the idea for the tape recorder? It was brilliant!"

She smiled weakly and shrugged. Warren added sympathetically.

"I just hope Sean gets the help he needs. He really is messed up, love."

Warren glanced at her briefly before shifting gears.

"I've read stories about these priests and how some have molested hundreds of boys. It really can screw up a kid for life if they don't get psychological help. I'm not starting a pity party for Sean, mind you. But can you see where his head is? Abuse becomes a vicious cycle."

Val nodded.

"I know. He does need help, which is why I wanted to make sure he gets it. Some people just talk about getting help. I want to make sure he DOES get it. I want to see proof that he means it. I'm also not going to be responsible for telling Granny and Siobhan. That's his responsibility. I don't want it on my conscience if anything happens to Granny. It's going to be hard enough telling this to my own mother."

"Do you feel better?"

"Warren, Caroline's still dead, and I can't bring her back. I wish I could just turn back time and intervene. But it's over now ... I have to go on without her. It's just incredibly sad."

Warren wound his way up the driveway to their house. He went around to open the door for her. They noticed milk bottles on the step.

"I forgot to bring those in this morning. I'm not use to having fresh milk delivered daily to my doorstep."

Warren bent to pick them up.

"No need to apologize. I'm sure they're still fresh. You look like you're in need of a backrub."

Val entered the house and dropped her purse on the kitchen table, heading straight up the stairs. Warren followed her. She peeled off her shirt and fell across the bed. Warren propped her up with pillows and slowly ran his fingers across her back. Val, with her face mushed into the pillow, sighed loudly, conveying how wonderful it felt.

She didn't mean to cry. It was a letting go, a visceral response to everything that had just transpired. Warren continued rubbing her back, knowing she needed the release, eventually falling asleep to the soothing feel of his touch.

Val and Warren spent the remainder of the week drawing up plans to get their house ready. She asked what he thought about making the dining room into the living room since the view was magnificent. He said he didn't mind moving things around and was looking forward to seeing what she could make of the place.

"And if you don't like it here, we can look for another house."

Val assured him that she loved the house, because it was his.

"Well, it will be 'ours' and I want you to be happy here."

She assured him that she would be and was looking forward to decorating their home. At present, it was rather stark and unimaginative. She insisted on paying for their new furniture and decorating costs.

"My Grandparents established generous trust funds for me and Caroline. They wanted the money to be used for life events like this. Since you already bought our house, it's the least I can do. It will also finance my future unemployment."

Warren chuckled at her reference to becoming a wife and mother.

Over the next few days, in an effort to keep busy, she and Warren went out and looked at fabric for curtains together.

"Granny has friends who are very talented at making curtains. I could have one of them come over and take the measurements for us. I remember as a little girl going with my parents when my mom picked out lace for curtains. Funny how life repeats itself."

Warren agreed that that would be a good project for her while he was flying the following week.

"It'll keep you busy. Decorating is more your thing than mine, love."

They spent Warren's last weekend off buying furniture, picking out a new dining room set, bedroom set, and a variety of living room pieces and lamps. Presently, the living room contained well-worn furniture from his college days. Val didn't tell him to throw anything out. She did what her mother told her she had done to her father.

"Just let him see what it looks like when the new things arrive; he'll see for himself the old stuff is junk."

Val had a Plan B if he still didn't want to part with it, and would suggest he keep it in his study or offer to have them reupholstered. She could live with that, and it would keep him happy.

She came up with colorful ideas for the kitchen, and knew exactly what she wanted for the walls and windows. She felt very happy and secure planning their future home life together. Saturday night, she called her mother and told her all about the house and the furniture they'd purchased that day, and about her plans to move to Ireland.

"Mom, I need a change. Since his work is here, that's what is easiest for him. I'm planning on keeping the condo on Commonwealth Avenue, though. I'll be home frequently, and Warren will stay there during his layovers in Boston. You won't hate me will you? If I leave, I mean?"

Grace chuckled.

"No, silly. But I will miss you! I'll just have to take advantage of those family flying discounts of your husband's!"

Valerie assured her that she could and would often.

"Honey, as it is, when you're working, I don't see you for weeks on end. It'll all work out. No worries."

She assured her daughter.

"Have you and Warren come up with a wedding date yet?"

"Right now, I'm busying myself with decorating ... fun stuff. It's a great diversion, Mom. We'll talk about it soon though."

Her mother was excited for her.

"Well, you have a great time, and I'll see you when you get home."

"Thanks, Mom. Love you!"

"Love you, too, Val."

Warren and Val went to church together on Sunday, but she seemed preoccupied and fidgety. She was like a little kid that couldn't wait to get out.

"I don't know what it was about that place today, Warren. I looked at that priest and didn't believe a word he said. I mean he could be the nicest guy in the world. But I looked around at all the kids staring up at him like he was God, and I just wanted to scream.

"You hypocrites! Didn't Jesus call them hypocrites?"

Warren thought about it.

"No. He actually called the Pharisees in his day 'White Washed Sepulchers'."

Val was impressed.

"Wow! How did you remember that?"

He shrugged.

"I don't know, maybe it was from one of those movies. I only remember him calling them that."

"Warren, I know that all priests aren't pedophiles. I get that in my head. But I'm afraid to trust them in my heart."

Warren nodded in understanding.

Val called Glynnis and Peggy when they got home and asked how they were doing. They assured her that they were fine, and asked her how her talk with Sean went, and if she left any bloody implements behind that could be used as evidence.

"Well, I think I scared the daylights out of him. He's admitting himself into a clinic this week. He seemed truly sorry. Though I still can't stomach being in the same room with him right now."

She went on to tell Glynnis how she'd threatened him with the tape recorder.

Glynnis seemed a little nervous.

"Val, I could never tell my dad. He was having chest pain after defending Peggy a little while ago. This would kill him."

Val reassured her.

"I know, Glynn. I wouldn't ask that of you. I just needed something to make him take what I was saying seriously and it worked."

Val asked if they'd have any time to come over for a few days to visit while Warren was away flying. Peggy said she really had to work in the gallery, but suggested that perhaps Glynnis could head over for a few days. It would do her some good to get away for a little while.

Glynnis told her she'd love to come and see her future home. Both Glynnis and Peggy were thrilled to hear that Valerie would soon be on their side of the Atlantic. Glynnis said she'd check into shuttle flights in the morning.

"I could come out as early as tomorrow and leave Wednesday. How does that sound?"

Val told her that would be great. She would drive Warren to the airport on Monday so that she could have use of his car.

"You can help me pick out some artwork for the walls!"

Glynnis told her that she was sure Peggy had something wonderful for her as a housewarming gift planned.

The women hung up, and Val jumped onto the bed next to Warren.

"She's coming over!"

He was reading a book.

"Who?"

She took the book out of his hands.

"Glynnis! She's flying over tomorrow. I may just wait for her shuttle when I drop you off. You don't mind if I use your car, do you?"

He shook his head no reminding her.

"You'll need to give me the keys to the condo. I might as well start my new routine and stay at your place this trip."

Val got up to get them right then, so she wouldn't forget, and then bounced back onto the bed.

"Are you happy?"

Warren kissed the top of her head as she reclined in his arms.

"What kind of question is that? Of course, I am! And you?"

She smiled and kissed his hand.

"Of course! You've been my anchor. I'm thrilled we're engaged. I can't imagine my life without you now."

He found her sentiments touching, and half-jokingly suggested.

"Why don't we just run off and get married tomorrow?"

Val thought about it.

"You know, if things were different, I just might do that. But I can't deny my mom this once-in-a-lifetime event. She's waited so long for something like this. I couldn't do that to her, Warren. Our wedding will be a huge bright spot in her life. Dare I say it will help get her through in some ways. She'll enjoy keeping busy helping me plan our wedding. It'll give her something to look forward to and hope for."

"My mother would probably never speak to me again either. Speaking of which, I'd better call her. We've got the engagement party Friday night, remember? I'll be home early Friday morning."

Val nodded, and as he reached for the phone, she whispered.

"Let me hear what she sounds like."

She put her ear to the phone when Warren started talking.

"Hi, Mam. It's me. What do you mean, 'ME WHO'? It's Warren, your fifth child, remember?"

Val stifled a laugh.

His mother talked quickly and cheerfully and asked after her future daughter-in-law. Warren had fun with her.

"Well, now let me tell you, she's right here beside me, on my BED, Mother. Can you believe it? Would you like to say hello?"

Val whacked him playfully for revealing their forbidden location and accepted the phone.

"Hello? Hi, Mrs. Cahill. It's nice to talk to you, too, finally. I'm standing up now, no longer on the bed. He's a brat for telling you that!"

After they were done chuckling, Warren's mother expressed her condolences about Caroline's passing.

"That was a horrible tragedy, dear. I'm sorry for your loss."

Val thanked her for the beautiful floral arrangement, at the same time winking at Warren, who gave her a grateful nod.

"I'm looking forward to meeting you this week, too."

Warren listened in as Mrs. Cahill offered.

"If you find you need anything while Warren's away, just have him write down my number for you, and we can come right over."

Valerie thanked her for her offer and said good-bye. She handed the phone back to Warren.

"Yes, Mother. She is wonderful ... in every way."

Val made an "aw" sound as he was hanging up.

It was after eight Sunday evening when Val asked Warren.

"So where are your flight pajamas?"

He brought her downstairs and showed her to a closet off the living room. His uniforms were all neatly arranged in plastic bags.

"You have them dry-cleaned?"

She had a dejected look.

He nodded.

"Yep. The airline pays for it. Not bad, eh? You won't have any ironing to do."

Val purposely stamped her foot like a kid.

"That's the one domestic thing I do well!"

He chuckled.

"Tell you what, while I'm gone, I'll leave you a few shirts to iron so you won't feel totally useless. How does that sound?"

She mocked him jokingly.

"Oh, Mr. Cahill, you're just too kind."

They went to bed, she being on the giving end of the backrub this time. He fell asleep within minutes. When she heard him snoring lightly, she whispered.

"Warren, you're just too easy."

She pulled the covers up over his shoulders and headed back to her room, falling asleep quickly.

Valerie got up at six o'clock on Warren's first day back to work. She went down to the kitchen and collected more milk off the front steps. It was starting to pile up in the fridge. They had more than they needed, and she was afraid it might go bad before they drank it all, especially with him being gone for a few days and her being the only one home.

She made coffee and then decided to bring him breakfast in bed. She got a few eggs out of the refrigerator and made him dropped-eggs-on-toast.

It was one of her favorites. She brought the tray, complete with juice and steaming hot coffee with fresh cream, up to his bedroom. As she opened the curtains to let the sunlight in, Warren turned over and put the pillow over his head.

Cheerfully, she announced.

"Darling, it's time to wake up. I made you breakfast."

Warren took the pillow off his head.

"What? I didn't hear the smoke alarm go off!"

She banged a pillow over his head.

"Oh, you are a brat!"

Warren reached out for her.

"Just kidding, sweetheart. You're spoiling me. Tell me, will you still do these things for me once we're old and married?"

Val pretended to mull over that thought.

"Hmmmm ... well, we are already old. But, yes, I will. I'll have nothing else to do but dote on you. I won't have a job!"

She set the tray up across his lap and took a bite of his toast. Warren sat up.

"Well, I could ask Maggie and Brian to hire you on to help with the cows. They could always use another set of hands."

Val reached under the sheets and pinched him.

"These hands can be used in other ways, my dear."

Warren nearly choked on his juice.

"Okay, okay, forget the cows!"

He took a sip of his coffee, and then asked a question that crossed his mind.

"Do you think you'll be bored, not working?"

Val shook her head adamantly.

"No. I'd like to get pregnant soon. I'm not getting any younger, you know. I'm thirty-five! I could give birth to my own grandchildren if I wait much longer!"

Warren laughed at her comment.

"So let's talk about a timeframe for the wedding."

Val had given it some thought already.

"Well, I love Chatham in the fall. I'd like to have our wedding at my mother's house, but nothing too elaborate. With the backyard overlooking the ocean, it's a perfect backdrop. We could have a tent set up. We'll have it catered, and I thought about having an old fashioned New England clambake down on the beach. How does that sound to you? We could stay at the Chatham Bars Inn for our wedding night. It's close by and that's where we could put up most of our out-of-town guests. Remember how lovely it was when we went to dinner there? Our guests would feel like royalty!"

"You've got it all planned out. This is great! How long does it take to actually pull something like this together?"

Val grinned.

"With me, my mom, and Auntie Sheila at the helm? Two weeks ... tops!"

He laughed.

"You're kidding me."

Val assured him that it wouldn't take very long at all.

"I envision about a hundred people or so. Many coming are family, friends, members of the ensemble, and a few people from work. What do you think? What would you like? You can invite anyone you want."

Warren said he'd need to make sure that his family all had their passports ready to go. Otherwise, it might take them an additional month. He was sure all but one of his brothers had theirs already. That was his only concern, as he'd like for them all to be there.

"Have you given any thought to a date? I'm in no way rushing you. I'll need to clear the time with work and give them some notice. I want you to feel comfortable, though. If you need more time to work through Caroline and Sean, I can wait."

Val drank the last sip of juice.

594

"To be honest, Warren, I'd like to get married soon, in September. It's quiet on the Cape after all the summer residents and tourists are gone. Indian summer is beautiful. I'd say the middle to end of September. It's only June. I'll give my resignation in August. It'll give me and my mom time to get out invitations. I know she'll love putting this together. Do you think that's too soon?"

"No, love. Like I said, I'd marry you tomorrow."

They chose Saturday, September 23rd as their wedding date. Val wanted to make sure it was after the anniversary of her father's death, which was in August.

Warren looked at the clock and told her he had to hit the shower.

"Do you mind us getting pregnant right away?"

"Nope. You want to start now?"

She shushed him.

"Wouldn't it be perfect if I conceived on our wedding night?"

He pretended to think hard about that.

"Could be a long night!"

Warren called up to her from downstairs to tell her that Glynnis had left a message. She was on her way, taking the 9:00 a.m. shuttle from London.

Val started rushing around, and offered to drive. They parked in general parking and walked into the terminal together. Warren looked incredibly handsome in his uniform. She was aware of the admiring glances from other women and it made her proud to be with him.

Since they'd gotten there early for his flight to the US, Warren walked with her to Glynnis's gate. She was surprised when she got off the plane, and they were both there waiting for her. They hugged and she gave Warren a kiss on the cheek.

"My! Don't we look handsome!"

Glynnis complimented him. He rolled his eyes.

"There really is something about a man in uniform, isn't there?"

She looked at Val, who glanced up at her handsome fiancé.

"There certainly is ..."

Warren shook his head.

"You're both great for my ego, but I must get going, ladies. Have a good time. Make sure to drive on the right side of the road!"

Valerie gave him a long and lingering embrace. Her eyes teared. She hated saying good-bye.

"Oh, love, don't do that. I'll see you in a few days."

He kissed her warmly and Glynnis turned away to give them their privacy.

"I love you, Mr. Cahill. Safe landings."

He tipped his hat to her and turned away, wheeling his flight case behind him.

"He's such a great guy, Val. I'm so happy for you."

Val hugged her friend, excited to have some time with her.

"C'mon ... I want you to see my new house!"

They practically ran out to the car park.

Val felt exhilarated. She watched as flights took off behind her in the rearview mirror and said a quiet prayer for Warren's safety. She and Glynnis talked animatedly all the way back to the house.

After the house tour, the women made a shopping list for food. Val begged Glynnis to teach her how to cook a few of her favorite dishes, like ginger beef and a delicious yet simple chicken pesto dish. Val talked about the plans for their wedding.

"This September? That's just a few months from now!"

Glynnis realized.

"Yes. I don't want to wait, Glynn. I love him dearly and we both want to start a family. There's been so much sadness lately; this is a real high-light for me."

Glynnis agreed that they all needed a happy occasion to look forward to. Val told her about the engagement party his family was having for them on

Friday. They talked about gowns and where Val thought she might purchase her dress. Warren called later that evening from her condo to say that he'd made it in safely. She heard him scratch the bow across her violin.

"You forgot to put it in the case."

She thought for a moment.

"I thought I did put it away ... it's always reappearing, it seems."

She told him that she loved him and that she looked forward to seeing him at the end of the week.

After two fun-filled days of shopping, taking long walks, and girl-talks lasting well into the night, Val reluctantly dropped Glynnis back at the airport on Wednesday morning. Glynnis was anxious to get back to help Peggy with the gallery. Business was booming and their friends, Joel and Carlos, were coming over to help Peggy design the second floor of the gallery. Glynnis wanted to be there to help her pick out lighting fixtures.

"We'll see you soon, hon. Call us and we'll work out the dress issue."

Glynnis reminded Val, who assured her she would.

When Val pulled back into the driveway, she noticed more milk bottles on the steps. As she put them away, she realized she had six full bottles of milk, with the open one only half gone. *This is a sin to waste*, she thought and decided to go visit with her neighbors the next morning and work out a new delivery schedule.

Thursday morning, she took four of the unopened bottles out of the refrigerator and placed them carefully in a basket and walked down the hill to visit with Brian, Maggie, and Eileen. Although it was only eight thirty, she knew they got up much earlier than that every morning. Maggie was happy to see her coming, but curious about the bottles in her basket.

"Everything okay with these?"

"Oh, fine, except that I'm afraid they'll go to waste. I had six bottles collecting in the refrigerator and only one that's opened. I think we'd do well with one bottle every two days. Until we have children, of course, then we'll just buy one of your cows!"

"Ok, I'll take them off your hands."

Maggie good-naturedly offered to carry a few of the bottles back inside for her.

"Come in and have a cup of tea. I'm due for a break."

Val followed her into the large, brightly lit kitchen. Eileen ran up to her and gave her a hug.

"Hi there, sweetie!"

Val put her arm around the little girl's shoulders. She looked at Val's ring longingly.

"Can I try it on again?"

Val smiled and nodded. She held out her hand and told her to make a fist once it was on. She did and admired it like it was the first time. She sat on Val's lap while the women talked.

"So how are the wedding plans coming along?"

Eileen offered her ring back and jumped down to chase after a tiny kitten bouncing along in the living room.

"We decided on September 23rd. We'll have it at my mother's house back in the States. I'm planning to give my notice at work in August. I can't wait."

Maggie listened with excitement.

"It's going to be such a different life for you over here. Do you really think you'll like it?"

Val replied without hesitation.

"I'm sure I will. I need the change. It'll be good for me."

Maggie smiled.

"It's a thrilling time, isn't it? Setting up house and planning a wedding."

Val set her cup down, showing her excitement.

"I'm enjoying picking out things for the house. We bought furniture last weekend! I'm having it delivered at the end of August."

Eileen bounded in, carrying a darling black and white kitten. Val scooped the tiny fur ball into her hands.

"Oh, this one is just adorable!"

Maggie told her she had five of those "adorable" kittens to find homes for. They wouldn't be ready to leave their mother for a few more weeks.

"Maybe I can talk Warren into having us take one! I don't know if he likes cats. But I love them!"

She nuzzled the tiny animal.

Eileen took her by the hand into the living room to the basket where the others were nursing.

"See, their mommy is feeding them."

Val bent to look more closely at them, and her heart was drawn to a tiny gray one.

"Oh, this other one is sweet, too. If I can convince Warren, do you think I may have that one when they're ready? Warren could keep it up at the house, but he'd have to bring it back down here when he flies until I'm back here in September permanently. Do you think that might work?"

Maggie nodded her head.

"Not a problem!"

She patted her daughter's head.

"Well, that's one down ... four more to go!"

Val told her she'd let her get back to work. On her way back up the hill, she stopped to collect the eggs. She had over a dozen of them. She needed to find a constructive way to use them. There were far too many for them to eat for breakfast and she made a note to get a cookbook with egg recipes in it. She had to laugh as she looked at what she was doing. Who would have ever imagined that she'd hang up her business suits and heels to carry dirty eggs in her sweater? But she wouldn't change it for the world!

She took extra care in putting on her makeup and doing her hair when Warren returned Friday morning. She put on a white linen skirt with a flattering, soft pink and white tunic top before she drove out to the airport to meet him. Glancing at her watch, she realized it was only 9:30AM in the morning, yet she'd already done so much it felt like noon.

She stood at the window as the ground crew guided Warren's plane in with their orange lights. Val's heart was bursting as he waved to her through the tiny window of the cockpit. She watched while all the passengers filed out, knowing it would take him a little longer to log everything. She sat once everyone was gone and looked about the busy airport. This was his life. It was everything she dreamed of, and she gave God a silent "thank you." She found it ironic that she actually did wind up being with a man who was a pilot. *He does work in mysterious ways.*

Warren finally appeared, rolling his flight case behind him. He set it down as she stood and gave him a huge hug.

"God, I've missed you."

He said.

They kissed as his copilot quickly moved past them.

"Congratulations!"

He called back, tipping his hat to Valerie.

"Thank you!"

She replied, waving, and turned back to Warren.

"Are you ready to go home?"

He nodded thankfully and took off his cap, placing it on her head.

Val talked endlessly about her visit with Glynnis, and the plans she and her mom were making for the wedding, and how she worked out a schedule with Maggie for their egg and milk situation. Warren laughed at her excitement, silently grateful to see her so happy. It confirmed for him that Ireland would be a good change for her.

"Oh, by the way, do you like cats?"

"Well, I grew up with three of them. They keep the field mice out."

Val told him about Maggie's kittens.

"Warren, they are the most adorable little things and I saw one that I liked, but I wanted to check and make sure you weren't allergic to them. I always had a cat growing up. They're wonderful pets."

He didn't object, but was concerned about not being there to take care of it when they were away.

"I've got that all worked out with Maggie. The kittens won't be ready to leave their mother for another two or three weeks. Maggie said she'd watch ours until I got back in September. You can take it when it's ready and just cart it down to Maggie's house when you leave on a trip."

Warren promised her he'd walk over with her to see their new addition at some point. At the moment, all he wanted to do was get home and relax.

Back at home, Val looked at him sympathetically.

"You're not faring too well with the abstinence thing, I'm afraid."

He made a mock pout and shook his head, then kissed her while she helped unbutton his jacket and shirt.

"Mr. Cahill, you are such a turn-on in this uniform ..."

He smirked at her.

Val gave him a backrub after he showered, and he quickly fell asleep. She lay next to him and closed her eyes, enjoying the sound of his breathing. Not ready for sleep yet herself, she quietly got up and went downstairs in search of the ironing board. She wanted to iron her dress for their party that night.

The phone rang and she jumped to answer it, so it wouldn't wake Warren up. Her blood ran cold when she heard Sean's voice.

"Val, I just thought I'd call to let you know that I've checked into the Knightsbridge Treatment Center in London. I'll be here a couple of months. I can't talk for long. I'm only allowed one call a day. They're pretty strict about that. Anyway, you can call your granny and Aunt Siobhan now."

"So you talked to them? How are they doing?"

Sean didn't say anything at first.

"Not well. I'm sporting stitches over my right eye from a punch Siobhan gave me. A great left hook that one has ..."

Val could easily picture her doing that.

"I'll call them in a few minutes. I sincerely hope you get the help you need there. Good-bye, Sean."

She hung up the phone. Her heart was racing. She looked at the clock; she had enough time to go to her grandmother's house while Warren slept.

She made it there in twenty minutes, and walked slowly up the steps, using her own key to open the door. Her grandmother was sitting at the kitchen table, her hands folded; shoulders slumped, looking blankly out the window. She turned when she heard the door close, and, to Valerie, she looked ten years older than she had the week before. She hurried over to embrace her grandmother, who cried softly, unable to speak.

"Granny, I'm so sorry. I never expected anything like this."

Her grandmother had always been as tough as nails, but the devastating impact of the latest news shook her.

"I could kill him, Valerie. Yet, on the other hand, I want to kill the priest who did this to him. I swear if it takes every pound I have, I'll track him down and prosecute! My poor Caroline!"

Siobhan walked in and joined the women.

"This just gets worse and worse, doesn't it? When will it ever stop?"

She sat down, dejected.

Val went into the bathroom to get them all tissues. Despite the direness of the situation, she tried to shed a positive light on it.

"I know this is hard for all of us. I wanted to strangle him when I got here. Thank God Warren was with me, or I may have."

Siobhan spotted her ring and held her hand.

"Oh, Valerie, it's beautiful! Look, Mam!"

Her grandmother held out her hand to see.

"It is a gorgeous ring, lovey. Congratulations."

Val thanked them and went back to what she was trying to say.

"Sean is getting the help he needs, which is a good thing. I have to be honest with you though. I'm not in a place where I can forgive him right now. Maybe, in time, but I just can't right now. I love you two to pieces and I don't want this to separate us. We've got to keep our family together."

Granny patted her hand.

"Valerie Jean, we love you. That'll never change. I'm just so ashamed of my son's actions. I don't know what to do about all of this. What bothers me the most is that I can't apologize to Caroline ... I can't!"

She started to cry again.

Val hugged her tightly and cried with her.

"Granny, it's not your fault, and Caroline is in a place where she can't be hurt anymore. We can take comfort in that."

She looked at Aunt Siobhan, who just stared out the window.

"I think you just need to give this time. It's such a shock for us all right now. I dread telling my mother."

Siobhan shook her head.

"Neil would have killed him."

Val replied.

"I don't think he would have tried it if Daddy was alive, but I think your reaction was pretty close to what his would have been. I hear you pack a pretty good punch!"

Siobhan was embarrassed.

"I just reacted. I wasn't even thinking ... something just welled up inside me, and it had nowhere else to go but in his miserable face!"

She quickly glanced at her mother and apologized for being insensitive.

Val stayed and had a cup of tea with them and told them of her wedding plans. Granny's eyes brightened when she heard that her only remaining granddaughter was moving to Ireland, and Siobhan was happy about it, too.

"Granny, I have to tell you that I'm not planning on inviting Sean to my wedding. Call it a form of self-preservation, but I don't want him there."

Her grandmother nodded in understanding.

"It's your day, love. It's okay."

Val finished her tea and realized she'd need to rush to get back in time. She told them about Warren's family engagement party that night.

"I've got to wake him up. I picked him up at the airport this morning. The poor man is exhausted."

Siobhan added.

"Not from flying, I'm sure ..."

Val gave her a quick smile and chuckled.

"Oh, you think you know it all, do you? It just so happens that we're 'keeping it holy' until we get married. Truth be told, it's killing us both!"

Siobhan laughed out loud. Granny smiled at her.

"Good for you, Val. It's nice to know someone is doing something right in this family! Enjoy your life, child. We've only got one to live!"

She kissed her grandmother and aunt and left. She sent another prayer heavenward for God to give them peace during their latest trial.

When she got home, she was surprised to see Warren up and about. She gave him the latest update.

"Sean called. He said he checked into a place in London. I wanted to talk to Granny and Siobhan."

He was concerned for them.

"How'd they handle it?"

Leaning against the counter, she looked at the ground, then at him.

"Well, they're in shock, of course, and are trying to decide whether to continue to love him, or hate him. I think a little of both right now, though Siobhan punched him and he has stitches above his eye and quite a shiner, from what I understand."

Warren rolled his eyes.

"That Siobhan's a tough one, eh? I best watch myself around you Callaghan women. At least, she didn't go for the butter knife option!"

They went upstairs to get ready for the party. Val packed her suitcase in order to be done with that task before her early morning flight. The two weeks had flown by, and already she felt immense sadness at the thought of leaving Warren the next day.

Mr. and Mrs. Cahill were kind and gracious. They commented to their son about how beautiful his future bride was. Val was introduced to all of his brothers and their wives and children. She felt she'd never keep track of all their names.

"Don't worry. They'll grow on you ... like moss."

Warren used Father Bruce's analogy.

There was a lot of laughter, music, and many toasts on their behalf. Val opened quite a few gifts. What she treasured most, however, was a family Bible that had been given to them, with their names already embossed on the front cover.

"We can add the wedding date now that we know it. I'll just rewrap it and give it to you again after the wedding."

Everyone laughed at Warren's brother Conor's comment. His wife slapped his arm.

"You'll do no such thing!"

The children were running in and out, taking all sorts of sweets off the tables. Val sat and talked with her future sisters-in-law. They wanted to hear all about her home in Boston and more details about Cape Cod. Val described her mother's house and the layout of the backyard overlooking the ocean.

"Oh, it sounds just lovely. We've not been on a trip in years. It'll be like a second honeymoon. The Cape sounds enchanting!"

Kerry exclaimed.

Warren was working on a special discount with his airline to bring his entire family and their children over. The group would number over thirty.

The evening was enjoyable. It was getting late when Warren announced to the group that he had to get Val home, as she had an early morning flight on Saturday. Valerie kissed everyone good-bye and thanked her future mother-in-law, telling her that she'd be calling her the following week to get addresses for the invitations.

"I'll put the list together tomorrow and get that off to you."

Val wrote down her address in Boston, and they copied it and passed it around to everyone.

Val and Warren talked excitedly all the way home.

"They're good people, Warren. I love your family already."

They went straight to bed when they got home.

Warren seemed rather quiet to Val the next morning. She wondered if he was upset about something. He told her yes, he was.

"I've grown to like having you here with me. I can't think of a better feeling in the world than seeing your smiling face at the airport or having you putter about the house."

"We'll manage, hon, and we'll actually get to see each other a little more now - when you stay over at the condo during your Boston lay-overs. Besides, you'll be happy to know that I've left you a whole list of projects for the house. You've got plenty of painting to do!"

"Ah, yes ... painting ... very good!"

He rolled his eyes and drew her in for a kiss. She reminded him.

"Don't forget to look in on our kitten. I didn't get a chance to get down there to show you. She's gray and looks like a pussy willow. I'm calling her 'Pearl'. Eileen will point her out to you."

He chuckled.

"We're going to have a cat named Pearl?"

She nodded emphatically.

"Yes. She's pearl gray!"

They drove quietly, holding hands on the way to the airport.

The announcement to board came all too soon. Val waved good-bye sadly and blew him a kiss. He stood at the window and watched her plane take off. He turned looking around the airport and thinking about their time together, and hating the thought of going home to his empty house.

Chapter Fifty-One

Chatham, Cape Cod, Massachusetts, Summer 1998

FATHER ROB COUGHLIN SAT PATIENTLY in the living room of the bishop's residence awaiting the car that would take him to Chatham, Massachusetts. The afternoon was clear and breezy, the temperature in the high seventies. His bags were carried outside and the driver opened the car door for him. Gathering his robes about him, he acknowledged him with a condescending nod and stiffly thanked him.

Heavy traffic slowed his journey. Rob grumbled to himself in the back seat. The driver, having heard only the tone of his displeasure, offered to make a rest stop for him, if needed. Peering over his glasses as if being disturbed, Father Coughlin flatly thanked him and went back to reading his book, Twisted, by Jeffery Deaver, book one in a collection of murderous short stories.

He set his reading glasses down as they crossed over the Cape Cod Canal. The view commanded his attention. He sensed a different spirit prevailed here, and he couldn't quite wrap his arms around what it was that made him uncomfortable. The canal was filled with boats; it being a perfect day for sailing. He smiled to himself, looking forward to discovering more about this new and coveted tourist destination to which he'd been assigned.

The driver eventually pulled up to the front of a stately residence and opened his passenger's door. The back of St. Bridget's Rectory overlooked an estuary and wildlife reserve. The open marsh stretched for miles behind the property. Turning around, he listened to the wind rushing through the high grass. The sound of flocking geese could be heard in the distance as the sun began its descent. Rob stopped to enjoy the warmth of the sun while his bags were being lifted and placed on the front steps. The door opened and a priest, about his age, came out to welcome him warmly.

"It is a pleasure to meet you, Father Coughlin. Welcome to Cape Cod."

Father Bruce Moriarty reached out in a friendly manner and shook his cold hand.

"Let me help you with those."

Father Bruce offered to carry his bags into the hallway.

"I'm sorry more aren't here to greet you."

He apologized.

"It's a rather busy time of year around here. Lots going on now with all the summer weddings. Soon enough, all the tourists will head back home and we'll have our sanity back!"

The new priest didn't respond.

He invited Father Coughlin out back to rest for a moment from his long ride, and poured him a glass of iced tea. They sat comfortably on cushioned patio chairs on the back deck overlooking the estuary. The patio was lined with a variety of colorful flowers. A small wind chime dangled in the breeze, occasionally emitting a delicate tune.

"Would you like more ice, Father Coughlin?"

Father Bruce asked graciously. Rob nodded, but didn't extend an offer to let him call him by his first name. He liked the way Father Bruce continued to address him by his title. He accepted the glass without thanks and asked a few questions about the surrounding seascape. Father Bruce gladly pointed out some of the local fauna and flora in their view.

"We lose a few feet of land to erosion each year due to the storms. Some of our families' homes sit dangerously close to the cliff's edge. For some, one more storm, and their home may land in the ocean. New England has seen its share of nasty hurricanes. Let's pray we don't have another one for a while."

Rob agreed, raising his glass.

"Father, I was hoping that I might ask a favor of you. I know you're just arriving and want to get settled in before you begin your duties. However, there is a matter that just came up in which I'd like to ask your help."

Wanting to show the priest his willingness to assist, Father Coughlin nodded.

"Yes, of course. What is it?"

"There is a dear family in our parish."

Father Bruce explained.

"They've suffered a number of significant losses over the years. Most recently, the loss of Grace Callaghan's twenty-eight-year-old daughter, Caroline, only a few weeks ago. It dealt a horrible blow to the entire family ... and to me. I've been staying in regular contact visiting with the family as they are like my own."

Rob remembered the familiar name from the financial contributions sheet. Feigning a sympathetic nod, he commented flatly.

"I can only imagine their grief."

Father Bruce went on to explain more.

"As if burying her youngest daughter wasn't enough, her late husband's anniversary Mass is coming up in August. I typically preside over the Mass and then join her for tea at the house afterwards. It's kind of our tradition. They're a delightful family. Grace is a talented piano player and has been a long-standing member of our ensemble. Her eldest daughter, Valerie, is an accomplished violinist, and just announced some good news: she's engaged and getting married soon."

"I've been asked, at the last minute, to fill in for a morning wedding on Saturday and must travel. The pastor who was to preside got called home due to an illness in his family. I know it's rather short notice, but would you be willing to serve Mass this Sunday and then perhaps visit with Mrs. Callaghan afterwards – just to check in on her? I'm sure she'd love to meet you. I'm not sure what time I'll make it back on Sunday."

Father Coughlin wanted to seize this opportunity.

"Of course. It would be my pleasure."

Father Bruce explained gratefully.

"I've left a message on her answering machine explaining the situation. She'll understand and will welcome you with open arms."

Father Coughlin assured him that he'd be happy to help out.

"I came at the right time, I see."

Father Bruce smiled.

"You sure did. Like I said, it gets pretty crazy around here during the summer months. But wait until fall, when the tourists leave. Life goes back to a normal pace, and it's relatively peaceful here again. You can actually drive to the store and be back within minutes. If you try it now, you're lucky to get back in an hour!"

They continued their conversation about the pros and cons of living in a resort community.

Rob finished his iced tea, and Father Bruce showed him to his room. The first thing Rob noticed was that the walls were wallpapered in different floral pastels and seascape designs. It had a French country look, a refreshing change from the pale pink stucco walls to which he'd grown accustomed. Father Bruce set his bags down in front of a door at the end of the hall.

"This was my room, but I wanted you to be able to enjoy the view."

Father Bruce offered, handing him the key.

Entering the room, Rob was struck by the panoramic view of the sun setting over the estuary. There were windows on three sides of the room. A wave of peace and tranquility rushed over him, and he smiled as he turned to thank Father Bruce for his sacrifice.

"This is not an easy room to relinquish. Thank you. I'm sure I'll find it very comfortable here."

Father Bruce left him alone to unpack, and went to prepare his sermon for Saturday's marriage ceremony.

He was getting tired of weddings, yet was truly looking forward to Valerie's. Grace had called him that morning to make sure that the church was available on September 23rd. Father Bruce had personally penned Val's wedding date into the book. He assured Grace that he wouldn't miss it for the world, and would prepare a special musical piece for Valerie and Warren with the help of the ensemble. He asked her to keep that a secret, and she assured him she would.

He'd contacted the members of the ensemble on Monday to arrange practice dates. He felt a twinge of sadness, thinking of Valerie leaving permanently for Ireland. He found it uplifting that Warren had come and asked him to bless Valerie's engagement ring. It was an elegant ring for a beautiful woman. He prayed in earnest for them as a couple, asking God's blessing upon them for a long life of health and happiness.

With the door to his room closed, Rob pulled his brother's remains out of his suitcase and set the box on top of his bureau. The bureau was adorned with a lace doily, overhanging the dresser on both sides. Rob turned the doily over and saw that it was made in Ireland.

He admired the pleasant scenic paintings which hung on the walls, and noted the fact that the cross was hung, not above the bed, but above the doorway to his room. There was a new, scented candle set on the bedside table. A chair was invitingly positioned in the corner with a handsome floor lamp beside it. Laid out on the floor was a soft, cream-colored area carpet, which beckoned him to take off his shoes and rub his feet in its plush comfort. He sat on the edge of the bed to receive the final confirmation of relative luxury. Peering under the bottom sheet, he saw that he'd be sleeping on a Sealy mattress; it was one of the most comfortable beds he'd ever had the pleasure of laying on.

He smelled a delicious aroma drifting up from the kitchen below. Roast beef was on the menu for dinner. He'd not had a meal like that in ages, and it was one of his favorite dishes. So far, he'd been very impressed with his new church. He laid back on the pillow with his hands behind his head thinking about how he was going to get rid of Father Bruce Moriarty ...

*   *   *

Val's plane had a tough time landing at Logan Airport. High winds made it necessary for the pilot to pass the runway twice before landing, causing Val to see firsthand what Warren had been talking about regarding wind shear. She gave a prayer of thanks when she finally touched down safely Saturday night.

She'd slept on the plane, so she wasn't too tired. She wasn't looking forward to the long drive down to the Cape, but she wanted to spend some time with her mother. She took a taxi to her house in Boston first, planning to leave her bag there before picking up her car and heading out. Heaving the suitcase on to the bed, she noticed a card on her pillow.

"Darling, when you see this we'll be apart. I miss you already and love you immensely. I can't wait for you to come home and be with me for good. All my love, Warren."

Her eyes teared reading his thoughtful note. Oh, how she loved that man!

Val looked for her mother's house keys, finding them in the Lazy Susan on the kitchen table. She also grabbed a few of her favorite CDs for the ride. She enjoyed violin sonatas and partitas, finding them peaceful to listen to while she drove. Depending on what mood she was in, she also enjoyed Billy Joel and Cat Stevens.

It was dark when she crossed the Cape Cod Canal. The June air was a little cool, and the winds had finally started to die down. Tomorrow it would be up in the eighties with a slight chance of rain, according to the radio weather report.

Val pulled onto the crushed seashell driveway, recalling an accident she had as a child in which she stubbed her toe, getting a piece of a seashell embedded deep underneath her toenail. She remembered screaming from the pain. It quickly became infected and she had to have it removed in the emergency room at their local hospital and was on an antibiotic for a week. Her father made it a point then to remind her to always wear her shoes when walking on the driveway. She loved the familiar sound of the car wheels driving over the crunchy particles. It was strictly a Cape Cod beach sound.

A light was on in the living room and Val saw her mother's shadow move across the room to the front door. The familiar crash of the screen door was heard when Grace ran out to greet her daughter. Val quickly climbed out of the car and hugged her mother. She proudly showed off her new engagement ring.

"Oh, Val! It's gorgeous!"

Grace gushed.

"He has great taste!"

Val put her hands on her hips.

"Of course he does, Mom. He chose me!"

Her mother laughed. It was so good to see each other. Val sat at the kitchen table as her mother bustled about, heating up the teakettle.

"Do you want something to eat? You must be starved."

Val shrugged.

"Sort of. I'll get it, Mom. You sit and relax."

Val poked her head in the refrigerator and popped open the lids on a few of the containers.

"You have a ton of food in here still."

Grace sat back.

"It's not gone to waste. I can tell you that. I've had so many people dropping by and they all bring food with them! By the way, tomorrow our new pastor is coming to visit after Mass."

Val looked at her quizzically.

"I didn't know we were getting a new pastor. Father Bruce isn't going anywhere. Is he?"

Her mother assured her that Father Bruce wasn't going anywhere soon, to her knowledge.

"I don't know all the particulars, only that the Archdiocese has assigned him here. The church has grown, and Father Bruce can't do it all. We don't know much about the new pastor, except that he came from out west somewhere."

Val took a fork out of the drawer and ate cold pasta from a container. Her mother asked her about the engagement party. Val told her all about Warren's brothers and what a large family he had.

"My future mother-in-law is very nice. She's really tall, Mom! I think she must be at least five foot ten, five foot eleven. I think you'll hit it off great with her. She's quite the homemaker, having raised five boys ... God-bless- her!"

Grace laughed at her daughter's use of the Irish expression.

"You talk like you've lived there for years already. You'll pick up their brogue quickly you know."

Val waved the fork at her mother.

"You know, Warren told me that same thing."

She set the empty container in the sink and told her mom she'd wash it in the morning.

"Mom, tomorrow I need to talk to you about a few things. I'm tired right now and just want to go to bed. But maybe some time in the afternoon we can chat, okay?"

Her mother nodded, assuming that Val wanted to go over wedding plans. Grace kissed her levelheaded daughter goodnight and told her not to bother to set the alarm for Mass in the morning, encouraging her to sleep in.

"Thanks Mom. I think I'll do that. The trip is quickly catching up with me."

The sound of percolating coffee followed by the mouthwatering smell of her mother's blueberry muffins woke her late Sunday. She heard voices down in the kitchen. Her stomach growled. She looked at the clock. It was 1:00PM. I've slept half the day away, she thought. Pushing the hair off her face, she quickly got up, only to get dizzy and sit back down again.

"Head rush ..."

Val mumbled to herself and got up slower. After showering and brushing her teeth, she put on a pair of shorts and a T-shirt. She dreaded talking to her mother about her uncle Sean. Her mom seemed so happy because she was there visiting. Val hated to break her heart yet again. *Damn him!* She muttered to herself.

She walked downstairs and swung around the banister like she'd done a million times as a kid. She and Caroline often got into trouble for sliding down the long banister when they thought no one was looking. Caroline once knocked the finial off at the end, falling on her behind. Val was laughing to herself while sauntering into the kitchen.

She stopped suddenly in the presence of the heavy priest balancing on the bar stool at the counter. His eyes shifted quickly from mother to daughter. He didn't smile, offer his hand, or even get up. Her mother graciously introduced him.

"And there she is ... sleeping beauty."

She greeted Valerie with a kiss.

Turning toward the priest, she continued.

"Valerie, I'd like to introduce you to Father Rob Coughlin, our new pastor at St. Bridget's."

Val couldn't help but stare at the overfed man barely able to fit on the stool. His name sounded familiar. She recovered and walked over to extend her hand reluctantly when he didn't make a move to get up.

Val disliked him immediately, though she lied and said it was a pleasure to meet him. Turning her back on him, she went around the counter to pour herself a cup of coffee. Val thought she caught a hint of an Irish accent in a few of the words he spoke. Her mother sensed her daughter's cool indifference but went on to fill her in on Father Coughlin's background.

"Well, Valerie, I was just telling Father here how you arrived late last night from Ireland."

Val turned and politely nodded, sipping her hot coffee and slowly becoming more alert.

"Ironically enough, Father Coughlin is from County Clare."

Val didn't want to appear rude to her mother's company, so she took a seat next to her, directly opposite him.

"Imagine that. Small world ..."

Val said dryly - he was no Father Bruce.

Her mother continued on pleasantly.

"Yes. As a matter of fact, his first parish as a young priest, not that you're old, Father, was St. Peter's and Paul's in Ennis. He taught at the same school your dad attended."

Val set down her mug and stared intently at the man across from her.

This couldn't be ... Her head began to reel. She quickly excused herself, feigning a wave of nausea (though it was in part real), and rushed upstairs. Pulling the small tape recorder from her purse, she hit the fast-forward button, trying to find a point in her conversation with Uncle Sean where he revealed what she was looking for.

"... When I was a boy, Neil and I attended a private, Catholic school. Neil was always the strong one, and smarter. I sometimes resented him always sticking up for me. I told him that I could fight my own battles. I was kinda jealous of him ..."

Val fast-forwarded some more.

"There was a young priest, new to our school, Father Rob Coughlin. He taught religious studies. Anyway, he was very nice to me and told me that he had an older brother that was a lot like Neil when he was younger..."

Val cut off the tape. She walked downstairs, in shock. Evil found it's way to her doorstep. A righteous anger and indignation welled up within her. She would not allow it to advance any further in their lives!

She rounded the staircase with speed and determination and stood unflinchingly in the doorway.

"Mr. Coughlin ..."

She began, but her mother politely corrected her.

"Val, that would be *Father Coughlin* ..."

"Mom, do you remember I told you we needed to talk today?"

Her mother nervously looked between her guest and her daughter embarrassed at Val's disrespectful tone and manner.

"Now?"

Her mother's voice was strained.

Tension was building, and Rob didn't like the sound of the young woman's voice. He was feeling uncomfortable and seized the opportunity to announce that he had to leave. He began to thank Mrs. Callaghan for her hospitality and delicious muffins.

Val blocked the doorway. Her mother was baffled by her daughter's strange behavior.

"Valerie, Father Coughlin is leaving now."

Val stared at him icily.

"No, Mom. He's not going anywhere."

Clenching her fists, Val seethed.

"Mr. Coughlin, can you answer a question please?"

Rob was getting perturbed at the insolent little bitch addressing him so flippantly. He made a move to brush past her. Val wouldn't give him an inch and barred the doorway. Raising her voice even more, Val asked.

"Did you happen to teach 'religion' at St. Christopher's Boys School in Ennis?"

He looked at her curiously, not knowing where her line of questioning was going.

"Yes. As a matter of fact, I did, for a number of years."

He tried to excuse himself, lying that he was late for an appointment and had to leave immediately.

Val ignored his excuse and wouldn't budge from the doorframe.

"Tell me then, sir, does the name Sean Callaghan ring a bell with you?"

Rob froze, and his mouth dropped at the name. Val seized upon the moment with lightning speed.

"You bastard!"

Grace's hand came from out of nowhere and slapped her daughter across the face.

"Valerie Jean Callaghan! NEVER have I ..."

Val pushed her mother to the side as she grabbed the fat pervert by the collar and shoved him back against the refrigerator.

"I bet you've screwed many little boys over the years, haven't you, FATHER Coughlin? You raped innocent children who trusted you!"

Grace grabbed hold of Valerie, begging her to stop. Val was enraged and wrenched herself free from her mother's grasp.

"NO, MOM! You don't understand!"

Grace was in shock. Turning, Val shoved her finger in Rob's face.

"I'm going to report you! You SON OF A BITCH! You're going to jail, and I hope they do to you in prison what you did to those poor children! I hope they rip you apart!"

She picked her coffee mug up off the counter and flung the hot liquid into his face, burning his eyes. He shouted in pain and fell back against the wall, covering his face with his hands.

Grace was holding her forehead and screaming for her daughter to stop. She rushed to aid the floundering priest. Valerie pulled her away from him and shoved him down the hall.

"Did you think that hurt? I bet it's nothing like the pain you inflicted on your victims!"

He was backed up against the wall, feeling his way along toward the safety of the front door. His vision was blurred from the hot liquid that burned his eyes. Grace was shaking her head, apologizing profusely to the priest for her daughter's behavior.

"MOM!"

Val warned.

"Don't say you're sorry to this animal. He's the one, Mom. He's the one who raped Uncle Sean as a boy."

Her mother didn't understand what she was saying and thought her daughter had finally cracked from the pressure of everything that had happened in the last few weeks.

Val was out of control. She lunged after Rob when he made it to the front door and kicked him from behind with all her might sending him right through the screen door and sailing off the front porch, face-first, onto the broken seashell driveway.

He didn't know what happened and didn't feel the pain at first. His face and nose were bleeding profusely as he lifted himself off the ground. Crushed shells were embedded deep within his face and had torn open the palms of his hands and knees of his pants.

Val stood on the porch, physically restraining her mother from going to help the badly bleeding man.

"NO, MOM! Go and call the police! Trust me, Mom! I know who he is. I know WHAT he is!"

Grace wouldn't leave.

Rob knew he had to get out of there fast. The authorities would be there within minutes. He stumbled getting into his car, his vision badly impaired, and sped off.

Grace, tears pouring down her face, her eyes wide with horror, searched her daughter's face, struggling to understand.

"VAL! What is wrong with you!"

She begged for some clue into her daughter's tirade.

"MOM! Go and call the police now! HURRY please!"

Grace ran to the phone and called 911. She gave them the details as best she could. She then telephoned the rectory to speak with Father Bruce. The housekeeper answering the phone asked if it was an emergency. Grace assured her that it was. The kind woman informed Mrs. Callaghan that Father Bruce was expected back shortly. Grace asked for him to come right over to the house as soon as he could.

From the porch, Val could still see the car swerving as the priest tried to get away. He was driving erratically and she knew the police would catch him soon. If she went after him again, she might kill him herself and be charged with murder.

She watched his car finally turn the corner and disappear from sight. She wouldn't ruin her future for the likes of him. She thought of Warren and Caroline and stayed planted on the front porch with her arms crossed as she caught her breath. Adrenaline was pumping through her body. She whispered her prayer heavenward.

"Lord, I ask you to go after him."

Came her simple, yet heartfelt plea.

Rob was shaking behind the wheel. Blood dripped into his already blurry and badly burned eyelids. His heart was pounding out of his chest. The past had caught up with him and his mind swirled with plans of escape. Speeding down the road, swerving, he didn't even know what direction he was traveling in. Making his way on to a main street he kept driving until he found signs for a highway, any highway. He followed the signs for Boston while wiping at the blood that was dripping from his brow.

Valerie turned and walked back into the house after his car was out of sight. She stood in the hallway as the realization of what had just happened hit her. Slowly, she slid down the wall into a heap, sobs wracking her body.

Her mother dove for her as she collapsed. Grace held her daughter, rocking her gently like a baby. She smoothed her hair with her hands and soothed her. They held one another on the floor.

Suddenly the doorway was darkened by a man's figure. He took off his sunglasses, opening the screen door, he bent to pick Valerie up off the floor. Father Bruce put his strong arm around her waist and led her to the couch, with Grace following nervously behind.

"Thank you for coming, Bruce. I don't know what's gotten into her!" Grace cried.

Compassionately, he asked Valerie to tell him what happened.

"I got your mom's message and came right over."

"Yes, Valerie, please explain. I can't piece all of this together."

Her mother echoed. Turning to Father Bruce, Grace added.

"All I know is that she flipped out and assaulted our new pastor, and I doubt he's ever coming back!"

Father Bruce took Valerie's hand in his.

"What happened?"

Val regained her composure and sat up. She reached for her mother's hand as she explained how she'd come to find out from Glynnis and Peggy about Caroline's abuse as a child. Grace cried out when she heard of Sean's involvement.

"Oh, my God! How could he do that to my baby? MY BABY!!!"

Father Bruce stood and held Grace, so she wouldn't collapse next, guiding her to a chair. Valerie went to her.

"Mom, that's why I took off on him like a maniac. I went to Ireland to confront Sean while Granny and Siobhan were still here with you. Warren came with me for fear of what I might ... well, what I just did here!"

Val remembered the tape recorder and told her mother and Father Bruce to wait a moment.

"I've got something that'll help explain the whole story — in his own words."

Val bounded up the stairs as the police pulled up to the house. She returned with the small recorder in her shaking hands. The officers had gathered with them in the living room. She quickly explained what happened to them and rewound the tape for all to hear.

Sean's voice explained the situation and the details. Father Bruce sat listening to Sean's confession, eyes closed, tapping his foot. It was a good thing Father Coughlin was gone. Had he known and arrived any earlier, Father Bruce would be on trial for murder.

Grace cried as she heard Sean's account of his being repeatedly raped as a boy. Father Bruce held her hand as the horror began to take shape in their minds. When Val stopped the tape, Father Bruce looked at them both.

"I will track that man down! I swear to you that I'll make sure the Archdiocese knows about this rapist and does something about it."

The police asked for the tape recording and got on the two-way radio to call in the make and model of the car the priest was driving. They left the house in pursuit, promising to notify them when they caught him. The tape would be used as evidence.

After they left, Val shook her head in disbelief and addressed Father Bruce's reference to the church.

"Father Bruce, they DO know about it and they HIDE it! It's an old schoolboy network. The church covers up for these predators until someone complains loudly to the media or when a victim comes forward and confesses; then they try and play it down and put the man away in rehab somewhere for a few months, eventually declaring him "cured" and move him on to another parish. Or they pay the family off to keep quiet."

"The entire church should be on trial for organized crime, in my opinion. My company, Sidebar, wrote an article on trying the clergy, taking on the church in court. It's pathetic!"

Father Bruce knew all too well about the politics involved. He stayed out of that choosing to focus on God's ministry. However, this had gone too far and now affected him personally and those he loved.

Val went on.

"Did you know that early on in Ireland, that the church actually encouraged priests to drink? It's true; they honestly thought it would kill their sex drive. That's why a lot of these priests became alcoholics."

"The church has a history of attracting men with sexual problems. They bring them in as young men, kids basically, who aren't developed sexually or who have identity issues. These guys try to ignore their sexuality and find they can't. Some of them end up abusing kids that are the same age or close to the age they where when they stopped developing mentally!"

Father Bruce nodded. Psychologically, he knew what she said made sense.

Father Bruce addressed Valerie.

"How would you fix things? I mean, how does the church fix this mess?"

He stood up and leaned against the mantle over the fireplace, cupping his hand over his mouth. He stared sadly at the photo of Caroline and lightly touched her image.

Valerie sat next to her mother and leaned her head against the back of the couch.

"There are no easy answers. I guess the first thing the church should do is admit disaster! In order for them to fix the system, they need to stop huddling among themselves and quit trying to protect the organization and work to heal their congregations."

"Personally, I wouldn't allow celibate men to run things. Present company excluded, of course! They need to involve more laity — men and women, MARRIED men and women even — to help them run the day-to-day operations of the church. They need a system of checks and balances ... you know like Democrats ... Republicans ... clergy and laity."

"They need to admit their mistakes and not try to cover them up. The congregation sees right through this. To them, many priests are nothing but a bunch of hypocrites and they don't want any part of it! Then the faithful leave the fold in droves! Why can't they do some sort of in-depth background check on these guys? Talk to their neighbors, friends, and teachers. The CIA does it! You can't afford not to!"

Val sat back, thinking, with her eyes closed.

"If I were Christ, and I had to look upon the atrocities that 'His' church is accused of committing, I'd be trembling right now. I mean, doesn't the Bible say something to the effect that 'Judgment begins in the house of the Lord'?"

Father Bruce nodded.

"Yes. It says just that."

Val stood.

"I wouldn't want to stand before Christ and give Him an account of this! The Christian church "universal" would come up seriously wanting. He'll bring it down, Father Bruce. If something isn't done soon, if the church doesn't 'repent' and change its ways, I'm afraid God will take it to its knees."

Grace had calmed down some and was listening intently to the wisdom of her eldest daughter. Father Bruce had his hands still clenched.

"I'm going to get to the bottom of this. I won't rest until that man is found and those who hid this crime are exposed."

Val hugged her mother.

"Mom, I'm sorry if I scared you. The last thing in the world I wanted to do was to see you hurt again. Sean is in rehab now. Granny and Aunt Siobhan are devastated by the news. They can't believe it."

Grace told Val that she'd call Granny in a day or so. She needed time to sort through it all.

Val looked at Father Bruce warmly.

"You know what?"

He looked at her sadly, not knowing what she was about to say.

"If I had to picture what Jesus looked like, I'd give him your face."

Father Bruce bent his head and cried. Val went and hugged him.

"It's not your fault. You followed your true calling. You've been a wonderful priest, Father Bruce. I know the whole church isn't filled with pedophiles like Rob Coughlin. There are many truly genuine, wonderful pastors out there, following their call to serve every day. But it is your responsibility, as a true man of God, to be vigilant and watch. You can sense those who are insincere and shady. Go with your gut."

Calmer, knowing that it was in the hands of the authorities; Val asked her mother if she'd be okay by herself. Grace nodded. Val had to get back to Boston as she had to work the next day. She was emotionally exhausted, but relieved after opening up to her mother.

Father Bruce walked her out to her car.

"I'll stay with her, Valerie. I'm so sorry for all of this."

Val put her hand on his.

"Pray for Uncle Sean, Father Bruce. He needs it. Pray for me, too, that one day, I might forgive him. Right now, I hate him and that Coughlin guy."

He nodded in understanding.

"I will. Are you okay to drive?"

Val assured him she was.

Police sirens were heard rushing in the distance.

Val waved to her mother, who was at the window, and proceeded to follow in the skid marks left by Rob Coughlin's car. She spoke more prayers to God on her ride home, asking him once again to find this criminal and bring him to justice.

Chapter Fifty-Two

Boston, Massachusetts, Summer 1998

ROB WINCED AS HE TRIED to wipe his face while changing lanes. He'd been driving for hours, not knowing where he was going. The shock was wearing off and pain was setting in. He caught a glimpse of his swollen and bloody reflection in the rearview mirror. He knew it was all over but wouldn't turn himself in. When he neared the bus station, he'd ditch the car.

Stopping into a small downtown coffee shop near the station, horrified people stared at him. Some whispered that he must have been mugged and offered to call him an ambulance. A woman standing in line noticed that he was a priest and rushed to help him, offering napkins. Waving the Good Samaritan off, he said that he'd slipped and fallen and would be okay.

Once he got into the bathroom, he hardly recognized his own face. His back, where that bitch had kicked him, was also killing him. He'd barely been able to get out of the car, let alone walk upright.

Excruciating pain nearly caused him to pass out when he splashed water over his face. His hands burned as pieces of sea shells were embedded deep within his palms and face. They would need to be removed soon.

Knowing he didn't have time to spare, he gingerly tried to pat it dry — then gave up letting the bloody water drip. Going to a local hospital was out of the question. He needed to get out of the state as fast as possible. He left the café quickly and stopped at an ATM, where he took out a couple of hundred dollars in cash on the card he'd been issued by the Archdiocese when he became the pastor of St. Bridget's. It was to be used for purchasing items for the rectory.

Keeping his head down, he slowly made his way to South Station to buy a bus ticket west. He'd return to his brother's cabin in Montana, the only place he could think of as a safe haven.

Sleeping on the bus was impossible because of the burning pain in his face and hands. He panicked inwardly when a police car surged past the large moving vehicle, with sirens wailing and lights flashing. He had purposely sat at the very back of the bus, and got up only to use the lavatory.

By the time he reached Chicago, his face was badly swollen and infection was setting in. In the bus's small bathroom mirror, he could see pus forming beneath the skin. His eyelids were nearly swollen shut and red from the hot coffee thrown at him. The vision in his right eye was still very blurry. He was frightful to look at and stayed slouched down in his seat until all the other passengers had departed.

He had a few hours to kill before his next bus connection arrived. He found a nearby Goodwill Store and went in to purchase a pair of civilian pants, a shirt, and an old jacket with a hood. He paid the woman, who took no pity on him. She figured him a disgusting drunken derelict who got beat up and only wanted to get him out of her store as quickly as possible.

He found the restroom and changed. Sneaking into the alley behind the store, he threw his priestly garments into a dumpster, knowing for sure his life in the clergy was over. He bought a cup of coffee from a pushcart at the bus station and went back to wait for the transfer that would take him on to Montana.

Security guards were searching under and between the buses with flashlights and dogs. He held his breath and boarded the bus making his way slowly to the back. Slumping down in the last seat, he pulled his hood over his head to avoid unwanted stares. Reaching in his pocket for cash, he realized that he'd left the rest of his money and charge card in the pocket of his priestly pants that were now resting in the trash behind Goodwill. He sighed at his stupidity. Penniless, he held tightly to the ticket that would take him to Montana.

More people began to board the bus. He turned away, hiding his face from a woman who was intent on staring at him. He wasn't a priest any longer, but a deformed and wretched man with an infected and disfigured face, who had no future to speak of. Rob thought of his brother Rich and how he was heading to Montana without him, his ashes left in a towel back on his bureau at St. Bridget's.

"Oh, frig him!"

He thought bitterly to himself. His older brother had never been there for him anyway.

The bus drove all night. He dozed sporadically, arriving in Montana a day and a half later. He was physically tired and beginning to feel sick having not eaten since he was in Chicago. Concentrating was difficult due to the hunger that gripped him. He tried to focus on a simple plan to get himself out to the cabin. With no credit card and money, he couldn't rent a car. He tried to hitch a ride, but only those with flatbed trucks motioned for him to jump on the back. He walked until he thought he'd collapse. He slept one night in a barn. He thought he'd make some progress when an old man with thick glasses and poor eyesight stopped to offer him a lift. When he got a closer look at his would-be passenger, it scared him and he sped off. Rob jumped back from the vehicle and fell as it peeled away, screaming in pain. It felt like his back was broken. He dreaded riding on horseback out to the homestead. He didn't know if he'd be able to even mount the animal. The jerking motion would probably kill him for sure, although, at this point, death would be welcomed.

When Rob finally neared the familiar reservation, he waited until the owner of the horses was out of sight. He knew they ran a fairly laidback, family business, still trusting a man by his word - the idiots! When the owner went inside, Rob untethered one of the horses and led it around back. He patted its nose in an effort to keep it quiet. The horse reared up, sending him crashing to the ground.

Rob's back cracked, and indescribable pain surged through his entire body. He breathed rapidly so as to not cry out. He lay on the ground, still clutching the horse's reign with his swollen hands. Struggling to get to his feet, he limped along pathetically, leading the horse through the adjacent woods. It would be dark soon and the air was becoming damp and raw. When he felt it safe enough, he tried to mount the stead. It reared slightly at first, but Rob, a seasoned horseman, was angry enough to nearly strangle the creature with his last bit of remaining strength. He took control of the animal and set off in the direction of the cabin.

The sky opened up and the rains fell with a vengeance. Loud thunder roared as lightning lit up the path before him. Rob felt a divine wrath working against him and was fighting the animal every few feet to stay on course. He was miles away from anyone who could offer him help, not that he'd find it. He remembered the Indian guide's story as he made his way through the potter's field. He thought also of the irony found in the Bible story about Judas and how, after he betrayed the Lord, he hung himself and was buried in a potter's field. The phrase today would describe a final resting place for the poor, indigent, and unknown.

After what seemed like hundreds of miles and countless hours, Rob arrived at the cabin feverish and cold. Shivering, he was resigned to his fate.

He didn't have a key. Taking a stone, he threw it through the window. Shattered glass crashed to the floor inside the cabin. He reached in and opened the window but couldn't lift his leg over the sill as his hip was badly sprained from the horse's throw. He struggled against the throbbing ache and forced his leg up, catching a glimpse of the snorting black stallion in a piece of fragmented glass still stuck in the casing. The beast, unprovoked, reared up, then pawed furiously at the ground. Rob was nervous that it might lunge at him. Quickly he hoisted himself up over the sill. Leaning over at the waist, he hurled himself forward in a half-somersault motion, landing with a thud on the wooden floor inside. There was a new searing pain where a glass fragment cut open the back of his thigh.

It was pitch black inside the cabin, except for an occasional lightning bolt that illuminated the room. He reached down with his hand and felt the warm blood seeping from the fresh wound. He dragged himself across the floor to the couch. His hand was barely visible in front of his face. Lightning crackled and illuminated the cabin momentarily, enough to let him make out where he was in the room. He made out the edge of the hearth and slithered his wet body across the floor toward the fireplace. Finding the box of long stick matches, he lit one and seized the lantern set on the edge of the hearth. The wind howled outside and whistled through the broken window. Indian spirits seemed to shout at him from every direction. He couldn't get the sound out of his ears and could barely see through the slits that were his eyes.

He squinted from the light of the lantern. Looking above the fireplace, he spotted his brother's hunting rifle. He'd never reach it. His entire body ached. He took the poker from the fireplace and was able to knock the gun down from the mount on the wall. It crashed to the floor. Rob checked the barrel. It was loaded. Hoisting himself up, he limped slowly to the front door and unbolted it.

A spectacular bolt of lightning struck, causing the horse to rear and tear away from the post. Rob cursed the animal as it took off into the night. He staggered out the front door, closing it securely behind him, and stood under the porch while the rain lashed in at him sideways. Even the dampness hurt his face. He stumbled out into the torrential downpour.

The ridge was barely visible up ahead. He felt himself moving beyond the pain as his mind played tricks on him. Rob ducked from what he thought was a large swooping black bird. They were all around him. Fever racked his broken and bloodied body. The cabin was out of view, and he quickly became disoriented, crying out in fear.

As Rob neared the ridge, he stumbled when his foot caught a rock, causing him to tumble over the steep edge. He rolled violently down the embankment, landing face up in thick mud, the back of his head slammed against a jagged rock. Unable to move his neck or legs, Rob looked up at the ridge from which he'd fallen. He'd not make it to where he'd envisioned. He no longer had the ability to pick himself up. His skull was pounding.

Feeling beside his head with his right hand, he removed a sharp object that cut into his ear. Recognizing it as a piece of pottery, he threw the ancient clay aside. The rifle had come to rest just below his left arm. Fumbling for the weapon, he positioned it toward his head. With his last bit of remaining strength, he pulled the trigger.

Chapter Fifty-Three

THE SNOWS COME EARLY TO MONTANA; leaves begin falling in late August and early September. Yet, on September 23rd, the spirit of Indian summer blew a soft warm breeze across Cape Cod, Massachusetts.

It was a delightful, bright, and cloudless Saturday morning. As Val lay peacefully sleeping in her childhood bedroom, the curtains breathed in harmony with the gentle zephyr. She stirred slightly.

Downstairs, Grace had risen early. The promised package had finally arrived from a Señor Miguel del Mar of Spain. He'd been distraught to learn of Caroline's passing and had informed Grace that his staff had located a picture frame and necklace which Caroline had apparently overlooked while packing.

The frame contained a beautiful photograph of Caroline, carefree, overlooking the ocean on a stop they'd made while biking. He had taken the picture himself and made an extra copy to keep. Caroline had chosen that one to put in the frame as a souvenir to give to Val when she got home.

Grace had given Señor del Mar her address and was going through the contents of the box, which had aptly arrived on Val's wedding day. She stared at the picture of her beautiful, deceased daughter, whose auburn hair shone brilliantly in the sunlight, giving her an almost angelic appearance. The teal blue ocean provided a stunning backdrop. She appeared serene, content. Grace delicately and lovingly ran her fingers over her daughter's beautiful image and allowed herself a quiet moment to cry. She decided to wrap the two boxes and give to Val as wedding presents. Taking a roll of gold wrapping paper out of the hall closet, she spent some time carefully decorating the small packages, finishing with little bows and ribbons. She'd wrapped many gifts recently for Val's wedding shower. She had received so many presents that she had to parcel them out, leaving some at her Boston condo and shipping whatever else she wanted back to Ireland.

Grace poured coffee and set it on the breakfast tray next to the elegantly wrapped presents. She walked upstairs to awaken her daughter. Leaning against the wall, Grace balanced the tray while opening the door.

"Well, young lady, this is it. Your BIG DAY. Do you feel like getting up?"

Val turned over slowly and, with her eyes still closed, yawned.

"I was having the nicest dream, Mom. Caroline was in it, and it felt so real. I didn't want to leave her to wake up."

Grace smiled, but a tear slid down her face.

"Speaking of which, I've a surprise for you. It just arrived. I'll leave you to your coffee and you can open them in private."

Val sat up, curious to know what was in the beautiful gift boxes. She thought it more gifts from Warren. Each week since they'd parted, he'd been sending her little mementos, counting down until their wedding day.

Grace left and Val pulled the tray up. She took a sip of the hot coffee and unwrapped the first tiny package. She opened the pink jewelry box, which revealed a gold seashell charm on a delicate matching chain. The bottom of the box was engraved with a Spanish name that she couldn't decipher. She placed the necklace around her neck and secured it. Reaching for the larger present, she tugged gently at the ribbon until it gave way. Her face lit up when she saw the picture of Caroline. In an instant, both joy and pain hit her simultaneously. It was just how her sister had looked in her dream!

Val felt a warm current run through her body sensing something supernatural happening. The chrome frame didn't seem to do the picture justice, until Val noticed a button on the bottom and what looked like a little speaker on the back. She pressed it and Caroline's voice became audible.

"Hi, Val! It's me. I wish you could see this place. It's gorgeous! I'm having so much fun. I miss you, sis. Here's wishing you a great day. Love you! Caroline."

Val was speechless. It was like Caroline was speaking to her from heaven. When she finally found her voice, she cried out.

"MOM! Mom, hurry!"

Grace nearly dropped her teacup bounding up the steps in response to her daughter's cry. She pushed through the door.

"What's the matter! Are you okay?"

Val nodded and showed her mother the frame. She couldn't stop shaking.

"It's Caroline, Mom. It's like she made a way to send me this message today ... listen."

She pressed the button again, and the message repeated itself.

Grace sat and held her daughter as the two cried in one another's arms. Grace, having not removed the frame fully from the box, didn't notice the button on the bottom.

"How'd you get this?"

Val asked her mother incredulously after catching her breath and clutching the photo tightly to her heart.

"A man Caroline befriended in Spain, Miguel del Mar, I believe was his name. She stayed at his hotel and he said she must have overlooked it when packing. She had it boxed with your name on it. He looked up our address and called me. He promised to mail it a few weeks ago. He took the photo while biking with Caroline. She mentioned to him that she wanted to give it to you ... and the necklace was to be a souvenir she wanted you to have. Something having to do with St. James ... he's the patron saint of voyages, I think ... pilgrimage. You can check that out with Father Bruce I bet."

"Mom, this is the best wedding present! I can't wait to show Warren and Father Bruce. They'll be so excited. This is definitely coming to Ireland with me. I don't want to press it too much. I don't want the battery to run out. I'll press it only when I need to hear her voice."

Grace beamed at her. It was her wedding day miracle.

Val and Warren were married at a candlelight Mass at St. Bridget's at four o'clock that afternoon. Glynnis, Peggy, Sheila, and Siobhan were her bridesmaids and were paired up with Warren's four brothers. Val walked down the aisle with her Uncle Tim to a song from one of her favorite Christian artists, Twila Paris's "The Body of Christ." She stopped briefly to hand her mother and grandmother each a rose. Warren had handed his mother one when he entered to meet Valerie at the altar.

Father Bruce was beaming from ear to ear. He was so excited that he messed up her surname and married name. Warren whispered to him that Val just married herself, and he broke out into a fit of laughter. He shared it with the congregation, who joined them in the chuckle.

The ceremony was relaxed and personal. Warren took great pride in reciting his vows and placing the wedding ring on Val's finger. She handed her flowers to Glynnis, who couldn't stop smiling through the whole ceremony. Val couldn't tell if it was because she was happy or just plain nervous.

She looked lovingly into Warren's eyes as she placed the ring on his finger. He gripped her hand, and they kissed before they were supposed to. Father Bruce pointed out that that wasn't in the script, drawing more rounds of laughter as he told them to stop getting ahead of the program.

He set down his Bible and, with outstretched arms, approached them as friends. In his own words, he prayed an unrehearsed blessing.

"Dear Heavenly Father, it is, indeed, a good day. We come to you today having been through some horrible storms and yet, somehow, you brought us through. When the waters rose, you led us to dry ground. Having come through such deep sorrow, we praise you for the joy this marriage brings.

Bless their love, Lord, may it abound more and more. Help them as they go forth in this life together as one, honoring you in this union. Bless their lives, Lord, and their children's lives. Extend your mercy, love, and protection about them from this day forward. In Jesus name we pray. Amen"

Turning to Warren, he told him.

"NOW you may kiss your bride!"

Warren looked into Val's eyes, and she brought her arms up around his neck. Their embrace lingered, and their kisses were warm and gentle.

Grace took her place behind the piano. Val noticed the special look of friendship and gratefulness that passed between her mother and Father Bruce. The ensemble began to play a beautiful piece that Father Bruce had prepared and orchestrated just for them. Warren and Val stood and listened, too moved by the music to walk away. It was as if the chords were written in heaven and sent to them for this, their special moment.

When the song ended, instead of turning to walk down the aisle, Val asked Warren if he'd wait just a moment. She ascended the steps to Father Bruce, who was standing up at the altar, and gave him a warm hug and a kiss on the cheek.

"I can't tell you how much you mean to me. I just wanted you to know that I love you."

Father Bruce had tears in his eyes.

"I love you, too, Valerie. Go now and have a happy life."

Warren reached out his hand to receive his wife. They walked down the aisle to the cheers of those in the pews. His brothers were up for a rip-roaring party. The reception wouldn't disappoint.

Everyone was instructed to go home and change into jeans or something comfortable. There'd be no formal "head table"; they'd be gathering on the beach for a classic New England clambake. The caterers had arrived hours earlier and dug pits in the sand, lining them with seaweed, to steam the lobsters and clams. The meal was then hauled up to the backyard, where picnic tables were covered in red and white-checkered tablecloths.

Everyone was given a plastic bib and various lobster-cracking utensils. Those who didn't like lobster had their choice of chicken or steak.

The band was made up of folks from the ensemble that played out on occasion at local bars and restaurants on the Cape. Later in the evening, a deejay stepped up the beat for dancing.

Val and Warren danced on the porch with several of their friends and relatives. It was a wonderful celebration. Val barely had a moment to sit with her new husband before she was dragged up on to the porch by her friends and asked to play something on the violin. She looked at Warren and rolled her eyes. She was a little self-conscious, being in front of her new family members, and decided not to fiddle at that time, instead choosing to play an old Irish love song. The tune was perfect, bringing tears to her new mother-in-law's eyes.

Everyone cheered when she was done, and Warren gave her a warm hug and kiss. It was well into the evening when, after another round of toasts, Warren announced that he was spiriting his new bride away to begin their honeymoon.

The guests formed two long lines and held their hands up over their heads to create a human tunnel. Warren and Val passed underneath, stopping to kiss everyone as they wished the happy couple well. Father Bruce was at the end and gave them both a hug and whispered to Valerie.

"I'll be praying."

He winked at her, knowing her desire to conceive soon. Warren was wondering what he meant by that. Val told him she'd fill him in later.

When they reached their hotel, a gentleman from concierge led them to their honeymoon suite. The room was decorated with dozens of sterling roses, which Warren had brought in special, knowing they were Val's favorite flower. She made Warren sit on the bed, and pulled the picture of Caroline out of her suitcase, hiding it behind her back. He was wondering what she was up to.

"Well, we knew that this was going to be a very special day, but it was made even more special for me this morning when I had a visit from someone very near and dear to my heart. Care to guess who?"

Warren couldn't begin to guess.

"I give up. Who?"

Val held up the picture of Caroline. Warren's eyes widened.

"Here ... listen."

She pressed the button.

Warren listened to her sister's message. He smiled at Val in amazement.

"How did this come about?"

She sat next to him on the bed and shared the story of Miguel del Mar, and how the package had arrived that morning, and of her early morning dream from which she didn't want to awake.

"She's with you in spirit, Valerie. What a blessing this is."

He looked at the photo of the beautiful young woman and handed it back to his wife. Val placed it back in her bag.

"I'm taking this to Ireland with us."

Warren motioned for her to come and lay beside him. He just wanted to hold her.

French doors, overlooking the ocean, lay open to the warm Atlantic breeze, caressing their skin. Warren held her close for the longest time as they drifted into a peaceful, quiet state. Val turned to him, and their lips found one another.

Val stared at his hand in the dimly lit room and was filled with joy as she saw the wedding band sparkle on his finger. It was a different sight on Warren, as he typically wore only his watch. She held up his hand to examine it more closely. He watched her amused expression.

"You like that, don't you?"

She laughed, nodding her head.

"I really do!"

He looked at her hand.

"You have much prettier hands than I ..."

Val shivered suddenly. Warren got up to close the doors.

"You need to get under those covers if you're cold."

Val looked at him seductively.

"I'm not safe under there with you now, am I?"

He shook his head.

"Noooo, ma'am, you're not."

Val undressed slowly, letting his eyes take her in.

"What if I don't want to?"

She teased.

Warren unzipped his pants.

"You really have no choice. It's in the contract. Written under the section called 'Marital Duties' in fine print."

Val chuckled.

"The things I do for you!"

She felt his lean body pressing against her. Warren held her tightly. The feel of her was enough to send him.

Valerie stared at him, and he read her thoughts.

"You really want this to happen tonight, don't you?"

She nodded and played with the hair on his chest. He already knew she was anxious to conceive. He lifted her chin and kissed her lips.

"I'll see what I can do."

Valerie smiled.

"I know you will."

Chapter Fifty-Four

Ennis, County Clare, Ireland, Summer 2001

WARREN PICKED HER UP AS she screamed with delight. Valerie came running down the stairs.

"What happened?"

Warren was carrying her like a sack of potatoes over his shoulder.

"She did it again ..."

He set her down, and she quickly scampered off.

Valerie caught up with her. Putting her hands on her hips she pretended to be stern.

"Uh-oh, Caroline ... tell Mommy. What did you do?"

She giggled and ran out into the kitchen, chasing after the cat.

"Pill! Pill!"

She shouted.

Val chuckled and waved her hand in the air.

"I just get a kick out of the way she says Pearl's name. Did she get you again?"

Warren nodded, wiping the messy egg yolk off his pants.

"I bet you taught her that little trick, didn't you?"

Val denied it vehemently.

"No way! She learned that all on her own."

Caroline had developed a habit of throwing eggs. It started a week ago when they'd decided she was old enough to let her help them collect the eggs from the hen house. At first, she just chased the birds around, getting them all riled up as she tried to capture them. Val patiently tried to show her how to reach in gently and retrieve the eggs. Caroline accidentally dropped one, causing Val to say, "Uh-oh!" From then on, it was "uh-oh" and she'd throw an egg on the ground, taking great delight in watching it splatter.

"She gets it from you."

Val told Warren. He reminded her that it was just her age.

"You know what they say about the terrible two's."

Val sat for a moment, and Caroline ran up and laid her head on her mother's lap. Val stroked her silky red hair.

"Can you hear the baby talking?"

Caroline put her head and little hands on her mother's stomach and nodded. She pretended to knock, then put her mouth on her mother's tummy to give the baby a kiss. Val placed her hand on the other side of her stomach.

"See? He heard you. Feel! He's kicking."

Caroline's eyes widened. She loved when he did that.

Warren knelt down beside his daughter and put his hand on his wife's stomach.

"Do you think he wants to come out and play?"

Caroline nodded and told him.

"He's stuck."

Val and Warren laughed. After their daughter toddled off, he whispered to his wife.

"I can't wait to come in and play."

"You, dear husband, must behave or you won't be allowed on the playground!"

He went over to the freezer and took out her ice cream.

"Well, just for that, you won't be needing any more of this!"

Caroline spotted the container he held and shouted.

"Shervert!"

Warren corrected her.

"It's SherBERT ... like in Ernie and BERT."

He picked her up and gave her a spoon.

Val walked into the kitchen and asked.

"Caroline, you'll share that with Mommy now, won't you?"

Showing her stubborn streak, Caroline shook her head mightily. Warren made a face and stuck out his tongue at Val, carrying a spoon-licking Caroline off into the other room. Val waved them off. She sat at the kitchen table, feeling the baby kick some more. She was sure it was a boy. It was such a different pregnancy than what she had with Caroline.

Warren walked back into the kitchen, announcing that their daughter was very happily watching a Sesame Street tape that Grace had brought over from the States.

"She's having a delightful time eating your 'shervert,' too."

He mentioned snidely.

Val hugged him as close as she physically could, given her big belly. He rubbed her stomach.

"What makes you so sure this one's a boy?"

Val smiled a knowing grin.

"I just am. Call it mother's intuition. I knew Caroline would be a girl, didn't I?"

Warren rolled the name over his tongue.

"Warren Neil ... I like the sound of that. But I actually like it better the other way around, Neil Warren Cahill. It flows better. Would you mind if we switched it?"

Val was surprised. She'd always told him that if they should ever have a son, she'd like to fit her Father's name in there somewhere. Warren didn't seem to mind the order.

"If you're sure, my mom would be thrilled!"

Val scooped up the cat as she walked by and snuggled her on her shoulder.

"She is just a sweetie kitty, aren't you, Pearl?"

The cat purred as if she understood. Warren scratched the cat under her chin, and peeked into the living room. Caroline had climbed up on his chair and fell asleep. He carried her upstairs for her nap. Closing the door quietly, he led his wife into their bedroom.

Val lay down on the bed, thankful to get off her feet for a few moments. She felt every bit her thirty-eight years. Warren rolled her on to her side and drew her in close beside him, rubbing her swollen belly.

"I still think you look great."

Val knew what he was getting at.

"Oh, stop! I can't possibly be attractive to you in this state."

Warren snickered, assuring her that the reason she was so attractive to him was that the pressure was off — no worries about whether or not they were trying to get pregnant. Val loved his sense of humor.

"Honey, if you can manage this, I'm all yours."

Warren was a master of adaptation. He found ways to not only make her feel comfortable during her pregnancies, but desirable at the same time. She was happy and fulfilled, carrying their second child.

It had been over three years since Caroline's death, and as Val lay listening to her contented husband breathing beside her, she counted her blessings. Her daughter, Caroline, not only resembled her sister, but Val would often catch that gleam in her eye, and it was as if Caroline was sending her a special wink from heaven letting her know that she was still there and would be with her always.

Val had asked Peggy if she would be their next child's godparent. Glynnis was Caroline's Godmother, and both were anxiously looking forward to the birth of her second baby. Grace was planning on coming over to Ireland for the summer, and staying with Granny and Aunt Siobhan. She wanted to be close by when her daughter gave birth.

Siobhan kept Val updated from time to time on Sean's progress in therapy. He'd moved out of the house as the tension and memories became too much for all under the same roof. He was still actively involved in counseling and was currently finding success using a drug called Lupron.

Siobhan explained to her that the medication inhibited the production of testosterone, thereby eliminating the sex drive. Though the mind can still fantasize, the actions are short-lived when the body refuses to respond. Sean was able to go about a fairly normal life, and, for the first time in many years, was not tortured by vivid fantasies and lewd thoughts. He'd remain on the medication for life.

Val thought about her own precious daughter, sleeping peacefully in the room next door. It scared her to think of anyone ever hurting her. Val remained vigilant and tried not to allow herself to become too paranoid. Warren had brothers, and though Val didn't fear for her child's safety around them, she always watched closely. Caroline was never far from her view.

She remembered what Sean had said to her a couple of years after he was involved in therapy. She had agreed to meet him for lunch. It was an odd get-together. She'd spoken to Father Bruce beforehand, who prayed with her over the phone for the strength she'd need. Father Bruce told her that in order for her to be free and move on, she'd need to forgive her uncle. At first she was indignant until he explained why.

"Val, unless you forgive him, you hold yourself in emotional bondage, as well as the one toward whom your unforgiveness is directed. It festers in your spirit and grows. Anger eats away at you little by little. Forgiveness sets YOU free."

Over coffee, she looked at her uncle and felt twinges of pity, concluding that he, too, had suffered horrible torments as a child. From somewhere deep within came the words, "I forgive you, Uncle Sean." He broke down in tears.

Father Bruce, at Grace's urging, made a special trip over to Ireland to meet with Sean, who, after years of therapy, was finally open to talking with a member of the clergy. Father Bruce apologized to him for the hurt the church had caused him, and listened quietly as Sean ranted against the system and its deception and hypocrisy. Father Bruce held him when he broke down and cried.

Sean's final advice to his niece, when she confessed to him how frightened she was for her own child's safety, stayed with her.

"The greatest tool in a predator's arsenal, Val, is his cultivated ability to listen. Your defense is communication. Be open with your children. Seize every opportunity to let them express what they're thinking and feeling. Let them know they're loved unconditionally. Make the bond between parent and child so strong that the gates of hell can't prevail against it, and pray - pray and ask God daily to put that invisible hedge of protection about them, making them invisible to the eyes of all those who'd seek to hurt them."

She was grateful for the continued advice, counseling, and friendship of "Father" Bruce.

The political structure of the church, though truly working to weed out those who hurt the flock, was not moving fast enough for his liking. He ran into continuous administrative and political roadblocks within the hierarchy and quickly became frustrated.

The search for Father Coughlin had long gone cold, and he found himself praying in earnest for the Lord to bring him to justice. Ultimately, it was Grace who spoke to him and, through love, helped him release the emotional burden he carried for her daughter.

The bonds they shared grew stronger with time, and through the many struggles, they discovered a love for one another that took them both by surprise.

Those who were close to him understood why he decided to leave the priesthood. His love of music was well known and recognized by St. Bridget's, who offered him a paid secular position to stay on as conductor of the Harbor Lights Ensemble.

Kathleen M. Urquhart

Val lingered in that peaceful place, somewhere between rest and sleep and smiled to herself thinking how ironic it was that the man to whom she'd referred to all her life as "Father" had this last year, literally, become her Dad.

* * *

Dear Reader,

I appreciate the time you've invested in reading this novel. It is my first self-published work (and greatest hope) that you found yourself on a riveting literary journey.

The trauma and effects of sexual abuse are being widely felt today. This crime against humanity has left in its wake a generational debris field of broken lives and families. It has reached epic proportions that can no longer be ignored.

If we can find anything "good" in this worldwide epidemic, it is this:

WE ARE AN ARMY!

We have come through a battle. We are stronger, wiser, and well equipped to turn the tables on our assailants. We have prevailed against tremendous odds and are VICTORS. I refuse the title of victim.

Our experiences can help by cutting off future access to innocent children. United, we have the strength and power to prevail. There are now more of us than them. We can, and must, expose these criminal violations for the future and safety of our children and grandchildren.

Through this poignant story, it is my desire to come alongside those who've experienced sexual abuse and empower them with the understanding that there is a future filled with hope and healing. Men and women who've experienced the pain and betrayal due to personal transgressions can embrace joy and success in all that they do.

If you would be so kind, please take a moment and go out to Amazon. com and write a positive review of **Pigtails and Potter's Field**. If you would also share an uplifting post and recommend this book to others on your Facebook page, Goodreads, Instagram, and Twitter you will help me circulate this novel far and wide. Many need to know that they are not alone.

This plague of perversion will be eradicated. It begins with your voice. In this war that we face, silence is not an option ...

Please visit my website: www.kurquhart.com
Email: Kathleen.urquhart@comcast.net

With deepest gratitude,

Kathleen